THE ANGEL OF MUSIC

THE ANGEL OF MUSIC

THE COMPLETE SERIES

C. DAVID STEPHENS

LLANO ESTACADO PUBLISHING

LLANO ESTACADO PUBLISHING
3521 50th Street #29
Lubbock Texas 79413

Covers design by Clarissa Yeo.
Cover train photograph by Carl Morrison.

First printed in the United States of America.

ISBN: 978-0-936158-08-2

10   9   8   7   6   5   4   3   2   1

"No one ever sees the Angel; but he is heard by those who are meant to hear him. He often comes when they least expect him, when they are sad and disheartened. Then their ears suddenly perceive celestial harmonies, a divine voice, which they remember all their lives. Persons who are visited by the Angel quiver with a thrill unknown to the rest of mankind. And they cannot touch an instrument, or open their mouths to sing, without producing sounds that put all other human sounds to shame. Then people who do not know that the Angel has visited those persons say that they have genius."

—Gaston Leroux, *The Phantom of the Opera*

TABLE OF CONTENTS

BOOK 1

SANTA MONICA

1

ANGEL

CHRISTINE DAAÉ, a beautiful child of twelve years, sat on a bench in the nearly deserted Greyhound station in Amarillo, Texas. It was drab and colorless, lit by banks of cold, harsh fluorescent lights hanging from a suspended ceiling, once white, now the color of dust. Christine's feet were pulled up behind her knees. A tattered backpack was tucked behind her legs, a strap looped over one of her legs above the knee. If anyone tried to snatch the backpack, she would know it immediately.

Christine's blonde hair, dirty and tangled, was draped over a man's shoulder. Her hands were stuffed inside the pockets of her cheap, puffy, polyester jacket. She was sound asleep.

The man was Viktor Daaé, her father, pale, gaunt, needing a shave. His clothes were dirty and somewhat the worse for wear, not as dirty and worn as the hardcore homeless, but there was a reason he and his daughter were in a bus station so late this night and not in a hotel. He dozed fitfully. One of his arms was wrapped around a tattered violin case, the other around his daughter. Between Viktor and the end of the bench were their worldly belongings: two duffel bags, a shopping bag, and a sleeping bag.

A janitor, wearing a uniform that was once a color somewhere between dark blue and dark gray, with a sewn-on name tag of white with red letters, listlessly pushed a dust mop across the hard, shiny floor. The creaking of the mop handle mingled with the slight buzz from the fluorescent lights as the janitor pushed past a line of plate-glass windows. A single bus was parked outside under the canopy, lights and engine turned off. It wasn't going anywhere tonight.

The ticket agent, a young man wearing a white shirt and black tie, with a plastic name tag above the pocket, stepped from behind the ticket counter and stopped at a bank of switches along the wall. He flipped some switches, some of the lights went out, and the glare on the floor was suddenly not quite as harsh. The janitor continued rearranging the dust on the floor.

The ticket agent approached the bench.

"Sir."

Viktor stirred and opened his eyes slightly. The ticket agent waited for him to respond.

"Yes?"

"The bus station is closing for the night. You can't stay here."

Viktor sat up straight, nudging Christine.

"Yes, of course."

Christine opened her eyes and seeing nothing of interest, closed them and snuggled against her father's shoulder. Viktor nudged her again.

"Wake up. We have to go."

Christine sat up straight and wiped her eyes. She looked around the empty room, and then at the ticket agent. He seemed to be someone in authority, and Daddy seemed anxious, so she disengaged the backpack from her leg and prepared to take leave of the bench.

The ticket agent hovered as Viktor stood and began gathering their belongings.

"Do you have a place to stay?"

"We will manage."

In the years behind the counter the ticket agent had heard many accents but this one was a bit different, Eastern European perhaps, or Scandinavian, but not one heard often in a bus station in the Texas Panhandle.

"There's a shelter, not far from here."

The ticket agent pointed toward the door. Viktor looked in that direction.

"Go one block, turn right, head south, turn left at the Santa Fe Building. It's in the next block after that."

"The Santa Fe Building?" Viktor asked.

"It's a tall old building. You can't miss it."

Christine reluctantly pulled on her backpack.

Viktor picked up the violin case and the rest of their belongings and eased Christine toward the door.

"Good luck," the ticket agent called behind them.

Viktor looked over his shoulder as he pushed open the door.

"Thank you, sir. Thank you very much."

The ticket agent watched as they turned to go. Definitely Scandinavian, he thought, probably Swedish, judging from the look of the blonde child. English was compulsory in Swedish public schools, he knew from years of voracious reading, and nearly all adult Swedes spoke very good English, with only a slight accent.

All travelers had a story to tell, especially those traveling by bus, and the ticket agent often passed the time behind the counter on the night shift by trying to guess what those stories might be. He assigned identities to individuals, and relationships to couples or groups. Criminals, spies, kidnappers, adulterers, runaways had all passed through the bus station on his watch, some no doubt, as he assigned them in his flights of fantasy, but almost all their stories were certainly more mundane.

No, the ticket agent decided, the man wasn't a kidnapper. The girl wasn't a runaway. It was obviously a father and daughter fallen on hard times. But these two were not the ordinary bus passengers sleeping on a bench. Although clearly destitute, or close to it, there was something about them, especially the little girl. He silently wished them well. He knew he would likely never see them again, never know their real story.

Snow blew in as Christine stepped through the door and into the night. She pulled the hood of her jacket over her head. She was accustomed to snow, and wind, but this night was particularly bitter, and having just awakened from a warm, comfortable sleep, even more bone-chilling. The snowflakes were dry, like tiny pellets, not big and wet and sloppy, and they scattered on the wind like white dust when they hit the pavement.

It frequently snows sideways in Amarillo, tonight blown by a stiff north wind. Fortunately, Viktor and Christine were headed south, so they pulled up their hoods over their heads, clutched their coats tightly, and walked briskly with the following snow. Christine wore her backpack and carried the shopping bag. Viktor lugged everything else.

Hardly anything was open in downtown Amarillo at night, and many of the storefronts were vacant anyway, a sad testament to years of suburban flight, consumers' preference for soulless shopping malls and strip centers instead of the vibrant downtowns of decades past.

The dry snow danced in little whirlwinds across the decades-old, well-worn, red brick streets. Small snowdrifts formed against all available surfaces. The traffic lights flashed, no drivers around to care. Up ahead was the Santa Fe Building, the top glowing like fire in the night sky, enormous red letters spelling out "Santa Fe" in all four directions. Christine looked up, not much impressed. It wasn't nearly as tall as the old buildings in downtown Chicago, and "Santa Fe" meant nothing to her.

Although long since eclipsed by taller, glass and steel boxes, the fourteen-story Gothic Revival building loomed large over downtown Amarillo. Completed in 1930, it once housed the headquarters of the Panhandle and Santa Fe Railway, a Texas subsidiary of the Atchison, Topeka, and Santa Fe Railway, but railroad operations had been consolidated, then merged, and the building stood vacant for years before being repurposed into county offices while retaining its historic character and standing tall as a reminder of a time gone by. It had been many years since a passenger train called at Amarillo. Somehow the bus didn't have quite the romance of the rails.

Viktor and Christine turned at the corner, and up ahead in the next block, as promised, was a neon cross glowing in the night. As they drew nearer, a small unlit sign became apparent: SHELTER.

Viktor tried the door. It was locked. He rang the doorbell and waited. Christine pressed her face into her father's coat for protection against the blowing snow. They stepped back as an older gentleman pushed open the door. His appearance, clothing, grooming, and manner indicated that he was not a resident at the shelter. Neither was he an employee. He was a volunteer, enjoying a comfortable retirement from a successful career, but he missed getting up and going to work every day, the interaction with others, and the feeling of contributing. Volunteering at the shelter provided him with all that, albeit without the paycheck. He had rather not work nights, but he took his turn on the night shift without complaint.

"Come in. Come in."

Viktor pulled the door open further and Christine stepped quickly under his arm and into the warmth. Relative to the cold outside, it was almost too hot, but it felt wonderful on Christine's rosy cheeks and nose.

"The man at the bus station said we might be able to stay here, just for the night," Viktor said hopefully.

"Yes, of course. Please come in."

Viktor followed Christine into the large dining room.

"We have an early bus in the morning."

"Where are you headed?"

"Los Angeles."

"Well, the weather will certainly be better than here," the volunteer said with a smile. "Are you hungry?"

Christine's head turned quickly. She didn't speak, but her eyes gave her away. Her stomach was growling.

"Yes, thank you, if it's not too much trouble," Viktor responded.

"We always have a pot of soup on in the kitchen." He looked at Christine. "Do you like soup?"

Christine smiled and nodded her head.

"Soup would be wonderful," Viktor answered. "Thank you."

"Have a seat."

Viktor and Christine dropped their baggage to the floor and sat down at the end of a row of folding tables. Viktor pulled her close to him and hugged her tightly.

A row of fluorescent lights came on. Viktor looked around the room. It was filled with long rows of folding tables and chairs. The walls were decorated with religious art and large posters with positive, uplifting slogans. Along one wall was a serving line opening into the kitchen. Along the opposite wall was a rudimentary stage with a couple of folding chairs and an old upright piano.

The kitchen door swung open, and the volunteer emerged with a tray. He stepped over to the table, put down the tray, and placed a large bowl of hot soup in front of each of them. There was a small carton of milk for Christine, a cup of coffee for Viktor, and crackers in little cellophane wrappers.

"We only have decaf this time of night."

Viktor blew on the coffee and sipped. "It's fine, wonderful. Thank you."

Soup was always good, but on a cold winter's night in a strange place, when you hadn't eaten all day, hot soup was indeed wonderful. Christine dived in. Viktor tore open a package of crackers and handed them to her.

"Is it hot enough?" the volunteer asked.

Christine nodded her head rapidly, and then slurped another spoonful.

"There's plenty more in the kitchen."

"Thank you," Viktor replied.

The volunteer quietly stepped back into the kitchen, leaving them alone with their soup.

Their bellies full, Christine and her father took advantage of the shelter's laundry room, heavy-duty commercial machines, but without the coin slots, no small thing, as the cost of one load of laundry and drying at a Laundromat would easily pay for two meals on the dollar menu at McDonald's.

Christine sat in a plastic chair in the laundry room, leaning against Viktor's shoulder, staring vacantly at the washer, trying to stay awake. Clean clothes would be well worth losing an hour's sleep, but the steady hum of the washer on spin cycle made it difficult to keep her eyes open.

She used to love helping her mother on laundry day, especially in the winter. She would dive into the warm, fluffy pile of laundry—freshly dried laundry always smelled wonderful—giggling as her mother picked pieces off the top and folded them carefully, finally revealing Christine's smiling face, buried in the pile. Now it was just a chore, done only when the opportunity presented itself, and always desperately needed.

When the laundry was dry, folded, and put away in their bags, they moved on to the bathroom, baggage in tow, locking the door behind them. Viktor took advantage of the bag of toiletries provided by the shelter and went immediately to the lavatory to shave.

Christine wasted no time stripping off and jumping into the shower. She looked up with anticipation at the shower head and turned the knobs. She tested the temperature, and then stepped cautiously into the stream of water. She closed her eyes and let the hot, steaming water cascade over her face. She turned and tilted her head back, soaking her hair. She missed their large old bathtub, and the thick, rich bubbles, but most of all she missed her mother washing her hair for her.

Viktor washed and dried his face, and then dug through the bag of toiletries. He found aftershave and a bottle of shampoo. He stepped over to the shower.

"We have shampoo."

Christine immediately poked her hand through the shower curtain and reeled in the shampoo, wasting no time in getting it on her hair and rubbing it into a luxurious lather.

Viktor splashed on aftershave and looked in the mirror, satisfied with his improved appearance. He normally showered first and then shaved, and he knew the aftershave would not survive his own forthcoming shower, but it felt good at the time.

While Viktor took his turn in the shower Christine vigorously brushed her teeth, and then tried to dry her hair with a towel while rummaging through their bags for clean clothes. She had no pajamas and decided she needed something to wear for the trip from the bathroom to wherever they would be sleeping. She settled on jeans and a T-shirt, along with her jacket, which would be easier to wear than to carry.

With clean bodies and clothes, and carrying and dragging their baggage, they followed the volunteer through a large, dimly lit room, filled with cots, nearly all of them occupied. Christine, wearing her backpack, continued toweling her hair.

The volunteer stopped near a corner where there were two empty cots.

"I'm sorry, but our family rooms are full tonight. We've been quite overwhelmed of late. Since you'll only be here for one night, you should be all right here."

Viktor dropped some of the bags onto one of the cots.

"Yes, this will do nicely. Thank you."

Christine dropped her backpack onto a cot, and then turned and looked out over the large number of people, mostly men, asleep on cots. Some of them tossed and turned. One of them, with a heavy, ragged beard, was awake, and stared at her. She quickly turned away and busied herself drying her hair.

"Breakfast is served from six to eight," the volunteer said.

"Thank you. You are too kind," Viktor replied.

The volunteer quietly disappeared into the darkness, between the rows of cots.

Viktor pushed their bags under the cot nearest the wall.

Christine finished drying her hair, as much as possible with a towel, and spread the towel on the end of the cot to dry, hanging over the edge. She opened her backpack and dug through it, pulling out a hairbrush.

Viktor sat on the end of the other cot, pushed back, and spread his legs. Christine smiled and sat between his legs on the edge of the cot. She handed the hairbrush over her shoulder to her father.

Christine looked out across the room as Viktor brushed her hair. Her eyes momentarily connected with the bearded man, and then she quickly turned away. Her head bobbed as her father pulled the brush through her still damp and tangled hair. A dad could never be as gentle with a hairbrush as a mom, but he got the job done.

Her mother used to brush her hair every night, just before going to bed. It seemed so long ago, sitting on the edge of her bed, her mother brushing her hair, both singing, while Viktor played the violin in the living room. There was no singing now, and no violin playing, and this huge room full of strangers was a long way from their small, cozy house in Chicago.

She missed her mother, and her happy life before this, but she didn't complain. She still had her daddy, whom she loved dearly, and he her, unconditionally. It would get better, he told her, and she believed him. It certainly couldn't get much worse.

The bearded man was still watching her, so she closed her eyes and heard her daddy's violin, and her mother singing, and she smiled, her head bobbing somewhat less as the tangles disappeared and the hairbrush now slid effortlessly through her golden hair.

Viktor handed her the hairbrush.

"That should do it. We need to get some sleep. We have to get up early."

Christine slid off the cot, put the hairbrush in her backpack, and then placed it under the cot by the wall. She sat on the cot and looked out across the room. Thankfully, the bearded man had turned over. She pulled off her pants, folded them, and placed them on top of her backpack. She quickly slipped onto the cot and pulled the covers tightly around her neck.

Viktor followed a similar routine, removing and folding his clothes, and then pushed all their things as far as possible into the corner under Christine's cot. He pushed his cot against hers and climbed on. He rolled over to face her. He kissed her and tapped her nose with his finger. She smiled and closed her eyes.

THE DINING ROOM was crowded and bustling, mostly single men, but several women, and a few families, a group of people content to have a warm bed and a hot meal before facing another grim day on the streets. Many of them obviously had not taken advantage of the shelter's laundry and shower facilities. Some sat alone, staring into space, ignoring those around them, robotically moving scrambled eggs from tray to mouth.

Some were more social. This was their home. These were their friends. But for the dirty, ragged clothes, scraggly beards, leathery skin, and general unwashed and unkempt appearance, they could have been any other group of men having breakfast at the local diner, talking of politics and sports.

Viktor and Christine sat at a table where there were families with children. Christine was relieved to see kids her own age for a change, and not just adults, especially men, most of whom were scary looking. She looked up and smiled at a little girl, about five, across the table. The girl's skin was soft and smooth, her cheeks rosy, yet undamaged by life on the streets. The little girl smiled back, and then sipped her milk.

Viktor and Christine ate in silence, quickly finishing their meals. She emptied her carton of milk. He gulped down the last of his coffee and then pushed back from the table. He picked up both their trays.

"Wait here with our things. I'll be right back and then we will pay our bill."

The father of the little girl looked up. "You don't have to pay."

"It's okay," Viktor replied. "We don't mind."

"But it's free."

Viktor smiled and walked away, carrying the trays. He dropped Christine's empty milk carton into a large trash can, and then placed the trays and silverware in a bus tub.

Christine pulled on her backpack and picked up the shopping bag. Viktor gathered up the rest. The little girl's father watched as Viktor threaded his way between the tables with Christine close behind him, headed toward the stage.

They deposited their bags near the stage. Viktor placed the violin case on the edge of the stage, opened it, and took out his violin and bow. The little girl's father watched curiously as Viktor stepped onto the stage, followed by Christine.

Viktor began playing "Angel," by Sarah McLachlan, on his violin. Christine stood silently behind him with her head bowed. A few people turned to look, and then some returned to their breakfast, not particularly interested.

In the kitchen, pots and pans stopped clanging as volunteers looked out over the dining room toward the beautiful violin music coming from the stage.

Viktor took a step back, still playing the violin, and Christine stepped forward, raised her head, and began singing. The chatter stopped. There was complete silence in the room, except for Christine's voice and her father's violin.

Volunteers stood and stared, captivated. Hardened, grizzled, homeless men stopped eating and looked toward the stage as the music washed over them.

Could that incredible sound really be coming from this little girl? It was the full, rich voice of a mature woman, but with the softness of a young girl, filled with innocence, tinged by pain. Christine, possessed by the music, scanned the room, through hand gestures and eye contact with everyone present, appeared to be singing directly to each of them. Just hearing that voice was one thing, but seeing it come from that small, beautiful child was an incredible experience for those in the room.

It was the voice of an angel, descended to Earth on a cold winter's night in the Texas Panhandle, in from the gloom, and now bringing tears to the eyes of those who were privileged to bear witness.

The front door opened and a young man with a full beard, wearing a desert camouflage field jacket, stepped in, expecting the typical noise and commotion and a hot meal. Instead, he found all eyes on this tiny angel. He closed the door quietly, turned toward Christine and stood silently. Like so many other young veterans of the wars in Iraq and Afghanistan, he was unemployed and homeless, adrift in a nation that had forgotten him. But here was this young girl, immediately turning to face him, arms outstretched, palms up, welcoming him in from the cold. He stood trembling, tears flowing.

The song ended, and Christine pulled her hands together and held them at her breast. She tilted her head slightly and smiled ever so sweetly. Whatever possessed her had departed, leaving only a little girl smiling on the stage.

The audience sat for a moment in stunned silence, and then nearly everyone rose to their feet, clapping and cheering loudly. The young man at the door wiped his tears and headed for the serving line. He wasn't sure what he had seen, and heard, but it had, temporarily at least, silenced the fury in his head.

Viktor packed away his violin. He and Christine gathered their things and made their way to the front door, saying nothing, going as unobtrusively as they had arrived, leaving in awe a group of homeless people and volunteers, whose lives had just been enriched, their spirits lifted, if only for a moment.

The snow had stopped, but the fierce wind out of the north was now in their faces as they trudged toward the bus station. Christine looked up and saw "Santa Fe" glowing brilliant red like a beacon in the dark.

2

THE BELEN CUTOFF

DANIEL WAS INVOLVED in a poker game in the lounge car of the *Scout*, which had only recently been reinstated after being suspended for lack of traffic during the depths of the Depression. He was far better dressed than the others in the game and smoked more expensive cigars. He had scarcely noticed that his eastbound train had been stopped at Gallup, New Mexico, for more than an hour. This was not unusual, as trains occasionally pulled over onto sidings to allow oncoming traffic on the same rails to run through, or to be passed by a train with higher priority. It mattered little to Daniel, as he was thoroughly enjoying the camaraderie of the game.

The Santa Fe stationmaster at Gallup made his way down the aisle, stepped up to the poker game, and put his hand on Daniel's shoulder. "May I have a word, sir?"

"Certainly," Daniel replied.

"In your car, if you don't mind."

Daniel stood up, leaving his money on the table, and followed the stationmaster through the train and into the last car, his own.

Private railcars, or business cars, were the private jets of the era. Everyone who was anyone, and most all companies of any size, especially the railroad companies, had their own private railcars. They were set up in a variety of ways, depending on the owner, and the usage. Typically, they had multiple bedrooms, crew quarters for the servants, one or more bathrooms, kitchen, dining room, and parlor. Today's private jets might be fast, even comfortable, but they pale in comparison to the luxury of a private railcar. Railroads went to every town or city of any size or importance, and private cars could be attached to any passenger train, always at the end so they could be quickly dropped off at their destination. It was easy revenue for the railroads—the cars were owned and maintained by private individuals or companies—and all the railroads had to do was haul them, at an insignificant incremental cost. Perhaps more important than the revenue, those who traveled by private railcar were often potential freight customers, and that was where the real money was for the railroads.

At a time when railcars were made of wood and even the best paint job tended to quickly fade in weather, private railcars were highly varnished. In the early twentieth century, the sixty-foot varnished wooden cars gave way to modern eighty-foot steel cars, but "private varnish," the term used by railroad men to refer to private railcars, stuck and is still used today.

Daniel had weathered the Depression better than most. His speculative investments took a hit, but most of his wealth was in railroads, mining, oil, timber, and real estate. Real estate was down, but he still owned a lot of it, and he had no doubt that it would recover. His own private varnish, of the eighty-foot steel variety, built shortly after World War I, was not nearly as opulent as some, and he wasn't crazy about the decorating his wife Clara had done, but it was well-appointed and served his needs nicely.

Daniel and the stationmaster made their way to his private car at the end of the train.

"The Raton Pass is closed by snow," the stationmaster said.

"Lucky for me the *Scout* uses the Belen Cutoff," Daniel replied with a smile.

"Yes, but I have a problem and hope you might be able to help me."

"How can I help?"

"An opera singer, on her way to Chicago, has removed herself, bag and baggage, from the *Super Chief*, and sits in my office, as we speak, demanding to be put aboard another train."

Daniel laughed, "An opera singer?" Why was his poker game interrupted by this frivolous business?

"She is scheduled to perform in Chicago tomorrow night, and several company executives are being dragged to the opera by their wives."

"Why don't you just reroute the *Super Chief*?"

"I don't have that authority. Apparently, the company believes the plows will soon break through the pass and traffic will resume, but even if Raton reopens within hours, the *Super Chief* will be delayed."

As a result of the Railroad Wars of the late nineteenth century, which occasionally involved armed conflict between corporations, the Santa Fe had lost the Royal Gorge, but won the Raton Pass, a well-known route from the Great Plains through the mountains following the Santa Fe Trail into the New Mexico Territory. The pass was at an elevation of more than seven thousand feet, however, with a three and one-half percent grade. As the Santa Fe quickly expanded westward, through acquisitions, swaps, and new construction, traffic increased, and they began to look for a better crossing over the Continental Divide. The Belen Cutoff was the result, opening in the early twentieth century, cutting off just southwest of Albuquerque, through Belen, and making the mountain crossing through Abo Canyon, at an altitude more than a half mile lower than Raton, and with a grade of only one and one-quarter percent, through the newly built railroad town of Clovis, across the Texas Panhandle, and rejoining the mainline in Kansas. Much of the transcontinental Santa Fe freight traffic immediately shifted to the new route, but most passenger trains, shorter and lighter than the freights, had less of a problem with the grade and continued to use the Raton Pass. Some passenger trains, including the *Scout*, were routed through the Belen Cutoff, allowing them to serve Amarillo, a city of growing importance to the Santa Fe, while trains remaining on the Raton route provided service to Colorado and Santa Fe.

Daniel was sympathetic to the stationmaster's situation. Even if the plows managed to reopen the Raton Pass within the next few hours, there would be trains backed up in both directions, multiple sections of some, which had been added as a result of the improving economy. Even if they gave the *Super Chief* priority, which they almost certainly would, there were only so many sidings to store trains, and only so much one could do with a single track through a high-altitude pass in a snowstorm. The opera singer, although completely ignorant of railroad operations, and who likely had no idea there was another route available to Chicago, had correctly guessed that her best option was to get on another train. Unfortunately, the *Scout*, consisting of more coaches than sleepers, and pulled by a steam locomotive, was at the opposite end of the spectrum from the luxurious, all-sleeper, diesel-powered streamliner, the *Super Chief*, which, although it had only recently entered service, was already the crown jewel of the Santa Fe line, having immediately been dubbed "The Train of the Stars."

"Even if I wanted to put her on the *Scout*, the sleepers are sold out, and I can't very well put her in a chair car," the stationmaster opined.

Daniel laughed. "No, that would not be wise."

The *Scout* was a train for the common people. Daniel was just as happy playing penny ante poker with traveling salesmen as higher stakes games with the elite, and, of course, he had his own private car at the end of the train, so it didn't really matter to him which train he was on. The Santa Fe didn't really want old, heavyweight private cars hanging off the end of the *Super Chief*—it upset the aesthetics of the sleek, modern stainless-steel streamliner—and on this trip time was not important to Daniel, so the *Scout* through the Belen Cutoff was fine with him.

"Yours is the only private varnish in the yard. I would consider it a personal favor if—"

The stationmaster needed say no more. Doing a favor for the railroad was one thing but doing one for a stationmaster was something else entirely. Daniel made it a point to maintain good relations with stationmasters all along the line, regularly passing out expensive liquor and Cuban cigars. If you needed your private car set out, and especially if you needed it stored for a few days while you went fishing or hunting with business associates, having it handled expeditiously, serviced properly, and watched by the railroad police was important. If a stationmaster asked for a personal favor, Daniel was only too happy to oblige.

"Of course," Daniel immediately replied, although in his limited experience, opera singers were not only fat and ugly, but insufferable. He would make a little small talk, and then as soon as the *Scout* was on its way to Belen, he would excuse himself and rejoin his poker game, leaving his porter to deal with the diva. Luckily, Clara insisted on keeping the car stocked with the latest magazines of interest to women, even though she was rarely aboard, preferring to stay at their Los Angeles estate while Daniel traveled on business.

The stationmaster quickly returned with the opera singer, and two porters bearing baggage. To Daniel's surprise, she was not at all fat, petite in fact, and not ugly but a stunning beauty. She was also quite young, not yet thirty.

Daniel never made it back to his poker game—the conductor scooped up his money and returned it to his private car some hours later.

Daniel was smitten by the time the *Scout* entered the Belen Yard. After the second bottle of champagne—the diminutive diva could hold her liquor— Daniel and his new companion, clearly of less than stellar moral character, were sharing a bed.

While the *Super Chief* was still crawling through the snow and the traffic jam over the Raton Pass, the engineer of the *Scout* suddenly found himself with track priority on a relatively level road and was highballing it across the High Plains, arriving in Chicago several hours ahead of the *Super Chief*.

Upon arrival at the Palmer House in Chicago, Daniel found, delivered to his suite, a bottle of Jack Daniels, a box of Cuban cigars, and two tickets to the opera, compliments of the Santa Fe. Due to his generous assistance, the company executives would be able to enjoy the opera tonight, along with their wives.

Daniel laughed out loud. He had no doubt that the executives would have preferred any number of other diversions for the evening—it was keeping their wives happy that was obviously the reason for the gifts. He opened the Jack Daniels and poured a glass for himself, and one for the opera singer.

"Not today," she said, "I'm working tonight."

Daniel had reluctantly accompanied his wife to the opera a few times and cared nothing for it. She had to continually nudge him in the ribs to keep him awake. On this occasion, however, he found he quite enjoyed it, certainly more so than the Santa Fe executives.

Soon after his return to Los Angeles, Daniel found an excuse to make a business trip to Europe. With war clouds looming, the Continent was no place for women and children, so he would regrettably have to sail alone, and Clara understood. He would not be alone, of course, but in the company of his young opera singer on her European tour.

The diva dumped Daniel for a baron, with his own castle, but by then Daniel had discovered an abiding passion for opera and had tired of the diva's drama. He continued across Europe alone, attending every available opera and symphony along the way. He also paid close attention to the political situation, decided that war was imminent, and that the United States would ultimately be drawn in. War always offered an opportunity for immense profits, and this was not lost on Daniel.

The last opera he attended, shortly before sailing for New York, was *Turandot*. He was especially moved by "Nessun Dorma." He resolved that night to become a patron of the arts, a decision which would no doubt thrill Clara, at least until she discovered how it came to pass. Upon his return to the United States, he immediately began making substantial contributions to opera companies and symphonies, primarily across the southwest, along the Santa Fe line. He also decided to open a music school for children.

And so, a high mountain pass, a major winter storm, a favor for a station-master, and an illicit affair with an opera singer resulted in the creation of the Belen Conservatory of Music in Los Angeles.

Daniel's surname was Titshaw. Although due to his wealth and position, no one dared make jokes about it, at least to his face, he had endured endless ridicule as a child, and did not wish to subject future generations of children to that same emotional trauma. He had briefly toyed with the idea of naming it the Estelline Conservatory of Music.

Estelline was not only the name of his young paramour, but also a stop on the Fort Worth and Denver Railway where the mainline between Fort Worth and Amarillo branched off to Plainview and Lubbock. Daniel had been through Estelline many times, with an occasional side trip by automobile for hunting and poker at the 6666 Ranch at Guthrie. As a young man just starting out in business, Daniel had met and been much impressed by Captain Burk Burnett, who had carved the fabled 6666 Ranch out of the wilderness. Daniel took note of how Burnett's wealth increased dramatically when oil was discovered on the ranch and made it a priority to learn all he could about mineral rights.

That bit of history would no doubt have been lost on Clara, whose private investigators would certainly have discovered that Daniel's opera singer was also named Estelline. She was aware of his dalliance with the diva but said nothing—this was not the first and it would not be the last. Divorce was not as easy, or as well accepted, at the time, and although she would have been independently wealthy, she would have lost her social position as the wife of such a prominent man. No, she would remain married—they hadn't shared a bed, or even a bedroom, for years—so it wouldn't be a problem. She was quite content with her ladies' clubs, her charity work, the arts, and her social calendar. Still, there was no reason to push it, so Daniel settled on Belen as the name of his conservatory, his wife didn't object, and that would be that.

Clara was indeed thrilled when Daniel laid out his plan to build a conservatory so that children might pursue an education in music. She explained to him that a conservatory was more of a college than a children's school, and that what he envisioned was probably more accurately called a children's music school, or perhaps an academy if it were to also include instruction in subjects other than music. He was adamant, however—it was his money— he would damn well name his school whatever he wanted, and it would be a conservatory, like they had in Europe, for children in grades seven through eleven. A twelfth grade was added some years later when high schools across the country began doing the same. He did not see how a college education would be of any consequence to a musician.

Clara did wonder why her husband had elected to build a children's music school, of all things. They had four children of their own, two sons and two daughters, none of whom had ever expressed more than a passing interest in music, and only the youngest, Alfred, was still in school. Perhaps he was thinking of grandchildren yet to be born. Their eldest son, Daniel Jr. had just last year married his college sweetheart, Frances, giving Clara a granddaughter, Marjorie, to spoil.

Work soon began, and the Belen Conservatory of Music was completed shortly before the attack on Pearl Harbor, which was fortuitous as vast resources were soon diverted from the private sector to the war effort and most non-war-related construction projects ground to a halt. Clara threw herself into the design and the decorating, traveling extensively across the Southwest, along the Santa Fe line in their private railcar, shopping, and spending Daniel's money freely for art and furnishings. This suited Daniel quite well, as he wanted only the best, and the school's construction and furnishings reminded him of the great Santa Fe hotels along the line. The timber for the massive wooden furniture came from his own forests, transported on railroads in which he had a financial interest.

Daniel's wealth expanded greatly during the war—which he had correctly predicted and positioned himself to profit from—and the boom that followed, and by the time of his death, the conservatory's endowment was such that for generations to come any qualified student would be allowed to attend tuition free if necessary.

3

TWO-GUN HARRY

As Viktor nodded off Christine stared out the window of the bus, looking for something, anything, on the featureless plain to break the monotony. There was the Cadillac Ranch, which she found amusing, but that was just west of Amarillo, only minutes into the trip, and they had a long way to go. There was a whole lot of nothing between Amarillo and Albuquerque, but after a couple of hours, nearing Tucumcari, a sign caught Christine's attention: HISTORIC ROUTE 66.

The movie *Cars,* which Christine had watched many times on DVD, introduced a whole new generation to Route 66, and now she was on it. The cars flying by on I-40 didn't look anything like those in the movie, of course, but still, it was Route 66, where her mother had promised to take her someday, all the way to California. It should have brought a tear to her eye, but she had already cried a lifetime of tears before her twelfth birthday.

Her mother had seemed to be an encyclopedia of knowledge about Route 66, and Christine tried to remember that silly song her mother would play on the piano and sing, "Two-Gun Harry from Tucumcari." Christine had loved to hear her mother tell the story about the real Two-Gun Harry.

"Daddy, look! It's Tucumcari."

Viktor looked out the window. A large green sign said TUCUMCARI.

"Yes. Your great-grandmother Stella worked in a café in Tucumcari for a brief time."

"I know." She stared out the window, but there was little to see other than motels and fast-food places along the Interstate. She quietly sang a few bars of the song.

Many years ago, Tucumcari, New Mexico, was an important stop for both the Southern Pacific and Rock Island railroads. Dozens of trains passed through daily, both passenger and freight. There were few railroad routes across the Continental Divide, and most of them were at substantial altitude. Tucumcari was the mid-point of the route between Chicago and Los Angeles that offered the most southerly and lowest-altitude crossing. This was of no small importance to those suffering from lung ailments, and in the days before antibiotics, there were many. Although the passenger trains operated by the Southern Pacific, and jointly with the Rock Island, were somewhat less prestigious than those of rival Santa Fe, the route had advantages, and accordingly Tucumcari was a familiar stop to a great many people.

Trains often stopped at Tucumcari for crew and equipment changes and passengers would disembark to stretch their legs and get a bite to eat, especially when traveling on trains without a dining car. A colorful local businessman, Harry Garrison, would meet the train, dressed in a ten-gallon hat, fancy chaps, and wearing two six-guns strapped around his waist, firing blanks, or at least Christine's mother hoped they were blanks, into the air. The passengers would follow him like the Pied Piper back to Harry's Lunch, a café just across from the depot, for a home-cooked meal that some said was itself worth the trip. At the time everyone traveled by train, and many important people, entertainers, politicians, and business tycoons, had eaten at Harry's Lunch in Tucumcari, and so was born the legend of "Two-Gun Harry from Tucumcari," immortalized in song by Dorothy Shay, a singer of some renown in the forties and fifties, who obviously had made the stop at Tucumcari at least once.

During World War II millions of men and women in uniform transited the continent by rail, both by regularly scheduled passenger service and on special troop trains, along with endless freights carrying tanks, trucks, cannon, ammunition, food, and all the other necessities of war. While Harry was equally at ease with celebrities and the common man, no customers at his lunch counter were more important to him than those in uniform. His younger brother Billy had been posted before the war with the Cavalry at Fort Bliss, near El Paso, just down the Southern Pacific line from Tucumcari, and then went on to fight in the Battle of the Bulge where he was captured by the Germans.

Christine's mother had promised they would stop in Tucumcari on their way to California, and they would sing that silly song together while walking down the platform at the depot on their way to Harry's Lunch, or at least what was left of it, a faded sign on a crumbling building.

Railroad passenger traffic had dropped off precipitously during the fifties and sixties—the great passenger trains had been replaced by airliners and automobiles. When Amtrak took over nearly all rail passenger service in 1971, Tucumcari was bypassed in favor of the Santa Fe route over the Raton Pass. Harry, ever the entrepreneur, converted his buildings into a second-hand store, with doors facing onto the street opposite the old platform where, not that long ago, Two-Gun Harry had greeted throngs of passengers.

Christine was ten when her mother died, and her memory was never completely clear as to Tucumcari's importance in her mother's stories. Her mother's illness further impeded those memories, and the stories about Tucumcari, having something to do with Christine's great-grandmother Stella, died with her.

STELLA HAD GROWN UP on a farm, one of several children helping her parents, Welsh immigrants, scrape out a living on the often-inhospitable Oklahoma plains. Like so many other children growing up during the Great Depression she longed to escape the dreary life of poverty and struggle. Her older brother had been a Marine in the Pacific war and had managed to survive relatively unscathed a series of landings which had become legend. He went to college on the GI Bill, took a job teaching high school in the nearby small town, and helped his father on the farm. Stella loved to sing, and sang with the church choir on Sundays, but could only dream of a career as a singer. As soon as she was able, however, the pursuit of those dreams won out and she headed west, along Route 66, bound for southern California. The bus ticket took her only as far as Tucumcari, by way of Amarillo, but that would be a start. It was hundreds of miles from the farm, and she was on her way. She took a room in town and quickly found a job. The hours were certainly better than farming, tips were good for a friendly, attractive young waitress at Harry's Lunch, and there was a steady stream of customers in 1951. The nation was once again at war, and troops and war materiel were streaming through Tucumcari on the way to the west coast for transshipment to Korea by sea.

Business was slow at Harry's one fall day, a lull between passenger trains, and the customers were mostly locals and a few railroad men. Stella was just outside the café on a short break—she had memorized the timetables and knew another passenger train was due in soon. Her attention was drawn to an unusual sight, for her at least, a steam locomotive and tender pulling a single passenger car and a caboose. The passenger car was an older one, a heavyweight, eighty-foot Pullman, dark in color, not like the modern, stainless steel streamlined cars that frequently passed through. The car was pulled by a road locomotive, not a yard switcher—Stella had worked at the café across from the station long enough to know the difference—which made it even more unusual. The short train stopped directly in front of Harry's and an impeccably dressed older gentleman climbed down from the railcar and strode purposefully toward the café.

Daniel didn't often get to Tucumcari, he was a Santa Fe man—he owned stock in the company—but he had oil and gas holdings in southeastern New Mexico, along the Southern Pacific line, and whenever he was in town he always stopped at Harry's for lunch.

Stella recognized a good tip when she saw one—he must be rich, he apparently had his own train—and she moved to open the door for the old gentleman, but he quickly seized it and held it open for her.

"After you, mademoiselle." Daniel clearly wasn't French, but Stella was impressed. He was in his sixties but looked positively ancient to Stella. Manners were in short supply among the younger men she encountered, so this was a pleasant surprise.

Daniel waved at Harry and selected a table. Stella quickly produced a menu and whipped out her order pad. Daniel studied her name tag and then bellowed, "Hey, Stella!" which drew a laugh from Harry and a few others in the room, at least those who had seen *A Streetcar Named Desire*, which was recently in theaters.

"I get that a lot. My name's Estelline, but I think Stella sounds more modern." She waited for him to open the menu, but he never did. "What are you having?"

Daniel handed her the menu. "Harry knows what I want." He motioned toward two men in overalls, the engineer and fireman from his train, and the conductor, just taking a seat at another table. "Put them on my check."

When Stella brought his meal, chicken fried steak, mashed potatoes, and black-eyed peas. Daniel said, "I knew an Estelline once." He smiled wistfully. "She was an opera singer."

"Oh, really? I'm a singer too, or want to be at least, but not opera. I'm trying to make it to Los Angeles to break into show business."

When he finished eating, Daniel left a very generous tip, even more than Stella had expected, and when he went to pay the check, Harry handed him a box lunch for his porter.

Stella noticed a big fat cigar in Harry's pocket and a smile on his face as she held the door for Daniel. She stepped outside for a moment and watched him board the private railcar. Only then did she notice that painted above the windows, where it might normally have said PULLMAN or the name of the railroad, was ESTELLINE.

Daniel's private train had barely cleared the tracks when a westbound passenger train pulled into the station, and passengers flooded across the platform toward Harry's Lunch. Among them was Walter Williams, a handsome, personable young Marine on his way to San Diego. He sat at a large table filled with other Marines and smiled at Stella as she handed him a menu. It was love at first sight.

After three weeks of furious and passionate letter writing, Stella received a telegram. Walter would not be shipping out immediately as expected, but would be remaining at Camp Pendleton indefinitely, and would she do him the honor of becoming his wife? She immediately accepted. He wired the money for a train ticket, and she caught the next train for the coast. It wasn't the *Golden State*, the streamliner jointly operated by Southern Pacific and Rock Island that sought to compete with Santa Fe's legendary *Super Chief*, but at least she was on a train headed toward her soon-to-be husband in sunny southern California, and it was better than the bus, even if she did have to spend the night sitting up in a chair car instead of lounging in a private sleeper compartment.

"If the Corps wanted you to have a wife, the government would have issued you one," was a familiar saying, and Stella had to meet with Walter's commanding officer to convince him that it was true love and they planned to stay married forever, and that yes, she did indeed realize that he could ship out to Korea any day and there was a war on and he could be killed and she would be a young widow. She stood her ground, the Marine captain signed off, they went to a justice of the peace along with a few of his Marine buddies as witnesses, and the government issued Walter a wife.

From San Diego, it was an easy run up the coast to Los Angeles, and soon the young Marine wife was singing club dates on weekends, always escorted by Walter and as many Marines as could pile into a car. She was very popular with both bands and audiences, a striking blonde with a beautiful voice, who could segue easily from the upbeat songs of the day to mournful ballads and bring tears to the eyes of even the most hardened grouch. When she wasn't working in nightclubs, she never turned down an opportunity to sing for free in the officer, NCO, and enlisted clubs on the Marine base.

She was deliriously happy, doing what she loved, and married to the love of her life. She did not yet know she was pregnant when orders came down and Walter shipped out for Korea. He had never met his infant son when he was killed in a human wave attack by the Chinese Communists on the frozen, desolate Korean Peninsula, in 1953.

Stella left southern California aboard the Santa Fe *Scout*. She had scraped together enough cash for a sleeper for her and her infant son, but not for the *Super Chief*, which would have been a more comfortable, and faster, trip to Chicago over the Raton Pass. Her husband rode in the baggage car, in a government-issue casket. The train took the Belen Cutoff route through the Abo Canyon, and on to Amarillo, a city she had passed through once before, on her way west. The route bypassed Tucumcari—she knew Santa Fe didn't go there—but she reminisced about the wealthy old gentleman she had encountered the same day she met her future husband.

She changed trains in Chicago, the easternmost terminus of the Santa Fe, and took the first available, and affordable, Pennsylvania Railroad passenger train to Cleveland. She met her late husband's family for the first time and found them to be quite distant, paying little attention to their new grandson. They cooled even further when they realized Stella was the beneficiary of her late husband's GI life insurance. There was a reason that all servicemen were required to review their notification and GI life insurance documents before shipping out to war. Stella's husband had already taken care of these matters, soon after their marriage.

Stella buried her husband in the family plot, hoping the government would make good on the marker—the family had made no plans for one—and returned as soon as possible to California, Los Angeles this time. The GI life insurance check arrived—it looked to her like a large sum at the time—and would surely last her until she was able to establish herself as a singer.

Here Christine was now, in Tucumcari, or at least zipping past it on I-40, the boring ribbon of concrete that had so rudely replaced the storied Route 66. She had never missed her mother more than now. Her father was sound asleep, so she closed her eyes and tried to sleep, but that song kept going through her head, "Two-Gun Harry from Tucumcari." She remembered that the stories about her great-grandmother had a lot to do with trains, and she wished they were on a train now, instead of the bus. Had her mother lived, maybe they could have made the trip to California on the train.

Just east of Grants, New Mexico, the Burlington Northern and Santa Fe mainline crossed I-40 and then danced with it for hundreds of miles to the west. There seemed to be a steady stream of mile-long freight trains, stacked high with large, drab-colored metal boxes, and pulled by a string of diesel-electric locomotives. She never wondered what was in the boxes, or where they were going, but there sure seemed to be a lot of them. That the names on many of the boxes were either Korean or Chinese meant nothing to her. She tried counting the railcars, but invariably lost count when something else caught her interest, if ever so fleetingly.

By happy coincidence, the sun was low in the western sky as the bus passed through the aptly named Red Rocks country. Christine awakened her father and they delighted at the spectacular scenery while they munched on overpriced sandwiches that took too much of their remaining money at their recent stop in Albuquerque.

Darkness fell just as the view outside the bus window was finally improving and the only thing left to see were the lights of passing cars and trucks, and the now familiar triangular pattern of the lights on the diesel-electric locomotives leading the long freight trains through the night.

It was much easier to sleep on a bus than an airplane. The seats were larger, softer, and instead of a perfectly smooth ride accompanied by the shrill whine of the jet engines, on a bus you swayed ever so gently with the road surface, while being lulled to sleep by the steady, low-pitched rumble of the diesel engine. Christine finally drifted off to sleep, pretending she was on a train. Trains had beds, or at least the ones did that she saw in the old movies on television.

The Greyhound droned on through the night. The sun was now at their backs as the desert turned into populated areas, and then the outskirts of the sprawling Los Angeles megaplex.

Viktor dozed. Christine, in the window seat, was wide awake, trying to see everything at once as the bus crawled along in rush-hour traffic, west-bound on the San Bernardino Freeway.

Christine marveled at the enormous Union Pacific rail yard just off the freeway, with parallel tracks as far as she could see, long freight trains crawling through the yard, more trains than she had ever seen at one time in her life. The bus slowed to a crawl in heavy traffic as it drew nearer to downtown Los Angeles, which was just fine with Christine, allowing her to look and look and look.

She turned her head to follow something of interest out the window and then suddenly gasped.

"Daddy! Daddy! Wake up!"

Viktor immediately sat up and looked around. "What's wrong?"

"Look!" Christine pointed out the window.

An enormous steam locomotive blasted past the bus, right down the middle of the freeway, pulling a string of private railcars, oblivious to the slow traffic on both sides.

"What is it?" she asked.

"It's a train," her father answered.

"I've never seen a train like that."

"It's a steam locomotive. There used to be tens of thousands of them, everywhere."

"Even in Sweden?"

"Even in Sweden." Her father smiled. "Everywhere."

"It said Santa Fe on the side," she said. "Like that old building in Amarillo."

Viktor smiled and nodded.

Trains down the middle of the freeway were a familiar sight in Los Angeles, but they were short Metrolink commuter trains. Santa Fe steam locomotive 3751, operated by a local nonprofit group, was occasionally seen in southern California, pulling excursion trains such as this one, but never failed to startle motorists when it suddenly appeared in the center of the freeway, just feet away from motorists, blowing steam and smoke. It was a thrilling sight.

"I wish we were riding on that train instead of the bus," Christine said as she watched the private railcars zoom past the window, too soon gone. There was so much to see that she did not notice the name painted on the old heavyweight Pullman car at the end of the train: ESTELLINE.

She sighed and settled back into her seat; the momentary excitement now gone. Viktor closed his eyes and tried to nap.

There was no more snow, just plenty of sunshine and palm trees, just like she had seen on television. Everyone seemed to have their own car, and somewhere to go in it. Up ahead she saw a big green sign: Downtown Los Angeles. The bus followed the arrows on the sign, through the downtown canyons of tall buildings, finally pulling into the bus station.

Viktor and Christine stepped out of the bus station and into the hustle and bustle of downtown Los Angeles.

"Where do you want to go first?" Viktor asked.

"The beach!" Christine didn't hesitate.

"And which way is that?"

Christine shrugged. She had no idea. Viktor turned to face the morning sun.

"The sun is rising in the east. We are on the west coast, so we go?"

"West!" Christine pointed west.

They walked west, carrying all their baggage.

"How far is it?" Christine asked.

"Too far to walk," Viktor replied. "We will need a ride, but we have some things to see first while we are downtown."

It never occurred to Christine to inquire as to how her father seemed to know his way around this huge and strange city. She just assumed that daddies knew everything.

They walked through the city, dodging traffic, lost in the crowds, passing the mundane and the fantastic. Christine gazed upward at the tall buildings, and into the shabby store fronts, many with signs in various languages other than English. They passed through street vendors, wandering homeless, street preachers, an endless sea of restless humanity.

Soon the clutter faded, and the buildings and the sidewalks were far better maintained. They rounded a corner and Viktor stopped suddenly.

"What's wrong?" Christine asked.

Viktor pointed up at a large banner hanging from the Dorothy Chandler Pavilion. It said simply: OPERA.

Christine beamed, swirling around, and then stopped, staring up at the banner. "Someday I'll sing here, Daddy."

"Yes, my child, someday you will. And I will play for you in the orchestra."

They continued walking and stopped at another building. It was unlike the others in the area, only two stories, of Spanish Mission style architecture, with a red tile roof and lots of wrought iron. There was a bit of landscaping, and it was immaculate.

Near the door was a sign: BELEN CONSERVATORY OF MUSIC.

4

VIKTOR

Viktor Daaé was born to a farmer and his wife in Sweden. The family lived in a large farmhouse with Viktor's grandfather, who owned the farm. Since his wife's death Grandfather had spent less time working the farm and more time alone in his room playing his beloved violin. This irritated Viktor's father, who was left to run the farm with little assistance.

Grandfather was a naturally gifted violinist with no formal training. Although with proper training and direction he might have performed with the greatest symphonies, he, like generations before him, had remained a farmer. He would play the violin on Sundays, for gatherings of family and friends, and occasionally for some event in the village, but the fingers that so gently and effortlessly summoned exquisite music from the violin were daily committed to milking the cows, plowing the fields, repairing barns, fences, and equipment, and harvesting the crops. He tried to pass on his love for music to his children, but only one, a daughter, was so inclined. Her instrument was not the violin, but the piano, which she taught in Stockholm where she lived with her husband, a low-level bureaucrat. A second daughter married a local farmer, the third daughter became a schoolteacher, and running the farm fell to Viktor's father, the only son.

Viktor's father had no use for music, or education for that matter, beyond what was necessary to run a farm. He tolerated Grandfather teaching Viktor the violin since the old man still actually owned the farm, but Viktor was destined to one day take over the family farm himself and that was that.

Viktor had other plans. Although he was not afraid of hard work, he had no desire to spend his life on a farm. The world was a big place and he intended to see it. He also loved music, and the violin, and dreamed of escaping the farm and playing in an orchestra. There was no music education in the local school, beyond the fundamentals, and his father forbade him to take lessons from anyone other than Grandfather. Going to university to study music was but a fantasy.

Grandfather spent many hours teaching Viktor to play violin and required him to spend many more hours alone practicing. Viktor found this not a task to be dreaded, but pure joy, and the more he practiced and played the more joy the violin brought him. It was an escape from the drudgery of the farm. He envisioned himself playing with a great symphony orchestra, wearing a tuxedo, performing great works by great composers.

When the weather allowed, Viktor and Grandfather would often slip away after supper, hike down to the lake, build a fire and play the violin for hours under the stars. Viktor loved listening to Grandfather tell stories, and his favorite was the one about little Charlotte and the Angel of Music.

"All great musicians," said Grandfather, "are visited at least once in their life by the Angel of Music." He promised to send the Angel to Viktor when he died. The Angel would not come to him, Grandfather warned, unless he practiced his scales, learned his lessons, and had a good heart. Although Viktor enjoyed Grandfather's stories, he didn't really believe there actually was an Angel of Music. It was just a story.

Grandfather died when Viktor was fourteen, leaving him his treasured violin. There would be no more lessons. To avoid infuriating his father, Viktor would wait until everyone was asleep and then slip out to the barn to practice. He cleared out a small room and stacked hay around it to deaden the sound and prevent his father from hearing as he played for at least two hours each night.

One night, after two hours of frustration with a new piece he had been learning, Bach's "Chaconne," he gave up and put away his violin. As he turned to go back to the house, he heard the piece played by an incredible violinist. He was at first frightened, but then began to look about for the source of the sound. He could not find it anywhere, in the barn, the loft, or outside. The house was dark, everyone was asleep, and could not hear the music. Viktor went back into the small room, took out his violin, and began to play, this time hitting every note perfectly in harmony with the unseen violinist. It was an experience like no other. The small room in the barn became a grand hall and Viktor soared. Was this really the Angel of Music? Had Grandfather been right all along? Logic and reason said otherwise, but Viktor could not deny having heard what he heard, and there was no question that his music improved immeasurably. He said nothing; telling his father would have only resulted in ridicule.

On the morning of his eighteenth birthday Viktor arose earlier than usual. When his father entered the barn shortly later, he was incensed to find that the cows had not been milked. He went looking for Viktor to vent his rage, but the boy was nowhere to be found. An examination of his room revealed a considerable amount of clothing and other articles missing, including Grandfather's violin.

Viktor had planned his escape for years, saving his money from the few odd jobs he was allowed to do outside the farm, along with a small sum Grandfather had secretly given him shortly before his death. He had carefully made lists of what he would need to take with him, and anything that would be incriminating he had hidden away from the house. When the appointed day came, he packed the few remaining things he would need, and Grandfather's violin, and simply walked away into the darkness. He debated leaving a note for his mother, but feared that it would be discovered too soon, leading to a potential confrontation with his father along the road. He decided instead to send her a letter when he was safely away from the farm.

It was a long walk to the nearest town with a railway station where he would not be recognized, but Viktor had traversed it several times, carefully timing each one so that he would know exactly how long to allow for the trip on the appointed day. He arrived early, having failed to account for the excitement and adrenalin, and took a seat on a bench on the platform until the station opened. Tucked under one arm was a duffel bag stuffed with clothes and everything else on his list he felt necessary. Under the other arm was his treasured violin.

Viktor was first in line at the ticket window when it opened, purchased his ticket, and returned to the bench to wait for the train. It was not his first train trip, but it was the first on his own, which he found exhilarating. There was one transfer from the local train to the mainline, which he handled like a seasoned traveler. He loved riding the train, watching the landscape pass by on his way to Stockholm.

Corresponding through a trusted friend's address, Viktor had gathered all the necessary applications for employment and a passport. He found work immediately, washing dishes on a cruise ship, with the promise of being promoted to waiter as soon as an opening became available. Dishwashers could be found anywhere, but a polite, presentable young man who spoke English was more difficult to come by and Viktor soon gained his promotion.

Viktor found life at sea agreed with him and was ideal for a young single man with no money and no place to go. Room and board were included. The tiny room was shared with another crew member, but it was adequate, and the food was good and plentiful. The crew was somewhat stratified depending on their duties. For those members of the crew who the passengers never encountered, the cruise line hired whatever third-world nationals were willing to work for the least money. For those who had contact with passengers, Viktor found many more young people like himself, adventurers and university students working a year, or a season, at sea, and then returning to their studies. Many languages were spoken among the crew and Viktor used the opportunity to brush up on his rudimentary French and Italian.

Days off for cruise ship waiters frequently came on port days, while most of the passengers were ashore and eating in the local establishments. This suited Viktor quite well, as it provided the opportunity to explore, either alone or with other crew members. His ship worked the lucrative Mediterranean market, allowing him to visit a great many ports along the Riviera. While other crew members preferred to spend their time ashore drinking, dancing, and hitting on the local girls, Viktor frequently took along his violin and sat in with various groups at cafés. He was always welcome as word spread of the young Swede who played an enchanted violin.

Viktor also sat in on jam sessions aboard ship, not only with the crew members who worked as musicians on the cruise, but others as well. The genres and styles of music were all over the map, anything but what was played on the upper decks for the passengers, and Viktor could play it all.

In his off hours Viktor would play the violin whenever he could. His roommate enjoyed his playing, but after a while in their small room it became too much, so Viktor would scout the decks available to the crew for a secluded place to play. It wouldn't stay secluded for long, however, as crew members quickly gathered. Passengers also leaned over the railing of their own decks to listen to the haunting strains from below.

Getting a job as a musician aboard a cruise ship was no easy task, and Viktor had resigned himself to being a waiter for some time to come. He didn't mind, as he found the music played for the passengers to be rather boring, and he much preferred the jam sessions aboard and sitting in with small combos ashore. Nevertheless, when a violinist in the main orchestra became violently ill and had to be evacuated by helicopter mid-cruise, Viktor was pressed into service, and so began his career as a professional musician.

Viktor spent several years at sea, on a variety of ships, in the Mediterranean, Caribbean, and Pacific, both north and south. He called at many ports and met a great many people, both crew members and passengers, as well as those ashore. He was particularly fond of Saint-Tropez, which he had first discovered while accompanying other crew members when their ship was docked at Cannes. It was far more laid back than Cannes, and so were the girls.

While in the employ of the cruise line he visited all the major cities on the west coast of the United States and spent some down time between ships in Los Angeles. In the South Pacific, he made it to Auckland and Sydney where an Aussie crew member had arranged discounted tickets to a performance at the Sydney Opera House.

Transferring between ships on the cruise line allowed him time off to make extended excursions outside the ports where the cruise ships called. He traveled extensively ashore, frequently by rail, and visited the great opera houses and music halls of the world. He witnessed incredible performances and wished that his grandfather could have accompanied him.

His dream to see the world had become reality, but eventually he tired of the cramped accommodations and the limited repertoire of music aboard the cruise ships. He longed to play in a great symphony, where the music itself was the attraction, and not just an accompaniment to food, drink, and dancing aboard a cruise ship. He had become enamored of an attractive young singer on board his most recent cruise ship, plying the Caribbean, and had returned with her to Chicago. The relationship didn't last, but he found Chicago to his liking. There was a large Swedish community, and lots of opportunity to play music. He played weddings, bar mitzvahs and gave lessons. The work wasn't steady, but there was enough of it, and conditioned by the sparse living conditions at sea, he didn't require much.

He fell in with a group of musicians in Chicago and expanded his repertoire considerably. He played fiddle for a time with a country and western group before it broke up after a fight over money or, he suspected, the drummer's girlfriend. His goal of playing in a major symphony eluded him, not because he hadn't the talent, but because the life of a freelance musician suited him. He enjoyed seeing different people in different settings every day and playing a variety of music. He was as happy playing fiddle in a dive bar as first violin in a small orchestra for a society wedding reception.

Life was good, and far from the farm in Sweden, but as all young men eventually do, Viktor began to think about having a family of his own, and after moving into his own small apartment, he began taking on more violin students. Teaching came naturally to him, and his reputation spread. He demanded much of his young students, but their parents received more than their money's worth.

The historic and elegant Palmer House became a frequent place of employment—those with the money to afford an event at the Palmer House usually wanted only the best musicians, and there was no better violinist in Chicago than Viktor Daaé. Not only were his musical abilities superb, but in playing weddings over the years he had developed enviable presentation skills, and he would often be directed by the orchestra leader, as they played "The Blue Danube Waltz," to step onto the dance floor with the bride and groom as they danced, sweeping around them while playing his enchanted violin, much to the delight of those in attendance.

It was at one such wedding reception, as Viktor played violin for the newlyweds and their guests, that he took note of a beautiful young woman wearing a black skirt, white shirt, and black bow tie, efficiently clearing tables with a smile on her face while swaying to the music. Her name was Rachel.

VIKTOR WAS IMMEDIATELY attracted to Rachel. She was beautiful, blonde, and vivacious, and reminded him of the girls back home in Sweden. He watched her happy in her work at the wedding reception at the Palmer House, clearing tables while he played with the small orchestra so that the well-to-do guests could dance. A fortune they were wasting, he thought, but he was happy to have a paycheck, as was Rachel.

During a short break, Viktor had made his way to the kitchen where he cornered Rachel, told her some of the musicians would be jamming after the reception at a club nearby, and invited her to join them.

"Unlike the musicians, who simply have to pack their instruments and walk away, some of us actually have to work for a living, cleaning up after the rich people."

"I will get for you the address and you will join us later."

She found his accent and fractured English charming. He was certainly handsome, looked harmless enough, and she was so inclined. He was older, not that it mattered. She didn't recognize the address of the club, which was hardly nearby, and she didn't have a car, so she brought along a friend from college for protection, and a ride. One would never guess by looking at him— he was a brawny redneck—but he could make a piano do things it was never intended to do, and Rachel was quite certain that he would someday be a great classical composer, unless he elected a more immediate payday by hitting the road with his rock band, which was quite good. Like her, he had ended up in Chicago with parents pursuing employment. Rachel and the redneck were left to work their way through a local college with a rather undistinguished music department.

As they pulled into the parking lot Rachel noticed an abundance of pickup trucks and soon realized the "club" was a country and western dive bar. They had come this far, she was intrigued by the Swede, both she and Jim Bob shared a love for an extremely wide range of music, so they parked and went in.

They could hear the music long before they opened the door, and as soon as they did Jim Bob let out a loud "Yee-hah!" and Rachel immediately questioned her decision to accept the Swede's invitation. Yet she soldiered on, and while Jim Bob purchased a pitcher of beer from the bar, Rachel stood in awe as Viktor burned up his violin—or was it a fiddle—playing "The Devil Went Down to Georgia." She was suitably impressed, the audience was stomping the floor, the dance floor was on fire, and everyone was having a grand time. Viktor looked a bit out of place in his tuxedo, although without the bow tie, among a very diverse group, playing a variety of instruments.

Rachel was not unfamiliar with country and western music—her father had listened to it often, once the sixties had worn off. Rachel's grandmother, Stella, during her infrequent visits when she was sober, had shared a great variety of music with Rachel, including "Two-Gun Harry from Tucumcari" along with her accompanying story; torch songs, country and western, classical, and many more, all to the consternation of Rachel's mother, who, as far as she knew, never listened to anything other than church music.

After a mug or two of beer Rachel and Jim Bob were boot scootin' to "Cotton-Eyed Joe," as Viktor fiddled and fretted that she had brought a man along. She was here, however, and that was a start.

Jim Bob recognized one of the musicians, with whom he had played a couple of gigs, and had soon mounted the stage and taken up position at the piano. Viktor seized the opportunity to make his way to Rachel's table and inquire as to the status of her friend.

"What? No, he's not my boyfriend. He's just a friend from school."

It was exceedingly difficult to hear, as Jim Bob's rendition of "Great Balls of Fire" would have made Jerry Lee envious, but Viktor and Rachel attempted to talk over it, while their heads bobbed with the music.

"You didn't really expect me to come to a dive bar alone, did you?"

Viktor smiled, relieved. She seemed to be enjoying herself, as did Jim Bob, who was a maniac on piano.

"He's my wingman," Rachel said, which confused Viktor. "I think he's tracking multiple targets of opportunity," she added, which Viktor found even more baffling.

Viktor returned to the stage and his violin. Jim Bob hit on unattached cowgirls, or at least he hoped they were unattached, with varying degrees of success.

It was getting late, time to wind down, and Jim Bob took Rachel by the hand, dragged her onto the stage over her protestations, had a quick conference with the musicians, and Viktor began playing "The Tennessee Waltz." The crowd roared its approval, quickly taking to the dance floor, the other musicians joined in, and Rachel had no choice but to step up to the microphone and sing. The response was enthusiastic.

5

THE BEACH

VIKTOR AND CHRISTINE watched as students arrived at the Belen Conservatory of Music, some walking from the bus stop or subway station, others dropped off by private car. Christine noticed that some were dressed rather wildly and creatively. Many were carrying musical instrument cases. They appeared to be a happy lot, chattering and greeting each other as they swarmed into the school.

"Here is where you will go to school." Viktor said.

The conservatory was the purpose of their trip. Christine was too young at the time to remember, but her parents had often discussed moving to Los Angeles so that Christine could attend the Belen Conservatory of Music. Her mother was a secondary school teacher, and although music was her field— a position at the Belen Conservatory would have been a dream come true— she could teach other subjects as well, so they were confident she could easily find work in the greater Los Angeles area. Viktor, of course, was a fantastic violinist, and surely there would be session work, or at the very least weddings and other events such as he had worked in Chicago. By age six, Christine was something of a musical prodigy, and they were willing to take any job that would allow them to relocate to Los Angeles and get her into the conservatory where she would fulfill her potential.

If only her mother could hear her sing now, Viktor thought as they stood here at the doorstep to their goal, it would confirm what they knew years ago, and reaffirm their efforts, and now his alone, to do whatever was necessary.

"Can we go in?" Christine asked.

"Not today. First, we must find a place to live, and a job. Then we will apply to the conservatory. You will audition, they will be amazed, and you will be accepted."

"When Daddy?"

"Soon, my child, soon."

Christine was downcast, but she understood.

"I thought you wanted to see the beach."

Christine nodded her head enthusiastically.

"Then let's go."

"How do we get there?" Christine asked.

"By train, if we have enough money." He pulled out a few dollar bills. "This should be sufficient to get us started on our way."

Christine was intrigued, and then thrilled. She looked around. "Where's the train?"

"It's underground."

"There's a train under the ground?"

There were trains under the ground in Chicago, of course, but Christine had never been on them, or even knew of their existence. She had sometimes accompanied her mother, father, or both, downtown, but they always went in their car. She had often seen the elevated trains in Chicago, leaning forward to look up through the windshield or rear window of the car as the trains roared overhead.

"Oh no! We're being run over by a train!" Viktor would shout as they drove under the elevated line. Christine would squeal and hide her head, and then come up laughing and watch as the train sped away.

Christine had never been on either the subway or the elevated trains in Chicago, or any other train for that matter. This trip continued to be full of surprises.

They gathered their things and descended into the Civic Center Metro station. Christine took in all the new and unusual sights below ground as Viktor studied the map and timetable for a moment, and then put much of the last of their money into a slot in a machine. Tickets emerged.

"We will take the Red Line to Hollywood," Viktor said.

"Cool." Christine had no idea what that meant, but it was fine with her. She was eager to continue her adventure.

Christine's anticipation grew as they waited on the platform along with other riders, an eclectic group to be sure. She heard the rumble of the train, increasing in volume, and was then startled by the wind that blew through just ahead of the train's arrival. Christine pushed ahead, eager to board, but Viktor held her back while passengers got off the train. Then they joined others in boarding and selected seats well away from other riders. Viktor pulled their baggage as close as possible, putting some under the seat and some in his lap. He had ridden enough subways to know that in some cities the police would ticket you for putting your bag in a seat even if there were plenty of empty seats available. The last thing he wanted was trouble with the police, and a ticket might cost the same as several days of food.

Christine watched excitedly as the doors closed and the train began to move. It wasn't what she had imagined, but it was a train. There was nothing much to see through the windows of a subway train, but Christine looked anyway.

They emerged from the subway into the brilliant sunshine on Hollywood Boulevard. Christine spun around, trying to see everything. She was in Hollywood!

"Which way is west?" Viktor asked.

"Um." Christine looked around in all directions. She had no clue, which she signified by shrugging her shoulders.

"Where is the sun?"

Christine whirled around and pointed at the sun.

"It's still morning, so the sun is where?"

"In the east!" She turned and pointed again. "And the beach is west!"

They had not gone far when Viktor stopped suddenly and looked around.

"What?" Christine asked.

"I can't find it."

"Find what?"

"Somewhere along here was a nightclub, where your great-grandmother sang a long time ago."

"Really?" Christine looked around, searching for any sign.

"Your mother mentioned it years ago. It was near the Pantages Theatre."

Christine excitedly pointed at the Pantages.

"Yes, near here. I wish now I had written it down. There are so many things I wish I had written down."

"What was the name of it?" Christine asked.

"I cannot remember."

They both looked around at the storefronts. There was no nightclub. Many of the buildings had been repurposed over the decades, along with much of the rest of Hollywood, and some were vacant, with plywood covering the windows.

HOLLYWOOD BOULEVARD WAS crowded with people and cars. The lights of the Pantages Theatre were ablaze as a Duesenberg touring car drove past. The car pulled up in front of a nightclub across the street and the doorman rushed out to open the back door. Daniel stepped out, immaculately dressed. People on the sidewalk stopped to stare, hoping to see a famous movie star. They were disappointed that Daniel was no one they recognized, maybe a producer or studio head, or maybe just a rich man. Their attention soon shifted to the doorman as he extended his hand for Daniel's companion, a stunningly beautiful young blonde. A low-cut dress displayed her ample assets. An expensive fur covered her bare shoulders. She smiled at the growing crowd.

Flashbulbs began popping as the young woman preened. Daniel allowed her a moment in the spotlight, and then, as if rehearsed, she stepped over and took his arm. The doorman rushed ahead to open the front door of the nightclub.

Inside, a big band played on stage, and Stella sang "I'll Be Seeing You." The dance floor was packed.

Daniel was shown immediately to his table, one of the best in the house. His young companion clung to his arm as she smiled, searching the crowd for a familiar face, or at least a fan.

A waiter hovered as Daniel pulled back a chair for his companion. Drinks were ordered and the waiter dispatched.

When the song ended, Daniel bellowed, "Hey, Stella!" There were a few gasps and chuckles from the crowd and on the dance floor as people turned and stared.

Stella lowered her head and covered her face for a moment, and then said, "I'm going to take a short break." As the band resumed playing, she threaded her way through the dancers to Daniel's table. He stood and kissed her hand. He then pulled back a chair and she took a seat.

"I love your movies," Stella said to the young woman.

"Thanks, but I wish the studio would give me better stories."

"I may have to get in the picture business," Daniel said, winking at the actress.

Stella placed her hand on Daniel's. "How long has it been, four years, five?"

Daniel nodded. "I see you made it to Los Angeles."

"Oh, yes. I married a Marine, spent a few months in San Diego before he shipped out to Korea, and here I am, singing on stage in Hollywood."

The actress was curious about the relationship between her date and the singer, but wisely said nothing.

Stella turned to the actress. "We met in Tucumcari. I was waiting tables at Harry's, near the station, when this gentleman arrived on his own train."

"You have your own train?" the actress asked.

"Just a private railcar," Daniel said. "We'll have to take a trip in it."

"I need to get back to work," Stella said, pushing back her chair. "It was so nice seeing you again."

Daniel stood. "Yes, it was." He pulled a business card out of his vest and handed it to her. "Let's stay in touch."

Stella hurried back to the stage, spoke briefly to the bandleader, and then launched into "Two-Gun Harry from Tucumcari."

VIKTOR SEARCHED ONCE MORE for the nightclub, shook his head, took Christine by the hand, and they continued west on Hollywood Boulevard.

"Maybe someday I can sing in a nightclub," Christine said.

"No!" Viktor scolded. "No nightclubs for you. You will sing in the great opera houses of the world."

Christine giggled. "I was just kidding, Daddy."

"And when you are a rich and famous opera singer you can buy for me a house on the beach where I will sit on the deck and play violin for the dolphins."

"Someday, Daddy, someday."

Viktor stopped at Hollywood and Vine, looked around, and pointed north. "There."

"What is it?"

"That round building, Capitol Records. Maybe someday you will make records for them."

"Why is it round?"

"It looks like a stack of records," he said.

They walked along Hollywood Boulevard and there was plenty to see, tourists from all over the world, and all manner of things for sale in the shops along the street, which they could not afford. They stopped frequently to look at the stars on the Hollywood Walk of Fame.

At the Dolby Theatre, Viktor extended his arm and Christine took it. They walked a few steps toward the entrance and then stopped and turned.

"I'd like to thank the members of the Academy," Viktor said.

Christine laughed. "Oh, Daddy, you can't get an Academy Award for playing the violin, can you?"

"I'll have to speak to the Academy about that."

They continued on to the Chinese Theatre. Christine, in the best tourist tradition, placed her hands in the famous handprints. Viktor looked around at the considerable foot traffic on the street and announced, "This looks like a good place."

Christine gathered all their belongings around her and sat leaning against a wall. Viktor opened his violin case and placed it on the ground, not far from Christine, where she could watch it closely.

He began playing "La Campanella," and people immediately began to gather and listen. Some were merely entertained, but others, who knew music, were amazed. Here was a violin virtuoso playing on the streets for donations. Many obliged, dropping money into the open violin case.

After picking up a few dollars at the Chinese, they boarded a bus and continued their journey westward, along Santa Monica Boulevard.

"Why can't we take the train?" Christine asked.

"There is no more train," Viktor replied.

"Why not?" Christine wanted to know.

Why not indeed.

Christine marveled at the sights along the way. Viktor pointed out places of interest.

"Rodeo Drive. Do you need to do some shopping?" he asked.

"Sure! I'll need an elegant gown to wear to the opera house." But, of course, she knew she would be doing no shopping in Beverly Hills anytime soon. The Metro Bus continued westward.

In Santa Monica they made their way to McDonald's on the Third Street Promenade, ordering from the dollar menu and sitting just outside to eat. Christine looked around and saw homeless men who looked much the same as those at the shelter in Amarillo. When she had a home, and plenty to eat, Christine, like most others, had paid little attention to the homeless. Now that she was one of them, she noticed them everywhere, and it saddened her.

"How far to the beach?" Christine asked, determined to think of something more pleasant.

"We're almost there. Did you bring your bathing suit?"

"Daddy! It's too cold to swim in the ocean." She took a bite. "Besides, I don't have a bathing suit."

After they had eaten, they walked along the Promenade. It was a winter weekday, light pedestrian traffic, just the usual mix of the well-to-do, the homeless, a few tourists, and a smattering of street performers.

"This looks like a good place," Christine said.

"Yes, yes it does," Viktor replied, "but better tonight maybe, and first we must see the beach. Is that not what you wanted?"

Christine nodded her head vigorously.

The sun was low in the western sky as they walked down Broadway. Christine could see the ocean and could barely contain her excitement. They crossed Ocean Avenue and made their way through the park towards the pier, across the bridge, and finally down the steps to the beach, which was deserted. They walked across the sand, stopping well short of the water. They dropped their belongings and stared at the ocean.

"Better in the summer, I think," Viktor said.

"Oh, Daddy, of course it will be better in the summer."

Viktor put an arm around her and pulled her close. She snuggled into his side.

"You will have by then a bathing suit."

Christine's blue eyes, wide with amazement, sparkled in the setting sun. It may have been winter, they may have been homeless, and she may have had no bathing suit, but Daddy had promised her the beach, and there it was. She was content.

IT WAS NIGHTTIME on the Promenade and the sidewalk cafés, warmed by propane heaters, were crowded. Lots of people strolled. Street performers of all types were more plentiful than during the day.

Viktor and Christine located a suitable spot and Viktor played "Zigeunerweisen" on his violin. Christine, with their baggage, waited nearby. People dropped money into the open violin case.

Christine immediately took notice as a policeman approached. She hunkered down, trying to be as unobtrusive as possible. The policeman stopped, listened to the music, and waited for Viktor to finish the piece.

"May I see your permit?" the policeman asked.

"Permit?" Viktor replied, tensing up.

"You need a permit to perform on the Promenade."

"I'm sorry, sir. I did not know."

"You'll have to move along."

"Yes sir. Of course."

There were a few boos from the crowd, who were very much enjoying Viktor playing the violin.

"Where would I go to get such a permit?"

"City Hall."

"Thank you, sir. Thank you."

More people dropped money into the violin case. Christine didn't move. Her eyes were glued to the policeman.

Viktor quickly put his violin in the case, on top of the money, closed it, and watched as the policeman walked away. Christine stood and pulled on her backpack. Viktor gathered the rest of their things and they moved along in the opposite direction of the policeman.

As soon as the policeman was out of sight, they ducked into McDonald's, stowing their baggage at a table outside, as far as possible from others. Viktor looked around furtively, then quickly opened his violin case, scooped up a few bills, and pocketed them. He closed the case and handed it to Christine. She sat at the table, guarding their belongings, while her father went to the counter to order.

Although Viktor's performance had been cut short, they had collected several dollars and so he splurged on dinner, ordering four items from the dollar menu, but no drinks, of course, only water. Water was free, and he had no intention of paying even a dollar for water with a bit of sugar and food coloring in it.

Christine never complained about what they had to eat or drink, but it pained Viktor to watch her eat ever so slowly, sipping water while all the other children in view had enormous tankards of soft drinks and walked away leaving behind on the tray, the table, or the floor, more food than Viktor and Christine had to eat. "Things will get better," he often told himself at times like this.

THE SAME SEA BREEZE that provided free air conditioning for Santa Monica in the summer now brought a chill over Palisades Park as Viktor arranged their baggage alongside a fence overlooking the Pacific. He spread out the sleeping bag and baggage on the lee side, as it were, of the fence.

Christine looked out at the Pacific, mostly shrouded in darkness but for the lights of a few container ships offshore, and then glanced over to the pier, ablaze in light. She turned and looked out over Ocean Avenue, at the cars, many of them expensive, whizzing by. There were people on the sidewalks, coming out of the fancy restaurants, shops, and hotels. It was a world apart from those setting up camp in the park. There were several other makeshift campsites, though probably none with such a young child.

Christine crawled into the sleeping bag, pulled off her shirt and tucked it into her backpack. She pulled off her pants, rolled them up, and placed them under her head, serving as a pillow.

Viktor looked around, checking everything, accounting for all their belongings, making sure Christine was as safe as possible in these circumstances, slipped into the sleeping bag, and then followed her procedure in undressing and making a pillow. He pulled the violin case into the sleeping bag beside him and zipped up the bag.

He put an arm around Christine, who snuggled close, and they looked up at the stars.

"A permit will cost money, and we need money for a room."

"We can sleep here, Daddy. I don't mind."

"This is not a good place for a young girl."

"I'll sing, Daddy. People always give us more money when I sing."

"You shouldn't have to sing on the streets. A man should be able to support his child."

"But I love to sing. You know that."

"And people love to hear you sing."

"And to hear you play, Daddy. They love to hear you play."

He pulled her closer and hugged her tightly.

"Tomorrow I will look for a job."

"Surely there's a symphony in a place this big. You could be first violin," Christine said, trying to encourage him.

"You don't just show up from nowhere and become first violin of a major symphony orchestra," Viktor replied. "I'll find something less grand to start."

He kissed her and tapped her nose with his finger.

Christine rested her head on his shoulder, closed her eyes, and sang softly, "Ar Hyd y Nos," until she went to sleep.

It took longer for Viktor to fall asleep. There was much on his mind. Although there was little to stay for in Chicago, he had just uprooted his precious daughter from the only home and friends she had ever known and dragged her, sometimes on foot, to Los Angeles to make good on a promise to his late wife. They were destitute and alone, having only each other. He hoped that was enough and that he had made the right decision.

He closed his eyes and saw himself playing his violin in the living room of their house in Chicago, listening as his wife sang "Ar Hyd y Nos." Rachel sat on the sofa with Christine between her legs, brushing her long hair while they both sang.

6

THE WHITE TRAIN

Fame and fortune eluded Stella, but she did manage to make a living as a nightclub singer for some years—she was quite good—dragging her young son Hudson across the country, by train, bus and automobile, and an occasional DC-3, from one club date to the next. Hudson always preferred the train and amassed quite a collection of railroad timetables. He was able to identify a great many locomotives on sight and used railroad names as if they were his friends.

There was also a succession of men, none of them keepers. By the time Hudson turned eighteen, he was ready to strike out on his own, and leave his mother in the company of her current musician boyfriend.

Unfortunately, Hudson turned eighteen at the height of the war in Viet Nam, and immediately faced the draft. He decided the best course was to get it over with rather than wait for the inevitable "Greetings" from Uncle Sam and enlisted in the Marines, like his father. He returned from Viet Nam with a Purple Heart and a Bronze Star with a "V" device.

He debated going to college on the GI bill but decided instead to follow up on a lead from a friend in the Marines about an unusual government job in Amarillo. His military service and war record were in his favor, and although his background investigation uncovered his mother's problems with drugs and alcohol, he had somehow managed to make it through the sixties unscathed, due in no small part to being in the Marines for much of the time, and so, after extensive psychological evaluation and training, became a guard on the White Train. Although it was painted a variety of colors over its career, and it no doubt had some official name, its original color was white, and it was never called anything other than the White Train.

When asked what he did for a living during that time, Hudson joked that he was a delivery boy. "What do you deliver, pizza?" was the inevitable response. Hudson would always laugh and say "Yeah, that's it, pizza."

Although a branch line was eventually built into Santa Fe to handle local traffic, the Atchison, Topeka and Santa Fe Railway mainline never actually made it to its namesake city. After crossing the high mountain pass through the Sangre de Cristo Mountains at Glorieta, the Santa Fe Railway struck out downhill toward Lamy and then westward, a far less difficult engineering challenge, than following the original Santa Fe Trail northwest along the mountainside into Santa Fe.

The tiny town of Lamy, New Mexico, had a very unusual distinction. Nearly every nuclear scientist, every technician, every soldier, every worker on the Manhattan Project, and many of their family members, alighted from a Santa Fe passenger train at Lamy, and then traveled by automobile or bus through Santa Fe to Los Alamos, where the atomic bomb was born.

Santa Fe's transcontinental route through New Mexico, by way of the Belen Cutoff, and on to Chicago, ran right past the Pantex plant, just northeast of Amarillo, where U.S. nuclear weapons had always been built, repaired, and disassembled. A labyrinth of tracks branched off the mainline into the plant where the White Train once picked up and delivered nuclear weapons during most of the Cold War.

There were special railcars for carrying the warheads themselves, with a considerable degree of security built in, but with such an incredibly high-value cargo each White Train included a guard car where armed guards ate and slept, with two of them always on duty, watching out through the gun ports in the guard tower on top of the car. The guards could lay down a withering amount of automatic weapons fire, if only to hold the would-be thieves at bay until relief arrived, in force. The government had no intention of losing cargo from the White Train.

Although the likelihood that one of the things would explode into a nuclear fireball was virtually nil, it would have been a public relations disaster to have a nuclear weapon in a ditch somewhere, so the White Train maintained a very low track speed, often taking weeks to complete a round trip between Amarillo and far-flung sites such as the submarine base at New London, Connecticut. Boredom was a constant companion for the guards on the White Train.

It was a good job for a young, single man, but Hudson soon met Ruth, an attractive preacher's daughter in Amarillo. She was aghast to discover what he did for a living, but true love won out, her father performed the marriage ceremony, and Hudson and his new bride bought a house in Amarillo using a VA loan. It wasn't long before a beautiful baby girl, Rachel, joined the family, and Hudson's life riding the rails delivering nuclear warheads came to an end.

Taking advantage of contacts made during his tenure on the White Train, Hudson found work with the Santa Fe Railway, and the little family began moving up and down the Santa Fe line as he worked his way up. As an only child, growing up on the road, Hudson wanted several children, and a stable home. His wife seemed content with just the one girl, and they finally put down roots in a suburb of Chicago, where the Santa Fe had its headquarters.

Hudson's wife was merely devout when they married, but over the years she became even more extreme in her manifestations of faith. Hudson had gone to church with her, mainly because it was the expected thing to do, but he had never been particularly religious. This began to change in Chicago, however, when he and his wife started attending a new church, far more radical than anything he had experienced before. His wife embraced it immediately, but it took a bit longer for Hudson to drink the Kool-Aid. Eventually coworkers at the railroad began to avoid him rather than endure his endless proselytizing. By the time she was a teenager, Rachel had become adept at nodding her head in agreement, while letting the religious propaganda roll off her like so much rainwater. Not surprisingly, her dating life suffered immeasurably, not only because her parents forbade it, but because eligible suitors, as well as casual friends, desired to maintain a safe distance from her parents.

Rachel thought she was dealing with it well, counting the days until she would go off to college, anywhere but Chicago, and was shocked to the core when, just after her seventeenth birthday, her father quit his job a few years short of eligibility for a full railroad pension, they sold the house, the cars, and all their possessions, and donated the money to their church, leaving Rachel with only as many of her clothes and belongings as she could pack into two suitcases. She had suspected for some time that their new church was really a cult, and so she bolted, probably wisely, with her two suitcases, and her parents left for unspecified missionary work in some unnamed place, without her. Rachel never heard from them again.

Rachel moved in with her best friend and insisted on getting a job to support herself, even though her friend's parents were happy to provide her with room and board until she graduated from high school. After that she was on her own. She found a room and worked a variety of jobs, usually several at a time, determined to put herself through college. She was working a catering job for a society wedding—the pay and tips were quite good—at the Palmer House in Chicago when she met a handsome Swede who played an enchanted violin, working the same wedding.

VIKTOR LEANED AGAINST the wall in a parking structure next to the door to the women's restroom, their baggage at his feet, with one hand resting on the violin case.

In the restroom, Christine brushed her teeth, her eyes darting over at a homeless woman washing her clothes in the next lavatory. The woman appeared a bit crazy, talking to herself and making bizarre gestures, so Christine hurried, spit out the toothpaste, rinsed her mouth, gathered her things, and darted quickly through the door.

"Let's go," Christine said as she came out of the restroom. "There's a crazy woman in there doing her laundry."

They made their way to Santa Monica City Hall, where Christine waited with their bags while Viktor waited in line.

"So many rules just to play music," Viktor said to Christine as he approached with a sheaf of papers. "We have to get photographs, which also will cost money."

They headed out of City Hall with the intent to violate the law in order to make some money by playing music, so they could buy the permit to be compliant with the law while making some money by playing music.

They walked along Ocean Avenue, headed toward the pier, where Viktor had learned they could obtain passport-style photos inexpensively.

Viktor stopped suddenly and turned.

"What is it?" Christine asked.

There was a sign in the window of a coffee shop: HELP WANTED.

They quickly entered the coffee shop and Viktor ushered Christine into a booth in the corner, along with all their bags, while he retrieved an application from the manager and went to work filling it out. After a few minutes of frustration, he walked over to the manager.

"I don't really have an address or a phone. We just got into town. But I am ready to work. I am a hard worker," Viktor said.

The manager looked over the application. "You really need an address, and a way to contact you."

"I'll be here every day. You can count on me."

The manager glanced over at Christine, sitting quietly. "Is that your daughter?"

"Yes sir."

"Where will she stay while you're at work?"

"We will manage."

"Have you eaten today?"

"We have to buy permits at City Hall to perform on the streets, and have our photographs made, and that will take all our money. I'm a musician, but I need steady work."

The manager looked again at Christine. "Well, it might work out. We close at three in the afternoon, and the best time for street performers is in the evening. I definitely need someone reliable, not another drifter."

"We are not drifters. We are staying. I plan to enroll my daughter in the Belen Conservatory of Music."

A waitress brought plates of hot food from the kitchen and while the manager was on the phone, after staring for a moment at the steaming plates of hot food, Viktor and Christine ate the best meal they'd had in a very long time.

"Get used to it, Mr. Daaé," the manager said as he returned to the table. "One meal per day is included. Employees can also take home leftover cooked food at the end of the day."

"Thank you. Thank you." Viktor started to stand, but the manager put a hand on his shoulder, and he sat back down.

The manager handed Viktor a slip of paper. "Here's the address of a motel that rents rooms by the week. It's not much, but it's close by, you can walk to work, and it should do until you can find something more suitable. They are expecting you. I'll cover the first week and take it out of your pay. You start at six tomorrow morning. Don't let me down."

Viktor jumped to his feet and shook hands with the manager. "I'll be here. I won't let you down."

The motel wasn't much, but it was far better than Palisades Park. There was a small refrigerator, a hot plate, and a microwave. There was an old television, and a clock/radio, but no phone. A small table and two chairs stood near the window. There was a heater, but no air conditioner. This was Santa Monica after all, where even many homes of the wealthy had no need for air conditioning.

The lavatory had rust stains and mineral deposits, as did the combination tub/shower, along with a dingy, moldy shower curtain. A small window above the toilet provided ventilation.

Christine plopped immediately onto the one double bed. She was still a child, Viktor told himself, and one bed was better than one sleeping bag, but soon she would be a young woman, and he must find a better place to stay, with a second bed. For now, however, this looked like the Palmer House.

7

SUO GÂN

AFTER UNPACKING THEIR bags at the motel, which didn't take long as they had so little, Viktor and Christine headed out to complete their mission for the day, go to the pier to obtain passport-style photos, and then back to City Hall where they turned over nearly all their money for two street performer permits. Now they were legal, but would soon be hungry again, so they immediately headed back to the Santa Monica Pier, with permits, and violin, in hand, to earn enough money for food. It would be a week before Viktor would be paid, and they would be deducting the cost of the room, so he knew it was essential that they make as much money as possible by performing on the street.

It was a wooden pier, a century or so old, with a roller coaster and Ferris wheel, various other carnival-like attractions, places to eat, and a collection of shops selling overpriced souvenirs. Having been featured in dozens of movies, television shows and music videos, it probably looked vaguely familiar to Christine, although she hadn't really seen that many movies, or much television, in the past few years.

Most of the pier was closed to vehicles, other than those making deliveries, which was a good thing, as it creaked and groaned under their weight, and was reserved for pedestrian traffic, which was quite heavy in the summer, not so much in the winter. The postcard photos were always taken in the summer, and at night, when the Ferris wheel and coaster were ablaze in colored lights, never on a gloomy, depressing winter's day, like today.

It was late afternoon when they returned to the pier. There were only a handful of street performers, and a few people strolled. There were a few fishermen at the rails where several weathered signs warned, NO CASTING, and so the fishermen dutifully lowered their lines into the water below, although some ignored the signs, whipped back their rods without so much as checking behind them to see if they were about to snag some unsuspecting passerby, and cast away, as if placing their hook a few feet further from the pier might somehow magically increase their yield.

Viktor played the violin, the case open for donations, and Christine, wearing a bright red scarf around her neck, sang "Suo Gân." People stopped and listened, amazed to hear those words, that sound, coming from this beautiful child who seemed possessed by the music, using her hands as much as her voice, accompanied by that incredible violin.

One of those who stopped to listen, with particular interest, was Zoe, a pale-skinned young woman of twenty-one, with heavy eye makeup, black lipstick, black fingernails, black hair, wearing an ankle-length black vintage dress, black shoes, carrying a large black parasol, seemingly from another era entirely, completely out of place. Then again, this was California.

Standing beside the Angel of Darkness was Raoul, thirteen, wearing a private school uniform with jacket and tie. He listened intently, watching Christine closely, following her eyes, her hands, her every move, enthralled by her clear, sparkling voice, although understanding not a word of the strange language she was singing.

As the song came to an end, people dropped donations into the case. Christine turned towards her father, and as she did, her scarf came loose and floated away on the gentle sea breeze. She shrieked and stretched out her arms, but the scarf was gone, headed out to sea.

Raoul quickly ditched his jacket and shoes. "It's all right! I'll get it!" He dashed toward the rail.

"No!" Zoe shouted as she realized what he was doing.

Zoe moved toward him, but it was too late. He was over the rail, dropping feet first into the ocean. Viktor and Christine joined Zoe at the rail, along with a few other spectators, and looked down below as Raoul swam toward the scarf, floating on the surf.

"Get out of there!" Zoe cried out, followed by an excited stream of what appeared to Christine to be French.

But Raoul was a man on a mission. He retrieved the scarf, waved it triumphantly, and set out for shore.

Viktor, Christine, and Zoe, carrying Raoul's shoes and jacket, scurried along the pier, watching as Raoul swam down below. They hustled down the stairs to the sand as Raoul struggled out of the Pacific and sprinted toward them with his prize.

As they met, Raoul held out the soaked scarf, breathing hard, quite pleased with himself, although shivering mightily—there's a reason California surfers wear wet suits even in warmer weather. Christine, rather bemused, accepted the scarf.

"What were you thinking?" Zoe demanded.

Raoul shrugged.

"Thank you, young man. It was her mother's scarf." Viktor said.

Christine looked curiously at her father, and then turned to Raoul and said, "Thank you."

She extended her hand to shake, but Raoul took it, bowed, and kissed it.

"I am Raoul, rescuer of young ladies' scarves."

Christine smiled and looked down at the scarf, dripping in her hand. No one had ever bowed and kissed her hand before, and she was at a loss as to the proper response.

"Hi. I'm Christine."

She then suddenly leaned forward and impulsively kissed him on the lips. He was speechless, gazing into those blue eyes as she backed away, smiling.

"Okay," Zoe said, "now we have met cute, but I really do have to get you home and dried off. Your mother will kill me. Maybe I can just put you in the dryer with your clothes and she will never know."

Zoe grabbed Raoul and pulled him away. He turned and called out, "What's your number?"

"I don't have a phone," Christine called after him as Zoe hustled him off the beach toward the parking lot.

CHRISTINE'S SCARF HUNG over the shower rod as she washed her face. She dried off and touched the scarf. It was still damp. She smiled. He was a foolish boy, but so very cute, and dashing.

She stepped out of the bathroom, wearing a T-shirt as a substitute for pajamas. Viktor brushed off a pair of his pants on the table.

"You have cereal for breakfast tomorrow, milk in the refrigerator, and a sandwich for lunch. I'll bring something from the café for dinner, and then we will go out and perform."

Christine opened a dresser drawer and pulled out a hairbrush. "Okay."

"I'll barely make enough at the café to pay for this room. We'll need more money."

"It's okay, Daddy. I love to sing."

"Stay in the room. I don't want you going out until I've had a look around the neighborhood. And don't let anyone in, except the maid, if there is one."

"Why did you tell that boy it was Mama's scarf?"

"A small lie, which hurts no one, but enhances someone else's self-esteem, cannot be a bad thing."

Christine sat in a chair in front of a mirror and started brushing her hair. "We got it at a thrift store."

"He doesn't know that." Viktor said as he took over the hair brushing. "He did a gallant thing, and we had nothing with which to reward him, so I let him believe his deed was more than it was."

"Actually, his deed was pretty stupid. He could have drowned," Christine replied.

"Yes, yes, he could."

"And that water must have been freezing," she said.

"He seemed quite taken by you."

Christine smiled. Of course he was.

CHRISTINE WAS SOUND ASLEEP in the double bed. Viktor, fully dressed, leaned over and kissed her. He wiped a tear and kissed her again, almost enough to wake her, but not quite, and then slipped quietly out the door, hoping that she would remember to put on the chain as soon as she got out of bed.

The coffee shop did a brisk breakfast business. Waitresses scurried about, carrying multiple plates and pots of coffee. Viktor, wearing a white apron, quickly and efficiently bused tables. He washed mountains of dishes, wiped down stainless steel tables and food preparation surfaces, and stayed very busy, determined to impress the manager, who he knew had taken a chance on him.

Viktor ate his free lunch, as well as snatching apparently untouched food from plates in the bus tub—every calorie he could eat for free at the café was another calorie for Christine later. He enjoyed the job. It brought back fond memories of his early days aboard the cruise ship, and he felt like they were finally making real progress toward their goal.

The café closed at three, but Viktor stayed at least another hour or two to clean up, which he did conscientiously. He hung up his apron, retrieved a bag of leftover food from the refrigerator, opening it and displaying it to the manager to make sure there was no suspicion he was taking something he was not entitled to.

He walked to the motel, carrying his small bag of food, humming a tune, quite satisfied. He climbed the stairs at the motel and knocked on the door. Christine, lying on the bed, feet in the air, reading a textbook and writing in a notebook, jumped up. She rushed to the door and opened it part way. Seeing her father, she closed the door, released the chain, and opened it wide.

Viktor stepped into the room, held up the bag, then leaned over and kissed her. Christine set the table while Viktor heated the food from the bag in the microwave.

With a white hand towel draped over his arm, doing his best impression of a waiter at an upscale restaurant, he stepped over to the table and placed food in front of Christine, and bowed. "Dinner is served, mademoiselle."

"Thank you, kind sir."

Viktor sat down and they ate.

"Your lessons?"

"English, history, math, social studies, and a little Italian."

"Your music?"

"Scales, scales, and let's see, more scales."

"Did you work on the new piece?"

"A little," she said. "How was work?"

"It was work, nothing more. But this evening, we will make together great music."

She tried to smile, nod, and fork food all at once.

It was busy on the Third Street Promenade after Viktor and Christine finished their dinner and headed out to perform. As Christine hovered nearby, closely watching the open violin case, Viktor played Chopin's "Nocturne in C# minor" on his violin. While the crowd was enchanted by Viktor's playing, Christine picked out a few of the larger denomination bills from the violin case and pocketed them, leaving the smaller ones for bait, then quietly backed away and sat on a bench while her father played. Christine knew from experience that people might drop a single into the case while palming a five on the way out. This was their food money, and she watched it like a hawk.

Professor Valerius, a distinguished-looking gentleman in his fifties, and his lovely wife, casually dressed in an upscale sort of way, stepped out of one of the sidewalk cafés and stopped to admire the music.

As Viktor finished the piece Professor Valerius applauded politely and nodded.

"Exquisite, sir," the professor declared.

"Thank you, sir." Viktor bowed.

Professor Valerius dropped a twenty into the violin case, which Christine
quickly retrieved as soon as the professor and his wife turned and strolled
away.

After rounding the corner, Professor Valerius paused for a moment to
listen to an angelic voice, singing "Casta Diva." He and his wife returned
to the Promenade and watched as Viktor played and Christine sang.

THERE WEREN'T MANY people on the Santa Monica Pier the next afternoon.
Raoul, in his school uniform, along with Zoe, still Goth, still dressed in black,
although not nearly as elaborate as before, searched the pier. Raoul turned
to her in frustration.

"Where could they be?"

"It's a weekday. Not many street performers on the pier."

"Let's try the Promenade."

"It's a weekday on the Promenade as well."

"We have to keep looking."

They piled into Zoe's car and set out to search Santa Monica, driving up
and down the streets in the area of the Promenade, Palisades Park, anywhere
they could think of.

A maid pushed her cart along the second-floor walkway of the motel
where Viktor and Christine were staying. She paused in front of a room and
listened to very loud singing. She crossed herself and continued her rounds.

Inside the motel room Christine danced, stark naked, on the bed, with her
arms, head and hair flailing, singing loudly and with great enthusiasm. It
wasn't classical, opera, pop, or even easy listening.

Zoe and Raoul had just turned off Ocean Avenue into a less-than-desirable
neighborhood when Raoul shouted, "Stop!"

"Why?" Zoe asked, slowing but not stopping.

Raoul rolled down the window. "It's her!"

"How can you tell?" Zoe asked.

"It's her. I know it is. Pull over."

Zoe reluctantly pulled over. Raoul leapt out of the car and dashed toward
the alley. He looked up at a small, open window on the second floor of a

motel. Zoe took the first available parking spot, got out of the car, and approached Raoul. He pointed at the open window. They could hear the singing coming from the window.

"You sure that's her?" Zoe asked. "That sounds like headbanger music."

"I'm sure."

He picked up a few pieces of gravel and started throwing them at the window. One finally found its mark.

In the motel room, Christine, song over, jumped off the bed and stuck the landing. Wet clothes hung from the backs of chairs and every other available surface.

Thonk! She walked toward the sound, coming from the bathroom. Another small stone struck glass. Thonk!

She stepped into the bathroom, which was also covered in wet clothing. It was laundry day. She was forbidden to leave the room, so she had washed absolutely everything, including what she was wearing. No one was to be allowed into the room so being naked was not a big deal, and very efficient as far as laundry day went. She picked up a pair of damp panties from the toilet lid, moved them to the lavatory, climbed on the toilet and peered out the window.

"Raoul?"

"Wait," Raoul shouted from down below. "We're coming up."

"No!" Christine exclaimed. "You can't."

Raoul raced around to the front of the motel, up the stairs, and rapped on the door. Zoe finally caught up.

"How do you know this is the right room?" Zoe asked.

"I counted the windows from the corner."

"But of course you did."

Raoul impatiently knocked again.

The door opened just a bit and Christine, bare shoulders, looked out without removing the chain.

"Can we come in?" Raoul asked.

"Daddy said to not let anyone in the room."

"Can you come out?"

"Daddy said to not go out."

"Can you at least open the door?"

Christine hesitated. "I'm like, naked."

Oops. Zoe decided to take charge. "We can wait while you put something on. He's been dragging me all over town looking for you. We have something to tell you."

"Okay, just a minute," Christine said, then turned and headed into the bathroom, forgetting to close the door, leaving it slightly ajar.

Raoul leaned in for a look, but Zoe quickly covered his eyes with her hand and whispered, "Avert your eyes you little perv."

Christine, wearing a towel, returned, took off the chain, and opened the door. Raoul moved forward.

"You have to stay outside," Christine warned.

Raoul stopped. "Is this where you live?"

"Yes."

"Cool."

Zoe elbowed Raoul.

"My parents would like to invite you and your dad over for dinner," Raoul said.

"He's not here. He's at work."

"You can ask him when he gets home."

"Okay."

"Do you have something to write on?" Zoe asked. "We'll give you our number."

Christine turned and looked for something to write on. Zoe glanced around the room. There were schoolbooks on the table. Dishes, canned goods, a loaf of bread, sat beside the microwave. It didn't take her long to evaluate the situation.

Christine returned and handed a notebook to Zoe, who wrote down their information.

"Do you have a phone number?" Zoe asked.

Christine shook her head.

"That's okay," Zoe said. "Have your dad call us or Raoul will be banging on your door again."

Zoe handed Christine the notebook.

"Okay," Christine said, taking the notebook. "I'll tell him."

Christine looked around the door as she started to close it.

"Wait," Raoul said, reaching out to stop the door from closing. "That song you were singing on the pier, it was really pretty. What's it called?"

"Suo Gân," Christine replied.

"What?"

"Suo Gân," Christine repeated.

"Is that Japanese?" Raoul asked.

Zoe smiled.

"No, it's Welsh," Christine replied.

"Where do they speak Welsh?" Raoul pressed on.

"In Wales, I guess."

"Where is Wales?"

"Next door to England."

"Is that where you're from?"

"No, I'm from Chicago."

"Oh, okay."

"Bye." Christine pushed the door closed.

"Bye. Call me." Raoul held up his thumb and little finger like a telephone.

Christine twisted the lock, put on the chain, turned, leaned against the door, and smiled.

"That's your song," Zoe said to Raoul as they walked away.

"What's my song?"

"Suo Gân," Zoe said. "That's the first song you both heard together. That Christine was singing it when you met is a bonus, or maybe a sign."

"Cool," Raoul concluded. A sign indeed.

8

RACHEL

Rachel was now regularly singing with Viktor's group, working weddings, bar mitzvahs, club dates. The money was decent, and they had soon moved in together and started talking about marriage and kids. She knew Viktor had a Green Card—she saw him show it when they signed on to work a wedding reception for a politician running for federal office—so she was sure he didn't just want to marry her for legal residency. Marriage was agreeable to her, and their plans suddenly accelerated when she became pregnant.

It was not easy finishing her last year of college while working and raising a new baby girl and paying off hospital bills—musicians and caterers going gig to gig were not covered by group health insurance. But graduate she did, with a teaching certificate, and before long they scraped together enough for a down payment and moved into a cozy little house in the Chicago suburbs. During the day Viktor was a stay-at-home dad with the infant Christine while Rachel taught at a nearby middle school. At night she took over diaper duty while Viktor ventured out to make music and bring home some desperately needed extra cash. Rachel stayed home with Christine, wishing she could be out singing with her husband, but relishing every moment with her beautiful daughter.

Christine had been a happy child, and when the time came, she dearly loved going to school where there were other children her own age. She wished there were more music lessons, or at least singing, but budget cuts always hit the arts first. She looked forward to the day when she could sing in the school choir—that was only for the older children—so she would have to get her music at home, and there was plenty to be had there. Rachel was a music teacher and Christine took everything she had to offer, quickly picking up piano, but singing was her passion.

The Daaé home was always filled with music. Musician friends would often stop by after dinner to jam, and Christine was always right in the thick of it, at least until her bedtime, although that was sometimes extended. It was not uncommon for a broke musician, or Jim Bob, to be sleeping on the sofa and Christine would delight in poking him awake in the morning and would then run screaming and giggling as he chased her down the hallway. Musicians were her extended family and she had never felt more loved and content.

Viktor and Rachel both wanted several kids, but first they had to pay off the hospital bill for the first one and put a few dollars away for the future. At least they were now covered by health insurance through her teaching job, but that wasn't nearly enough when Rachel was diagnosed with breast cancer and thoughts of more kids suddenly evaporated.

Viktor and Rachel were amazed, and outraged, at how much money hospitals could demand over and above what the insurance company paid. When Christine was eight, Rachel became unable to work and lost her health insurance altogether, not that it mattered because the bills were already insurmountable. Being unable to pay several hundred thousand dollars wasn't much different than being unable to pay ten thousand.

Viktor did the best he could, working part-time jobs in addition to performing at every opportunity, scraping together cash wherever he could, to try and maintain a semblance of a normal home life for Christine, who increasingly knew that something was very wrong. Rachel was weak and sick, and while Christine's friends laughed and played, she took on ever more of the cooking and cleaning and tried to nurse her mother back to health, a huge responsibility for a ten-year-old.

Rachel had eclectic tastes in music, as did Viktor, which they passed on to Christine. When she should have been resting, Rachel worked with Christine on her music, teaching her songs, helping her with technique, phrasing, and intonation. Easy work, to be sure, as Christine soaked it up like a sponge. She also revealed a facility for languages, and Rachel soon introduced her to Italian opera, or at least arias, which Christine dearly loved to sing.

It was obvious to both Viktor and Rachel that Christine had a rare gift. Not only did she have perfect pitch, and the ability to pick up any genre of music effortlessly, she had the voice of an angel. Grown men wept when she sang.

When Viktor came home one day, exhausted from his jobs, the girls surprised him with a new song Christine had learned, "Con te partirò." He immediately declared it his favorite song in all the world, and his aches and pains were suddenly gone. They ate the fast food he had brought home and played the violin and piano and sang into the night. It was one of Christine's favorite memories.

CHRISTINE WAS ELEVEN when her mother died. The adults told her that her mother had gone to a better place, to live with Jesus, to be with the angels, or some other euphemism, but to Christine her mother was just gone, no amount of flowery language would change that, and she cried and cried and cried.

Teachers from Rachel's school took up a collection to buy a casket and two grave spaces, but there was no money for a headstone, so a simple metal marker would have to do. Who knew dying could cost so much? They held a graveside service, which Viktor expected to be small, but dozens of Rachel's friends from college, fellow teachers, the caterers and banquet workers and others whose lives she had touched attended, a few of Christine's classmates with their parents, along with many of the musicians Viktor had worked with at all those weddings and bar mitzvahs.

Christine was so overwhelmed by her mother's death that Viktor did not even suggest that she sing at her mother's grave. Instead, he let go of her hand long enough to play "Nigun" on his violin and Christine leapt into Jim Bob's arms, flung her arms around his neck, wrapped her legs around his waist, and cried her eyes out.

One of Rachel's friends from her catering days was now the catering manager the Palmer House, and she was able to arrange a small banquet room at no charge, so the funeral party gathered there for a wake of sorts. There were enough musicians to put together a small orchestra, which seemed to fluidly morph into a rock band, or country and western, depending on their mood, and who had the microphone.

Even the music could not lift Christine from her sadness, and the endless stream of adults coming over to express their condolences as she sat with her father only made it worse. Viktor noticed this, put his arm around Christine and said, "Let us go up and make together some beautiful music. Maybe you will feel better."

Christine nodded agreement, mounted the stage and a hush fell over the room. With Jim Bob on piano, Viktor on violin, and an assortment of musicians backing her, she began to sing, segueing from one song, and genre to the next, as fast as the musicians could reconfigure. The audience watched in astonishment as she switched effortlessly from "Ombra mai fu" to "The Tennessee Waltz" to "The Way You Look Tonight." Well-dressed people began to slip through the doors, coming from other events in other banquet rooms, joined by catering staff and the kitchen help, just to listen to this incredible voice. Soon the crowd spilled in through the doorways and ringed the perimeter of the room, trying to not intrude on whatever it was that was going on in there, but still drawn to the angelic voice of that beautiful child on stage, surrounded by a motley group of outstanding musicians. The general manager, who remembered Rachel as a cheerful and hardworking catering employee putting herself through college, also stepped in. He had reluctantly agreed to comp the room but was now so very glad he did. The Palmer House, in more than a century of existence, had hosted some of the greatest performers in the world, from opera to punk rock, and had no doubt seen some legendary jam sessions, but none, he was sure, could touch what he was witnessing at this moment.

Christine sang, in her own world, completely detached from her surroundings, except for the few seconds it took to relay her next selection to the musicians. She would then turn back to the microphone, assume the persona of her mother, or her great-grandmother, whom she never really knew, or someone else entirely, and enthrall the audience with one beautiful, moving song after another.

It was "Angel" that brought down the house.

VIKTOR HAD TRIED to find Hudson and Ruth when Rachel died, but to no avail. Rachel had not heard from Stella since shortly after Christine was born, and presumed her to be dead, probably from drugs or alcohol, and so Viktor was on his own.

On advice of a friend, Viktor had stopped making the house payments even before Rachel died. The theory was that it would take months for the bank to foreclose, and then even more time after that to file an eviction notice. In the meantime, it would benefit the bank, although they would never admit it, to have the owner in the house, mowing the grass, keeping the pipes from freezing and making it look occupied. Although a few vengeful homeowners would trash the place before they left, most wouldn't, and would leave the house in much better condition than if it had been sitting vacant for months, a magnet for vandals and squatters.

Viktor met with a bankruptcy attorney, who wanted fifteen hundred dollars in advance, and then there was the matter of being required to pay a "nonprofit" debt counseling service to show him where he had gone wrong in managing his finances. Insanity, Viktor concluded, and decided to let fate take its course.

Eventually the eviction notice was posted on the front door, and Viktor and Christine packed what they could in the car and left. They lived out of the car for a while. He would drop her off at school, and then go to one of his part-time jobs until time to pick her up from school. There was no money for childcare, so at night, while he played gigs, Christine would wait as quietly and unobtrusively as possible, with the musicians' hats and coats and purses and instrument cases. She listened and learned and memorized many songs of various genres. If the event was informal enough so that her clothes weren't totally inappropriate, Christine would occasionally sing with the group, which always brought an enthusiastic response. After the performance, there were usually plenty of leftovers to eat, and some to take home, or rather to the car.

Viktor and Christine worked as street performers whenever possible. His violin alone didn't bring too many donations, but Christine's singing certainly did. The coming of winter severely limited their earning potential on the streets, however.

Viktor gave private violin lessons. The money was good, but they were so much more difficult when he no longer had a home, or any other place to host them. He responded by offering to give lessons in the customer's own home, but this required him to park around the corner, so they wouldn't see that he was living out of his car, and worse, to leave Christine alone in the car during the lesson, which worried him no end.

His cell phone was vital for booking private lessons, weddings, and other gigs, and too often it came down to buying minutes for the phone, gas for the car, or food for Christine. The bill collectors had somehow gotten hold of his cell phone number and were burning up his minutes harassing him on the phone. They always masked their real numbers, however, and he had to take all incoming calls in case it was paying work. He knew that he had reached rock bottom one winter's day when he stopped at a convenience store, put five dollars' worth of gas in the car, which would only take them a few miles, and then had to decide on sandwiches for his daughter or minutes for his cell phone. He bought the sandwiches, tossed the cell phone into a trash can, and drove to the nearest pawn shop.

Christine had been wearing her mother's wedding ring on a string around her neck. She went into the pawn shop with her father, pulled it off and put it on the counter. Viktor removed his own wedding band and placed it on the counter beside his wife's. He declined the pawn ticket. He wouldn't be returning to pick them up, he just wanted the money. The pawn broker did as requested. Viktor scooped up the cash, and they walked out. They stopped at the cemetery, and Christine placed a small bouquet of flowers, rescued from last night's wedding reception, on her mother's grave. Viktor cried, apologized for selling their wedding rings, and swore he would get their daughter to Los Angeles and enroll her in the Belen Conservatory of Music, as they had planned for all those years.

Just as in her mother's stories, and the trip she had promised Christine, Viktor and daughter set out from Chicago on Route 66, The Mother Road.

When their car broke down just outside Kansas City, there was no money to repair it, and so they took what they could carry and left the car where it had died. They had been on foot, carrying everything they owned, ever since.

9

HANNAH

HANNAH WAS A California girl to the core. A tall, lean stunner with a long brunette mane and a sharp wit, she could have easily become a top fashion model, but she preferred surfing and hanging with the guys, with whom she was enormously popular. She was also valedictorian of her high-school class, and as a reward, her working-class parents came up with the money for her to join her best friend, Kayla, backpacking across Europe the summer before entering university as a pre-med major in the fall.

Backpacking and staying in youth hostels were part of a time-honored tradition, no matter one's means, and Hannah and Kayla were determined to squeeze every drop from the experience. Saint-Tropez was, they discovered, a small town with a large reputation, and getting there was not all that easy, especially with their limited, but improving, French. They finally arrived, and after a night's sleep in a crowded hostel, they set out to partake of the local culture, right after hitting the beach.

They were sunning themselves, topless, as was the local custom—they felt so sophisticated and well, European—when their sun was blocked by two young Frenchmen. Then they felt suddenly naked and were unsure of the protocol in such a situation. Lying topless on the beach in complete anonymity among many others similarly situated was one thing, but were you supposed to discreetly cover yourself when near a stranger, especially when being spoken to, or just leave them on display? They elected the latter—the Frenchmen were quite handsome—and they certainly didn't want to appear bourgeois, or American.

Alain, who was, Hannah had already decided, the hotter of the two, spoke, directing his comments to her. His English was remarkably good, more so than the average French playboy plying his trade on the beaches and in the nightclubs along the Riviera. Such men were to be watched out for, both sets of parents had warned, as these playboys were as plentiful as tourists in the summer, seeking out especially the naïve young American girls. Nothing of lasting benefit ever came from these summer flings, but for many young girls on their own for the first time the fling itself was benefit enough.

Hannah and Kayla were invited to a party that very evening aboard a small yacht, conveniently moored just over there, Alain had said, and the girls had accepted immediately as the Frenchmen's eyes stared one last time at their bare breasts before taking leave. The girls resolved to discover the close-in topless protocol before the next such encounter, although they agreed that it had been rather exhilarating, and sexy, unlike their experiences on the southern California beaches.

The girls were unsure of the dress code for such an event, and backpacking left a young woman with a very limited wardrobe from which to choose, but surely the Frenchmen were aware of that, and less would probably be better than more, so they settled on bikini bottoms with no tops, but flowing, brightly colored cover-ups which would leave some air of mystery. That ship, they decided, had already sailed, at least for the two Frenchmen in question, but they liked the way they looked, bare shoulders with no straps, and they slipped into some flip flops and were on their way.

Once aboard Hannah and Kayla felt perhaps overdressed. There were nubile young girls, some of them no doubt younger than themselves, wearing thongs and absolutely nothing more, dancing topless on the deck. American Puritanism won out, however, and Hannah and Kayla kept their cover-ups tightly knotted.

The small yacht, it turned out, was anything but small. It also belonged to the family of the other boy; the one Kayla was with. No matter, Hannah thought, her own young Frenchman was more handsome and charming even if he wasn't rich, and—she knew the drill—this would be but a summer fling, a brief one to be sure, as they had only a few days in Saint-Tropez before moving on to Spain, or whichever country was next on their crowded itinerary. In any event, Hannah was well-protected, at least in a reproductive sense. She was no dummy, she would be starting her pre-med studies in just a few short weeks, and nothing was going to slow her trajectory.

BY HER SENIOR YEAR at the university Hannah was spending summers at the Chagny estate in the French countryside. Alain's family's yacht, far larger than his friend's yacht at Saint-Tropez, had been moored that summer at Monte Carlo, where his parents were vacationing. Hannah's French was by then serviceable, and she knew she was being vetted by Alain's parents for possible marriage to their son. They were not at all happy he had chosen an American girl, but she was beautiful, tall, extremely intelligent, focused, and charming. Alain's father, the comte de Chagny, was in failing health and wished to see his son, and heir, settled in marriage before assuming his title.

The expected marriage proposal came soon enough, and it was exceedingly romantic. Hannah was prepared, and the negotiations began. She loved Alain very much, and had no problem being the wife of a count, and all that entailed, but she would forgo neither medical school, nor the practice of medicine. Her chosen field—she was an adrenaline junkie—was trauma surgery, which was fortunate, as it would allow her a flexible schedule. She would work in the emergency room, patching up all manner of gunshot wounds and other traumatic injuries, and then go home. There would be no office hours. No one would call for an appointment before being shot, assaulted, or mangled. There would be no follow-up care. Someone else would handle all that. Her patients would arrive suddenly and unexpectedly by ambulance. She would save their lives and move on to the next.

Since his business could be handled from anywhere in the world, Alain agreed to maintain a residence wherever her practice required, as well as apartments in New York, London, and Paris, as well as the various family estates.

Hannah graduated from university summa cum laude, breezed through medical school at the top of her class, and while her classmates pursued plastic surgery, dermatology, and such, she was one of the few women who went into trauma surgery. After her residency, she hung out her shingle in Los Angeles.

HAVING ABANDONED MOST of their clothes when they left their home and much of the rest when they left their car in Kansas City, neither Viktor nor Christine had anything suitable to wear to dinner with well-to-do people, so they found a thrift store and went shopping.

In the dressing room, Christine slipped on a dress, and went out to look at herself in the mirror. It would do, she decided, there were no curves to accentuate, no cleavage to display, and the boy had already seen where she lived, and how she dressed, so he could not possibly be expecting much.

She stepped back into the dressing room, pulled off the dress, put her own clothes back on, and then found her father, trying on a dark suit jacket. She approved. He checked the price tag on both the suit and the dress, and they headed for the cash register.

Viktor counted out money on the counter. The clothes, inexpensive as they were, put a serious dent in their budget, and so they went immediately to the Third Street Promenade to try and recoup this unexpected expense.

THE CHAGNYS ESCHEWED Beverly Hills, Bel Air, and Malibu for a large old two-story on a corner lot in Santa Monica. They had no need to impress anyone, and they all quite liked the little beach community, especially Hannah, who had grown up in the area and was very familiar with the town. Ogden Hall Preparatory Academy, Raoul's private school, was nearby, as was Hannah's hospital.

When Viktor, in his dark suit, white shirt and tie from the thrift store, and Christine arrived, Raoul complimented Christine on her dress, which, after the episode at the beach, confirmed to her that he was either the ultimate gentleman or a complete fool. She returned the compliment—Raoul was impeccably dressed in a sport coat and tie.

Introductions were made. The other guests were Professor Valerius, who had taught music for many years at UCLA, and his wife. Hannah served as the ideal hostess, making everyone comfortable in her lovely home. Christine was in awe of the art on the walls and the furnishings. It was light years from what she was accustomed to, especially for the past two years. Viktor had come prepared to endure anything to allow his daughter the opportunity to accept Raoul's dinner invitation and was impressed that no one seemed condescending to him and his daughter, although they were all clearly of superior social and economic status.

Viktor noticed the grand piano in the living room and wondered if it were merely decorative or if this was, perhaps, a musical family, as that might provide common ground for conversation. Not that it mattered, he decided, they had been invited as a courtesy, they would make small talk, thank Raoul again for rescuing Christine's scarf, they would go back to the motel, and that would be that. Raoul's youthful crush would pass, and he would return to his little rich friends and find a girl more suited to his station in life, who would, Viktor was certain, be nowhere near as beautiful, talented, honorable, or lovable as his own Christine. *C'est la vie.*

Alain, quite distinguished looking, now formally the comte de Chagny following his father's death, sat at the head of the table. At the other end of the table was his wife, Hannah, now Doctor Chagny, slightly younger than her husband.

Viktor sat on one side, next to Professor and Mrs. Valerius. Across the table were Raoul, Christine, and Zoe. Viktor and Christine were still unsure of exactly who Zoe was, an older sister, a cousin, an aunt? No explanation had been offered during introductions. She was certainly mysterious, all Goth and dramatic in black. Despite her appearance, she was quite well-spoken, charming, funny, and obviously played some part in the family.

Viktor noted, when wine was poured, that the label said "Chagny." These people not only had their own wine but their own wineries, and their own vineyards, among their extensive holdings.

"Christine and I were very much impressed by Master Raoul's gallant retrieval of her scarf from the sea," Viktor offered during dinner.

"It was my mom's," Christine added.

Viktor smiled. The child learned quickly.

"We are quite proud of him," Chagny said, and then looked at Raoul. "Although jumping off the pier was not the wisest thing, young man."

"Sorry, Dad."

"You would have probably done the same thing at his age, dear," Hannah said. "You were quite the romantic."

Chagny raised his wine glass. "Had the young lady been you, my dear, of course I would."

There was a round of polite laughter.

"We do have to give credit to Zoe," Hannah said. "With my husband traveling so often on business, and me at the hospital so much, she is practically raising Raoul."

"And doing a very good job," Chagny added.

"Yes, she is," Hannah said.

"Are you brother and sister?" Viktor asked, deciding he may as well get right to the point.

Zoe chuckled.

"Oh no, Raoul is an only child," Hannah replied. "Zoe is our, well, I'm not exactly sure what she is. 'Babysitter' is out of the question. It would crush Raoul's self-esteem. 'Nanny' doesn't seem quite right either. It's 'governess' when we're in Europe, but that seems rather pretentious for Los Angeles.

'Au pair' might be the technically correct term." She paused for effect, taking a slow sip of wine. "What exactly are you, Zoe?"

Zoe dabbed at her mouth with her napkin and replaced it in her lap. "Raoul liked 'girlfriend,' but the other kids weren't buying it. We briefly considered 'mistress.' It actually has multiple meanings, but that was lost on most people, especially kids."

The kids snickered. Viktor looked at Zoe, puzzled.

"I liked 'concubine,'" Zoe continued, "but hardly anyone knew what that was, so we settled on 'co-conspirator.'"

"I like it," Hannah concluded.

"With a driver's license," Zoe added.

"Don't let the Goth look fool you, Mr. Daaé," Professor Valerius said. "Zoe is one of my finest students at the university, in composition, graduating this year, and hopefully continuing in our graduate program. We have a pool in the department on what her look will be from year to year."

"Last year it was punk," Mrs. Valerius said.

"Ah yes," Hannah said. "Zoe and Raoul made quite the couple around Santa Monica, Zoe with her spiked red hair and Raoul in his school uniform."

"Where do you go to school, Christine?" Mrs. Valerius asked.

"Daddy teaches me."

"You are home-schooled?" Mrs. Valerius asked.

"I guess," Christine replied, having no idea what that meant.

"You could go to my school!" Raoul offered.

Viktor was eager to change the subject. "What type of music do you compose, Miss Zoe?"

"Classical is my passion. I dabble in opera. I'm going for a master's in composition for visual media."

"Visual media?" Viktor asked.

"I plan to score movies and television. A girl has to make a living."

"If Wagner were alive today, he would be scoring films," Professor Valerius said.

"Yes," Viktor said, thinking about it. "I imagine he would, and doing quite well at it."

The professor chuckled.

"Wagner would be the most sought-after composer in Hollywood, living in a multi-million-dollar beach house in Malibu, with a line of Grammys and Oscars on the mantle above the fireplace, and a bevy of bikinied beauties around the pool," Zoe said, eliciting a few laughs. "And I would be his assistant."

After another round of laughter, Professor Valerius asked, "Have we met, Mr. Daaé? You look familiar."

Mrs. Valerius put her hand on his. When he glanced in her direction, she shook her head slightly.

"I don't believe we have, sir," Viktor said. "We only recently arrived in Los Angeles."

"Perhaps you and Mr. Daaé are kindred spirits, Professor," Zoe said. "He plays an enchanted violin."

Professor Valerius suddenly realized where he had seen Viktor but said nothing. He was not sure what anyone else at the table knew, and he didn't want to embarrass Viktor.

"And Christine has the voice of an angel," Zoe added.

Raoul turned to Christine. "Could you sing for us? And your dad could play the violin."

"Of course," Viktor said quickly. "We don't mind singing for our supper."

"Oh no," Chagny protested. "You are our guests. We wouldn't dream of asking you to sing for your supper."

"A figure of speech, comte," Viktor said, smiling. "We would be happy to perform, but I didn't bring my instrument."

"You can use mine!" Raoul volunteered. "And Christine can sing."

"Very well," Viktor said. "But perhaps first you should play for us, Master Raoul."

"Excellent." Chagny concluded.

"It's settled then," Zoe said. "Raoul and I will be the opening act."

The group moved into the living room with their coffees, and it became clear to Viktor that the grand piano was not merely decorative as Zoe sat on the bench and Raoul took up a position nearby with his violin. Christine's eyes were on Raoul as he played "Bruch Violin Concerto, Third Movement." There was enthusiastic applause when he finished the piece.

"What do you think, Mr. Daaé?" Hannah asked. "He will be auditioning again this year for the Belen Conservatory of Music, so don't just be polite. We need real feedback."

Viktor did not hesitate. "He has good command of his instrument. His bowing and fingering need work. His presentation shows promise. If he has the commitment, he can become an excellent violinist."

Hannah looked at Professor Valerius, who smiled and nodded his head, validating what Viktor had said.

"Thank you, Mr. Daaé, for that honest evaluation," Hannah said. "Now we know what we need to work on, don't we, Raoul?"

"Yes ma'am."

"Are you available for private lessons, Mr. Daaé?" Hannah asked.

"I don't really have the facilities for students."

"You could come here, sir," Raoul offered.

"I suppose I could."

"And Christine could come with you."

"Splendid. We'll work out the details later," Chagny said.

"After Christine sings and Mr. Daaé plays," Raoul said, as he handed his violin to Viktor.

Christine stepped over to the piano and searched through sheet music with Zoe. Raoul received his first lesson as he watched Viktor tune the violin, and then found a good spot on the floor and sat down.

Viktor raised the violin and bow and began to play "Dark Waltz," soon joined by Zoe on piano.

Christine sang. Raoul was transfixed. The Chagnys and the Valeriuses were very much impressed. There was no doubt to any of them that they were witnessing something incredible in Christine's performance. There was enthusiastic applause when the song ended.

Raoul leapt to his feet. "Brava! Brava!"

"Oh my, Zoe, you were right. This child does have the voice of an angel," Hannah said.

"Encore! Encore!" Raoul shouted.

"Please, Daddy?" Christine said.

Viktor nodded. Christine turned and whispered to Zoe.

Raoul resumed his position on the floor and waited in anticipation.

Zoe and Viktor began playing, "O mio babbino caro." Christine sang. Raoul was enraptured.

"Very good," Professor Valerius said when the song ended. His wife nodded in agreement.

He turned to Zoe. "What do you think, Zoe?"

"Very good indeed."

"Well, Raoul," Chagny said. "Perhaps the scarf you rescued from the sea belongs to your future classmate at the conservatory." He turned to Viktor.

"Have you considered the Belen Conservatory of Music for Christine, Mr. Daaé?"

"Oh, yes," Viktor replied, smiling. "It is the purpose of our trip to Los Angeles. I believe Christine has a future in music."

"An understatement, to be sure," Chagny said.

"She is how old?" Professor Valerius asked.

"Twelve."

"Are you interested in opera, Christine?" The professor asked.

"Yes sir, but I do understand the difference between singing an aria in a small room and an entire opera on a grand stage."

Professor Valerius nodded.

"One more!" Raoul said. "One more, please."

Christine looked at her father. He nodded. She turned to Zoe and whispered in her ear.

"I know it, but are you sure?" Zoe responded.

Christine smiled and nodded enthusiastically.

Zoe began to play "La mamma morta." Christine sang.

There was stunned silence when the song ended. Zoe looked at Professor Valerius as a sly smile appeared on his face.

Raoul leapt to his feet. The others joined in his enthusiastic applause.

"That was incredible," the professor said. "One can only imagine what wonders are in store when she matures, although I don't see how it can get much better than this."

"She has much to learn," Viktor added. "Her mother provided her with an excellent foundation. I can help with her music, but singing is not my field."

Professor Valerius nodded his head, his mind racing at the possibilities of this prodigy standing before him. "Perhaps I can be of assistance in that area. Singing is not my field either, but I know an extraordinary singer when I hear one, and I have colleagues who do specialize in singing. The conservatory is the place for her, for now, but I'll be happy to advise."

While the adults sipped brandy in the living room, and talked about grownup things, and no doubt music, Christine joined Raoul in his room for some hard-core video gaming, reverting easily to normal tweens, music the farthest thing from their minds. Raoul didn't press her, and she volunteered little about her life. She and her father were clearly of limited means. The girls at his school wore more expensive, and fashionable, clothes and shoes. Her nails were far from manicured. Her hair was luxurious, but she had not recently been in an upscale salon. She wore not a trace of makeup. He was smitten.

Zoe poked her head through the open door far too soon. "Raoul, our guests are ready to leave. It's time to return Christine to her father."

The kids jumped up to go.

"I'm glad you came," Raoul declared.

"Me too," Christine responded.

They hustled past Zoe and bounded down the stairs as the adults said their goodbyes.

It was apparent to Professor Valerius as Viktor and Christine walked down the sidewalk, leaving the Chagny home, that they were not headed to their car. He pulled over and rolled down the window. "Mr. Daaé, do you need a ride?"

Viktor paused and turned. "We're fine. We like to walk. It's not far."

"Please, let us drive you."

Viktor reluctantly accepted the offer, and he and Christine climbed in the back seat of the Valerius's car. It was, of course, more than "not far" to their motel.

"Daddy, why did you call Raoul's dad comte?" Christine asked.

"He is, I believe, a French count. Is that not correct, Professor?" Viktor said.

"Yes, actually, he is," Professor Valerius said. "The family goes back centuries and is one of the most distinguished in France. Raoul will one day inherit the title, and if the two of you should marry, Christine, you will be comtesse de Chagny."

Christine liked the sound of that. "Cool."

"There will be no talk of marriage, my child," Viktor said. "You are only twelve years old."

"Oh, Daddy, I know that."

"She did practically ask for the boy's hand in marriage tonight, 'oh my dear papa,'" Professor Valerius said.

"Your Italian is quite good, Professor," Viktor responded.

Christine smiled as Professor Valerius drove on.

"It is right up there on the left, the motel," Viktor said.

Mrs. Valerius looked over the motel with concern as the professor pulled into the parking lot. Viktor and Christine stepped out of the car.

"Thank you for the ride, Professor," Viktor said.

"Let's stay in touch, Mr. Daaé." He handed him a business card.

Viktor took the card, nodded, turned, and followed Christine toward the stairway. Professor Valerius's car pulled away.

Viktor started coughing, paused, and leaned against the railing. Christine turned and rushed to him. "Daddy, are you okay?"

"Yes, my dear. It's just a cold I think."

As they waited for traffic, Mrs. Valerius watched Viktor and Christine enter their room.

"We simply cannot allow that dear, sweet child to live in a transient motel," she said.

"No, my dear, we cannot."

10

THE LITTLE COTTAGE

THE VALERIUSES WERE college sweethearts and had been together ever since. After graduation, she taught music in public school while he completed his master's degree. As he worked his way up in position, prestige, and salary at the university, she quit her regular teaching job, they converted the small guest house behind their modest home in Santa Monica into a music studio, and she began taking private students. She had not gone to college to be a housewife, and this would allow her to continue teaching music at home even after they had children. She envisioned her baby in a crib nearby, being lulled to sleep by the sound of music, although it occurred to her that the screeching of a bad student might be counterproductive to instilling a love of music in her own child.

The children never came, the Valeriuses decided to not seek a medical solution, but let nature take its course, and so remained childless. Her young music students provided something of a substitute for a while, but they went home after their lessons and left a void. Eventually she lost her passion for teaching music, and busied herself with other activities, including charity work, and found herself falling into a rut as the wife of a noted professor of music.

The guest house began to accumulate furniture removed for newer and better, empty boxes, obsolete electronics, Christmas decorations they no longer used, mountains of clothes, gifts for which they had no use but never got around to returning or donating to charity, and all the other residue of a middle-class existence in a disposable culture. It began to resemble a storage locker, yet they continued to push more stuff through the door.

They stood in the open doorway surveying the scene.

"Why don't you stop at the motel on your way to campus and I'll get started on this," Mrs. Valerius said.

"What if he refuses our offer?"

"This needs to be cleaned out anyway. We've been avoiding it for years."

The professor nodded in agreement and set out on his mission.

The electronic age had not yet arrived at the motel, and so the desk clerk thumbed through a box of cards. "They checked out this morning, early."

"Did they leave a forwarding address?" Professor Valerius asked.

"No, nothing."

"Did he say anything? Any idea where they might have gone?"

"Sorry. Looks like they were paid up for a week, in advance, through last night."

ZOE TREKKED ACROSS CAMPUS. Wagner's famous notes, "dah dah dah dah" erupted from her cell phone. She answered. "What's up, Professor?"

Professor Valerius filled her in.

"I'm on my way," she said. "Try the Promenade and the pier. They might be busking. It's early, but it's worth a shot."

The professor's mission seemed more important than class, so she reversed course, hopped in her car, and quickly covered the short distance to Ogden Hall, where she persuaded the office staff to allow her to pull Raoul out of class. Private schools were considerably more lenient with such matters, especially when the student in question was the son of wealthy and generous parents.

Zoe and Raoul huddled in the hallway.

"I think her dad is a dishwasher," Raoul said.

"Do you know where?"

"Sort of. I think it's a coffee shop. I'm coming with you."

"No, you have school."

Raoul was nothing if not persuasive and the pair soon picked up Professor Valerius from the sidewalk at a city parking structure in Santa Monica.

"Turn right," Raoul said.

Zoe turned right.

"Pull up over there."

"We come here all the time, Raoul. You could have just told me."

Zoe took the first available parking space.

"Then you wouldn't have let me come," Raoul said as he opened the door and leapt out.

Raoul raced toward Christine, asleep on a pile of baggage, against a wall in the alley.

"Christine!" Raoul shouted as he jostled her.

Christine woke up and rubbed her eyes. Raoul was right in her face. "Christine!"

Zoe rushed up. "Are you okay, honey?"

Christine, now mostly awake, sat up. "What are you guys doing here?"

"Looking for you," Zoe said. "Professor Valerius wants to talk to your dad."

"He's at work," Christine responded. "You can't bother him at work. He could get fired."

In the coffee shop, Viktor carried a bus tub full of dirty dishes, with Professor Valerius following closely.

"Thank you, Professor, but I really can't discuss it right now. I must work. I can't lose this job."

"Of course," the professor replied. "I need to get to class myself. But we can't leave Christine on the street. At least let Zoe take her, and your things, to my home, where she will be safe. My wife is there. I'll pick you up after work and we can talk."

Viktor glanced at the coffee shop manager, and then back at Professor Valerius. "Very well, I will trust to you my daughter. I get off around four o'clock." He turned and pushed into the kitchen.

"I'll be here," Professor Valerius called after him. "Christine will be fine."

Viktor opened the back door to the alley. "Christine, you will go home with Professor Valerius. I'll see you there after work."

"Yes Daddy."

Viktor started to close the door, but Raoul surged forward. "I'll take care of her, Mr. Daaé."

Viktor paused briefly, "Thank you, Raoul," and then closed the back door.

Inside the coffee shop, as Professor Valerius moved toward the front door, the manager approached. "Is there a problem, sir?"

"Oh no," Professor Valerius responded. "I just needed to speak to Mr. Daaé about a matter of some urgency. I'm sorry if I kept him from his duties. It was not his fault. It was mine."

The manager followed Professor Valerius at a distance, stood at the corner and watched as the professor, Zoe, Raoul, and Christine walked by, laden with baggage and Viktor's violin.

———

PROFESSOR VALERIUS AND Viktor stood just inside the door of the guest house. While Mrs. Valerius had made considerable progress, there was still much to be done.

"My wife used it as a music studio years ago when she taught piano. Now it's just, well, you can see."

Viktor looked around. All he could see was piles of clutter.

"It was originally built as a guest house, I believe, or possibly a rental back when that was allowed, so there's a bath and a kitchenette, more suitable for one person, but it has to be better than a motel room. There's only one bed, but the sofa pulls out. We'll get it cleaned out, of course. There are things here that we should have thrown out long ago."

"What does your wife think of this?"

"It was her idea."

Viktor remained unconvinced.

"I'm sure you are a proud man, Mr. Daaé, but think of your daughter."

The two men looked through the open doorway into the back yard. Christine sat on a bench with Raoul, talking quietly, and then she burst into laughter.

"We aren't accustomed to accepting charity," Viktor said. "We have tried hard to make our own way."

"It's hardly charity, Mr. Daaé. Your daughter has a talent far beyond her years. As a professor, and lover of music, I consider it my duty to do what I can to both encourage and nurture that talent." The professor paused, and then continued. "My wife and I were never blessed with children. Let us spoil Christine like a grandchild. We would be happy to be allowed to provide for her education. Perhaps we could get her into Raoul's school until she can audition for Belen. I'm sure you are doing a very good job of teaching her, but she needs to be around other children, and certainly not on the streets."

The professor made a good case. Viktor looked again at Christine and Raoul, having a grand time.

"I would insist on paying something in rent."

"The city won't allow us to rent it. You'll just have to be our guests. It would be our privilege."

"With me working full time, I suppose it would be better for Christine to be in school, and to have someone around to look after her."

"About that, Mr. Daaé, you already have one violin student, Raoul, whose father will pay quite well, and I'm sure there will be more to come when word gets around that you are available for private lessons. You could teach violin here, in the guest house."

"It wouldn't disturb your wife?"

Professor Valerius laughed. "On the contrary, she'll be scheduling your appointments, serving refreshments, copying music. You'll have to shoo her away. She misses music and she misses having children around."

They stepped through the doorway into the back yard. "Christine!" Viktor shouted.

Christine jumped up. "Yes Daddy?"

"Would you like to live here in this little cottage?"

"With you?" With the recent turmoil, and all the sudden attention from adults, Christine had some concerns as to what, exactly, had been decided.

"Of course, with me."

Christine rushed forward and leapt into her father's arms, kissing him repeatedly.

"Yes! Yes! Yes!"

Zoe and Mrs. Valerius, watching through the back door of the main house, stepped into the yard. Raoul pumped his fist, and then high-fived Zoe.

VIKTOR AND CHRISTINE slept in the spare bedroom in the main house while the little cottage was cleaned out, which did not take long after Zoe arrived with several college students and a truck. Enough furniture, pots and pans and the other essentials were procured from thrift stores, or mined from the clutter, and Zoe and Mrs. Valerius set about decorating. When it was finished, Viktor was overwhelmed, and Christine was thrilled.

Raoul rightfully had the honor of becoming the first music student in many years to receive private lessons in the little cottage. Mrs. Valerius quickly began filling openings for Viktor, although he told her to not move too quickly, as he must keep his promise to not let down the coffee shop manager. He continued arising before dawn for a few weeks and busing tables until a replacement was found and trained and Viktor was satisfied that his commitment had been honored.

Just as the professor had predicted, Mrs. Valerius took charge of Viktor's schedule, baked cookies and made hot chocolate, which were always enjoyed by the students. She even found herself taking on the occasional piano student in the main house, where the piano had been moved long ago, and both the house and cottage were once again filled with music, not always the most beautiful, but they were helping children to learn, and there was always the hope that one of them might go on to greatness.

Mrs. Valerius began tending her flower garden in the back yard, which had gone to seed, putting her even closer to the music than the open kitchen window. She loved the music, and she especially loved it after the students had gone home and Viktor played the violin and Christine sang. She and the professor would sit on the bench in the back yard and enjoy their private concert. Having children around reinvigorated their marriage.

Chagny made a phone call and Christine suddenly went from the bottom of the wait list to the top at Raoul's private school. A check to the activity fund was also no doubt part of the package, but it was a price he was willing to pay for his son's happiness. He was quite pleased at how Raoul had taken the initiative and gone out of his way to help Christine and her father. He was being groomed to be a leader, to one day take over the family business and estates along with Chagny's title, and he was showing great promise in that regard.

Christine was immediately declared a co-conspirator and Zoe would pick up both kids every day after school and they would rush off on whatever adventures they could fit in before their music lessons back at the little cottage. Zoe, it turned out, was Queen of the Thrift-Store Shoppers and helped Christine fill out her wardrobe outside of her private school uniforms. Raoul would tag along and offer a man's perspective, being frequently overruled.

Raoul improved immeasurably on the violin, finally mastering "La Ronde des Lutins," greatly increasing his chances of being accepted on his second audition to the conservatory, which would be during the upcoming summer. His mother was quite content to allow him to follow his musical bent, but Chagny, while agreeing in the interim, believed that long-term, Raoul needed to get into a good university and position himself to one day become comte de Chagny, take over the family estates and business interests, and that would not be accomplished through the violin.

While Viktor tutored private students in the little cottage, Zoe and Mrs. Valerius would work with Christine on the piano and her singing. Everyone expected Christine to also be auditioning for the conservatory in the summer.

The Valerius home had long been a gathering place for music students from UCLA, which reminded Christine of her home in Chicago. There were great jam sessions, with both Viktor and Christine participating, and Raoul whenever he could convince his parents to let him stay late after practice. The university music students were much impressed by Christine, and Zoe had no trouble securing assistance from her friends who were vocalists to work with Christine on improving her technique. Talent, she had in abundance, but all those qualified to know agreed that Christine needed training, which she dove into with enthusiasm. Singing had always come as naturally to her as breathing, but when she discovered how much she could improve, and extend her range, by controlling that very thing, breathing, she improved greatly.

There was opera, which Christine studied closely, and she would later corner the opera singers and quiz them on technique, which they freely shared.

Mrs. Valerius stayed busy, preparing hors d'oeuvres for the crowd, cleaning up after, with the help of Viktor and Christine, but loving every minute of it. Her home was filled with laughter and music, and the blonde child was at the center of it all.

One night, after all the musicians had gone home, Christine climbed into bed. Viktor kissed her, tweaked her nose with his finger, and she felt happier than she had in years. As she lay awake in the darkness, however, she could hear him coughing and she was worried. Colds didn't last that long.

THE CO-CONSPIRATORS DESCENDED upon the pier and came away with a passport-style photo for Raoul, and then made their way to City Hall, where Zoe handed over the photo, a completed form, and some money, and then turned to Raoul and said, "Congratulations, you are now a licensed busker."

"A licensed what?" Raoul asked.

"A busker," Zoe replied. "One who busks. Street performing, also called busking, is a time-honored tradition around the world and across all cultures, going back centuries."

"Cool," Raoul said.

They went immediately to the Promenade, where Raoul played violin, and Christine sang, quickly attracting a crowd. Zoe hovered nearby, keeping a close watch on the open violin case. They continued playing and singing, collecting a considerable amount of money, which Zoe counted and divided between Raoul and Christine. As they walked along the Promenade, the kids passed out the money to the homeless. They continued over the next few days, especially on weekends, when crowds were larger, trying out different acts, different genres, seeing which generated the most donations.

Zoe took them thrift-store shopping, outfitted Raoul as a 1950s rocker in blue jeans and leather jacket and found a sweater and poodle skirt for Christine. Their new act was a smash hit on the Promenade, with Zoe, in black leather on the drums, Raoul on guitar, and Christine singing. They collected a lot of money, which they immediately passed out to the homeless, but as word spread, there were ever more homeless standing around, waiting for a share of the loot.

Inspired by the kids' enthusiasm in their work for the homeless, especially Christine, who was not that far removed from the streets herself, Zoe began composing an original piece, somewhat classical, at least musically, with lyrics that dealt with the plight of the homeless, and those who had so little, surrounded by those who had so much.

11

OGDEN HALL

WHEN THE OGDEN HALL orchestra began rehearsing a new piece Raoul immediately recognized the melody, if not the name. It was "Suo Gân," the same lovely and haunting lullaby Christine was singing on the pier when he first laid eyes on her. The sheet music included the lyrics, in English, which would be performed by the choir.

Immediately after enrolling at Ogden Hall, Christine had joined the choir, although she intentionally throttled herself so as not to attract attention. It wasn't that difficult, she discovered, much like working on a new piece, where she would hold back, so as not to unduly stress her vocal cords while still learning the lyrics and melody. While the others in the choir put all they had into it, Christine held back, making it look like she was really singing. The choir teacher never had a clue, and never asked Christine to sing a solo.

Although commonly sung in Welsh by children their age in the United Kingdom, apparently "Suo Gân" was too much for rich, spoiled California kids, and so they sang an English translation to the same music.

"Those aren't the words," a girl whispered to Christine as they sang. She pointed at her sheet music for good measure. "That doesn't even sound like words."

"Oh, sorry," Christine said, lifting her own sheet music to find the English words. She had been singing in Welsh, just as she had learned it from her mother, who had learned it from her own grandmother, Stella, on her infrequent visits. Rachel had sung it to Christine many times when she was a small child. Christine had memorized the lyrics as soon as possible, struggling with the rather difficult language, but by the time her mother died she had mastered it thoroughly and sang it often, always accompanied by her father on violin. Christine was not at all interested in the English translation, so she just lowered her voice to a whisper and continued singing the Welsh lyrics. No one noticed or cared.

Ogden Hall sat on a few manicured acres, complete with palm trees, on a bluff overlooking the Pacific Ocean. It was quite unlike anything Christine had experienced before—a world away from suburban Chicago. She was overwhelmed by the physical beauty of the place, which was sometimes a problem, depending on the orientation of her current classroom, as the views out the window were often spectacular. The cafeteria opened onto a courtyard, and the weather was often such that the kids ate their lunch outside in the open air.

Many of the students were children of wealthy, famous, infamous, or important parents—heads of studios and music companies, multi-national corporations, actors, rock stars, politicians, consular officials from foreign countries, and the merely rich. Black SUVs arrived every morning in an endless stream, dropping off these children of privilege. Some of them, by virtue of extreme wealth or position, or an occasional credible threat, were accompanied by bodyguards. The bodyguards were themselves, by their very presence, a topic of interest at the school. The private ones tended to be very large, and unarmed, since it was rather illegal to carry a firearm in a school. Others though, smaller, better dressed in suits and ties, and usually wearing some sort of lapel pin, were rumored to be official, Secret Service, off-duty cops, state police, or whatever, and armed, although no one had ever actually seen one of the firearms. At least one of them was rumored to be Mossad. She certainly looked the part and was a constant companion in the classrooms, hallways, even the girls' restroom, of a very beautiful, mysterious fourteen-year-old girl with dark, curly hair, who few boys even dared approach, for fear of being taken out by a single finger to the eye, or worse, from the lady bodyguard, who was quite hot herself, in a dangerous, exotic sort of way.

The bodyguards had their own table in the cafeteria, or the courtyard, and always carefully positioned themselves so they could keep an eye on their charges. The Mossad lady ate alone at lunch—no one dared join her—at a table just a few feet from the dark-haired mystery girl and her small circle of friends.

There were also several students at the school who were themselves celebrities—their parents would have otherwise been nobodies. These were child actors. At other schools, regular working kid actors, recognizable but not yet famous, were often bullied or ostracized by other students, while those who had achieved some level of success had to put up with the fawning of those who sought fame by association, as well as those shoving head shots and audition tapes into their backpacks. At Ogden Hall the most famous child actor in the world could walk the halls in peace and have regular friends, even though going to the mall together might require coordination between bodyguards, chauffeurs, nannies, and publicists.

"Is that who I think it is?" Christine asked Raoul one day at lunch.

"Yep, that's her," Raoul replied. "She's in my English class."

"I haven't seen her here before."

"She's a migrant film worker."

Christine laughed. "A what?" She had learned about migrant farm workers at school in Chicago, but this was something entirely new.

"She just returned from Vancouver, shooting a movie. That's were most American movies are made, in Canada, with German money. Sometimes they go to Louisiana, or New Mexico," Raoul added. "I think Georgia is the new kid on the block, so that's where everyone is going now." He explained how states and foreign countries lavished taxpayer money on the studios, owned by multi-billion-dollar, multinational conglomerates, in order to get them to come make films in their state or country. It was all very confusing to Christine. Like most other people, she thought movies were made in Hollywood.

"She's the first movie star I've ever actually seen in person," Christine said.

"It's LA. You'll get used to it."

"We're wearing the same outfit."

Raoul laughed. They were all wearing the same outfit, school uniforms. He pointed at a boy across the cafeteria, "His dad's studio is making the movie." He turned and pointed at a girl. "Her dad's directing." He pointed toward a boy. "His mom's scoring."

"Scoring?" Christine asked, puzzled.

"Writing the music for the movie."

"Cool," Christine said, turning back to stare at the young actress for a moment. "She looks prettier in person."

"Yeah," Raoul was unimpressed.

"And smaller," Christine added.

Christine assumed that her tenure at Ogden Hall would be brief—the Belen Conservatory was her destination. Accordingly, she resolved to get through it without making too many waves. She had been forced to abandon the few friends she had in Chicago and didn't want to get too close to the kids at this new school. Not that it mattered, because they didn't exactly welcome this new girl with open arms. Most of them had been at the school since kindergarten and saw Christine as an interloper. It didn't help that Raoul seemed to be, if not her boyfriend, then her only friend at school. Although Christine was small, and just on the edge of puberty, she was very pretty, and a real blonde, and therefore a threat to the other girls who had been jockeying for position, and staking their claims to the hot boys, or at least the boys most likely to succeed, or inherit their fathers' success, hopefully both.

Being a year apart in age and grade, Christine and Raoul had no classes together, but were often seen together in the halls, and always at lunch, which upset the social order. Girls sat together in well-defined groups—which group you were in mattered greatly. Boys sat together apparently based on whatever video game they were playing. While there were a few mixed gender tables, they always consisted of some shared experience, such as theater, art, or music. Couples sitting alone at a table were quite rare for this age group. The significance of Raoul lunching daily with Christine was not lost on the girls at the best tables—even at thirteen Raoul was already considered a catch. Not only was his family at least as wealthy as any other at Ogden Hall, but Raoul himself was a French viscount, the vicomte de Chagny.

Kids of that age were already starting to pair up and pretend to be teens pretending to be adults. They used the term "going out" as a synonym for dating, although none of them actually dated, or even "went out," at least in twos. If Johnny "liked" or even said something nice about Susie, they were suddenly "going out" in everyone's eyes. In reality, they went on group dates, a dozen or so at a time, offering the protection of the pack, while only flirting with dating.

Christine felt out of place in all this. She wore no makeup, had yet to be fitted for a training bra, had never had a professional manicure, and had never even been to a hair salon. Her mother had cut her hair as long as she was able, and Viktor had trimmed it a couple of times since. She washed it and brushed it and occasionally adorned it with a ribbon or hair clip, and that was it. The other girls in her classes at Ogden Hall obviously had standing appointments at the hair salon, nail salon, and spa to have their legs waxed. Christine and her father could have eaten, and eaten well, for what some of these girls spent on grooming.

Legs suddenly took on new importance to Christine. She had rarely worn a skirt or dress—pants or jeans were the "uniform" at her previous school, or shorts in the fall and spring when the weather was willing. Dresses were reserved for church, which the little Daaé family attended rarely, her mother's funeral, and thereafter very occasionally when Christine would sing at a wedding or other function with her father's small orchestra. But skirts for girls were part of the uniform at this school. They were short, well above the knee, and required a completely new skill set for a twelve-year-old girl— crossing her legs modestly and swinging them out of a desk or chair without exposing anything. Compared to the limitless freedom of pants or shorts, this took some getting used to.

With all the bare legs on display, Christine noticed that those of nearly all the other girls in her classes were quite smooth and hairless. Fortunately, the hair on her own legs was fine and blonde, but there it was, marking her as a little girl and not a young woman. Oddly enough, these things were noticed by, and mattered only to, other girls. Boys at that age were far more interested in killing things on their video screens, making crude jokes, playing pranks, and generally being—boys. It was quite different in the upper-class corridor, where hormones raged, and the students were often indistinguishable from young adults.

It helped that everyone wore uniforms at Ogden Hall. Christine would not be embarrassed by her clothes, even though Mrs. Valerius had been taking her shopping to upgrade her wardrobe. Christine still preferred the funky findings from her forays to the thrift stores with Zoe. The school uniforms were made of natural fiber, wool, and cotton, rather than the polyester that Christine was accustomed to, and it made her feel more sophisticated and grown up. She found it odd that girls as well as boys wore ties, and she never quite mastered tying the things, but always loved sitting between her father's legs while he put his arms around her and tied it for her, without even using a mirror.

Christine had always been a good student—she was smart and caught on quickly—but the curriculum at a public school in Chicago was not the same as at this private school in California. In addition, she had been out of school for some time, tutored by her father, which rarely matched the track other students her age were on, but she applied herself and was able to keep up.

Christine settled into a routine at Ogden Hall, trying to get along, while she and Raoul counted the days as spring wore on and the school year wound down, looking forward to long, lazy days on the beach during the summer, busking on the pier and Promenade for the homeless shelter, and as Viktor constantly reminded them, preparing for their auditions at the conservatory.

Raoul, under Viktor's tutelage, continued to improve on the violin. Christine tried different genres and received lots of advice on what would most impress the committee at the conservatory. It was almost like a talent show—go for a familiar and popular piece, or one that shows your technique and range? Most agreed that showing technique and range was the preferred choice—the committee would, after all, be a collection of highly experienced music educators, and not a bunch of rubes sitting in front of the flat-screen, repeatedly texting in votes for their favorite song, regardless of who was singing it.

After months of homelessness, and continual change, Christine found herself settling into a new routine. Few knew of her past, none apparently at school, other than Raoul. The pair spent a lot of time together—Raoul always found a reason to dally after his violin sessions with Viktor. Christine enjoyed the attention. Life was not the same as when her mother was alive, but she and her daddy had a roof over their heads, food to eat, and clothes to wear. Viktor was earning decent money teaching violin, most of which went into savings for the future.

A soft sea breeze gently disturbed the curtains on the window of the little cottage and ruffled the corner of Viktor's newspaper. Angelenos complained about the spring chill, especially near the beach, but Viktor quite enjoyed it. After a winter on the streets of Chicago and on the road, he found it quite comfortable.

"Oh, no," Christine exclaimed.

Viktor stepped over to the bathroom door.

"What's wrong?"

"Nothing," Christine replied from behind the door.

"Did you hurt yourself?"

"It's nothing really, just a little blood."

Viktor froze. The moment had come. How he wished his wife were still alive and here to deal with this.

"Is there anything I can get for you?" He knew there was nothing on hand.

"Do we have any bandages?"

"Bandages?" Viktor was confused.

"I kinda like cut myself."

"I'm coming in," Viktor said, opening the door.

"No! I'm in the tub!"

He pushed through the door anyway. Christine tried to cover herself, not that there was much to cover. It hadn't been all that long ago that her daddy seeing her naked was not a big deal, but things were changing. She had one hand over her breasts, and one covering a cut on her shin, blood running down her leg and dripping into the water.

Viktor grabbed a towel and tossed it at her. She covered herself with the towel as much as possible. He picked up a washcloth and applied pressure to the cut. "How did you cut yourself? Did you break something?"

"I was shaving my legs."

He saw his razor, the heavy metal kind with removable blades, sitting on the edge of the tub.

"Why?"

"There was hair on them."

"There is hair on your head. Do you shave that?"

She started crying.

"Why are you crying?"

"All the other girls at school shave their legs. I feel like a freak."

"Well, I suppose that time comes in every young girl's life. But I think you need the proper equipment, not a man's razor. I'll speak to Mrs. Valerius. Perhaps she can help you."

"What about Zoe?"

"Very well then, Miss Zoe. Perhaps that would be better. She's a young woman. I assume she shaves her legs."

He moved his hand away from the cut. "It has stopped bleeding, for the moment. Dry off, and try to not get blood on the towel, then I will put a bandage on it."

She looked at him but didn't move. He stood and chuckled. "I'll wait outside. Call me when you're ready."

Zoe didn't shave her legs, she had them waxed, indulging herself in a small luxury for a girl working her way through college. When Mrs. Valerius received news of Christine's plight, she quickly arranged for a girls' day out at the spa, her treat. Raoul was not invited, nor did he want to be—while he enjoyed Christine's company there were some places men were just not meant to go. Instead, he received an extended violin lesson from Viktor in the little cottage.

Christine began to question just how important smooth legs were when the hair was ripped from hers by the attendant at the spa. "Ouch!" Shaving wasn't that bad, she decided, at least until you lacerated yourself, but here it seemed the pain would never end. Mrs. Valerius and Zoe seemed to endure the pain much better, and Christine hoped that if she decided to try it again—apparently the results of waxing lasted but a few weeks—it would get easier.

There were also massages, which Christine found a bit unnerving but relaxing; facials, something Christine's soft, smooth skin needed not at all, but fun nevertheless; and manicures, which every girl can always use. Christine decided against anything fancy and went with clear polish. After a few hours at the spa, waxed, kneaded, peeled, buffed, and polished, Christine felt all grown up, and limp.

There was another matter—which Viktor had related to Zoe, with some degree of embarrassment—that needed attention. Mrs. Valerius berated herself for failing to recognize the developing issue, but then she never had children of her own, and it had simply not occurred to her that Christine needed a bra. Viktor and daughter cooked and ate most of their meals in the little cottage. The weather in late winter and early spring was, as usual, quite cool in Santa Monica, and so Christine was often wearing a jacket when Mrs. Valerius saw her, but there were times, in the house, singing with Zoe, that Mrs. Valerius now distinctly remembered Christine wearing little T-shirts. Had it been her own daughter, she would have immediately acted. She resolved to make up for it, and to pay more attention to the child's needs in the future.

They hit the shops. While Zoe normally haunted the thrift stores and discounters, she knew full well how to shop at the upscale boutiques and department stores where Mrs. Valerius took them. Once more Christine missed her mother, as this was clearly a rite of passage every young girl should share with the woman who brought her into the world. While that was on her mind, however, there were more immediate concerns, the measuring, the fittings, the trying on, and the selection of the proper bra. Some of the girls at Ogden Hall were child models, and Christine quickly realized what they must go through every day on the job—this was exhausting, and embarrassing. They finally settled on an assortment of bras—although one style would have easily sufficed, and Christine left the store wearing one of them, now definitely feeling all grown up, although a bit odd with this thing around her chest, and the realization that it, or one like it, would be there for decades to come. Suddenly being a little girl didn't seem so bad.

————

Hannah, dressed in scrubs, having just come from the emergency room where she performed a minor miracle on a young man mangled in a construction accident, walked down the hallway of the hospital. Doctor Gaston, another surgeon, caught up to her.

"Doctor Chagny," Doctor Gaston said.

Hannah slowed and turned her head. "Doctor Gaston."

He caught up and they walked, both too busy to stop and chat.

"I saw Raoul on the Promenade."

"Behaving, I hope."

"Oh yes. He was playing the violin and a very pretty young blonde girl was singing."

"That would be his new best friend, Christine."

"I'm no expert, but she seemed quite good."

"She is."

"I gave them a couple of dollars."

Hannah suddenly stopped. "They were soliciting money?"

"Oh yes. Your nanny was passing the hat, as it were."

"I'll have to speak to Zoe about this."

"Oh no, you don't understand. They were giving their earnings to the homeless."

Doctor Gaston pulled a wad of bills from his pocket and peeled off a hundred. "I didn't have much cash on me at the time, so please give this to Raoul."

He handed her the hundred, which she hesitantly took.

"That's quite a young man you are raising. I am very much impressed. Let me know when they will be performing again. I'll bring my wife. She's an opera fanatic. Well, you know that, of course."

At dinner that night, Hannah quietly slid the hundred across the table toward Raoul.

"What's that for?" Raoul asked.

"Doctor Gaston, a colleague of mine at the hospital, said he caught your performance on the Promenade a few days ago. He said he was a bit short of cash at the time and wanted to make an additional donation."

Raoul stared at the hundred, and then shifted his eyes toward his father. Chagny stared back for a moment, in complete silence and then asked, "Is there something you wanted to tell us, Raoul?"

"Okay, I've been busking on the Promenade with Christine and Zoe."

"Busking?" Chagny asked.

"I have no idea how to say it in French," Hannah said. "It's hardly a word that comes up in everyday conversation, but what he is trying to say is that he is a street performer."

"I have a license and everything."

"Street performer? License?" Chagny grew even more confused.

"Where did you get a license?" Hannah asked.

"At City Hall. Zoe—"

"Ah," Hannah said, "the co-conspirator."

"It was Christine's idea."

"Don't try to blame the girl," Chagny said, becoming irritated. "Be a man and accept responsibility, for whatever it is that you are doing." He looked at Hannah. "What exactly is it that he's doing?"

"You've seen street performers on the Promenade, my dear, whenever we go there to eat. That's what he's doing. He plays the violin and Christine sings, and people give them money."

"Sometimes I play electric guitar and Zoe plays the drums."

"Is your allowance not enough? Do you not have everything you need?" Chagny asked.

Hannah burst into laughter. "Okay, enough. He's donating the money to the homeless, at least according to Doctor Gaston." She turned to Raoul. "That is what you are doing with the money isn't it?"

"Yes ma'am. We were passing it out as we earned it, but the cops made us stop because the crowds of homeless people following us were starting to annoy people. So now we just collect the money and take it to the Santa Monica Shelter." He reached out and grabbed the hundred. "Tell Doctor Gaston thanks."

"Well, I am quite impressed, Raoul," Chagny said. "I'll match whatever you collect."

"Cool!"

"When our friends see you busking, especially if they give you money, please tell them what you are up to," Hannah said. "I don't want them to think we have fallen on hard times."

12

THE FIRST DATE

It had been a particularly arduous lesson in the little cottage. Viktor watched silently as Raoul put away his violin. He knew the last piece needed work, and expected some harsh, but needed, criticism. Instead, there was nothing. Did that mean that his teacher liked it? Doubtful, Raoul thought, as Viktor was a master violinist and expected nothing short of perfection from his students. He had only been taking lessons from Mr. Daaé for a short time, and while he knew he was improving, there was always something said at the end of the lesson.

"Needs work," Viktor finally said.

"Yes sir, I know."

"You will play it four times tonight at home and we will try again tomorrow."

"Yes sir."

Raoul picked up the violin case and stood nervously. Viktor gathered and stacked sheet music, finally turning toward Raoul.

"Is there something more?"

"Yes sir." Raoul paused, silently rehearsing yet again what he would say next. He had to get it just right.

"Well?"

"I would like to take Christine to dinner, sir, with your permission."

"Dinner?"

"Yes sir."

"With your family?"

"No sir, just me and Christine."

Viktor looked down at him and raised his eyebrows.

"For Valentine's Day," Raoul added, upset with himself that he had left out that important bit of information.

"Valentine's Day?"

"Yes sir."

"You two are lovebirds already?" Viktor toyed with the boy.

"No sir, well, I mean I like her and stuff." Raoul struggled for the right words. "It's just dinner."

"My daughter is far too young to be going on dates with boys."

Raoul was dejected.

"How would you take her to dinner, on the bus?" Viktor asked.

Raoul perked up. "No sir, Zoe would drive us."

"It would be a double date, this Valentine's dinner, with your governess and her gentleman friend?"

"No sir." Raoul wasn't expecting that. "I don't think so. Zoe didn't say anything about bringing a date. She's just driving us."

"So, Miss Zoe would drop you off and it would be just you and my Christine at dinner?"

"Yes sir."

"Alone, just you and my precious daughter?"

"No sir, there would be lots of other people at the restaurant."

"Where is this restaurant?"

"It's here, sir, in Santa Monica."

"Hamburgers, hot dogs, what kind of place is this restaurant in Santa Monica?"

"It's a French restaurant, sir. My family eats there often. It's very nice."

Raoul waited for an answer that seemed an eternity in coming.

"I will take it under consideration, speak to Miss Zoe, and let you know my decision."

"Thank you, sir." Raoul said.

Smiling hopefully, Raoul snatched up his violin case and bolted through the door, racing across the yard, into the back door of the main house and through the kitchen.

"Whoa, slow down," Mrs. Valerius said. "Have a cookie."

She held a cookie sheet filled with freshly baked cookies. Raoul screeched to a halt and grabbed a couple.

"Thank you, ma'am."

He headed toward the living room, and then turned and grabbed another. "For Christine," he said, again turning away.

"Don't forget Zoe," Mrs. Valerius said, but he was already through the door. "Never mind, I'll bring them in."

Christine looked up from her homework and Zoe from the piano as Raoul dashed into the living room. He quickly dropped his violin case onto a chair, shifted the hot cookies into his other hand, and handed one to Christine.

"What did he say?" Christine asked, taking the cookie.

"He said he would take it under consideration, or something, and speak to Zoe."

"To me?" Zoe asked, turning away from the piano.

"I told him you'd be driving us. He asked if we'd be double dating."

"Did you tell him my love life is nonexistent at the moment?"

"I didn't know what to tell him, so I just said you would drop us off at the restaurant and there would be lots of people there."

"Works for me," Zoe said.

Mrs. Valerius stepped in, having transferred the cookies to a serving tray. She stepped over to the piano and Zoe took one.

"I'll go to the gym later," Zoe added, taking another.

Zoe took a bite. She looked up, noticing both kids staring at her.

"What?"

"Go talk to Mr. Daaé," Raoul pleaded as Christine nodded her head enthusiastically.

"Now?" Zoe took another bite. "These cookies are to die for." She looked at Mrs. Valerius, who smiled back.

"I think we should let him come to me in his own time," Zoe said, turning her attention to Raoul.

"I already have reservations," Raoul said. "We don't have any time to waste."

"Well, at least let me finish my cookie."

Mrs. Valerius extended the tray and Zoe took another. They both enjoyed watching the kids squirm.

All heads suddenly turned toward the sound of the back door closing. A moment later Viktor stepped into the room.

"Mrs. Valerius, I could smell your cookies all the way out to the little cottage."

"They are your favorite, I believe, Mr. Daaé."

"Yes madam, they are."

Mrs. Valerius held out the tray and Viktor took two cookies as the kids watched intently.

"Daddy, isn't there something you wanted to talk to Zoe about?"

"Ah yes," Viktor said, savoring a cookie. "I read your piece, Miss Zoe. It is superb. I look forward to playing it."

"Thank you, Mr. Daaé."

"Isn't there something else, Daddy?" Christine slipped over beside her father and put her arms around him, looking up with those beautiful blue eyes.

"Go out to the little cottage and practice your scales. I will be out presently," Viktor said. "I need first to speak to Miss Zoe."

"Yes Daddy." Christine beamed as she glanced over at Raoul and then scurried out of the room.

Zoe pulled a large wad of keys out of her bag and handed them to Raoul. "Go wait in the car."

Raoul grabbed the keys and his violin case and darted toward the front door.

"You can start it, but do not move it," Zoe called after him. She turned to Viktor. "He fancies himself a Formula One driver. Hopefully he'll grow out of it."

Viktor and Zoe stood facing each other, rather awkwardly, until Zoe realized he was waiting for her to sit first. She obliged, taking a seat on the piano bench. Viktor sat in a nearby chair.

Mrs. Valerius stepped in with a teapot and three cups on a tray. Viktor immediately stood. "Please sit down, Mr. Daaé, and I'll pour the tea."

Viktor sat back down, and Mrs. Valerius poured two cups of tea. "Should I leave the two of you alone?"

"No, please stay," Viktor said. "Your opinion will be welcome. Master Raoul has asked my Christine out to dinner, a date, as it were."

Zoe smiled.

"Apparently I am the last to know of this plot," Viktor added, taking a sip of tea.

"I'm afraid so," Zoe said. "Raoul had already asked Christine when he came to me to work out the logistics."

"And my daughter obviously accepted his offer of this date to dinner."

"Actually, she told him he would have to ask your permission first."

Viktor smiled slightly, quite pleased.

"It seems you have raised her well," Mrs. Valerius said.

"Thank you, madam." Viktor paused, collecting his thoughts. "I had not planned on this moment coming so soon, and without her mother here to help with the decision and the preparations."

Mrs. Valerius stood and refilled Viktor's teacup. "We are here to help in any way we can."

"This is a fancy restaurant, where Master Raoul proposes to take her?"

"It is fairly upscale," Zoe replied. "The Chagnys eat there often."

"Christine has only one dress, other than her school clothes, the one she wore when we were invited to dine at the Chagny's."

"Please allow us," Mrs. Valerius quickly said.

"No, madam, you and the professor have done too much for us already, the little cottage, her tuition, and school uniforms."

"Raoul is smitten, Mr. Daaé," Zoe said. "I don't think he will care what she wears."

"But we cannot embarrass the count. You said he and his wife dine often at this fancy restaurant." Viktor sipped his tea. "I am taking on a new student this week. I can spare a few dollars for a dress for my Christine."

"As a college student who will be paying off student loans for years to come, I know all the best places to shop for bargains," Zoe said. "I will be happy to take Christine shopping for a new dress that fits your budget."

"Thank you, Miss Zoe. I would very much appreciate that."

Zoe stood up. "I'll take Raoul home and then come back and pick up Christine, if that's okay with you, Mr. Daaé, and we will go shopping tonight." She moved toward the door.

Viktor quickly stood. "Miss Zoe." She stopped and turned. "Christine is so young, and not nearly as worldly as Master Raoul. I fear she knows nothing of boys. Am I doing the right thing in allowing her to go on this date?"

"Relax, Mr. Daaé. It wasn't that long ago that I was her age. I know plenty about boys and I know Raoul. Christine is a smart girl and seems to have her head on straight. She will be fine, but if Raoul is anything less than the perfect gentlemen, he'll deal with me even before his father gets ahold of him."

"I grew up on a farm in Sweden, so this is all new to me. Do children their age in California normally go out on dates?"

"They go out on group dates," Zoe said. "As far as I know, this will be Raoul's first actual date alone with a girl."

"I see." The concern showed on Viktor's face.

"It's just puppy love."

"Puppy love?"

ZOE'S CAR WAS RUNNING, the heater on, and it was quite toasty as she slid into the driver's seat.

"Well," Raoul asked impatiently. "What did he say?"

"You're in like Flynn."

"Huh?"

"He said yes, although he does have some reservations."

"What reservations?"

"Christine has had a difficult life. She hasn't even been around other kids her own age for a while, so you must be on your best behavior."

"But she can go?"

"She can go."

"Yes!"

Zoe pulled away from the curb.

"Let's go shopping," he said. "I need to get her a gift."

"That won't be necessary."

"Why not?"

"You're taking her to dinner at a fancy French restaurant. How many young girls get that for Valentine's?"

"I don't know, lots of them?"

"In your world maybe, but not hers. This is all new to her."

"Okay, if you say so."

"If you get her a gift, she will feel obligated to get you one, and she and her father definitely do not have the money for such things. Trust me. Dinner is more than enough."

She drove for a moment, and then turned to Raoul.

"There is something you can get for her."

"What is it?"

"We'll work on it tomorrow."

ZOE EXPERTLY FLIPPED through a rack of dresses in the large thrift store, finally selecting one, pulling it out, and draping it over the rack.

"This one's nice."

Christine reached for the price tag, looked, and nodded her head.

"Do you want to try it on?"

Christine nodded again and they set off toward the makeshift dressing rooms.

"What about shoes?" Zoe asked.

"I have shoes."

Zoe suspected she had only the pair she wore to dinner at the Chagny's, but those would do with this dress.

"Do I have enough money, with tax and stuff?"

"Just enough," Zoe replied. It wasn't much, and she knew it was more than Mr. Daaé could afford, but she was committed to finding the best dress for the money. "There might even be enough left over to get him a card."

"I made him a card already," Christine said as she stepped through the curtain.

"Perfect," Zoe said.

"Will the card be enough? Should I get him a gift, candy, or something?"

"Boys give girls candy for Valentine's, not the other way around. The card will be enough, even better since you made it yourself. You don't need to get him anything else."

Zoe nudged Christine's shoulder, spinning her around so she could get a good look at the dress.

"This will work. Unfortunately, there's not a lot available for a girl your age."

"You mean a girl with no boobs," Christine said, looking in the mirror, somewhat dejectedly.

Zoe laughed.

"You'll get there. Don't be in such a rush."

Zoe took another look at the dress.

"What do you think? Do you want to get this one?"

Christine nodded her head, slipped through the curtains, and peeled off the dress.

"There is one thing you could get him, and it won't cost a penny," Zoe said.

"What is it?"

"We'll work on it tonight when I get you home."

"Tell me! Please!"

"Patience, my dear, patience."

———

CHRISTINE SAT ON THE piano bench, fidgeting, her feet dangling above the floor, wearing her new thrift-store dress. Her father sat nearby. Christine's head turned quickly toward the sound of the doorbell.

Professor Valerius stepped over and opened the door.

"Good evening, Professor," Raoul said.

"Good evening, Raoul. Please come in."

Christine was already on her feet, quite eager. Viktor slowly stood but did not move away from the chair. Mrs. Valerius stepped in from the kitchen, wiping her hands on a towel. Zoe slipped in and Professor Valerius closed the door behind her.

A normal thirteen-year-old boy might be intimidated, but Raoul was a man on a mission. He smiled at Christine and then strode purposefully across the room to Viktor, who stood.

"I am here to collect Christine, sir, with your permission."

"Very well, Master Raoul, have her home by ten o'clock, no later."

"Yes sir."

They shook hands. Raoul stepped back and turned toward Christine, who rushed past him and into her father's arms.

"Thank you, Daddy."

"I wish your mother were here to see how beautiful you are."

He hugged her tightly and stroked her hair.

"You have a good time and mind your manners."

"Yes Daddy."

"And you as well, Master Raoul. My Christine is the most precious thing in my life."

"Yes sir. I will."

"You all have my cell number," Zoe said. "I'll call if we run into traffic, but otherwise we will be back by ten."

Christine kissed her father and broke away, wiping tears. Raoul extended his arm and Christine eagerly took it, the tears turning into a broad smile.

Zoe snapped a photo with her cell phone.

"They make such a cute couple, don't you think? I'll email you copies."

Professor Valerius held open the door as Zoe and the kids hurried through it, and then closed it behind them.

"Well," Viktor said, "I have to prepare for tomorrow's lessons."

"Nonsense," Professor Valerius said. "You will have dinner with us."

"I could not impose."

"You won't be imposing," Mrs. Valerius said. "I've prepared dinner for the three of us. And then we will all wait together for Christine to come home. We are just as nervous as you."

"Very well. After dinner perhaps I will fetch my violin and we will make music to occupy the time."

"An excellent idea," Professor Valerius said.

Viktor looked at the front door. "My daughter is so young and innocent. I hope I am not making a mistake. I remember when I first went out with her mother. How I wish she were here tonight."

"Mr. Daaé, we have known the Chagnys for years and Raoul has always been well-behaved. I recommended Zoe for the position as his nanny. If she trusts Raoul with your daughter, then I have to believe she is in good hands."

13

ZOE

Zoe's birth was completely unplanned, or more likely, as she came to suspect years later, the result of one six-pack too many. Her two older brothers were in high school by the time Zoe started to school in a barren, dusty, although quite prosperous small town in the Permian Basin. Her father worked in the oil fields, where the money was good, when work was available. Her mother drank.

The oil business had always been one of boom-and-bust cycles, and hardly anyone bothered to squirrel away a few acorns during the booms to be able to weather the busts. A popular bumper sticker in Midland, Texas, during one such bust summed it up: "Please Lord, let there be another oil boom, and this time I promise to not piss it all away."

Kitty, Zoe's mother, pissed it all away. Zoe's father was one of those hardworking blue-collar guys who handed over his paycheck to his wife and let her handle the bills. As long as he had a good truck, food, beer, a place to sleep, and pocket money, he was happy. He made good money and assumed his wife was spending it wisely. They had a roof over their heads, the kids had clothes to wear and food on the table, so as far as he was concerned, all was right with the world.

With two big brothers Zoe had little choice but to become a tomboy. She was frequently knocked down while trying to keep up with them, but she jumped up and kept going, a lesson learned early that had served her well over the years. She also quickly became a daddy's girl. As soon as she could climb up into his truck, she went with him. There was no reason to stay at home—her mother showed far more interest in her cocktails than her daughter.

After both brothers got their own apartments, and jobs as roughnecks, Zoe spent even more time with her daddy, which wasn't much, as he worked lots of overtime. Drilling oil wells is hardly a nine-to-five job and he would often not come home until long after midnight. Neither did her mother. She wasn't working, she was clubbing, leaving her daughter home alone, which was fine with Zoe. She spent the hours practicing on the cheap keyboard her father had bought for her at a pawnshop. It wasn't a real piano, but the keys were in the right position, and it made the right sounds, so it served her purposes. She was composing her own music by age ten, which she performed for her father who declared it wonderful although he had no idea what it was. It certainly wasn't country and western. Kitty offered no opinion. She just threw her head back and downed another Manhattan.

Puberty visited Zoe early. Before her eleventh birthday her grandmother bought her a much-needed bra during her annual summer trip from California. Kitty had either not noticed or not cared, and Zoe's father really didn't want to know about such things. That was one more thing his wife should have handled. The boys in school noticed, reinforcing Zoe's desire to remain a tomboy, continuing to dress in jeans and baggy shirts so as to not attract attention to her new curves. She had little interest in the local boys, anyway, finding them crude and uninteresting. Most of them considered rap, or hip-hop, or whatever they called it, to be music and that alone was reason enough to have nothing to do with them.

While the money was good working in the oil field, the money was even better being killed in the oil field. Zoe was twelve when a well blew out and her father was impaled on a section of drilling pipe. He was killed instantly, and Zoe's life was instantly changed, her mother's, not so much. Kitty continued drinking, and as soon as her husband was in the ground, she went back to clubbing.

The life insurance check arrived soon enough, and Kitty set about spending what was left after the burial expenses. The settlement with the oil company took a bit longer.

Zoe suggested she use some of the windfall to go to cosmetology school and open her own salon, something she had once talked about doing. Kitty expected the settlement to be substantial, even after the lawyers took a huge chunk, so why in the world would she want to work in a beauty salon, or own one? Some of that money could also have sent Zoe to college, but the thought never crossed Kitty's mind.

Without having to worry about her husband coming home unexpectedly

Kitty had less reason to go out clubbing. She just moved the party home and there were plenty of partiers. It also reduced her risk of yet another DUI, since she could drink until she passed out and not have to drive home.

The endless parties seriously impacted Zoe's treasured alone time. She barricaded the door to her room, but it was impossible to play, or compose music with all the noise and debauchery. She cried a lot on those nights, not only for her father, but also for the miserable state of her young life.

For as long as Zoe could remember the lock on the bathroom door had not worked, and it had mattered not at all, at least not until a succession of men, mostly oil-field workers, started staying over. More than once the door had suddenly opened just as she was stepping out of the shower. There was always an "Oh, sorry, I didn't know anyone was in here," but their eyes never left her naked body while the words came out. She rummaged through her father's workshop, found a latch, and the required tools, and installed it on the bathroom door.

Zoe had long run around the house in panties and a T-shirt, but that changed quickly with new and interested eyes following her every move. Even after she started wearing baggy clothes at home, the eyes followed her. There was no disguising her blossoming boobs. By twelve she was turning heads wherever she went.

Kitty had all but burned through the insurance money when the settlement check finally arrived, in the low seven-figure range, and her spending shifted into high gear. Her first major purchase was a brand-new Mercedes, the same one the wives of the oil company executives drove, and the second was a house in Midland. Zoe could not understand why they suddenly needed a five-bedroom, four-bath brick house with a four-car garage for just the two of them, but she didn't question the need for the hot tub and in-ground pool. Those she could use, even more if she had friends, of which she had few, and fewer still now that they were moving into Midland. There was also what must have been the Cadillac of outdoor grills, but Zoe had never seen her mother attempt to cook outdoors. Daddy always did that, on his cheap little grill that he had bought at a garage sale.

Her mother had rarely taken her shopping anywhere other than Walmart, but matching bikinis, in honor of the new pool, were soon purchased from an upscale boutique in the Midland Park Mall. Few women in their forties and girls of twelve have the bodies for matching bikinis. Kitty and Zoe were no exception, and neither had any business wearing those barely-there creations, although for completely different reasons.

Kitty spent thousands on furniture for the new house. Zoe didn't particularly like it—she was quite happy with what they had. She was also disappointed that with all the money being spent on furniture it never occurred to her mother to buy a piano.

The move to Midland also meant a new school for Zoe, just as she was entering seventh grade, a terrible time to change schools. She was never particularly popular at her old school, but she had been with the same group of kids since kindergarten, had a few friends, and had learned to deal with the others. The new school was culture shock. It was far larger, and the kids were far richer and snottier than she had known before. Being the new girl was never easy. Being the new girl in seventh grade with the body of a high-school cheerleader was fraught with peril, from both sides of the gender divide. Zoe resolved to make it in this new school, however, and was somewhat comforted by the fact that they had an excellent music department—there was so much oil money that even after lavishing piles of it on athletics there was plenty left over for the arts. Zoe quickly immersed herself in music, found a few kindred spirits, and made it through the school year relatively unscathed.

Zoe even had a date to the spring formal with the son of a petroleum geologist whose fractional points on several successful wells had left him rather well off. She managed to catch her mother sober long enough to buy a new dress. It was too low-cut for Zoe's tastes, especially since she had been hiding them ever since starting at the new school, but Kitty insisted that if you have it, you should flaunt it. Kitty certainly did. The geologist's son, unfortunately, took easily to being a rich kid and was convinced that certain privileges accompanied wealth. His eyes were on Zoe's ample cleavage all during the dance, as were many others, and in the limo on the way home he made his move, bolstered no doubt, by the contents of the flask in the pocket of his tuxedo. She had not objected when he put his arm around her shoulder and pulled closer, but suddenly the other hand was on her knee, and then felt its way upward, while he buried his face in her cleavage.

She pushed him so hard he bounced off the door, and on the rebound her fist was waiting for his nose, which she promptly broke, splattering blood on his starched white shirt. The limo driver hit the brake and looked in the mirror, and quickly determined that no action was required on his part other than driving immediately to the young lady's home. The boy was cowering against the door, as far as possible from Zoe, whose knuckles hurt like hell.

Kitty never questioned why there were blood splatters on Zoe's dress or why her hand was bruised, and Zoe never said anything about it. She knew her mother wouldn't have cared, she had handled it herself, as always, and that was that.

ONE MISERABLY HOT DAY in the summer of her fourteenth year, Zoe was lounging by the pool, quite topless. She was alone, so it didn't really matter. Kitty and her newest boyfriend, whom Zoe had not yet met, were in Ruidoso at the horse races, or more likely, Zoe assumed, at the casino bar. Either way Zoe had the house to herself for the weekend and relished the solitude. Classical music played over the state-of-the-art sound system on the patio by the pool, so she didn't hear the garage door opening.

Having seen what the sun had done to her mother's leathery skin, or was it the booze, Zoe sat up and applied the highest available SPF sunscreen. Rather than just slather it on, she did it slowly, imitating the TV commercials she had seen, and it felt rather sensuous.

It also looked rather sensuous, through the blinds in the kitchen, as Kitty's new boyfriend feasted his eyes on this unexpected delight. He knew that Kitty had a daughter, fourteen as he recalled, but surely this wasn't her. This must have been a cousin, or a friend, or maybe a college girl house-sitting.

The boyfriend stepped into the living room, where Kitty was busy opening a bottle of booze at the bar. "Do you have any steaks in the freezer? I'm going to go out and fire up that fancy grill out by the pool."

"Okay," Kitty replied.

Zoe glanced up at the large thermometer. It was 110 degrees in the shade, so she dived into the pool and swam a length underwater, returned and was just coming up the steps out of the pool, holding the rail, as the boyfriend walked across the patio.

"Oh, sorry," he said. "I didn't realize anyone was out here." His eyes never left her breasts, which she quickly covered with her hands. Rather than turn around and go back into the house, he watched her dash over to the lounge chair and pick up a towel, which she quickly wrapped around herself, after turning around to deprive him of one last glimpse.

Kitty barely looked up as Zoe raced through the house, dripping wet, clutching the towel to her breast. Instead, she walked out onto the patio and changed the music.

Steaks were grilled. There was no explanation for the early return from the mountains, nor any mention of the boyfriend seeing Zoe topless at the pool. He did, however, position himself at the table directly across from her. She wore an oversized flannel shirt, which her mother thought was ridiculous on such a hot day.

The new boyfriend wasted no time moving in and Zoe soon began calling him "the creeper," not to his face, of course. That it pissed off her mother was a bonus, but Kitty never asked for an explanation.

Zoe had a private bathroom off her bedroom. Both had locks. If the creeper tried to pull the bathroom stunt, he would have to go through two locked doors. Surely he wasn't that stupid.

It never occurred to Zoe that there was a difference between a privacy lock and a security lock. A security lock required a key to enter, but bathrooms and bedrooms typically had privacy locks, which could be easily opened with a flattened paper clip or small screwdriver. Zoe never knew which the creeper used. All she knew was that she woke up to find his hand where it had absolutely no business being, and that he reeked of alcohol. Her screams went unheard—Kitty, as usual at this time of night, was passed out.

Zoe pulled away and rolled off the bed, tearing herself away from the creeper's grasp. She grabbed the Louisville Slugger that one of her brothers had left behind, and swung for the fences, connecting solidly with the creeper's left temple. He staggered backward, crashing into the keyboard her father had bought for her, destroying it.

When the first responders responded, they found Zoe standing in the front door, wearing nothing but a T-shirt, tightly clutching what was left of the Louisville Slugger—she had broken it on the creeper's skull. There were no tears. She seemed quite calm and composed.

"He's in my bedroom," Zoe said, pointing with the bat. "Second door on the left."

"Is there anyone else in the house?" the cop asked.

"My mom. She's unconscious."

The cop's eyes went immediately to the half bat.

"Natural causes," Zoe added.

The creeper came out of a coma a few days later. Zoe had never heard of a plea bargain but was told that one was being negotiated and that she would not have to testify, which was just fine with her. Once more she had handled it herself and that was that.

Kitty soon had a new live-in boyfriend, who steered very clear of Zoe and always looked the other way when she entered a room. Zoe had had enough, however, and her brother Greg arrived one Saturday morning to load her and all her things into his F-250 pickup truck for the trip to Granny's house. He also gave her a shiny new aluminum baseball bat, unbreakable, he assured her.

They took I-20 and drove straight through to Los Angeles, stopping only for fuel, food, and restrooms. Although she had no license, Zoe took the wheel on long straight stretches through the desert while her brother napped. After unloading Zoe and her things and eating his fill of Granny's chicken-fried steak and mashed potatoes, Greg slept a few hours and hit the road. He had to be back at work in the oil field on Monday morning.

Zoe never knew what happened to the creeper, nor did she care. She was out of it, and now living with Granny in sunny southern California. It was a new start, but the shiny new aluminum bat was beside her bed just in case.

GRANNY HAD GROWN UP in Lubbock, Texas, and had graduated from Lubbock High School in 1955. She married her high school sweetheart and, after completing a course at the local business school, went to work as a secretary and put him through the petroleum engineering program at Texas Tech. After four years of ROTC, he was commissioned a second lieutenant in the Air Force and they soon left for a tour in Germany, where he oversaw fueling airplanes, not exactly his field, but it was petroleum. When his Air Force obligation was up, he went to work as a petroleum engineer for an oil company in Midland, where he and his wife started their family. Once the kids were grown, he took a job with a southern California oil company.

Granny also went back to work, as secretary at the Belen Conservatory of Music. She didn't need to work, her husband assured her, but she wanted to stay busy, and music was, after all, her first love. She continued in that position even after her husband died.

Zoe arrived in Los Angeles assuming she would go to whatever school was near Granny's house and dreading changing schools yet again. She would be a freshman in high school, and all the other freshmen would be new to that school as well, or so she hoped.

Granny had other plans, however, being aware of Zoe's musical talent, and suggested that she audition for the Belen Conservatory of Music. Zoe had never heard of it, never imagined that such a thing existed, and had only a few short weeks to prepare an audition. Granny working there provided an inside track, but it would be all up to Zoe. Fortunately, Granny had a piano in her living room, and Zoe plunged into finishing her latest composition, which she would play as part of her audition. The rest of it would be the headmaster and staff poring over the composition itself, dissecting every note.

On the wall in the living room were several photographs from Granny's younger days. Taking a break from the piano one day, Zoe studied them carefully.

"Is that you?" Zoe asked.

"That's me." Granny laughed. "I was quite a dish back then. We were hanging out at the Hi-D-Ho."

"Who are the dudes?"

"That's J.I.," Granny said, pointing them out one by one. "Joe B., Sonny, and the one in the glasses is Buddy, but I guess you figured that out already."

"Buddy who?"

"Sit down, Zoe," Granny commanded. "Your musical education is about to begin." She stepped across the room to a vintage record player, carefully removed a genuine vinyl record from the stand, and gingerly placed it on the turntable.

"Words of Love," by Buddy Holley floated from the record player. Zoe was mesmerized, and she was quite certain that was a tear sliding down Granny's cheek.

Granny kept changing the records, and Zoe kept listening, curled up on the floor in front of the record player. When Granny had spun the last disc, she reminisced for hours about her days in Lubbock. Zoe was full of questions, and they talked as they prepared and ate dinner, and then started through the stack again, with Zoe making notes and organizing her favorites. She was even more thrilled when Granny pulled out sheet music and they sat down at the piano.

LUNG CANCER FORCED Granny to retire from her job at the Belen Conservatory of Music when Zoe was a junior there, and she died before Zoe graduated, but not before she arrived by ambulance to hear dozens of students she had known for years perform Zoe's senior composition, clearly classical, but heavily influenced by Buddy Holley and the Crickets.

It took some months for Granny's estate to be settled, and Zoe simply stayed in the house and went to school and hoped no one would notice. She had never known for sure if Granny had become her legal guardian, so she tried to fly under the radar until she turned eighteen. Granny left all her memorabilia, including her treasured 1955 Lubbock High yearbook, her car, and piano, to Zoe, with the remainder being divided equally among Zoe and the rest of the grandchildren.

When the house sold Zoe moved into an apartment near campus, with far too many roommates. There was no room for a piano, so she sold it cheap, carefully evaluating each offer and deciding on the best home for it. Zoe's share of the remainder of the estate was enough to provide a buffer as she struck out on her own. She found a job at a restaurant near campus where the main attraction was waitresses in Daisy Dukes and unbuttoned checkered shirts tied under the breasts.

"May I take your order," Zoe asked.

Professor Valerius looked up, as surprised to see her as she was him.

"Zoe, I didn't know you worked here."

"A girl's gotta make a living."

Professor Valerius turned to a younger man at the table.

"Zoe is one of my first-year students in composition."

The younger man seemed more interested in her other attributes. "You are a composer?"

"Someday, hopefully."

"I'm trying to sell the professor my music notation software. I'll leave him a demo. Maybe you'd like to try it out."

"Sure."

The next day Zoe was summoned to the professor's office, ostensibly to review the young salesman's software, but she dreaded the meeting following the encounter at the restaurant.

"I wanted you to know that I don't frequent restaurants like that," Professor Valerius said. "I had never been there before, but the salesman insisted the food was good."

"It's not a place I prefer to work, but I need the money."

"Oh no. I didn't mean to impugn—"

Zoe laughed. "That's okay. My boobs have caused me no end of grief since I turned twelve, so I decided to put them to good use. The tips are good, great if you bend over, far more than I could make playing piano at wedding receptions and bar mitzvahs."

"College has become obscenely expensive. I washed dishes and bused tables twenty hours a week to pay my way. That doesn't work these days."

"It certainly doesn't." She grinned. "Although there are a few girls on campus who get by working twenty hours a week at the strip joints near LAX, and they'll graduate with no debt."

"No names, please."

"The guy said something about a music notation demo."

"You can try it if you like, but it's no great shakes. I believe he was mainly looking for investors."

"He was mainly looking at my boobs."

Professor Valerius laughed. "If you are looking for a career change, I have friends, a very well-do-do and respected couple, with a young son in need of a nanny."

"I don't know if I'd be any good on diaper duty," Zoe replied.

"I think this one has already been potty trained," Professor Valerius replied. "He walks and talks and even plays a serviceable violin."

"Sounds interesting, but I doubt it pays as much as I'm making in tips."

"Maybe not, but it's live-in, free room and board, and you wouldn't be ogled and pawed by jerks."

"Where?"

"Santa Monica. Did I mention they have a grand piano and season tickets to the opera, ballet, and symphony?"

The Chagny's background check on Zoe turned up nothing of interest, other than the fact that she had moved to California when she was fourteen to live with her grandmother but enrolling at the Belen Conservatory of Music shortly thereafter seemed to explain the sudden move. There was no mention of batting practice on the creeper's cranium. They had no idea what she had been through, and no idea they had just hired a nanny who would make certain their young son was raised to be a gentleman who treated ladies with respect.

Raoul's previous nanny had graduated from college and moved on. She was a dour young woman whose piercings and tattoos increased each year as she squatted in the room next to Raoul. The only good thing about her was that she mostly ignored him, spending her time fingering her phone, raging on social media. She was happy when he started catching rides to and from school with friends—less work for the same pay.

Raoul feared the worst when Zoe arrived at the Chagny house. She wore cowboy boots, a checkered shirt, buttoned and tucked in, along with Levi's. A red bandana tied her hair into a ponytail. He was immediately thrown into the lion's den on the first night when his parents went out and left him to have dinner alone with the newcomer.

"The other girl was a freak," he said.

"I'll try not to be freakish, although I have been known to dress rather oddly."

"When she was a junior, she changed her major to gender studies."

"I'm a music major, composition."

"Oh, yeah. Mom said you were recommended by Professor Valerius." She nodded.

"I think she was trying to chemically castrate me," he said.

"Your mom?"

"The other girl. She kept making me hot tea. I don't even drink hot tea."

"Your *cojones* are safe with me."

"You're weird."

"Austin is weird. I'm from Midland."

"Are you a cowgirl?"

"I am from Texas but never did much cowpunching. I do sometimes listen to country music, but only the classic stuff, not the crap they play now. And I have been known to boot scoot when the spirit moves me."

"Boot scoot?"

"Dance to country music."

"Yuk."

"Don't knock it until you try it. There's some pretty hot chicks in Levi's and cowboy boots."

"My mom wants me to take dance lessons."

"I can teach you to dance."

"None of that sissy stuff."

"What sissy stuff?"

"Ballet."

"You don't like ballet?"

"My parents take me. It's not bad. I like the music. But there's no way I'm wearing tights."

"I was thinking ballroom, waltz, tango, cha-cha."

He shrugged.

"Girls dig it," she said.

The Chagnys could hear "Cotton-Eyed Joe" as they opened the front door. When they stepped into the living room, they found Raoul playing the violin and Zoe dancing. After the initial shock wore off, they found Zoe to be a good influence on Raoul. She not only drove him to the park to practice soccer, but she joined him. She was a girl, so he tried not to be too aggressive, but she quickly disabused him of that notion, knocking him on his butt more than once. She also drove him to his games and stood on the sidelines, cheering loudly, shouting encouragement, and freely dispensing unsolicited advice to the coach.

She taught him to dance and enlisted help from her friends in the dance program at UCLA to teach him the more exotic dances. His friends from school were jealous when they discovered he was tangoing with college girls. The lessons paid off in spades at the spring formal where he was the beau of the ball. Zoe was right. Girls dug it.

14

FRENCH FRIES

ZOE PULLED UP in front of the French restaurant and turned toward Raoul and Christine, in the back seat, sitting close together.

"I'll be at the bookstore. Call me when you're ready to be picked up, or I'll be here at nine-forty-five."

"But Mr. Daaé said ten o'clock," Raoul protested.

"Travel time, my boy, travel time, and you do not want to get Christine home late on your first date."

"Oh yeah, that." Raoul opened the car door. "Okay."

He stepped out and extended his hand.

"Thanks, Zoe," Christine said as she slid across the seat, taking Raoul's hand, and stepping onto the sidewalk.

Christine took Raoul's arm and they walked into the restaurant, just like they knew what they were doing.

The maître d' stepped forward to greet them. "Master Raoul, it's so good to see you again." He turned and bowed slightly toward Christine. She had no idea how to respond so she just smiled and clutched Raoul's arm even more tightly.

The maître d' looked over Raoul's head, and then down at Raoul.

"Will your parents be coming later?"

"No sir, just us. My dad decided to take my mom to Palm Springs for Valentine's, and he said we could use his reservation."

"But of course. Right this way. Your table is ready."

Christine just stood there as the maître d' turned and walked away. Raoul gently nudged her, and she followed, looking over her shoulder trying to discover why Raoul was following rather than walking beside her.

Christine tried to take it all in as they followed the maître d' through the restaurant. Everyone looked so elegant, all dressed up. Even the waiters were well-dressed. She had seen waiters in tuxedoes before, but always in the kitchen or service hallways, never from this vantage point.

She glanced over at a young woman in a long gown playing the piano. She didn't recognize the piece, but it was beautiful and added to the mood.

The maître d' stopped, turned, and motioned toward the table. Raoul immediately stepped forward and pulled out a chair for Christine. She smiled as she sat down, again not knowing the proper response. The maître d' pulled a linen napkin out of the empty water glass in front of Christine, deftly unfolded it and placed it gently on Christine's lap, somewhat startling her. She felt Raoul pushing on the chair and slid forward, bewildered by all the attention.

The maître d' moved into position as Raoul took his seat, placing a hand on the chair as Raoul sat down and slid forward.

"Thank you." Raoul said.

Raoul placed his own napkin in his lap. His father felt the napkin ritual was appropriate for the ladies, but not for the gentlemen, and Raoul had learned his lessons well.

The maître d' handed Raoul a menu. "Your waiter will be with you shortly. Enjoy your dinner."

"Thank you."

"It's all so elegant, and formal. I've never been anywhere like this."

Christine's feet dangled above the floor and swung nervously as she soaked up this completely new environment. A busboy suddenly appeared and dropped to one knee. Christine turned immediately to see why this young man was looking under the table, when she felt a pillow under her swinging feet. The busboy stood, bowed, and disappeared.

"Wow," Christine said. "That was amazing."

She had no way of knowing, and certainly no point of reference, but their table was the best in the house, occupied by two children, which raised a few eyebrows. Nor did she know that hers was the best seat at the best table, providing an excellent view of the entire restaurant.

"This is the table where my father proposed to my mother," Raoul said.

"And they were supposed to be here tonight, at this table, for Valentine's" Christine said. "How romantic."

"My father always reserves this table."

Another busboy filled the water glasses and removed the excess place settings.

Raoul opened the menu. Christine looked around for hers. "Don't I get a menu?"

Raoul closed the menu, smiled, and handed it across the table.

"You can use mine."

Christine took the menu and opened it.

"It's in French."

"It's a French restaurant," Raoul said, holding out his hand for the menu, which Christine handed over with a frown. "In restaurants like this the gentleman normally orders for the lady anyway, so they just bring one menu."

"Oh, okay. What am I having?"

"What would you like?"

"I don't know. The menu is in French."

"Well, you're in luck. I speak French."

The waiter appeared and bowed. "Good evening, Master Raoul. I understand the count and your mother will not be joining us this evening."

"No, it's just us."

"Then I suppose we can dispense with the before-dinner drinks."

"Yes, and the sommelier."

The waiter smiled slightly. They were making light of it, but the lack of drinks and more importantly, wine, meant a smaller tip. Nonetheless, this was the son of one of their best customers and would receive impeccable service.

Christine leaned forward to Raoul, "What's a sommelier?"

"The dude who brings the wine."

"Oh, yeah, we don't need him. I've never had wine."

"Would you like to order now, or should I come back later?" the waiter asked.

"We'd better order now, curfew and all."

"But of course. Might I recommend the duck? It is particularly tasty today."

"Ew," Christine said, making a face. "Ducks are so cute. I couldn't eat one."

"What about salmon?" Raoul asked.

"You mean like salmon patties?"

"Not exactly," the waiter said.

"Do you like steak?" Raoul asked.

"Who doesn't like steak?"

"I think filet mignon for the lady," Raoul said to the waiter and then turned to Christine. "Medium?"

"Sure, not too big."

Raoul and the waiter both smiled.

"Perhaps I'll tell the chef to err on the side of medium well," the waiter said in French.

"*Oui,*" Raoul said. "And I'll have the salmon."

They then spoke for a moment in French with Christine understanding none of it.

"And french fries," Christine said as the waiter turned to go.

"Pardon?" the waiter said, turning back to the table.

"French fries for the young lady," Raoul said.

"I'll see what I can do," the waiter said hesitantly as he turned to go.

Christine extended her arm across the table. "Pinch me."

"Why?"

"So I'll know if this is real or a dream."

Raoul took her hand and held it but didn't pinch her.

"It's real." He released her hand. "If you'll excuse me for a minute, I need to go to the little boys' room."

"Oh, okay." She seemed a bit taken aback.

"Unless you need to go first. I can wait."

"No, go ahead. I'll go later."

He stood and placed his napkin on the table. "I'll be right back."

As Raoul passed by the kitchen on his way to the restroom, he could hear heated words between the chef and the waiter.

"French fries? Not from my kitchen."

The maître d' entered the fray. "But she is the guest of Count Chagny's son."

"Never!" the chef responded. "The count will understand."

Christine heard none of this and turned her attention to the other diners. There were no other kids in the entire restaurant, and she suddenly felt very much out of place. This was not at all her world.

As she looked around, she heard a familiar melody coming from the piano. She turned quickly toward the music. The young woman was gone, and Zoe was at the piano, playing "Quand on n'a que l'amour."

"Oh no, not now," Christine whispered to herself as she pushed back her chair. She started to stand, then stopped as she heard violin music and looked up to see Raoul, walking toward her, playing his violin.

All conversation stopped and all eyes were suddenly on Raoul, and then on Christine as he approached and began circling their table. Christine blushed and smiled as she listened for a moment, and then stood and began singing, in French.

Raoul was surprised, obviously not expecting her to sing, and missed a couple of notes, but Zoe covered him on piano.

There were now audible gasps from the diners as Christine's beautiful soprano filled the room, floating above the piano and violin. Raoul continued circling her slowly and she turned to face him, giving everyone a perfect view of this beautiful child with an angelic voice.

When the song ended there was thunderous applause and cheers. Raoul bowed. Christine curtsied, and they took their seats. Raoul carefully placed his violin in an empty chair.

The chef, waiter, and maître d' watched transfixed as the applause continued, along with calls for an encore.

"This is the insolent child who had the audacity to order french fries from my kitchen?" the chef asked, wiping a tear.

"The very same," the maître d' replied.

"She will have her 'french fries.'"

Zoe swooped in and retrieved Raoul's violin.

"Now I really am going to the bookstore."

"You tricked us," Christine said.

"It wasn't me," Zoe replied. "It was cupid." She turned to go. "Nine-forty-five. Be ready."

Zoe paused on the way out to kiss the maître d' on the cheek.

"Thank you."

"No, Miss Zoe, thank you. Our guests enjoyed it immensely."

The other diners had returned their attention to their meals, and Christine no longer felt their stares.

"I didn't know you were going to play the violin," Christine said.

"I didn't know you were going to sing. Zoe told me she would sneak in through the back door with my violin and wait in the kitchen until I went to the restroom, and then we would surprise you."

"I was definitely surprised," Christine said. "She told me the same thing, except for the part about you and the violin. She was supposed to sneak in and start playing the piano, and then I would sing. When you went to the bathroom and then she started playing I didn't know what to do."

"I thought you didn't speak French."

"I don't. I just sing it. I don't speak Italian either, but you've heard me sing in Italian. And Welsh."

"So, you don't know what the words mean?"

"Oh, no, I do. Zoe translated the lyrics for me. I can't sing it right if I don't know what it means."

"*Quand on n'a que l'amour,*" Raoul said. "When we only have love."

Christine blushed. "I wanted to get you a gift, but I didn't have any money, and Zoe said the song would be better."

"It was the best gift ever."

The waiter arrived with their meals.

"Filet mignon, medium well, for you, mademoiselle," he said, placing the plate in front of Christine.

"And the salmon for you, monsieur."

"Thank you."

"And french fries for the young lady."

"Thanks," Christine said.

"Enjoy." The waiter backed away and was gone.

"Wow, that's salmon?" Christine asked.

"Would you like to try it?"

"Sure," she said.

Raoul cut off a piece and Christine reached across the table and grabbed it with her fork.

"Um, it's good," she said.

She cut off a piece of the filet mignon.

Raoul watched as she took a bite.

"How is the steak?"

"It's amazing. I never had anything like this."

She picked up a french fry with her finger. It was very thin, skin still on it, causing it to curl, and obviously seasoned with something. She tilted her head back and dropped it into her mouth.

"Yum."

They chatted through dinner, laughing and giggling, occasionally drawing smiles from the other diners.

"That was wonderful," Christine said as the busboy cleared their plates.

"But wait, there's more!" Raoul announced.

"More?"

"We haven't had dessert."

"Do we have time?"

He checked his watch. "Barely."

"Will you be having coffees with your dessert?" the waiter asked, appearing from nowhere.

Raoul and the waiter both turned their attention to Christine.

"My daddy doesn't let me drink coffee," she said. "Do you have hot chocolate?"

"I'm sure the chef can whip something up."

"Coffee for me," Raoul said. "Thank you."

"House blend?" the waiter asked.

Raoul nodded.

Dessert appeared in short order with a cake in the shape of a heart, oozing chocolate, and topped with fresh strawberries. The waiter placed it in the middle of the table.

"Compliments of the house," the waiter said. "The staff very much enjoyed your performance. You have the voice of an angel, mademoiselle."

"Thank you," Christine said, dipping her head, slightly embarrassed.

The waiter slipped away.

"Do you like chocolate?" Raoul asked.

"I love chocolate. What are you having?"

Raoul smiled. "I thought we'd share."

"Oh, yeah." Christine laughed. "It looked awfully big for just me."

They ate directly from the cake plate, ignoring the empty saucers directly in front of them.

"Um, chocolate," Christine said as she both ate and sipped the delectable treats.

The cake was almost gone when the waiter slipped the folder containing the check beside Raoul's plate.

"I don't mean to rush you, but it's nine-forty-five, and Miss Zoe is waiting outside."

"Sure, thanks," Raoul said, quickly opening the folder. He looked at the bill, filled in the tip, signed, closed the folder, and handed it to the waiter.

As soon as they finished the cake, coffee, and hot chocolate they scurried toward the door, to a smattering of applause along the way.

Zoe was waiting in the car, the valet holding open the back door. Christine dove in, followed quickly by Raoul.

Zoe looked in the mirror. "Well, how was it?"

"It was amazing. Those were the best french fries ever!" She leaned over and kissed Raoul on the cheek. He grinned. Best kiss ever.

15

THE FUNERAL TRAIN

Following the death of his wife in 1948, Daniel had retreated to the family ranch near Santa Fe. The death certificate listed "stroke" as cause of death, but Daniel knew it was grief. She had gone into mourning following the death of Daniel Jr. and had never recovered.

Although he had a wife and young daughter, which might have enabled him to avoid the draft, at least for a time, Daniel Jr. answered the call of duty and joined the Navy in 1942, soon completed officer training school, and was assigned to the destroyer USS *Johnston* on her commissioning in October 1943.

The *Johnston* went to work immediately in the Pacific, engaging in several actions before sailing on October 12, 1944, to join Taffy 3, a task group consisting of several escort carriers, destroyers, and destroyer escorts. On October 20th, the U.S. Sixth Army, under the command of General Douglas MacArthur, landed on Leyte, charged with retaking the Philippine Islands from the Japanese. Japan could ill afford to lose the Philippines, and quickly dispatched a large naval force, intent on destroying the American landings. The American ground forces were protected by warplanes flying off Taffy 3's escort carriers, and these carriers were in turn protected from the Japanese Navy by the *Johnston* and other destroyers and destroyer escorts in the group.

After inflicting enormous damage on the enemy in the Leyte Gulf, Admiral Bull Halsey's fleet carriers and battleships had steamed out to sea in pursuit of what turned out to be a decoy. The Japanese Navy's Center Force, thought to be retreating with other enemy forces, slipped back into Leyte Gulf under cover of darkness, and threatened to destroy the American forces on the beaches. All that stood between the powerful force of heavy battleships and cruisers was Taffy 3, including USS *Johnston*, to defend the American troops on the beaches.

Johnston and other destroyers immediately began laying smoke to hide the escort carriers from enemy guns. Already under attack from the enemy's longer-range guns, *Johnston*, without awaiting orders, broke formation and raced into the attack, facing a line of seven destroyers, followed by four cruisers, and finally four battleships, including *Yamato*, the largest and most powerful battleship on Earth. The five-inch guns on a destroyer were little more than a nuisance against the armored hulls of the battleships and cruisers, so the captain of the *Johnston* did what any small, scrappy fighter would do against a far larger and more powerful opponent—poke out his eyes. Quickly closing the range, *Johnston* opened fire, aiming for the superstructures of the heavy ships, inflicting considerable damage. As soon as she was in range, she fired all ten of her torpedoes—there was no shortage of targets in the water—and blew the bow off one of the heavy cruisers. Other destroyers, destroyer escorts, and warplanes from the escort carriers in Taffy 3 soon joined the attack and fought so furiously that the Japanese commander thought he had encountered Halsey's main fleet of carriers and battleships and broke off the attack with substantial losses.

The little group of destroyers had turned away a much larger and better armed enemy force, saving the American forces on the beach. Unfortunately, *Johnston* was hit multiple times by big guns from the Japanese cruisers and battleships and was heavily damaged. The bridge was abandoned and when the destroyer escort USS *Samuel B. Roberts* passed by on her way into the attack, her crew saw the captain of *Johnston* at the stern of the ship, shouting orders down through an open hatch to crewmen below who were turning the rudder by hand. Enemy destroyers began circling and shelling the crippled ship, finally knocking out all power.

Lying dead in the water, on fire, with gunners crying out for more ammunition with which to continue the attack, the order was given to abandon ship, and USS *Johnston* went down on October 25th, just two days short of a year since she was commissioned. Of the 327 crew on board, 186 were lost, including the captain and Daniel Jr.

PASSENGER RAIL TRAFFIC was already in decline even before the Great Depression, spurred by automobiles rolling off the assembly lines in Detroit and the ever-expanding network of highways across the nation. Railroads were still the preferred method of travel for long trips—highways of the era left much to be desired—but local traffic dropped precipitously. World War II saw an enormous resurgence in passenger rail traffic, however, as automobile production in Detroit ground to a halt and factories were converted to building tanks and trucks and Jeeps for the war effort. Gasoline and tires were rationed, so even those who already owned automobiles couldn't go very far in them. Then there was the matter of the thirteen million or so men and women in uniform, almost all of whom were transported by rail at some point during the war, from their hometowns to their basic training bases, and ultimately to one of the coasts where they boarded ships bound for one of the theaters of war. Far too many of them also returned home by rail, in a government-issue casket in the baggage car.

After the war, the railroads made a valiant effort to hold on to passenger traffic, but the die was cast. Despite a surge in passenger traffic, and profits, during the war, there were several war-related factors that combined to spell the death of passenger rail service, at least by private railroads.

Millions of Americans, in their shiny new cars from Detroit, which had quickly retooled immediately after the war, took to the rapidly expanding Dwight D. Eisenhower National System of Interstate and Defense Highways, modeled on the German Autobahn, which had so impressed General Eisenhower upon his arrival in Germany, and the railroads' long-haul passenger service suffered greatly. The death blow for passenger rail service, however, came from one of the companies that had helped win the war.

Boeing built the B-29 Superfortresses that dropped the atomic bombs that brought World War II to a conclusion. Boeing also quickly retooled after the war, and a few years later the Boeing 707 signaled the end of long-haul passenger rail service in the United States. A coast-to-coast trip that took three to four days on even the fastest streamliners with the best interline connections, or driving hard on the Interstate, now took a mere six hours by air. Daniel considered it a badge of honor that he had never set foot aboard one of those infernal flying machines. His private railcar, now named *Estelline*, was parked on a siding at Lamy, New Mexico, ready to carry him wherever he needed to go, attached to the back of a Santa Fe passenger train.

Although he was a loyal railroad man, Daniel was well invested not only in Boeing and airlines, but also in a chain of truck stops along the Interstate. With the rapid decline of passenger rail service, however, his private railcar was increasingly resigned to the siding at Lamy. There were very few passenger trains through Lamy that could take it anywhere. It didn't really matter, his younger son Alfred, had taken over the family businesses and investments, Daniel was content at the ranch with the livestock and his memories, and rarely traveled.

Johnston Caldwell was twelve, and a student at the Belen Conservatory of Music, when his great-grandfather died, fittingly perhaps, on May 1, 1971, the day Amtrak, a government-owned corporation, took over passenger rail service from the railroads. Johnston was a legacy at the Belen Conservatory—his mother, Marjorie, had been a student there.

In his retirement, Daniel had become a patron of the fledgling Santa Fe Opera, and had beamed with pride when his granddaughter Marjorie, Daniel Jr.'s only child, first stepped onto the stage to perform.

Johnston volunteered to travel to Santa Fe with his father to escort his great-grandfather's remains back to Los Angeles for the funeral and burial. They arrived in Albuquerque on a Boeing 707, where they were met by staff for the drive up to the ranch.

Alfred had been in Europe on business when word came of his father's death, and he arrived in Albuquerque by private jet. He was accompanied by the greatest available tenor of the time, a burly, bearded Italian who went by only one name, Rinaldo. Alfred had offered to send him on to Los Angeles aboard the private jet and let him rest at a luxury hotel until the funeral, but he preferred to stop off in Santa Fe for a brief visit with friends at the Santa Fe Opera.

Johnston joined Rinaldo on the trip to the opera house where preparations were underway for the coming season. He was very familiar with the place, having been there many times with Daniel. Johnston was, by his own admission, a passable musician, enough to gain admission to the Belen Conservatory of Music. He was far more interested in the business of music than the actual performance. By virtue of his great-grandfather's patronage, Johnston had relatively free run of the opera house, and haunted the shops and stages and dressing rooms and offices, soaking up everything that was offered, eagerly running errands for the singers and technicians. Since its inception the Santa Fe Opera had offered an apprentice program where young singers, and later technicians, could work and gain experience in their chosen field with a professional opera company. Johnston had his sights set on the technician program although he had been warned, in no uncertain terms, that his family connections would carry no weight when it came to consideration of his application.

Daniel's burial instructions were quite specific. As a Navy veteran of

World War I, his remains, in a government-issue casket, were to be transported by rail in a baggage car, "the same as a common soldier," as had been Dwight D. Eisenhower, whom Daniel greatly admired. In the confusion over Amtrak's assuming control of passenger rail services no one at the ranch was exactly sure how to arrange such a thing. Having been well taught by his father, Alfred placed a call to a top executive with the Santa Fe Railway, and when the hearse and limousines arrived at the siding in Lamy, there was a short train consisting of a matched pair of Santa Fe diesel-electric locomotives, wearing the famed Warbonnet livery, an old Santa Fe heavyweight baggage car, the *Estelline*, and a caboose.

Johnston had played on the *Estelline*, along with his cousins, whenever they could persuade one of the ranch staff to drive them to Lamy and unlock it, but he had never actually ridden on it. He had heard stories, and notwithstanding the circumstances, he was looking forward to a trip on the old private railcar.

Having been parked for several years, the *Estelline* was a bit musky smelling, but still in good shape for a fifty-year-old railcar. Daniel had not retained regular crew for the car for quite some time, so the ranch staff improvised. Alfred had fond memories of trips on the car from his own youth and as a young man after the war, shadowing his father on business trips, and was able to instruct the ranch staff on the car's operation. No one particularly trusted the kitchen, so after a late afternoon departure from Lamy, they stopped at the Santa Fe depot in Albuquerque just long enough to load take-out from a nearby restaurant for those on the *Estelline* as well as the train crew. "It's what Dad would have done," Alfred laughed.

There was plenty of wine on board, but no women, and as the funeral train rolled westward into the night, the men, and Johnston, chowed down on authentic Mexican food, the real deal, not what was found in the upscale restaurants. Rinaldo was quite impressed by the food, less so by the California wine, but still it was wine, and he didn't turn down any refills. Johnston was allowed a splash of wine in his water glass—the European way—and eagerly listened to the stories that began to flow as easily as the wine. Johnston had always known his great-grandfather was a larger-than-life character and was all ears when Rinaldo asked Alfred point blank about the young opera singer, Estelline.

"The rumors are quite true," Alfred admitted, and then went on to relate the story, as told to him, after his mother's death, by Daniel. No stranger to dalliances himself, Alfred completely understood.

"What happened to Estelline?" Rinaldo asked. He was familiar with a great many sopranos in Europe, but had never heard of her, other than the rumors.

"She left my dad during her European tour for a baron," Alfred explained. "Unfortunately for her, he was a German baron, and he lost his castle and his fortune in the war. I have no idea what happened to her after that."

The funeral train had headed south out of Albuquerque, rather than directly west, per Daniel's instructions, detouring through Belen, where several railroad men and retirees stood on the platform, hats held over their hearts, as the funeral train rolled slowly past. The trip through Belen also provided an appropriate entrée for Alfred to confirm the story of how the conservatory came to be named.

"So that's really how Grandpa became interested in opera?" Johnston asked.

"That's really how," Alfred replied. "Before that, Mother had to drag him to the opera. The affair with Estelline lasted only a few weeks, but it incited in him a love for opera, and for music, that lasted a lifetime."

"Wow," Johnston said, "and I inherited it."

"Just your love for music," Alfred said. "Hopefully, when you marry, you will be faithful to your wife."

"While he was in Europe, after she dumped him, Dad went to a number of operas." Alfred paused and took a breath. "At a performance of *Turandot*, I don't recall where exactly, he heard 'Nessun Dorma' performed by a truly great tenor, again I don't recall exactly who, and he loved it. He wrote in his burial instructions, and told me personally, more than once, that 'Nessun Dorma' was to be performed at his funeral by 'the greatest available tenor of the time.'" He raised his glass toward Rinaldo. "Hence, our very special guest on this trip."

Johnston slept in the children's room and dreamed of how much fun it must have been for Daniel Jr., Alfred, and their sisters to have traveled by train and slept in this very room. Great Uncle Alfred pointed out Daniel Jr.'s bunk, and that, of course, was the one Johnston elected to occupy on this trip.

The men stayed up a bit longer—there was more wine, more stories, and the inevitable poker game—a tradition on the rails. It was penny ante, so the lone staff member on the car could join in, which would have suited Daniel just fine.

The funeral train was met at Union Station in Los Angeles by a hearse, several limousines, and family members. Marjorie rushed into Rinaldo's arms, and they hugged and kissed the air.

Rinaldo insisted on going to rehearsal—not that he needed it, but the Belen Conservatory was providing a large orchestra and chorus to accompany him. Rinaldo promptly named Johnston his aide-de-camp and they set off in a limousine for the conservatory.

To Johnston's surprise, Rinaldo was not the least bit difficult in rehearsal, patiently waiting as the maestro worked with the orchestra and chorus, and then repeating his performance, or portions thereof, until the entire group's performance was, although not perfect, acceptable given the time constraints and the experience level of the musicians and singers. After rehearsal, Rinaldo answered questions of the students, and teachers, regaling them with his exploits with the great opera companies of Europe. His aide-de-camp served as moderator, selecting which student, or teacher, would be allowed to ask the next question, a role he relished.

Daniel was never big on church, but a big church was required to hold all the mourners. Many of his contemporaries were dead or too frail to make the trip, but both he and Alfred had worked for years to protect the family fortune after his death—no small feat in those times of confiscatory taxes—and a great many people came to show respect, if not for Daniel, then for the wealth. Most of the students from the Belen Conservatory, who were not already part of the proceedings, were in attendance, along with many of their parents, grateful to the man who had generously provided not only the conservatory, but the no-tuition scholarships where necessary. The parents also appreciated the fact that no one, other than a third-party accounting firm that handled tuition payments, knew which students were on scholarship, making all students equal, at least in that regard.

Johnston had remained stoic throughout the eulogies and awake during the sermon that preachers always manage to slip into a funeral service, but "Nessun Dorma" had him weeping openly. He understood immediately his great-grandfather's love for the piece. Rinaldo's performance was stirring and flawless. Johnston's classmates in the orchestra and chorus also acquitted themselves well.

16

JOHNSTON

THE SPANISH MISSION style architecture from the exterior of the Belen Conservatory of Music was carried through to the interior. The hallway was rather dimly lit, with shafts of light from the windows piercing the darkness and reflecting off the shiny, hard-surfaced floor. The walls were tiled up to about Christine's height, and then plaster above that. The arched ceilings were high, and illuminated by sturdy, wrought-iron chandeliers.

It seemed somewhat spooky to Christine, like an old church or something she had seen in movies, not at all like her school in suburban Chicago which had suspended ceilings with rows of fluorescent lights which lit up everything below with hardly any shadows. The teachers at her old school had decorated the walls of every classroom, as well as the hallways, with bright, colorful signs and graphics. Here everything was earth tone and muted.

At her old school there was constant chatter and laughter, even though the acoustics were designed to capture such sounds. Here there was a very faint sound of music, both vocal and instrumental, coming from various directions.

Christine marveled at the paintings that adorned the walls but was particularly interested in the railroad theme throughout the building, or at least what she had seen so far. There were paintings of old trains pulled by steam locomotives, driving hard through the snow over mountain passes, passing by the red cliffs of western New Mexico, which she recognized, and of depots and stations along the Santa Fe line, including Belen, New Mexico. The Atchison, Topeka and Santa Fe's livery, which itself had a distinct southwestern flair, was incorporated into much of the artwork.

On the wall next to the trophy case was a large oil portrait of Daniel Titshaw Jr., Lieutenant j.g., United States Navy, in uniform. Beside it was an oil portrait of USS *Johnston* (DD-557), gallantly on the attack in the action off Samar on October 25, 1944. Small brass plaques identified both portraits, but no further description was given, or necessary.

There were massive, well-worn benches made of dark wood in the hallway, the seats polished by the bottoms of countless children over the years. Christine's feet did not touch the floor as she waited with Raoul and Zoe.

"I wish my daddy could be here," Christine said.

"He had an appointment," Zoe replied. "We're just picking up an application. He will be here for your audition, and when you are accepted, he will be here for the grand tour."

Christine continued to swing her feet for a moment, then suddenly jumped off the bench, scurried across the hallway, and stared intently for a moment at an oil painting of an old Santa Fe railroad depot. Memories suddenly flooded over her, and she launched into an impromptu rendition of "On the Atchison, Topeka and Santa Fe."

Zoe immediately stood and joined in the singing, and they began to dance. Raoul had no idea what had come over them.

The school secretary stepped through a door and approached Zoe and Christine. They quickly stopped singing and dancing.

"Sorry it took so long; the phone just wouldn't stop ringing." She handed Zoe a thick stack of papers, folders, and brochures. "This will get you started. An audition will be required, of course, and I will schedule it when the completed application is returned and reviewed."

"We'll get right on it," Zoe replied, taking the stack of papers, and glancing through them.

"What was that song you were singing?" the secretary asked.

"'On the Atchison, Topeka and Santa Fe,'" Zoe replied. "Judy Garland as I recall."

"Ah, yes," the secretary said. "I saw that movie on TV."

"My mom used to sing it to me when I was little," Christine said.

Zoe turned toward the click-clack of shoes on the hard floor. A distinguished man in his sixties, with just the right amount of gray in his well-coiffed hair, approached. He wore expensive jeans, a tailored jacket with an open collar shirt, making him look like anything but the headmaster of a children's music school.

AFTER HIS GREAT-GRANDFATHER's funeral, Johnston's trips to the ranch at Santa Fe became fewer. Daniel was the glue that held the family together, although one or more of the families still made it there every summer, providing adult supervision for the cousins who were happy to be there with or without their own parents. While the other cousins were content to ride horses on the ranch and drive the tractor, Johnston spent as much time as possible at the Santa Fe Opera.

The *Estelline* was returned to its siding at Lamy—no one knew exactly what to do with it—but as the cousins became older, they had less interest in exploring aboard it, although as a result of his trip on the funeral train, it would always have special significance to Johnston.

Johnston graduated from the Belen Conservatory of Music and went to a top university, where he minored in music and majored in business. During his senior year of college, he submitted his application to the Santa Fe Opera's apprentice program, using a false name so there could be no charges of favoritism. He was accepted, revealed his true identity, and spent the summer after graduation working as a technician harder than he ever thought possible, and loving every minute of it.

He then set out to conquer the music business, and did so with considerable success, eventually starting his own label. He had the opportunity to record an album featuring duets with his mother, Marjorie, and Rinaldo, which pleased him greatly. His music business expanded to include producing live performances and television specials. He delighted in discovering young, struggling acts in the clubs and promoting them into superstars. He also devoted a great deal of time and money, to the opera and symphonies, mentored young performers, and was often called to speak at the Belen Conservatory—any musician planning on a professional career was encouraged to learn something about the music business, as there was an abundance of sharks ready to take advantage of them.

Cousin Franklin Titshaw, Alfred's grandson, persuaded Johnston to join him in restoring the *Estelline* to her former grandeur, a task he eagerly undertook. Private railcars were all the rage among the nouveau riche. They were perfect for taking your friends to the football game. Southern California was a great place to own a private railcar, with several Amtrak routes terminating or connecting in Los Angeles. The cousins had a leg up—the family trust already owned a private railcar, a historic one, with special significance to the family.

They had the car pulled by a freight train from Lamy over the Raton Pass to a private facility in the Midwest that specialized in such restorations. There it underwent a complete overhaul, replacing parts as needed, repairing rust and other damage. The plumbing and wiring were brought up to date, and it was wired for head-end power so that it could be pulled behind Amtrak trains, about the only available method for traveling by private railcar unless you owned your own railroad. A generator was installed so that power could be maintained when not connected to a train.

The wives insisted on handling the decorating, although the cousins persuaded them to follow the original décor whenever possible. It was, after all, a restoration of a historic private railcar, one of the oldest still in service, as they had discovered during the restoration.

Work was finally completed on the *Estelline*, a little used siding in an industrial area in Los Angeles was leased, and a metal building constructed, where the car would be parked out of the weather, safe from vandals, when not in use. The car easily passed its inspection and was certified to roll behind Amtrak trains. In addition to trips up the coast to the bay area, behind the *Coast Starlight*, where it could be set out at Oakland for trips into Napa, its frequent destination would still be the siding at Lamy, as the cousins envisioned family trips to Santa Fe to enjoy the family ranch, now held in trust for future generations, and the Santa Fe Opera, where the family held season tickets. It would be pulled by Amtrak's *Southwest Chief* which still used the route over the Raton Pass, conveniently passing through Lamy.

Johnston ultimately became disillusioned with the music business. He was tired of the divas, the jerks, the drug-addicted rock stars, the trashed hotel rooms, the late-night calls to handle an overdose and keep it from the media, the pregnant groupies with lawyers, the infighting that threatened to break up successful acts, the endless lawsuits, with or without merit, and the general "assholism" he encountered in the industry.

Although hip-hop was generating huge profits for other labels, Johnston refused to record "rap talkers," as he called them, and bristled when they had the audacity to call themselves "hip-hop artists." "What art?" he asked. "It's not even music. It's just some street thug wearing a jogging suit, prancing around the stage while spitting into a wireless microphone. All that's required to be a hip-hop 'artist' is a rhyming dictionary, a handgun, and a bunch of nitwits willing to buy your albums." He had enough trouble already with acts on his label. He certainly didn't need them gunning each other down on the streets, although album sales always did seem to increase whenever a star met an untimely death.

Buying albums had also become a problem, as the younger generation showed absolutely no compunction about stealing music. In the digital age it was simply too easy. Calling it "sharing" or "downloading" instead of "stealing" apparently assuaged some of the guilt. Record stores, a favorite haunt of Johnston since childhood, along with millions of others, began dropping like flies, and the recording industry began retrenching. Johnston decided it was time to sell his label to one of the majors and retire to his beach house in Malibu.

His retirement was short-lived, however, when the headmaster at The Belen Conservatory suffered a massive heart attack and plopped face down at his desk. Despite the heroic efforts of his long-time secretary, he was dead before the paramedics arrived. It was quite an exciting day at the conservatory, as rumors spread quickly—assisted immeasurably by the ubiquitous cell phones—and parents swarmed the school to pick up their children, fearing everything from an outbreak of the plague to a terrorist attack. It was nothing more than a dead headmaster, they eventually learned, and before long, things were back to normal.

Johnston agreed to take over as headmaster, at a salary of one dollar per year—he hardly needed the money—until a suitable replacement could be found and groomed. Six years later he was enjoying his tenure and making no special effort to name a successor, although his third wife was pressuring him to make a decision on retiring to Santa Fe, where she had already built, furnished and decorated a small hacienda with a large north-light studio for her art, just outside town, and he could spend his days volunteering at the Santa Fe Opera and working with the young people in the apprentice program, "which is what you wanted, right dear?"

"ZOE, HAVE YOU returned to haunt our hallowed halls?" Johnston asked.

Zoe hugged Johnston. "No, Headmaster. I am bringing you a potential new student." She motioned for the kids to stand.

"Are you trying again this year, Raoul?" Johnston shook hands with Raoul.

"Yes sir."

"How are your parents? I haven't seen them in months."

"They're fine."

"We must get together soon."

Raoul turned to Christine. "This is my friend, Christine. She sings like an angel."

Christine blushed and extended her hand. "How do you do, sir?"

"Very well, thank you. I'm Johnston Caldwell." Johnston shook Christine's hand and then turned to Zoe. "Is this—?"

Zoe nodded.

"Professor Valerius called about you, Christine," Johnston said. "It takes a lot to impress him."

"Thank you, sir."

"He also speaks highly of your father. I believe he called him 'the first violin of the world.'"

Christine smiled and nodded.

"Mr. Daaé has been teaching me," Raoul added.

"Excellent. I look forward to both of your auditions."

Zoe drove them home, detouring along Melrose for some window shopping, and ice cream.

Viktor walked down the sidewalk and stopped just as Zoe pulled up in front of the Valerius home. Christine jumped out of the car and ran into Viktor's arms. "Where have you been?" she asked.

"I had an appointment."

"With who?"

"It's not important."

Zoe stepped up. "I could have driven you, Mr. Daaé."

"The bus is fine. I like to walk. It's a beautiful day." He turned to Christine. "Did you get the application?"

"Yes Daddy."

"Then we must get to work on it right away," Viktor said, and then spotted Raoul standing on the sidewalk with his violin case, "right after Raoul's lesson."

THE CHAGNYS HAD some family commitment, which Raoul was required to attend, giving Zoe the night off. She offered to come along with Christine and Viktor, busking for the homeless, but Viktor encouraged her to spend her rare free time with her friends from college, and she did. Christine and her father headed out for the Promenade with street-performer permits in hand. They selected a good spot near a movie theater and Viktor began to play the violin. Christine worked the crowd with a bucket, clearly marked "Donations for the Santa Monica Shelter," which increased the take. It also helped that word had spread about the beautiful blonde girl and her friends who performed on the pier and the Promenade and donated their earnings to the homeless.

There was a continuous stream of people into and out of the movie theater, peaking when a popular movie started or ended. At one such time,

Robbie and Andy came bounding down the steps from the theater, stopping long enough to snicker and point at Christine. She recognized them from Ogden Hall, and quickly turned and walked away.

When Viktor finished his piece, he asked, "What was that all about, those two boys?"

"It was nothing, just some jerks from school."

"What did they say?"

"Nothing. They didn't say anything. They were just being jerks. That's what boys do. Don't worry about it."

It had been a good night, they had collected a substantial amount for the shelter, which Christine and Raoul would deliver tomorrow on the way home from school. Viktor was not feeling well, and so they walked home.

PROFESSOR AND MRS. VALERIUS, Viktor, and two lawyers sat at a conference table. The mood in the room was somber. Viktor read a document while everyone else waited patiently and politely—English was not his first language.

"Okay," Viktor said, lifting his head as he finished reading.

"Do you understand everything?" one of the lawyers asked.

"Yes. Yes, I understand." Viktor signed the document and slid it across the table toward the lawyer. The lawyer in turn pushed it over to the Valeriuses.

"Are you sure this is what you want to do?" Professor Valerius asked.

"I am sure. Very sure. It is the best thing."

"Very well," Professor Valerius said as he signed the document and then passed it over to his wife, who also signed.

Viktor wiped a tear, pulled out a handkerchief, and wiped his nose. "Thank you. Thank you very much." He stood, and the Valeriuses quickly stood also.

Viktor shook hands with the lawyers, and it was done.

17

THE FLASH MOB

CHRISTINE WALKED THROUGH the hallway of Ogden Hall with Raoul. They came to a sudden stop. Robbie and Andy stood shoulder to shoulder, blocking their path.

"Hey, Chagny," Robbie said. "We saw your girlfriend begging on the street."

Christine froze and gritted her teeth, her face flushing.

"That's where you found her, isn't it," Andy added, "on the street?"

Raoul plowed into them, fists flying. Christine screamed. A crowd quickly gathered. Although perhaps not as common as in public school, it was still a fight, and none of the kids were going to miss it.

"Raoul, no!" Christine begged, to no avail. All three boys were now on the floor, with Raoul on top. None of the bystanders made a move to break it up—they just wanted to watch and film it on their expensive phones. Fortunately, one of the private bodyguards stepped in and snatched Raoul from the pile and the fight ended quickly.

Zoe was in class when the text message arrived, and she rushed immediately to Ogden Hall. This could not be good.

Raoul and Christine sat solemnly in chairs along the wall of the school office. One of Raoul's eyes was already starting to turn black.

Christine looked up in nervous anticipation as Zoe and the headmistress stepped out of her office. Raoul didn't flinch. He had done what he had to do, and he was ready to take whatever was coming.

"The count," Zoe paused for emphasis, "is in Paris on business and Raoul's mother is in surgery, saving someone's life. As soon as one of them is available, I can assure you they will be in immediate contact."

"We simply can't have behavior of this type in our school," the head-mistress said. "This is a very prestigious institution, as you are aware. We have quite a number of children of very important parents."

"Yes ma'am," Zoe responded. "It will be dealt with."

"We've never had a problem with Raoul before," the headmistress added. "I just don't understand it."

"Where are the other two boys who were involved?"

"In the nurse's office."

Christine choked back laughter. Zoe pointed her finger and Christine straightened up.

"I'm on her list too, so I may as well take them both."

"Very well."

Zoe motioned for the kids to get up. "Scoot."

Raoul and Christine headed for the door, glad that this part was finally over.

"Violence is never the answer, young man," Zoe scolded as they walked through the door, making sure the headmistress heard her. "Just wait until your father gets home."

As soon as they were through the front doors, and onto the sidewalk outside Ogden Hall, Zoe asked, "Okay, what really happened?"

"They insulted Christine and I pounded them," Raoul stated flatly.

"Both of them?"

"They both insulted her."

"So, you were defending your lady's honor?"

"Of course."

"Exactly," Christine confirmed.

"You are so my hero," Zoe said. "Your father will be proud, your mother, not so much."

She stopped, took Raoul by the chin, and turned his head so she could get a closer look. "That's going to be a humongous shiner."

"I'll wear it like a badge of honor."

As they got into Zoe's car, she said, "Oh, by the way, you're suspended indefinitely."

"What about Christine?"

"Innocent bystander," Zoe replied. "She's good to go."

"Cool," Raoul said.

———

IN THE LITTLE COTTAGE the next morning, Christine, wearing her private school uniform, tied her shoes. Raoul, not in uniform, took his violin out of the case.

"I get suspended, and I still have to go to school," Raoul complained.

Christine giggled.

"More time to practice for your audition," Viktor said.

"If you can't do the time, don't do the crime," Zoe added.

Christine jumped up and grabbed her backpack. She kissed Viktor. "Bye, Daddy." She turned to Raoul. "Later."

"Bye. I'll be here, slaving away on the violin."

Christine laughed, and she and Zoe darted through the door.

CHRISTINE WALKED ALONE in the school hallway, somewhat leery, the object of a great many stares and not a little bit of whispering. She stopped suddenly and looked up, concerned, facing two boys, both thirteen. Her mind raced. What now?

"I'm Teddy. This is Greg."

"Okay," Christine said warily.

"One of us will walk you to class every day, or anywhere else you need to go," Teddy said.

"Anybody bothers you, let us know and we'll pound them," Greg added.

"Good to know," Christine replied, still uneasy.

"Where are you going now?" Teddy asked.

"Choir."

"We'll take you."

They started to walk.

"Who are you guys?"

"Raoul sent us."

Heads turned as Christine, escorted by Teddy and Greg, headed toward the choir room.

Raoul's lesson, he was happy to learn, did not last all day. Zoe swung by and picked him up for lunch. Viktor had some unnamed appointment, to which Zoe offered to take him, but he had already made arrangements.

After lunch, Zoe dropped Raoul off at home. "You are under house arrest, young man. Business is apparently very good today in the emergency room and your mother is rather busy, but she insists that you stay in your room until she gets home. I have class."

"What about Christine?"

"Don't worry about Christine. I'll pick her up from school."

Mrs. Valerius, reading one of the tattered year-old magazines that always adorn medical waiting rooms, waited beside Viktor, who stared straight ahead at the wall.

A door opened, and a nurse stepped through. "Mr. Daaé?"

"I'll wait here," Mrs. Valerius said, "unless you want me to come in with you."

Viktor shook his head and followed the nurse through the door.

Raoul was immersed in a video game when Zoe and Christine entered his room.

"Okay, slugger," Zoe said. "The count cut a deal, and no doubt a check. You're getting off with time served and community service."

"Community service? You mean like picking up trash on the beach?"

"Actually, I was thinking flash mob, but I suppose you could pick up trash if you prefer."

"Noooo!"

"What's a flash mob?" Christine asked.

Inciting a fight had considerably improved Christine's street cred at Ogden Hall, and in its wake her work for the homeless was revealed, impressing all but the most cynical of the little snots. When Zoe, with the grudging acquiescence of the headmistress, approached the students about her plan, there was an overwhelmingly positive response. Well, almost overwhelming, there were a couple of boys with bandages on their faces who weren't so enthusiastic, but they were given no choice.

The Third Street Promenade was bustling early Saturday evening, filled with pedestrians and street performers. The weather was excellent, as usual, in Santa Monica in the spring. The sidewalk cafés were full and over-flowing. There were uniformed police officers among the crowd, more than usual.

Teddy and Greg, along with some helpers, set up a keyboard and stool. Nearby they placed a plywood box, about three feet square and eighteen inches deep.

The Chagnys, Valeriuses, Gastons, and Viktor sat at a table in a sidewalk café, conveniently located right in front of the impromptu stage.

Zoe sat at the piano, set up sheet music, and began playing "Lovers," by Shigeru Umebayshi. Raoul and Christine, in their Ogden Hall uniforms, strolled along the Promenade. He played violin.

Teddy stepped forward and extended a hand to help Christine onto the plywood box. She began singing as Raoul circled.

The number concluded, Christine curtsied, and there was loud applause from the growing audience. Robbie and Andy, faces bandaged and bruised, worked the crowd carrying five-gallon buckets with signs, "Donations for the Santa Monica Shelter."

Raoul handed off his violin and bow to Viktor for safekeeping, helped Christine off the stage, and they rushed into the crowd, gathering fistfuls of money, which they dropped into the boys' buckets.

More students, in Ogden Hall uniforms, filtered through the crowd and lined up in rows. The choir director took up position in front of the choir. He turned toward Christine, who handed her money to Raoul and dashed onto her box between the choir and the director.

Zoe began playing "Suo Gân." While the choir sang the English translation, Christine sang in Welsh.

There was huge applause and cheers from the crowd when the song ended. Robbie and Andy, under the close watch of police officers—there was a lot of money in those buckets—solicited donations.

Zoe changed her sheet music, turned to the choir director, and nodded. Just as the choir director raised her baton Raoul called out, "Wait!"

Zoe froze. What in the world was he up to?

Raoul rushed forward and stood beside Christine, who was also curious to see what Raoul was going to do.

"The reason we are all here today is because of my friend, Christine, who sings like an angel."

Christine blushed.

"She inspired me, all of us I guess, to give something back. All the donations today go to the Santa Monica Shelter, so dig deep when my friends come by with the buckets."

There were a few chuckles from the crowd as well as performers, who knew why his "friends" had black eyes.

"This next song was composed by my friend Zoe." He bowed toward Zoe. "It's called 'Christine's Song.'"

Christine looked at Raoul, clearly surprised. He kissed her on the cheek, stepped over to Zoe at the keyboard and said, "I thought of a name for your piece."

"You did indeed. I like it."

Raoul stood near the keyboard, affording him a good view of Christine.

The choir director raised her baton and Zoe began to play. Christine and the choir sang.

Robbie, Andy, Teddy, and Greg quietly solicited donations, and there were many. In addition to cash, many people, including Count Chagny, Professor Valerius, Doctor Gaston, and the parents of many of the students, deposited envelopes containing checks in the collection buckets.

By the time the piece ended, and the kids took their bows, many of those assembled were in tears. Zoe and Christine hugged and kissed, and then found themselves in a three-way bear hug with Raoul.

THE SANTA MONICA SHELTER was busy. There were long rows of tables, full of homeless, eating breakfast, with more standing in the serving line.

Raoul and Christine approached the shelter manager, followed by Robbie and Andy.

"Good morning, guys," the manager said cheerfully. "Have you been busking for us again, I hope?"

"Yes sir," Raoul said, grinning ear to ear.

Raoul nudged Christine and she handed a paper bag to the manager. He looked inside, smiled, and withdrew a stack of cash and checks. "You've been busy."

"We had a good weekend," Raoul said.

"And a lot of help," Christine added.

Zoe, along with dozens of students in their school uniforms, swarmed through the door.

"What's all this?" the manager asked.

"We thought we'd put on a show, if you don't mind," Christine said.

"Not at all."

"Okay, guys, hit it!" Raoul said.

Zoe took a seat at the piano. The students spread out and formed a choir, who, along with Christine, sang "Christine's Song." The diners, the manager, and the volunteers, were very much appreciative.

In the kitchen, Raoul, Robbie, and Andy washed dishes as the music, and Christine's angelic voice, filled the room.

18

HABANERA

Mrs. Valerius, elegantly dressed herself, zipped up Christine's recently purchased strapless dress, and then admired her in the mirror in the Valerius bedroom. Christine beamed.

"Wait," Mrs. Valerius said. She opened a jewelry box on the dresser and searched, removing a gold necklace. She stepped behind Christine and put the necklace around her neck.

"What do you think?"

"It's beautiful."

Mrs. Valerius clasped it in place.

Viktor and Professor Valerius, both in tuxedoes, waited patiently in the living room. Mrs. Valerius entered the room and stepped aside so that Christine could make her entrance.

Christine swirled around, modeling her new dress.

"You look so beautiful," Viktor said.

Christine rushed into her father's arms, and he hugged her tightly, trying to not muss her hair or new dress.

Viktor looked over Christine's head to Mrs. Valerius. "Thank you, madam."

"Why won't anyone tell me where we're going?" Christine asked.

"Then it wouldn't be a surprise," Mrs. Valerius said.

"My little girl is becoming a young woman," Viktor said. "You look so much like your mother."

The doorbell rang and Professor Valerius stepped over and opened the door. Raoul, in a tuxedo, and Zoe, in a long, black, quite gothic gown, entered.

Raoul's eyes were drawn instantly to Christine. "Wow!"

Christine blushed.

"Your chariot awaits, my lady," Zoe said.

Christine stepped over to pick up her wrap off a chair, but Raoul quickly took it from her and spread it out. Christine hesitated, not really knowing what to do, but finally turned, and Raoul placed the wrap gently over her bare shoulders.

Raoul offered his arm—he had been trained well. It took Christine a moment to catch on—this was a new experience—but she had seen it in the movies, so she took his arm.

A stretch limousine stood in the street, motor running. The chauffeur closed the trunk, stepped around to the side, and opened the back door. The Chagnys waited inside.

Raoul, with his lady on his arm, proudly led the procession down the sidewalk, followed by Viktor and Zoe, and then Professor Valerius and his wife.

The limousine pulled up in a line of others at the Dorothy Chandler Pavilion. Raoul hopped out and offered his hand to Christine. She stepped out and looked up. Huge banners hung from the overhanging roof: CARMEN. Christine burst into tears and Raoul eagerly took her into his arms. She cried for a moment, then turned toward Viktor. "Daddy, it's the opera!"

"Bizet, no less," Viktor said.

Christine pulled away from Raoul and rushed into Viktor's arms. "Thank you, thank you, thank you."

"You can thank Count Chagny," Viktor said, "not me."

Christine rushed into Chagny's arms, hugging him tightly. "Thank you, sir. Thank you so much."

Chagny was taken aback but chuckled and enjoyed the hug. "You are welcome, mademoiselle."

The sidewalk was covered by fellow opera goers, elegantly dressed and so sophisticated. Christine could barely contain her excitement as she took Raoul's arm—she now had the hang of it—and joined the group headed into the Pavilion.

Raoul beamed, and why not? He was thirteen, with a beautiful girl on his arm, who was not his sister or cousin.

The Chagnys and Valeriuses shook hands and air kissed with others on the sidewalk. They had been here before.

Everyone seemed to know each other in the upstairs foyer. Chagny schmoozed with other obviously wealthy and important people. Professor and Mrs. Valerius introduced Viktor around. Hannah introduced Christine to Doctor Gaston and his wife.

"When will you be performing again on the Promenade, Christine?"

"I don't know, sir. We're there quite a bit."

"We really enjoyed the flash mob," Mrs. Gaston said.

Zoe, away from the crowd, conspired with Jacqueline, a young staff member, wearing an earpiece with a tiny microphone attached, and carrying a clipboard.

A page walked through the crowd, ringing a small bell. The crowd began moving toward the doors.

The group took their seats in Founders Circle. Christine's eyes darted back and forth, taking it all in.

"These are pretty good seats," she whispered to Raoul.

He smiled and nodded. "Have you ever been to the opera?"

"No, this is my first time."

The lights went down.

The opera began.

Every note played on Viktor's face and Zoe's as well.

Raoul's eyes darted quickly between the stage, the orchestra, and Christine, who was entranced, silently mouthing the lyrics. It was spectacular, her first real opera, in a grand opera house, and she was wearing such a beautiful dress. She could not have been happier. This was a long way from the cold, harsh streets of Chicago. It must be a fantasy, she thought, and she wished it would never end.

At intermission, everyone retired to the foyer and the schmoozing continued. Raoul and Christine chattered excitedly, until Zoe interrupted them. They looked up to see Jacqueline approaching.

"Would you like to go backstage?" Zoe asked.

Raoul smiled and turned to watch Christine's reaction.

Christine nodded her head enthusiastically. "I'll have to ask Daddy."

"I've already cleared it with Mr. Daaé," Zoe said.

Christine turned to Viktor who nodded and smiled. Christine waved back, grinning.

"Coming down now, sir," Jacqueline said into the tiny microphone.

Zoe, Christine, and Raoul followed Jacqueline through the crowd.

As they arrived backstage, they slipped quietly through the frenzy of activity. Zoe pulled out her cell phone. "Triple-check all cell phones."

Raoul pulled out his phone and they both confirmed the phones were off.

Christine didn't have a phone to turn off and was too busy looking around anyway.

"Absolute silence," Zoe commanded. "You talk to no one. Don't get in anyone's way. If someone is coming toward you, become one with the wall. Got it?"

Raoul and Christine both nodded emphatically.

"Are we okay here?" Jacqueline asked.

"We're good. Thanks," Zoe replied.

"Okay, gotta go. Be back later," Jacqueline said as she turned to go, hustling away, through a growing crowd of cast members, and assorted stage people. Raoul and Christine lapped it up.

The orchestra began playing. The cast rushed onto the stage. The opera continued.

Raoul and Christine, with Zoe hovering, watched and learned. Christine continued to mouth the lyrics, clearly familiar with the opera. Raoul was more interested in the rigging, the lights, and all the support activity.

The kids backed into the wall as performers hustled past, and then quickly retook their positions, drinking it all in, missing nothing.

When the opera came to an end there was considerable applause, bows on stage, and then more applause.

In the foyer, some people headed for the stairs, others milled around. Jacqueline located Viktor, who nodded toward Professor Valerius and followed her through the crowd.

The Chagnys worked the room, talking quietly to a few people, who turned and looked, and then eased their way back toward the seats.

The opera house manager approached Chagny, "Do you want to wait until the house is entirely cleared, count?"

"It's not necessary," Chagny answered. "If people want to stay and listen, it's fine."

"As you wish."

"They won't be disappointed," Chagny said.

The manager nodded, unconvinced.

"And neither will you. Trust me," Chagny added.

"Of course," the manager answered.

Backstage, Jacqueline and Viktor approached, followed by a page carrying two violin cases.

"Did you have a good time?" Viktor asked.

"Daddy! It was wonderful! We got to see everything!"

Raoul took one of the violin cases from the page. Viktor took the other.

"But it's not over," Raoul said.

"It's not?" Christine asked, wondering what else could possibly happen to top this.

"No, you are going to sing, for a small private audience, but in a grand opera house," Raoul told her.

"And Raoul and I will play with the orchestra," Viktor added.

"The orchestra?" Christine asked, confused.

"Your orchestra awaits, prima donna," Zoe said, leading Christine toward the stage.

Christine looked out at the nearly deserted house. The orchestra remained in place. The conductor bowed.

Christine burst into tears. She looked up. The Chagnys, Valeriuses, Gastons, Professor Dodge and her husband, along with many other people—word had spread—were seated in Founders Circle. She rushed into Viktor's arms. "Oh, thank you, Daddy."

"Don't thank me. It was all Master Raoul's doing," Viktor said.

Christine rushed Raoul, planting kisses all over both cheeks.

"Actually, it was my dad who pulled the strings, and Zoe did all the leg work, but I'll gladly take the credit, and the kisses."

Christine planted one on his lips. "Thank you so much!"

"Enough with the kissy-kissy," Zoe said. "You'd better warm up, and quickly."

In the lobby, people heard the orchestra tuning up, a bit odd after the performance was over, and turned back toward the auditorium. Among them was Alfonso, a handsome boy of thirteen, with black, curly hair. He wore a black shirt and pants, not nearly as well-dressed as the others, but drew little attention. He was alone, and took a seat in the center, a few rows back from the front. He glanced around as others streamed in.

Shortly later, Christine, followed by Viktor and Raoul, stepped onto the stage. The boy turned toward the loud applause from Founders Circle, his interest piqued.

Christine took her position, center stage, with Viktor and Raoul a couple of steps behind her.

Curiosity seekers took seats in the auditorium. Something was going on and they wanted to see what it was. No one told them to leave, so they stayed.

Viktor bowed to the conductor. Raoul quickly followed suit.

The conductor nodded his head, and then raised his baton. Viktor and Raoul raised their bows.

The orchestra, Viktor, and Raoul, began to play "Habanera."

The opera house manager, standing at the back of Founders Circle, near the door, braced for the worst.

Christine began to sing.

The opera house manager was stunned. So was Doctor Gaston's wife. There was murmuring and disbelief among the other invited guests in Founders Circle.

Stagehands and members of the opera company, including the dark-haired mezzo-soprano who played the role of Carmen and had just sung the same aria on the same stage a short time before, gathered backstage to watch and listen.

When Christine finished, the crowd, what little there was, jumped to its feet and roared approval. Even the orchestra stood and applauded.

"Brava! Brava!" shouted Alfonso.

Christine, not knowing exactly what to do, curtsied.

Viktor and Raoul bowed.

The diva stormed away, livid. How could they have insulted her in this way? It was a child, a child, and a skinny blonde one at that!

Christine, trembling, crying, turned to Raoul, who quickly handed his violin and bow to Viktor, and she rushed into his eagerly waiting arms.

19

CALON LÂN

Zoe worked on a piece on the piano in the Valerius living room, with Viktor and Raoul on violin and Christine singing. Zoe suddenly stopped playing, followed by everyone else. She leaned forward and wrote on her sheet music.

Viktor leaned in and pointed at the sheet music. "See what she did there. That's good. That's very good, Miss Zoe. You will be someday a great composer."

"Thank you, Mr. Daaé, but I have a long way to go," Zoe replied.

Professor Valerius stepped through the front door.

"I look forward to playing your symphony," Viktor said.

Professor Valerius dropped his briefcase on a chair. "And I look forward to hearing it." He leaned over and kissed his wife, who entered bearing cookies.

"Mr. Daaé," Professor Valerius continued. "The music department is having our annual spring fling, cookout, and bonfire at the beach this weekend. Would you and Christine like to join us?"

"We wouldn't want to intrude," Viktor said.

"Intrude? We would be honored to have you. Bring your instrument. It will be an incredible jam session."

"But university students, is it a place for children?"

"I'll be there," Raoul said.

"He's my plus one," Zoe added.

"Oh yes," Professor Valerius said. "The faculty always brings their kids. It's very much a family affair, at least until the old, and very young people leave. After that, we don't want to know what happens."

"We're not that wild, Professor," Zoe said.

"I remember my college days all too well," Professor Valerius said, putting an arm around his wife, who smiled, also remembering.

CHRISTINE STILL DIDN'T have a swimsuit, so she headed out shopping with Zoe and Raoul in one of the funky shops at Venice Beach. She held up a one-piece for Zoe's inspection.

"I like this one," Christine said.

Zoe put it over her arm with some others to try on.

Raoul held up a string bikini. Christine covered her face. The bikini would have covered hardly anything.

"In your dreams," Zoe said.

Raoul reluctantly put the teeny bikini back on the rack.

"I think we should get you a Speedo," Zoe said. "You are half French, after all."

Christine laughed.

"No way. I'm wearing my Jams," Raoul insisted.

THE BEACH PARTY WAS, as promised, a family affair. There were lots of children, both older and younger than Christine and Raoul, but they would have been quite happy had it been just the two of them. Christine wore a one-piece swimsuit that she and Zoe had selected, over Raoul's objections. Christine took a pro forma dip in the ocean, accompanied by Raoul, but found it quite chilling and ran wailing for a towel. She had soon added knee-length shorts and a T-shirt to her outfit. Raoul stuck with his Jams and a pullover shirt with a clothes-for-cool-kids logo above the left breast.

Zoe managed to come up with Goth beach wear, which somewhat resembled Victorian swimwear, all black, of course. She wasn't that much out of place, as she was surrounded by musicians and artists, not accounting majors, and so there were some fairly outrageous outfits.

There was beach volleyball and various other games, along with plenty to eat and drink. Weenies were roasted on the campfire.

Professor and Mrs. Valerius, Viktor, and many of the other adults, lounged in beach chairs near the fire, watching the children play, engaging in a spirited discussion of music.

As dusk approached, instrument cases appeared, musicians gathered around, and a rather large jam session ensued. Viktor and Raoul joined in on violin, and after a few songs, Raoul pulled Christine into the group and she sang "Calon Lân," her voice soaring into the night air.

Professor Dodge, a female colleague, leaned over to Professor Valerius and whispered, "Is she Welsh?"

"Her father is a Swede," Professor Valerius responded. "Her mother died a couple of years ago and I don't really know anything else about her, other than she was a middle school music teacher."

The children, with whom Christine had been playing silly games not long before, were amazed. The faculty members, who had not previously heard her sing, were very impressed. Professor Valerius was quite pleased, as his colleagues would no doubt credit him with the discovery of this delightful young prodigy. There was loud applause as the song ended. Christine giggled in delight at the audience's reaction.

"Did I lie?" Professor Valerius asked.

"Her voice is quite beautiful, and beyond her years, but a Welsh rugby song is hardly a stretch," Professor Dodge replied.

"This is like a vacation for Christine, like a four-year-old singing 'Mary Had a Little Lamb,'" Professor Valerius said. "She is even better in Italian. She moves effortlessly between genres, and she truly loves to sing. To call her a prodigy would be an understatement."

"Well, I would like to hear more."

"She hasn't yet the lungs for opera, but she acquits herself quite nicely with arias in several languages. She has Puccini for breakfast. She's only twelve and will be auditioning soon for the Belen Conservatory."

"And she is living with her father in your guest house?"

"Yes, and I do hope they stay on. Her father gives private lessons on the violin and business is picking up."

"Who coaches her?"

"Her father works with her on her music, but she's never really had a voice coach, other than Zoe's friends at school. Could you suggest someone?"

"Let's see how it goes at Belen. If she gets in, then we will conference with Johnston and her voice teachers there and decide on the best course. Do keep me posted."

Professor Valerius nodded and smiled.

"A most interesting child," Professor Dodge said.

Christine began singing "True Love Ways," soon joined by the strings. There was loud applause when the song ended.

"Was that for my benefit?" Professor Dodge asked.

"No." Professor Valerius chuckled. "I suspect that was Zoe's doing."

"Zoe?"

"You should ask her someday to show you her grandmother's 1955 Lubbock High yearbook."

"Autographed?"

"Of course."

"Oh my," Professor Dodge said, looking over at Zoe. "I never knew Zoe was a Buddy Holley fan."

"You have no idea," Professor Valerius said.

There was no need for violins on the next selection, and so Viktor took his seat and Raoul took Christine by the hand. Massed guitars kicked in with a vengeance, and a college student burst forth singing "Oh! My Head." Raoul and Christine started dancing, more like flailing, and were quickly joined by all the other kids and the scene soon bore an eerie resemblance to *Lord of the Flies*. The kids were having a grand time, even if they had no idea what the music was.

As soon as the song was over, and the kids fell to the sand, feigning exhaustion, another young man stepped up, wearing the requisite glasses, playing a guitar, and launched into "Rave On," joined quickly by any other musician who cared to participate, and there were many, whether the song called for their instrument or not. Christine and Raoul sat in the sand, holding hands, raving on to the music.

As the jam session wound down and parents began packing to go, the children, including Christine and Raoul, gathered around the campfire, listening as Viktor told stories. A young girl moved closer to Viktor, "Another story, please, Mr. Daaé."

"Very well," Viktor agreed.

He took a dramatic pause, and then began. "Little Charlotte was a good girl. Her hair was as golden as the sun's rays and her soul was as clear and blue as her eyes."

Raoul looked at Christine, only inches away, blonde hair and blue eyes sparkling in the firelight.

"She was a good student, helped her mother, was kind to her doll, took great care of her dress and her little red shoes and her violin, but most of all she loved, when she went to sleep, to hear the Angel of Music."

"The Angel of Music?" the young girl asked.

"Every great musician receives a visit from the Angel at least once in his life. Sometimes the Angel leans over their cradle, as happened to Little Charlotte, and that is how there are young prodigies who play the violin better at six than grown men."

His young audience was captivated.

"Sometimes the Angel comes much later, because the children are naughty and won't learn their lessons or practice their scales."

The children giggled. They were all from musical families and knew all about practicing their scales.

"And sometimes, he does not come at all, because the children have a bad heart or a guilty conscience."

Now the children were worried.

"No one ever sees the Angel, but he is heard by those who are meant to hear him. He often comes when they least expect him, when they are sad or depressed. Then their ears suddenly perceive celestial harmonies, a divine voice, which they remember all their lives."

The children "oohed" and "aahed."

"Those who are visited by the Angel quiver with a thrill unknown to the rest of mankind. And they cannot touch an instrument, or open their mouths to sing, without producing sounds that put all other humans to shame."

"Have you heard the Angel, Daddy?" Christine asked. She already knew the answer, but she played along for the benefit of the other children.

Viktor nodded his head slowly, and his eyes lit up.

"Yes, my child, I have, and you will hear him one day as well. When I am in Heaven, I will send him to you."

All the children's eyes turned to Christine.

Viktor went into a fit of coughing.

"Daddy!" Christine put her arm around him, worried.

Raoul rushed to a cooler, brought back a bottle of water, and handed it to Viktor. It seemed to relieve the coughing, if only for a moment.

20

THE RENAISSANCE FAIRE

CHRISTINE AND RAOUL continued busking for the homeless in their free time. Summer vacation was tantalizingly close, and they had big plans for some summer fun. Now that they thought about it, busking was itself fun. They were outdoors making music. People applauded and gave them money, for the homeless shelter, of course, but it was an enjoyable way to spend an afternoon.

Raoul's audition to the Belen Conservatory, having been scheduled months in advance, came up first, before Ogden Hall was out for the summer. He acquitted himself well, and was accepted, which relieved him greatly, as he was certain that Christine would be accepted, and they would be going to the same school once more.

While Zoe worked hard to finish up her senior year at UCLA—there was so much to do, finals, papers, compositions, all manner of loose ends to wrap up—Raoul threw himself into helping Christine with her upcoming audition. His father reminded him, however, to pay attention to his own studies. Finals were coming up at Ogden Hall as well.

Christine and Raoul, along with the Chagnys and Valeriuses attended Zoe's graduation, with honors. The kids cheered loudly as her name was called to walk across the stage. Zoe had already decided to pursue at least a master's, if not a doctorate, in composition, and she had been accepted. Her meager inheritance and her jobs only went so far, and she graduated, as do so many others, with a considerable amount of student loan debt. She now had to find a way to pay for post-graduate school and her living expenses. Raoul would soon be fourteen and she expected her tenure as co-conspirator would be coming to an end. She had been a latchkey kid much younger than that, and the Chagny housekeeper was always around during the day anyway.

At her graduation party at a fancy restaurant, however, Zoe was pleasantly surprised when the Chagnys offered to continue her employment for two more years. The increased demands of graduate school would no doubt occupy more of her time—which would require Raoul to take on a bit more responsibility for himself—but that was a good thing, they felt. Zoe would continue to transport him to and from school, and provide supervision and structure as required, but she was to concentrate on her own studies. Raoul was quite pleased with the arrangement—he still had a driver whenever he needed one, which made it easier to hang out with Christine, and more freedom. He already looked on Zoe as more of a big sister than a nanny.

"You'll still be coming with us to Saint-Tropez," Raoul reminded Zoe.

"Of course," Hannah added.

"And Christine can come too, right?" Raoul continued.

"Really?" Christine was amazed.

"We will first need to discuss it with Mr. Daaé," Hannah said.

"Daddy, please!"

"I will think about it," Viktor said, "but first you must concentrate on your audition."

"If I get into the conservatory, then I can go?" Christine asked.

"I would not make being accepted a requirement. That would not be right. I would only require that you do your work in preparation, and do your best at the audition, that is all. But there are other things to consider."

Neither Christine nor Raoul could possibly imagine what else there was to consider. It sounded like a plan.

"Do you have a passport, Christine?" Hannah asked.

"I don't think so, ma'am. I'm not even sure what that is."

Raoul smiled. He had been an international traveler for so long that it never occurred to him that most kids his age didn't have passports. All his friends from Ogden Hall had them, of course, and all in their own name, not grouped with their parents, so that they could accompany friends to exotic locations around the world every summer. Then there were the professional children at school for whom a passport was an occupational necessity.

"Zoe," Hannah continued. "Can you take care of that, with Mr. Daaé's permission, of course? It will need to be expedited. Alain's office can help you there. And there will be additional documents necessary to take someone else's minor child out of the country."

"Perhaps you might join us, Mr. Daaé?" Chagny asked. "We will have plenty of room, won't we, my dear?"

"Of course, that's a brilliant idea, why didn't I think of it?" Hannah said. "It's settled then, you both must join us, and that will solve the documentation problem."

"We will see," Viktor said.

"I recall you mentioned you had been to Saint-Tropez," Chagny said.

"Yes, in my younger days when I was a musician aboard a cruise ship. I always managed to get ashore and sit in at a few of the small clubs."

"Perhaps we have met before. I haunted quite a few of those small clubs myself."

"You did indeed," Hannah said. "He was quite the French playboy when I met him."

"Yes, count, perhaps we did." Viktor smiled, something he so rarely did. "Those were good days, were they not?"

Chagny laughed and nodded his head. "Yes, yes, they were."

Hannah turned to the Valeriuses. "You two should join us as well. We will have a glorious time. The food, the music, you will love it."

"I do have this summer off," Professor Valerius said. "Someone else is handling the summer programs for a change. What do you think, dear?"

"I agree with Hannah," Mrs. Valerius said. "It's a brilliant idea."

"Ah, the beach," Zoe said. "I definitely need to hit the gym."

Raoul leaned over to Christine. "The beaches are topless in France."

Christine was horrified. "Do I have to go topless?"

Raoul enthusiastically nodded his head.

"Of course not, my dear," Hannah said. "Ignore Raoul. He's a teenage boy. You can wear your top if you like."

Christine was relieved.

"No topless for you." Viktor settled it, rather grumpily. "You will wear a top. Maybe I will go with you shopping for a bathing suit, a one-piece."

There was some polite laughter.

Christine leaned over to Zoe and whispered, "Are you going topless?"

Zoe smiled but did not answer.

Raoul snorted. He obviously knew the answer.

"We could always drop you off in Paris, young man, and you could spend summer vacation with your grandmother," Hannah scolded.

Christine giggled. Raoul straightened up.

"Since everyone's here, I have an idea for a short break with Raoul and Christine," Zoe said.

This was news to both Raoul and Christine, who were immediately interested, no matter what it was.

"I've been thinking about it for some time but hadn't mentioned it because we've been so busy with finals and auditions," Zoe continued. "It's a road trip, up the coast, but I think it would be a good cultural experience for the kids, very educational."

"What is it?" Raoul asked.

"It's a Renaissance Faire. We'll go in costume. I have a friend who works in the costume shop at UCLA. There will be lots of buskers and lots of customers, so maybe we can even make a few dollars for the shelter."

"Cool," Christine said.

"And it's a road trip?" Raoul asked.

"It's on the central coast, so it would be overnight, probably two nights as we'll be exhausted from a day at the faire."

"We will have to see about that," Viktor said.

They discussed it and the parents agreed that the kids had been working hard and deserved a short weekend break, provided they kept up with their studies, both were prepared for finals at Ogden Hall, and Christine was prepared for her audition at the conservatory.

Zoe drove Christine and Raoul to the costume shop, where the kids darted between rows of assorted costumes.

"Over here, guys," Zoe called out.

Christine and Raoul rushed over. Brenda, a college student working at the costume shop, pulled a Renaissance-era dress off a rack, and held it up in front of Christine.

"Do you have anything a bit more upscale, like nobility?" Zoe asked.

"Let's see," Brenda replied. She headed down the aisle, with the others following. She pulled out a dress and held it up. "Something like this? It will be a lot fuller when we stuff it with petticoats."

Christine's eyes lit up.

"I like it," Zoe said. "And for the young viscount?"

"What about this?" Brenda said, pulling a suit for Raoul.

"It looks like a dress," Raoul protested.

"It was all the rage among young noblemen of the era," Brenda said dryly.

"Just go with it," Zoe said, "Nobody you know is going to see you in it."

"You and Christine will see me in it," Raoul said.

"We promise to never tell," Christine said.

"And no cell phone pictures," Raoul said. "I don't want this all over the Internet."

"What are you going as?" Brenda asked Zoe.

"A wench, of course."

"But of course."

"We'll need shoes and stockings and unmentionables, and all the rest," Zoe said.

"Unmentionables?" Raoul asked.

VIKTOR WAS IN BED in the little cottage, coughing, not feeling well at all. Zoe and Raoul waited nearby as Christine hovered over the bed. "I should stay here and take care of you."

"No, you go with your friends and have a grand time."

"But Daddy, you're sick."

"I'll be okay. It's a Renaissance Faire. It will be fantastic. I wish I could go with you."

"Next year we'll go together," Christine said.

"Next year, with you I will go," Viktor said. "I promise."

Zoe stepped forward. "We don't have to go, Mr. Daaé. It's not that big a deal."

"I will be fine. A young girl should be with her friends, singing, playing music, experiencing life, not stuck here with an old man who has a miserable cold. Mrs. Valerius will bring me soup and get whatever I need. It's only two days. Go."

"Yes Daddy." She leaned over and kissed him. "I love you."

"I love you more," he responded, hugging her tightly.

Raoul and Christine piled into the back seat of Zoe's car, excited and ready to go. Zoe slid into the driver's seat and looked in the mirror. "No making out in the back seat."

The kids giggled.

Raoul had seen it before, but Christine fell in love with the scenic beauty along the Pacific Coast Highway, which was probably better than making out. The 101 would have been much faster, though infinitely uglier, and Zoe felt everyone should experience the drive up the coast at least once. It was worth the additional time on the road. Not a bit of studying for finals was done on the trip up.

They checked into a chain motel, not the bottom of the rung, but clean, and the rooms were large. Chagny offered to put them up in far more luxurious accommodations, but they were kids and Zoe didn't want to spoil them. Besides, this was an adventure, not a weekend at a luxury resort. All they needed were beds and a bathroom and a fast-food place, which there always were near a cluster of motels. There had been discussion over how many rooms, and it was decided that one room with two beds would be the most practical from the standpoint of adult supervision, and most importantly, safety. Zoe leaned her aluminum baseball bat against the wall between the beds.

Zoe stepped out of the bathroom, wearing whatever it was that Goth girls wore to bed. It was black, and interesting, Christine thought.

Raoul and Christine were already in bed, the same one, on their backs, covers up around their necks, all eyes on Zoe, if only to gauge her reaction.

"Uh, no." Zoe declared. "Boys in this bed, girls in this one."

Christine giggled. "There's only one boy."

"Then he gets a bed all to himself. Scoot."

Christine slipped out of the bed and scooted into the other one. Zoe motioned for her to move over. Christine moved over next to the wall and Zoe got into bed beside her, reached over and turned off the lamp between the beds. There was more giggling in the dark.

The next morning there were bags, clothes, and stuff piled on every surface. Zoe cinched up Christine's corset.

Raoul came in from the bathroom, wearing tights and a wig. "Do I have to wear this wig?"

"Of course," Zoe answered.

He held up a codpiece. "What's this thingy?"

"A codpiece."

"Where does it go?"

"Give me a minute and I'll show you, but first I have to build some bosoms for the fair maiden."

"Bosoms?" Raoul asked.

"Boobies," Zoe said.

Christine giggled, making cinching the corset even more difficult.

"Okay," Raoul said slowly, drawing the word out, backing away, and then turned and went back into the bathroom.

Zoe pulled and pushed and tugged, trying to build some bosoms with what she had to work with.

"Oh, okay." Raoul said from the bathroom. "I get it."

Zoe and Christine burst out laughing.

RAOUL, CARRYING HIS VIOLIN, and Christine, fully decked out in fashionable Renaissance apparel for a young noble boy and his lady, and Zoe, their wench, headed into the faire, stopping at the entrance.

"Performers aren't allowed to use cell phones inside the faire," Zoe explained. "They kind of ruin the atmosphere." She pulled out her cell phone and checked it. "Cell phones off." Raoul followed suit. Christine still didn't have a cell phone, nor a place to put one at the moment.

"Did they have violins back then?" Raoul asked.

"Yes, actually, the modern violin came into being during the Renaissance, so you are completely authentic."

Christine felt a bit naked in the low-cut dress, which wouldn't have been so bad if everything she had on her chest hadn't been cinched up in the corset, leaving most of what she had, or didn't have, on display. "Are you sure nobody can see anything?"

Raoul immediately looked. There was nothing to see.

"You're fine," Zoe said. "It's what all the girls are wearing. Look around."

Christine looked around. It was indeed what many of the young girls, at least those in costume, were wearing. The older girls and women, on the other hand, who had something to see, were displaying rather generous cleavage, including Zoe, who made a wicked wench.

"You look nice," Raoul said to Christine.

"Thank you, kind sir," Christine answered. "You do too."

"I look like a fool," he answered.

"What about me," Zoe asked. "Do I look like a slut?"

"I wasn't going to say anything," Raoul said, "but yeah, you kinda do."

"Thanks, that's exactly what I was going for."

They checked out the sights, strolling musicians, jugglers, dancers, and performers of all kinds, along with lots of civilians. They passed by a young man in stocks, being punished for who knew what.

They watched jousting. They saw the king and queen. A magician did a trick for Christine.

They sat at an outdoor table along with several other people and ate with their hands as serving wenches refilled their goblets.

After lunch they found a suitable location and began busking. Raoul played the violin and Christine sang "Quanto sia lieto il giorno." They drew a crowd—Christine was quite convincing as a young Renaissance girl. The money was good, especially since Zoe solicited donations by hiking up her skirt and stuffing the money in her garter belt.

They took their act on the road, and strolled through the faire, playing and singing, with Zoe collecting money, and stuffing some of it into her ample cleavage.

Zoe estimated the time at a sundial. "I'd better go check my messages. I'll meet you by the stocks," she said. "By the stocks, not in them, so try to stay out of trouble."

Christine and Raoul walked, holding hands, such a sweet young Renaissance couple, headed toward the stocks.

"Are you having a good time?" Raoul asked.

"I'm having a wonderful time." Christine put her free hand over her chest. "Is anything hanging out?"

Raoul glanced. "No, you're good."

"I can't believe girls had to wear all this stuff back then."

"Girls? What about boys? Look at me!"

Christine looked and laughed. "You do look kind of funny, but cute."

Raoul and Christine sat on a bench and watched as a young woman was dragged, kicking, screaming, and protesting, to the stocks and locked down. The crowd roared its approval.

Raoul looked up and saw Zoe, skirt hiked up with both hands, running toward them.

"Christine!" Zoe shouted.

"Oh no, something's wrong," Raoul said. He grabbed Christine's hand. They jumped off the bench and ran toward Zoe.

ZOE DROVE SOUTH on the 101. Speed, not scenery, mattered now. Raoul and Christine sat in the back seat, holding hands, grim. There had been no time to change clothes. Everyone was still in their Renaissance costumes.

On arrival at the hospital in Los Angeles Zoe whipped into the parking garage and found a spot. They jumped out of the car.

"Bring your violin," Christine said.

The elevator door opened, and Christine came out singing "Con te partirò," followed by Raoul playing his violin, and Zoe, pulling out her cell phone.

Viktor lay in bed in a hospital room, barely conscious, connected by tubes and wires to an IV and instruments. Professor and Mrs. Valerius stood nearby. Hannah stood at the end of the bed, looking over the chart.

"I hear the Angel," Viktor said weakly.

"Yes, Mr. Daaé," Professor Valerius said, "I believe you do." His cell phone rang, and he answered it.

Doctor Gaston and everyone else in the hallway turned to watch in amazement as Christine walked briskly, singing "Con te partirò," followed by Raoul playing his violin, both in full Renaissance costume, with a wench on a cell phone bringing up the rear.

Professor Valerius stepped out into the hallway and waved. Christine rushed toward him, swept into the hospital room, and rushed to her father's bedside, still singing. She took his hand and pulled it to her breast. He opened his eyes as she abandoned the song.

"Daddy!"

"It's time, my child."

"No, Daddy. I need you."

"Raoul," Viktor said.

Raoul stepped forward quickly. "Yes sir."

"You will watch out for my darling daughter?"

"Yes sir, of course I will."

Viktor motioned for Christine to come closer. She leaned forward, in tears.

"I will send to you from Heaven the Angel of Music," Viktor said.

"No, Daddy, please. I want you, not the Angel."

Viktor did not respond. Hannah stepped over, looked at the instruments, and checked her watch.

Zoe leaned against the wall and cried softly in the hallway, listening to Christine's sobs and wails from inside the room. She suddenly felt utterly out of place dressed as a wench.

Raoul watched, stunned, as Christine sobbed over her father's body. Professor Valerius pulled her away. "He's gone, Christine."

Christine broke free and kissed her father. Professor Valerius pulled her away once more and she turned and fell into Raoul's arms. He comforted her, caring not in the least about how foolish he looked wearing tights and a wig.

———

Raoul and Christine sat in the hospital waiting room, holding hands. Christine was still crying softly. Zoe sat on the other side of Christine. Professor and Mrs. Valerius sat in a facing row of chairs. Christine composed herself somewhat and looked up.

"Will I have to go to an orphanage?"

"No, of course not," Professor Valerius assured her.

"You will live with us," Mrs. Valerius said. "We'll move your things into the other bedroom in the main house."

"Why can't I stay in the little cottage?"

"You can't stay out there all by yourself, dear," Mrs. Valerius said.

"She can stay with us," Raoul said.

"Christine, your father knew his time was drawing near, and he asked us to be your guardians when he was gone," Professor Valerius explained.

"Why didn't he tell me?"

"He didn't want you to worry. You were so happy in school, with your new friends, and he didn't want anything to interrupt preparation for your audition. He insisted that you get into the conservatory."

"He should have told me. I would have understood. I'm not a little girl anymore."

"No, my dear, you are not," Mrs. Valerius said.

"I can never replace your father, but I will be here for you, whatever you need," Professor Valerius said.

Chagny rushed up to the group. Professor Valerius stood, and they shook hands.

"I came as soon as I heard," Chagny said. He dropped to one knee in front of Christine and took her hand. "I am so sorry, Christine. Anything you need, you let me know."

"Thank you."

"Raoul, you will stay by her side for as long as she needs."

"Yes sir."

Chagny stood, put a hand on the professor's shoulder and they stepped away a few feet. "I understand you will be caring for the girl."

"Yes, Mr. Daaé made the arrangements a few weeks ago. We will be her legal guardians. She doesn't really have any other family."

"Her schooling, the conservatory, university?" Chagny asked.

"We will take care of it."

"Of course. But I am here if you need help, with anything."

"Thank you."

"At least allow me to handle the funeral expenses. I'll make all the arrangements."

"That would be very generous of you."

Chagny turned and looked at the kids. "Christine brings out the best in
Raoul. I am so very glad she came into our lives, and her father as well. He
was a most interesting gentleman. Raoul adored him."

21

CON TE PARTIRÒ

Viktor's funeral was a small gathering in a large church. The casket was modest, as was his wish. There were lots of flowers. Many students from Ogden Hall were in attendance along with many of Viktor's violin students, and their parents. Near the back of the church were quite a few homeless—word had spread quickly on the streets—along with several staff and volunteers from the Santa Monica Shelter.

The Ogden Hall choir occupied the choir loft. All the students wore their school uniforms. Viktor's violin was prominently displayed on a stand. There were many floral arrangements.

As the choir performed "Suo Gân" in English Teddy led a short procession, followed by Christine tightly clutching Raoul's arm, and then Greg bringing up the rear. Teddy and Greg escorted Christine and Raoul to their seats, alone on the first row—Christine was the only family member in attendance—and then took up positions just off the dais on opposite sides, as if guarding Christine from some unseen menace.

Although her father loved playing it and hearing her sing it, "Suo Gân" would not have been Christine's choice to be sung at his funeral. She had been too consumed by grief over her father's death and uncertainty over her own future to object when Raoul chose the song.

Christine, choking back tears, and Raoul, sat holding hands. Christine wore a black dress, Raoul a black suit, white shirt, and tie. His suit was custom made in Paris. For most boys his age, the collar of their dress shirts never fit properly, but Raoul's certainly did, rising high above the collar of the jacket, just like his father's. Christine was far too young and inexperienced to notice such things, but Zoe did. She sat directly behind them, along with the Chagnys and Valeriuses. Zoe was dressed in black, not at all Goth, but conservative and appropriate for the occasion.

The music came to an end. Then there was silence for a moment as Professor Valerius made his way to the podium.

"I had the privilege of knowing Mr. Daaé, although for far too short a time. He was a gentleman to a fault. I wish I could have known him better, but he was a private man. He and his daughter Christine lived in our guest house for the last few months of his life, where he taught violin to private students, and brought music back into our home, from which it had been missing for far too long. Although his students did not always produce the most pleasing sounds from their violin," Professor Valerius paused for some polite chuckling from the parents of the students in question, "Mr. Daaé was a man of infinite patience and worked with them until they improved. He was a master violinist, in my opinion the first violin of the world. He played an enchanted violin. He loved music, but more than anything else in the world he loved his daughter, Christine. He gave up everything to bring her to Los Angeles in hopes that she might receive a first-class education in music. He honored my wife and me by allowing us to help fulfill the dream that brought him and his daughter into our lives. He will be missed, but he, and his music, will live on in Christine."

Raoul stood and extended his arm. Christine took it, and he escorted her to the casket. The funeral director placed Viktor's violin and bow in the casket, carefully arranging them beside Viktor's body.

Raoul choked back tears as Christine leaned in and kissed her father, and then touched the violin. "So you can play for the Angel of Music, Daddy." She remained composed, there were few tears, and nothing left but grief. Although she was surrounded by others who cared about her, she had never felt more alone.

IT HAD TAKEN DAYS, and considerable effort, for Viktor and Christine to make the trip from Chicago to Los Angeles, but the return, in the Chagny's luxurious Gulfstream, took only hours. Christine was nervous about boarding the plane—she had never flown before—and her first flight would be in a private jet.

The Valeriuses and Zoe accompanied the Chagnys on the flight. Although there was a flight attendant on board, Zoe insisted on helping her serve drinks and snacks, if for no reason other than to keep busy. She had been quite fond of Mr. Daaé, enjoyed talking, and making music with him, and it deeply affected her to see Christine suffering so.

The Chagnys and Valeriuses sat in facing seats. Zoe knelt in the aisle and spoke to Professor Valerius. "I should never have taken the kids to the Renaissance Faire. I had no idea Mr. Daaé was so sick. He kept saying it was just a cold."

"He didn't want anyone to know, especially Christine. She had been so happy with you and Raoul. He wanted her to go on that trip and enjoy herself."

"She should have been with him. We barely made it back in time."

"No one knew exactly how long he had, even the doctors. But maybe he knew it was time and he didn't want her there to see him die, so that she could remember him as he was, and not in the hospital."

"But she did see him die."

"Yes, she did, but I think the bit of joy and peace it gave him to see her one last time was worth the pain it caused Christine. She's hurting now, but someday she will appreciate that moment."

Christine sat in silence with Raoul. It had already been a long and tiring day and helped along by the drone of the jet engines she soon dozed off and the pain went away, if only for a short time. She was awakened by the screeching of tires on the runway.

As they checked into the Palmer House, the manager, who had been awed by Christine's singing at her mother's wake, approached her. "Miss Daaé, we are glad to see you again at the Palmer House, although I wish it were under happier circumstances. I am so sorry for your loss. If there is anything you need during your stay here, please let me know."

"Thank you," Christine answered quietly.

The others in her party were puzzled that Christine seemed to know the manager of this luxury hotel but said nothing.

No one wanted Christine to be alone during the night, and the Valeriuses thought it too soon to ask her to sleep in their room, so it was arranged for Zoe to share a room with her. Raoul protested that he should also be allowed to stay in the room with the girls—they had all slept in the same room just a few days ago on their trip—but Chagny insisted that it would be inappropriate in these circumstances. As a compromise, Raoul would have an adjoining room and the connecting door would remain open so that he would be readily available should Christine need him during the night.

With the two-hour time change it was rather late when they arrived in Chicago. Chagny ordered a light supper from room service, but Christine paid little attention to her food, and was already in her pajamas when the room's phone rang. Zoe answered and listened for a moment. "Who may I say is calling?" She seemed a bit puzzled, and then turned to Christine. "Some guy said to tell you there's a redneck in the lobby, and then he hung up."

In an instant Christine was up, out the door, and down the hallway.

"Raoul," Zoe called out. He immediately appeared in the doorway. "Christine went down to the lobby. Go catch her. I'll be down in a minute."

Zoe dialed her phone. "Professor, we have a situation."

The elevator door opened, and Christine raced through the lobby. Jim Bob spotted her and ran to meet her, catching her as she flew into his arms, wrapping her legs around his waist and hugging him tightly.

"You've grown, Squirt," he said.

Christine wouldn't let go, squeezing as hard as she could. Raoul was on the next elevator, and he rushed forward to defend his lady, although he had no idea from what. Christine didn't seem to be in any distress, clinging tightly to Jim Bob.

"Who are you?" Raoul demanded.

"The redneck," Jim Bob said. "Who are you?"

"Raoul Chagny. I'm here with Christine."

Zoe arrived next. "Christine, are you okay?"

Christine finally released her death grip on Jim Bob and slid to the floor, put her arm around his waist and buried her head in his chest. "I'm fine. This is the redneck."

"Hi, I'm Jim Bob Butrell. I was a friend of Christine's parents, and the squirt." He squeezed the squirt and she reciprocated. "I called the funeral home and they said this was where she was staying."

"I'm Zoe, Raoul's—driver."

"Driver? Okay," Jim Bob said, not exactly sure why the boy would have his own driver.

The Valeriuses and Chagnys stepped up. "This is Professor Valerius and his wife," Zoe said.

Professor Valerius and Jim Bob shook hands. "How do you do?"

"Jim Bob, family friend."

"Mr. Daaé appointed the Valeriuses guardians for Christine," Zoe added.

"Ah," Jim Bob said, "I was worried about that. I'm glad to see he made arrangements."

"Apparently there was no other family," Professor Valerius said.

"Yeah, I think that's right," Jim Bob said. "I don't know if Viktor's parents are still alive, he never talked about them, and the way I heard it, Rachel's parents kind of abandoned her for some cult when she was in high school. Nobody's heard from them since."

"This is Count and Doctor Chagny," Zoe said. "Raoul's parents." There was more handshaking.

"You knew the Daaés well?" Professor Valerius asked.

"I went to college with Rachel. I was her wingman the night she met Viktor, in a country and western dive bar."

"A dive bar?" Hannah asked, "Oh my."

"She actually met him here, at the hotel. Rachel and I were working catering and Viktor was playing violin for a wedding reception. He had a gig playing fiddle after the wedding and invited her to come by. She had never heard of the place, so she brought me along for protection."

"He was playing fiddle?" Raoul asked. "I thought he played violin."

"A fiddle is nothing but a violin without a case, son," Jim Bob said. "As I recall, he was playing 'Devil Went Down to Georgia' on the fiddle, and it was smokin'. He actually did have a separate fiddle, a cheap one, for the redneck bars so he wouldn't burn up his violin, which was quite an instrument."

"Yes sir, it was," Raoul said.

"I had to explain to him what a wingman was—he thought I was Rachel's boyfriend. We hit it right off after that. I stood up at their wedding. I used to change Christine's diapers."

Christine, embarrassed, buried her face in his side.

"We had some legendary jam sessions at their house, and I would end up crashing on the couch."

"You're a musician?" Zoe asked.

"Yes ma'am, I've been accused of that, and worse."

"I love your accent," Zoe said. "Tennessee?"

"Texas, east Texas, almost Louisiana, maybe a bit of Cajun."

Jim Bob looked at Christine in her pajamas. "Well, it looks like it's past your bedtime, young lady. I'd better be going."

"Will you be coming to the cemetery tomorrow?" Chagny asked Jim Bob.

"I'll be there."

There were handshakes all around as Jim Bob prepared to leave.

"I have a little group and we'll be playing a gig tomorrow night. Most of the old gang has scattered, but some of them will be sitting in. It won't be nearly what we had for Rachel here at the hotel, but if you can make it, we'd love for you to come. We all intend to raise a glass or two for Viktor."

"We were planning to leave right after the services," Chagny said.

"I understand," Jim Bob said.

"Christine has to work on her audition piece for the conservatory," Mrs. Valerius said.

"Oh yeah, that," Jim Bob said. "I guess that means you're not in yet?"

Christine shook her head.

"You'll make it."

He looked up. "I assume you are all aware that she sings with the voice of an angel."

Heads nodded in agreement.

"I'm never singing again," Christine declared.

Jim Bob looked up and around the opulent hotel lobby.

"We had Rachel's wake here. There were lots of musicians. Christine sang and brought down the house. The hotel manager was in tears. I haven't been here much since."

WHATEVER COMPOSURE CHRISTINE had regained since the funeral she lost at the graveside service. Seeing her father's casket sitting on the platform next to her mother's grave was almost too much for her. Raoul stood ramrod straight, trying to hold back his own tears while holding on to Christine.

There were a few other people in attendance, some of the teachers from Rachel's school, and a smattering of musicians. The service was brief. Christine declined to sing—she had declared her intent to never sing again—so Jim Bob stepped up and sang "Amazing Grace," which brought a flood of tears to Christine's eyes and most of the others as well.

When the services were over, Chagny and the local funeral director approached Jim Bob. "Mr. Butrell," Chagny said, "could I impose upon you for a favor?"

"Of course, what do you need?"

"Would you be so kind as to pick out an appropriate headstone for both of Christine's parents? The funeral director will make the arrangements for engraving and placing it and will bill me for it."

"Absolutely."

As the group prepared to leave, Christine and Raoul were still sitting silently in the chairs in front of the casket. Jim Bob stepped over and knelt in front of Christine.

"Honey, I know you're hurting right now. I know you said you'd never sing again. I lost my dad when I was in high school, so I know a little bit of what you are going through. I was older, and I still had my mom, so it wasn't as bad, but it looks like you have some people here who care about you." He looked up at Raoul. "I'm not exactly sure who you are in all this, boy, but she seems to like you, so if you hurt her, I'll become your worst nightmare."

Raoul stiffened up but didn't respond. Clearly Jim Bob was quite capable of doing just that and Christine seemed quite attached to him.

"Christine, you have a gift that comes along maybe once in a generation, or a century. Just hearing your voice is incredible, but seeing it come out of such a beautiful little girl is a transcendent experience. Grown men weep."

"A trans what?" Christine asked.

"You can look it up later. I don't want to push you into anything. It's your life. You can take whatever path you like, but I think you love to sing. I know you love to sing, and you're damned good at it, and the world would be a better place if you continue to do it. Both your parents wanted you to go to that conservatory thing in Los Angeles. Your daddy went to enormous lengths to take you there. Give it some thought before you decide. On second thought, don't listen to me. I've heard you sing. To hell with everybody else. They don't deserve you. Your beautiful voice is burned into the soundtrack of my mind, so I'll just keep you to myself."

She almost laughed. He kissed her, and she kissed back, hugging him, and not wanting to let go.

"Okay, I have to go and try to teach some music to a bunch of lunkheads at the community college. You call me, honey. Someday I might even make it to La La Land. We can hang out and hit up some clubs. I'll teach you how to dance. And I hear there's this thing out there called a beach, sounds like a great place to pick up chicks."

Having finally coaxed a smile out of her, he broke away, and left. He stopped for a moment and handed Zoe a piece of paper. "I understand you have to get back, but I wrote down the address for tonight, just in case. I put my number on there also. If Christine needs anything, you call me. I love her like a daughter, and I'll do anything for her, anything."

Christine stood beside Zoe and watched as Jim Bob drove away in his battered pickup.

"I would have never guessed he could sing like that," Zoe said.

"You should hear him play piano," Christine said, her grief, at least for the moment, in remission.

ON THE WAY BACK to the hotel Christine decided she wanted to go see Jim Bob play and no one dared deny her in her fragile state. Fortunately, they had not yet checked out of the Palmer House, so they decided to stay another night. The Gulfstream crew had already left for the airport, but they were accustomed to changes in itinerary and would not mind another night in Chicago on the clock. One brief phone call from Chagny was all that was required.

After lunch at the hotel, Christine insisted that everyone should go see the sights of Chicago or whatever, but it would not be necessary to sit around keeping her company. She had friends in the hotel to see anyway. Raoul immediately declared that he would accompany her. Both Hannah and Mrs. Valerius decided the hotel spa would be an ideal way to spend the afternoon, and perhaps Zoe would join them? Zoe declined. She thought a brutal workout in the health club would be just the thing for her, and she instructed Raoul to keep his cell phone on him as she would check with him periodically. Hannah added that the kids were not to leave the hotel without first getting permission.

"What about the gentlemen?" Chagny asked.

"Surely you boys can find something to do, my dear," Hannah replied. "Find a poker game. Go to a ball game. They do play ball here, don't they? I know you have friends in Chicago who are members of private clubs—go hang out there and drink brandy and act all British."

"Christine," Chagny asked, "Are you sure you will be all right?"

Christine nodded firmly.

Hannah leaned over and whispered to Chagny, "It's the best thing for her. She doesn't need all of us fawning over her."

Chagny nodded in agreement, and then turned to Christine. "Very well, Christine, we will leave you in Raoul's capable hands." He pointed a finger at Raoul, "Raoul, be a gentleman."

"Dad!"

"We will meet back here in time for dinner at seven, and then go to this club," Chagny said, and everyone agreed.

Christine and Raoul roamed the hotel. Raoul had seen plenty of grand hotels from the guest side and was fascinated by all that went on behind the scenes. Christine knew all the cool places, and before long she seemed like her old self, although Raoul knew she would never be the same. She found old friends in the kitchens and hallways and employee areas and hugged and hugged and hugged. The kids sneaked into a wedding reception and corporate meetings, giggled a bit, and slipped away in search of their next adventure.

AFTER DINNER, THEY discovered their driver didn't need directions—it was a well-known blues club—and he was no stranger there himself. Even before they stepped out of the limousine Chagny was beginning to question his decision to stay over. It looked like a dump—not in the way upscale blues clubs try to use carefully aged building materials as decorative items—it really was a dump.

It took two one-hundred-dollar bills, one for each of the kids, to persuade the doorman/bouncer to allow minors into the club, along with Chagny's assurance that neither of them would be drinking anything stronger than soft drinks. The price for those would be the same as alcohol, he informed him, knowing this would not be a problem—rich people trying to be cool often slummed in the club, and the club's owner was quite happy to take their money.

Additional folding money got them a large table, well-located. Chagny discovered later that Jim Bob had already reserved it for them in case they changed their minds. As they sat down, Zoe's attention was drawn to the stage. She quickly understood why Christine had said earlier, "You should hear him play the piano."

There was a saxophone player whose day job was defensive tackle for the Bears. The man was huge and fearsome looking but handled that sax like it was his lover. A large black woman stood behind the microphone, singing the blues the way the blues should be sung. Jim Bob waved at them from the piano, which made Christine smile.

It was obvious to Chagny fancy drinks were not part of the bartender's repertoire, but drinks were ordered, with expensive soft drinks for the kids. Christine appeared to be, if not happy, then far less distressed.

The blues continued. Several musicians, friends of Viktor's, sat in for a song or two, and all of them made their way to Christine's table to hug her and comfort her and offer their condolences. She bore up well. Everyone had come prepared to endure the evening in deference to Christine, but discovered they rather enjoyed the music, currently "Ain't Got No, I Got Life."

As the adults began checking their watches—it would soon be time for the kids to go to bed—Christine leaned over and whispered something to Raoul. He dutifully got up, walked purposefully to the stage, and spoke to

Jim Bob. Jim Bob nodded, and at the end of the song in progress, the singer announced she was taking a break and alerted the bartender, which brought considerable laughter from the audience. Jim Bob leaned over and spoke into his own microphone. "Ladies and gentlemen, we have a special guest with us tonight, a very good friend of mine. I went to school with her mama, and I played a lot of gigs around town with her daddy, who was one hell of a fiddle player and quite a gentleman as well. Her daddy passed this week and a lot of his old friends have been sitting in with us here tonight. I had hoped she would join us on stage, and she has agreed to sing just one song, so give a big round of applause for Miss Christine Daaé."

There was considerable applause until Christine got up and walked onto the stage. A heckler shouted, "That skinny little white girl gonna sing the blues?" Some of the applause turned to laughter. The huge saxophone player slowly stood and shambled up to the microphone, shoulders alternately dipping and rising, head stable and glaring at all those who faced him, not unlike the view of an opposing quarterback just before the lights went out. Christine had to move over to allow room. He leaned down—it was a long way down to the microphone—and a hush fell over the crowd. "This skinny little white girl gonna blow your doors off, so you just shut your face and listen." That settled it, and a huge round of applause followed. He then leaned down even further so Christine could reach up to hug him tightly around his enormous neck. He stepped back and motioned for her to step up to the microphone. She did, he waved his finger at the audience, returned to his custom, reinforced chair, and all eyes fell on Christine.

"I'm sorry I never learned to sing the blues—I'm only twelve," Christine said into the microphone.

The audience, having been duly warned, waited in silence. The musicians took up their instruments.

"This was my daddy's favorite song in all the world, and he knew a lot of songs. I was singing it to him in the hospital, but I didn't get to finish it because he died."

There was an audible gasp from the audience, now somewhat ashamed of their previous behavior. Christine turned and nodded to Jim Bob, who began playing "Con te partirò." She began to sing, in Italian. As her voice floated over the room, the bartenders and waitresses stopped and stared. Glasses stopped clinking. No one moved. No one spoke. It wasn't the blues, but the audience was stunned and even the doorman/bouncer was in tears by the time Christine finished the song, as was the big saxophone player.

There was total silence in the room as Christine stepped over and kissed Jim Bob, and then quietly left the stage, where Raoul proudly waited to take her arm and escort her back to the table.

"I'm ready to go," Christine said. Chagny had already settled the bill, with a very generous tip, and everyone immediately stood to go. Only then did the thunderous applause begin, accompanied by a standing ovation, as the crowd parted to make way for the skinny little white girl who had just blown their doors off.

22

NESSUN DORMA

The seats on the Chagny Gulfstream were even larger than first-class seats on a commercial airliner, which came in handy as Christine and Raoul shared one while robotically playing a video game on the screen in front of them. Mrs. Valerius had fretted over allowing this, but they seemed so innocent, and far more interested in their video game than in exploiting the intimacy of their seating arrangement. Chagny assured her that they would be required to occupy separate seats for landing, and for the moment, Christine seemed content.

Zoe sank into the deep upholstery of her own seat, listening to classical music on large, state-of-the-art headphones, not the tiny little plastic tubes they rented on airlines.

The Chagnys and Valeriuses occupied the lounge seats, quietly discussing Christine's future, both immediate and long-term, over drinks. Her audition for the conservatory was coming up all too soon, and her announcement that she might never sing again concerned them all.

Christine and Raoul, engrossed in their video game, and with the monotonous hum of the jet engines, heard none of it. For a short time at least, the video game took Christine's mind off the loss of her father and her uncertain future.

"You have to audition," Raoul said as he killed something on the screen.

"Why?"

"So you can get into the conservatory."

"I don't care about that anymore," she said.

"What are you going to do?"

"I'll just go to regular school."

"And then what?" he asked.

"And then what what?"

"Are you going to be a schoolteacher, a nurse, work in a department store?"

"Maybe I'll work on a cruise ship."

"Really?"

"My daddy did it, and he liked it."

"A cruise ship?"

"Yeah, he played in the orchestra. He got to see the world. What's wrong with that?"

"You're going to be a singer on a cruise ship?"

"No, a waitress, or a maid, or maybe a cruise director. I'm never singing again."

"Don't be silly."

"I'm not being silly."

Bam! She killed one of his guys.

"You love singing. Singing is your life."

"My daddy was my life."

"Okay, then it's settled."

"What's settled?"

"If you aren't auditioning, then I'm not going to the conservatory. We'll both stay at Ogden Hall."

"But you've already been accepted."

"So?"

"It's what you wanted. You tried so hard to get in."

"I'm pretty good, but I'm not a great violinist. It's just something I like to do. Mostly, though, it's just to piss off my dad."

"I thought your dad wanted you to get into the conservatory."

"He wanted me to win, to succeed, to achieve a goal, to get in. He doesn't really want me there. He wants me to stay in private school, maybe a prep school, get into a good university, get an MBA, and take over the family business someday."

Christine dropped her game controller into her lap and looked at him, processing this revelation.

"I love music," Raoul continued, "but it's not my life. I'm not going to play with a great symphony, and I'm not going on some world tour as a soloist. I'll take over the family business, become a patron of the arts, maybe play violin in a small string combo on Friday nights at a wine bar in Paris."

"Well, that sucks."

"Yeah, it kinda does."

They went back to their video game.

CHRISTINE AND HER father had arrived in Los Angeles with only the clothes on their backs and what they could carry. They had acquired little more since, but at least the little cottage was cozy and it was theirs, more or less. It was also rather cheery and always filled with music. Sheet music was spread everywhere. Christine had often sung in the shower while her father accompanied her on violin in the other room. They had sung together as they prepared meals, and then laughed as they sat down to eat when they realized they had been singing. The spare bedroom in the Valerius house, by contrast, was cold, depressing, and eerily silent.

Christine knew she was lucky to have a room, a home, decent people to look after her, provide food, clothing, and shelter. She would soon turn thirteen. It would be five years, almost half the time she had spent on Earth, before she could hope to make it on her own. Younger children faced with the loss of both parents, no matter how heartbroken and terrified, simply expect someone to care for them. Christine was old enough to worry about it, to fear the future, to realize that major adjustments would have to be made. She had faced hardship and uncertainty with her father, but she had him, and he always assured her things would get better, and they did, much better, until now.

"It will be better when you get the rest of your things in here," Raoul said. "I'll help you move."

Christine sat on the bed, staring at the wall. "I wish I could stay in the little cottage."

"Yeah, that would be really cool." Raoul's mind raced as he looked out the window at the cottage. "Maybe when you're older they'll let you." Now his mind really raced. "We could have some killer parties out there."

Christine laughed. "Yeah, right." But laughing hurt and the sadness quickly returned.

Raoul sat down on the bed next to her. "I don't know what to do."

"What do you mean?"

"You're so sad, and I don't know what to do about it."

"There's nothing you can do."

"I can't imagine losing my mom or dad, definitely not both. It must really suck."

"It really sucks." She managed a little smile, but a laugh didn't quite come.

He looked around the room, not knowing what to do. He took her hand and she squeezed it tightly.

"You don't have to do anything," she said. "Just be here."

"I can do that."

She leaned her head on his shoulder and he quickly put an arm around her and squeezed ever so slightly. They sat for a moment in complete silence. No words were necessary.

"What will I sing for my audition?" Christine asked quietly, looking straight ahead.

"I thought you weren't going to audition."

"Well, I might as well do it. Maybe I won't even get in. They said most kids don't on their first audition. You didn't, and you're pretty good on the violin."

"You'll get in. In case you haven't noticed you're an incredible singer."

"Nah." She nudged him.

"Yeah." He nudged back.

"But if I get in, you'll have to go too, right, even if it's only to piss off your dad?"

"If you'll go, I'll go."

"Deal."

It took the adults a moment to notice Christine and Raoul standing in the doorway from the hall into the living room.

"I'm going to help Christine move some of her things out of the cottage and into her new room," Raoul announced.

"Don't be long, we need to go," Chagny said.

The kids quickly disappeared out the back door and the adults returned to their conversation.

"I didn't know what to do about her father's clothes and things," Mrs. Valerius said quietly, "so I just left them where they were. I hope it doesn't upset her to see them out there."

"We'll let her decide in her own time," Professor Valerius said.

"When my dad died it took my mom years to get rid of his clothes," Hannah said. "She finally had to deal with it when we persuaded her to downsize and move into a condo. I'm sure it's even more difficult for a child to make that decision, but I agree with the professor, leave it up to her. She's a strong young girl."

———

Christine gathered her things while Raoul looked around the cottage. "Wow, it's weird being here without your dad teaching me."

"I know."

"Sorry, I just meant—"

"I know what you meant. Stop apologizing. He's gone and we both miss him."

Raoul plopped down on the bed and looked around the room. "I never really noticed before but there's only one bed."

"The sofa makes a bed."

He looked over at the sofa.

"It's a hassle to pull out and make up, so when we first came here, we both slept in the bed."

"Really?"

"Yeah, we slept in the car, in the same sleeping bag in the park, on cots in homeless shelters, and in the same bed in that motel, the one where you threw rocks at me."

"I threw rocks at the window, not at you, and it was gravel. I just wanted to get your attention."

Christine laughed. "I know. I was kidding."

"And you weren't wearing any clothes. That was weird."

Christine covered her face in embarrassment. "It was laundry day. I decided to wash everything at once, including my underwear."

"Cool." Raoul pondered the image.

"I guess that's never a problem at your house."

"No, the maid always does the laundry. I just open the dresser drawers and there's clean underwear."

"Must be nice."

"It is, I guess. I never really thought about it."

Christine sat on the bed beside Raoul and showed him a little scar on her leg. "See my scar."

"Where?"

Raoul moved in for a closer look as Christine pointed to the scar.

"Right there."

"What happened?"

"I was shaving my legs."

"Ugh. Girl stuff. Sometimes it's really nice to be a guy."

"It was the first time I did it and I wasn't very good at it, so I cut myself. It bled, and I screamed and my dad like, freaked out and started banging on the bathroom door. I told him not to come in, because I was like all naked in the tub and stuff, but he came in anyway."

"Wow. That must have been embarrassing."

"You have no idea. It used to be like, no big deal, I was just a kid, so what did I care? But then since we came out here, I started, you know, developing, so I was trying to like, cover up, and Daddy just threw me a towel."

"Developing?"

"Boobs and stuff."

Raoul looked at the boobs and stuff. She put her hand on his face and pushed him away. "Don't look!"

"Sorry. I'm a teenage boy. That's my job."

She crossed her arms over her chest and stared at him.

Raoul laughed. "I was just messing with you. I think you look really nice."

"After that Daddy started sleeping on the sofa."

Raoul took another look at the sofa.

"It's really small and so am I," she said, "so I told him he could have the bed and I would sleep on the sofa, but he insisted."

Chagny knocked on the door to the cottage. "Raoul, it's time to go." There was no response, so in increase in volume was called for. "Raoul!"

The door opened slightly, and Raoul peered out. "I'm staying here with Christine."

"It's late. Christine has to go to bed. You can't stay."

"I'm helping her with her audition," Raoul said, closing the door.

"You can come back tomorrow and help her then. We have to go."

"I'm not coming out until it's time for Christine's audition."

Chagny tried to turn the doorknob. It was locked. "Raoul!" There was no response.

Chagny returned to the house and stepped into the living room. "I suppose the good news is that Christine has decided to audition."

"And the bad news?" Hannah asked.

"Raoul refuses to leave."

"Well, you did tell him to not leave her side," Professor Valerius said, smiling.

"I didn't think he would take it literally."

"I guess he could sleep in the spare room," Mrs. Valerius said.

"He means to stay in the guest house with Christine," Chagny said. "He slammed the door in my face and locked it."

"I'll go get him," Hannah said. "They certainly can't stay out there together. Puberty has already reared its ugly head, for Raoul at least, and Christine doesn't seem too far behind."

"No, wait," Zoe interrupted. "What can happen? They're kids. Christine's grieving. Her audition is day after tomorrow. They will be rehearsing. Raoul has been nothing but honorable toward Christine, and I can't imagine he would do anything improper. He's closer to her than anyone else and she needs him right now. I think you should let him stay." She turned to Professor and Mrs. Valerius. "With your permission, of course, Christine is now your responsibility."

"This is certainly uncharted territory for us," Professor Valerius said.

"I'll go get my things and come back and I'll take the spare room, if that's all right," Zoe said. "If anything comes up, I'll be right here."

"I think that sounds like a wonderful idea," Mrs. Valerius offered.

"Well, I suppose so," Hannah said, "And you can bring Raoul some clean clothes."

Zoe's phone buzzed. She checked it and smiled. "Raoul says to bring his violin."

Chagny looked at Professor Valerius. Both men shrugged. The decision was made. Hopefully, Raoul was indeed a young man of honor.

ZOE AWOKE IN THE spare bedroom to the sound of Raoul's violin and Christine singing coming in through the open window. She smiled. All was right with the world, or at least improving. She rolled off the bed and followed her nose into the kitchen where Mrs. Valerius was cooking breakfast.

Zoe and Mrs. Valerius prepared a tray with breakfast for the kids, which Zoe placed by the door outside the cottage. "Breakfast! You can't make music without fuel." She returned to the kitchen for her own breakfast.

In the little cottage, Raoul and Christine ate heartily.

"Maybe you could rap," Raoul suggested, jumping to his feet. He immediately started rapping. Christine quickly joined him, two white kids trying to rap. They were young and limber enough to mimic the moves, but their delivery wasn't quite "street." Nevertheless, it got their blood pumping, and it was fun for a moment. They dropped back into their chairs at the small table.

"Somehow I'm guessing that won't go over too well," Christine concluded.

"Well, it can't be pop either, so classical? Opera?"

"English or Italian?" Christine pondered.

"What about French?"

"Italian sings better, for me anyway."

"I never really thought about language on the violin, it's just music, but I guess it's important in singing," Raoul said.

"Duh."

"No, I mean it's important like to the headmaster and the committee. If you sing in Italian, will they think you are just trying to impress them?"

"I am trying to impress them."

"You know what I mean."

"Yeah, I know, but if the piece is written in Italian, I'm singing it in Italian, I'm not going to sing an English translation. That would be dumb."

"What about the song that blue chick with the tentacles sang in that Bruce Willis sci-fi movie," Raoul said.

"Who is Bruce Willis?"

ZOE WORKED ON A composition at the piano. Mrs. Valerius tended her flowers in the back yard as Raoul played and Christine sang in the little cottage. The breakfast dishes were put outside the door. Lunch was brought in. Work continued on Christine's audition piece, which had yet to be determined.

Professor Valerius stepped into the kitchen as Zoe and Mrs. Valerius prepared dinner. "Any progress?"

"We seem to have settled on an aria, in Italian," Zoe said.

"We have not yet decided which one, although Puccini is our current favorite," Mrs. Valerius added.

"Puccini is good," Professor Valerius nodded, "and would probably be well received by the audition committee, especially since Christine will nail it. Johnston, if I'm not mistaken, has a particular fondness for Puccini."

"It could be a long night," Zoe said.

"At least she's singing again," Professor Valerius said. "I hope that means she's healing."

He walked out back to the cottage and knocked on the door. "I'm home, guys. Let me know if you need anything."

"We're cool, thanks, Professor," Raoul shouted.

RAOUL AND CHRISTINE were sprawled on the bed sound asleep, just like a couple of kids. The covers were tangled. If there was anything improper going on, someone forgot to tell them.

Raoul's violin sat on a desk, atop a mountain of sheet music and note-books. The wastebasket overflowed with empty water bottles. The room was softly illuminated by moonlight.

The window was open, and the curtain billowed softly in the cool sea breeze.

A magnificent tenor sang "Nessun Dorma," a cappella.

Christine stirred and sat up. She looked around the room but saw no one. She got out of bed, went to the boom box and checked it. It was turned off. The singing continued as she frantically searched for the source. Nothing, there was no one there. She looked out the open window. No, it was coming from within the room. She turned and looked again. Now rather spooked, she rushed over to the bed and shook Raoul. "Raoul, wake up!"

Raoul rolled over, "What?"

"Can you hear it?"

"Hear what?"

"The man singing, can you hear it?"

"I don't hear anything. You're losing it. Go back to sleep."

He rolled over and covered his head with the pillow.

Christine jumped up, swirling around, lost in the music. "It's the Angel. Daddy sent the Angel."

Raoul sat up, groggy.

"Who?"

"The Angel of Music. Daddy sent him to me from heaven, just like he said he would."

"What did he say?"

"He didn't say anything. He just sang."

"Well, what did he sing?"

She turned on the light and darted across the room to the desk and started rifling through sheet music. "It's very familiar, maybe Puccini. I have to find the sheet music."

"For what?"

"Didn't you hear it?" She was becoming irritated. "Get up, we have to practice."

Raoul decided to humor her and reluctantly got out of bed.

"Here it is!" Christine declared.

Raoul staggered toward her, wiping his eyes. She put the sheet music on a music stand, and then handed him his violin and bow.

"Can you play this?" Christine asked.

He leaned over and looked at the sheet music. "This is written for an orchestra."

"Can you play it or not?"

"I can take a shot. Are you going to sing a duet with the ghost?"

"It's the Angel, not a ghost. And besides, he already stopped singing."

Raoul remained unconvinced, but after looking around the room for the ghost, or Angel, he took up his violin and bow and began playing as he scanned the sheet music.

Christine stood closely beside him, reading the lyrics.

PROFESSOR VALERIUS, HIS WIFE, and Zoe, all in their night clothes, streamed out of the house, across the back yard and stood at the door of the guest house. From behind the door, Raoul played violin, and Christine sang "Nessun Dorma."

"Is that Christine?" Professor Valerius asked quietly.

"Who else could it be?" Zoe whispered.

Mrs. Valerius was puzzled. "What in the world are they doing up at three in the morning?"

"Surely she can't be planning to sing 'Nessun Dorma' for her audition," Professor Valerius said.

"It sure sounds like it," Zoe said.

"Well," Professor Valerius said, "there's always next year."

"It's her audition, and her choice," Mrs. Valerius said. "We must support her."

23

THE AUDITION

RAOUL SLIPPED QUIETLY out of bed, trying to not awaken Christine. He watched her sleep for a moment, and then went into the bathroom. After showering, he turned off the water and reached for the curtain before realizing he was not alone.

"What are you doing in here?" he asked from behind the curtain.

"I'm brushing my teeth," Christine responded.

"I'm in the shower!"

"Obviously. Just keep the curtain closed."

"Don't worry."

"Why didn't you wake me up?"

"I thought I'd let you get your beauty sleep while I was in the shower, but that didn't work."

A moment later Raoul cautiously pulled back the shower curtain ever so slightly and peered out. The coast was clear, but the door was open. He quickly stepped out of the shower and grabbed a towel, just in time to cover up as Christine appeared in the open doorway.

"Hurry up. I have to shave my legs."

"Women," he muttered softly to himself. If only he knew.

Raoul pulled the door closed, quickly dried off and pulled on his briefs, and then checked his face. Shaving would not be necessary, so he brushed his teeth.

Christine rummaged through the small closet. There wasn't much of a selection of appropriate clothing for the audition. She hadn't given it the slightest thought, otherwise preoccupied for the past few days, and now suddenly realized that she had to find something, and quickly. She wore black to the funeral and burial, and she briefly debated over whether to wear one of those dresses to the audition.

"What are you wearing?" Christine asked as Raoul stepped out of the bathroom.

"Black."

"Really?"

"I'm background. It's your audition."

The boy had a point. She would not wear black, but that didn't leave much choice.

"Wear something white, or off-white, all innocent and angelic like."

"Since when do boys know anything about women's fashion?"

"I hang out with Zoe all the time. I know tons of stuff about women."

Again, the boy had a point, but that further limited the already limited selection. Frustrated, she stepped away from the closet and headed toward the bathroom.

"I'm going to shave my legs. I'll pick something later."

"There's not much later left. We have to bounce," he said as he pulled on a pair of black pants.

Zoe, carrying a dress in a plastic bag emblazoned with the name of some upscale store, knocked on the door to the guest house. Raoul opened the door. Zoe looked him over from head to toe. He wore black shoes, black socks, black pants, black shirt, and a black tie.

"Well, good morning, Johnny Cash," Zoe said.

"Huh?"

"Where's June Carter?"

"Who?"

"Christine."

"Who is June Carter?"

"Never mind," she said, not bothering with an explanation, which he probably wouldn't understand anyway. "Where is Christine?"

"She's shaving her legs."

"Oh, okay, good. Mrs. Valerius and I went out last night and picked up a dress for her audition." Zoe handed the dress to Raoul. "We had to guess at the size, so tell her to try it on and we can pin it up if necessary."

Raoul took the dress and lifted the plastic. "Off-white, perfect."

"Hurry every chance you get. I'll need to do something with her hair. You should eat, both of you, before you go. Never audition on an empty stomach," she called out as Raoul closed the door.

"Who was that?" Christine asked, coming out of the bathroom.

"Zoe. She brought you a dress for the audition."

"Oh, good." Christine plopped onto the bed and feverishly applied lotion to her freshly shaved legs.

"Did you cut yourself?"

"No, I'm getting pretty good at it. Let me see the dress."

Raoul dutifully removed the plastic bag from the dress, swept one hand up under it, and displayed it in the best tradition of Paris couturiers.

"I love it!" Christine gushed. "It's perfect."

She leapt to her feet and took the dress, holding it up and admiring it. It was indeed perfect, off-white, with a black sash at the waist.

"Turn around."

Raoul turned around. Christine spread the dress onto the bed, whipped off her T-shirt and slipped into the dress. "Zip me up."

Raoul turned once again and zipped her up. Then he tied the sash. The significance of the black sash was lost on them both, but obviously not on Zoe, who had selected the dress.

Christine turned and modeled the dress, beaming.

"You look hot," Raoul said.

"Hot? I can't look hot for my audition. I'm twelve."

"You look beautiful."

She threw her arms around his neck and hugged him tightly. "Thank you."

"And you smell good," he said, with a face full of blonde hair.

"You do too. Is that my dad's aftershave?"

"Uh, yeah, sorry, I wasn't thinking."

She hugged him even more tightly than before, and then pulled away slightly, face to face, wiping a tear. "It's okay. Take it home with you and use it. Whenever I smell you, I'll think of Daddy."

She kissed him briefly on the cheek, and then wiped another tear.

"Did you shave?"

"No, not really."

She laughed. "Let's go, we're going to be late. Get your fiddle and the sheet music."

Professor Valerius and Zoe sat at the kitchen table, eating breakfast. Mrs. Valerius stood at the stove, tending eggs. Christine and Raoul, carrying his violin and sheet music, entered.

"Are you hungry?" Mrs. Valerius asked.

"Yes ma'am," Raoul said.

Christine shook her head. "I'm not hungry."

"Are you ready," Professor Valerius asked.

"Yes sir, we're ready," Christine said.

Professor Valerius stood. "I have some things to attend to at school, but I will be there in time for your audition." He leaned over and kissed Christine on the head. "You look beautiful, my dear." He then extended his hand to Raoul. "Thank you, Raoul, for all that you have done for Christine. We certainly appreciate it." They shook hands.

"I'm going with Zoe and the kids," Mrs. Valerius said. "I'll save you a seat." They kissed, and the professor departed.

Mrs. Valerius and Zoe immediately began pulling and picking at Christine's dress. It fit perfectly. There was nothing left to do.

"Hurry up and eat," Zoe said. "I'll try to do something with Christine's hair in the car on the way."

"That's okay," Raoul said. "I called my mom last night and she's sending a hairdresser to meet us at the conservatory. I guess we need to get there a little bit early."

"Oh, my," Zoe replied. She put her arm around Raoul's neck and pulled his head into her breast, and then looked at Christine. "This one's a keeper, honey."

"And my dad is sending a car."

Christine and Raoul sat together in the limo, holding hands. Zoe and Mrs. Valerius sat facing them.

"Are you nervous?" Zoe asked.

"I wasn't until you asked," Christine answered.

"Oh no, sorry."

Christine laughed. "Just kidding."

Zoe was relieved.

"I won't be nervous until I step onto the stage."

The limo drove on through the canyons of downtown Los Angeles, approaching the Belen Conservatory.

Raoul leaned over to Christine and whispered, "Do you know who June Carter is?"

"I have no idea."

The limo pulled up in front of the Belen Conservatory and everyone piled out onto the sidewalk and started inside, except Christine, who stood firm.

"Give me a minute," she said.

Everyone froze, more than a bit worried.

Memories flooded over Christine, standing in the same spot she stood with Daddy, not all that long ago, looking at the beautiful building, watching all the students, happy and chattering, streaming in. Now it was her turn. She gritted her teeth and took a deep breath.

"I'm ready."

Backstage, Zoe hovered as the hairdresser worked quickly. There wasn't much that needed doing but fussing over her hair made Christine feel rather special and pretty, and that was what it was all about. The hairdresser knew that and was happy to have the work. Her regular job was hair and makeup in television and, compared to a day of covering up too much hard living and too much plastic surgery, working on the flawless skin and thick, glossy hair of a young girl was like a vacation.

Raoul sat nearby, studying the sheet music, trying to concentrate while another potential student performed just a few feet away. Raoul jumped to his feet as Christine, flanked by Zoe and the hairdresser approached.

"Wow," Raoul said, looking Christine over. "You look even better than before."

Christine stepped forward and reached out to hug him.

"Wait! Stop!" Zoe announced. "Save all the hugging and kissing until after. We don't want to mess up her hair and makeup."

There really wasn't much makeup, but there was a bit of definition on the cheekbones, and lip gloss with a hint of color. Raoul took Christine's hands, they air kissed on both sides, "Muh, muh," and then Christine giggled. If she was nervous, it didn't show.

Johnston and the others on the audition committee sat in a nearly empty auditorium. A student finished performing and bowed.

"Thank you, Mr. Shaw," Johnston said. "Well done. We will let you know."

The student bowed again and walked off stage, passing by Zoe, Christine, and Raoul, waiting in the wings.

"Are you sure you don't want me to accompany you on piano?" Zoe asked.

"I'm sure," Christine said.

"Okay, I'll just go out and watch with everyone else."

Christine nodded.

"Go," Raoul said, "I've got it covered."

Zoe walked onto the stage, around the curtain, and down the stairs into the auditorium.

"Zoe, what brings you here?" Johnston asked.

"Christine Daaé is up next. I'm with her." Zoe slipped down the stairs and headed toward Mrs. Valerius, already seated, along with the Chagnys, two rows behind Johnston and the committee.

"Ah yes," Johnston said.

Zoe waved her hand. "Over here, Professor."

Johnston stood and turned as Professor Valerius came down the aisle on the other side of the auditorium, accompanied by Professor Dodge.

"Professor Valerius, Professor Dodge," Johnston said, "what a nice surprise."

"Do you mind if we sit in?" Professor Valerius asked.

"Not at all. We are honored by your presence."

Professor Valerius, Professor Dodge, and Zoe converged on Mrs. Valerius and the Chagnys and took their seats following the requisite handshaking and air kissing, and then Johnston turned and sat back down.

Raoul picked up his violin and bow and stood beside Christine in the wings, who stared out onto the stage in intense concentration. He didn't know what to say, so he said nothing.

"It wasn't really my mom's scarf," Christine said, staring straight ahead.

"What?"

"The scarf that you rescued from the sea. It wasn't my mom's. We bought it at a thrift store."

"Okay," Raoul said, puzzled.

He waited in the wings as Christine stepped on stage and approached the microphone.

Christine took a deep breath. "Christine Daaé, sir, vocalist."

"What will you be singing for us today, Miss Daaé?" Johnston asked.

"'Nessun Dorma.'"

"'Nessun Dorma?'"

"Yes sir."

"Are you sure that's what you wish to sing?"

"Yes sir."

"Miss Daaé, 'Nessun Dorma' was written for a tenor, an adult male. It is one of the best-known arias in all opera. Surely you know that."

"Yes sir."

"I presume you are a soprano."

"Yes sir."

"And obviously a female child, or an adolescent."

"Yes sir. I guess. I'm a soprano, but I don't know what adolescent means."

There was some restrained chuckling in the audience.

"You only get one audition per year. Are you sure you wouldn't rather pick something more suited to your circumstances? We are aware of your personal situation, with your father, and would allow you to reschedule if you need a few more days."

"No sir. I'll sing 'Nessun Dorma.'"

"Very well. Will Zoe be accompanying you on piano?"

"No sir."

"Did you bring a backing track?"

"No sir."

"Are you going to sing the piece a cappella?"

"No sir."

Johnston was becoming extremely frustrated. Professors Dodge and Valerius whispered back and forth.

"I brought a violinist," Christine said, motioning for Raoul to come on stage.

"A violinist?"

"Yes sir."

Raoul took up his position behind Christine.

"A single violinist?"

"Yes sir. He's pretty good."

Zoe choked back a laugh. Johnston turned.

"Sorry," Zoe said.

Johnston turned back toward the stage. "Very well, Miss Daaé, it's your audition. Please proceed."

Christine turned and nodded to Raoul, who began to play "Nessun Dorma" on his violin.

Christine turned back toward the small audience and began to sing. The committee was immediately impressed, as was Professor Dodge. Johnston looked directly at Christine, becoming engrossed as the sound washed over him. He stared, mouth agape, as the small, beautiful girl tackled a difficult piece of music, written for an adult male, and made him believe. She didn't belt it out like an inexperienced child who tries to use volume to make up for lack of skill. She simply opened her mouth, and an incredible sound came out, perfect pitch, perfect intonation, perfect phrasing. It was a near-perfect rendition of "Nessun Dorma," only with a twelve-year-old girl, singing with the voice of an angel, rather than an adult tenor.

Every word sung by Christine played on Zoe's face as she swayed to the music, feeling it deeply, silently mouthing the words herself.

When Christine paused for a break in the vocals, Raoul was a man on a mission, playing an enchanted violin and trying to make it sound like the large orchestra for which the piece was written. The Chagnys were pleased. Never had they heard Raoul play so well, so intently, with such emotion.

As Christine sang the finale Johnston was stunned. Tears flowed down his face. The others on the committee made notes, but there was no question what their vote would be.

When she finished, the audience, Johnston and the committee stood and applauded loudly. She curtsied.

Zoe wiped tears of joy.

Professor Valerius was now convinced that he was witnessing a musical talent that came along once in a century. He was her guardian, and with that came an enormous responsibility. He looked forward to the challenge of helping her become all that she could be. His wife saw all that and more. It would now be up to her to be mother to this beautiful, gifted child, and it was a role she relished.

Professor Dodge leaned over to Professor Valerius and whispered. "Oh my, you were quite right about the girl. Johnston is in tears. This is the place for her."

"Brava! Brava!" shouted Chagny.

Raoul lowered his violin and bowed toward Christine.

Christine tilted her head slightly and smiled sweetly. She had nailed it, and she knew it. The audience was hers.

24

THE CONSERVATORY

CHRISTINE MOVED INTO the main house immediately following her audition but avoided dealing with her father's belongings for as long as possible. The time had finally come. She and Raoul had laid out all Viktor's clothes on the bed. Raoul lined up two pairs of shoes beside the bed and turned toward the bathroom door when he heard Christine softly crying. He stepped over and put his arm around her shoulder as she held her father's razor in her hands.

"This was my daddy's. It's the one I was using when I cut my leg. I'm keeping it," she said.

"Do you want me to bring back his aftershave?"

She wiped a tear, smiled, and shook her head. "No. You can keep it."

She turned off the light. Raoul stepped aside as she stepped out of the bathroom and placed the razor in a small box on the bed.

"Are you guys ready to roll?" Zoe asked as she stepped through the open doorway.

"Just about," Christine said. "We need to stop by the shelter and drop off Daddy's things."

"No problem," Zoe said, "but you may want to wait a couple of minutes."

"Why?" Christine asked warily as Mrs. Valerius stepped in, carrying a large envelope.

"It's from the conservatory," Mrs. Valerius said.

"You got in!" Raoul said.

"How do you know?" Christine asked as she took the envelope.

"The envelope is huge, stuffed with welcome material. If you didn't get in it's just a regular envelope."

"Really?"

"Trust me. I've gotten both."

Christine ripped open the envelope, her smile growing as she read the cover letter.

"Told you," Raoul said. "We should celebrate."

"We'll go out to dinner, wherever you want," Mrs. Valerius said.

"Pizza!" Christine replied.

"Pizza it is." Mrs. Valerius clearly had something better in mind. "And we'll need to shop for new school clothes. You won't be wearing a uniform any longer."

"That will be easy," Zoe said. "Funky is the uniform of the day at the conservatory. We can hit the thrift stores."

Raoul nodded in agreement.

"Except for performances," Zoe said. "You can splurge on those."

"What should I do with my school uniforms," Christine asked. "I won't be needing them, and I don't think the shelter could use them."

"You can donate them to Ogden Hall," Raoul said. "Some of the scholarship kids can use them."

"Like me?"

Raoul winced.

"Your father paid for yours," Mrs. Valerius said, thinking quickly. She and the professor had paid for them, but a little white lie would not hurt. "You can do with them as you like."

"Ogden Hall," Christine said, nodding. "They're practically new, so some girl can use them."

"I do want to get photos of you in your uniform first," Mrs. Valerius said. "Kids always look so good in school uniforms."

"I know someone from school," Zoe said. "She's very good, works cheap, and has good cameras and lights, but she prefers available light."

"Excellent," Mrs. Valerius said. "Perhaps in the back yard."

Viktor's clothes were dropped off at the shelter. Christine settled into her new room. A compromise was reached on the celebratory dinner. Christine just wanted pizza. Raoul just wanted to be with Christine. The adults settled on the most upscale pizza place on the Westside, with unimaginably thin, crisp crust and the most decadent of toppings. To Christine, it was just pizza, although very tasty.

———

ZOE'S FRIEND WAS indeed very good, professionally posing and photographing Christine and Raoul, in their Ogden Hall uniforms, together and separately, all around the back yard and the little cottage. Everyone was thrilled with the results—children did indeed look so good in school uniforms. Chagny insisted on paying the photographer. Christine selected a photo of her sitting on the bench with Raoul. She and Zoe paid fifty cents for a frame from a thrift store, and she hung it on the wall of her new bedroom, right next to a photo of herself at age six, along with her mother and father.

Raoul joined Christine and Zoe as they made the round of thrift stores buying school clothes. He was looking forward to not wearing a uniform, or the expensive, designer clothes in his closet. He doubted his mother, and especially his father, would approve, but he filled sacks of regular kid clothes, second-hand, some well-worn, just the ticket for the conservatory, according to Zoe. No one would be able to distinguish the rich kids from the scholarship kids by their clothing alone.

Christine and Raoul stood just outside the dressing rooms in the last thrift store, both wearing shorts, hers considerably shorter and cuter than his, and T-shirts, hers tighter and showing a bit of belly.

"Perfect," Zoe said. "You'll fit right in. You'll also need something kind of dressy for your first recital, which we need to start working on, by the way."

"Recital?" Christine said.

"After school on the first day, around seven so parents can come. All new students have to perform in their chosen specialty."

"I'm already working on my violin piece," Raoul said.

"And you have plenty of dress-up clothes," Zoe said to him.

"I can wear my audition dress," Christine said.

"No, you'll want to wear something different," Zoe said. "And you should go shopping with Mrs. Valerius. I think she feels a bit left out."

Christine smiled and nodded.

"Let her get you something really nice."

"And hot," Raoul added. Christine elbowed him.

"It's important to knock it out of the park at the first recital," Zoe said. "Be full of confidence. Everyone will be watching like a hawk, especially the girls, especially the sopranos. It can get really competitive."

"Oh, no," Christine said. "Just like Ogden Hall."

"Not really," Zoe said. "I'm sure there are still plenty of mean girls, but at the conservatory, talent wins out. There are cliques and jealousy and back-stabbing, but if you can bring it to the stage, which I know you can, you'll get along just fine."

"Don't worry," Raoul said. "You'll knock 'em dead."

ZOE SWOOPED INTO the Chagny house, carrying recycled plastic bags stuffed with clothes, which she dropped onto a sofa in the living room.

"We bought school clothes for Raoul."

Hannah began rummaging through the bags.

"Oh, dear. Did he pick these out?"

Zoe nodded. "He wants to fit in. At Ogden Hall he was a prince among princes. At the conservatory he'll just be a kid who plays a pretty good violin, with a really cute girlfriend."

"Girlfriend?"

"They've been inseparable lately."

"I've noticed. Where is he, by the way?"

"At the movies. I dropped them off on the Promenade."

"What about dinner?"

"Fast food. He has cash, and a credit card."

"This is moving awfully fast."

"It's summer, and Christine doesn't really have any other friends. I don't think they're getting too serious, at least not when I'm around."

"But they're alone right now, at the movies."

"I see you remember your teenage years."

"Indeed. I spent a lot of time at the AMC on the Promenade, making out, and then married a French playboy I met on the Riviera."

"And I spent a lot of time at the mall in Midland. We both turned out okay. Well, the jury's still out on me."

Hannah laughed. "I'm sure you'll be fine. And I have faith in Raoul. You've been a positive influence on him. We don't thank you enough."

"I can text him and say I'll pick him up for dinner."

"No, that's okay. Alain won't be here anyway. He just left for Paris."

"I didn't know he was gone."

"They are running tests, but it looks like his mother may have cancer. I offered to go with him, but he said to wait until they have the results."

"Oh, no. I'm so sorry."

"She has excellent doctors, so let's hope for the best. There has been remarkable progress in the last few years."

"If you need to go, I can hold things down here."

"Thanks. We'll see how it goes." She rifled through the bags of clothes for a moment. "Unless you have other plans, it will be girls' night."

"Works for me."

"With wine."

"Even better. Raoul can take an Uber."

WITH THE CHAGNYS' permission, Zoe had taken a part-time job during the summer as a personal assistant to a composer, so Raoul, and Christine, increasingly took an Uber around town, or the train, or bus. Raoul felt quite grown-up squiring his lady around town with a "chauffeur" who was not frequently checking the rearview mirror to see what was going on in the back seat. There was not that much going on anyway, other than holding hands, which couldn't be seen in the mirror. Both Zoe and Hannah were happy to see that it wasn't all fun and games. Although summer was off-season for the opera and symphony, the kids attended music events, both high- and low-brow, along with visits to museums, galleries, and the theater. And, of course, there were movies, theme parks, and the beach.

They sat on the beach as the sun dipped slowly into the Pacific, thin clouds turning a brilliant orange. In the distance, an enormous ship, piled high with colorful containers containing countless consumer commodities, steamed slowly toward the Port of Los Angeles.

"The sunsets are much better here than Saint-Tropez," Raoul said.

"Really? I thought it was supposed to be so beautiful there."

"It is, but the beach faces east, so the sun just disappears behind a hill."

"East? Then why do they call it the south of France?"

He leaned forward and drew in the sand with his finger. "There's a bay. Saint-Tropez faces north, into the bay, not the Mediterranean. The best beach is Pampelonne, here, and it faces east."

"Do girls really go topless on the beach?"

He grinned and nodded. "Oh, yeah."

"I'm not sure I'm ready for that."

He looked at her chest. She elbowed him.

"Don't look!"

"Sorry."

She glanced down at her chest. "There's not much to see anyway."

He took another look and grinned.

She covered herself with both hands. "Boys!"

His grin faded. He opened his mouth to speak but didn't.

"What?" She lowered her hands.

"My grandmother is sick, so Dad says we aren't going to the beach house this summer."

She was clearly disappointed. "That's okay. Not that I have anything to compare it to, but this beach isn't bad, and I can keep my top on."

He chuckled and they both sat in silence for a moment, staring into the distance.

"Is your grandmother going to be okay?"

"I don't know. She has cancer."

"Oh, no. Cancer sucks."

"She's starting chemo so Mom's going over."

Christine turned toward him. This could be very good or very bad.

"She wants me to go with her."

It was very bad.

"Sorry." He shrugged.

"When are you going?"

"In a few days. Mom has to wrap up some things at the hospital, and the house, although Zoe can handle that."

"Will you be back in time for school to start?"

"I hope so. I don't even want to go. I told her I could stay here with Zoe, or maybe just go over for a week or two, and be back in time for orientation, and to work on my recital piece."

"That would work."

"She said I can practice the violin in Paris just as easily as Santa Monica."

Clearly not what Christine wanted to hear.

"Zoe will have the house to herself, if you want to hang out with her."

"We can work on my song for recital."

"Have you picked one?"

"Not yet, but apparently now I'll have plenty of time to get it done."

"We can Skype. Do you have a laptop?"

"I'm using one of the professor's castoffs. They're getting me a new one before school starts. Mrs. Valerius said we saved so much by buying school clothes at the thrift store we can splurge on a laptop. Zoe's nerd friends are specking it out and one of them will go shopping with us to negotiate."

Raoul laughed. "Whatever it is you need, Zoe has a friend."

"She does, doesn't she? Then they'll load it up with software, remove all the crapware, whatever that is, and tune it up for peak performance, not that I really need all that much. I never had a computer before, hardly know how to operate one."

"Zoe has a friend for that, too."

She laughed. "I'll be sure and tell them I need Skype."

"And a webcam."

"That's already on the list, along with a headset, both wired and wireless. They're still arguing over whether to get a cheap one for regular stuff and then a good one for recording."

"You can use the studio at the conservatory for recording."

"Oh, yeah. Cool."

"Although Zoe probably has a friend who can sneak you into the best recording studios in town and operate all the gear."

"I'm going to miss you."

"Me too, but I'll be back."

"Soon, I hope."

She leaned over and put her head on his shoulder, as the sun sank deeper into the Pacific.

ORIENTATION AT THE conservatory was held on Saturday morning before class started on Monday. Raoul had promised to be back in time but was nowhere to be seen and Christine faced her first day at the conservatory alone. She was happy to see that Zoe was right about the dress code—her thrift-store wardrobe fit right in.

Upperclassmen were on hand to staff various posts as the new students toured the school, marveling at the state-of-the-art facilities. Although the building itself was more than seventy years old it had been continually upgraded with the latest technology.

Christine was particularly interested in the recording studios. While the more technically inclined drooled over the mixing board and equipment, Christine stood at the microphone in the booth, impressed by the complete silence. In addition to the booth, one of two, for soloists, there was a larger room, for small groups, and the control center was also wired directly to the auditorium, where an entire orchestra could be recorded.

Every classroom had a huge flatscreen television connected to a small studio equipped for live broadcasts and able to feed just about anything to any or all rooms from racks of equipment.

The classrooms for regular academics looked much like those at any other school, but nearly every music classroom was equipped with a piano, as were all the rehearsal spaces. Dozens of music stands were scattered throughout the building. More stands, or any other equipment, could be ordered and dispatched aboard rolling carts from an enormous storeroom.

The tour ended in the auditorium, which was far too large for the number of students at the school but designed for performances in front of an audience. Unlike auditoriums in regular schools, the acoustics were superb, tuned by the finest in the business.

The stage floor had not been replaced since the conservatory opened decades before. Daniel Titshaw had spared no expense, and the thick red oak floorboards, hauled across the continent by rail, worn by thousands of young feet, still had several sandings and refinishings left in them. The curtains were thick and heavy—even when open they contributed to the acoustics. Christine marveled at the rigging above the stage and noticed openings high above the seats at the back of the auditorium where spotlights could be operated. She smiled as she stood on stage. Soon that spotlight would be on her. If only her daddy could be here to see her sing her first song at the conservatory.

There were dressing rooms, a cavernous costume room, a scene shop, storage rooms. Even the best performing arts schools in the country were no match for Daniel's vision, and wealth.

The new students were herded into the auditorium. Christine debated over where to sit—the front row might make her look like a suck-up, too far back might brand her as antisocial. She took a seat several rows back from the front and a girl immediately plopped down beside her and extended her hand.

"I'm Sue."

"Christine."

"What's your deal?"

"My deal?"

"Your musical thing."

"Oh. I'm a singer."

"You don't play an instrument?"

"I play piano, but I'm no prodigy. I just sing."

"You can guess what instrument I play."

"I can?"

"Asian chick."

Christine was confused.

"Violin. Duh. Although I blow a trumpet for fun."

"Cool."

"You from LA?"

"Chicago. I came to LA a few months ago with my daddy to try and get in here."

"What does your dad do?"

"He played violin."

"Played?"

"He died a couple of months ago, just before my audition."

"Oh shit. Open mouth, insert foot. Sorry about your dad. What about your mom? Is she a musician?"

"She died a few years ago."

Sue covered her face. "Mouth, meet foot."

Christine smiled. "It was always their dream to move to LA so I could go to the conservatory. My mom was going to get a job teaching and Daddy was going to be a session musician."

"Wow. My story's rather boring, compared to that. My parents own a convenience store in Koreatown."

"What's Koreatown?"

"Where the Koreans live." She pointed. "Not far from here. I can ride the bus to school."

"I probably will too, once I figure out how. Mrs. Valerius brought me today and will pick me up."

"Who's that?"

"My guardian."

"Valerius. Professor Valerius?"

"You know him?"

"Every musician in LA knows him. He's a bigwig at the Herb Alpert School of Music at UCLA, but I guess you knew that already."

Christine smiled and nodded.

"Herb Alpert is my hero. I have all his albums. Dude can blow horn."

"Then why do you play violin instead of the trumpet?"

"Asian chick, remember? Korean parents. I play violin."

"Oh, okay, I get it." Christine looked around the room. "I see a lot of violin players."

"Soprano?"

Christine nodded.

"Watch out for the mean girls. I hear the competition is fierce between the sopranos."

"Yeah, I heard that too."

Christine raised up and looked around.

"What are you looking for?" Sue asked.

"My friend, Raoul. He had to go to Paris." Christine checked her phone. "He was supposed to be back today for orientation, but he hasn't called or texted."

"He *had* to go to Paris?"

"His grandmother has cancer."

Sue winced. "I really need to work on my social skills."

Christine smiled. "That's okay."

"Is your friend French?"

"His dad's French. His mom's from Santa Monica."

"So, he's bi-hemispherical?"

"Uh, yeah, I guess. And bilingual."

"Is he cute?"

"Pretty cute."

"My parents probably won't let me date until I'm eighteen."

"We aren't really dating. It's complicated."

"Isn't it always."

The volume of chatter began to lower as several people, including Johnston Caldwell, stepped onto the stage and took their seats.

"What's your recital piece?" Sue asked.

"'Dove sono.'"

"Do you have an accompanist?"

"My friend Zoe on piano, and Raoul on violin, but if he doesn't show up, I'll have to use a backing track."

"Better with live music." Sue pantomimed playing the violin. "I can sit in if you want."

"Really, you'd do that?"

"Sure, why not?"

"Do you know the piece?"

"I've played it. I'll just need to scan the sheet music once or twice."

"Do we have time to rehearse?"

"Do you have a piano at your place?"

"Yes."

"It's easier to carry a violin than a piano, so I can come over, if your pianist is available."

"I'm sure she is. I'll call Mrs. Valerius and see if you can come for dinner, if that's okay with you."

"Can she make hamburgers?"

"I guess."

"Then I'll be there. We only eat Korean food at home, so I have to sneak out to get hamburgers, or anything else good."

The chatter stopped suddenly as Johnston stepped up to the podium.

"Welcome to the Belen Conservatory of Music."

25

DOVE SONO

Christine and Sue stood on the sidewalk outside the conservatory as cars lined up to pick up students. They started walking toward her car as Mrs. Valerius pulled up. Christine opened the back door and leaned in.

"This is Sue."

"Hi, Sue."

"Hi."

"We're going to rehearse my recital piece. She's going to accompany me on violin."

"I thought Raoul was accompanying you."

"He didn't show up for orientation, and he hasn't called, so I don't know if he'll be here Monday or not."

"I hope nothing's wrong."

"I asked Zoe if she had heard from him, and she seemed kind of weird."

"Weird?"

"Like she didn't want to talk about it."

"Oh, dear. Surely he'll call tonight."

"It's already late in Paris," Christine said. Raoul had installed an app on her phone that showed the time in both Los Angeles and Paris.

The girls got into the car.

"We need to stop and pick up Sue's violin," Christine said.

"It's in Koreatown," Sue said. "Is that too far out of the way?"

"Not at all," Mrs. Valerius said as she pulled away from the curb.

"Can Sue stay for dinner?" Christine asked.

"Of course."

"Can we have hamburgers?"

"Wouldn't you rather have something nicer for your new friend?"

"I like hamburgers," Sue said.

"It's a cultural thing," Christine said as she and Sue giggled.

"We'll have to stop at the store," Mrs. Valerius said.

Sue had hoped to hop out and grab her violin, but Mrs. Valerius insisted on going in and meeting her parents. Sue was Christine's first new friend at the conservatory and there would hopefully be dinners and sleepovers in the future, so Mrs. Valerius wanted to start off on the right foot.

The cheapest hamburger ingredients would have been fine with the girls, but Mrs. Valerius stopped at Whole Foods and bought Angus beef patties, whole-grain buns, and Dijon mustard, along with lettuce, tomatoes, and pickles. The professor was not a fan of french fries, so the girls filled the cart with various upscale chips.

IN HER BEDROOM, Christine downloaded sheet music from her laptop and printed it out. She handed it to Sue, who scanned it for a few seconds and said, "Piece of cake."

Sue was playing the violin when Raoul popped up on Skype.

"Who's that?" he asked.

"That's Sue," Christine said. "You abandoned me, so I got a new accompanist on violin."

Sue leaned in and waved. "Hi, I'm Sue. You must be Raoul."

"Yeah."

Sue leaned toward Christine and covered her mouth but did not lower her voice. "He *is* cute."

Raoul grinned. Sue stepped back and resumed playing.

"She's good," Raoul said.

"Why didn't you show up for orientation? Is everything okay?"

"Not really. My mom can't leave yet, and she won't let me fly commercial by myself. She's really good."

"Your mom?"

"Your friend."

"Why can't you just take the jet?"

"It's not available. Dad's in Australia on business. That's why Mom has to stay here with my grandmother."

"Will you be here by Monday?"

"I hope so."

Sue stopped playing and leaned in. "Look, dude, if you can get here, I'll totally bug out. Otherwise, I've got it covered."

"That's okay. You can accompany her. I'd rather watch from the audience anyway. That way I can see Christine's face instead of the back of her head."

Christine covered her face. Sue laughed.

"Well, I'll let you get to it," Raoul said. "I'll call or text and let you know when we're leaving."

"Okay, bye."

"Bye."

And he was gone.

"The jet?" Sue asked.

"His dad's kinda rich. He has a private jet."

"Cool. Have you flown on it?"

"Once. When we went to Chicago to bury my daddy."

"Shit. I did it again."

Christine laughed. "It's okay. I can pop off some real zingers myself."

"How was it?"

"How was what?"

"The private jet."

"Oh. Good, I guess. I'd never been on a plane before."

"I fly to Seoul every summer to see my grandparents. In coach. The cheap seats. I'd love to fly on a private jet, or even first class, or business."

MRS. VALERIUS LISTENED intently to the sound of "Dove sono" coming from the bedroom as she crossed the living room to answer the door. Zoe stepped in, carrying two bottles of Chagny wine.

"You didn't need to bring wine," Mrs. Valerius said, examining the labels. "Especially expensive wine, for hamburgers."

"I'll explain later. Do you need help in the kitchen?"

"It's under control. He insists on grilling in the back yard, but he hasn't used that thing in years."

"So, who is this new friend?"

"Sue. She plays violin. Quite well from what I've heard so far. I am just so thrilled that Christine met someone right off the bat."

"The conservatory is like that. They all have a common interest, unlike public school."

"Her parents own a convenience store in Koreatown. I met them when we stopped by to pick up her violin. They seem like very nice people, and very normal."

"Normal?"

"Christine has had a bipolar life so far, from living on the streets to hanging out with rich people and flying on private jets."

"I know exactly what you mean."

The professor successfully resurrected the grill, donned a chef's apron, and happily grilled hamburgers. Zoe and Mrs. Valerius did the rest in the kitchen and the girls tore themselves away from rehearsal and tore into the hamburgers and fries at the picnic table in the back yard.

"How long have you been playing violin?" Professor Valerius asked.

"Since I was three," Sue said. "I started taking lessons when I was six."

"I look forward to hearing you play Monday evening."

"No pressure," Zoe said.

"I look forward to your critique," Sue said.

"Don't worry," Christine said. "He won't hold back."

"Good. Bring it."

"With the possible exception of Itzhak, Christine's father was the finest violinist I've ever heard," the professor said.

"Really?"

"Raoul took lessons from him when we lived in the little cottage," Christine said.

"I wish I could have met him," Sue said.

"When Christine was at school, and Mr. Daaé had no students, he would stand just outside the door and play," Mrs. Valerius said, pointing at a bench. "I would sit on that bench and enjoy a private concert."

"I wish we had recorded him," the professor said, taking Christine's hand. "You always think you have time."

Christine looked at him and smiled.

CHRISTINE'S PERFORMANCE DRESS was laid out on her bed. She sat at the dresser, in shorts and T-shirt, touching up her makeup, not that she needed any, but she had learned long ago that even perfect skin needs makeup on stage. She heard the doorbell ring and quickly stood and slipped on the dress. Zoe knocked briefly on the partially open door and stepped in.

"Where's Raoul?" Christine asked.

"His plane was delayed."

"What?"

"Don't worry. He should be here in time for the performance. I didn't want to get stuck in traffic from the airport, so he'll grab a cab, or Uber, and meet us there."

Christine was not happy. "Let's go. We have to stop and pick up Sue."

"Isn't she coming with her parents?"

"I told her we'd pick her up. Her parents will come later."

"No problem."

Christine sat in the back seat, her dress hanging from a hook above the door, as Zoe followed GPS instructions to the convenience store. Sue was watching from the window of the store as Zoe pulled up. Sue rushed out of the store, carrying a bag and violin case. Her mother was close behind, carrying a hanging bag, talking rapidly in Korean. She switched to English long enough to greet Zoe and Christine, then waved as Zoe sped away.

"Where's your boy thing?" Sue asked.

"His flight's delayed," Christine said, checking her messages once more.

"Is he going to make it?"

"I don't know. I haven't heard from him."

"Good thing we rehearsed."

Sue whipped out her phone. "What flight's he on? I have Flight Tracker on my phone."

"I have no idea."

"He's on the Gulfstream," Zoe said. "They're landing at Van Nuys. I told Raoul to call or text as soon as he gets in."

"Wow," Sue said. "Boy sure wants to hear you sing, or something."

The long-awaited text arrived simultaneously on Zoe's and Christine's phone just as they entered the conservatory.

Backstage, as usual, was controlled pandemonium. Christine and Sue set up shop in the girls' dressing room and quickly got dressed and made up. The stage manager checked his clipboard and then watch, calling out, "Thirty minutes."

Christine spotted Raoul through the crowd.

"Is that him?" Sue asked.

"That's him."

"Boy sure knows how to dress."

The boy did indeed, gray slacks, white shirt, navy blazer, all of it custom made. He made his way through the crowd and hugged Christine, careful to not smudge her makeup.

"I didn't think you were going to make it," Christine said.

"I'm here."

"Where's your violin?"

"We need to talk."

"Okay."

"After the show."

Christine was about to speak when a handsome boy with curly black hair approached. Sue took notice.

"Are you Christine?" the boy asked.

"Yes."

"I'm Alfonso." He looked at Raoul. "I hope I'm not interrupting."

He clearly was. "Raoul." The boys shook hands.

"This is Sue," Christine said. Alfonso nodded at her, then turned his attention to Christine.

"I heard you sing."

"You did?"

"At the Chandler Pavilion."

"You were there?"

"My uncle works there, and they let me sneak in if there are empty seats. I heard something was up, so I stuck around. I'm glad I did. You were amazing."

"Thanks."

"I was also working in the scene shop during your audition. I recognized the voice immediately and went to investigate. I watched from the wings. You made the headmaster cry."

"I did?"

"You did. And you were fantastic." He noticed Raoul was getting antsy. "I don't want to keep you from your friends, so I'll get right to the point. My duet partner graduated, and I need a new one."

"You want me?" Christine asked, surprised.

"I want you."

"There are lots of sopranos here."

"I've heard the rest and sung with most of them. I want the best."

"Wow."

"Think it over and we'll hook up later. I'm looking forward to hearing you tonight."

He stepped forward, took her by both hands, and planted air kisses on both cheeks as Raoul fumed.

"Babe and a half," Sue said softly as she watched Alfonso walk away.

She turned back and watched for a moment as Raoul and Christine stared at each other. "I'll just go and check my violin," she said, and away she went.

"We'll talk now," Christine said, as if the past few moments had never happened.

"I don't want to upset you before you perform."

"And this is how you don't upset me?"

Raoul looked around. "Not here." He took her by the hand and led her away.

They sat on a bench in the hallway, a suitable distance from the people streaming into the auditorium. He took her hand.

"I'm not going to school here."

"What?"

"We're moving to Paris."

Christine was stunned.

"When?"

"Right away. My mom is at the house, packing clothes and stuff."

"Why can't you just stay with Zoe?"

"I tried. I really tried. But they wouldn't go for it. Zoe will be house-sitting anyway. I don't know why they wouldn't let me stay here."

Christine took deep breaths.

"Are you coming back when your grandmother gets better?"

"I don't know. I hope so. They probably wouldn't let me in the conservatory, but I could go back to Ogden Hall."

Christine started to cry.

Raoul pulled out his pocket square, a real one, and handed it to her. "You'll ruin your makeup."

"I don't care." She choked back tears. "We were supposed to go here together. You promised."

"I'm sorry, but there's nothing I can do. I can't exactly run away from home."

"Everything I care about gets taken away. Everything."

She leapt off the bench and ran down the hallway.

"Where have you been?" Sue asked as Christine rushed up to her and Zoe backstage.

"You knew!" Christine said to Zoe. "You knew and you didn't say anything."

"It wasn't my place to tell you," Zoe said. "And I didn't know for sure until yesterday. I didn't want to upset you before your performance."

"Well, that didn't work out too well, did it?"

"Fix your makeup," Zoe said. "We're on in a few minutes."

Christine dashed into the dressing room.

"What just happened?" Sue asked.

"She can tell you later. Let's just concentrate on the performance. She needs to do really well tonight."

The Valeriuses had promised to save him a seat, but Raoul sat near the back, hoping to avoid eye contact with Christine. He told himself it was so she wouldn't be distracted, but he really wanted to avoid the invisible daggers thrown his way.

"Is this seat taken?" Alfonso asked.

"No, go ahead," Raoul answered.

Alfonso sat down. "Sorry for butting in backstage. Apparently, I stepped into some drama."

"What drama?"

"I saw you two in the hallway later."

"It was nothing."

"She was crying."

"It was personal."

"I hope it doesn't affect her performance."

"It won't. Nothing fazes her once she steps on stage."

They watched in silence as the acts progressed. Sue took the stage and played "Zigeunerweisen." There was loud applause when she finished and took a bow.

"She's good," Alfonso said.

"Yes, she is."

"You play violin, don't you?"

"Yeah. How did you know?"

"Chandler Pavilion, remember? That was you with Christine, wasn't it?"

"That was me."

"I thought so."

Raoul stared at him.

"Why aren't you accompanying her tonight?" Alfonso asked.

"I didn't know if I was going to be here."

Sue remained on stage as Zoe sat at the piano and Christine, without a trace of a smile on her face, stepped up to the microphone. There were murmurs of anticipation in the audience.

"Do you speak Italian?" Alfonso asked Raoul.

"No, why?"

"Just asking."

"I speak French."

"I believe she's singing in Italian tonight."

"She sings in several languages."

Alfonso smiled.

Christine looked out at the audience, took a deep breath, and then sang "Dove sono," followed by thunderous applause and a standing ovation.

Alfonso and Raoul stood shoulder to shoulder, applauding enthusiastically.

"Brava! Brava!" Alfonso shouted. He turned to Raoul. "Do you need me to translate the lyrics for you?"

"No, that's okay. I know the piece."

BOOK 2

SAINT-TROPEZ

"What had this Erik to do with Christine's sighs and why was she pitying Erik when Raoul was so unhappy?

—GASTON LEROUX, *The Phantom of the Opera*

1

HOLLYWOOD CANTEEN

CHRISTINE STOOD NERVOUSLY backstage in the auditorium of the Belen Conservatory of Music. She shuffled her feet on the decades-old boards where now-famous musicians and singers had once stood awaiting their turn on stage. The curtains had not yet opened but she could hear the crowd murmuring as the stragglers took their seats. The excitement was building on both sides of the curtain.

The band members, all wearing black pants and matching blue blazers, were in position on stage. This was a one-time gig, and the budget was miniscule, so the podiums were made of foam board. They were so lightweight they had to be taped to the floor to keep them from falling over, and the band members warned to watch their knees. A contest had been held to select the name, and the winner, "The Belen Beats," was displayed prominently on the podiums.

Ricky, the stage manager, scurried about the stage, checking every detail. Christine smiled as he appeared to be proofreading the big sign: HOLLYWOOD CANTEEN. Yes, it was still spelled correctly and, no, it had not moved from where they had installed it yesterday. He scanned the floor, checking for scraps of anything someone might trip over. Satisfied, he headed for the wings.

Christine turned to watch him as he swooped past her and into the midst of a group of dancers. All the boys and some of the girls wore World War II uniforms of all the military branches from the era. The rest of the girls wore wartime fashions, including stockings with lines down the back.

Christine hadn't even thought of the dancers, it was someone else's idea, and the rather large expense of the costumes almost derailed it. Fortunately, this was Los Angeles, and the father of one of the students worked for a major studio. He said he would donate the money for the costumes, rented from a local costume house, but most likely the expense ended up as a line item on someone's movie budget, leaving producers wondering why there was a bill for World War II uniforms in a contemporary romantic comedy. Whatever, the kids looked great.

This was a private music school, and they had briefly considered asking the public performing arts school to provide the dancers, but instead just held auditions and picked the best twelve dancers from their own ranks. This was their show and they intended to do it themselves. Even the bandleader was a student, although he had plenty of coaching from the faculty, and most importantly, from an elderly retired faculty member who had actual experience from the big band era.

As Christine turned her attention back to the stage, she felt a hand on her shoulder. She turned to look.

"Headmaster Caldwell," she said. "I thought you were watching from the audience."

Johnston Caldwell and Christine did something of a sideways hug so as to not smear her makeup. She didn't normally wear much, if any, makeup, and certainly didn't need it, but all performers, male and female, recognized that you needed plenty of it when going on stage under bright lights.

"I gave up my seat to a paying customer," Johnston said. "We're sold out, standing room only. They're bringing in folding chairs."

"Wow, that's cool."

"Don't be so modest, Christine. You draw a crowd."

"It's a group effort," she said.

"It was your idea, and you've done an excellent job bringing it all together on short notice."

Short notice, indeed. The students had already done their spring concert and for many, individual recitals. Now they were concentrating on finals and looking forward to summer vacation. But they were a group of overachievers—they had to be just to be admitted to the Belen Conservatory of Music. They all loved music. For many it was their entire life, their very reason for being. They relished the opportunity to perform music completely outside their normal repertoire. That it was another of Christine's charitable endeavors didn't hurt. Most of them had been roped into others more than once.

There weren't that many World War II veterans left, but the music from that era was instantly identifiable, and everyone agreed with Christine that it would make a great show to raise money for various charities benefitting veterans from more recent wars. During her own time on the streets Christine had encountered several homeless veterans. She knew that many others suffered from catastrophic wounds, both physical and mental. She discovered that there were nonprofits set up to help them and decided the least she could do was to put on a show to raise money.

"Why do they call it a big band?" Christine asked. "There's only twenty guys. That's not very big."

"I don't know, actually," Johnston said. "You could call it a swing band if you like. I think Glenn Miller called his group an orchestra, even though he didn't really have a lot of strings."

He didn't mention that the big bands of the era also didn't have any women, except the girl singer, and few minorities, unless it was the entire band. None of the kids even questioned this as they formed the Belen Beats, white, black, Hispanic, Asian, boys and girls. All they cared about was making music. One of the boys wondered aloud if the girl members of the band should wear skirts. The girls just laughed, and everybody dressed the same.

The bandleader was elected. Christine was the girl singer by acclamation. It bothered some of the older girls that she was just a freshman, but no one doubted her voice, and no one doubted her ability to sell out a house, so they settled for being members of the girl group—a knockoff of the Andrews Sisters. Their songs didn't exactly require extraordinary singing ability but were sure to be crowd pleasers. Their uniforms, much like the Andrews Sisters, were era-appropriate, not at all sexy, or what a teenage girl would wear today, but they reminded themselves that it was for charity. There would also likely be people who mattered in the audience, people who could launch their careers.

Christine, on the other hand, wore a stunning, strapless, ankle-length gown, also era-appropriate, but very sexy indeed. Blonde hair cascaded over her bare shoulders, and she suddenly felt a bit self-conscious at showing so much skin when all the other girls were completely covered. She instinctively reached for her chest to make sure she wasn't falling out. She had been a late bloomer, but there was now at least enough there to hold up the strapless dress, with the aid of a good bra. She also felt a bit of a chill, unsure if it was a draft or nerves. She wished the headmaster was still there to snuggle up against for warmth, but he was busy encouraging the others. Actually, she wished her daddy was there, so she could bury her head on his shoulder, not even worrying about her makeup, and he could kiss her on the forehead and squeeze away all the nerves.

The audience suddenly went silent, and everyone backstage knew that meant the house lights had just gone down. Ricky took a couple of steps onto the stage and counted down quietly, "Three, two, one."

He pointed at the bandleader and then backed away as the band started playing "In the Mood." They may have been a bunch of teenagers, but their sound was exquisite.

There was loud applause and cheering from the audience as the curtain opened. Christine smiled, relieved. It was going to be a good night.

The saxophone players stood and rocked it. It might not have been the kids' kind of music, but the beat was infectious, and they worked it.

Another round of applause and cheers rang out as the dancers swarmed onto the stage. What they lacked in talent they made up for in enthusiasm. Who knew swing dancing could be so much fun?

Christine peeked out from behind the curtain and then quickly pulled back, bumping into Ricky. "Oh my gosh," she said.

"What's wrong?" Ricky was ready to panic.

"There are old people dancing in the aisle."

"That's a good thing, right?" Ricky asked.

"Yeah, definitely," Christine said as she took another look. "And they're pretty good at it too."

The trumpet players were on their feet now and Christine watched as Sue, her jet-black hair pulled back in a ponytail, stepped out front for a solo. Christine's friend Sue was a violin prodigy. Although she sometimes soloed with major symphony orchestras on weekends, her parents insisted that she not miss a day of school. They also weren't too thrilled that she played the trumpet for fun, and to blow off steam after a long day of practicing on her violin. They were both in the audience however, beaming with pride as their daughter blew the horn in true big band tradition.

The dancers were all out of breath as they scurried off the stage while the auditorium thundered with applause.

"Good job, good job." Ricky fist bumped and slapped backs as the dancers got out of the way of the girl group, ready to go on.

Sue remained on her feet in front of the band, waiting for Ricky's signal.

Ricky checked his clipboard just in case but had long ago committed the set list to memory. He waited for the applause to die down and then pointed at Sue, center stage. She immediately launched into "Boogie Woogie Bugle Boy" on her trumpet.

"Go Sue!" Christine shouted, and then quickly covered her mouth when she realized how loud that was.

The girl group danced onto the stage and surrounded Sue, who joined in the dancing as she played. The drummer kicked it with a throbbing beat, and then the rest of the band joined in as the three girls began to sing. Sue's parents were not accustomed to seeing their daughter in such a performance, but the audience seemed to love it.

Christine smiled as she watched the girls watch Alfonso as he walked on stage to join them in the next number. Alfonso was a tall, dark, exotic sophomore with an incredible voice who made all the girls go weak in the knees. He spoke Italian fluently along with serviceable French, and often helped Christine understand the lyrics she was singing, along with the pronunciation. No one other than Christine appeared to notice that his accent seemed to come and go depending on the situation.

As far as anyone knew, Alfonso had never dated anyone at the conservatory. There were plenty of rumors—he was dating a girl from another school, a college woman, a famous Disney princess, one of the teachers. While most of the other kids dressed like slobs for school, Alfonso was always impeccably dressed. He was also quite polite and oh, so very charming. He kissed more than a few hands, including teachers, which would have probably gotten him expelled from a public school for sexual harassment, but things were a bit more relaxed at the conservatory. There was plenty of cheek kissing in the European fashion and no one complained. Christine's own cheeks had been kissed many times by both boys and grown men, including visiting conductors astonished at her singing ability. She didn't mind. It made her feel sophisticated.

Alfonso often sang duets with Christine, which made the other girls jealous. They made a gorgeous couple, at least on stage, and the music they made was magic. They held hands and looked longingly into each other's eyes while singing love songs that perhaps a couple so young should not be singing. They once kissed spontaneously, completely unrehearsed, at the end of a particularly beautiful love song. There was complete silence from the audience until Christine turned and smiled, and then the two took a bow, followed by applause. It wasn't all that passionate a kiss, but apparently enough to draw the ire of the other girls. For several weeks afterwards, Christine endured their stares at school.

Backed by the girl group, Alfonso sang "Don't Fence Me In," which was quite popular with the audience. Then the girls left the stage and Alfonso stood alone. The set list had been carefully ordered to flow between fun, light pieces, and more serious ones. It was time for serious, and Alfonso was the man.

After a short intro from the band, and in the finest tradition of crooners from the era, he launched into "I'll Get By," drawing immediate applause. Christine silently sang along, swept up in the music.

The girl group stood next to Christine, watching, wishing, hoping. When he briefly cast his glance in their direction, they were all certain he had eyes only for them. Christine knew better. He was messing with her head again. He was also going to be a tough act to follow.

Ricky inserted himself between the girls and Christine. "Are you ready, voice all warmed up?"

Christine shrugged. "It's not exactly opera."

Alfonso walked calmly off the stage amidst loud applause. "Go get 'em kid."

Christine took a deep breath and said softly to herself, "Showtime."

There was even more applause, and cheering, as Christine walked onto the stage. She turned and faced the audience. There was complete silence as everyone waited in anticipation. She smiled and then turned and nodded at the bandleader.

A hush fell over the audience as Christine sang "I'll Be Seeing You," followed by a standing ovation.

The intro tipped the audience to what was coming next, and they quickly started applauding. Christine turned and gestured toward Sue as she stood and blew her trumpet, and then the audience fell silent as Christine began to sing "It's Been a Long, Long Time." She looked over at Alfonso once while singing—she might as well mess with his head too. It served him right.

There had been much discussion, and research, for her next song. Christine had been perfectly willing to sing "Lili Marlene" in German, but they decided to go with English, for a variety of reasons. That suited her just fine—she didn't really consider German all that beautiful a language for singing. Whatever the language, it brought down the house. She smiled as she walked off the stage—it was going well.

The girl group, joined by three boys, followed her, singing "Mairzy Doats" and "On the Atchison, Topeka and Santa Fe."

There was a rush for the restrooms during intermission. Christine had been taking small sips of water so she wouldn't have to deal with all that dress in a small stall. She spotted Johnston headed her way.

"I've been working the room," he said. "We're a hit. You're a hit. They love it. We have to do this again sometime."

"Okay, sure," Christine said. "I'm in. There's a lot of songs we had to cut."

It didn't take much to get the audience back after intermission. The band played "Sing, Sing, Sing," the dancers danced onto the stage, and the audience poured in, lots of them dancing in the aisle as they made their way to their seats.

"How can you not dance to that?" Alfonso asked.

"Okay, let's go," Christine responded, grabbing his hand.

Alfonso laughed. "Save your breath. Those kids are going to be beat."

The dancers were burning plenty of calories on stage. "Sing, Sing, Sing" could go on indefinitely, but the bandleader kept checking to see if the audience had returned, and mercifully cut it short before the dancers collapsed. They had only a few seconds to catch their breath before the band segued into "Moonlight Serenade," but at least they could now slow dance.

Christine felt Alfonso's hand on her back. She turned to him, he took her into his arms, and they danced onto the stage, joining the other dancers. They had danced a respectable distance apart during rehearsal, but they were now much closer. She didn't know if he was pulling her closer or if it was her. She didn't care. It felt good, and probably looked good, which was even more important. She put her head on his shoulder and it felt even better. She didn't even worry about her makeup, smudging it or getting it on his jacket. It simply didn't matter. She was completely at ease.

They were glued together as they swirled around to the music. When the song ended the other dancers quickly left the stage, leaving Alfonso and Christine alone, dancing without music for a few beats. He was supposed to take a step back, bow, kiss her hand, and then leave the stage. She looked up, waiting for him to release his grip on her. But instead, he kissed her fully on the lips, to hell with the makeup. He still didn't release her, and she held her breath for a moment as they stared into each other's eyes.

The girls backstage fumed as Alfonso released Christine, bowed to the audience, and then walked by, smiling.

Christine wanted badly to check her lipstick, bright red and plenty of it, which was the style of the era, but the band was already starting her song, and so she just started singing, "We'll Meet Again," hoping it wasn't too smudged.

She had no opportunity to confront Alfonso over the kiss—one of them was always on stage for the rest of the concert. She decided it didn't matter anyway. Maybe he was messing with her head, maybe it was real. Whatever, it was fun, and quite nice to have a little attention from a boy, especially a smoking hot one. Her love life had been nonexistent. Not that there was that much of it for any of the other kids in school her age. Not many of them were paired off, and not many of the boys interested her anyway. There would be plenty of time later for boys, but right now it was all about the music.

All the singers took the stage for "When the Lights Go on Again," but it was basically a duet with Christine and Alfonso, with the others singing backup. Christine had insisted that the song be the finale, with everyone on stage, everyone participating, even the dancers. But there was one more song to sing, and everyone agreed there was only one among them to sing it.

Once again alone, center stage, Christine sang "The White Cliffs of Dover" and the tears began to flow.

Christine was pushed into taking two curtain calls to loud applause, everyone on their feet, before saying "I am not going back out there again by myself." While the crowd shouted "Encore! Encore!" Alfonso quickly took her arm and said, "Let's go, everybody out there."

The curtains opened, everyone took a bow, and then began singing "Comin' in on a Wing and a Prayer."

The curtains closed, but the audience was not finished. "Encore! Encore!" Unfortunately, the kids had prepared only one encore. Ricky was frantic. "What are we going to do?"

"'Danny Boy,'" Alfonso said.

"Who's going to sing it?" one of the girls asked.

"Alfonso, of course," Christine said, not at all flippantly. As far as she was concerned, he was the clear choice.

"Christine," Alfonso said. There were lots of nods in agreement.

"Do a duet," Ricky said.

"No, Christine," Alfonso said.

"It should be everybody," Christine said. "We can do it together."

"Yeah, that would be cool, but we haven't rehearsed it," Alfonso said. "It would be a mess. It's better as a solo anyway."

"Then you do it," Christine said.

"Better if a girl sings it," Alfonso said.

Alfonso turned to Johnston. "What do you think, sir?"

"It's your gig," Johnston said, extending his hands in a gesture to make sure they understood he meant all of them.

The bandleader stepped up. "We don't have sheet music."

"No problem," Alfonso said. "She can do it a cappella."

"Can you?" Ricky asked.

Christine shrugged. "I guess so, but I haven't rehearsed."

"I'll accompany her." All eyes were suddenly on Sue.

"On the trumpet?" Ricky asked.

"Sure, why not? Lots of people do it as a trumpet solo." Sue looked at Christine and smiled. "I blow, you sing. Easy work."

"Okay," Christine said reluctantly.

"I'll play an intro and you can come in whenever the spirit moves you."

Christine nodded. "I hope I remember all the words."

"No problem, I'll cover you."

Everyone started to scatter. "No wait," Christine said. "If I'm going to do this, everybody stays on stage. We're all in this together."

The band stayed in their seats, and all the others formed a half circle around Christine and Sue, center stage. A hush fell over the audience as the curtains opened. There were a couple of proud Koreans in the audience as Sue blew. Everyone else just held their breath until Christine stepped forward and started to sing.

In the audience, Zoe leaned over to Professor and Mrs. Valerius and whispered, "They're winging it. They did not rehearse this."

There was not a dry eye in the house, or on stage, as Christine's soaring soprano filled the room. It also didn't hurt that she was a stunning beauty with remarkable stage presence and possessed by the music.

2

VINYL

CHRISTINE SAT ON the bench in the hallway outside the office at the conservatory, staring at the shiny floor. When she sat on the same bench two years ago her feet didn't touch the floor. Now they did, barely, but they did.

"Christine," the school secretary called out through the open door, "the headmaster will see you now."

Christine was more than a bit nervous as she headed for the headmaster's office.

"Am I in trouble?" she asked as she sat down.

"Have you done something to be in trouble for?"

"Not that I can think of, but you never know."

Johnston chuckled. "I was just about to mail the checks to the nonprofits and wanted you to see the results from the concert." He handed her a piece of paper.

"Wow. That's a lot. We did good, huh?"

"You did well, as your English teacher would put it."

Christine just smiled and nodded.

"Some of the expenses were covered by parents, so the net is even more than we had projected."

"Great."

"I'm very proud of you, Christine, for coming up with the idea and organizing everything."

"I had a lot of help."

"Yes, you did, but it was your initiative."

"Is that it?" Christine started easing off the hot seat, ready to get back to anywhere but here. No student wanted to spend any more time than necessary in the headmaster's office.

"What are your plans for the summer?"

Christine wasn't expecting that but was fairly sure "hanging at the beach" wasn't the proper response. "The professor is lecturing at some symposium in New York. I'm supposed to go with them."

"Excellent. You certainly need to spend more time working on music and not just singing."

"I think it will be way over my head."

"Christine, your singing is outstanding. Your audition piece was better than what most seniors present for graduation. How old were you then?"

"Twelve, well, almost thirteen."

"We can't teach talent. We can't teach you where to find that amazing voice you have. We can only teach you how to use it, and improve it, and you are coming along very well. You have the ability to become one of the greatest singers of your generation, or the century for that matter."

"No pressure, huh?"

He smiled. "No pressure. Have you given any thought to the direction you want to take, opera, classical?"

"I was thinking rap."

"Get out of my office."

"Hip-hopera?"

It was a game they played. He smiled. "Well, whatever direction you choose for your voice, your knowledge of music needs to keep up, and, frankly, it hasn't been."

"Sorry, but it's so dry, and boring. I just want to sing. I don't need to read music or write it. Just play it for me on the piano and I'll take it from there."

"What would your father say?"

"Huh?"

"Could your father read music?"

"Sure."

"Could he write music?"

Christine nodded.

"I understand he went to great lengths to bring you to Los Angeles for the sole purpose of enrolling you in this institution."

"Yes sir."

"So that you could just continue to do what you could already do, sing?"

"No sir."

"Your father was a smart man, and I'm told, one of the greatest violinists to ever pick up an instrument. If he were still alive, would he be satisfied that his beloved daughter was lagging behind her classmates in music and composition at the school he struggled to get her into?"

"No sir."

"Then we will be doing better in the fall semester, won't we?"

"Yes sir."

"You can make a career, even make a lot of money, singing other people's songs, but that's just performing music, not making music. I love hearing you sing Puccini, and please don't stop doing it. But give some thought to making your own music. You might like it. You might even be good at it."

"Yes sir."

He stood up. She took that as her cue to do the same.

"What are you doing this summer," she asked.

"We'll be in the south of France for a few weeks, and then Santa Fe for the season."

"The season?"

"Opera, perhaps you've heard of it."

Christine nodded.

"One more thing," Johnston said as he reached for the credenza.

Christine stopped and turned. Now what?

"When we were putting the concert together you mentioned that your great-grandmother had recorded some of the same songs."

"Yes sir."

"But you had lost her records."

"When you're walking to Los Angeles a lot of things get left behind."

"A friend of mine sells used records. He keeps them in a huge warehouse, not far from here. The major labels sometimes call him when they can't find copies of their own recordings. The place looks like a mess, row after row of piles and piles of records, but he somehow knows where everything is and can find it within a few minutes. I asked him if he had any Stella Williams."

Christine looked at him hopefully.

"He only had one, 'I'll Be Seeing You.'" He handed her a vinyl album. "It's yours now."

Christine gasped for breath as she took the album.

"Ooh, real vinyl. Thank you so much." She threw her arms around him and hugged him tightly.

"I'm quite sure Professor Valerius has the proper equipment for listening to an antique like this."

She nodded vigorously while reading the jacket. "Definitely."

"I listened to it a couple of times myself and made a digital copy. Please don't tell the piracy police."

"Oh, I won't."

"It appears you inherited the music gene from both sides of your family."

She nodded again.

"But you seemed to have been channeling Vera Lynn at the concert," he said. "I'm not sure where that comes from."

"Youtube."

3

THE JUNE GLOOM

THE JUNE GLOOM had descended and held hostage the coastal cities. It was a mild gloom, as glooms go, today a band only a couple of miles wide. On the 405, cars crawled along, bathed in sunshine, and in the Valley, temperatures were already starting to creep up. Tourists found this odd—the sun was always supposed to shine in California, especially during the summer, and certainly at the beach.

A light drizzle was falling in Santa Monica, just enough to wet the streets and make them glisten in the morning sun. It was days like this that Zoe regretted not spending the money to repair her interval wipers, so she resigned herself to manually turning them on for a couple of strokes whenever the view through the windshield became mildly obscured.

Christine was oblivious. Like most teenagers riding in a car, her ears were stuffed with ear buds, and the music was too loud. Zoe didn't bother to say anything, as she would just have to repeat it after Christine removed the ear buds and said "what?"

They parked in a city parking structure near the Promenade, which was gloriously empty this early in the morning. Once Christine packed away the music, they debated over whether it was drizzling hard enough for an umbrella, of which they had only one. They decided it wasn't and set off in search of coffee. Zoe refused to pay three-fifty for a cup of coffee, and Christine didn't care one way or the other, so they stopped at McDonald's on the Promenade.

They hadn't eaten breakfast, so they ordered from the dollar menu and found a table outside sufficiently protected from the drizzle.

"We ate here our first day in LA," Christine said.

"I eat here all the time."

"My daddy really knew how to eat cheap. We always had water to drink because it was free, and we always ordered off the dollar menu."

"Been there, done that."

Zoe checked her watch. They lined up for free refills and set off toward the mall.

"Rain stopped," Zoe said.

"Cool."

They strolled along the Promenade, headed for the mall. It was too early for the street performers, too damp, and too few tourists, but the Promenade was coming to life. Stores were opening, awnings were unfurled, tables and chairs arranged on the patios of the cafés, awaiting the lunch crowd.

There were a few walkers. Some strolled, some walked purposefully, and some race walked, which Christine found funny.

Zoe and Christine arrived at the upscale department store just as the doors opened, and quickly found the right department. With practiced hands, they flipped through dresses on the rack.

"So, do I have to call you Doctor Zoe now?" Christine asked.

"Why in the world would you call me that?"

"Aren't you getting like, a music doctor thingy?"

Zoe laughed. "Just a music master's thingy, which took two years. A doctorate would take even longer."

"Well, you've come this far, you might as well go all the way."

"It's tempting, and someday I might do it, but I have to make a living, and the free rent is about to come to an end."

Christine turned her attention from the dress to Zoe. "Free rent?"

"The Chagnys have put the Santa Monica house on the market."

"When did that happen?"

"A couple of weeks ago."

"Why didn't you tell me?"

"I guess it just never came up until now."

"Where are you going to live?" Christine asked. "I know. You could move into the little cottage. They still don't trust me to be out there by myself."

"I have a gig, so I'll get an apartment."

"What kind of gig?"

"I'm scoring a small independent film for Konrad Krueger."

"Who's he?"

"A composer. A famous one."

"Never heard of him."

"I'm sure you've seen the movies he's scored. He's very much in demand."

"If he's a composer, why doesn't he score it himself?"

"He wanted to. It's the directorial debut of a friend of his, but he's too busy with a big blockbuster and there's a waiting list after that one, so I'm scoring the small film under his supervision, and in his style. It's an incredible opportunity."

They picked through a few more dresses, but nothing excited them.

"Have you heard from Raoul?" Zoe asked.

"Raoul who?"

"The boy who rescued your scarf from the sea, your first date, your first kiss, your first love, and I hope not your first more-than-that."

"Ew! I was twelve, maybe thirteen, depending on what I'm being accused of."

"Well, at least we've established who Raoul is."

"Why would I be hearing from him?"

"We've been invited to spend two weeks with them in Saint-Tropez."

"Who's we?"

"You and me, kid, you and me."

"Why didn't he invite me himself?"

"Well, the Chagnys called the Valeriuses first to get their permission. Then Raoul called and asked me to feel you out about it."

"Feel me out? Is that like feeling me up?"

"You know what it means."

"So feel me."

"Raoul doesn't want to ask you if he knows you're going to say no."

"No."

"It's the south of France. How could you not want to go?"

"He invited me two years ago. How did that turn out?"

"You know what happened. His grandmother was diagnosed with cancer."

"We were supposed to go to the conservatory together, but he dumped me and fled the country."

"He didn't dump you. He called, he texted, he Skyped."

"He hit on French girls."

"And you know this how?"

"Girl talk. I'm still in touch with a few of his friends from Ogden Hall."

"Well, he's not inviting any of them. He's inviting you."

"Whatever."

Exasperated, Zoe, holding a dress in her hand, turned to a girl browsing nearby. "Excuse me, miss." The girl turned toward Zoe. "I need a teenage girl's opinion. Could you help me out?"

The girl looked older than Christine, but still a teenager. She had dark hair, shoulder length and straight. Her skin was olive, probably a result of tanning beds, Christine surmised, and not ethnicity.

"Sure," the girl said. "That dress is ugly. Put it back."

"It's not about the dress but you're right, it is ugly."

The girl stepped toward them while Zoe hung the dress on the rack.

"My friend here, Christine, has been invited to spend two weeks in Saint-Tropez, but she would rather go to a symposium in upstate New York. What do you think?"

"Duh. Saint-Tropez."

"What's so great about it?" Christine asked.

"Well, let's see, boys, the beach, boys, the beach, shopping, sailing, oh, and boys. You can go topless on the beach. That attracts boys. There's also the yachts, but my mom won't let me on them until I'm eighteen."

A well-dressed woman approached. "I won't let you do what until you're eighteen?"

"Go on the yachts at Saint-Tropez."

"Definitely not," the woman said. "I was a teenager once. I know what goes on out there."

"This is Christine," the girl said. "She's been invited to Saint-Tropez for the summer, and she doesn't want to go."

"Of course you want to go dear, properly chaperoned."

"That would be me. I'm Zoe."

"How do you do, Zoe? I'm Alexandra Cummings, and this is my daughter, Connie."

"Pleased to meet you," Zoe said.

Christine feigned disinterest.

"Have you been?" Alexandra asked.

"Yes, several times," Zoe said. "I was a nanny, more or less, for the Chagnys."

"Count Chagny?"

"Yes," Zoe said.

"Oh my. The Chagnys have quite an estate in Saint-Tropez, don't they?" She turned to Christine. "It's in the hills overlooking Pampelonne Beach.

We've attended a soirée or two there." She turned her attention back to Zoe. "I can't imagine Raoul would need a nanny. What is he now, seventeen?"

"Sixteen. They moved to Paris two years ago when Raoul's grandmother got sick, and I've been house sitting for them while I finished graduate school."

"Raoul will be quite the catch, handsome, rich, a real little gentleman as I recall, and he will inherit his father's title. A girl could do worse." Alexandra looked at Connie. "My daughter, of course, wasn't interested."

"I like bad boys," Connie said.

"Raoul has invited you, Christine?" Alexandra asked.

"Yeah, we kind of have a history."

"A history? Spill!" Connie said.

"I thought we were soul mates, then he dumped me. I haven't seen him for two years. His grandmother got all better but he's still in Paris."

"Then you have to go. You have a great bod. Pick out a killer bikini, or at least the bottoms, and rub his nose in it." Connie glanced at her mother. "Well, not literally, of course."

"Maybe I will go," Christine said.

"Great. Let the old ladies pick out dresses. We'll hit the swimwear department."

Connie grabbed Christine's hand and off they went, soon ripping through bikinis at a blistering pace. Connie held up a string bikini.

Christine covered her face. "I could never wear that."

"Why not?" Connie asked.

"People can see your butt."

"So? Everybody has a butt."

Unconvinced, Christine continued searching.

"Do you really go topless at the beach in Saint-Tropez?" Christine asked.

"Of course. Americans are such prudes."

"And your dad doesn't mind?"

"He's pretty open-minded about stuff like that, and everybody does it. Actually, you stand out if you don't go topless."

"I don't know if I could do it."

"It's easy. Well, I was a little nervous the first time, mainly because I didn't really have much to see, but after that it seemed completely natural."

Christine glanced at Connie's chest. She clearly had plenty to see now, or she had a lot of padding stuffed in there.

"Do the boys stare?" Christine asked.

"They try not to, but they do. But it's not like here, where boys are obsessed with boobs, looking down your shirt when you bend over, hoping you turn over at the beach while your top's untied. Over there it's no big deal. Once they've seen them, the mystery is gone."

Connie held up a bikini. "You should totally get this one."

"I don't have any money. I'll have to ask my guardians."

"Your guardians?"

"My parents are dead."

"Oh, sorry."

"My dad arranged for Professor Valerius and his wife to be my guardians until I'm eighteen."

"So, is that a bummer?"

"Not really. They're pretty cool, for old people, and way into music. He's one of Zoe's professors at UCLA, or was, she's graduating."

"Well, that's good, I guess."

"They're going to New York for a couple of weeks. He's lecturing at some symposium thingy. I was trying to decide whether to go with them or hang here in Santa Monica with Zoe, but then the Saint-Tropez deal came up."

"Saint-Tropez, girl, no question."

"How do you know Raoul?" Christine asked.

"We went to school together at Ogden Hall."

"I went there," Christine said.

"I don't remember you."

"I was only there a few months, and then I got into the conservatory. So did Raoul, but then he bailed."

"O-M-G! You're that girl!"

"What girl?" Christine asked, somewhat defensively.

"You're the girl Raoul pounded those two jerks over!"

"Guilty."

"Maybe he is a bad boy after all."

"He said he was defending my honor."

"Then you were in the flash mob on the Promenade. I heard you guys raised like a shitload of money for a homeless shelter or something."

"Yep, that was me."

"You sing really good. That's not my kind of music, but old people seem to like it."

"Thanks." Christine took a moment to process, and then added, "I guess."

———

ALEXANDRA AND ZOE searched through dresses while keeping an eye on the girls, laughing, giggling, holding up bikinis.

"We normally try to go to Saint-Tropez every summer," Alexandra said. "We have friends who let us use their house. But my husband just had a series picked up for the fall season, so he's already in Vancouver. We'll join him as soon as school is out."

"What does your husband do?" Zoe asked.

"He's a producer."

"I like this one," Zoe said, holding up a dress.

"For you or Christine?"

"For me. I'm getting my master's in music composition from UCLA."

"Well done. Do you plan to teach?"

"No. I plan to score movies and television."

"I'll have to put you in touch with my husband. I hope you work cheap."

Zoe laughed. "Everybody has to start somewhere."

"My husband started out reading scripts and fetching coffee. There are a lot of overnight success stories that took decades. We've been quite lucky."

Alexandra held up a dress. "I like this one."

Zoe checked the price tag. "I like the price."

Alexandra looked over at the girls and smiled. "Those two seem to have become instant best friends."

"Yes, they have," Zoe said. "Christine doesn't make friends easily. She's a special child."

"Oh, I'm so sorry."

"No, it's not anything like that. She's something of a musical prodigy."

"Oh, really? What instrument does she play?"

"She sings a bit."

NEARLY EVERY BIKINI Connie held up was far too revealing for Christine, but they continued down the rack.

"What do you do at a conservatory, just study music all day?"

"No, we have regular classes too, but music is pretty much the reason for being there."

"So, everybody is pretty good at music, huh?"

"Yeah, you have to be just to get in. Raoul auditioned twice, some kids even more than that. A lot of kids don't ever make it."

"How many times did you audition?"

Christine dropped her head and mumbled, "Once."

"You go, girl."

"I kind of got lucky and picked the right audition song."

"What was it?"

"'Nessun Dorma.'"

"Nissan? Like the car?"

Christine laughed. "No. It's Italian."

"You speak Italian?"

"Not really, well, a little bit. I just sing in it. It's no big deal."

"Wow. I'm flunking Spanish."

"For singing, you don't really have to speak the language. You just learn the song phonetically and read the English translation, so you'll know what you're singing about."

"So, what's this Nissan song about?"

Christine smiled. "It's from Puccini's opera, *Turandot*. This dude, Calaf, is in love with a beautiful princess."

"So, you're like the beautiful princess?"

"No, I'm the dude."

"The dude? Get out."

"It's kind of complicated, but basically the princess can either marry Calaf the next day or kill him, and so that night he sings 'Nessun Dorma,' which translates to 'none shall sleep' in English."

"How old are you?" Connie asked.

"Fifteen. How old are you?"

"Sixteen, and you are so not normal."

"Thanks?"

"Not many kids our age listen to opera."

"I don't either, not a lot anyway, but I sing it, or at least arias. I've never tried to sing a whole opera. I listen to regular stuff too, well, some of it."

"Why are you singing the dude's part?"

"It's a really beautiful song. It's normally sung by a tenor, a guy, an adult guy, but I just fell in love with it."

"Seems like a weird choice for an audition."

"We had just got back from Chicago and my audition was coming up, and I didn't have much time."

"Why didn't you pick a girl song?" Connie asked.

"I kept looking and trying different things, but nothing seemed to work, so I just went to sleep and then it came to me."

"Like, in a dream?"

"Sort of, but I could still hear it when I woke up."

"Hear what?"

"It was a tenor, with the most beautiful voice I had ever heard, singing 'Nessun Dorma,' a cappella."

"Was it on the radio or something?"

"No, it was just there, everywhere, but I couldn't tell where it was coming from. I woke up Raoul, but he couldn't hear it at all."

"Whoa! Whoa! Slow down. You woke up Raoul?"

Christine nodded.

"You were in bed with Raoul?"

"Yeah, I guess, but we were just sleeping."

"You were just sleeping, with Raoul?"

"We weren't doing it. Ew! We were just kids. I was like, twelve."

"I was right. He's not a bad boy."

"He was just helping me with my audition. We kind of locked ourselves in the little cottage."

"What's the little cottage?"

"It's like a guest house. My daddy and I lived there for a while before he died."

"Then you and Raoul shacked up there?"

"No. We just wanted to get away from everybody, and we were trying to find the perfect audition piece. It wasn't like we were making out and stuff."

"Whatever. So, who was singing the Nissan song while you were in bed with Raoul?"

"The Angel of Music."

4

TRAIN À GRANDE VITESSE

MRS. VALERIUS CHECKED and rechecked Christine's bags as they waited at the LAX Air France counter. "Are you sure you didn't forget anything?"

"I don't think so," Christine said. "I don't really need much, a couple of bathing suits, shorts, T-shirts, flip-flops, toothbrush, deodorant."

"And underwear. Did you pack enough underwear?"

"I'll be fine. Surely they have a washing machine."

"They have people for that," Zoe said.

"See," Christine added. "Stop worrying. They have people for that."

The line inched forward.

"What about sunscreen?" Professor Valerius asked.

"I want to get a tan."

"You don't want to get skin cancer," he said. "One good burn at your age could come back to haunt you decades later."

"Don't worry," Zoe said. "I have plenty and I'll see that she uses it."

"Thank you, Zoe." Professor Valerius turned back to Christine. "Do you have enough money?"

"I guess," Christine said. "I doubt they'll make me pay for food."

"Yes, but you might want to do some shopping." He reached in his pocket and peeled off three hundreds.

Christine's face lit up as she reached for the money. "Wow, thanks."

She folded the money and stuffed it in her pocket. "Are you guys going to be okay?" she asked. "Maybe I should go with you instead."

"Nonsense," Mrs. Valerius said. "You would be bored to tears in the Catskills. Go to Saint-Tropez and be with your friends."

"But the professor will be lecturing every day," Christine said. "What will you do?"

"Well, let's see, golf, a few good books, long walks by the lake, haunting all the little shops and bookstores in town, lunch with friends, dozing off in a hammock on the porch. Don't worry about me. I'll be fine."

"Okay," Christine said, not convinced.

"And then there are the nights," Mrs. Valerius said with a sly smile.

"What happens at night?" Christine asked.

Mrs. Valerius looked over at her husband, who also smiled.

"Ew!" Christine said while making the appropriate face.

Zoe laughed.

"Since you couldn't go with us, we decided to turn the trip into a second honeymoon," Professor Valerius said.

"Our first was in Niagara Falls," Mrs. Valerius said, turning to her husband. "Maybe we should drive up there and see if we can find that little motel."

"Okay, enough!" Christine said, holding up her hands. "I'm getting on the plane and going to France."

They finally worked their way up to the ticket counter. Christine and Zoe presented their tickets and passports. The ticket agent studied them for a moment and then looked up. "You are traveling together?"

"Yes," Zoe said.

"Your relationship?"

"Friends, why?"

"She's a minor and this is an international flight."

"Oh yes, sorry," Professor Valerius said, stepping forward. He pulled a folded paper out of his pocket and handed it to the agent. "We are Christine's guardians, and this is our permission for her to leave the country. I used the airline form. It's notarized. I hope it's sufficient."

The ticket agent smiled and read the form. "Excellent. Everything seems to be in order."

They checked their bags, and the agent handed over their boarding passes. "Have a nice flight and enjoy your time in France."

The Valeriuses accompanied the girls as far as security, and then there were hugs and kisses all around. They waited until the girls had cleared security and then waved as they headed down the concourse.

"It will be strange, just the two of us again," Mrs. Valerius said.

"Yes, yes it will. It's been quite an experience having a teenage girl in the house. At least I'm hip to all the lingo so I'll know what the freshmen are saying behind my back."

Mrs. Valerius laughed, and they walked away, arm in arm.

Christine and Zoe continued the trek to their gate.

"Why don't we get to go on their private jet?" Christine asked.

"There's just the two of us, and those things cost a fortune to operate."

"He doesn't think we're worth it?"

"Relax. Don't try to read anything into it that's not there. Besides, business class on Air France is hardly the bus. Trust me."

Zoe was right. It was hardly the bus. Christine took the window seat and immediately flopped back the seat. She was somewhat startled when the seat extended almost into a bed. She threw her head back and sprawled out over the seat.

"Wake me up when we get there."

"Please return your seat backs and tray tables to their original upright position for takeoff," Zoe said. A passing flight attendant smiled.

"There will be plenty of time to sleep later, after dinner and a movie," Zoe said.

Christine righted the seat and craned her neck to look around the cabin as people found their seats and stuffed their baggage into any available space.

"I guess this is cool."

It was indeed cool, but it was also a long way to Paris. The fine French food was wasted on Christine, but Zoe enjoyed it and the wine, very much. After a couple of movies, video games, and music, Christine drifted off to a fitful sleep.

CHRISTINE TEETERED, trying to stay awake, as Zoe spoke rapidly in French with a ticket agent at Charles de Gaulle Airport.

"Are we there yet?" Christine asked as Zoe turned away from the counter.

"Not even close. Our flight to Nice has been cancelled."

"That's not nice," Christine said. "Get it, Nice not nice?"

"Yes, I get it." Zoe smiled at Christine's little pun. "And the other flights for the rest of the day are booked solid."

"So, we're going to get a motel and sleep, right?"

Unbeknownst to Christine, she had just fallen into the airline-hotel-jet-lag vortex. International flights arrive in Europe early in the day, but check-in time at hotels isn't until late afternoon, and jet lag causes people to stumble around like zombies until they can find a bed.

"No, we're going to take the TGV to Marseille." Zoe said as they walked away.

Christine grudgingly followed, her backpack and duffel bag gaining weight by the step. "What's a TGV?"

"*Train à Grande Vitesse.*"

"So, it's a train?"

"Yeah, it's a train."

"Why didn't you just say so?"

"You'll see."

CHRISTINE WAS CURLED UP, contentedly watching the beautiful French countryside fly by when she suddenly shrieked and sat upright.

"What was that?"

"We just met another train," Zoe said without even glancing up from her book.

"How fast are we going?"

Zoe looked up. "Probably just under three hundred kilometers per hour."

Christine gave her that teenage-girl stare for a moment. "So, how fast are we going?"

Zoe smiled. "About one hundred seventy-five miles per hour."

"Why didn't you just say so?"

"We're in France. They don't do miles. Stop being so American."

"So that's like, really fast, right?"

"Yes, that's like, really fast. It's also a lot more comfortable than flying, and you can look out the window and actually see something."

"If you look really quick."

Christine settled back and tried to count the electrical poles zipping past, but soon gave up and pulled out her smartphone. A few flicks of the fingers and she was studying a map of France.

"How far is Marseille from Saint-Tropez?" Christine asked.

"Doesn't your phone tell you?"

"Yeah, but it's in those kilometer thingies."

"It's a couple of hours."

"American hours or French hours?"

Zoe laughed. "Hours are hours."

"Are we taking another train to Saint-Tropez, or a bus?"

"Doctor Chagny is sending a car."

"Cool. Will Raoul be there to meet us?"

"Um, no. He's in Moscow with his father."

"Moscow?"

"He's being groomed to take over the family business," Zoe said, "so he travels a lot with his father."

"He invited me to his house in France, but he's not even home?"

"He'll be there tomorrow. It's not like we were all planning on going out tonight. I'd think you'd want to sleep, jet lag and all."

"I wonder what he looks like."

"The same, probably taller. I guess he's shaving now, or maybe he's trying to do that cool, unshaven look." Zoe glanced over at Christine's phone. "Don't try to tell me you haven't googled him."

"Yeah, pictures of him and some rich, snotty French girls."

"They're not all French."

"They're not?"

"His dad does a lot of business in Eastern Europe. Lots of really stunning young women, and teenage girls, there."

"That jerk."

"He invited you here, not them. Give the boy a break."

"Do you think he wants to get back together?"

"I have no idea what goes on in teenage-boy minds."

"Me either."

Zoe went back to her book. Christine snapped a selfie. A few hundred more electrical poles zipped past.

"I am so not showing my tits," Christine suddenly blurted out, capturing Zoe's attention.

"Where did that come from?"

"That's probably why he asked me to come. Then he'll want to go to the beach."

"Uh, yeah, we will almost certainly go to the beach at some point while we're here. That's one of the main reasons to vacation in the south of France."

"They go topless on the beach."

"Yes, I believe they do." Zoe smiled. "Definitely they do."

"He just wants to see my tits. What a pig."

"You are allowed to go topless on the beach. It's not required, and Raoul is not a pig."

"How do you know? You haven't seen him lately either."

"I practically raised him, and I certainly hope I had some positive influence on him. Then again, he is a teenage boy, raging hormones and all, and half French."

"There you go."

"I was kidding. I doubt he's much different than the boys you go to school with. Are they all pigs?"

"Mostly, yeah, or gay."

Zoe smiled and tried to go back to her book, without success.

"If a gay guy sees you naked, are you supposed to be all 'ew!' or is it the same as another girl seeing you naked?" Christine asked.

Zoe laughed out loud.

"It's not funny," Christine said.

"No, it's not. I never really gave it a lot of thought, and I did plenty of musical theater, so I'm sure some gay guys saw my boobs along the way." She frowned. "So did some straight guys, and probably not by accident."

"Yeah. I know what you mean."

"Why all this sudden concern about somebody seeing you naked?"

"I'm fifteen. Weren't you concerned about it when you were fifteen?"

"If you only knew."

"Knew what?"

"Never mind," Zoe said. "Look, it's your body, your decision, usually anyway. If you don't want to go topless on the beach, don't do it."

"A lot of the girls at school think Alfonso is gay."

"He's not."

"How do you know?"

"I've seen the way the boy looks at you, and other girls."

"Maybe he's just acting."

"Sparks fly when you two sing love songs together."

Christine grinned. "Yeah, they kinda do, don't they?"

"I'll say."

"Did you see the way he kissed me at the Hollywood Canteen?"

"I did."

"He wasn't supposed to do that. He was supposed to kiss my hand. That's how we rehearsed it."

"Did you call him out for it?"

"Nope. I kinda liked it."

"Do we need to turn back so you can make out with Alfonso for the summer?"

"Nah. We're just friends. I wouldn't want to ruin a good duet. And it's fun messing with the girls who have a crush on him."

Zoe was finally allowed to get back to her book.

Christine stared out the window. "Daddy would have loved this train."

5

CAFÉ AU LAIT

The morning sun streamed through the large window, illuminating all in its path, the tile floor, the plaster walls, the chairs, dresser, and bed, with the rest falling into shadow. Christine, sprawled face down on the bed, got a bit of both, bare legs in full sun, white T-shirt blending into the sheets of the same color. Her hair looked a bit darker in the shadows than in the spotlight on stage. She was dead to the world.

"Wake up!"

Christine didn't move. Connie kept pushing and punching her until she finally did.

Christine rolled over, or at least as much as she could with Connie straddling her.

"Wake up, bitch!"

"Connie?" Christine rubbed her eyes.

"In the flesh." Connie crawled off enough to let Christine roll over the rest of the way and pull herself up into a sitting position.

"Where am I?" Christine asked.

"Saint-Tropez. Where do you think?"

"I thought you were in Vancouver."

"Mom and I decided to dump Dad there and popped on over. We've been here a couple of days."

"I didn't know you were going to be here."

"We're going to own this town, if you ever get your ass out of bed."

"Are you staying here?" Christine asked.

"No, at some friends' house, the same one we always use."

"Where is everybody?"

"Everybody and his dad are inspecting vineyards or whatever," Connie said. "Everybody's mom and Zoe went into town to shop."

"How long have I been asleep?"

"I don't know, hours and hours. Jet lag, baby, jet lag. It's not as bad going the other way, so you have that to look forward to."

"What time is it?"

"About ten, I guess. I've been here a couple of hours."

"Did you see Raoul?"

"Yeah, he wanted to wait for you to wake up but had to go with his dad."

"Did he see me?"

"He looked in on you."

Christine quickly checked what she was wearing. It could have been worse.

"At least you were wearing panties." Connie said.

Christine covered her face. "Oh my gosh!"

"What's the big deal? What were you wearing when you slept together?"

"We didn't sleep together, not like that anyway."

"Whatever."

"And we were just kids," Christine said. "Now we have stuff, or I do. I guess he does."

"He does."

"I'm starving. Is there anything to eat?"

"Sure, I'll go make some coffee while you throw something on."

"What should I wear?"

Connie pointed to herself. "This is the uniform of the day, pretty much every day actually, shorts and T-shirt over a bikini."

"Cool."

"Get a move on," Connie commanded as she darted through the door. "We're wasting sun."

Christine took a quick shower and could smell the coffee as she dug through her duffel bag looking for the appropriate uniform.

"How hungry are you?" Connie asked as Christine stepped into the kitchen.

"Pretty hungry. I was too exhausted to eat anything last night."

Connie opened the refrigerator. "Well, the French are pretty squirrely when it comes to breakfast, so this will have to do until lunch."

She put a croissant on a saucer and plopped it on the table beside a bowl, then added a jar of jelly.

Christine studied the dark liquid in the bowl in front of her. "I need a spoon for the soup."

Connie laughed as she poured milk into a cup and put it in the microwave. "It's not soup. It's coffee."

"Why is it in a bowl?"

"You're in France, deal with it."

Christine tried to pick up the bowl with one hand.

"You can use both hands," Connie said. "Nobody will complain."

Christine took a sip, using both hands. "Yuck, it's strong!" She put down the bowl.

Connie handed her a spoon, retrieved the milk from the microwave and poured some into the coffee.

"Presto, *café au lait*, more or less. You're supposed to use steamed milk, but I don't know how to do that, so I just nuked it."

Christine stirred and took another sip. "Much better."

Connie pulled the tip off the croissant and dipped it in the bowl of coffee. "This is why they use a bowl." She wolfed it down.

"What a mean thing to do to coffee," Christine said, but tried it anyway.

"They use regular cups for dinner, with handles."

"Good to know."

Christine finished the croissant. Connie looked at the clock on the microwave. "We need to get going."

"Get going where?"

"You'll see."

"Shouldn't we wait for everybody to get back?"

"Why? They have their deal, we have ours."

"My deal was sleeping until I was so rudely interrupted."

"You can sleep when you're dead. You're in Saint-Tropez. That's your deal."

Christine stood up, still unconvinced.

"They'll be back this afternoon," Connie said. "Throw on a bikini and let's roll."

Connie sat on the bed while Christine threw on the uniform of the day.

Christine squinted in the brilliant sunshine as they walked outside into the courtyard. She followed Connie to a small motor scooter parked in the driveway.

"Isn't there a bus or something?" Christine asked.

"There's a bus, if you want to wait, like forever, but this is much better.

We can go anywhere we want, when we want. Plus, they're way cool. All the kids ride them."

"Are you sure you know how to drive it?"

"I drove it over here."

"How fast does it go?"

"Not very fast. It's not like a hog."

"A hog?"

"Never mind. Just get on behind me and hold on."

"Hold on to what?"

"Me."

Christine hesitantly climbed on.

"It's a lot more fun behind a boy," Connie added as they putted away, Christine holding on for dear life.

Connie was right. It was way cool. They headed into town, careening around some tight turns on very narrow roads.

"Why are all the houses behind walls?" Christine asked.

"I don't know. They just are."

"It must be a French thing."

"Yeah, that."

Christine drank in the sights. The Mediterranean shimmered in the distance. It was beautiful, unlike anyplace she had ever been before. She was already glad she came, and even more glad that Connie was there too. This was much better than the Catskills, whatever those were, or even Santa Monica.

The walls, hedgerows, and fences faded into rows of houses and apartments as they neared town, much like a coastal town in California, except the street signs were in French.

As they entered the center of town they wound through very old buildings, tightly packed, on narrow streets, swarming with tourists.

Christine gasped as they approached the marina. "Wow, look at all those yachts."

"Those aren't yachts. Those are boats. The yachts are anchored out inside the breakwater. They're too big to get into the marina."

Connie parked the motor scooter and they set off on foot, soon arriving at a small sailboat, tied to the pier.

"Where are we going?" Christine asked as they boarded the boat.

"Lunch."

"On the ocean?"

"Not exactly."

"I've never been on a sailboat. This is a sailboat, right?"

"Uh, yeah, that's why it has a mast and sail. Can you swim?"

"Sure." Christine thought for a moment. "We aren't going to fall in, are we?"

"Not unless you want to."

Connie untied the boat and pushed it away from the pier.

"Are we stealing this boat?" Christine asked.

Connie laughed. "No, it comes with the house."

Connie started the motor.

"If it's a sailboat, why does it have a motor?"

"It's kind of hard to sail away from the pier and even harder to sail into one, at least without getting shipwrecked."

Christine nodded. It made sense.

"And we can get back if there's no wind," Connie said.

Once they were out of the marina, Connie had Christine take the tiller and she hoisted the sail.

"Where did you learn to sail a boat?" Christine asked.

"My dad."

"Do you have a sailboat at home?"

"Yeah, we have a small one at Marina del Rey. My dad also crews on a racing yacht owned by some rich Internet guy. You have to be rich to own one of those. They are totally awesome."

With only a little instruction, Christine was already handling the tiller like a pro, as they sailed out of the marina and into the harbor.

"A little to the left," Connie said.

Christine moved the tiller to the left, the boat turned to the right, away from a large yacht anchored just ahead.

"No, the boat's left. Move the tiller to the right."

"I don't want to hit that big boat."

"That's a yacht, and we're not going to hit it."

Christine pulled the tiller the other way and the sailboat turned toward the yacht.

"Is that where we're having lunch? I thought we weren't supposed to go on the yachts."

"We aren't stopping, just doing a drive-by. I spotted some hot boys on there yesterday."

"Come aboard," one of the hot boys shouted from the deck of the yacht as the girls sailed by.

"Can't, we have other plans," Connie replied.

"But I want you."

"No, you want these," Connie said as she pulled up her T-shirt. There was no bikini top underneath, and her breasts were fully exposed. The boys on the yacht cheered loudly.

Cristine shrieked. "What are you doing?"

Connie lowered her shirt. "Just goofing on them."

"Do you know them?"

"No."

Christine hid her face as they sailed away. "I can't believe you did that."

"Loosen up. It's Saint-Tropez. There's topless chicks everywhere, even on that yacht."

Christine turned to look. Sure enough there were topless girls, laughing and waving.

They sailed on for a while, Christine becoming even more confident in her abilities as a sailor. They hugged the coast and came around a point of land jutting out, forming a little cove.

"We're here," Connie announced.

"Where?"

Connie struck sail. The sailboat's forward progress stopped, and they just bobbed for a moment.

"Lunch. That's my mom." Connie pointed toward the beach, where her mother, wearing a painter's smock and beret, had an easel set up.

"How did she get here?"

"She drove."

"Where's her car?"

"Up there behind the trees. This is her favorite place to paint. She comes here all the time when we're in town."

"It's beautiful."

Connie moved toward the stern. "Trade places with me."

Christine moved forward while Connie started the motor.

"Why didn't we just ride with her?"

"And miss all this?"

"Yeah, I guess it's hard to flash your boobs at boys from a car while your mom's driving."

"No it's not."

"You are so bad."

Connie beached the boat. Christine shrieked. "What happened?"

"We ran aground."

"Is that bad?"

"No, that's how you park a boat on the beach."

Connie turned off the motor and hopped into the water. "Come on if you want to eat. My mom doesn't have sail-through service."

Christine slid over the side and followed Connie.

Lunch was an absolute feast compared to breakfast. There was a wicker picnic basket and a cooler. They spread out on a blanket and gorged themselves on sandwiches with foot-long French bread, packed with everything in the cooler. There was also plenty of fresh fruit.

After lunch Christine helped Alexandra clean up while Connie spread towels on the beach. "Thank you for lunch, Mrs. Cummings. It was wonderful."

"Alexandra, please. And yes, it was quite good, wasn't it? It's amazing how quickly teenagers can get weaned off fast food when they have the real thing available."

Connie peeled off her T-shirt, and then her shorts. At least she was wearing half a bikini.

"What are you doing?" Christine asked, somewhat surprised.

"Bagging some rays. Are you coming?"

"You'd better bag your boat. I think it's trying to escape."

Connie turned to look as the sailboat slipped away from the beach. "Oh shit!" She ran for the boat. "Come help me!"

Christine jumped up and ran to help her. They splashed into the water and pulled the boat back onto the beach, both laughing.

"That was close," Christine said.

"Nah, it wouldn't have gotten too far. Come on, let's get some sun before I have to have you back at Casa Chagny, or whatever *casa* is in French."

"I have no idea."

Alexandra had everything picked up when the girls returned. "*Maison* is French for *casa*."

"Works for me," Connie said.

"Oh yeah. I learned that from Alfonso."

"Alfonso?"

"A guy at school."

"A guy at school named Alfonso?"

"Sometimes I call him Alfie, and sing a little of the song, just to mess with him."

"What song?"

"'Alfie.'"

Connie shrugged.

"Dionne Warwick," Alexandra said.

Still nothing.

Christine sang a few bars, which meant nothing to Connie.

"Let's get back to Alfonso," Connie said. "Are you two an item?"

Alexandra returned to her easel while the girls sat on the beach towels.

"Oh no, it's nothing like that," Christine said. "We're just friends. We sing a lot of duets together. He's a really good singer."

"With a name like Alfonso he has to be a total babe."

"He is, or at least the girls at school think so. He's Italian, but he speaks some French."

"How old is he?"

"Sixteen."

"And you're just friends."

"Yeah."

"So, if you don't want him, can I have him?"

"I guess."

"You can hook me up when we get back to LA."

"I used to think maybe he was gay, but not so much anymore."

"Why not?"

"We were dancing, like really close, and I think he got a, you know."

"No, I don't know. He got a what?"

Christine couldn't say it.

"A boner?" Connie asked.

Christine nodded.

"And then he kissed me."

Connie took a moment to process. "Now who's the bad girl?"

"We were on stage. It was a performance."

"Sounds like he performed just fine."

Christine grinned. "Yeah, he did." She took off her T-shirt and shorts.

"Are you sure you don't want him? Seems like he likes you."

"Or it was just a biological reaction. Guys do that, or so I've heard."

Christine dug in her bag, pulled out a tube of sunscreen and offered it to Connie.

"Nah, don't use it. You'd better, though. You're white as a ghost."

Connie clearly no doubt already had a generous helping of sun, or more likely a tanning bed in Los Angeles, as it was all-over, at least as far as Christine could tell.

Christine slathered sunscreen on her legs, stomach, and shoulders.

"Aren't you going to take off your top?" Connie asked.

"I don't think so."

"It's just us girls."

"Maybe later."

"Yolo. You might as well get it over with, that way it will be easier next time, when there are boys around."

Christine shrugged, untied the string of her top and let it slip away. "I guess you're right."

She felt not at all uncomfortable with her breasts on display. Nobody was looking anyway.

"Turn over and I'll do your back," Connie said.

Christine turned over and Connie spread sunscreen on her back.

"So, you were dancing with Alfonso, who may or may not be gay. He got a boner, so he's probably not gay, and then he kissed you. What's up with that?"

"It was a concert. It was no big deal."

"Like a rock concert?"

"No, we were doing the concert. It was part of the act. Everybody was dancing, and then they all left the stage but me, and then I sang."

"What did you sing?"

"'I'll Be Seeing You.'"

"Never heard of it. Who sings it?"

"I did."

"Duh, who else sings it? Somebody famous."

"Peggy Lee, Vera Lynn, lots of people."

"Who are they?"

"It's a really old song. I guess they are too."

Connie slapped her on the butt. "There, all sunscreened up."

"I think I'll take a nap."

"Don't do that. You won't be able to sleep tonight. You need to stay awake as long as you can, then maybe by tomorrow you'll be on French time."

Christine reluctantly turned over and sat up. She gazed out over the water. "It's so beautiful."

"What?"

"The ocean."

"We have an ocean in LA."

"Yeah, but it's not as pretty as this one."

The girls sunned, frolicked in the sea, rescued the sailboat again, and then sunned some more.

"It's getting late," Alexandra called out as she packed her things. "You girls better shove off. Christine probably needs to get back to the house."

The girls stirred but were in no hurry to move.

Christine tied on her bikini top.

"That wasn't so bad, was it?" Connie asked.

"No, it was pretty cool," Christine said, pulling on her T-shirt. "But there weren't any boys around."

"It's better with boys. Everything's better with boys."

They gathered their things and headed towards Alexandra, who was just slipping her work-in-progress into a portfolio.

"Oh, I wanted to see it," Christine said.

"Maybe later," Alexandra said.

"She doesn't let anybody see her stuff until it's finished," Connie said.

They loaded up and trudged up the hill, the two girls carrying the cooler. Christine made a mental note to wear better shoes next time.

"You should have dumped the ice on the beach," Alexandra said. "It wouldn't be nearly as heavy."

"Now you tell us," Connie said as they dropped the cooler on the ground beside the car.

"Give my regards to the Chagnys," Alexandra said as they finished loading.

"Yes ma'am, and thanks for lunch," Christine said.

The girls watched as Alexandra drove away, and then headed down the hill to the beach.

"You are so flashing the yacht on the way back," Connie said.

"Not going to happen."

The yacht had sailed by the time the girls returned to the marina and Connie kept her shirt on. On instructions from Connie, just like she had seen in the movies, Christine hopped out onto the dock, and tied up the boat. She was quite pleased with herself.

6

MOONLIGHT SERENADE

CONNIE'S MOTOR SCOOTER pulled into the Chagny driveway and Christine hopped off.

"Do you want to come in?"

"Nah, you and Raoul have lots of catching up and smooching to do."

"Catching up yes, smooching no."

"Yeah, right."

"I had a good time. Tell your mom thanks again for lunch."

"Later," Connie called out as she chugged away.

Christine stood in front of the heavy wooden door, unsure whether to knock or just go on in. She knocked. After what seemed forever, Zoe opened the door.

"You don't have to knock, just come on in."

Christine stepped in. "Is everybody back?"

"The gang's all here. Did you have fun?"

"Yeah, we rode a motor scooter, sailed a boat, and had lunch with Connie's mom."

"Glad you came?"

"So far."

"He's out by the pool." Zoe pointed and then walked away.

Christine didn't move. Two years. What did he look like now? She had changed, a lot. Surely he had as well. She badly wanted to take a shower, wash her hair, and put on something a bit less grungy than shorts and T-shirt. But that might seem like she was overdoing it. If he was out by the pool, then he probably wasn't all dressed up. Connie did say the French ate dinner late, and it wasn't all that late, so he was probably all casual. She glanced down at her wrinkled T-shirt. Well, maybe not this casual. She ran her fingers through her ratted hair and felt the sand dribble out. She turned, determined to have a shower first, and put on something more appropriate. Then she stopped. This was Raoul. He had seen her at her best on a grand stage, and her worst, dirty, hungry, and homeless, and even in her underwear. This was probably the only boy in the world for whom she didn't have to change clothes, wash her hair, or anything else. This was Raoul, the boy who had jumped, fully clothed in a school uniform, into the frigid Pacific Ocean to retrieve her thrift-store scarf.

"Showtime," she whispered. She took a deep breath and walked out onto the pool deck. It was a stunning view, a large pool surrounded by immaculate landscaping, and the late afternoon sun shimmered on the Mediterranean in the distance. She dumped her bag on the deck. She looked around. No Raoul. No anybody. This was a good excuse to have that shower. She turned to go, and then heard the muted splashing of water. She turned back and watched as Raoul walked up the steps out of the pool.

"Hey," he said. "Where are you going?"

"Hey, yourself. I didn't think there was anybody here, so I was going to take a shower. I'm all grungy from the beach."

He stepped toward her, dripping wet. He had grown and changed. He was always taller than she, but now much more. The boy was also buff, more muscled than before. She glanced down and noticed his brightly colored Jams.

"I thought French guys wore Speedos."

He laughed. "I don't like those things. It's like guys are showing off their stuff."

She laughed a little. They stared at each other for a moment, both having a good look while trying not to be too obvious. He moved closer, put a hand on each of her shoulders, kissed her on both cheeks, and then backed away slightly.

"Don't I at least get a hug?"

"I don't want to get you all wet."

"I won't melt."

He reached out and pulled her in. She buried her head in his chest. Yep, he was taller, and more muscular. She liked it. She started crying.

"What's wrong?"

"I don't know. It just brings back memories, of Daddy, and bad times."

"But good times too, I hope."

She pulled back and wiped her tears. "Yeah, good times too."

He kissed her on the forehead.

"Daddy used to do that."

"I know."

"Do I have time to take a dip before dinner?"

"Sure."

He watched with interest as she peeled off the T-shirt. She was suddenly glad that she had taken the time to put her bikini top back on before leaving the cove. She dropped the shorts. He took an even longer look.

"What are you looking at?" she asked.

"You've grown."

"You too."

"Yeah, we're not kids anymore."

Christine dove headfirst into the pool and swam the length underwater. She surfaced at the far end and watched as Raoul slowly walked down the steps into the water. Then she swam up to him and stood up, putting her arms around his waist and her head once again on his shoulder. No one spoke for a moment.

"Don't think I'm not still mad at you."

"For what?"

"For dumping me and running off to Paris. I had to go to the conservatory all by myself. I didn't know anybody there."

"I didn't really have a choice."

"I know, but I'm still mad."

"Sorry."

She didn't move, her head still on his shoulder, but turned just right so that she could see the Mediterranean.

She flinched as his hands slid down her waist, over her bottom, and onto her thighs. Her legs went around his waist as he lifted her. He started walking, carrying her as she held on, with her head darting around to see where they were going.

He grabbed a raft and she shrieked as he dumped her on it. He then pulled it over to the steps, climbed a couple, and eased onto the raft. It was built for one, but easily held them both quite comfortably, if not cozily, but then, that was probably the idea.

There was much they both wanted to say, but for the moment they just drifted quietly in each other's arms.

———

THE WARM WATER felt wonderful as it cascaded over Christine's head in the shower. Their first meeting after two years had gone well enough, she thought. They hadn't kissed, but maybe that wasn't a bad thing. She didn't want him to think she was letting him off easy, or that she was easy, for that matter.

As she toweled off, she realized that she had no clue what to wear. Breakfast and lunch had worked out well, but this was her first dinner in Saint-Tropez, and these people were rich and lived in this fabulous house. They didn't even live here—it was just their vacation house. She could only imagine what their house in Paris looked like.

Christine wrapped herself in a towel, opened the door and peeked out. The coast was clear. She tiptoed down the hallway.

"Going somewhere?"

Oops. It was Raoul.

"I was looking for Zoe's room," she said.

"It's down that way."

She turned and started the other way.

"But she's in the kitchen. Did you need something?"

"It's a girl thing." She clutched the towel tightly.

"Oh," he said, somewhat surprised. "I suppose I could run into town and get you something."

"No, it's not that, and ew! I just wanted to ask her what to wear to dinner."

"I don't know. Whatever you want, I guess. I kind of like the outfit you're wearing."

"I'm wearing a towel."

"Yeah, I guess it would be kind of hard to sit down, and you would have to keep checking to make sure it didn't fall off at the table."

"Ya think?"

"Well, this is what I'm wearing. You could do the same."

"You're a boy. You're wearing pants and a shirt. Maybe I should wear a dress."

"My mom's wearing pants, jeans actually, if that helps."

"Yeah, that helps."

He followed her back to her room.

"You can go now," she said, shooing him away.

HANNAH, RAOUL'S MOM, was indeed wearing jeans, although they probably cost a thousand dollars American. Her shirt was also made of pure silk. Zoe wore a dress, a simple one, all flowery and summery, but she often did that, once her Goth phase was history.

Christine had selected jeans and a T-shirt, a nice one, form fitting, not like the baggy one she wore to the beach, and it showed a bit of midriff. Raoul's dad was elegant as usual, even if he was just wearing pants and an open-collared shirt.

The sliding glass doors were open, providing not only a view of the pool and the Mediterranean beyond, but a gentle sea breeze. After brief chitchat, they all gathered around a large table. Raoul conveniently positioned himself beside Christine.

Hannah filled Raoul's glass with wine. "Would you like some wine, Christine?"

"I don't know if I'm allowed."

"I checked with Professor and Mrs. Valerius when we spoke to them about the trip, and they agreed it would be okay. It's the European way."

"I guess I'll try it, then."

"Here, let me," Zoe said. She was seated beside Christine, closer than Hannah. She poured half a glass for Christine.

"Well, go ahead and try it," Raoul said.

Christine picked up her glass, and Raoul clinked his glass against hers. She took a sip and then made a face.

"But it's one of our finest Chardonnays," Chagny said.

"Sorry, sir," Christine said, putting down her glass.

Chagny laughed. "Don't worry, Christine. It's an acquired taste."

"I've never had wine before."

Chagny lifted his glass. "A toast then, to Christine's first time."

Raoul snickered.

Christine watched, unsure of what to do, as everyone raised their glasses and toasted.

"Just remember," Hannah said, "all things in moderation."

Christine tasted her food. "This is delicious. What is it?"

"Sea bass," Hannah said. "It's local, and fresh. Zoe and I picked it up today at the market downtown."

"French food is all new to me, especially the coffee bowls," Christine said.

"The what?" Raoul asked.

"The bowls of coffee. Connie had to show me how to dunk the croissant in it."

"Oh yeah, that. I'm a bacon-and-eggs man myself. I never did like continental breakfasts."

"Do they have a McDonald's here?"

"Thankfully, no," Chagny said.

"There's one in Gassin," Raoul said. "It's not far. Let me know when you need a fix and I'll take you."

"How do you know the Cummings?" Hannah asked.

"Who?" Christine said, and then thought about it. "Oh, Connie and her mom. We met them at the mall when we were shopping for Zoe's graduation dress."

"I'm sorry we didn't make it over, Zoe," Hannah said, "but things were just so hectic in Paris."

"That's okay," Zoe said. "You have done far too much already to help me get that piece of paper."

"It's the least we could do."

"Did you have fun at the beach with Connie?" Raoul asked.

"Uh huh," Christine said. "It was a lot of fun. We went sailing in a boat and she let me drive. Then we met her mom for lunch at a little cove."

"Be careful. She's a wild child."

"Yeah, I know. She flashed some guys on a yacht."

Raoul laughed. "That's Connie. She nearly got kicked out of Ogden Hall more than once. Does she still go there?"

"I think so."

"How is the conservatory?"

"It's okay. Some of it's kind of boring. I wish they would just let me sing."

"Have you made a lot of friends there?"

"A few."

"Anyone special?"

"Yeah, there's Sue. You met her. She's probably better than you on violin, but we'll never know, will we?" She couldn't resist the dig.

"I guess not."

"Do you still play?"

"Not very much. I'm kind of busy with school and learning the business. Anyone else?"

"There's Alfonso. He's Italian. He also speaks a little French. Oh, that's right, you met him too, didn't you?"

"Yeah, we met."

"We sing duets together."

"Do they ever," Zoe added.

Christine shot her a glance.

"He's an incredible tenor," Zoe said. "He reminds me of a young Rinaldo."

"Who's that?" Raoul asked.

"One of the greatest tenors of the last few decades," Zoe said, turning to Christine. "Johnston has some of his early vinyl."

"I heard the 'Hollywood Canteen' show was a smash hit," Hannah said.

Christine nodded. "It was sold out, standing room only. We made a lot of money for charity."

"Were you the headliner?" Raoul asked.

"It was a group effort."

"She was definitely the headliner," Zoe said.

"Alfie and the girl group had just as many songs as I did."

"She could go on tour with a swing band tomorrow, if those still existed," Zoe said.

"There are a few that play in clubs in Paris and along the Côte d'Azur," Chagny said. "I wish we could have been at your show, Christine."

"Mr. Caldwell thinks we should do it again in the fall."

"Do let us know," Hannah said. "We'll try to come over now that Raoul's grandmother is better."

"Did you have a duet with 'Alfie'?" Raoul asked.

"Not really. Sort of. 'When the Lights Go on Again' was an ensemble, but mainly me and Alfonso."

"And you danced with him," Zoe said and then hummed a few bars from "Moonlight Serenade." Christine glared at her.

"'Moonlight Serenade'?" Chagny said.

"Yes," Zoe said. "One of my favorite big band songs."

"Mine as well. They played it on our honeymoon, remember Dear?" Chagny said.

"I remember it well," Hannah said. "And I remember the kiss at the end."

Zoe hummed some more of the song. Christine wanted to strangle her.

AFTER DINNER ZOE quickly assembled a playlist from the Hollywood Canteen concert to provide music as the adults had drinks in the living room. Christine and Raoul went out to the pool and sat side by side in a large lounge chair, watching an enormous moon over the Mediterranean.

"Are you dating anyone?" Raoul asked.

"Not really. Sometimes I go out with a group."

"What about Alfonso?"

"Sometimes he goes with us." She looked at him for a moment. "He's not my boyfriend."

"You gave Zoe the evil eye every time she mentioned him."

Christine laughed. "She was just messing with me."

"About what?"

"Alfonso. He's like a total babe. All the girls at school are all googly eyed over him, and jealous of me because we sing duets together."

"That's it, just duets?"

"Well, 'Moonlight Serenade' is an instrumental, so Alfie and I joined the other dancers on stage at the concert, sort of like featured dancers, although I'm not that good a dancer, but Alfie is. At the end of the song, he was supposed to bow and kiss my hand and exit stage right, as a segue into the next number, where I sang 'We'll Meet Again.' Get it? We'll meet again."

He nodded. "I don't know the song, but I get it."

"Vera Lynn. It was huge in World War II. People in the audience were bawling."

"Okay."

"But instead of kissing my hand, Alfie bent me over backwards and really planted one on me."

Not what Raoul wanted to hear.

"He completely caught me off-guard and mussed up my makeup, or at least lipstick."

"You should have slapped him."

"No way. It totally worked and the audience loved it."

"Did you?"

She smiled and shrugged.

"We're not dating if that's what you want to know. Sometimes he goes out with me and Sue, to the movies, or concerts, the beach, stuff we used to do." She paused a moment after the intentional dig. "Actually, he's dating an actress, but her publicist wants to keep it on the downlow."

"Why?"

"She plays a goody-two-shoes on TV and the network doesn't want her image ruined, so they set her up with soy boys for premieres and stuff."

"Soy boys?"

"Not Alfonso. Definitely not Alfonso."

Raoul remained confused. "Who's the actress?"

Christine pantomimed zipping her lips. "Google it. There are lots of rumors. Pick one."

Raoul nodded.

"We did go out on an actual date once, well, a double date with Sue and a Chinese cello prodigy. It was the spring dance at the conservatory a few months ago. The actress's publicist sent paparazzi. It was a real hoot."

"I saw the pics online."

"We looked really good together, didn't we?"

"I hate to say it."

"Speaking of pics online."

"Okay, you caught me."

"You're a man about town in Paris with lots of beautiful young girls on your arm."

"Mostly daughters of my parents' friends."

"Uh huh. Hot daughters."

"Eastern European chicks are really hot."

"Your parents have friends in Eastern Europe?"

"Business associates."

They watched as a cloud floated in front of the moon.

"Why am I here?" she asked.

"I invited you. You came."

"You abandoned me and ran off to Paris. I haven't seen you for two years."

"Yeah, about that. It's a long story."

"I have lots of time."

He took a deep breath. "My parents thought we were getting too serious."

"Too serious? We were kids. I was twelve, well, thirteen when you bailed."

"And they thought we were too young."

"I guess, but we were just having fun. It wasn't like we were making out."

He took her hand. She looked down. "Just that."

"Then there was my grandmother. We thought she was going to die."

"How is she?"

"In remission, doing better, and just as feisty as ever."

"Feisty?"

"She's quite a character."

"So, she's better, but you never came back."

"I wanted to. I really did. I tried to talk them into letting me live with Zoe and go to the conservatory."

"That could have worked. Just the two of you in that great big house."

"Yeah, then we could have really made out when Zoe was in class or at work."

"Nuh-uh."

"That's what my parents thought, anyway."

"Well, maybe a little, later, when we were older."

"Like now?"

She looked at him. "Like now."

They stared into the distance, lost in their thoughts.

"You never even came back for a visit," she said.

"I thought it would make things worse."

"How could it do that?"

"You were just starting a new school, where you could make new friends, maybe meet a guy. We were five thousand miles apart and I couldn't do anything about it. It wouldn't be fair to you, either of us, really, to pretend we were a couple."

"We never really were a couple, were we?"

"Maybe we could have been, someday."

He put his arm around her, and they sat in silence for a moment.

"Remember when we were in the motel with Zoe, and we were in bed together, and she made us switch?" Christine asked.

"Yeah, I definitely remember."

"I wonder if she ever figured out we were just fooling with her."

"I don't know. That was a fun trip, wasn't it?"

"Yeah."

"Well, until—"

"Those people at the hospital must have thought we were crazy, me singing, you playing the violin, and all of us dressed in those funny costumes."

"That was a beautiful song. I listen to it a lot. I wish I had a recording of you singing it."

"'Con te partirò.' It was Daddy's favorite song."

"I miss him," Raoul said.

"Yeah, me too."

They sat quietly for a while.

She giggled.

"What?" he asked.

"I was just thinking about your codpiece."

"Don't start."

"It's kind of like a Speedo."

"I guess, same deal, showing off your stuff. Maybe that's where they came up with 'package.'"

"Yeah, probably."

He kissed her on the forehead. "How's your vacation going so far?"

"Well, let's see. I flew business class on Air France, rode on a really fast train, a motor scooter, drove a sailboat, drank coffee from a bowl, went to the beach, had some lunch, bagged some rays, oh, and a French boy groped my bottom."

"Who?" Raoul asked, surprised. "I'll kick his ass."

"It was you, dummy."

"When?"

"In the pool."

"I groped your bottom?" He thought about it. "Oh, that. That wasn't groping. I was just picking you up."

"By the bottom."

"Sorry, I didn't realize."

"I wasn't complaining, just making conversation."

He smiled. They snuggled.

"Where do we go from here?" she asked.

"I don't know. I thought you would find someone else and forget about me."

"I could never forget you. You rescued my scarf from the sea. You rescued me from the streets. When my daddy died all the grownups did what grownups are supposed to do, but you're the one who took care of me, stayed by me all the way." She wiped a tear. "We slept together! Maybe your parents were right. We were getting too close."

"They let me invite you here."

"For two whole weeks."

"Maybe they changed their mind."

She turned and looked toward the house. Zoe had disappeared and Raoul's parents were dancing.

"That's 'Moonlight Serenade.' Your parents are dancing."

When she turned back Raoul was standing with his hand extended.

"May I have this dance."

She smiled, stood, and he took her into his arms. They danced in the moonlight, closely, her head on his shoulder. When the song ended, he bent her over backwards and kissed her like she had never been kissed before. She had waited two years for it, and it was worth the wait.

7

JE SUIS MALADE

CHRISTINE SLEPT FAR better her second night in France. She was half asleep, with a smile on her face, perhaps from a pleasant dream, when she heard a soft knock on the door. She waited, unsure. There was another knock.

"Christine. Are you awake?"

Now she was. "Who is it?"

"It's me."

"Me who?"

"Raoul. Are you up?"

"No."

"I'll come back later."

"That's okay. You can come in."

He opened the door, stepped in, and quietly closed it. She covered a bare leg and pulled the sheet up around her neck. He watched for a moment, smiling, and then climbed onto the bed beside her.

"What are you doing?"

"Reminiscing about that night in the little cottage."

"Your mom will have a cow if she comes in."

"She's still in bed."

"What about your dad?"

"He left early for the winery, and Zoe went for a run."

"Don't get any ideas."

He grinned. She pulled the sheet up further.

"I was thinking we could go out for breakfast, real breakfast, not croissants and jam," he said.

"Sounds good to me."

He didn't move.

"Well—" Christine said.

"Well what?"

"Get out so I can put on some clothes."

"Oh, yeah, that." He sat up. "I'll wait for you outside."

CHRISTINE STEPPED OUT the front door, small bag slung over her shoulder. She had selected a cute little sundress with spaghetti straps. She felt very sexy in it. Hopefully it would have the same effect on Raoul.

Raoul leaned against a motor scooter.

"We're going on that?" she asked.

"Yeah, is there a problem?"

"I'm wearing a dress. I was expecting a car."

"This is a lot easier to get around on, and park," he said. "All the kids ride them."

"So I've heard."

"Do you want to change?"

"No, that's okay. I see girls in dresses on scooters all the time in movies. It looks kind of neat, all Audrey Hepburn."

"Who?"

"Audrey Hepburn, Gregory Peck, *Roman Holiday?*" she said.

He shrugged.

"Never mind," she said.

He climbed on. She hesitated. Audrey Hepburn's dress was almost to her ankles. Hers was well above her knees. She hiked up her skirt and climbed on behind him. Now the dress was even shorter, much shorter. Too bad he wouldn't get the full effect of the visual, she thought.

He checked the rearview mirror. "Nice legs."

"Thanks." She smiled. Mission accomplished. She looked down at her bare legs, thankful that she had gotten some sun yesterday.

She held on and they took off. Connie was right—it was way better behind a boy.

Her dress blew up around her waist and she was sure everyone was getting a good look at her underwear, but she didn't care. It was exhilarating, just like in the movies, and this was Saint-Tropez. She buried her head in Raoul's back as her hair, and dress, trailed in the wind.

They took a different route than she had yesterday with Connie, away from town. They were soon on a larger road, again reminding Christine of

California. There were gas stations, parking lots, commercial buildings. Raoul slowed and pulled off the main road.

"Oh!" Christine shouted. "It's Mickey D!"

Raoul pulled in.

"What's a McDrive?" she asked.

"Drive-through."

"Oh yeah, duh."

"But we're going in, sit down and have a proper breakfast."

They went in and Christine found everything very familiar, except the menu. Fortunately, it had pictures, and she had a translator.

"They don't have as big a breakfast menu as they do in the states," Raoul said, "but I'm sure we can find something other than croissants and jam."

"That's okay," she said.

He ordered, they picked up their food and found a table.

"How is it?" Raoul asked.

Christine couldn't answer because her mouth was full, so she just smiled and nodded. After she swallowed, she picked up a foam cup of coffee and pointed at it. "Look, one hand." She took a sip.

They sipped their coffee for a moment.

"You know what's weird?" she said.

"What?"

"I've had a different person in my bed both mornings I've been here."

"Huh? Who?"

"Yesterday Connie was sitting on my butt when I woke up."

"Really?"

"She got tired of waiting and woke me up."

"She was sitting on your butt?"

Christine nodded. "Then she put sunscreen on my back at the beach and slapped me on the butt. You don't think she's a lesbian, do you?"

"Connie? No way. She likes boys. She *really* likes boys, but who knows? Maybe she's omnisexual." He took a sip of coffee. "She slapped you on the butt?"

"After she put on the sunscreen, she was like 'there, all done,' so probably no big deal. Maybe I've just led a sheltered life, well, at least since we slept together."

Raoul grinned.

"She didn't offer to do my front," Christine said. "Now that would have been weird."

"Huh?"

"We didn't have on any tops."

"Whoa," he said, choking on his coffee. "You were topless at the beach?"

"Yeah. That's like a thing here, right?" Christine said casually. "When in Saint-Tropez, do as the Saint-Tropezians do, or whatever."

"Yes, but I thought, I mean—"

"You thought what?"

"I just wish I had been there."

"It was just us girls, so I decided to try it out. Don't get your hopes up."

"How was it?"

"It was kind of, what's the word, exhilarating, sort of naughty, but not really, it was kind of natural. Then again, there weren't any boys around."

He smiled wistfully. A guy could dream, couldn't he?

BACK ON THE MOTOR SCOOTER, Christine was even less concerned about her dress blowing up around her waist. "I'm having a wonderful time," she said as they zipped through the hedgerows on the narrow, winding road. The commercial buildings turned into farmland.

They pulled into a parking lot. There were several cars, a small tour bus, and a line of people at the door to a beautiful stone building. It looked to Christine like it was a thousand years old.

"I'm not even going to ask where we are," Christine said as they dismounted. "Surprise me."

Raoul took her hand and they headed for the door.

"Don't we have to get in line?" she asked.

"No, actually, we don't."

"Why not?"

"You'll see."

Raoul bumped fists with the young man at the door and they swept right in. He positioned himself beside the door guy and pulled Christine alongside. He began greeting guests as they entered.

"*Parlez-vous français?*" Raoul asked the next person in line. Even Christine knew what that meant.

"No, we're American," the woman said.

Obviously, Christine thought.

The woman's husband nodded, and their two kids, a boy, twelve and a girl, ten, just looked bored.

"We're from Oklahoma," the woman said.

"I am Raoul Chagny. This is my friend, Christine. Welcome to our winery."

"Hi," Christine said, waving.

The twelve-year-old boy was checking her out, a leering smile on his face, no longer bored.

"Our winery?" Christine whispered to Raoul as the next couple approached.

He nodded and smiled. "Yes, get to work."

"*Bonjour*," Christine said, hoping her accent didn't suck too badly.

Raoul worked the entire line. Christine helped where she could, but she decided customer service was not her calling.

Raoul took her by the hand, and they went exploring.

"I've never been in a winery before," she said.

"Anything special you want to see, or do?"

"I want to stomp the grapes."

Raoul laughed. "That's only in the movies, and *I Love Lucy*. We use machines now, and the grapes aren't quite ready anyway."

"Well, boo. That looked like fun."

"It would have been fun to watch."

She lifted her dress, probably more than she would have otherwise dared, and danced around. He laughed, and never took his eyes off her bare legs.

"Let's duck into the tasting room before the tour gets there."

"What's a tasting room?"

"A room where you taste the wine."

"Cool."

Attendants were setting up as Raoul and Christine swept in. Raoul picked up a bottle and poured a small amount into two large glasses, monogrammed with the name of the winery. He handed one to Christine. She started to drink.

"Wait. First you swirl it around in the glass." He demonstrated. She copied him.

"Then you smell it." He showed her again how it was done. "And then you taste."

They both sipped their wine. Raoul reached for a stainless-steel spittoon and spit.

"What's wrong?" Christine asked. "Didn't you like it?"

"You taste, and then spit."

"Ew, gross."

"If you taste a lot of different wines you don't want to get drunk."

"Sorry, I swallowed."

"That's okay, you're not driving."

"Good point."

"So how was it?" he asked.

"I liked it better than the one we had last night."

"I thought you would. It has more residual sugar."

"What does that mean?"

"It's sweeter."

"Yes, definitely."

"Last night it was very dry," he said.

"Seemed pretty wet to me."

"Dry just means that all the sugar was converted to alcohol during fermentation."

"Got it," she said. "I'm turning into a real wino."

"We prefer the term wine connoisseur," Chagny said, appearing seemingly from nowhere.

"Oh, hi," Christine said. "I liked the wine."

"Thank you," Chagny said. "Are you enjoying the tour?"

"Yes, very much."

The tour group caught up with them and they stepped away to let the group up to the tasting table.

"Can I have some wine?" the Oklahoma boy asked.

"No, of course not," his mother answered.

"That French girl has some," he said, pointing at Christine.

"She works here."

"If you'll excuse me," Chagny said to Christine.

Chagny began working the room. Raoul took Christine by the hand and led her through the growing crowd. She suddenly flinched and looked over her shoulder.

"What's wrong?" Raoul asked.

"My butt just got groped again."

"I'm sure it was just an accident."

"It was no accident. It was that little creeper."

The Oklahoma boy had a big smile on his face.

"Do you want me to beat him up, or throw him out?" Raoul asked.

"Nah, it probably made the little creep's day."

Raoul took another look, really wanting to do something.

"My butt sure is getting a lot of action since I've been here."

Raoul laughed.

"But by Americans," Christine said. "I thought it was French guys who were gropers."

"You've only been here a couple of days. Give it some time."

"Great," she said.

Christine was very impressed by the next stop on her private tour.

"Wow," she said as they stepped into the large room.

"This is the barrel room."

"I wonder why."

"This is where—"

"The barrels are." Christine finished his sentence.

He smiled. "We age the wine in oak barrels."

"How long?"

"A couple of years, depends on the wine."

"It's kind of empty. You need more barrels."

"Actually, we have warehouses for aging the wine. This is more for show. People rent this room for weddings, receptions, parties, dances, whatever. But there really is wine in the barrels."

"It's beautiful." She sang a few notes. "And the acoustics are pretty good, probably better with a lot of people in here."

"Wow, did you learn about acoustics at the conservatory?"

She nodded.

Raoul took a small bow and extended his hand. "Would you like to dance?"

"We don't have any music."

"We'll make our own music. It's been two years since I heard you sing." He took her into his arms, and they began dancing to imaginary music.

She sang "Je suis malade," and they danced, sweeping all over the floor. He wanted to pull her closer, but felt she needed room to breathe, and sing.

She was right, the acoustics were pretty good, and her voice easily filled the room. Neither of them noticed as the tour group slipped in quietly. They just kept dancing.

Toward the end, as the song became more intense, Raoul let her go and stepped back, giving her room to work. It was obvious from her performance that she had sung this song before on stage. This time she had only eyes for him, ignoring the growing audience.

She curtsied to him after she finished the song, and the tour group broke into enthusiastic applause. She seemed a bit embarrassed by the attention and curtsied again, this time to the audience. Raoul stepped up, bowed, and kissed her hand.

Chagny pushed his way through the group, shouting "Brava! Brava!" He kissed Christine on both cheeks. "Now everyone will expect such a performance when they tour the winery." He turned to the audience, extended an open palm toward Christine, and then bowed to her. She didn't know what to do so she curtsied again amidst continuous applause.

Raoul slipped his hand around her waist. "We'd better get out of here before they ask for an encore."

"Good idea," she said, as they headed for the door.

"Do you know what the words mean, or were you just singing it phonetically?" Raoul asked as they approached the motor scooter.

"Phonetically, but Alfonso translated it for me."

Raoul raised his eyebrows.

"Don't let it go to your head," she said. "I just think it's a really beautiful song."

"Yes, it is, very beautiful."

8

BIKINI BOY

After leaving the winery, Raoul took Christine on a whirlwind tour of Saint-Tropez and the surrounding area, including spectacular views of the Mediterranean from various vantage points. She even thought she recognized the little cove where she had lunch with Connie and her mom.

He let her have a hand at driving the scooter, in a remote area with no other traffic. She got along well enough by herself, but his weight behind her made for a rather wobbly ride. That was fine with her, as she much preferred riding behind him, so closely that she could feel his heartbeat, and no doubt he, hers, among other things.

They were on one of the narrow roads outside town when he slowed and turned through a gate. There was a house, much smaller than the Chagny estate, but quite charming.

"We've been summoned by Connie," Raoul said as they dismounted.

The door swung open, and Connie burst through, kissing Raoul on both cheeks, and then throwing her arm around Christine's neck, bending her over, practically choking her. "About time, bitch."

"Is this your house?" Christine asked.

"It belongs to some friends. We always stay here."

"Cool."

"I love your dress," Connie said. "Well come on in, *mi casa* is *su casa*. Oh wait, that's Spanish, which I'm flunking."

The house was also much funkier than the Chagnys', and cluttered, with the living room serving as a temporary studio for Alexandra's art, which was scattered everywhere.

"Oh look," Christine said. "It's the winery." It was a watercolor of the

Chagny winery and a very good likeness indeed, sitting on a table, leaning against the wall.

"Your mom is pretty good," Raoul said.

"I guess." Connie turned to Christine. "He took you to the winery?"

Christine nodded. "Yeah, it was fun."

Connie partly covered her mouth and fake whispered, "He takes all his girlfriends there."

Christine gave Raoul a rather dirty look.

"I do not!" Raoul said. "Tell her I don't."

"Okay, he doesn't, just the hot ones."

Christine was still unsure. Raoul was not amused.

"Okay, okay," Connie said. "I'm kidding."

Connie looked at Christine. "Raoul should know that by now. We've known each other forever."

"What's this one?" Raoul asked, changing the subject, as he reached to lift a cloth that was covering a painting on the easel.

"Oh no!" Connie said, reaching out to grab his hand. "You can't look at that one. Mom doesn't like people to see her work-in-progresses or whatever, especially this one."

"Sorry," Raoul said, dropping the cloth.

"Come on," Connie said, "we're having lunch on the patio. Patio's the same in English, Spanish and French, right?"

"I think so," Raoul said.

"Is it time for lunch already?" Christine asked. "I'm still stuffed from breakfast."

"We had a big breakfast," Raoul said.

"It was wonderful," Christine added.

"Great, that works out well," Connie said. "We're having a light lunch, some kind of salad thingy."

They stepped out onto the patio as Alexandra placed a large bowl of very exotic looking salad on the table.

"Oh hi," Alexandra said, followed by a lot of double-cheek kissing. "Sit down, sit down."

"It looks great," Christine said. "I'm going to get so fat while I'm here."

"We'll go jogging later," Connie said.

They all sat down and dug in.

"How are your mom and dad, Raoul?" Alexandra asked.

"Fine," Raoul said.

"We'll have to have them over for dinner, and Christine and Zoe, of course, but I need to clean up my mess first. I get caught up in painting and scatter my stuff everywhere. Connie is no help. Do not go into her room."

"It's not that bad," Connie said.

Lunch was good, Christine thought. The salad was heaped full of little shrimps. She watched the others for a moment before tearing off a piece of bread and dipping it in a bowl of olive oil. A strange concept, but rather tasty.

"I'll help with the dishes," Christine said after lunch.

"Oh, don't bother," Alexandra said. "We'll just put them in the sink, and I'll get them later."

"Are you sure?"

"She's sure," Connie said.

"Well, I guess I'll be going," Raoul said.

"Where are we going next?" Christine asked.

"Oh, you're staying here, with Connie," Raoul said.

"I am?"

"Didn't she tell you?" He turned to Connie. "I thought you two had this all worked out."

"We're going shopping," Connie said.

"We are?"

"And doing girl stuff."

Christine looked at Raoul, a bit confused. "You said you had the day off."

"I have errands for my mom. I'll see you tonight. Go do your girl stuff."

There was more double-cheek kissing.

"Goodbye, Mrs. Cummings," Raoul called out to the kitchen. "Thanks for lunch. It was delicious."

"Okay, spill," Connie demanded immediately after closing the door behind Raoul.

"Spill what?" Christine said.

"Did you get lucky last night, or maybe this morning?"

"Lucky?"

"You know."

"I know what?"

"Sex, bitch, do I have to spell it out?"

"Ew!"

"So that's a no?" Connie asked.

"That's a no."

"Did you at least make out, or get some clothes off?"

"We went swimming, so I guess we got some clothes off."

"Topless?"

"He was. I had on a bikini. He was in the pool when I got there."

"And?"

"And what?"

"Did you make out?" Connie kept pressing for details.

"Not really, we just sort of cuddled on a raft in the pool, and then after dinner he kissed me."

"With tongue?"

"No, well, not much, but it was nice."

"So, are you two an item again?"

"I don't know. Who cares?"

"I care. I haven't bagged a boy since I've been here, so I'm living vicariously through you and Raoul."

"Ew!"

They made their way back out to the table on the patio and sat down.

"I thought we were going shopping," Christine said.

"Later. Mom needs you for a few minutes."

"For what?"

Alexandra appeared, wearing her smock and beret. "Swap seats. I need Christine over here."

"What's going on?" Christine asked.

"Mom's painting you."

"She is?"

"She started it yesterday at the cove but needs to do some more work on your face, or something."

"Okay, I guess." Christine was uncertain. "What do I do?"

"Just sit and talk," Alexandra said, moving her easel onto the patio. "Pretend I'm not here."

"So those boys on the yacht yesterday were hot, weren't they?" Connie said. "Who knew group sex could be so much fun?"

Christine was stunned. "What? Mrs. Cummings, we didn't do any such thing."

"She's kidding, Christine."

"Oh, okay," Christine said, and then smiled. "Oh, okay. I get it. You said to pretend you're not here."

The girls chatted and giggled while Alexandra painted. Christine occasionally looked over in her direction, somewhat self-consciously, and then the giggling resumed.

They were finally dismissed by Alexandra, but Christine was still not allowed to see the painting.

CONNIE PARKED HER motor scooter in what Christine was convinced was not even a parking space, but Connie said it was okay, and they scooted across the street into a trendy boutique.

"They have the coolest shit," Connie said as they entered.

"What are we shopping for?"

"Bikinis."

Connie looked around. The place was deserted.

"Do you need a new one?" Christine asked.

"Not me, you."

"I didn't bring any money," Christine said. "Well, I did, but I left it at the house. I wasn't planning on going shopping."

"No problem, Raoul is paying."

"He is? Wait, what's going on?"

Connie started browsing.

"He had the whole day planned, breakfast, the winery, the tour, lunch and then he was going to take you shopping for a bikini."

"So why isn't he here?"

"I told him it would be weird for a boy to go bikini shopping with a girl."

"What would be weird about it?"

"Nothing, but he went for it. Boys don't like to shop, but I do. Trust me, honey. I'm doing you a favor."

Connie picked up a bikini. "Here, try this one on."

"It's kind of skimpy."

"Which is why you don't want him here today," Connie said.

"I don't?"

Connie followed Christine into the dressing room, which really wasn't big enough for two people.

"Oh, sorry," Connie said, backing out.

Christine closed the curtain, what there was of it.

"Why don't I want Raoul here?"

"You want to save the big reveal for tomorrow, at the beach."

"The beach?"

"We're going to the beach tomorrow. Raoul will be there. You need a suit that stuns, a bikini that bedazzles."

"How do you know Raoul will be there?"

"We talk."

"How do you know I will be there?"

"It's all arranged, just roll with it."

"Who else is going to be there?"

"Zoe, the Chagnys. That's about it. Just one boy, and he's yours, but I'll manage. Maybe Zoe and I can bag a couple of college boys, or Russians."

"Russians?"

"Saint-Tropez is crawling with Russians this time of year."

Christine stepped out, wearing the bikini.

"That's hot," Connie said. She looked around. "I don't think there's anybody here. We should just grab a bunch of bikinis and bounce."

"Please don't. I'd have to chase you down and drag you to the *gendarmes*." It was a male voice, with a bad French accent. Connie whirled around.

"Do you work here?" Connie asked.

"Yes," the guy said.

"I was expecting a girl."

He shrugged. Both girls stared. He was tall and handsome, dark hair, with that little bit of beard stubble that looked so sexy, especially on Europeans, but probably scratched when you made out.

Christine, suddenly feeling almost naked, fidgeted.

"That suit's not for you," the guy said.

"It's not?" Christine asked, looking down at herself.

"No, try this one. It suits your body better. You're very slender, petite, as the French would say."

"Everybody says petite," Connie said.

"But very nice *lolos*," he said, looking at Christine.

"Nice what?" Christine asked.

"Tits," Connie said.

Christine's hands immediately covered the objects of discussion.

"You're kind of rude," Christine said, "and your accent is like, totally fake. You're not even French."

"You got me," he said, dropping the fake accent. "I'm from New York."

Christine reached for the bikini. "Give it to me. I'll try it on."

He handed her the bikini and she headed for the dressing room.

"Do you really work here?" Connie asked.

"I'm just watching the store for Colette."

"Who is Colette?"

"She works here."

"Where is she?" Connie asked.

"She had, how do you say, a rendezvous."

"Connie, can you come in here a minute?" Christine asked from behind the curtain.

Connie stared at the guy for a moment, then took a few steps and pulled back the curtain of the dressing room.

Christine shrieked. "What are you doing?"

"You said come in."

Connie stepped in and closed the curtain.

"I didn't say rip open the curtain so that creeper could see me naked."

"He's not looking."

"Yes he is," Christine said, tugging at the curtain.

"Whatever."

Christine held up the bikini and showed Connie the price tag. "This is way too expensive."

"That's francs, not dollars."

"Oh. So how much is it?"

"I don't know. I'm no good at math. Divide that by four or five or something."

"Oh, okay," Christine said, then did the math. "It's still too much."

"Chill. You're dating a rich kid. Get used to it." She peeked out through the curtain. "Now he's looking."

"Well then close the curtain!" Christine said. She turned around as she wiggled into the new bikini.

"He is smoking hot. How old do you think he is?"

"I don't know, nineteen, twenty, maybe."

"Just right."

"Oh no. You are so not going to hit on some guy you met in a bikini store."

Connie shrugged. "Why not?"

The guy waited for them to come out. "Perfect. That is the suit for you, mademoiselle."

"Do you really think so?" Christine asked, looking down at herself.

"Trust me, I'm a guy."

She turned and looked at a full-length mirror. "It is kind of hot and it fits really good."

"You should definitely get it," Connie said.

Christine went back to the dressing room.

"What brings you to Saint-Tropez?" Connie asked.

"Same as you, I guess," the guy said.

"Boys?"

He smiled. "Girls."

Connie browsed suits while Christine changed.

"I think I'll try this one on," Connie said.

"It's nothing but strings," he said. "How could it not fit?"

"You make a shitty salesgirl."

Connie went into the dressing room as Christine came out carrying her new bikini.

"Okay, I'll take this one," Christine said, handing him the bikini.

"Christine is a pretty name, very feminine."

"How do you know my name?"

"I heard the other girl say it."

"You were eavesdropping on us?"

"I work here, remember?"

"No you don't."

"Close enough."

"Whatever. We didn't see you."

"I'm like a ghost."

Connie came out, modeling a very skimpy string bikini.

"What do you think?"

"I think it doesn't leave much to the imagination," Christine said.

Connie whirled around.

"I can see your butt," Christine said.

Connie turned again.

"And the top barely covers your boobs."

"The top is adjustable," the guy said.

Connie looked down at the tiny little triangles covering her breasts. "That's okay, I won't be wearing the top much anyway."

"I hope you like it," he said, "because you'll have to buy it."

"Why?" Connie asked.

"You're supposed to keep your panties on when trying on a suit like that."

"A suit like what?" Connie asked as she turned her back to him and looked over her shoulder.

"One with a string that goes up your butt crack," he said. "What if someone else already tried it on with no panties?"

"Ew!" Christine said.

Connie went to change.

"Where are you from?" he asked.

"California," Christine said.

"What part?"

"Santa Monica."

"I haven't seen you there," he said.

"You said you were from New York."

"I'm bicoastal. My mom's in New York and my dad's in LA. I hang out on the Promenade when I'm in town."

Christine needed no further explanation. Many of the kids at both the conservatory and Ogden Hall were children of divorce and constantly shuttled back and forth. At least they were building up lots of frequent flier miles.

"I hang out on the Promenade a lot too," she said, and then added, "with my friends."

"Maybe I have seen you then." His eyes scanned her head to toe and back up again, pausing at her chest.

She looked at the dressing room, as if that would make Connie hurry. She was getting tired of small talk with this weird dude. The curtain was half-open, no doubt intentionally, she thought, and although Connie was completely nude, he wasn't even looking. He never took his eyes off Christine.

"Where do you go to school?" he asked.

"The Belen Conservatory," she answered before thinking about it.

"Is that like a reformatory?"

"No, it's a music school."

"What instrument do you play? No wait; let me guess, piano."

She shook her head.

"Violin?"

She hesitated. "No."

"Oboe, bassoon, drums?"

She shook her head.

"I give up."

"I sing."

She glanced again at the dressing room. Connie was getting dressed.

"Do you play an instrument?" Christine asked.

"I play a little guitar."

"You mean like a ukulele?"

He laughed. "No, I play a big guitar a little bit."

"I know what you meant," she said. "I was just messing with you."

Connie finally returned with the tiny string bikini in hand. "We'll take them both." She handed him a credit card.

"Raoul gave you his credit card?" Christine asked.

"No, he gave me cash. This is my mom's card."

They followed the guy to the sales counter, where he swiped the card. "Sign here." He put the two suits in a bag and handed it to Connie. "Come again soon."

"Do you have a name, or should we just call you Bikini Boy?" Connie asked.

"Erik," he said.

9

PAMPELONNE

TWO BEACH ATTENDANTS had six beach chairs set up with an umbrella and little table between each pair. Unlike the cheap, folding aluminum ones Christine had seen on the beaches in southern California, these were made of wood, very sturdy, and took two people to move. Like Connie said, she was dating a rich kid, so she may as well get used to it.

Chagny slipped a few bills to the two attendants, and the group staked out their territory and dropped their bags, the Chagnys, Zoe, Raoul and Christine. Connie took the end, where it was obvious she wasn't with Raoul, and she could have first dibs on hot boys passing by.

Christine looked around, surveying the beach and everyone on it. She was nervous but tried not to show it. Many of the females on the beach were topless, although some of them were face down, which she assumed didn't really count—girls did that everywhere. Some were wearing tops, and some even one-piece suits. Clearly topless was optional, so she waited for the ladies in her own group to take the lead. She decided to apply sunscreen, delaying the decision, and peeled off her T-shirt and shorts.

"Nice bikini," Raoul said. "Is it new?"

"You know it is, and thanks." She kissed him on the cheek. "I really like it."

"You're welcome. It looks good on you."

"That's what the guy at the bikini store said." Maybe that would make Raoul just a little bit jealous.

Connie was the first to shed her top, and she didn't even bother to do it unobtrusively, but standing up on full display, while looking around, casually checking out the action. She stayed on her feet to apply sunscreen, slowly, sensuously, it seemed to Christine, like an R-rated movie.

Christine watched both Raoul and his dad to see their reaction. It wasn't much—nothing at all from the count—but Raoul took a good look. She assumed he had seen Connie topless before, but he was a teenage boy after all, and could not help but look. At least it was just a glance. Connie had nice boobs, Christine thought. It would be hard for a boy to not look. Zoe and Hannah were next, almost simultaneously.

Christine felt her face flush. She had run through it over and over in her head, but the moment of truth had come. It wasn't just girls this time. There were boys, and men, all around. This was a major deal, she felt, especially with Raoul. Other than Raoul and his dad, she didn't even know any of the other guys within eyesight and would probably never see them again, so they didn't count.

"Do my back," Connie said as she spread out on the beach chair.

Christine eagerly accepted the bottle of sunscreen as it delayed her decision by at least a couple of minutes. She glanced at Raoul, who was adjusting an umbrella, and then sat down on her own beach chair and went to work on Connie's back. When finished she slapped Connie on the butt and said, "All done."

"Thanks."

"Do you want me to do your back?" Raoul asked.

"Sure," Christine said.

Connie turned her head so she could watch.

Christine handed the sunscreen over her shoulder to Raoul. Her first instinct was to lie face down and just untie the strings on her back—standard procedure on non-topless beaches—everybody did it, no big deal. But caught up in the moment, she suddenly decided to take her top off and then lie face down. That would seem natural, she thought. Raoul might get a little glance as she lay down, but it would be quick, and she could still stall off the inevitable reveal.

Christine swept her hair up off her neck with both hands and held it over her head. "Can you untie me?"

She thought this would be good strategy, forcing him to make the decision. Would he untie just the strings around her back, assuming she would keep the top on, while not leaving a tan line, or also the strings around her neck, causing it to fall off completely?

Raoul didn't speak, but she felt his hands untying the strings on her back.

The strings fell to her sides. He paused. She held her breath. Connie stared, clearly realizing what was going on.

Christine held her hair up as Raoul untied the strings around her neck. The bikini top fell into her lap. Connie grinned. Christine didn't even think to look to see if anyone else was looking. She dropped her hair, picked up the top and deposited it on the table, and then lay face down in one smooth motion. She turned her face away from Raoul, preferring to imagine his reaction, or maybe to hide her embarrassment. She wasn't sure if Raoul caught a glimpse or not. Connie watched, but didn't speak, and Christine was thankful that she somehow managed to hold her tongue and not make some snide comment.

Christine felt Raoul's hand on her back. It felt nice. His hands were much larger and stronger than Connie's, although it did seem he was trying to be gentle. She wanted to purr but restrained herself. She didn't want it to stop. It didn't. After finishing her back, he went to work on her legs, something she had not expected—surely he had seen her doing them herself. She did not protest. Maybe she had missed a spot or two. He started with her feet. She debated over whether to spread her legs as he worked his way up. Would that come off as an invitation? No, she decided, it would come off as practical, allowing him to spread the lotion between her thighs. After not nearly enough time had elapsed, he slapped her lightly on the butt and said, "All done."

"Well played," Connie whispered.

Christine smiled. It was well-played indeed.

"Do you want to do my back?" Raoul asked.

"Checkmate," Connie said.

Christine turned her head and looked at Raoul. "Okay."

She waited for him to lie down. Even if he kept his head turned toward her, he wouldn't be able to see everything all the time; or at least she didn't think he could, but he would get a better view than he already had.

He made no move to lie down. He just sat there, looking at her, smiling, waiting, no doubt anticipating.

"Oh well," she said. She sat up and swung her legs off the beach chair. She tossed her hair over her shoulders, extended her hands, palms up, and let him have a good long look. She even remembered to sit up straight and arch her back—a girl wanted to look as good as possible at times like this.

He looked, of course, much more than a glance, and then smiled. Then he looked right into her eyes, holding up the bottle of sunscreen.

No one else noticed, at least as far as Christine could tell. Chagny was immersed in his cell phone, Hannah and Zoe in their paperback books. People passing by just kept passing by, oblivious to the teenage rite of passage just yards away.

Raoul finally lay face down on the beach chair and Christine went about her task. She quickly noticed that boys had much more acreage than girls. Luckily this one wasn't too hairy.

When she finished with the sunscreen she slapped him on the butt, very hard, definitely not just a love tap. It was loud enough to get Zoe's attention.

"Ouch!" Raoul said.

Zoe looked for a moment, shook her head, and then went back to her book.

"All done," Christine said.

"Thanks."

She lay back on the lounge chair and replenished the sunscreen on her front as Raoul tried to watch without being too obvious.

They sunned for a while and Christine was surprised at how comfortable she was. After the initial reveal Raoul didn't really look at her any differently than if she were wearing a top. As Connie had said, once the boys had a good look, it was no big deal.

Connie sat up. "I think I'll take a dip." She stood, looked out at the water, and then turned back. Christine noticed that her back was arched. "Anyone want to come?"

Raoul looked at Christine, who gave no indication one way or the other. "Maybe later," Raoul said.

Connie scurried off toward the water.

Chagny stood and took a step toward Raoul. "Your friend is quite the exhibitionist, isn't she?"

"Yes, she is," Raoul said.

Hannah wrapped herself in a sarong.

"We're going up to the club," Chagny said. "Will you join us?"

"No, we'll hang here," Raoul said.

Chagny and his wife strolled away toward the club, arm in arm.

"He was talking about Connie, wasn't he?" Christine asked.

Raoul laughed and nodded.

"She seems to relish attention," Zoe said.

"We need to find her a boy," Raoul added.

"I think she's already working on that," Christine said.

Connie didn't land one and after a few minutes came out of the ocean, shoulders back, hips swinging. She stopped just in front of them and wrung out her hair. Then she plopped down on the chair.

"How was it?" Christine asked.

"Great," Connie said. "You should try it."

Christine looked at Raoul.

"It's up to you," Raoul said.

"Let's go in," Christine said.

Christine stood up, trying not to be an exhibitionist. Raoul took her hand, and they ran into the water.

They swam and splashed and played and Christine felt not a bit self-conscious. Raoul grabbed her and tossed her and picked her up by the butt. She wrapped her legs around his waist, her arms around his neck and they hugged, cheek to cheek, breast to breast, and it was wonderful. She felt a million miles from Santa Monica. This was a different world, and she loved it.

Raoul adjusted the umbrellas when they returned. The noon sun was the worst, he explained, and they huddled in the shade, talking, laughing.

"Well, that wasn't so bad," Christine said.

"What?" Raoul asked.

"Going topless."

"I kind of liked it."

"I'll bet you did."

"She's been obsessing about it," Zoe said.

"No, I haven't," Christine said.

"Oh, really?" Zoe asked.

"Okay, so I have, just a little bit, but this stuff is all new to me."

"So, you liked it?" Raoul asked.

Christine feigned disinterest, shrugged, and nodded. "It's okay."

"Told you," Connie said.

Raoul reached for his cell phone and read a text message. He stood up and walked a few steps out toward the water, waving his arms over his head. He checked his phone again and then sat back down.

"What was that?" Christine asked.

"There are some friends on that boat out there. They're coming to join us."

"Any boys onboard?" Connie asked.

"Yes, actually, there are."

Christine looked at the boat, a sleek, modern cabin cruiser. It was moving very slowly, but suddenly picked up speed. "It looks like they're leaving."

"They're going to tie up at the pier, down there," Raoul said, pointing.

Christine wondered about the protocol for the impending arrival of Raoul's friends. After all, boys were specifically mentioned. What boys? They couldn't be boys she knew. Strangers would be better anyway, like the guys walking past on the beach, barely noticing her, and why should they? There were topless girls all over the place. She felt anonymous enough. Nobody was staring, not even Raoul. She lay back on the beach chair, closed her eyes, and dozed off.

"Tits!" Raoul shouted.

Christine jumped and instinctively covered her breasts. Connie made no such effort.

"Shaggy!" a boy shouted as a small group of people approached.

Raoul grabbed the boy in a bear hug, and then turned to Christine. "Christine, this is Frankie Titshaw, but I call him Tits."

"And I call him Shaggy," Frankie said, as he collared Raoul and gave him a noogie.

Frankie was tall and gangly, rather average looking, Christine thought, much like most of the boys she knew. She debated over whether to stand, but Frankie leaned over to shake her hand. "Pleased to meet you, Christine."

She had no choice but to extend her hand, exposing herself. She decided to go for it, released both arms, and shook hands. Frankie also looked, but it wasn't quite as weird as Christine had expected.

"This is my girlfriend, Meg," Frankie said.

Meg could not be described as beautiful, but the alabaster skin, thick, dark brown hair and sparkling green eyes gave her a certain appeal. She was slender, narrow hips and small breasts, and she moved gracefully. Christine glanced down at her feet—she stood like a dancer, with one foot at a right angle to the other.

Meg threw out her arms for a hug and Christine decided it would be less awkward if she stood.

"Hi!" Meg said. "I've heard so much about you. I just know we will be the best of friends."

"This is my friend, Connie," Christine said.

There was more handshaking, and more staring at breasts, which didn't bother Connie one bit.

"Christine?" It was a familiar voice, a man's voice, and Christine suddenly froze and immediately knew that her face had turned fire-engine red. Her hands flew up to her face to cover her embarrassment, and her arms conveniently covered her bare breasts, or at least somewhat.

"Oh, no!" she said.

It was Johnston Caldwell, standing right in front of her. He didn't offer his hand to shake; ordinarily she would have hugged him without a second thought, but she was almost naked, wearing nothing but half of a bikini on her bottom and a look of abject horror on her face, standing there paralyzed.

She finally took a step and leaned forward, her arms firmly planted on her chest and face. He reached out and hugged her. She buried her face in his chest and closed her eyes, hoping it would all just go away. She felt his hands on her bare back. He didn't squeeze or pull her closer; his fingers touched her only lightly, but it was weird enough.

He leaned down and whispered. "This is as embarrassing for me as it is for you." He released her. She pulled away slightly and looked up.

"No, I'm pretty sure it's not," she said.

He smiled. "You remember my wife."

Christine backed away a bit more and looked at Mrs. Caldwell.

"How are you, ma'am?"

"Fine," Mrs. Caldwell said, thankfully neither offering her hand or a hug, and more importantly, changing the subject. "I absolutely loved your concert, Christine. Well, I love all of them, but there was something about this one. It was quite different for you, wasn't it?"

"Yes ma'am, but it was fun."

"This is my son," Johnston said, "Erik," putting his arm around Erik's shoulder.

Christine and Connie stood and stared. Erik smiled and shook hands with Connie, unabashedly on display, with a wicked grin on her face.

"Nice bikini," Erik said.

"Thanks," Connie answered.

He offered his hand to Christine. Without thinking, she shook hands, and only then realized that she had also lowered her left hand and was quite exposed. Erik looked and smiled.

"Hannah and Alain are at the club," Zoe said.

"I guess we'll go up," Johnston said, taking his wife's arm.

"Nice lolos," Erik said.

Christine pulled her hair over her shoulders, covering herself somewhat. She took a step toward Raoul, and he put his arm around her shoulder.

Meg peeled off her T-shirt. She wasn't even wearing a bikini top. She and Frankie took the Chagnys' chairs.

"Let's get another chair," Raoul said.

"No need," Erik said. "I'll just sit here." He sat on the sand directly in front of Christine's chair.

Raoul sat down and lay back.

"So, what was that all about?" Connie asked.

"All what?" Christine replied.

"With that old guy."

"That old guy is the headmaster of my school."

Connie burst out laughing. "Awkward!"

"Ya think?"

"I am telling this story like, forever," Connie said. "That is priceless."

Christine and Connie sat down and lay back. Erik leaned back on his hands, eyes on Christine.

"I didn't know Mr. Caldwell had a son," Christine said.

"He does," Erik said.

"Obviously."

"How old are you?" Connie asked.

"Seventeen."

"You look older."

"It's not the years. It's the miles."

Connie watched him for a moment, but he never took his eyes off Christine. Suddenly feeling quite naked, Christine sat up and pulled on her T-shirt.

"Let's go in," Connie said, standing and taking a step toward Erik. He didn't budge. She leaned down, cupped a hand beside her mouth, and whispered into his ear, "She's taken."

Erik turned his head, her bare breast right in his face. He smiled and stood. "Anybody else want to come in, Meg, Tits, Meg's tits?"

Frankie and Meg took him up on the offer and they all followed Connie into the water.

"That dude's weird," Christine said.

"Who?" Raoul asked.

"Erik."

"It was just a joke."

"Do you know him?"

"We met once at the ranch in New Mexico. He's Tits's cousin."

"Could you not call him Tits?"

"Okay, he's Frankie's cousin. He seems okay, a little wild. He's perfect for Connie. If they get married their kids will be holy hell."

Christine laughed. "But beautiful."

"He's the black sheep of the family," Zoe said, looking up from her book.

That got the attention of Raoul and Christine, who immediately turned and waited for more.

"Well, spill," Christine said.

"He's from one of Johnston's previous wives. I don't remember which one. Erik lives with her in New York, but from time to time she ships him to LA. He's been kicked out of private schools on both coasts. Military schools won't even take him."

"What's wrong with him?" Christine asked.

"Is he dangerous?" Raoul asked.

"Not that I know of," Zoe said. "I think it's mostly 'crimes against property,' as the cops would say, along with alcohol, probably drugs, and all the other rebellious teen things."

"How do you know all this?" Raoul asked.

"I stayed in touch with Johnston after I graduated from the conservatory. We mostly talked about music, but sometimes he talked about Erik. He didn't know what to do with him."

"We met him yesterday," Christine said.

"You what?" Raoul asked, surprised.

"At the bikini store."

"What was he doing in a bikini store?" Raoul asked.

"That's where the girls are," Zoe said.

"He said he was watching it for the girl who worked there," Christine said. "Maybe he kidnapped her and had her tied up in the back room. He sold us the bikinis."

"I hope Connie's was half price," Zoe said. "She didn't get very much bikini."

Christine laughed.

"I like it," Raoul said.

Christine slugged him. "You would."

10

HYMNE À L'AMOUR

Christine and Raoul strolled, hand in hand, along the waterfront, following the Chagnys and Zoe. The gentlemen wore jackets and ties, the ladies, summery dresses. Christine felt all grown up.

Lights from boats bobbing in the marina glistened on the dark water. There were a lot of people out on a beautiful summer night, and a lot of activity in the marina and around the clubs and restaurants. They could hear music up ahead.

There were several people waiting for tables as they entered the chic restaurant. Johnston spotted the Chagnys and made his way through the crowd.

"Have you been waiting long?" Chagny asked.

"No, we don't even have drinks yet. The place is packed."

"I don't think it will be much longer."

"Christine," Johnston said. "Do you have a minute?"

"Sure," she said.

Johnston put his arm around her waist, and they stepped away from the group. "About the beach—"

Christine dropped her head and covered her face. "I am so embarrassed."

"Don't be. It was my fault. I didn't know you were going to be there, and you obviously weren't expecting me. It was a most unusual situation."

"Definitely. It was my first time topless on the beach, well, with boys around, and I wasn't expecting the headmaster of my school."

"It was a situation I don't often find myself in with a student."

"I hope not."

"Never, really, until now. I guess what I'm trying to say is, what happens in Saint-Tropez stays in Saint-Tropez. We will just pretend it never happened, and never speak of it again, especially at school."

Christine tapped him firmly on the chest with the palm of her hand.

"Okay, Johnston, works for me."

He smiled. "And I'll try to not be on the beach at the same time as you. I'm sure you and your friends would probably prefer to not have a bunch of old people around anyway."

"That's okay. I was just caught off-guard. We don't have to avoid each other, but it definitely stays in Saint-Tropez."

They exchanged cheek kisses and he returned her to Raoul.

"What was that about?" Raoul asked.

"School stuff."

Raoul was unconvinced.

A distinguished-looking, well-dressed Frenchman appeared from nowhere, bowed to Chagny, and they shook hands.

"Your table is ready, comte."

"Thank you, Rémy. It's good to see you again."

Rémy kissed Hannah on both cheeks, and then shook hands with Raoul. "You have grown so much, Raoul. You are becoming quite the young man."

"Thank you, sir." Raoul put his arm around Christine's waist. "This is my friend, Christine."

Rémy's elegant manner suddenly disappeared. He looked like he had seen a ghost. "This is Christine?"

Chagny nodded.

"Christine Daaé?" He stared at her, agape. "Your father was Viktor?"

"Yes sir," Christine said slowly, apprehension growing.

Rémy lunged forward, pushing Raoul aside, pulling Christine into his arms. He hugged her so tightly she could barely breathe.

He pulled back long enough to look at her face, then kissed her on the forehead and pulled her head into his chest. "Your father and I played together in the orchestra aboard a cruise ship. He was my best friend."

He finally released Christine, and now had her undivided attention.

"What times we had," Rémy said. "I loved him dearly. He wrote to me about you. He never lied to me, but he failed to fully describe your beauty."

Christine was embarrassed by the attention.

"But then, you have grown," he said. "If only he could see you now. It's been what, two years?"

"Yes sir."

"I didn't know for weeks that he had passed away. I was devastated by the news. I would have been there, of course, had I known."

"It happened rather suddenly," Chagny said.

"Yes, so I hear."

The rest of Johnston's party, along with Connie and her mom, gathered around.

"We promised each other that the survivor would play violin at the funeral," Rémy said. "I wished to die first, as I would have received the better performance."

"Raoul studied violin with him for a few weeks," Christine said.

"Ah, yes, Raoul," Rémy said, turning to Raoul. "He wrote me that you were his student. Such a small world."

"Yes sir," Raoul said. "He taught me a lot."

"What happened to his violin? He treasured it so."

"We buried it with him," Raoul said.

"Perfect," Rémy said. "Thank you, Raoul." He turned to Chagny. "A fine young man you have here, comte."

Chagny nodded.

"I am so sorry," Rémy said. "Pardon me for taking up your time."

"Not at all. We admired Mr. Daaé a great deal, and we think the world of Christine."

"Well, right this way."

Rémy showed them to their table, the best in the house, and the only one empty. He snapped his fingers, and servers with drink trays swarmed around.

A group of musicians, consisting of a pianist and a few strings, played Vivaldi on a small stage.

With several couples, the Chagnys, the Caldwells, Frankie and Meg, Raoul and Christine, it didn't take long to select seats. Connie made sure to sit between Christine and Erik. Alexandra and Zoe, then the only remaining singles, sat together.

Drinks were served, orders taken. The menu, of course, was in French, but Christine trusted Raoul to order for her, although he went out of his way to translate the entire menu and ask her preferences.

Christine, along with a few others, applauded when the music stopped. Rémy stepped up and spoke quietly to Marcel, the piano player. Marcel immediately looked in Christine's direction. He scrambled off the piano bench and faced the room. "We will take a short break," he said in French.

Rémy and Marcel stepped up to the Chagny table. Rémy leaned over and whispered to Chagny. Marcel waited in anticipation, eyes on Christine.

Chagny turned to Christine. "Christine, this gentleman would like to speak with you."

Christine was puzzled. Who was this guy?

"Mademoiselle Christine," Marcel said, and then bowed.

"Yes sir?" Christine said.

"Marcel does not speak English very well," Rémy said, "so I will translate."

Marcel spoke rapidly in French, pausing occasionally for Rémy to translate.

"My brother plays violin in the Los Angeles Philharmonic. His son, Arnaud, attends the Belen Conservatory."

Christine nodded and smiled. "Yes, I know Arnaud."

"When I visited Los Angeles, we attended a concert at the conservatory. Arnaud played. I was very impressed."

Christine waited to see where this was going.

Rémy struggled to keep up as Marcel gushed. "And then this beautiful child, with hair as golden as the Beauce wheat fields in autumn, and eyes as blue as the Mediterranean sky on a clear spring day, came down from the heavens to grace us with her presence, the voice of an angel walking on the Earth."

Tears formed in Christine's eyes.

"It was you, mademoiselle, it was you."

Everyone at the table stared in rapt silence as Marcel bowed.

"Thank you," Christine said.

Marcel and Rémy turned away and whispered in French. Rémy shook his head firmly.

"What is it?" Chagny asked.

"He asked if Christine could sing for us, and I told him no. I would not presume to ask."

"Well, it won't hurt to ask," Chagny said. "Christine, this gentleman, who is obviously enamored with your singing, has asked if you would like to sing for us."

Raoul nodded enthusiastically.

"Okay, sure," Christine said, and then smiled.

Marcel was thrilled. *"Merci! Merci!"*

"I will delay your orders in the kitchen," Rémy said, "so that you may enjoy Christine's singing undisturbed."

"Thank you," Chagny said.

Christine kissed Raoul on the cheek. "BRB."

Marcel rushed toward the stage. Rémy extended his arm, Christine took it, and he escorted her onto the stage as the other musicians regrouped. She huddled with the musicians and Rémy. Marcel nodded vigorously in agreement and sat at the piano. Rémy stepped off the stage and took up a good vantage point.

Other than the Chagny table, no one paid much attention as the musicians began playing. Everyone paid attention when Christine began singing "Hymne à l'amour."

There was loud applause when she finished the song. She smiled at the audience.

"Good grief," Connie said to Erik, whose eyes were on Christine. "She really can sing."

"You have no idea," Raoul added.

Next Christine sang "Lili Marlene," in French. Again, there was enthusiastic applause from the audience. Diners ignored their dinners, and waiters dared not move while she sang.

Raoul shouted "Brava! Brava!"

Christine smiled and started to leave the stage.

Erik stood and shouted, "Encore! Encore!" Others joined in.

Christine returned to the stage, leaned over, and spoke in halting French to Marcel. He nodded and began playing. Tears flowed in the audience as she sang "Non, je ne regrette rien."

After a standing ovation, Christine was finally allowed to leave the stage. Rémy, tears streaming down his face, kissed her on both cheeks, hugged her tightly, and then escorted her to her seat.

Christine sat down first, and then everyone else in the room.

A waiter poured wine for Raoul, and then looked at Chagny, who nodded. The waiter poured wine for Christine. Chagny watched as she picked up her glass, swirled the wine around, sniffed, took a sip, and tasted. He smiled.

Dinner was served, with an added flourish from the waiters, who were now convinced they were in the presence of a famous young American singer and her entourage. Diners frequently glanced in Christine's direction, amazed that such a sound had come from that young girl, who was now laughing and giggling with her friends like any other teenager.

"Christine, I understand you had a concert at your school, big band music," Alexandra said.

"Yes ma'am."

"I wish I had known. We would have been there. My husband and I like to support veterans, and we love music from the big band era."

"We may do it again. It was fun."

"My daughter has no idea what we're talking about."

"Band music?" Connie said. "I know what band music is."

Christine smiled.

"I should add that the whole thing was Christine's idea," Johnston said. "She pulled it together in a very short time."

"You go girl," Connie said.

"I had a lot of help," Christine said. "Everybody pitched in."

"That was amazing," Meg said. "I wish I could sing like that."

"Do you sing?" Christine asked.

"No, I dance."

"How many languages do you sing in?" Erik asked.

"I don't know," Christine said, "a few."

"Do you also speak them?" Erik asked.

"No, not really, a little bit of French. Raoul and Zoe helped me. My daddy made me study Italian, so a little more of that, but mainly I just learn the lyrics phonetically. It's not that hard."

"Which do you prefer?"

"Italian, definitely. It's such a beautiful language for singing, and there's a ton of stuff available, but I also like French."

"What about Spanish?"

"That too, but I haven't done much in Spanish. I guess I should, being in LA and all."

"At the conservatory we insist that the singers, all the students actually, study the English translations so they will understand what they are performing." Johnston said. "That reminds me, Christine, I had never heard 'Lili Marlene' in French. Where did you find the lyrics?"

"Youtube."

"But of course."

"Alfonso helped me."

"The song has an interesting history," Erik said. "It originated in Germany, a marching song, but the Allies co-opted it, first in German, and then Vera Lynn recorded it in English. That's probably the definitive version, or at least the most popular."

Christine looked at Erik. He might be weird, but the boy knew music.

"Wow," Connie said. "How do you know all that?"

"He's an encyclopedia of music, when he wants to be," Johnston said.

Erik continued. "The French version was recorded in 1941, after they had already surrendered, so they may as well have just used the German version."

Johnston glanced at Chagny, who was obviously not pleased, but holding his tongue.

"Well, enough music history," Johnston said. "Let's just celebrate good friends, good food and good wine." He raised his glass of wine.

"Hear, hear," Chagny said, raising his own glass. Everyone else followed suit and toasted.

Erik raised his glass. "And here's to Christine for an amazing performance. I didn't realize I was in the presence of greatness."

"Hear, hear," Johnston said as everyone raised their glasses.

Christine reached for her glass, but Raoul took her hand and whispered, "You don't toast yourself."

"Sorry, I didn't know," she said.

"That's okay," he said, holding her hand as he raised his own glass.

After the toasts, the table was cleared, and dessert was served. A waiter poured coffee for Christine.

"That's coffee, right?" she asked Raoul.

"Right."

"Do I have to dunk something in it?"

"No, it's dinner, small cup, remember? You can just drink it."

"Okay, good." She took a sip of coffee.

Chagny summoned a waiter and asked for the check. The waiter disappeared and Rémy soon stepped up and pulled Chagny aside.

"Your money is no good here tonight, comte."

"What do you mean?" Chagny asked, surprised.

"Christine has honored us with her incredible performance. I could not possibly expect to be paid as well."

"But we are so many. That's a lot of money."

"It is done. I will not accept payment. Did you see all the people with their portables? Christine's performance will be viral within hours. My restaurant will be famous. I will make plenty."

"You already make plenty," Chagny said, smiling.

Rémy shrugged.

"Very well," Chagny said. "As you wish."

"What was that about?" Hannah asked as Chagny sat back down.

"Apparently someone has paid for our dinner."

"Who?"

"Christine."

"Christine? How could she? This place is very expensive."

"She sang for our supper. Rémy refuses to accept any further payment. I'll send over a case of wine tomorrow."

"You'll send over more than one case, and of our best."

"Yes, dear, of course."

Christine paid no attention to the conversation. She was holding hands with Raoul, her head on his shoulder, as talk swirled around them, lost in her own world.

11

LA MALAGUEÑA SALEROSA

CHRISTINE AND MEG sat on the tailgate of a pickup truck parked at the Chagny winery, swinging their legs. Both wore shorts and T-shirts.

"Do you and Frankie go to school together?" Christine asked.

Meg laughed. "No, not hardly."

"What's so funny?"

"He's a rich kid from LA. I'm a poor kid from Santa Fe."

"Oh, so kind of like me."

"Really? I thought you were one of them."

"I was homeless when I met Raoul."

"Seriously?"

"Seriously. My mom died, and we lost our house in Chicago, and then Daddy and I went to LA so I could enroll in the Belen Conservatory. We met Raoul and Zoe the first day we were there, and the Chagnys have been really good to me ever since."

"How did you meet?"

"He rescued my scarf from the sea."

"Come again."

"My daddy and I were busking on the Santa Monica Pier. Daddy played the violin, and I sang. People gave us money. Anyway, my scarf came loose and blew away and Raoul jumped off the pier into the ocean, fully dressed in his school uniform, and got it."

"Wow. My story's not quite so dramatic. My dad split when I was little, and my mom works in the ticket office at the Santa Fe Opera. That's where I met Frankie. The Titshaws are big supporters of the opera. They have a ranch outside town."

Raoul and Frankie appeared, each carrying a case of wine. The girls cleared off the tailgate and the boys loaded the wine into the truck. Erik appeared, carrying two cases.

"We're just supposed to deliver three cases," Raoul said.

"And that's all we will deliver," Erik said, smiling.

Raoul nodded his head and they bumped fists. Raoul checked the cases. "Three cases of our best for Rémy and one case of table wine for us. Works for me."

"No sense in wasting expensive wine on a bunch of kids."

"Good thinking. And it's less likely to be missed."

"Let's roll," Erik said, and headed for the driver's door. Everybody else piled in the back, along with the cases of wine, sacks of groceries, coolers, blankets, and other gear.

They bounced along the winding roads, trying to keep everything, and everyone, from sliding around.

"So, Mr. Caldwell is your uncle?" Christine asked.

"He's like an uncle," Frankie said, "but he's really a second cousin or something. Mom keeps up with all that. My great-great-grandfather was Daniel Titshaw."

"He's the guy who founded the conservatory?"

"Yeah."

"Why is Johnston's name Caldwell?"

"His mom was Daniel Junior's daughter, his only child. He was killed in World War II. When she grew up, she married a guy named Caldwell. The marriage didn't last but she kept the name."

"Oh, right. Daniel Junior's the guy in the picture at the conservatory, in the uniform."

"Yes. And the picture next to it is the USS *Johnston*, the destroyer he was on when he was killed."

"Which is where Johnston got his name," Christine said, quite satisfied with herself.

"You got it."

"Well, that explains a lot. I always wondered about those pictures. No wonder Johnston jumped all over our World War II song thingy."

Christine pondered for a moment.

"So, your last name is Titshaw and that's why Raoul calls you Tits?"

"Yeah, and I get razzed about it constantly."

"Really, Tits, you get razzed about your name?" Raoul said.

"Screw you, Shaggy," Frankie said.

"Well thank your great-great-grandfather for the scholarship to his conservatory."

"You're welcome," Frankie said. "The old man would have thought it was money well spent. He had a thing for beautiful young opera singers."

"I'm not really an opera singer."

The pickup slowed down and stopped. Erik leaned out the window. "Is this it?"

Raoul stood up and looked over the cab. "Yeah, this is it." He sat back down as Erik pulled through the gate. Everybody waited in the truck as Erik knocked on the door to the house.

Alexandra answered the door. "She's in her room selecting the proper outfit. Tell everybody to come in. It could be a while."

Erik turned around, "She's not ready. Everybody out."

The kids swarmed into the living room / art studio.

"Does she need to bring anything?" Alexandra called out as she went into the kitchen.

"No ma'am," Christine said. "We stopped at the store. We have everything."

Erik lifted the cloth covering a painting on an easel. "Wow, cool."

Christine gasped and covered her mouth.

"Oh no!" Alexandra said, rushing into the room. "I didn't mean for anyone to see that just yet."

Connie stepped in. "What's wrong?" She saw the painting. "Oh shit!"

It was an oil painting, at the little cove, with the sailboat in the background. Connie lay face down on a beach towel. Christine sat beside her, leaning back on her hands, looking out at the sea. Both girls were topless.

Alexandra grabbed the cloth and covered the painting. "I'm so sorry, Christine. I wanted you to see it first, before I decided what to do with it. I shouldn't have painted it, but the composition was perfect, the light was perfect, the subject was perfect, the mood was perfect. I just couldn't resist. I'll burn it, or you can have it. Tell me what to do. I feel like such a shit."

"What's the big deal?" Erik said. "All the great painters painted nudes."

"It's beautiful," Christine said.

"Really?" Alexandra said. "You like it?"

Christine nodded her head. "Can I see it again?"

"Are you sure?" Alexandra asked.

Christine nodded. Alexandra pulled back the cloth and everyone took a good look, especially Erik.

"Wow, it is beautiful," Meg said.

"It would have probably been less perverted if it was my own daughter sitting up showing her tits and you were face down and unrecognizable," Alexandra said.

"Yeah, that would totally rock," Connie said. "You could paint my face over Christine's." She studied it for a moment. "But you'd have to make the tits bigger."

"Connie," Alexandra said. "Don't be such a bitch."

"Do you like it?" Christine asked Raoul.

"Of course. I love it."

"But what do I do with it?" Alexandra asked. "It's probably illegal in the states. We Americans are so uptight about such things."

"You could hang it in a gallery here in town," Frankie said. "Somebody will buy it."

"Yeah, some pervert," Meg said.

"I'll take it," Erik said.

"Like hell you will," Raoul said.

Alexandra pulled the cloth back over the painting. "Christine, you decide. And I really will burn it if you want me to. Just let me know."

"I'll think about it," Christine said.

"And you're absolutely sure you're not angry?" Alexandra said.

"No, not at all, just a little surprised," Christine said. "I wasn't expecting it, that's all. It really is beautiful, but I don't think I could take it home. They might not understand."

"There's a simple solution," Frankie said, leaning in for a closer look. "Now that I've had a good look, just paint a top on her."

Christine elbowed him.

"Why didn't I think of that?" Alexandra said. "I guess I got all worked up over nothing."

"You could give it to Mr. Caldwell," Connie said. "He could hang it in his office at school."

Christine laughed.

"Why in the world would he do that?" Alexandra asked.

"You had to be there," Connie said. "It was friggin' epic."

———

ERIK AND FRANKIE each held a case of wine as they stood in front of Rémy in the kitchen of his restaurant. The girls waited outside by the truck.

"I told your father I would not accept payment," Rémy said.

"It's not payment," Raoul said. "It's a gift."

Rémy leaned over and looked at the label on one of the cases. "A very expensive gift. This is one of your finest wines."

"Yes sir."

"Either you take it, or we drink it," Erik said, "and I like fine wine."

"In that case, I will accept it," Rémy said, smiling. "I will not be responsible for teenage drunkenness."

"Great," Frankie said as he put down his case. Erik followed suit.

"I trust you will thank your father on my behalf."

"Yes sir," Raoul said. "Of course."

The boys turned to go.

"Raoul, a moment," Rémy said.

"Yes sir?"

"A cruise ship will be in port in Cannes later this week. Some of Viktor's old friends are aboard, in the orchestra. They would like to meet his daughter. I suggested that we have a small concert, more of a jam session, maybe."

"Here?" Raoul asked.

"Outside. I'll speak to the mayor. We'll block off the street. It will be free. People will bring a picnic."

"I'll ask Christine."

"Ask me what?" Christine said as she stepped up.

Rémy kissed her hand.

"Some of your father's friends from his cruise ship days will be in town and want to meet you," Raoul said.

"Okay."

"And he wants to have a free concert, outside, in the street," Raoul said. "He didn't say, but I assume he wants you to sing."

Rémy shrugged.

"Sounds fun," Christine said. "I've been working the streets since I was a kid."

Raoul chuckled. Rémy was confused.

Christine smiled. "My dad and I performed on the streets. He played. I sang. People gave us money."

Rémy nodded, and then kissed Christine on both cheeks. He turned to Raoul, "And you will play violin."

"I don't have my violin with me."

"We will find you a violin. You were Viktor's student. You are one of us."

"He'll play," Christine said.

THE KIDS LUGGED coolers, wine, groceries, and gear down the hill toward the beach.

"You didn't tell us we had to scale a cliff," Frankie said.

"Suck it up, wimp," Connie said.

"We could have taken the boat," Erik said. He was carrying more than his share and had a guitar case slung over his shoulder.

"No problem," Raoul said, "we're nearly there."

"Looks familiar," Erik said when they reached the beach.

"It's where Connie and I had lunch with her mom," Christine said.

"Oh, yeah, the painting."

"You mean you actually looked at the background?" Connie said.

"Of course. I'm a connoisseur of fine art."

"Admit it," Frankie said. "You're a connoisseur of fine boobs."

"I am a boob man."

"Can we talk about something other than boobs," Christine said, "especially my boobs?"

"What are you going to sing for the concert, or jam session?" Erik asked.

"I don't know."

"You two should do a duet," Meg said.

"Yeah, right," Raoul said.

"The boy can sing, Shaggy," Frankie said, "when he feels like it anyway."

"Really," Christine said. "You sing?"

"Meh," Erik said. "Let's build a fire. I'm starving."

"He inherited his grandmother's talent," Frankie said. "We still don't know where the rest of the shit came from."

"My dad can be a dick," Erik said.

They gathered sticks, built a small fire, and formed a circle around it. Erik broke out the wine and filled plastic cups. They roasted wieners and made hot dogs, with funny-looking buns, but then they were in France.

Christine had worn a bikini under her shorts and T-shirt, the uniform of the day, every day, according to Connie. She wasn't exactly sure what Connie and Meg had on under their shirts and shorts, but neither took anything off. Maybe there was a different protocol after the sun went down. Whatever, it was fine with her.

"Raoul," Meg said, holding up her plastic cup of wine. "You're the expert here on wine. Is this the correct wine for hot dogs?"

"It'll do," Raoul said, "although my dad would probably turn up his nose."

"The way only the French can," Frankie added.

Christine laughed.

They ate and drank and laughed and cuddled and watched the sun go down. It was magnificent. Christine was entranced as Erik played several classical guitar pieces.

He stopped playing and sipped some wine. Connie clapped loudly. "That was great!"

"What's the name of that last song?" Christine asked.

"La Malagueña Salerosa," Erik said.

"Mariachis play it all the time in Santa Fe," Meg said. "I love it."

"Are there lyrics?" Christine asked.

"It's been covered hundreds of times, some with lyrics. I kind of like the Chingon version."

"What's that?"

"Tex-Mex group from Austin. They really kill it."

"Okay, let's hear it." She moved over and sat directly in front of him, far too close for Raoul's liking. Connie liked it even less.

Erik shrugged and played it again, more aggressively, and sang the lyrics.

"Can you teach me?" Christine asked when he finished.

"Can you hold a note for a really long time?"

"Longer than you just did."

"It's a love song. Written for a man to sing to a woman."

"I don't care. I sing boy songs all the time."

"She sang 'Nessun Dorma' for her conservatory audition," Raoul said.

"Yeah, I know," Erik said. "Dad told me."

"I guess it worked," Christine said. "I got in."

"If you really want to learn it, we can work on it later."

"Great."

"Listen to the Nana Mouskouri version. That's the one you want to sing. It's a lot slower and sexy as hell."

"Sing something from the concert at school," Raoul said.

"We don't have a band," Christine said.

"We have a guitar player," Erik said.

"I really wanted to sing 'I'll Walk Alone' but it got cut for time."

"Hit it," Erik said.

"Do you know it?"

"Dad has all that old shit on vinyl. Martha Tilton, right?"

"Impressive," Christine said.

"I like hers better than Dinah Shore."

"She had a big band. Can you play it on guitar?"

"You start and I'll follow."

Connie suddenly stood and announced, "I'm going in." She ripped off her T-shirt. There was no bikini top, of course. She peeled off her shorts, not much of a bottom either, then raced into the water with all male eyes following.

When the Connie show was over Christine began to sing and Erik soon came in on guitar. There was applause when the song ended.

"Are you going to perform in the concert?" Christine asked.

"I thought the concert is just guys who played with your dad," Erik said. "And you."

"You could play with me," Christine said.

Meg laughed.

"Oh wait," Christine said. "That didn't come out right."

Everybody laughed.

"You know what I mean," Christine said defensively.

"We'd have to rehearse," Erik said. "I was just winging it tonight."

"You should probably pick something you both already know," Raoul said, looking at Christine. "It would save a lot of rehearsal time."

"We'll have to rehearse either way," Christine said.

"You can come over to the house," Erik said, "and we can pick something out and run through it."

Raoul shot him a look, clearly not thrilled with the idea.

"I'm sure my dad will have some ideas," Erik said.

"Great," Christine said. "Do you do music, Frankie?"

"Not a bit," Frankie said. "I'll handle promotion. That's my thing."

"If you need a dancer, or a backup singer, I'm in," Meg said. "Otherwise, I'll help Frankie."

No one noticed that Connie had returned, dripping wet. "What are you guys talking about?"

"The concert, or jam session," Christine said. "Are you in?"

"I couldn't carry a tune in a bucket." She made no effort to pick up a towel or her T-shirt, which the boys appreciated. "I'll be in charge of the after-party."

Connie finally put on some clothes and the gang hauled up the hill to the pickup. Connie planted herself by Erik, with the others in the back.

Raoul put his arm around Christine and pulled her close, hoping Erik would see it. Christine put her head on Raoul's shoulder.

Connie scooted over close to Erik as he started the pickup.

Christine sang "Long Ago (And Far Away)" as they drove home.

12

LA ROMANCE DE NADIR

CHRISTINE AND RAOUL floated peacefully on a raft in the pool at the Chagny house, looking out over the Mediterranean.

"Yee Haw!"

Christine looked over her shoulder and then scrambled off the raft, knocking Raoul off in the process.

Jim Bob, wearing a Hawaiian shirt, knee-length shorts, and a cowboy hat, threw out his arms. Zoe stood nearby.

Christine plowed through the water like a Marine storming a beach, up the steps, and leapt into Jim Bob's waiting arms, throwing her legs around his waist, squeezing hard and kissing him repeatedly on the cheeks.

Jim Bob lowered her onto the pool deck, and she stepped back as Raoul came up out of the pool.

"Oh, I got you all wet," Christine said.

"That's okay, honey, I won't melt."

Jim Bob and Raoul shook hands.

"Is this boy treating you all right?" Jim Bob asked Christine.

She smiled and nodded her head. "Pretty good."

Jim Bob took a step back. "Good Lord girl, look at you, all grown up, boobies and everything."

"Don't look at my boobies." She hugged him again. "I didn't know you were coming."

"Well, I heard there was going to be a jam session with your daddy's old friends. I couldn't miss that now, could I?"

"How did you hear about it?" Christine asked.

"This boy here called me. He might be a keeper."

Christine looked at Raoul, impressed.

"That was some fancy airplane," Jim Bob said.

"Air France?" Christine asked.

"Air Shag Nay," Jim Bob said. "I think those Frenchies called it a Gulf-stream. I couldn't understand much of what they were saying, so I just put on my headphones and rocked out. Oh, and I drank a lot of their fancy beer."

Christine turned again to Raoul. "Your dad sent the jet?"

"It was in Los Angeles with some of our execs," Raoul said. "They just made a stop in Chicago to pick up Mr. Butrell."

"Jim Bob. Mr. Butrell was my daddy."

"Or you can just call him the redneck," Christine said.

"That works," Jim Bob said. "I brought your fiddle."

"My violin?" Raoul said.

"We landed in Paris. The suits got off and some guy brought your fiddle out to the plane and told me to bring it to—where the hell are we anyway, Sant Tropay? It's in the house." Jim Bob pointed over his shoulder. "I saw your daddy at the airport. He got on as I got off. Now that's the way to travel."

"He has meetings tomorrow in Paris," Raoul said.

"Are you staying with us?" Christine asked, hopefully.

"I don't know. I just showed up. I can sleep on the couch, just like old times, huh kid?" He pulled Christine close and hugged her again.

"Yeah," Christine said, "just like old times."

"Hell, I can sleep on that floaty thing there."

"We have plenty of beds," Zoe said.

"Well, I guess I better find one," Jim Bob said. "My ass is whipped."

"Jet lag," Christine said knowingly. "It's not as bad going the other way."

"I'm going to take a nap, then hit the beach. I hear they're swarming with nekkid girls."

"Just topless," Christine said.

"Wait a minute, you haven't been—"

Christine shrugged.

"Well, your daddy grew up in Sweden," Jim Bob said. "They hang out nekkid in saunas there, so I guess he wouldn't mind, or is that Finland?"

"What the hell is *he* doing here?" Raoul asked.

Everyone turned to look. Erik stepped out from the house onto the pool deck.

"Nobody answered the door, so I just came on in," Erik said. "I hope that's all right."

"Oh no," Christine said. "What time is it? We were supposed to rehearse."

"I'm early," Erik said. "No rush."

"Jim Bob Butrell," Jim Bob said, shoving his hand toward Erik.

"Erik Caldwell." They shook hands, eyeing each other warily.

"I'll go dry off and put on some clothes," Christine said, and then scampered toward the house.

"You look fine the way you are," Erik said, eyes following her.

"Rehearsing for what?" Jim Bob asked.

"The concert," Erik said.

"I thought it was a jam session," Jim Bob said.

"Whatever, Christine wants to rehearse."

"Did you know Christine's daddy?"

"No, but she asked me to perform. I think she wants to do a duet."

"You sing?"

Erik shrugged, "and play the guitar."

"Well, all right."

Raoul and Erik stared at each other for a moment. "I guess I'll wait for Christine in the house," Erik said.

"Why don't you just rehearse here?" Raoul asked.

"We have sheet music and stuff at the house," Erik said. "My dad has some ideas, and he can accompany us on piano."

"Zoe can play piano," Raoul said.

Erik shrugged and went into the house.

"What was that all about?" Jim Bob asked.

"I just don't like the idea of Christine being alone with that guy," Raoul said.

"Hell, boy, I wouldn't either."

CHRISTINE HELD ONTO Erik tightly as the motor scooter scooted through the hills. He was going much faster than both Connie and Raoul.

"Who is this Jim Bob character?" Erik shouted over his shoulder.

"A friend," Christine said.

"He's kind of old."

"I've known him all my life. He knew my mom and dad before I was born, in Chicago."

"What's he doing here?"

"He's here for the concert. He used to play gigs with my daddy."

"Long way to come for a concert."

"Raoul called him, so he came."

"He looks like a hick. Sounds like one too. What does he play?"

"Piano, guitar, trumpet, probably other stuff. He's pretty good."

"I would have never guessed."

"Wait till you hear him."

JOHNSTON SAT AT the piano, sorting through sheet music. "What about 'Caruso'?"

"Oh, yeah!" Christine said. "I sing that with Alfonso. I love it."

Erik looked at the sheet music. "It's Italian. Sounds like a lot of work."

"The girl does all the heavy lifting," Johnston said. "All you have to do is keep professing your undying love."

"I can do that," Erik said.

Mrs. Caldwell answered the door. It was Zoe and Jim Bob.

"What are you guys doing here?" Christine asked.

"I had forgotten we were meeting friends for drinks at the beach club," Johnston said. "So I called Zoe and asked her to come over and accompany you."

"Jim Bob Butrell," Jim Bob said, shaking hands with Johnston.

"Johnston Caldwell. You knew Mr. Daaé?"

"Oh yes, knew him well. The stories I could tell."

"I thought you were going to crash," Christine said.

"I was too wired from all that French coffee, strong stuff, so I tagged along. Zoe drove, and it's a good thing—those French folks drive like maniacs."

Zoe and Jim Bob followed the Caldwells to the door. "Thank you for coming," Johnston said.

"No problem," Zoe said. "They will be in good hands."

Zoe closed the door behind the Caldwells.

"What about this one?" Erik asked, starting a song playing on his phone. They listened for a few seconds.

"No way, cowboy," Jim Bob said.

"What's wrong with it?" Erik asked.

"She's not singing that with you," Jim Bob said.

"But '*je t'aime*' means 'I love you,' doesn't it?" Christine asked. "I sing love songs all the time."

"That ain't no love song," Jim Bob said. "It's a porn song."

"Do you speak French?" Erik asked.

"Don't have to. I've read the English translation."

"Erik, there are quite a few songs with *'je t'aime'* in the title," Zoe said. "Perhaps you meant to play the one by Lara Fabian. This is a different one. There's a big difference."

"Huge difference," Jim Bob said. "It was banned in Britain back in the day."

"Well, this isn't Britain, and it isn't back in the day," Erik said. "I think we should sing this one."

"And I think I'll drop kick your ass across the Mediterranean into a sand pile in Algeria," Jim Bob said.

Christine laughed.

"Are you going to listen to them?" Erik asked.

Christine nodded her head.

"Let's just do 'Caruso,'" Christine said. "It's a beautiful song, and it's okay, right? Alfonso translated it for me."

"Yes, that one would be okay," Zoe said.

"'Caruso' works for me," Jim Bob said. "Love it."

Erik and Jim Bob stared each other down as Zoe sat at the piano and began to play "Caruso."

Christine sang beautifully, and then Erik came in for his part.

"No, no, boy," Jim Bob said. Zoe stopped playing. "Sound off like you got a pair," Jim Bob continued.

Christine giggled.

"Do you love this girl or what?" Jim Bob said. "Sing it like you mean it."

"I don't want to overpower her," Erik said.

"You can't overpower her. She's just holding back because it's rehearsal. She'll blow you off the stage if you can't keep up. Zoe, take it from the top, please ma'am, and I'll show this boy how it's done."

Zoe took it from the top. Jim Bob waited patiently while Christine sang, then he boomed out the male part. Christine came back in, and they finished the song in each other's arms. He kissed her on the cheek.

Christine turned to Erik. "Like that."

"But without the kissing," Jim Bob said.

"That was going to be the best part," Erik said.

Jim Bob pulled out his cell phone. "I need to look something up on the Internet. Is this going to cost me three hundred dollars a minute or something?"

Zoe laughed. "Use mine. It's local."

She handed him her phone.

"Well, you kids rehearse 'Caruso,'" Jim Bob said. "I'll be out by the pool surfing the net."

Christine and Erik continued rehearsing, running through it several more times.

"That's more like it," Jim Bob said, coming in from the pool. "Let's take a break. You have any beer?"

"Do you want one, Zoe?" Erik asked.

"No thanks," Zoe said.

Erik went to the kitchen.

"I couldn't remember the name, but I finally found it," Jim Bob said. "I think it might work for you, honey."

Erik returned with two beers, handed one to Jim Bob and took a sip of the other.

"Well, let's hear it," Christine said.

"This is an old recording, prewar," Jim Bob said. "It has that plaintive quality that stuff had back then, but don't think you have to sing it that way. Do your own thing. It's in French, so that might appeal to the locals. This guy sang in clubs along the Riviera back in the thirties. That's where we are, right, the Riviera?"

"Indeed," Zoe said. "Who's the singer?"

"Tino Rossi."

"Ah, yes. Be still my heart."

"Well," Christine said, "are you going to play it or what?"

He played it. Within seconds Christine was transfixed.

"What do you think?" Jim Bob asked when it was over.

"I love it. I want it. It's mine."

"It's a dude," Erik said.

"So?" Christine said.

"Whatever floats your boat."

"It's Bizet," Zoe said. "From his opera, *Les Pêcheurs de Perles*."

"Yeah, that's it, *The Pearlfishers*. Who knew people fished for pearls?" Jim Bob said.

"I don't know the official name of the aria, but everybody calls it 'Nadir's Romance' or 'La romance de Nadir' in French." Zoe said.

"That's it," Jim Bob said.

"Do you have the lyrics?" Christine asked.

"Right here," Jim Bob said, showing her the phone. "We can print them out and Zoe can help you with the French." He turned to Zoe. "You speak French, right?"

Zoe smiled. "I speak French."

"Are the lyrics dirty?" Christine asked. "They can't be dirty. It's too beautiful."

"No, not at all," Zoe said.

"We have a computer and printer," Erik said. "I'll go print the lyrics. I assume you want the sheet music also."

"Yes, please," Zoe said, "at least for piano. We can get the rest later if we need it."

"Play it again," Christine said.

Jim Bob played it again. Christine closed her eyes and slipped into another world.

No one saw the Caldwells as they entered quietly. They stood and listened as Christine sang "La romance de Nadir," accompanied by Zoe on piano.

"Brava! Brava!" Johnston said as they applauded.

"Thank you," Christine said, lowering her head. "We're still working on it."

"Do you aspire to be a tenor when you grow up?" Johnston said.

"I just like singing boy songs."

"It was absolutely beautiful," Johnston said. "Where did you come up with it?"

"The redneck found it online."

"The redneck?"

"Jim Bob. My mom called him the redneck."

"You hardly have redneck tastes in music, Mr. Butrell."

"Jim Bob," Jim Bob said.

"Wait till you hear him play some shitkicker stuff," Christine said.

"Christine, language!" Zoe said.

"Oh, sorry. Wait, we're not in school, and what happens in Saint-Tropez stays in Saint-Tropez, right, Johnston?"

Johnston laughed, and then put his arm around Christine. "Right, Miss Daaé, and I do believe shitkicker is a legitimate genre of music."

"It's late," Zoe said. "We should be going. I'm sure Jim Bob is ready to find a bed. He just got in from Chicago."

"I'll give Christine a ride back," Erik said.

"She can ride with Zoe and Jim Bob," Johnston said.

13

POKING THE BEAR

CHRISTINE RAN SCREAMING down the hallway of the Chagny house, with Jim Bob, wearing nothing but boxers and a T-shirt, in hot pursuit. Raoul raced from the kitchen to investigate the cause of the commotion. Just before Christine reached him, Jim Bob caught her, scooped her up and slung her over his shoulder. She screamed and pounded on his back, but he wouldn't let her go.

"Do you want her?" Jim Bob asked.

"Nah, you caught her," Raoul said. "You keep her."

Jim Bob lowered Christine to the floor.

"Well, thanks a lot," Christine said to Raoul. She put an arm around Jim Bob's waist and her head on his shoulder. "I guess you can keep me."

"Love to, honey," Jim Bob said, "but you're too much woman for me, so I'll have to cut you loose."

"You'd better hit the shower," Christine said. "You need to go to rehearsal with Raoul."

"Are you saying I stink?"

"I'm saying you need a shower."

"Well, clear out, unless you want to take a shower with me."

Christine shrieked, covered her face, turned, and cleared out, with Raoul close behind.

"What was that about?" Raoul asked.

"It's a thing we used to do in Chicago."

"Take a shower together?"

"No! Ew! He used to sleep on our couch sometimes and in the morning,

I'd poke the bear and wake him up and he'd growl and roar and chase me down the hallway."

Jim Bob stared at the bowl of coffee on the table in front of him.

"It's coffee," Christine said.

"Where's the handle?"

"You get those at dinner."

"Do you want milk in it?" Raoul asked, holding a cup of milk.

"Hell no," Jim Bob said, covering the bowl of coffee. He picked up the bowl and sipped. "Damn, it's strong."

"You should have gotten the milk," Christine said.

"Nah, I'm tough," he said, taking another sip. "Did you ever notice that the closer you get to the equator the stronger the coffee gets?"

"Now that you mention it," Zoe said.

"And they always have to doctor it up with milk and sugar and who knows what else," Jim Bob said.

"Are you sure you don't want to go to McDonald's?" Zoe asked.

"Nah, I'm in France so I'll just eat whatever the Frenchies eat," Jim Bob said.

Zoe placed a saucer containing a croissant in front of him. Christine pushed a jar of jam and a dish of butter across the table.

"That's it?" Jim Bob asked.

"That's it," Christine said. "That's what the Frenchies eat for breakfast."

"I'm gonna need a couple more of them funny looking biscuits," Jim Bob said.

Christine showed him how to dunk a croissant in his bowl of coffee.

"Are you sure you'll be okay alone at the house?" Raoul asked Christine.

"I'll be fine. I'll work on my new song. I need the practice. Unlike you guys, I won't have the sheet music in front of me."

"I'm sorry my mom had other plans, and my dad had to go to Paris."

"Don't worry about it. I'm a big girl. I know where the kitchen is."

"Okay, but call me if you need anything."

Christine, wearing a bikini with the top untied, lay face down on a lounge chair by the pool, looking at a tablet computer, listening to the music, and singing along to "La romance de Nadir."

Erik slipped up quietly from behind, sat down beside her and lightly touched her thigh. She shrieked and sat up, clutching her bikini top, strings dangling.

"Sorry, I didn't mean to scare you," Erik said.

"Then why didn't you make some noise instead of groping me?"

He made no effort to turn away, so she did, and reached behind her back to tie the strings.

"What are you doing here?" she asked.

"Everybody else was at rehearsal. I'm not in the orchestra, so I thought I'd stop by."

She stood up, took a couple of steps, and turned to face him.

"How did you know I didn't go with them?" she asked.

"I saw them."

"What about Connie?"

"I saw her too."

"Where is she?"

"Putting up handbills with Frankie and Meg," he said.

"Why aren't you helping them?"

"I saw them. They didn't see me."

"How did you get in?"

"The housekeeper let me in."

"You're lucky she didn't call the cops."

"Why would she do that?"

"Do you often go into other people's houses and grope young girls?"

"I didn't grope you. I just tapped you, on the leg."

"You could have tapped me on the shoulder."

He shrugged. She picked up the tablet.

"Well, as long as you're here, we might as well rehearse."

"Or we could take a dip in the pool."

"You aren't wearing a swimsuit."

"I don't need one."

"Uh, yes, you do."

She walked toward the house. "Or you would, if we were going swimming, but we're not, so get in here and let's rehearse before Jim Bob gets back and drop kicks your butt across the Mediterranean."

He got up and followed her.

"I'm so scared," he said.

"You should be."

———

THEY REHEARSED FOR a while in the living room, both "Caruso" and "La romance de Nadir."

"Let's take a break," Christine said. "Are you hungry?"

"Yeah, we could go down to the beach club."

"Or we could just fix a sandwich here."

"You can order anything you want at the club. I'll charge it to my dad. Or you can charge it to Raoul's dad."

"I don't want to be gone when everybody gets back."

"Why not?"

"Zoe would be worried."

"Zoe or Raoul?"

"Zoe is my chaperone while I'm here."

"You could text her."

Christine headed for the kitchen. "Do you want a sandwich or not?"

"I guess it will have to do," he said, following her, "but only if you make it."

She fixed sandwiches and they sat at the kitchen table.

"How long have you been at the conservatory?" he asked.

"Two years."

"Do you like it?"

"It's okay. What about you?"

"I don't go there."

"I know, doofus. Where do you go to school?"

"Nowhere at the moment."

"Duh, it's summer. Where will you go in the fall?"

"Who knows? I think my parents have run out of options. I guess I'll go to public school in New York, or just blow it off and be a bum."

"Why don't you go to the conservatory?"

"It's a little late. I'm a senior, or will be."

"Why didn't you go when you were younger? You seem to be pretty good at music."

"Are you kidding? My dad is the headmaster."

"Oh yeah, I guess that would suck."

"This sandwich is pretty good."

"Thanks. I'm not much of a cook."

"Let's run 'Caruso' again."

"I think we've got it."

"One more time," he said. "I don't think we quite have the passion we're looking for."

They went back into the living room, turned on the music, and sang "Caruso" again. When they finished, he took her into his arms, and they looked into each other's eyes.

And then he kissed her.

She pushed him away, but he pulled her back and she didn't resist. She felt his powerful hands on her back, squeezing the air out of her lungs. He moved in to kiss her again, but she turned her head and tried to push him away. He held on.

She pushed harder. "There's a car."

He released her. She scrambled for the tablet, restarted the music, and immediately launched into "Caruso," staying a respectable distance from him.

"What's going on?" Raoul asked as he, Zoe and Jim Bob entered the house.

"We're rehearsing," Christine said, and then turned off the music.

Raoul sized up the situation. "In a bikini?"

"She was at the pool when I got here," Erik said. "She didn't know I was coming over."

"Why did you come over?" Raoul asked.

"To rehearse," Christine said. "I told you."

"Well, I think we have it, so I guess I'll bounce," Erik said.

Jim Bob eyed him warily as he walked away.

"I don't trust that boy," Jim Bob said.

All eyes were back on Christine.

"Good grief. We were just rehearsing. It's not like we were making out or something."

She stormed out of the room. Raoul started to follow. Zoe stopped him. "I'll go."

Christine's door slammed just as Zoe got there. Zoe knocked. "Christine, it's me."

"Go away."

"I'm coming in."

She opened the door and stepped in.

"Why is everybody getting all bent out of shape?" Christine asked.

Zoe sat on the bed.

"Do you know why Jim Bob and I came over to the Caldwell house yesterday?"

"Johnston had to leave, and we needed a piano player."

"He doesn't trust Erik with you."

"He what?"

"Erik has some problems."

"I thought you said he wasn't dangerous."

"He's not, as far as we know. He's been in fights with boys. We don't know that he's ever assaulted a girl, but we would rather you not be alone with him."

"Who's we?"

"Me, your guardians, his dad."

"He's just flirting."

"He's used to getting his way and has been with a lot of girls. He's older than you and a lot bigger and stronger."

"So is Raoul."

"I helped raise Raoul. If he treated girls the way Erik does, he'd be singing castrado."

Christine laughed. "I know he's weird and all, but Erik hasn't tried anything. Actually, he's been nicer to me than a lot of other guys."

"He's a charmer."

"You can say that again."

"But you are Raoul's guest. Maybe you shouldn't spend time with some other guy while you are here. Better yet, spend time with the whole gang, less chance of something happening you didn't plan on and that you'll regret later."

"We were just rehearsing."

"I know. I should have warned you earlier about Erik."

"Okay. I'll keep my guard up."

"I'm responsible for you while you're here. I promised the Valeriuses I would look out for you. Don't get me in trouble." She stood to leave. "Oh, you're going shopping tomorrow."

"I am?"

"Hannah insists on buying you a new dress for the concert."

"You said I should bring some dresses, so I did."

"She loves to shop, and her tastes are impeccable, and expensive. Take the dress. Don't disappoint her."

"Are you going with us?"
"No, I'm taking Jim Bob to the 'nekkid' beach."
Christine smiled. "Ooh, sounds like fun."
"I don't have to worry about him, do I?"
"Jim Bob? He's a big teddy bear."

14

THE CONCERT

The excitement was building as the shadows lengthened and the sun slowly sank. As promised, the mayor had blocked off the street in front of Rémy's restaurant. There were hundreds of people, locals and tourists alike, crowded around the makeshift stage, sitting on blankets and lawn chairs, and bobbing in boats in the marina. Children scampered and played. Young lovers kissed.

People brought picnics, both simple and extravagant, and plenty of wine. Rémy had a finger-food buffet set up outside his restaurant and was doing a brisk business, as were his competitors and the street vendors.

Backstage, Johnston made his way through the crowd to the kids. He shook hands with Raoul. "Good luck, Raoul. I'm looking forward to hearing you play again." He shook hands with Erik. "Son, I'm proud of you. Have fun out there." He hugged him. Then he took Christine by both hands. "Christine, I have absolutely no responsibility here this time so I'm just going to watch from the audience." They exchanged kisses on both cheeks. "I can't wait to hear it."

The sun's rays soon disappeared behind the hills and the streetlights came on. Scattered applause broke out as the small orchestra took the stage and began tuning up. Rémy made a speech, which went on far too long, about Viktor and how his friends had assembled here tonight in his honor, as well as thanking the mayor, Count Chagny, and various others, for arranging this free concert. "We are honored to have Viktor Daaé's beautiful young daughter, Christine, to sing with us tonight. Those of you who do not know her or were not among those lucky enough to be in my restaurant a few days ago when she sang for us, are in for a real surprise."

He bowed to the conductor, and took his position as first violin, next to Raoul. Zoe was on piano. The conductor raised his baton. The orchestra played an instrumental number to get the audience in the mood and allow everyone to settle.

After a round of enthusiastic applause, Jim Bob, in an open-collared tuxedo and cowboy hat, stepped onto the stage, carrying a trumpet, and with Christine on his arm. She looked radiant in a slinky, spaghetti-strap dress that must have cost a fortune—she was afraid to ask. She also felt somewhat naked without a bra, but Hannah and the salesgirl assured her this was the proper way to wear the dress. And it was Saint-Tropez, after all.

Christine kissed Jim Bob on the cheek. "Hi, y'all," Jim Bob bellowed. Many in the audience began to wonder if they had been suckered. He took a couple of steps back.

Christine smiled sweetly as Jim Bob lifted the trumpet to his lips and began blasting out "La vie en rose." The audience broke briefly into applause. All eyes turned to Christine as she began singing. Erik watched from the wings.

Christine next sang "Je suis malade," turning occasionally to smile at Raoul. She took a break while the orchestra played an eclectic mix, much of it from Viktor's cruise ship days, although Jim Bob insisted on a few from their gigs in Chicago honky-tonks, which was a big hit with the audience, especially the American tourists.

Christine and Erik sang "Caruso," which brought thunderous applause as he leaned in and kissed her, and not on the cheek. It was not nearly as passionate as before, at the Chagny house, but it was enough to piss off Raoul. Fortunately, Erik released her before she could push him away, so it appeared to the audience to be just part of the show.

Rémy reached out and grabbed Raoul to keep him in his seat. "Let it go, son. Let it go."

Christine waved and smiled, holding hands with Erik as they left the stage.

"What the hell was that?" she demanded as soon as they were off the stage.

"I got caught up in the song," Erik said.

"Raoul was sitting right there."

"So? It was a performance. The audience loved it."

"You practically stuck your tongue down my throat. Did the audience love that?"

"You did."

She slapped him, hard, and stormed away. He raised his hand to his stinging cheek and smiled.

Christine had only a few minutes to compose herself and fix her lipstick before returning to the stage. The conductor waited for her signal, but it did not come. "Raoul," she said, motioning for him to join her on stage. Raoul looked at Rémy, who just shrugged, also not knowing what the girl was up to. Raoul put his violin on his chair and joined Christine on stage.

"My French is not good, so my friend Raoul will translate." She waited for him to translate, and then continued.

"Thank you all so much for coming tonight. I hope you have enjoyed it as much as I have. I'd like to thank Rémy, the mayor, the police, my friends, and everyone else who pitched in to make this happen on short notice."

She wiped a tear from her cheek and took a minute to compose herself. She motioned toward the orchestra. "Everyone in the orchestra tonight was a friend of my daddy. He played with many of them aboard cruise ships, before I was born. They played in clubs all along the Côte d'Azur, including here in Saint-Tropez, so this night would be so special to him. My friend Jim Bob, who has been there for me all my life, is here all the way from Chicago to play with us tonight. My friend Zoe, who helped me through some very tough times, is on piano."

All of this was unplanned, unscripted, unrehearsed, so Rémy and everyone else on stage just waited quietly to see where it was going.

"I'd like to thank Count and Doctor Chagny for inviting me here, to Saint-Tropez, to their lovely home, and for this beautiful dress, certainly not something I would wear to school in California, but I love it so." The audience erupted in laughter and applause.

"And finally, there's Raoul, the boy who jumped off a pier to rescue my scarf from the sea and then rescued me from the streets. He stayed by my side, literally, when my daddy died. There is so much to say about Raoul, and not enough time." Raoul was a bit embarrassed trying to translate glowing praise about himself but soldiered on. "So I'll just say this." She kissed him. He happily joined in, taking her into his arms, to roaring applause from the audience.

"Go get your fiddle and let's do this," she said.

Raoul retrieved his violin and rejoined Christine.

"This was my daddy's favorite song," she said.

The orchestra began playing and Christine sang "Con te partirò."

Zoe and Raoul were both in tears as they played, as were many in the audience.

When it was over Christine received a standing ovation. She took a bow and left the stage. Jim Bob followed her.

"You killed it, honey." He bear-hugged her. "I wish your daddy could be here."

"Me too. I miss him so much."

"Encore! Encore!" the audience shouted.

"That means you, kid."

Christine wiped the tears from her eyes and took his arm. They returned to the stage, arm in arm. He kissed her on the forehead, left her center stage and rejoined the orchestra. She turned to the conductor and nodded. The orchestra began playing, and Christine sang "La romance de Nadir." The audience was overwhelmed. Her voice, so clear and pure, soared into the night air.

Christine was sure her cheeks would be bruised from all the kissing after the concert. Her daddy's old friends just couldn't get enough of her, and she felt she owed them that much. She was also sure her ribs would be cracked from all the hugging.

Frankie, Meg, and Connie made their way backstage and hooked up with the others.

"Oh my God," Connie said, hugging Christine. "You were amazing. How do you do that?"

"The Angel," Christine said.

"Okay, gang," Zoe said. "We talked it over, and the good news is you guys will be allowed to go to a club." That brought a round of approval from the kids.

"What's the bad news?" Christine asked.

"Jim Bob and I are going with you," Zoe said. "And it will be just dancing, no drinking." That was not so well received, but there would be dancing, at a club, so there was that.

"It's non-negotiable," Zoe said. "No booze, and we go with you, or you all go home right now."

The club, they were assured, was the hottest spot in town. It was crowded with handsome young men and stunningly beautiful young women, and girls, obviously underage. There was a lot of bare skin.

The music was pounding, the dancers throbbing. The group made their way through the bedlam to a reserved table. "How the hell did we get a table?" Jim Bob asked Zoe. "This place is packed."

"The count is well connected. And our drinks are on him."

"That's okay. I can buy my own drinks."

"Wait until you see the prices."

"That bad, huh?"

"That bad. These aren't locals. They're rich kids, big rich, from all over the world. We could probably both retire on what was spent on the clothes they're wearing."

"Some of them aren't wearing much." He looked around. "Crap-on-a-stick, we already lost them."

"They're dancing. I've got my eye on them."

Jim Bob turned to watch. There they were, all six of them, coupled up, clearly enjoying themselves.

"Erik and Connie look like a live sex show."

Zoe laughed. "Let's just hope they keep their clothes on. At least she's distracting his attention away from Christine."

"Say what?"

"He's been hitting on her. I don't know if it's just to piss off Raoul or if he's really interested."

"Boy rubs me the wrong way."

"He has some issues. I'll tell you later when it's not so noisy."

"Do you have a boat?"

"I can get one. Why?"

"And concrete blocks?"

She laughed. "Hopefully it doesn't go that far."

"I hope not, but good girls are always attracted to bad boys."

A very beautiful young waitress in very short shorts stepped up and leaned over the table. Her shirt fell open and Jim Bob could see all the way to her shorts.

They ordered, and the waitress left. "Did you see that?" Jim Bob asked.

Zoe laughed. "Yes, I saw them."

"She looked like a swimsuit model."

"They have some pretty hot waitresses here. They make a fortune in tips. Some of them make an even bigger fortune after hours."

"No shit?"

"We're not in Kansas anymore."

"I'm beat," Christine said as she and Raoul sat down at the table during a lull in the music. The others soon joined them, all out of breath.

"Where's Jim Bob?" Christine asked.

"Up there," Zoe said, pointing at the stage.

Jim Bob, wearing his cowboy hat, sat down at the piano and played "Whole Lotta Shakin Goin On." Playing probably wasn't the right word—he attacked the piano. The band kept up with him and the dancers went wild, arms, heads and hair flying.

"Wow," Erik said. "That dude can play piano."

"That's nothing," Christine said. "You should see him shred."

"Come on," Raoul said, taking her hand. "We have to get back out there."

The waitress arrived just as the kids headed for the dance floor. "I guess I'll come back later."

"No wait," Zoe said. "Just bring six whatever kind of soft drink you have."

"Are you sure? It's the same price as alcohol."

"I'm sure. Count Chagny is picking up the tab. Just make sure the kids don't get any booze. Bring me another of these and send another of those to that lunatic cowboy on piano."

The waitress smiled. "I'll take care of it."

Zoe was still alone, sipping her drink, trying to keep an eye on six teenagers on the dance floor. The band wouldn't let Jim Bob leave the stage. He seemed to be a big hit, especially with the ladies.

Raoul and Christine plopped down, exhausted. "I need to go pee," Raoul said. "Will you be okay?"

"Sure," Christine said.

"Do you need to go too?"

"No, I'm okay."

Frankie and Meg sat down. "That was so much fun," Meg said.

"Your friend is a maniac on piano," Frankie said to Zoe.

Jim Bob stepped up to the microphone and the girls let out a cheer.

"Let's slow it down a bit," Jim Bob said, then turned to the band and nodded. They started playing. He sang "There! I've Said It Again."

"Let's go," Meg said, grabbing Frankie by the hand, headed back to the dance floor, passing by Erik on the way.

"Would you like to dance?" Erik asked Christine.

"Where's Connie?"

"Bathroom."

Christine slid off her chair. Zoe did not look pleased. "Relax," Christine said. "We're just dancing."

But it was slow dancing, and it was very close. Erik's shirt was drenched in sweat, and the fabric in Christine's dress was very thin, and hormones were raging. Erik managed to dance them through the throng and out of Zoe's sight.

"What are we doing?" Christine asked, looking up at him.

"Dancing," Erik said.

"No, we're not," she said, and put her head back on his shoulder.

His right hand slid down her back. He didn't grope, he just let his fingers dangle lightly on her bottom.

She felt tears running down her cheeks. This was wrong, so wrong, but she didn't want it to stop. Clearly, he didn't either. When the song ended, as everyone else broke apart and applauded, they just stood there, glued together by some unholy force, hearts beating as one.

15

THE COVE

CHRISTINE'S REMAINING DAYS in Saint-Tropez flew by all too quickly. Trying to avoid Erik, she spent more time alone with Raoul, drifting in the pool, holding hands, riding his motor scooter, long walks on the beach, and more than a little smooching. He didn't push her, and she was glad for that.

She was also glad that Connie was determined to defend her claim to Erik. Not that she loved him, it was probably just a summer thing, but he was a teenage boy and Connie was hot and wild and sexy, so she kept him occupied, and out of Christine's hair, and arms.

Zoe and Jim Bob had been spending a lot of time together, which Christine found cute, and helpful in that it provided her more alone time with Raoul without the benefit, or restrictions, of a chaperone. Not that she needed a chaperone; Raoul remained the perfect gentleman. Perhaps too much of a gentleman, Christine sometimes thought.

The gang had planned one last outing before Christine's departure, a day on the Caldwell's boat. It wasn't really a yacht, Connie had explained to her mother, just a boat. Exactly how much could happen in the mostly open cabin of a cabin cruiser? It wasn't like a multi-deck, multi-stateroom, ocean-going yacht, so Alexandra reluctantly agreed. Besides, she rationalized, if so inclined, teenagers would find a way and a place and there wasn't much she could do to stop it.

They provisioned the boat with purloined wine and a sumptuous picnic feast provided gratis by Rémy. "My restaurant is booked solid for the rest of the summer," he said, "all thanks to Christine and her amazing voice."

After crawling through the marina and past the breakwater, Erik opened it up and the cruiser cut through the water, throwing up a whitewater wake behind them. Christine didn't know where they were going, but it was exhilarating, the wind blowing through her hair, blue skies, and emerald water up ahead. She was in Raoul's arms, her back to him, his arms around her waist, just like a TV commercial for some tropical resort, she thought. She felt very content.

Connie and Meg quickly stripped down to bikini bottoms and sprawled out on the deck to catch some sun.

Christine found herself out of uniform—she was just wearing shorts and a T-shirt—her bikini was in her bag. "I'll be right back," Christine said, pulling away from Raoul. She slipped into the cabin, looked around to make sure none of the boys could see her, and stripped naked.

She saw Erik out of the corner of her eye as she pulled on her bikini bottoms and turned away.

"Erik! What are you doing?" She covered her breasts with her hands and arms.

"Taking a piss."

"Who's driving the boat?"

"Frankie."

"Couldn't you have waited just a minute?"

"Not really."

"I'm changing clothes. Do you mind?"

"Not at all. Don't let me stop you."

"Jerk." She turned her back to him and reached for her bikini top.

"Why are you avoiding me?" he asked.

"Why do you think?"

She tied the top strings of her bikini.

"I don't know what to think."

He took over tying the strings around her back. She let him.

"You're with Connie."

"No I'm not."

"She certainly seems to think so."

"That's her problem."

"What's going on?" Raoul asked, stepping into the cabin.

"Her strings were in a knot," Erik said. "I was just helping her get it undone."

"I thought you were going to take a piss," Raoul said.

"I was. Here. She's all yours."

He dropped the strings. Christine continued to hold the top over her breasts, turning to watch until Erik was in the head, and then removed the bikini top and dropped it into her bag. "I think I'll get some sun," she said as she walked past Raoul.

Raoul followed her out of the cabin. She continued onto the deck, waving as they passed a yacht. Connie and Meg sat up when they heard the cheering and catcalls coming from the yacht and they both waved at the young men on deck. The boys took a good look at the topless girls on the yacht.

Christine took up a position with the other girls. They lay back and soaked in the sun, providing an excellent view for Raoul and Frankie on the bridge. "Now that's what I'm talking about," Frankie said. "I love Saint-Tropez."

THE SUN WAS already low in the sky as they beached the boat at a very secluded cove and unloaded. Neither Connie nor Meg made any attempt to put on a shirt or their top, so Christine reluctantly went along. By this point the thrill was gone, she assumed, and indeed, the boys didn't seem to be making any additional effort to look. This was her last day, and last night, in Saint-Tropez, so she may as well make the most of it. In a few days she would be back in Santa Monica, and it would be nothing at all like this.

The boys built a fire, although there was nothing to cook. The picnic was sandwiches, gourmet, but cold. The food and wine were delicious, and the conversation spirited and laced with laughter.

Darkness fell quickly. The girls were still topless, and Christine felt it was strange, since they couldn't use tanning as an excuse, but she didn't want to be the odd girl out and she felt completely at ease sitting beside Raoul so very closely.

Raoul leaned back onto a beach towel and Christine followed in his arms. They kissed and kissed some more, and she didn't even notice that Frankie and Meg had disappeared. She could still see Erik and Connie out of the corner of her eye. They were doing much more than kissing and didn't seem to care who was watching.

Raoul's hands roamed a bit and Christine felt no urge to push them away. She was breathing heavily and could tell he was as well when they mutually decided to come up for air. She looked around. Frankie and Meg had returned, sitting quietly in each other's arms, staring at the fire.

Erik and Connie were now gone. Raoul poured some more wine.

"When are you guys going back?" Christine asked.

"Couple of days," Frankie said.

"I really need to get back to dance class," Meg said. "After all this time goofing off it's going to hurt like hell."

"What are you going to do for the rest of the summer?" Frankie asked.

"I don't know," Christine said. "Hang out, hit the beach."

"The LA beaches will kind of suck after this," Frankie said.

Christine laughed. "Totally. Could you imagine going topless on the Santa Monica Beach? Well, I guess you do anyway, but you know what I mean."

"I know what you mean," Frankie said, grinning.

Connie crossed in front of the fire, looking somewhat flushed. Erik was right behind her. "Your turn on the boat," he said to Raoul. He sat down beside Connie and looked at Christine.

She had been suspicious before, but now Christine realized what was going on. Her body stiffened.

"That's okay," Raoul said. "We're good."

Christine was relieved, not that she hadn't thought about it, but when the time came with Raoul, if it ever did, she expected it to be much more private, certainly not with two other couples waiting just a few feet away, knowing full well what you were doing in the boat.

Meg finally broke the uncomfortable silence. "Christine, how did you learn to sing like that?"

"I don't know, I just do."

"You do realize that you are incredible," Meg said.

"Nah, not really."

"I've heard lots of opera singers, world-famous ones. Trust me, you are incredible."

"It was the Angel of Music," Raoul said.

"The what?" Meg asked.

"Oh yeah," Connie said, suddenly coming to life, "when you and Raoul were sleeping together."

"Whoa, sleeping together?" Frankie asked. "When was this, Shaggy?"

"We were just sleeping," Raoul said. "After her dad died."

"And she heard the angel sing," Connie said.

"What angel?" Erik asked.

"The Angel of Music," Christine said. "It's just a silly story my daddy used to tell."

"Well, let's hear it," Erik said.

Christine suddenly felt uncomfortable talking about her daddy while mostly naked. She reached for her bag and pulled out her T-shirt.

"You tell it Raoul," Christine said, putting on her T-shirt.

"I can't tell it like your dad."

"Then forget it," Christine said. "It's just a fairy tale anyway."

"No," Connie said. "I want to hear it."

Frankie and Meg also encouraged him, and Raoul relented.

"All right," Raoul said. "I only heard it once, on the beach in LA, around a campfire, just like this, only a lot more people."

"Get to it, Shaggy," Frankie said.

Raoul began, doing his best to imitate Christine's father. "If you are a good kid and study hard and obey your parents and practice your scales, you might, *might*, someday be visited in your sleep by the Angel of Music, and then you will be blessed with musical talent beyond belief for the rest of your life."

Erik laughed. "And you believe that bull?"

"We had been looking at music and practicing for hours but couldn't find anything for her audition piece for the conservatory. She woke me up saying someone was singing. I couldn't hear it, but she could."

"It was the most amazing tenor," Christine said, "singing 'Nessun Dorma.' I couldn't see him, but I could hear him. It was the Angel of Music."

"We spent the rest of the night practicing it and she performed it the next day for her audition," Raoul said. "I accompanied her on violin."

"And it worked?" Erik asked.

"Your dad was crying. Christine was accepted, so yeah, I guess it worked."

"You probably just imagined it."

"Yeah, probably," Christine said, no longer interested.

"We should get back," Raoul said. "Christine has to get up early tomorrow. It's going to be a long day."

Connie and Meg finally put their shirts back on, probably more because of the chill in the night air than modesty as they sat on the deck while the boat knifed through black water.

Erik drove and Frankie stood nearby, helping navigate in the darkness.

Christine and Raoul sat in the back of the boat, cuddling, their time together slipping away, and they both knew it.

"Why didn't we take our turn in the boat?" Christine asked.

Raoul was surprised. "Did you want to?"

"No, yes, no, you know."

"That's why," he said. "I want you to be sure."

She looked up at him. "Thanks." She kissed him briefly.

He grinned. "We still have a few minutes before we get to the marina."

She slugged him on the arm. "In your dreams."

"It will definitely be in my dreams."

They cuddled for a moment.

"In case I forget to tell you tomorrow," she said. "I had a really good time."

"Me too."

She looked up at him. He kissed her, really kissed her, a kiss she would never forget.

16

THE PROMENADE

With Sue stuck in Seoul, summer in Santa Monica sucked for Christine. She had always thought it was a cool place, but after Saint-Tropez, it was just the same old same old. Raoul texted, and occasionally called, but it was not the same as feeling his warmth next to her, not to mention the kisses, too few, too brief, but fondly remembered.

The beach blew. These people had no idea. Even the food didn't taste any good. She searched out croissants and couldn't find a decent bowl of coffee anywhere. She shuffled through the days, constantly reminiscing about her glorious two weeks in the south of France. She even like saying, "the south of France," and had to remind herself to not overuse the phrase, lest others think her snobbish.

Mrs. Valerius assured Christine that her depression was quite normal. She and the professor suffered the same letdown after their trip to upstate New York, although she did concede that their trip was not nearly as exciting as Christine's. Mrs. Valerius barely asked about Raoul, and Christine suspected that she didn't really want to know because that would mean she would have to deal with it if the relationship blossomed. What if Raoul showed up in Santa Monica? Would she be allowed to go out with him alone? Thoughts of the future only deepened her blue mood.

She had not heard from Erik, and that was just fine with her. She didn't want to think about him. He was in New York and would hopefully stay there, although it had been mentioned that he was occasionally shipped to Los Angeles. She hadn't given him her cell phone number, or any contact information at all, for that matter, other than she lived in Santa Monica. She occasionally looked over her shoulder—maybe he was stalking her on the Promenade. He had made mention of it, after all.

He obviously knew where she went to school, so maybe he would show up there. It would certainly look innocent enough—his father was headmaster. But the fall semester was weeks away, time enough for Erik to forget about her and move on to someone else. He was obviously into Connie, literally into her apparently, so maybe that would continue, and he would leave her alone. The fact that she still thought about him was disconcerting, and she wished those thoughts would go away.

There had been one bright spot since returning home. She was lying on her bed listening to music on her headphones when Mrs. Valerius tapped her on the shoulder. "There's someone here to see you," Mrs. Valerius said, after waiting for her to remove the headphones.

Clearly the music had been too loud. She didn't hear the doorbell, and she didn't hear Mrs. Valerius call her.

"Who is it?" Christine asked.

"Come and see for yourself."

Random faces flashed through Christine's head as she scurried down the hallway. Could it be Connie, or hopefully Raoul? Surely it was not Erik.

It was Jim Bob. She flew into his arms, and they hugged.

"Are you stalking me?" Christine asked.

"Christine," Mrs. Valerius scolded, "where are your manners?"

"It's all right," Jim Bob said. "We hadn't seen each other for three years and now I turn up on two continents in three weeks."

"What are you really doing here?" Christine asked.

"I came to help Zoe move into her new apartment."

"You came all the way from Chicago to help Zoe move?" Christine asked.

"When you drive a pickup truck people expect you to help them move. Keep that in mind in the future. It will save you a lot of money. You do have to buy the beer, though."

"She doesn't have that much stuff," Christine kidded. She knew exactly why he was in town.

"I got used to that Mediterranean weather, and she said it was the same here, so I thought maybe I'd hang around awhile."

"Oh, good, you can stay in the little cottage."

"The what?"

"The guest house, out there." She pointed. "Daddy and I lived there for a while."

"That's okay, honey. I've got a place."

"You do?"

"Zoe and I have been kind of, well you know."

"Shacking up?"

"Is that okay with you?"

"It's really none of my business, but yes, it's way okay with me."

"Well, that's a relief. I was afraid you might think it was weird."

"I think you two make a cute couple."

"Well, we both love music and we both love you."

He hugged her again.

"Does she need me to help move?" Christine asked. "I'm kind of bored."

"Nah, like you said, she ain't got much stuff. We already got it all moved. Now she's just putting it all away. Apparently, girls don't want guys sorting through their underwear."

"No, probably not," Christine said.

"She also had a lunch meeting with her new boss, Konrad Krueger, so I got some time off. I really want to meet him, though. That guy can score."

"Well, if you stick around, I'm sure Zoe can arrange it."

"Are you hungry? I'm buying, unless you have other plans."

"What other plans? I have no life."

CHRISTINE AND JIM BOB pigged out on hot dogs on the Third Street Promenade.

"What do you think?" Christine asked, taking a big bite.

"It's not bad, but it's not really a Chicago dog. I wouldn't starve if I lived out here, though."

"So, you're thinking about staying?"

"I'm thinking about it."

"Kind of depends on Zoe, huh?"

"Kind of."

"I think she likes you."

"And I like her, and I like LA. Is the weather like this all the time?"

"Near the beach, yeah. It gets colder in the winter. Well, the locals think it's cold. It's nothing like Chicago, but you do need a sweater. Actually, some people need a sweater at night in the summer."

"All the girls on that Santa Monickey Beach had their tops on. What's up with that?"

Christine laughed. "It's not like Saint-Tropez, is it?"

"No, it ain't, but I could get used to it."

"Daddy was going to try to get some session work when we first came out here. Maybe you could do that."

"It's definitely something to think about."

"You can also make money busking, right here on the Promenade."

"No kidding?"

"That's what Daddy and I did when we first got here. That's how I met Raoul and Zoe, actually. We were busking on the pier. Then the cops caught us on the Promenade, and we had to get a permit."

"You have to have a permit to play music?"

"That's exactly what Daddy said. So, we got a permit and did pretty good. People always gave us more money when I sang. I guess a cute little girl helps, but you could do pretty good with your guitar."

Jim Bob turned and looked around the Promenade. "Right out there?"

"Right out there," she said. "It's a lot busier at night and on weekends, a *lot* busier. The place is packed with locals and tourists, and they have money in their pockets."

"I might have to check it out."

"I can show you where to get a permit."

"Do you still busk?"

"Sometimes I play with my friends from school and give the money to the homeless."

"Cool."

They finished their food and strolled along the Promenade.

"I would have taken you," Jim Bob said.

"Taken me where?"

"When your daddy died, I would have taken you in."

"Really?"

"No judge would have ever gone for it, a single man who played shitkicker music in dive bars, and completely unrelated. That's no life for a twelve-year-old girl. I'm sure that's what your daddy was thinking about when he set things up with the Valeriuses."

"I thought I would have to go to an orphanage."

"I would have snatched you up and run if it came to that. We'd have probably got caught and I'd have gone to jail, but I would have never let them put you in an orphanage."

Christine smiled and nodded. "That might have been fun, except the jail part."

"Your daddy was right. You needed a real home, and some stability. Looks like it worked out all right."

"They're really good to me. I can't complain. Well, I'm a teenage girl, so I do complain, but it's not bad. They make me do chores and stuff, but all my friends at school have chores too, except the rich kids, they have people for that."

"I'm sorry I wasn't here for you since your daddy died. I wanted to be, but time just gets away from you. It goes faster when you get older, so watch out for that."

"That's okay. You're here now."

"I don't know anything about little girls, but I know plenty about women, and you're almost a woman, so if there's anything you need to know, I'll be here."

She laughed, put her arm around his waist, and hugged him. "Good to know."

"Did they ever tell you why they're just your guardians, and didn't adopt you?"

"No," she said, "but I wondered about that."

"Your daddy never had any contact with his parents after he left Sweden, and your mama said her parents pretty much abandoned her and joined some cult when she was a teenager. If it went to court, they would have probably tracked down your grandparents and they might have demanded custody. Apparently, your daddy didn't want you sent to a farm in Sweden where you didn't even speak the language and he damned sure didn't want you raised by a bunch of religious nutcases in some commune or whatever."

"Wow. I guess I got pretty lucky."

"It could have been a lot worse, but like I said, this crazy redneck would have snatched you up and gone on the lam."

"We could have gone to France, and they would have never found us. We could have lived in a little cottage on the Côte d'Azur."

"I could have been a pearl fisher and we could have played little clubs at night."

"Totally."

Christine's cell phone rang. She answered.

"Connie? Are you back?"

"We're back in town for a few days before heading north, ugh," Connie said.

"Bummer."

"Your mom said you were on the Promenade. Oh shit, Mrs. Valerius, sorry."

"Yeah, I had lunch with the redneck."

"Who?"

"Jim Bob, from Saint-Tropez, remember?"

"Oh yeah, that guy. I'll be right there."

"Okay, see you in a minute."

Christine shoved her phone in her back pocket.

"That was Connie. She's going to catch up with us."

"How does she know where we are?"

"There's an app for that."

They walked in silence for a moment and then Connie swooped up from behind and slapped Christine on the butt.

"Hey bitch," Connie said.

"Ouch!"

They hugged.

"I need to ask you something," Connie said, "but don't get mad."

"Why would I get mad?"

"When we were packing to come home, my mom couldn't find the painting."

"What painting?"

"The one of you, and me."

Christine was visibly concerned. "What do you mean she couldn't find it?"

"She couldn't find it. We looked everywhere. You didn't take it, did you?"

"No, of course not." Christine was indignant.

"Don't get mad."

"I'm not mad, just concerned."

"My mom told you she would give it to you if you wanted it."

"I would never just take it without asking."

"That's what I told her."

"Did she paint a top on?"

"Nope. That's why she's worried."

"She also said she would burn it. Maybe she just dumped it and forgot."

"Whoa. I'm lost," Jim Bob said. "Paint a top on what? Burn it? What's the dealio?"

"I was kind of naked."

"Naked?"

"Well, topless anyway. We were at the beach and Connie's mom was painting."

Jim Bob laughed.

"It's not funny," Christine said. "It was beautiful, actually, but we didn't know what to do with it. I couldn't very well bring it home."

"Well shit," Connie said. "If you didn't take it then who did, Raoul?"

"No, he would have never taken it without permission."

"What about Erik? He had the hots for you the whole time we were there."

"No he didn't. I thought you two hooked up."

"I was just using him for sex. Besides, boys always want what they can't have."

"Nekkid pictures, hooked up, sex, what were you girls up to over there?" Jim Bob said.

"It's not like that," Christine said.

"Erik did mention it that day, but I thought he was just kidding," Connie said.

"When could he have taken it?"

"He was at the house a couple of times after that. I guess he could have snagged it without anybody noticing."

"How would he get it home? It was kind of big. He couldn't just shove it in a duffel bag."

"Easy," Jim Bob said. "Use a pocketknife to cut the painting out of the frame, then roll it up. Happens all the time."

"And you know this how, Mr. Cat Burglar?" Christine asked.

Jim Bob shrugged. "Movies."

17

WORDS OF LOVE

CHRISTINE'S MOOD WAS brightened considerably by having Jim Bob around. It wasn't as good as having her daddy, but it was close. He loved her unconditionally and she found it comforting, especially with her love life so uncertain after returning from Saint-Tropez.

Zoe's apartment was small, so they decided against throwing a big apartment-warming party, and it was just Zoe, Jim Bob, and Christine. Outdoor grills weren't allowed, so Jim Bob did the best he could in the tiny kitchen. He cooked hamburgers, genuine hamburgers, not those silly sandwiches with secret sauce people in Los Angeles tried to pass off as hamburgers. Jim Bob and Zoe had beer. Christine settled for Diet Mountain Dew. It reminded Christine of their little house in Chicago when Jim Bob would spend the night.

After dinner Zoe played some of the score she was working on. Christine thought it was wonderful and thought about what Johnston meant by making music and not just performing it. The last few weeks had certainly made it clear where love songs came from, and the wide variety of them. She had even found herself humming melodies and making up lyrics. Yes, Johnston had a point, and she resolved to do better in school.

CHRISTINE FELT GUILTY spending so much time with Jim Bob, but the Valeriuses didn't complain and after all, she was a teenage girl, and it was summer. It wasn't like she was running around with a teenage boy. She had adult supervision, although it might not seem that way to the casual observer—Jim Bob could be outrageous, and fun.

Christine leaned out the window and looked up as Jim Bob parked his truck near the Santa Monica City Hall.

"What are you doing?" Jim Bob asked.

"Reading the signs," Christine said.

"Why?"

"You have to be really careful about parking in Santa Monica. A parking ticket costs a fortune."

"So, are we good?"

"We're good, for two hours anyway. Check your watch."

Jim Bob checked his watch.

Standing in line to get a street performer permit brought back memories for Christine. When she and her daddy got theirs, it had taken the last of their money and they had to immediately start performing if they wanted to eat. Jim Bob didn't look quite that desperate, she thought. He had money in his pocket, a truck to get around in, and a place to stay.

"Well, let's go try it out," Jim Bob said after receiving his permit.

"Now?"

"Sure, why not?"

"Works for me," she said. "Do you have your guitar?"

"Of course. It's in the truck."

They had to park on the very top level of the parking structure, and she assured him that was a good sign—the Promenade would be crowded with tourists.

They found a spot, Jim Bob took his guitar out of the case, and Christine positioned the open case for optimum tips.

"What are you going to play?" she asked.

She plopped down beside the guitar case so she could keep an eye on the money when it started dropping in. She had learned well while on the streets with her daddy.

"I have no idea," he said. "What works in Californey?"

"Who knows?" she said. "It's summer, so there's lots of tourists from everywhere, so I guess it's up to you."

Jim Bob opened with "Fort Worth I Love You."

Christine, almost embarrassed, certainly surprised, asked, "What the heck was that?"

"A little Michael Martin Murphey. I've got a pirate track of Allen Damron singing it in Lubbock."

"Never heard of them."

"That's okay, they never heard of you either."

She made one of those teenage-girl faces, obviously not impressed with his song selection.

"It sounds better drunk," he said.

"Singing drunk or listening drunk?"

"Both, actually."

"Whatever."

Jim Bob played "Mr. Bojangles," attracting a small crowd.

"Now, I've actually heard that one," Christine said when he finished.

"Yeah, everybody and their brother covered it. I kind of liked the Dirt Band's version, and Nina Simone hit it a pretty good lick, but there's nothing like crying in your beer in some cheap bar in Austin, listening to the original, Jerry Jeff."

Christine clearly knew none of those people.

"How about some Buddy Holley?" he asked. "Have you heard of him?"

"Sure, Zoe turned me on to him."

"I knew I liked that girl," Jim Bob said and then played and sang "Take Your Time," without attracting much attention.

"Was that Buddy Holley?"

"Yeah, one of his lesser-known tunes, obviously."

"What else you got?"

He smiled. "Here's one just for you."

He sang "Crying, Waiting, Hoping," while looking directly at her.

That one resulted in a few bills dropping into the case.

"Jerk," she said when he finished the song.

Jim Bob laughed. "The thing about love songs is they nearly always fit the situation, or at least you think they do at the time."

As Christine pondered that bit of wisdom, a strikingly handsome man in his thirties, casually dressed, wearing designer sunglasses, approached Christine. Jim Bob watched him warily.

"Will you be singing today, Christine?"

"No sir, not today. I'm just here with my friend."

"Well, that's a shame, although your friend is very good." He nodded at Jim Bob.

"We might try to put something together next week when Sue gets back," Christine said. "Check the website at the conservatory."

"I'll do that." He dropped a twenty in the guitar case and strolled away.

"Is that—?" Jim Bob asked.

Christine smiled sheepishly and shrugged. "Yeah, there's a lot of famous people on the Promenade."

"Wow."

She picked up the twenty and handed it to Jim Bob. "Better put this in your pocket."

Jim Bob smiled as he took the money. "You know all the tricks."

"When it's your food money, you watch it like a hawk," she said. "Daddy taught me that."

"Twenty bucks," Jim Bob said as he pocketed the money. "Not bad."

"Not everyone is that generous, but it adds up."

"What do you want to hear next?" he asked.

"Surprise me."

He selected "Words of Love," and Christine loved it. So did the gathering crowd. Christine thought it was funny that this guy who was old enough to be her father was singing love songs to her and wondered what all these people thought. It didn't matter—she was happy.

"What?" Jim Bob asked when the song was over.

Christine looked like the cat who ate the canary, watching Zoe step up behind Jim Bob. He flinched as Zoe put an arm on his shoulder and her lips to his ear. "I'm hard at work and you're singing love songs to a hot young blonde?"

"You got me," Jim Bob said, turning to kiss Zoe, "but it looks like I'm the only one working here."

Jim Bob noticed that Zoe was with a man, so he stood up and extended his hand. "Jim Bob Butrell."

"This is Konrad Krueger," Zoe said. "We're just taking a short break for lunch."

They exchanged pleasantries. "Are you a Buddy Holley fan?" Konrad asked, with a slight German accent.

"I guess you could say that," Jim Bob said. "I often wonder what might have been."

"Don't we all," Konrad said.

Christine kept an eye on the money dropping into the guitar case, not enough yet to gather, so she just left it.

"And this is Christine," Zoe said.

Christine scrambled to her feet. Konrad kissed her hand. "I've heard a lot about you, Miss Daaé. I look forward to hearing you sing. Zoe assures me I will be impressed."

Christine ducked her head.

"I'm not easily impressed," Konrad said.

"You should put her on one of your soundtracks," Jim Bob blurted out. "She has a voice for the ages."

Konrad smiled.

"Well, I'd better get to work before somebody moves in on my spot," Jim Bob said, launching into "Not Fade Away."

Zoe and Konrad faded away as Jim Bob played and sang. More money dropped into the guitar case. Christine checked it and pulled out a business card, which she handed to Jim Bob.

"Konrad Krueger," Jim Bob said, reading the card.

"He didn't leave any money."

"This is better than money."

"It is?"

"He might have some session work."

THE PROMENADE WAS packed, and the sidewalk cafés were doing brisk business as the sun dropped into the Pacific and the buildings cast long shadows. It was a beautiful, cool evening in Santa Monica. Street performers were out in force.

Johnston shook hands and spoke with Sue's parents, who were sitting at a table on the patio of a restaurant. The Caldwells and Valeriuses then sat down at a nearby table. They watched as Alfonso and Jim Bob set up a keyboard for Zoe just outside the short fence. Sue carried her violin and trumpet. Christine put a sign identifying her cause du jour on Jim Bob's open guitar case.

"Are you sure this is a good place?" Jim Bob asked. "There's a guitar feller right there, and some more musicians over that way."

"Don't worry," Sue assured him. "They always clear out when the blonde girl sings."

"All righty, then. Let's kick it."

They started out with selections from their recent "Hollywood Canteen" concert.

As soon as Christine began singing the other musicians did indeed clear out in search of better pickings.

Jim Bob was very impressed with the amount of money being dropped into the guitar case, as well as the frequent applause. He was also impressed as Sue played trumpet and Christine sang "La vie en rose." He fist bumped with Sue when they finished the song, and she picked up her violin.

"There's your boss," Jim Bob said to Zoe.

Zoe looked up as Konrad and a strikingly beautiful young woman in her early twenties sat down at the table with the Caldwells and Valeriuses.

"Is that his daughter?" Jim Bob asked.

Zoe laughed. "Hardly. She's probably an actress, or an aspiring singer. Konrad likes them young, and hot."

"So I see," Jim Bob said.

They began playing "Caruso," and Christine and Alfonso stepped forward and sang. When the song was over, he bowed and kissed Christine's hand during a rousing round of applause. Several people stepped forward and dropped even more cash into the guitar case. They were by now surrounded by a large crowd, and a policeman was looking concerned.

"Let's wrap it up," Zoe said, "one more song. Do you want to do 'La romance de Nadir'?"

Christine nodded enthusiastically, and then turned to Alfonso. "I learned this song in Saint-Tropez. You could totally kill it, so pay attention."

She sang "La romance de Nadir," and the applause at the end was loud and enthusiastic.

Everyone took a bow, and then insisted that Christine take another, and another. Shouts of "Encore!" were heard, but the policeman began motioning for people to move along as the group packed up their instruments.

"Good Lord!" Jim Bob said as he looked at his guitar case. "That's a lot of dough."

"We did pretty good," Christine said, stacking the money.

CHRISTINE COUNTED MONEY in the back seat of the car as Professor Valerius drove to the shelter to drop off the day's take.

Mrs. Valerius leaned over the seat. "The Caldwells have asked us to stay with them in Santa Fe for a couple of weeks before school starts."

"Okay, have fun," Christine said without looking up from her work.

"You too. Mr. Caldwell thought it would be good for you to hear some opera performances."

"You mean like summer school?"

"No, like enjoying the opera in a wonderful house. People do that, you know."

Christine was perturbed. "I lost count." She put down the money. "Will Erik be there?"

"Erik?"

"Johnston's son. He was in Saint-Tropez."

"So it's Johnston now?"

"Yeah, at least until school starts. We kind of bonded over the summer."

"Bonded?"

"Don't ask."

Mrs. Valerius looked at her husband, who seemed somewhat bemused, and then back over the seat.

"I don't know if Erik will be there or not. I didn't ask."

"Can Connie come? Sue has to work at the store."

"She wasn't invited."

"Well, when you call Johnston to ask about Erik, maybe you could ask about Connie too."

"I thought she was going to Vancouver with her mother."

"She hates Vancouver."

"Does she like opera?"

"I doubt it, but we could hang out and it wouldn't be totally boring."

"Well, I guess it wouldn't hurt to ask, but I don't know if they have the room."

"We can share a room, or even a bed. We're girls, so no big deal. Her dad will buy her plane ticket, so it won't cost anybody anything, except maybe food, but she has a credit card."

"Or we could take the car," Valerius said. "It's a very beautiful drive, most of the way."

"Whatever," Christine said.

18

THE ESTELLINE

The Valeriuses walked through Union Station in downtown Los Angeles, followed by Christine and Connie, both engrossed in their respective cell phones. A porter brought up the rear, pushing a cart piled high with baggage.

Christine looked up. "Is this the airport?"

"No," Professor Valerius said. "It's Union Station."

"Are we taking the bus?" Christine asked.

"The train. It was supposed to be a surprise."

"We're going to have to sit on a train all night?" Connie said. "Well, that sucks."

"Surely they have sleepers," he said. "I can't imagine Johnston would have booked an evening departure otherwise."

"I checked on the Internet," Mrs. Valerius said. "This is the only daily departure and Amtrak does have sleepers. It sounds like fun. Have you girls ever been on a train before?"

"Yeah, sure," Connie said. "It sucked."

"I was on the subway with Daddy, when we first got here," Christine said. "Oh, and in France, I was on a train with Zoe. It was really fast."

"Probably the TGV," Valerius said.

"Yeah, that's it."

"There they are," Valerius said.

"Oh look," Connie said, "there's Tits."

Christine elbowed her. "Frankie."

There were greetings all around, and then the combined group, and their porters, headed toward the train.

"Are you going with us?" Christine asked.

"Yeah," Frankie said. "My parents have a thing in town and will be up in a couple of days, but I thought I'd travel in style, and with a couple of young hotties."

"In style?" Christine asked.

"You'll see."

It wasn't long before they did see. They walked past several Amtrak *Superliners*, and at the end of the train was the *Estelline*, a vintage private railcar.

"Oh my," Valerius said. "Is this yours?"

"It belongs to the family trust," Johnston said. "It was originally my great-grandfather's. The cousins got together a few years ago and had it restored. We love it."

They boarded the car and were greeted by the attendant.

"Abby?" Valerius said.

"Professor," Abby said, smiling. "How are you?"

"You two know each other?" Johnston asked.

"She's one of my students."

"Yes, of course," Johnston said. "We have a list of college students who work as attendants. Music seems to be the common denominator."

"Abby is one of our favorites," Mrs. Caldwell said.

The private railcar was a rolling palace, fully restored to its 1920s grandeur.

"There are three bedrooms, plus a room for the attendant," Johnston said, taking them on a tour of the railcar. "It has a full kitchen, so we won't have to bother with the dining car. We're fully self-contained."

Johnston opened the door to one of the rooms. "The kids can bunk in here. This is where my grandfather slept, with his brother and sisters when they were kids. It sleeps four."

"What about Frankie?" Valerius asked.

"It has bunk beds," Frankie said.

Valerius looked at Christine, who shrugged. "Okay with us."

Connie nodded, unconcerned.

Valerius was not convinced.

"Maybe Abby could bunk with the girls and Frankie could take her room," Johnston said.

"I've already seen—" Frankie began to say.

Christine cut him off, "He's already seen us in our bikinis."

"Yeah, that," Frankie said. "I'm sure their pajamas cover up a lot more."

"It's not like we're going to have a three-way," Connie said.

Christine closed her eyes and wished Connie would occasionally think before speaking.

"I'm kidding," Connie said.

The Valeriuses reluctantly agreed to the sleeping arrangement and moved on toward their own room.

"Who wears pajamas?" Connie asked as she dumped her duffel bag onto a bunk bed. Christine giggled.

The kids claimed their bunks, unpacked, and then joined the adults in the parlor where Abby served drinks.

"I'll have a martini," Connie said.

"Nice try," Abby said. "How about a club soda?"

"Whatever."

"These were the private jets of their day," Johnston said. "The railroads went everywhere that mattered and you could go anywhere in your private railcar. Most of them had been parked and abandoned or scrapped over the years as rail travel fell out of favor. There's been a resurgence of interest and now we can go anywhere Amtrak goes. It's great, as long as you're not in a hurry."

"I could get used to this," Mrs. Valerius said.

"Take it up the coast, sometime," Mrs. Caldwell said. "We often do."

"Or to Santa Fe," Johnston said. "Actually, Lamy is as close as Amtrak gets to Santa Fe, but it's close enough."

"Well, girls, what do you think?" Valerius asked.

"It's cool," Christine said.

Connie shrugged.

Abby passed out menus, just one sheet. "I think we have plenty of everything," she said, "so just let me know. I'd recommend the grilled salmon, by the way."

The adults were on their second drink and the kids were getting bored by the time dinner was served.

"Can we have some wine?" Connie asked at the earliest opportunity. Abby had already poured a glass for Frankie.

The Valeriuses were taken a bit aback. She was their responsibility on this trip.

"Do your parents allow you to drink wine?" Mrs. Valerius asked.

"Sure. And we all had wine in France."

"Well, this isn't France," Valerius said. "It's California. Your parents aren't here and made no mention of wine when we spoke."

Connie was not happy.

"Oh my," Mrs. Valerius said, "the salmon is wonderful."

"That's why we like Abby so much," Mrs. Caldwell said. "She should open her own restaurant. I'll invest if she's so inclined."

"A degree in music should come in handy for running a restaurant," Valerius said, followed by a round of subdued laughter.

"She's very organized," Mrs. Caldwell said. "This is a big group for one person to handle, but she does it with ease."

"Quiet, dear," Johnston said, "or she'll ask for a raise."

There was another round of polite laughter.

"Johnston, I understand you and Christine bonded in Saint-Tropez," Mrs. Valerius said.

"Yes, actually, we did."

Christine looked up from her dinner, afraid of where this was going.

"I don't often get a chance to socialize with students outside of school, but I certainly enjoyed my time with Christine on the Côte d'Azur."

Christine was near panic mode. Connie loved it.

"I think Côte d'Azur is French for beach, isn't it?" Connie asked. "Did you tell them about the beach?"

"She sang for our supper one night, in an elegant restaurant," Johnston said. "It was quite extraordinary."

Christine breathed a sigh of relief.

"And then there was an impromptu concert at the marina," he continued. "She learned a new song, on short notice. I was very impressed."

"Do I get extra credit?" Christine asked.

"We'll see," Johnston said. "Perhaps along with a paper on the operas you are about to discover in Santa Fe."

"Oh goody," Christine said sarcastically.

"We want to discover some boys in Santa Fe," Connie said. "Can you hook us up, Tits?"

"Frankie!" Christine said.

"Oh, sorry," Connie said. "I forgot there were grownups present."

The Valeriuses were confused.

"It's an unfortunate play on the family name," Johnston said, "Titshaw."

THE KIDS' ROOM was rather small, so they stayed in the parlor after dinner, even though they were denied after-dinner drinks. The train had wi-fi and they quickly became occupied with their electronics.

"Who is Estelline?" Mrs. Valerius asked. "I noticed the name on the car when we boarded."

Johnston smiled. "Ah yes, Estelline." He took a sip of cognac. "There's an interesting, although rather scandalous story about that, and also the name of the conservatory."

Christine's attention was suddenly diverted from her cell phone.

"My great-grandfather was something of a scoundrel," Johnston said, "although probably no worse than any other man of his position at the time, or any time, for that matter."

Christine changed seats, moving closer to the conversation. Frankie and Connie never looked up.

"As a result of the Railroad Wars near the end of the nineteenth century, the Santa Fe Railway won the rights to the Raton Pass over the mountains between New Mexico and Colorado."

"Railroad Wars?" Christine asked. "I must have missed that in history class."

"It doesn't get much coverage in school but that's really another story. What matters is that on a cold winter's night, not long before World War II, Daniel Senior was traveling from Los Angeles to Chicago aboard this very railcar."

Christine looked around, suddenly connected to history.

"The Raton Pass was closed because of heavy snow, and they didn't know if the plows would have it open by the time the Santa Fe *Super Chief*, Santa Fe's most luxurious train, was due at the pass. It was stopped in Gallup, New Mexico, just ahead of Daniel's train, also Santa Fe, the *Scout*, which was taking a more southerly route, at a lower elevation, through Clovis and Amarillo."

"Amarillo," Christine said. "I've been there, with my daddy, on the bus, and there was this big building that said 'Santa Fe' on the top."

Johnston smiled and continued. "Yes, Amarillo was a regional headquarters for Santa Fe at the time. There was an opera singer aboard the *Super Chief*, trying to get to Chicago for a performance which was to be attended by several Santa Fe executives and their wives. In Daniel Senior's experience, opera singers were old, fat, and ugly, not to mention demanding and entitled. Nevertheless, he agreed to take her aboard his private railcar as a favor to the Santa Fe, and to the stationmaster at Gallup. To his surprise, the diva was quite different than he had envisioned."

"She was hot, right?" Christine said.

"Yes, she was hot, young, beautiful, charming, and also, how should I put this, a woman of less than stellar virtue."

"A slut."

Johnston smiled. "Within hours, my great-grandfather had fallen in love, or lust."

"And they got married and lived happily ever after," Christine said.

"Not exactly. Daniel Senior was already married, and had four children, including my grandfather, Daniel Junior."

"What happened to the opera singer?"

"He followed her across Europe on tour, and then she dumped him for a rich European with a title. But it didn't matter because he had also fallen in love with music and opera. He resolved to build a conservatory of music."

"And the opera singer's name was Estelline," Christine said.

"Yes. It was almost the name of the conservatory, but he was afraid his wife would find out about the affair. The route the train took that night was called the Belen Cutoff, and that's where our school got its name. He did at least have the decency to wait until after my great-grandmother died before putting name of his mistress on his railcar."

"Wow," Christine said.

"You are not to repeat this story to any of my students at the conservatory," Johnston said.

Christine pantomimed zipping her lips.

Johnston continued. "Daniel Senior retained his love of opera and became a major patron of the arts, which pleased his wife greatly. He died at the ranch in Santa Fe and left instructions that his body be transported to Los Angeles by train in a baggage car. He also wanted his favorite aria to be sung at his funeral by the best available tenor at the time. My uncle flew in from Europe with just such a tenor, Rinaldo, a most interesting fellow, who joined us for the trip from Santa Fe to Los Angeles, aboard a private train, consisting of just this car and a baggage car."

"What was his favorite aria?" Christine asked.

"'Nessun Dorma,'" Johnston said.

Christine gasped. "Oh no!" Tears formed in her eyes. "I am so sorry. I didn't know."

Johnston stood, stepped over and took her hand. "Know what, Christine? What's wrong?"

"I sang your granddaddy's song for my audition. You probably thought I did it on purpose."

"No, of course not. How could you have known? It wouldn't have mattered anyway. It's a beautiful aria."

She looked up, relieved, stood, and threw her arms around him.

"What's that all about?" Connie asked.

"I have no clue," Frankie said.

Johnston put his arms around Christine and squeezed her tightly. "It's okay, Christine, it's okay."

"Are you sure?" Christine asked, wiping tears.

"I only thought I had heard 'Nessun Dorma' sung until I heard you sing it. My great-grandfather would have loved it, and he would have loved you dearly. We are honored to have you at his conservatory. You are why he built it."

Mrs. Caldwell was a bit confused, but the Valeriuses needed no explanation. They had been there.

THE ADULTS HAD already gone to bed, but the kids stayed up late with strict instructions to keep out of the liquor cabinet. Abby counted the bottles and noted all the levels before she retired for the evening. It wasn't all that long ago that she was a teenager herself. She knew all the tricks.

"Do you travel on this thing a lot?" Christine asked.

"Yeah, I guess," Frankie said. "My mom and dad love it. They go to football games and stuff and use it for business. It's pretty cool."

"I'll say."

"Do they ever let you use it by yourself?" Connie asked.

"Not really. I've been back and forth to Santa Fe a couple of times, or on positioning moves."

"What's a positioning move?" Christine asked.

"Moving the car where somebody needs it. Like now, when we get to Lamy, Abby will spend the night on the car and hook onto a train back to LA the next day. Then my mom and dad will come back on it in a few days."

"Couldn't they just fly?" Christine asked.

"They could, but like I said, they love the train. Sending this car back to pick them up is actually cheaper than firing up a jet."

"So, like, a hundred years ago, your great-great whatever banged a hot young opera singer on this train car?" Connie asked.

"I thought you weren't paying attention," Christine said.

"I wasn't until he started talking about sex," Connie said.

"You would," Christine said.

Connie looked around and nodded her head. "We could party like rock stars on this bad boy."

"It's tempting," Frankie said. "Erik and I have definitely considered it, but there's no way we could get it hooked onto a train, too much paperwork. It's not like sneaking your dad's car out for a joyride."

"Is Erik going to be there?" Connie asked.

"Where?" Frankie said.

"Santa Fe."

"Nah, he's in New York with his mom."

"Bummer," Connie said. "He knows how to party."

"Don't worry," Frankie said. "Meg and I can hook you up. We know all the coolest places in Santa Fe."

"Great," Connie said.

"So, who's going first?" Frankie asked.

"Going where?" Christine asked.

"Do you ladies want to go change or do you want me to go first?"

"Change into what?" Connie asked.

"Pee-jays," Frankie said.

"I sleep in the nude," Connie said.

Christine's jaw dropped.

"Well," Frankie said. "This is going to be interesting."

"I guess we'll go first," Christine said.

Frankie stepped out and Christine closed the door behind him. "Nude?"

"I was just jerking him around," Connie said. "I'll throw on a T-shirt or something." She grabbed her duffel bag. "Boxers or briefs?"

"Huh?"

"Frankie, do you think he wears boxers or briefs?"

"Briefs."

"I'll go with boxers. He's kind of a dork."

Christine giggled.

"What about you?" Connie asked.

"What about me?"

"Do you actually wear pajamas?"

"T-shirt," Christine said, "and panties."

"Oh yeah," Connie said. "That's what you were wearing when I woke you up in Saint-Tropez."

The girls had just finished changing when there was a knock on the door. "Are you decent?"

"Yes," Christine said. "You can come in."

"That's okay," Frankie said. "I'll come back later, when you're not."

Christine opened the door.

"Wiseass," Christine said.

Frankie stood there in his boxers.

"Ha," Connie said. "I win."

"Win what?" Frankie asked.

"Boxers or briefs," Connie said.

Frankie looked down and smiled.

"You guys should take the lower bunks," Frankie said. "If you've never slept on a train before you might get motion sickness. This is a pretty good track, though, so maybe not."

"Where's the bathroom?" Christine asked.

Frankie pointed. "Next door. You can take a shower if you want, but not too long. We're carrying the water with us in a tank."

"I can wait until Santa Fe to take a shower," Christine said. "Can I at least brush my teeth?"

"Sure. There's plenty of water. You can wash your face, your butt, your whatever."

"Ew!" Christine said.

"Just don't stand in the shower and let the water run for twenty minutes, at least not without me."

"Double ew!"

"I'll take this one," Connie said, "and you can sleep on top of me."

"Sounds good to me," Frankie said.

Christine shook her head and headed for the bathroom.

19

CASA CALDWELL

The Caldwell house was classic Santa Fe—thick, rust-colored adobe walls with large wooden beams protruding from the roof. There was no grass, just lots of dirt and gravel and native plants. It sat perched on a hillside on the edge of town.

Everyone dropped their baggage in the living room and took the tour. The floors were tile, the furniture, rugs, and art, very southwestern. A grand piano enjoyed prominent placement.

It was cozy, designed for retirement, not for raising a family. Christine and Connie quickly noted that there was no pool. This was Santa Fe, Johnston explained, not southern California. There was a patio, paved with brick. There were awnings, tables and chairs, an ideal place for quiet contemplation, which was of course, the opposite of what the girls were looking for.

Mrs. Caldwell showed them her detached studio, just off the patio. "It's north light."

"I hope she doesn't want to paint us naked," Christine whispered to Connie.

"I don't know. It could be fun, and it is north light, whatever that means."

Christine and Connie followed Frankie into a bedroom. There was a queen-sized bed, dresser, a chair, not much more. It was obvious from the posters and clutter that it was a guy's room. There were also several pencil sketches, both on the wall and scattered about.

"This is your room," Frankie said.

"Where are you going to sleep?" Connie asked.

"In the middle."

"Nuh-uh," Christine said.

"Just kidding. I'll be out at the ranch."

"I thought your parents weren't coming for a couple of days," Christine said.

"They aren't. You guys can come out and keep me company if you like."

"We might do that," Connie said.

Frankie began digging through the clutter.

"What are you looking for?" Christine asked.

"Drugs, porn, rubbers, stuff he wouldn't want you ladies to see."

"He, who?" Christine asked.

"Oh shit," Connie said. "Is this Erik's room?"

"Yeah," Frankie said, smiling. He gave up his search. "Screw it, if you find anything good, let me know." He turned toward the door. "I smell fajitas."

They had dinner on the patio, taking advantage of Abby's cooking for one more meal before she returned to Los Angeles.

Abby brought out large platters of steaming fajitas, followed by Mrs. Caldwell bearing fresh, hand-made tortillas.

"We're not in France anymore," Connie said, digging in. "Just like home."

"Abby makes the best fajitas," Frankie said.

"I grew up in East LA," Abby said.

"When you open your restaurant," Mrs. Caldwell said, "I think you should specialize in southwestern cuisine."

"Music is still my first love, but it is something to think about."

"It's hard to make a living in music these days," Johnston said, "not that a restaurant would be any easier."

"You could always teach music, Abby." Valerius said. "It's not rock-star money, but it's stable."

Christine unpacked her duffel bag and tried to find an empty drawer. Connie dug through piles of papers on the dresser.

"What are you doing?" Christine asked.

"Digging through Erik's stuff. What does it look like?"

"You shouldn't do that. You wouldn't want some boy going through your stuff."

"Some boy isn't in my bedroom tonight." She looked behind the dresser. "You could help me."

"Why would I want to do that?"

"It's your painting I'm looking for, remember, the one with your tits showing?"

"So, you think Erik took it?"

"Could be, and this is his room, so we might as well look for it while we're here."

"How do you know he's been here? Maybe he went straight back to New York, where he actually lives."

"Well, shit. So much for that idea." She picked up one of the pencil drawings. "The boy does like naked girls. Look at all these."

Christine looked at the sketches hanging on the wall. Many of them were of young women, and many of those were in various states of undress.

"He must have seen *Titanic*," Christine said.

"LOL. Good one."

Christine leaned in to look at one of the drawings. "He's pretty good."

"A pretty good perv."

"I wonder who all these girls are?"

"Conquests, probably, or a vivid imagination."

Connie went back to rummaging through Erik's stuff.

"I thought we decided he hadn't been here," Christine said.

"Oh yeah," Connie said, picking up a guitar. "He had a guitar in Saint-Tropez," Connie said. "So, he has been here."

"It's a different guitar."

"How do you know?"

"I just do. I watched him play the other one. This isn't it."

"Whatever."

Connie opened a dresser drawer and held up a pair of briefs. "Briefs."

"I would have thought you already knew that."

"Did you already know that?" Connie asked.

"How would I know what kind of drawers the dude wears?"

"He's hot to trot for your hide. Admit it."

"It wasn't me he took a turn with in the boat."

"Wow. Be a bitch, why don't you?"

"I'm just saying."

"You could have taken a turn in the boat with Raoul."

"Now who's being a bitch?"

"You started it."

"Let's just drop it," Christine said. "The whole idea was a girl getaway, no boys. I'm sick of all the drama. Let's just hang out and go to the opera."

Connie stuck her finger down her throat.

"And eat Mexican food, and go shopping," Christine said. "There's tons of stuff to do, art galleries, whatever. And there's the ranch. Maybe they have horses."

"I hope they have a pool. There sure aren't any beaches around here."

CHRISTINE WOKE UP, angry with herself for dreaming about Erik. She was even angrier that the dream was so real, so vivid, and so pleasant. She was also not happy that Connie was mashed right up against her back with an arm draped over her waist. She decided to let it go and closed her eyes.

But Connie was on the other side of the bed, wasn't she? Christine opened her eyes and looked, but it was too dark to see anything. Maybe Connie had gotten up during the night to use the bathroom and climbed back in on the wrong side of the bed.

Christine wiggled a bit. Maybe that would wake her up and she would move. It didn't really feel like a girl behind her. She felt the arm over her waist. Was Connie's arm really that hairy? She had never paid any attention. She felt behind her. It was definitely not a girl, so she did what any teenage girl would do in the same circumstance. She screamed.

Arms and legs flailing, she scrambled for the other side of the bed, kicking whoever was back there onto the floor, and then climbing over Connie while making her escape.

"What the hell?" Connie said, suddenly awake.

Christine turned on the lamp beside the bed and pointed.

Connie looked. There was nothing there.

"There was a guy in the bed," Christine said, shaking.

"You're dreaming, girlfriend. There's nobody there."

"Frankie, if that's you I'll kick your ass."

The door opened and more lights went on just as Erik, wearing white briefs, got up off the floor and onto his knees, leaning over the bed, rubbing his eye.

"Ouch!"

Johnston, wearing nothing but boxers, stood in the open doorway. "What's going on in here?"

"She hit me in the eye," Erik said.

"You what?" Connie asked, looking at Christine.

Valerius, in pajamas, crowded in beside Johnston.

"He was in bed with us!" Christine said.

"Apparently he was in bed with you," Connie said. "I was just minding my own business."

"I thought you were in New York," Johnston said.

"I had a fight with Mom, and I split," Erik said.

The two women, wearing robes, pushed in behind their husbands.

"Oh my God," Mrs. Caldwell said.

"Your mother didn't call," Johnston said.

"She doesn't know I left," Erik said. "She's shacked up with the asshole."

"Then why didn't you call?" Johnston said.

"I thought you were in LA."

"I'm very sorry," Johnston said to the girls. "I really did not expect him to just show up like this."

"That's okay," Connie said. "We needed a little excitement. Nothing like a boy in the bed."

"Come on, Erik," Johnston said. "You can sleep on the sofa tonight and tomorrow we'll decide what to do."

Erik stood and headed toward the door, turning to smile at the girls on the way out.

The adults made their retreat. Johnston closed the door behind him.

"So much for no drama," Connie said.

Christine was disgusted. "How could he not know there was somebody in the bed?"

"Of course he knew. That's why he got in on your side."

"Maybe he was drunk."

"He didn't look drunk to me. He looked like he was enjoying himself, until you punched him in the eye."

"Enjoying himself?"

"I notice things like that."

"Like what?" Christine was thoroughly confused.

"Hard to hide a hard-on in tighty-whities."

Christine gasped. The girls climbed back in bed and straightened the covers. There was a knock at the door and Johnston opened it slightly. "May I come in?"

"Sure," Christine said.

Johnston was now wearing a robe. "Sorry about before. When I heard the scream, I didn't take the time to put on a robe."

"That's okay," Christine said. "What happens in Santa Fe stays in Santa Fe."

Johnston smiled. "Thanks. And let me apologize once more for my son."

"It's not your fault."

"But it's my responsibility. I really thought he would be in New York with his mother. I would have never asked you to come if I had known he was going to be here."

"No problem," Connie said. "Don't worry about it. We know how to handle boys."

"Not this one. Christine, did he, do anything?"

"What do you mean?"

"Touch you, assault you in any way?"

"Ew! No, I don't think so. I was kind of asleep. Sorry I elbowed him in the eye."

"He deserved it. You should have kicked him in the gonads."

Christine shrugged. "This is his room, isn't it?"

"Yes."

"And his bed."

"It wasn't an accident. He wouldn't have come in and slipped into bed without turning on any lights or making any noise."

"He probably just thought it would be a funny joke. Kids do stuff like that. Don't make a big deal out of it."

"Thank you, and again, I'm sorry."

"No problem."

Johnston started out the door.

"Oh, and Johnston," Christine said.

He paused and turned.

"Nice boxers."

He smiled, flipped off the light switch, and closed the door. The girls turned off the lamp and went to bed.

"Did you know he was coming?" Connie asked.

"Who?"

"Duh, Erik."

"No."

"Are you sure?"

"Of course I'm sure," Christine insisted. "I wouldn't have come if I had known he was going to be here."

"Is there something going on between you two?"

"What? No way. Paranoid much?"

"So why didn't you want him to be here?"

"He's a jerk, that's why. You heard what his dad just said."

———

Christine responded to the call of nature during the night. She sat on the toilet and looked over at the door, wishing she had locked it. It was the middle of the night, so surely no one would come in. She finished her business, flushed, washed her hands, opened the door, and found herself face to face with Erik.

"Crap!" Christine said, too loudly.

"No, I just need to piss," Erik said.

"And I'm supposed to think it's a coincidence?"

He stepped in. She started to go around him and leave, but he closed the door behind him. She felt trapped momentarily but made no effort to push her way out.

"Well, at least you didn't just barge in while I was peeing."

"I waited until you finished."

"Ew! Pervert."

He leaned against the vanity.

"I thought you had to pee," she said.

"Are you going to watch?"

"Uh, no."

"There's the door."

She stood facing him. "Why are you here?"

"I told you, or I told my dad. I had a fight with my mom and split."

"And it never occurred to you to go to a friend's house, or to LA, or to the ranch. You just came here and climbed in bed with me?"

"It is my bed."

"Why didn't you get in on Connie's side?"

"You were on my side."

"Yeah, right."

"I thought we made a connection in Saint-Tropez."

"There was no connection."

"You could have fooled me, especially at the club."

"We were dancing, no big deal."

"I believe your exact words were 'no, we're not.'"

Christine clenched her teeth. He was right and she knew it. Words were doing her no good.

"Are we dancing now?" he asked.

She shook her head, slowly, not taking her eyes off his. He reached out, put his hands on her hips and pulled her to him. Her heart was pounding even before he kissed her.

Thoughts raced through her head, the unlocked door, Connie in bed only a few feet away, all the adults just down the hallway, Raoul half a world away. What was she doing? This was so wrong.

But it felt so right, for moment, and then she pushed him away and fled.

20

CIELITO LINDO

THERE WAS TENSION in the air at breakfast. Connie was quite cool to Christine, and everyone was on edge about Erik's presence, most of all his father. Johnston was uncomfortable with Erik being in the house with two teenage girls, especially Christine, who, he felt, was quite innocent, and as his student, somewhat his responsibility. On the other hand, Erik was his son, and this was their home, or one of them, and he couldn't very well kick him out.

"I think I'll go bunk with Frankie at the ranch," Erik suddenly announced.

"Are you sure?" Johnston asked. "We could set up a bed in the studio."

Christine was both relieved and disappointed but said nothing.

"Nah, that's okay," Erik said. "More room at the ranch. I'll probably be out there most of the time, anyway, might as well just crash there."

"Well, I guess that would work," Johnston said. "You're still welcome here."

"What about meals?" Mrs. Caldwell asked.

"We'll just grab a couple of burritos while we terrorize the town."

"Terrorizing the town?" Connie said. "Count me in."

"Frankie's on his way over," Erik said.

"You've already spoken to him?" Johnston asked.

Erik held up a cell phone with one hand while shoveling eggs into his mouth with the other.

The doorbell rang.

"I'll get it," Mrs. Caldwell said, pushing away from the table. "I assume it's Frankie."

"Do you have plans for the day?" Johnston asked.

"Not really, hang out, whatever," Erik said.

"Hi, Frankie," Christine said as Frankie sat down at the table.

"Have you eaten?" Mrs. Caldwell asked.

"I had a burrito, or two, on the way over but some coffee would be great."

Mrs. Caldwell retrieved a cup and poured coffee.

Frankie looked at Erik's black eye. "Gang-related?"

"Huh?" Erik asked.

"You have a shiner."

"I got beat up by a girl." Erik glanced at Christine.

"Occupational hazard," Frankie said.

"I don't know that I want the two of you out at the ranch alone," Johnston said.

"Alone?" Frankie said. "The place is crawling with people. We're staffing up for the gala."

"What gala?" Christine asked.

"It's a big fund raiser for the arts, dinner and dancing, black tie," Johnston said. "You are all invited, of course."

"I don't have a black tie," Christine said.

"The boys wear black ties," Connie said. "The girls wear sexy, low-cut dresses and show lots of cleavage."

"Cool," Christine said.

"That's what I'm talking about," Frankie said.

"Is Meg going?" Connie asked.

"Oh yeah, she'll be there."

"You did bring dresses, didn't you?" Mrs. Caldwell asked.

The girls nodded.

"If Meg is your date, then we'll need another boy," Connie said.

"Why?" Christine asked.

"Unless you want to fight over Erik," Connie said.

"Ladies, ladies," Erik said. "There's enough of me to go around."

"It wouldn't be the first time he showed up with two dates," Frankie said.

"So many women, so little time," Erik said.

Neither Christine nor Connie found that funny.

"Meg's working tonight," Frankie said, "so you two can fight over me and Erik can have the loser."

"What's tonight?" Connie asked.

"The opera," Frankie said.

"What's playing?" Erik asked.

"*Fidelio*," Johnston said.

"Oh, goodio," Christine said.

"I thought you would like it," Johnston said.

"What's so 'goodio' about it?" Connie asked.

"A girl dresses up as a guy to rescue her husband from prison or something, and another girl falls in love with her," Christine said.

"So, there's lesbians?"

"Not really. The other girl thinks the main girl is a guy."

Connie laughed.

"It's a great opera," Johnston said. "I'm looking forward to it. I haven't seen it in years."

"So, it's two girls and one guy," Connie said. "What could possibly go wrong?"

"We better bounce," Frankie said, gulping coffee. "The chef wants me to hit the farmer's market and pick up some other stuff."

"Your cook sent you on an errand?" Connie asked.

"No big deal. I was coming to town anyway to pick up Erik."

"I'll get my stuff," Erik said.

Frankie finished his coffee and stood. "Are you guys coming with us?"

"Coming where?" Christine asked.

"Running errands, the ranch."

"I guess," Christine said, and then looked at the Valeriuses. "Is it okay, or did you have plans?"

"We were going to take the tour of the opera house," Johnston said, "but we can go today, and you girls can check it out later."

"You definitely want to take the tour with Erik and me," Frankie said. "We know all the trap doors and secret passageways, and where all the bodies are buried. The regular tour is for tourists."

"Oh, my," Mrs. Valerius said.

"So, it's okay?" Christine asked again.

"Sure," Professor Valerius said. "Have fun but be sure you're back here in plenty of time to change."

"And remember, we have to be there early for tailgating."

"Tailgating?" Connie said. "At the opera?"

"The Santa Fe Opera," Frankie said. "They dance to the beat of a different orchestra."

"We'll come out and pick you up so you can change," Johnston said. He looked at the Valeriuses. "You can see the ranch before the hordes arrive."

"And I can look over the menu," Mrs. Caldwell said, "and check out the chef."

"Do you have horses?" Connie asked.

"Of course, it's a ranch." Frankie said. "Do you ride?"

"I've been known to."

"Western or English?"

"Whatever you've got."

"A woman after my own heart."

"Bareback works too."

Erik reappeared, with a backpack, duffel bag, and with his guitar case slung over his shoulder.

"Let's roll."

FRANKIE SPOKE RAPIDLY in Spanish to a vendor at the farmer's market. All that Christine could understand was "*¿Con permiso?*"

The vendor nodded and said, "*Sí, sí.*"

Frankie used his cell phone to take pictures of the vendor and his wares.

"What in the world are you doing?" Christine asked.

"Taking pictures."

"Obviously, but why?"

"The chef wants to know who has what available. Then he'll come back and put in his order."

"Sounds like a lot of trouble."

"There are some very rich and influential people coming to the gala. They expect the best. If the chef can't get it locally, he'll make some calls to people he trusts and have it flown in."

"Wow. Rich people are weird."

"We do need to pick up some actual food for lunch, onions, peppers."

"What's for lunch?"

"Onions and peppers."

"Well, they definitely have a lot of peppers."

"It's New Mexico, where peppers come from."

"Where's Connie?"

"I don't know," he said. "I guess they wandered off."

"I don't think she's having a very good time."

"Why not? I love it here."

"Me too, but I think she liked Saint-Tropez a lot better."

"Raoul's not here," he said.

"Raoul? What does he have to do with it?"

"Erik likes you."

"Erik likes anything with lolos."

"In Saint-Tropez Raoul was there to keep you occupied. That gave Connie a better shot at Erik."

"A better shot? It looked to me like she scored, or he scored, or whatever."

"Just because you've already ordered doesn't mean you can't read the menu."

Christine looked at him, befuddled. "Huh?"

"He's my cousin, but Erik is a horn dog. He'll hit anything that moves, at least female, or at least I think only female, but that doesn't stop him from ordering the next thing on the menu."

"And that would be me?"

"For now, yeah."

"Well, he can't have me, so he might as well just order some more Connie. She's easy."

"And that's the problem."

"What's the problem?"

"She's easy. You're not, as far as I can tell, anyway."

"I'm not."

He smiled.

"So, if I put out, he'll move on to dessert?" she said.

"I didn't say that."

"But that's what you meant."

"Actually, you might *be* dessert."

"One more time, huh?"

"I've seen him chase a lot of tail, but you seem to be different."

"Tail?"

"Girls. Maybe he wants to stop ordering off the menu and have dessert. Maybe he thinks you're the one."

"It doesn't matter. I may swear off boys altogether. I'm too young for this crap."

"That won't help."

"Why not?"

"Because in case you haven't noticed, you're a stone fox. You attract boys like flies to honey."

"Are you hitting on me now too? I'm calling Meg and ratting you out." She pulled out her cell phone.

"No, no way. I'm just stating facts. You are gorgeous, great legs, beautiful hair, sparking eyes, and you're really sweet."

"You didn't mention my lolos."

"I didn't want to get punched in the eye." He glanced at her chest. "But those are nice too."

She put away her cell phone, grinning.

THE RANCH HOUSE was imposing, to say the least, although it was designed to fit into the landscape, which was itself spectacular. Thick stone walls were topped by a red tile roof. There were balconies with black cast-iron railings on the second story rooms. There was a commanding view below of Santa Fe and the surrounding area.

Frankie's truck pulled up and the kids piled out.

"Wow." Christine said. "This is your house?"

"It's the ranch house. It belongs to the family trust. Daniel Senior built it."

"It's huge."

"The old man entertained a lot back in the day and people came in by train from all over the country, so he patterned it after the great railroad hotels of the day, lots of guest rooms and a big ballroom."

"It looks kind of like the conservatory."

"Same architect," Erik said. "She also designed some of the railroad hotels."

"What's a railroad hotel?" Connie asked.

"Before sleepers, people would ride the train all day, spend the night in a hotel right next to the station, and then take the first train the next morning. The Santa Fe Railroad built quite a few across the southwest."

"If you couldn't afford a hotel," Frankie said, "or were in a hurry, you just slept in your seat on the train and rode all night."

"Like on an airplane," Connie said.

"Or a bus," Christine said.

"Exactly," Frankie said.

"And then George Pullman came along," Erik said.

"Who's he?"

"He invented the sleeping car. The *Estelline* is a Pullman."

"You guys sure know a lot about trains and stuff," Connie said.

"It's in our blood," Frankie said. "Daniel Senior owned a lot of railroad stock, back when railroads were the biggest and richest corporations there were."

Christine gasped as they entered the house. The great room went all the way to the roof, with a grand staircase and a balcony all the way around. The fireplace was enormous. Rugs, no doubt old and expensive, dotted the hardwood floor. The furniture was massive, much of it covered in leather, glowing with a patina resulting from decades of well-tended use.

"The ballroom is this way," Frankie said, leading the way.

"Party house!" Connie said as they stepped into the ballroom.

Workers were busy setting up tables around the periphery, leaving an area for dancing in the middle. At the far end was a stage. Large windows and French doors covered most of three walls.

"This is like the movies," Christine said, eyes darting around, trying to take it all in.

"Wait till you see it full of people dancing, with a big band on the stage," Erik said.

"Like I said, the old man liked to entertain," Frankie said.

"I love it!" Christine exclaimed. "Can I live here?"

"Sure, why not?" Frankie said. "It sits here empty most of the year, except for the caretaker."

"I could be the caretaker," Christine said.

"We have an old couple for that, retired military," Frankie said. "Works out well, but don't ever come up here at night unannounced. He might blow you away."

"Homes," Carlos, one of the young men setting up tables, said, bumping fists with Erik. "*¿Qué es?*" he asked, pointing at Erik's black eye.

"Pissed-off husband," Erik said.

"Pissed-off papa more likely," Carlos said.

Christine rolled her eyes.

Erik smiled and nodded. "Later, man."

"The pool is out here," Frankie said, leading the way through French doors onto the covered porch, which wrapped around the house.

"Kind of old school," Connie said, "but it will do."

Old school indeed, with lots of tile and rock. Daniel Senior had added it onto the house in the fifties, due in no small part to the desires of his grandchildren who spent summers at the ranch. As age had taken a toll on his body, he found himself enjoying the pool more and more, and added an adjacent indoor pool so he could swim year-round once he retired permanently to the ranch.

The porch extended from the house along one side of the pool, creating one long cabana filled with tables and chairs. At the end of the porch was a pool house. There were heavy lounge chairs on the deck, much like the ones Christine had seen in Saint-Tropez.

"Is it heated?" Christine asked.

"Of course," Frankie said. "At this altitude it nearly has to be."

THE KITCHEN WAS HUGE, and bustling. Christine stood next to Juanita, a middle-aged Mexican woman, both rolling flour in their hands.

Connie swooped through the swinging doors. "What are you doing?"

"Making tortillas," Christine said.

"Don't they have people for that?"

Juanita gritted her teeth and continued her work.

"I wanted to learn, so Juanita is teaching me. It's pretty fun."

"Fun?" Connie said, raising her eyebrows. "Whatever. Erik is looking for you."

"What does he want?"

"Well, he has a guitar, so I'm guessing he wants to serenade you."

"I'm busy. He can serenade you."

Connie shrugged and left the kitchen. Christine tossed a tortilla on the grill. As she flipped it over, she heard a guitar in the ballroom.

"'La Malagueña Salerosa,'" Juanita said, smiling. "The boy likes you. You should go out there."

Christine reluctantly went out into the ballroom. Erik sat in a chair on the stage, playing the guitar and singing. Connie sat at a table, watching and listening, while the workers continued placing chairs.

Erik stopped playing when he saw Christine. "Did you learn the lyrics?"

"More or less."

"Get up here. Let's hear it."

"Sounds like you're doing a pretty good job by yourself."

"I want to hear you sing it."

"You said it's a song a man sings to a woman."

"And you said you like to sing boy songs."

"Whatever," Christine said, stepping onto the stage.

Erik began playing from the beginning. Christine watched him play, waiting for her cue.

"Okay," he said, "here it comes."

She began singing, attracting the attention of everyone in the room. Juanita and others came out of the kitchen to watch and listen. Christine was startled as Carlos shouted, "oowee, oowee."

There was loud and enthusiastic applause from the sparse audience.

"Why did that guy yell at me?" Christine asked when the song was over.

Erik chuckled. "He didn't yell at you. That was a *grito*. That means he liked it."

"A *grito*?"

"If you're going to sing in Spanish, or Mexican anyway, get used to it."

Erik began playing "Cielito Lindo."

"Do you know this one?"

"No."

"Carlos, *ayúdame*," Erik shouted.

Carlos strolled over, singing loudly.

"Come on, Christine, everybody knows the chorus," Erik said.

Christine knew he was right—you couldn't live in southern California without hearing the song—and joined in on the chorus, along with many of the others in the room, getting most of the words right, listening closely to Erik, and improving the next time around.

"Oowee, oowee," Frankie shouted.

Christine smiled. This was fun, and now she had another song she needed to learn.

There was more applause, and *gritos*, when the song ended.

"Lunch is in the kitchen," Juanita announced loudly. "I'm not a waitress."

Everyone lined up at the kitchen door.

"Smells great," Frankie said.

"It should," Christine said. "I made it, or at least the tortillas."

They filled their plates with enchiladas, tacos, tamales, rice, beans, the works, including onions and peppers Frankie had bought, and sat down at the large round tables in the ballroom.

The chef put down his plate and sat beside Frankie. "So, how is it?"

"Fantastic. Is this what you're serving for the gala?"

"Hardly. Rich people want rich people food. This is poor people food."

"Then I guess I'm poor people."

"Me too," Christine said. "Juanita, can you teach me to cook this stuff?"

"Sure. You see what the fancy chef is eating."

The chef laughed. "You know I love your cooking, Juanita, but the rich man wants what the rich man wants, and I'm happy to take his money."

"Mrs. Caldwell will be over later, to check the menu and get all up in your business," Frankie said. "Just nod and smile and when she's gone, go back to doing whatever it is you do in there."

"No problem. It happens all the time. It never occurs to them that they're pissing off the guy who handles their food."

Frankie and the chef bumped fists.

"How's it going out here?" the chef asked.

"I'll count again, but I think we have all the tables and chairs set up." Frankie said. "At the price these people are paying for a seat, we sure don't want them to have to eat in the kitchen."

21

NORTH LIGHT

THE STABLES WERE whitewashed adobe, not nearly as elaborate as the main house, but still quite impressive.

Erik, Frankie, and Connie saddled horses while Christine watched.

"Have you ever been on a horse?" Erik asked.

"Not really," Christine said.

"Do you have any Shetland ponies?" Connie asked.

"No, but we have a buggy," Frankie said.

Erik ignored them. "This is our gentlest horse. It's great for virgins."

"Virgins?" Christine said, defensively.

Connie laughed.

"First-time riders," Erik said.

Frankie and Connie quickly mounted, obviously well experienced.

"Come on, slow pokes," Frankie said as he and Connie rode away.

Erik held the horse by the reins. "Grab the horn with your left hand and put your left foot in the stirrup."

"Where's the horn?"

Erik put his hand on the saddle horn. "This is the horn." He pointed at the stirrup. "That's the stirrup."

"I know what a stirrup is." She grabbed the horn tightly and cautiously put her foot in the stirrup.

"Now climb aboard," Erik said, putting his hand on her butt and pushing.

"Way to cop a feel."

"I didn't want you to fall."

"Right."

He handed her the reins. "Hold the reins in one hand. You can hold onto the saddle horn with the other if you have to, but that's kind of amateur, so as soon as you feel comfortable, let it go. If you're right-handed, you'll probably use your right hand for the reins."

"Got it."

"You just kind of gently tug one way or the other and the horse will go that way. Pull up and he'll stop, hopefully."

"Hopefully?"

He smiled. "This one will stop. Don't jerk the reins. He knows what to do, so go easy. We'll take it slow until you get used to it."

"Ten four," she said.

Erik mounted his horse and made a clicking sound with his mouth. His horse started walking. "Hear that?" He began walking his horse in a circle. "That's usually enough to get your horse to go, or just tap him gently with your foot."

Christine tried to make the clicking sound and kicked at the same time. Her horse jumped. She shrieked.

"Pull up on the reins."

She pulled up and the horse stopped and then started backing up.

"Easy on the reins," Erik said.

Christine eased up on the reins and her horse stopped.

"Don't kick, just barely tap him. Squeeze with your legs, sort of like when you're—never mind, just squeeze."

After a bit of practice in the corral, they were ready to ride.

"We'll never catch up with them," Christine said as they rode away.

"That's okay. It's not a race."

They rode slowly, Christine becoming increasingly more comfortable.

"This is fun," she said. "How long have you been riding?"

"Since I could walk. Frankie and I have spent summers here forever. Sometimes we pack bedrolls and go out for two or three days at a time."

"You sleep outside, like cowboys?"

"Yeah, or in the line shack."

"What's a line shack?"

"When cowboys are tending herds too far out in the boondocks to get back to the bunkhouse at night, they sleep, and eat, in line shacks, sort of like little cabins you see in cowboy movies. We don't really run a lot of cattle anymore, and they use four-wheelers instead of horses, but some of the old shacks are still there."

"Cool."

"Frankie and I know this territory like the back of our hands, all the streams and waterholes and caves and secret hiding places."

"Secret hiding places?"

He smiled. "Look, there's the opera house."

"Where?"

"Down there." He pointed. "Just off the highway."

"Wow. It's big."

"It's pretty impressive. Wait until you see it up close."

"I'm looking forward to it."

They rode on for a while and then dismounted to rest the horses. They sat on a rock and gazed at the scenery.

"Who are you and what have you done with Erik?" Christine asked.

"Excuse me?"

"You've been an actual gentleman all day and haven't even tried to jump me. Well, you did grope my butt, but I guess you get a pass on that one."

"It's still early."

"And we're back."

He laughed. "I'm really not that bad. Or at least that's what my shrink tells me."

"Your shrink?"

"Yes. I'm not stupid. I realize I have problems."

He checked his watch. "We'd better head back. Dad will be pissed if we're not there when he comes to pick you up."

"Good idea," she said. "My butt's getting sore anyway."

CHRISTINE AND ERIK entered the main house through the back door.

"Would you like to see the upstairs?" Erik asked.

"What's up there?"

"Bedrooms."

"I've seen beds."

"And ceilings?"

Christine stopped and turned. "Do you have to work at being a jerk, or does it just come naturally?"

"It comes naturally, but I do get a lot of practice."

"What time is it?"

"It's still early. Frankie and Connie aren't even back yet."

He followed her into the great room.

"Maybe you could pose for me," he said.

"Come again?"

"You could pose for me. I'll sketch you."

"I am not taking off my clothes."

"Why would you take off your clothes?"

"I saw the drawings in your room."

"Oh, those."

"Yeah, those. Is that how you get girls?"

"Yes, actually."

"And it works?"

He shrugged. "Seems to."

"Well, it's not working this time."

"It's just a drawing. You can keep your clothes on."

Erik collected his drawing gear and he and Christine stepped through the French doors from the ballroom onto the balcony. Christine took in the view. Erik leaned over and looked at her face.

"What are you doing?" she asked.

"Checking the light. Let's go around the corner."

"Why?"

"North light."

"What's so special about north light?" she asked as they walked around the corner.

"We are in the northern hemisphere, so the sun is pretty much always in the southern sky. South light is therefore directional, which makes it harsh. Ever notice how people always want you to look at the sun while they take your photograph?"

"Yeah, so?"

"So they're idiots. The light is harsh and ugly, with deep shadows that make you look bad. And you squint."

"Oh yeah, now that you mention it."

"North light is reflected light, so it's much softer, more diffuse, and much more flattering, especially to women. The shadows are much gentler and pleasing."

"Wow, I never thought about it."

He pointed at the railing. "Here, back up to the railing."

"Sit on it?"

"No, just lean back and plant your butt on it. Don't fall over or I'll have a lot of explaining to do."

He fluffed her hair, positioned it to his liking, put his hand on her chin and turned her face for the best light. "Perfect."

He backed away, sat on a table, and began sketching. He worked furiously, looking up for a moment, and then back to his pad.

"Did you take the painting?" she asked

"What painting?"

"The one that Connie's mom painted, of me."

"Why would I do that?"

"Oh, I don't know, you've been stalking me, so maybe you wanted something to take home."

"I have not been stalking you."

"Plus, you said you would take it."

"Did someone actually take it?"

"Well, it's gone, so yeah."

"Maybe Connie took it," he said. "I think she has the hots for you."

"Yeah, right."

"Maybe her mom is a lesbian and she kept it and said someone stole it."

"Are you serious?"

"What about Raoul?"

"No way."

"Did you ask him?"

"I don't have to ask him."

"But you had to ask me."

"Yes, I did."

"Why would I need a painting of you when I can make my own, like I'm doing right now?"

"Hers was topless."

"How do you know mine isn't?"

She grabbed the sketch pad and looked. She was wearing a shirt. She handed him the pad.

"I'll erase the shirt later and fill in the rest from memory," he said.

Christine glared at him and then stormed away.

"What's wrong?" Frankie asked as Christine walked quickly through the ballroom.

"Your cousin is an asshole."

"What did he do?"

Connie watched as Christine went into the kitchen.

"What did you do?" Frankie asked as Erik approached.

"I was sketching her, and she got all pissed."

"Let me see," Connie said.

Erik handed her the sketch pad.

"At least she had her clothes on," Connie said. "You're losing your touch."

Christine came out of the kitchen with a bottle of water and a cordless phone, which she handed to Frankie. "It's for you."

"Who is it?"

"I don't know. Juanita took the call and got all excited and said to give you the phone."

"Hello." He listened. "He's not here. This is Franklin Junior. I'm his son."

He listened for a while and was not happy.

The Caldwells and Valeriuses stepped into the ballroom. Mrs. Caldwell made a beeline for the kitchen.

"Okay, I'll tell him," Frankie said.

"Who was that?" Erik asked as Frankie hung up the phone.

"The band."

"What band?" Christine asked.

"The one that was supposed to play for the gala."

"Supposed to play?" Johnston asked, stepping up.

"They're on a cruise ship in the Caribbean."

"I know. They dock tomorrow and fly straight here."

"Yeah, about that. There was a fire in the engine room."

"Are they okay?"

"They are, but the ship is dead in the water and they're waiting for a tow."

"Will they make it in time?"

"Probably not, especially since they are drifting into a tropical storm."

"Why didn't he call your dad?"

"They said they only had the number for the venue." He started to dial. "I'd better call him."

"Wait," Christine said. "I have a band."

Frankie smiled. "Thanks, but this is serious."

"I am serious."

"These people are paying big money and they're expecting a professional band, a swing band, like Glenn Miller, old-people music, for dancing."

"No problem."

"These are rich, important people. We can't just throw together a show like we did in Saint-Tropez."

"Hear her out," Johnston said.

"We can do the Glenn Miller thingy," Christine said.

"Weren't you at the Hollywood Canteen night at the conservatory?" Johnston asked.

"No, I was studying for finals," Frankie said.

"Old people were dancing in the aisles," Christine said.

"Is this for real?" Frankie asked Johnston.

"It's for real. You've heard Christine sing, and the rest of the cats ain't bad."

"Cats?" Frankie asked.

"They really are good," Professor Valerius said. "I think it's a great idea."

"I should have thought of this sooner," Johnston said.

"That's why you have me, Johnston." Christine tapped him on the shoulder.

"What's the name of your band?" Frankie asked.

"The Belen Beats," Christine said. "From the school that Daniel Senior built. This is his house. We are his kids. You should have called us first."

"Can they really do it?" Frankie asked Johnston.

"They can really do it, provided we can round everyone up on short notice."

"It won't even cost you anything," Christine said. "We work for free. Well, you'll have to get them here, and a motel, and food and stuff."

"And make a generous donation to the school's activity fund," Johnston added.

"Oh yeah, and that," Christine said.

"The Belen Beats," Frankie said. "That's perfect. There's a local connection and to the conservatory."

"Call your dad," Johnston said. "Tell him what happened and that I'm trying to arrange a replacement band. Christine and I will start working the phones and I'll call him in a few hours and let him know if we can pull it off."

"Here goes nothing," Frankie said, dialing the phone.

Christine was already on her cell phone. "Sue."

"Sup? How's Santa Fe?"

"Great, but we have a problem."

"What?"

"They're throwing a big gala for the opera in a couple of days and the band is stuck on a broken-down cruise ship and can't get here in time. They need a band that can play old-people music and dance stuff."

"If only you knew where to get such a band on short notice."

"That's why I'm calling. I'm going to the opera tonight, so can you start calling the cats in the Beats?"

"Sure."

"You don't mind, do you?"

"Mind? If it gets me out of the store to blow horn and party for a few days with my girl in Santa Fe I'm all over it."

"Great. I'll call you later with the deets."

"What's the opera?"

"*Fidelio.*"

"Coolio."

22

FIDELIO

Tailgating was a time-honored tradition at the Santa Fe Opera. Many opera goers arrived early and set up folding tables and chairs in the parking lot. For some it was just a couple with a small table and two chairs behind their car with the trunk open. For others it was a major production, with several tables in a reserved space. It was all quite elegant, and somewhat bizarre to the uninitiated. It was reminiscent of picnics in an earlier time—elaborate wicker picnic baskets were in abundance. It was a world apart from the raucous, smoky, inebriated exuberance of the tailgate crowd at a football game.

Local hotels, resorts, and restaurants provided turn-key service for well-heeled tailgaters and the caterers were already out in force.

When Johnston's extended family was in full entertaining mode their spread was quite elaborate. Tonight's group was relatively small, so their tailgate party used only two parking spaces, one occupied by a battered old pickup with the tailgate down. White tablecloths covered the folding tables, and a feast, along with bottles of expensive wine, was laid out by Juanita and helpers.

The ladies wore elegant dresses, the men tuxedos. The girls wore considerably less jewelry than the women and their dresses were shorter.

"Okay, I've been to tailgate parties but nothing like this," Connie said.

There was a steady stream of people stopping by—Johnston and his wife seemed to know everybody. Some of them glanced at the kids, their gaze lingering on Christine.

"Why are those people staring at me?" Christine whispered to Frankie.

"They're music people. Johnston is talking you up. He doesn't want

Connie to feel left out, so he's not making introductions. That will come later if they're interested."

"Wow. He must still think he's running a label."

"He kind of is. He has lots of young talent at the conservatory and it's his job to promote them to the industry, especially the good ones. You don't really need much promotion once they hear you sing."

Christine grinned.

Juanita was already wrapping up when Johnston announced it was time to go into the opera house. The ladies had already donned wraps or jackets, but Frankie took a stack of blankets out of the pickup and started passing them out to the men.

"What are those for?" Connie asked.

Frankie grinned. "It can get really chilly here at night."

"Don't they have heat inside?"

"They don't even have walls."

"What the hell?"

As promised, the opera house was even more impressive up close. Christine was amazed at the sweeping lines of the roof. She was caught up in the excitement as people swarmed in. She gasped as they entered the theater. She threw her arms around Johnston. "Thank you so much!"

"The opera hasn't even started."

"It doesn't matter. This is amazing."

"Couldn't they afford walls?" Connie asked.

"Why would you want walls when you have all this?" Johnston said, waving his hand across the panorama. "It is quite spectacular when there's a thunderstorm behind the stage."

"That would be perfect for Wagner," Christine said, waving her arms over her head. "Boom! Boom! Boom!"

"Yes, it would be," Valerius said, imagining such a thing, and amused at Christine's interpretation.

"Actually, it is," Johnston said. "Unfortunately, you can't book weather in advance like you can operas, so it's a rare treat."

"I love it," Christine said.

"Whatever," Connie said.

The group found their seats, and despite Christine's attempts to the contrary, Erik placed himself between her and Connie. His hand occasionally brushed against her bare leg making her wish she had worn a longer dress.

Fortunately, Connie didn't seem to notice, or if she did, she didn't acknowledge it.

Christine followed the action closely, sometimes silently singing along, drawing Erik's attention.

Connie had no idea what the people on stage were singing, or saying, as *Fidelio* droned on and on. She checked the time on her cell phone, wondering how much longer this torture would last. Everyone else seemed to be enthralled or at least paying attention.

At intermission both Christine and Johnston went immediately to work on their phones, checking messages and returning texts.

"Do people actually like opera," Connie asked Erik, "or do they just say they do because they think it makes them look cool?"

"Some people actually like it."

"Do you?"

Erik shrugged. "I'll admit it's an acquired taste, but it doesn't suck. Some are better than others. This isn't one of my favorites."

Meg rushed up, kissed Frankie, and greeted the others. "Sorry I couldn't go in with you, but I had to help my mom in the box office."

"Can you come in for the second half?" Frankie asked.

"No, but that's okay. I already saw dress."

"Second half?" Connie asked.

"This is intermission," Frankie said.

"Kill me now," Connie said.

"Okay, boss," Christine said to Johnston, "We're just waiting to hear from three kids, and I have to go to the little girls' room."

"Great. I'm still working on permissions and chaperones."

Connie was engaged in conversation with Meg and didn't notice that not only Christine, but also Erik had slipped away.

Erik waited for Christine outside the ladies' room when she came out.

"Are you stalking me again?" she asked.

"Even stalkers have to pee."

"This is the ladies' room."

"And the men's room is right over there. I thought I would be a gentleman and escort you back to your seat."

She took his arm. "So, escort."

"We still have time," he said, leaning against the wall.

She released his arm. "This isn't going to work."

"Peeing?"

"No, whatever it is you're doing, or trying to do, or think I'm going to do."

"Why not?"

"Because I'm with Raoul."

Erik looked around. "I see no Raoul."

"You know what I mean."

"He lives in Paris. You live in Santa Monica."

"And you live in New York, so what?"

"It's a lot closer than Paris, and I'm in LA a lot."

"We talk. We text. We Skype. It doesn't matter how far it is."

"Do you kiss the screen?"

"Huh?"

"When you Skype, do you kiss the screen?"

"Ew! No."

"So he can't do this," he said, taking her hand, "or this." He pulled her into his arms and kissed her.

She let it go on for too long, and then pushed away. "Stop it."

He did not let go of her hand.

"Would he move to Santa Monica for you?"

"I don't know, probably not. He has family stuff."

"I'd move there for you, today, tomorrow, whenever you want."

"What about Connie?"

"I wouldn't move for her."

"You two seem to have something going on, or did, in Saint-Tropez."

"The thrill is gone. I think she's done with me."

"Then find somebody else. You seem to be good at it."

"I found someone else, you."

She tried to release his hand, but he held on. She used her other hand to break his grip and walked away.

He began to sing, "My Heart Belongs to Only You," doing a very credible Bobby Vinton impersonation.

Christine stopped and turned, incredulous. He was drawing a crowd, with varied reactions, some miffed, some bemused, a few snapping pictures or shooting video with their cell phones. She turned and walked briskly away, covering her face, lest she end up on the Internet.

"Who is that singing?" Mrs. Valerius asked when Christine rejoined the group as they started toward their seats.

"Some fool," Christine said.

"Where's Erik?" Connie asked.

"How should I know?"

CONNIE FEIGNED A headache and went to bed as soon as they returned to the Caldwell house. Mrs. Caldwell and the Valeriuses had drinks in the living room. Johnston and Christine sat at the kitchen table with their cell phones and notepads.

"Is that everybody?" Johnston asked.

"One of the horns and one of the dancers are out of the country, but everyone else is confirmed. We can get by without a dancer, and I'll try to find another horn, although Sue said she could just blow louder."

Johnston laughed. "I'm sure she can. That girl is amazing."

Christine nodded.

"I'd like to have more chaperones, but this will probably do," he said. "These are good kids, right?"

"You're asking me? I'm one of them."

"Yes, I guess you are, but I like to think that my students would be less likely to get into trouble on a field trip than various other groups."

"You're probably right. Most of us are dorks."

"That's not what I meant."

"I know what you meant," she said, choosing her words carefully. "I don't think you have to worry too much about them sneaking into each other's motel rooms."

He smiled. "Good."

"Although musicians are passionate people," she said. She leaned closer and whispered. "And we go topless on the beach."

"Oh, no. Maybe I do need more chaperones."

She laughed. "Do you really think we can pull this off? It sounds like it's a big deal."

"It is a big deal, but we can pull it off. Just do what you did in the concert."

"There should probably be less vocals and more instrumentals, so they can dance, right?"

"They can also dance while you sing," he said. "That's how big bands worked back in the day, dance music with a girl singer."

He stood and extended his hand. "I'll be seeing you."

"Huh?" She was confused, but then smiled. "Oh, okay."

She took his hand and stood. He put a hand on her waist, and they danced as she sang "I'll Be Seeing You."

"Are you leaving me for a teenager?" Mrs. Caldwell said when she entered the kitchen.

"We're working on the set list for the gala," he said. "We need songs people can dance to."

Mrs. Caldwell shrugged, filled an ice bucket, and left the room.

"What about Alfonso?" Christine asked.

Johnston sang "I'll Get By" while they continued to dance.

"What are they doing in there?" Professor Valerius asked when Mrs. Caldwell returned to the living room.

"Working on the set list, and dancing."

The professor looked toward the kitchen.

"You should do a duet with Alfonso," Johnston said. "Why didn't we do one before?"

"We rehearsed 'At Last' but it got cut for time."

"We'll put it back in."

"Great. I love that song, and we already have the sheet music. Alfie and I will need to rehearse a little."

Johnston paused a moment. "That was Erik singing, wasn't it?"

"When?"

"Tonight, at intermission."

She nodded.

"To you?"

She nodded again. "He was just goofing around."

"Like when he got in bed with you?"

"Yeah, like that."

"Is there something going on between you two?"

"Not really, but I think he wants there to be."

"He's my son and I love him dearly, but he's not the boy for you."

"I know."

"This is really none of my business, and completely inappropriate as the headmaster of your school. I'm sorry."

"That's okay. I think we both know there's more than a teacher-student thing going on here."

He looked alarmed.

"In a good way," she added. "Although your wife might be suspicious."

He laughed.

"What about Raoul? You two seemed to be getting along well in Saint-Tropez."

"We did. It was good, but I'm not sure where it's going, long-distance relationship and all, on two continents, and we're still kids, so it makes it kind of hard."

"It's been a long time since I was a teenager, and no doubt it's even more difficult these days, so I can't pretend to understand what the kids at school are going through."

"It's tough being a kid."

Johnston chuckled. "Well, young lady, it's probably past your bedtime, and I need a drink." He pulled her into his arms. "Be careful with Erik. And you can always come to me, about anything."

"Thanks. I will."

CHRISTINE WAS GLAD that Connie was asleep, or at least faking it, when she slipped into bed beside her. She was sure Erik's behavior, and singing, at the opera did not go unnoticed by Connie and she didn't want a confrontation. Why couldn't he have just stayed in New York? She got along great with Connie when there were no boys involved.

What was she going to do about Erik? Everyone, including his own father had warned her about him. Why were girls attracted to bad boys? Raoul was a perfect gentleman. Anyone else would have taken a turn in the boat or at least tried, but he didn't. He was willing to wait. Why couldn't she just put Erik out of her mind and stick with the boy who treated her so well?

Or did he? Raoul abandoned her two years ago, at a terrible time in her life. Maybe it was his parents' fault, maybe it wasn't. He wasn't there for all that time and now he was back. Or was he? She was in Santa Fe. He was in Paris. Erik was here, professing his love for her, or at least desire. But maybe that was just an act. She needed look no further than the sketches of all the girls in his room, or even to Connie. Had he told Connie he loved her? Like Frankie said, Erik would hit anything that moved.

She had a decision to make, and as she lay there waiting for sleep to put her out of her misery, she made a list of the good and bad, reasons for and against. But love didn't work that way. Desire didn't work that way. It was nice when Raoul kissed her, but it was exciting when Erik did. Her body spoke a different language than her head.

Finally sleep took over. Her decision would be delayed another day.

23

THE SKETCH

When Christine awoke it was clearly late. The morning sun streamed in through the window. Connie was not in bed.

Christine rolled over, in no hurry to get up. She felt something under her arm. It was a piece of heavy paper, rolled up and tied with a ribbon. She pulled at the ribbon, unrolled the paper, and looked. It was Erik's sketch of her at the ranch, finished, and a thing of beauty.

She smiled. He had not erased her shirt.

The house was quiet. Apparently, everyone had deserted her. She showered, checked the hallway, still no one, and scampered naked to her room. She danced while playing loud head-banger music. Finally, she got dressed and went to the kitchen in search of food.

"Oh! You scared me," she said, on finding Johnston in the kitchen, pouring coffee.

"Sorry."

"I didn't know anybody was here."

"Just me."

"You didn't see anything, did you?"

"See what?"

"Never mind."

"Do you want some breakfast?"

"Do you have any cereal?"

"I suppose," he said, opening a cabinet.

She chose a box of cereal, found a bowl, and got milk.

"Where is everybody?"

"Connie went to dance class with Meg. Everyone else went to see some galleries and shop at the street vendors."

"Why didn't you go with them?"

"I still had a lot of work to do, getting everything arranged for the Beats."

"So, it's just you and me?"

"Just you and me, kid."

"Cool."

She shoveled cereal into her mouth. He fiddled with his phone.

"So, if I marry Erik, you'll be my father-in-law."

That got his attention, and not in a good way. "Yes, I suppose so, but please don't."

"Either you or Count Chagny. You don't have any titles do you, like prince or baron or something?"

"Not that I know of."

"That's okay. I don't really care about stuff like that."

"Good to know."

"And if I had a baby, you would be his grandfather."

"Yes, I guess I would, provided Erik was the father, of course."

"Of course."

"What brought all this on?"

"Just thinking about stuff, the future."

"Well, why don't you just enjoy being fifteen for a bit longer? There's plenty of time for other stuff."

"Or my future father-in-law could be some guy out there I've never met."

"That's a distinct possibility. And he will be a lucky man."

She smiled and went back to her cereal. He sipped coffee. "Do you have plans for the day?"

"I need to go out to the ranch and check on some stuff," she said.

"What stuff?"

"The stage, dressing room, stuff like that, make sure everything is set up right. Too bad Ricky's not here. That's really his job."

"We could fly him out early."

"That's okay. I can handle it."

"I have no doubt you can."

"Can you give me a ride?"

"Of course, and I can check on things myself. Frankie seems to be doing a good job, but I'm like you—I want to see for myself."

"Was Erik here last night, after I went to bed?"

"No, why?"

She shrugged. "Just wondering."

JOHNSTON PULLED UP to the ranch house and stopped.

"What's wrong with Erik?" Christine asked.

"Could you be more specific?"

"Is he bipolar, schizo, or just a jerk?"

"Nobody knows for sure. I've spent thousands of dollars on psychiatrists, and they can't come up with anything definitive. Years ago, boys like him were sent to military school to straighten out, but that doesn't work anymore. Hell, we tried, but we couldn't find a military school that would take him. Hopefully he will grow out of it."

"He's only a jerk some of the time. Like yesterday, we went riding and he was really nice. It was the first time I'd been on a horse, and he took all the time in the world to help me. Well, he also grabbed my butt, but that was just to get me up in the saddle."

Johnston smiled and shook his head.

"What?" she asked.

"Nothing."

"And then he started sketching me, and then he made some smart-ass remark and pissed me off."

"That's my boy."

"And then last night at the opera he was all nice again, and then he wasn't, and then he sang that stupid song, which has probably gone viral by now. Oh, I meant to check. Did you check?"

"No. Were people filming it?"

"Duh."

They sat silently for a moment.

"Actually, it wasn't a stupid song," she said. "It was beautiful. I need to get the lyrics and learn it. Alfonso too."

"It was already an oldie when I was your age, but yes, it is beautiful. I danced many times to that song. Bobby Vinton set a lot of hearts aflutter."

She flung open the door. "Why do good girls like bad boys?"

"I wish I knew."

FRANKIE WAS COUNTING chairs in the ballroom one more time. Johnston was convinced the boy was going places.

"Where's Erik?" Johnston asked.

"Out riding, I think."

"Everything under control here?"

"I hope so. We squeezed in two more tables for late reservations, but we'll have to cut it off."

"Christine and I are going to check out the stage and the dressing room for the band."

"Okay. We don't really have a dressing room. I figured they would show up wearing clothes."

"Better to change here and not get their clothes all mussed up on the bus," Christine said.

"Are there any wardrobe changes during the show?" Frankie asked.

"I have one or two, and maybe the girl group. Oh no. I need my dresses."

"Not to worry," Johnston said. "Zoe is going by your house to pick them up."

"And my strapless bra."

Johnston and Frankie grimaced.

"I assume Zoe will know about things like that," Johnston said. "If not, you can always go shopping."

They checked out the stage, stepping it off for distance, visualizing where all the band members would sit, looking out over the ballroom. They went out through one of the French doors onto the covered porch.

"We could set up some curtains out here and use this for a dressing room," Christine said. "I don't think anybody is going to get naked."

"I certainly hope not," Johnston said.

"Except me, well, nearly."

"We can use a couple of the bedrooms for people who need more privacy," Frankie said. "Let the other kids change on the porch."

"Good idea."

"What about dinner?"

"What about it?"

"The kids will probably be here early to get everything ready, so we could set up some folding tables out here and feed them. That way we won't have to clean and reset any tables in the ballroom."

"Sounds good."

"I'll talk to the chef."

"Talk to Juanita. We don't need anything fancy."

Frankie nodded.

"Well, you two seem to have everything under control, so I guess I'll head out," Johnston said. "Do you need me to come pick you up?"

"I'll see that she gets home," Frankie said.

CHRISTINE SPOTTED ERIK returning to the ranch on horseback and went to the stables to meet him.

"You should have gone riding with me," Erik said as he dismounted.

"You didn't ask."

"Would you have if I did?"

"I don't know. I slept late, so probably not."

"And there you have it."

"There was something in bed with me when I woke up."

"Connie?"

He went to work unsaddling his horse.

"No, she was gone," Christine said.

"Where did she go?"

"Dance class with Meg, or so I'm told."

"Who told you?"

"Your dad. What difference does it make?"

"It doesn't. I'm just trying to make conversation that doesn't get you mad at me."

She followed him as he carried the saddle into the stable and put it away.

"So how did the sketch get in my bed? Your dad says you weren't there last night."

"It must have been a ghost."

"Yeah, right."

He held up a finger to his lips, and then cupped his hand over an ear. "The ghost wants to know if you liked it."

"Yes, I did. And thank the ghost for not erasing my shirt. Now I can actually put it up in my room at home."

"The ghost is pleased."

He picked up two brushes and handed her one.

"What's this for?" she asked, following him back into the corral.

He started brushing the horse's neck.

"You might as well make yourself useful."

She started brushing on the other side.

"Stay away from the tail end," he said. "You might get kicked."

She laughed.

"What's so funny?"

"I could give you the same advice."

He stopped brushing for a moment and thought about what she said. "Oh, I get it, cute."

"Everybody tells me I should stay away from you."

"They're probably right."

"They are?"

"Sure. I'm no good. I'll probably drop out of high school if I don't get kicked out permanently. No college will take me, not that I give a damn. I'm pretty much a bum."

"You're not that bad, are you?"

"Well, my trust fund kicks up when I turn eighteen, enough to live on, so everybody can just kiss my ass."

"You can be really nice when you want to be. Why don't you just try harder?"

"Would it help?"

"Help what?"

He led the horse to its stall. She followed.

"Help convince you that I'm the guy for you."

"I don't know, maybe, but it might help you even if you're not the guy for me. We've only known each other for a few weeks. How do I know you're not just looking for another naked drawing on your wall or a turn in the boat?"

"We don't have a boat here."

"How about a roll in the hay then."

"Okay, since you're offering."

She rolled her eyes. They didn't speak for a moment.

"Would you really move to Santa Monica for me?" she asked.

"Of course, in a heartbeat."

"Saint-Tropez and Santa Fe are some weird places, like a fantasy. Santa Monica is real life."

"This is real life."

"No it's not."

"I'm not ready for whatever it is you want."

"I can wait."

"No, you can't. You'll find somebody else and forget all about me."

"I will never forget about you."

He leaned against the wall and pulled her into his arms. She waited for what she knew was coming, but it never did, not really. He kissed her lightly on the cheek, laughed, and walked away.

CHRISTINE OPENED THE refrigerator and found something to drink.

"Boys suck."

"It's good you find that out now, *mi hija*, before it's too late," Juanita said.

They both turned toward the sound of a guitar. Christine walked away in the direction of the music.

"It's too late," Juanita said quietly.

Christine stepped into the great room and listened. Erik sat in one of the oversized chairs, with his feet propped up on an ottoman, playing his guitar and singing "Can't Help Falling in Love."

Frankie joined her and they stood and listened for a moment.

"Can you give me a ride home?" Christine asked.

"How about to Johnston's house. Santa Monica is a long way."

Christine laughed. "Yeah, that."

24

THE SOUTHWEST CHIEF

CHRISTINE AWOKE EARLY for the big day—the band was arriving, and excitement was building. She and Connie barely spoke. Indeed, Connie showed no interest at all in the band, or the gala, and Christine wondered if inviting her on the trip was a good idea. Maybe if Erik hadn't shown up it would have been different. But that was out of Christine's control, and there was nothing she could do about it. What she could do was to see that the band put on a great show tomorrow night. She was also looking forward to seeing her friends, especially Sue and Alfonso.

"Are you going to dance class with Meg?" Christine asked as they ate cereal and drank coffee in the kitchen.

"I don't know," Connie said. "I haven't really given it much thought."

"Do you want to go with us?"

"Us who?"

"Me and Frankie and Erik," Christine said. She was suddenly thankful that she had inserted "Frankie" between "me and Erik," and wondered if there was some subconscious intent.

"Go where?"

"To pick up the band."

"Wow, big fun."

"So, I guess that's a no."

"That's a no. I'll just hang out at the ranch."

CHRISTINE LOOKED OUT from the back seat of the pickup driven by Frankie. Erik was in the front.

"Where are we going?" Christine asked.

"Pizza run," Frankie answered.

"I thought we were picking up the band."

"We are."

Christine grew more worried as they drove on. "That sign said 'Albuquerque.'"

"Yes, it did," Frankie said.

"We're going all the way to Albuquerque for pizza?" Christine asked.

"Sure, why not?"

"Am I being kidnapped?"

"Now there's a thought," Erik said. "But what would we do with you?"

"I'm sure you'll think of something."

"What kind of pizza do you want?" Erik asked as they exited the freeway in Albuquerque.

"This is crazy. Don't they have pizza in Santa Fe?"

"Sure," Erik said, "but we want Albuquerque pizza."

"Well, I'll order when we get there, wherever there is," Christine said.

"Suit yourself," Erik said.

Christine was getting nowhere with the boys, so she just sat back and hoped everything worked out. Surely they weren't stupid.

Frankie pulled into the Albuquerque Amtrak Station.

"This is the train station," Christine said. "I thought we were making a pizza run first."

"Yes ma'am, it is," Erik said.

"What's going on?"

"I told you, pizza run," Frankie said.

Frankie pulled around behind the station, near the tracks, and parked beside a mobile pizza truck. There were folding tables under an awning, and workers busily making pizzas.

The boys piled out, dropped the tailgate, and pulled out large coolers, while Christine watched, even more confused.

"Are we picking them up here instead of Lamy? Don't we need a bus, or more cars, or something?"

"Let's take pity on the poor girl," Frankie said, as he and Erik deposited coolers under the awning.

"Okay," Erik said. "The train stops here for a few minutes, and we're delivering pizza for everyone. Well, not everyone, just the band."

"Hot and fresh," Frankie said, pointing to the pizza truck. He showed Christine his phone. "I'm tracking the train by GPS. It's about thirty minutes out."

"Cool," Christine said.

"Your friend Ricky is taking pizza orders and texting them to these guys, and they're making custom, individual pizzas, right here on the spot. They'll pull them out of the oven just as the train rolls in."

"And they'll throw in a few extras, just in case," Erik said.

"Now that's what I call a pizza run," Christine said.

"We've used these guys before for parties at the ranch," Frankie said. "Beats the hell out of delivery."

THE AMTRAK *Southwest Chief* pulled into the station at Albuquerque and stopped. Kids piled out of the two *Superliners* and a lounge car ahead of the *Estelline* at the end of the train.

Sue came running toward Christine, both screaming and happy dancing on the platform.

"What are you doing here?" Sue asked. "They said we were just stopping for pizza."

"I'm the pizza guy," Christine said.

"Check out our rock-star ride. It's like a tour bus on steroids."

Alfonso hugged Christine. "More like summer camp on wheels."

Christine tried to listen to Sue gush while greeting the other kids.

"Redneck!" Christine shouted as Jim Bob lifted her off the ground.

"Did you miss me?" Jim Bob asked.

"I didn't know you were coming!" Christine said.

"We brought your dress," Zoe said.

"You could have just sent it with Sue," Christine said, hugging Zoe.

"We're wrangling this herd," Jim Bob said.

"Johnston talked us into being chaperones," Zoe said. "There's one other couple helping us out."

"So, are you officially a couple?"

"I guess so," Zoe said.

"Look at that rig," Jim Bob said, looking at the pizza truck. "That's what I call pizza delivery."

Sue pointed at a train car. "That one's the lounge car, where we all hang out, and those two are sleepers."

"You all slept in there?" Christine asked.

"Yeah, there's lots of rooms," Sue said. "Some of them have their own bathroom, and some of them you have to go down the hall. We made the boys take those. I am so not running up and down the hall in my underwear."

"Smart."

"We have to have a sleepover tonight on the train. We have an extra bunk in our room."

"You're staying on the train?"

"That's what they said."

"Okay, sure. Sounds fun."

"Sleeping on a train is so cool, especially when it's moving."

"I'll bet it is."

"It kind of rocks you to sleep. That one at the end is called private varnish. It's an old-timey train car. It's really cool. They let us go back two at a time and look, as long as we didn't touch anything."

Christine smiled and nodded.

"The private car belongs to that guy over there," Sue said, pointing. "He's the one that's putting on the whole gala thingy."

Christine turned to look. The guy was talking to Frankie.

"We rocked that train last night," Sue said. "We had a badass jam session in the lounge car."

"People from the other part of the train came and listened," Alfonso said. "It was wild."

"Oh," Sue said excitedly, "there were a couple of cougars—"

"Drunk cougars," Alfonso added.

"They were hitting on Alfonso," Sue said. "The boy was working his crooner act and those chicks were eating it up. It was hilarious."

"Yes, it was," Franklin Titshaw said, extending his hand. "You must be Christine."

"Yes sir," Christine said, shaking his hand.

"I'm Franklin Titshaw, Frankie's dad, and this is my wife, Mona."

Christine shook hands with Mona.

"We've heard a lot about you," Mona said.

Christine smiled.

"If last night's jam session is any indication, we are in for a real treat at the gala," Franklin said.

"Wait till you hear the blonde girl sing," Sue said.

"I'm looking forward to it. Johnston assures me you are something to behold, Christine."

"I've learned a lot at the conservatory."

"Well, we'd better get our pizzas," Franklin said, checking his watch.

"I believe Abby already has them, dear," Mona said.

"Will you be riding the train the rest of the way, Christine?" Franklin asked.

"I don't know. I didn't even know we were coming to Albuquerque."

"Oh, you have to ride the train," Sue said.

"Okay, sure."

"Excellent," Franklin said. "Have pizza with your friends and then come back when you can. I'd like to visit with you before everything gets under-way."

"Yes sir," Christine said.

The Titshaws walked away.

"He'd like to visit with you?" Sue asked. "What was that all about?"

"I have no idea."

The girls stepped over to the pizza table, where Frankie and Erik were passing out pizza and drinks. Sue found hers, one of the few remaining.

"This is my friend Sue, from school," Christine said. "This is Frankie. That was his mom and dad you just met. And this is Erik, he's—" Christine had only recently discovered Johnston had a son and didn't know if he wanted that information made public.

"Frankie's cousin," Erik said.

"I'm going to ride the train, if that's okay," Christine said. "Do I need a ticket?"

Frankie laughed. "We chartered the railcars, so you definitely do not need a ticket."

"All aboard!" the conductor shouted.

Kids, carrying pizza and drinks, scurried for the train.

"Oh no," Christine said. "I forgot to order a pizza."

"Do you like everything on it?" Erik asked, handing her a pizza.

"Is it yours?"

"Yes, but I doubt I'll have any problem getting another one, or two."

"Okay, thanks," Christine said, turning to go. The girls raced to the train.

LUNCH IN THE lounge car was a raucous affair, with Christine trying to catch up on all the latest gossip, as well as answering questions about why she was in Santa Fe and how did she know these people and various forms of "Thanks for getting us the gig. This totally rocks!"

As soon as they could break away, Sue led Christine to her room on the sleeper. "It's just me and Willow in here, but it sleeps three," Sue said, pulling down a bunk. "See, pretty cool, huh?"

"Pretty cool."

"There's the bathroom. It's kind of small, but it's all ours."

Christine nodded and smiled.

"Alfonso's right," Sue said. "It is kind of like summer camp on wheels."

"I guess we'd better go see what Mr. Titshaw wants."

"You want me to go with you?"

"Sure."

They headed for the *Estelline*, by way of the upper deck of the lounge car. "You can chill out up here and watch the scenery," Sue said.

"This is Sue," Christine said as they sat down in the parlor of the *Estelline*. "She's a violin prodigy, but she blows horn in the Beats."

"How are you enjoying the trip?" Franklin asked.

"It's great," Sue said. "Everybody loves it. It totally beats the bus."

"How are the rooms?"

"Fine, kind of small, but that's okay. We're kids."

"We had hotel reservations for the other group, but there are more of you, and rooms are hard to come by this time of year, so we would have had to scatter you out all over town. That would have required even more chaperones, and a lot of logistics, so Frankie suggested I just charter a couple of cars from Amtrak and let you stay on the train."

"Works for me," Sue said. "Most of the kids have never even been on a real train before, much less slept on one, so this kind of rocks."

"Oh, hi," Abby said.

"Hi," Christine said.

"Can I get you anything, wine, beer?" Abby touched Franklin on the shoulder. "Just kidding."

"I'm good," Sue said.

"I could use some water," Christine said. "I had pizza."

"Oh, me too," Sue said.

"Christine, Frankie tells me this was all your idea," Franklin said.

"I guess," Christine said, lowering her eyes. "All I did was suggest it. Frankie and Johnston kind of took it from there."

"Well, it's an excellent idea. I was out of the country for your benefit concert, or I might have thought of it, although I guess we had already booked the other group."

Abby returned with bottled water, not the kind from the supermarket.

"Are they okay?" Christine asked.

"Who?" Franklin asked.

"The band, on the cruise ship."

"Last I heard the towline broke and they're still a couple of days out of Miami," Franklin said, taking a sip of wine. "How was Saint-Tropez?"

"It was great, better than great. It was so much fun."

"We intended to be there. We try to go every year," Franklin said, "but there were just too many obligations, business, social, so we let Frankie go with Johnston. I doubt he cared whether we were there or not. Did he behave himself?"

"Yes sir. We had a lot of fun together. He's a really nice guy."

"I heard about your impromptu concert there. How do I keep missing these things?"

Christine shrugged.

"You sang 'Caruso'?" Mona asked. "It's one of my favorites."

"Yes ma'am, with Erik."

Franklin smiled. "The boy can sing, can't he?"

"Yes sir."

"He has a gift for music, and art," Mona said.

"He certainly does."

"I just wish he would stick with something, anything."

The train slowed to a stop.

"Looks like we're in Lamy," Franklin said.

Christine stood up. No one else did. "Isn't this where we get off?"

"Ordinarily, yes. The *Estelline* has parked here off and on for nearly a century. That's fine for an empty car, but we didn't want the kids to be stuck out here with nothing to do, so I've arranged for a locomotive to pull us into Santa Fe on a short line and keep us powered up." He looked at Sue. "You'll be right in town, near restaurants, entertainment, movies, galleries, anything you need."

"Cool," Sue said.

No sooner than Christine and Sue had left the *Estelline* did the grilling begin. "Do you know that girl?"

"What girl?"

"The one who brought us the water."

"She's the attendant on the private car. She cooks and stuff."

"So where do you know her from?"

"I think she's one of the professor's students."

"You think?"

"Okay, I came out here on that train car."

"No way."

"With Frankie."

"Just you and him?"

"No, ew! Connie was with me, and my guardians, and the Caldwells."

"The Headmaster Caldwells?"

"Yep. We're staying at his house in Santa Fe."

"No way."

"Yes way. He knows Professor Valerius."

"The headmaster is that guy's cousin?"

"What guy?"

"The guy in the private car, Franklin."

"He is."

"So, let's review," Sue said. "You came out here on a private train car with the headmaster, and you're staying at his house."

"Can't put anything past you."

"What about Saint-Tropez? I thought you went with Zoe."

"I did."

"What was the headmaster doing there?"

"He was just there, with his wife, and Frankie, and Frankie's girlfriend. They have a house there."

"You called him Johnston."

"I did? When?"

"Back there in the private car."

Christine smiled and shrugged.

"Did you stay at his house in Saint-Tropez?"

"No. Zoe and I stayed with the Chagnys. She used to work for them."

"The Chagnys?"

"Raoul's parents."

"The Raoul?"

"The Raoul."

"You stayed with Raoul?"

"I stayed at his family's huge beach house," Christine said. "Raoul was also there."

"How could I not know all this?"

"You were in Korea, doing family stuff. I told you I went to Saint-Tropez with Zoe. I just left out some of the details."

"Girl, you have this whole other life. I am so jealous."

FRANKIE AND ERIK waited with the pickup at the Santa Fe depot, along with Johnston in an SUV. A charter bus was parked nearby with the baggage bays open. The kids piled off the train with their instruments and headed for the bus.

"Hold on guys," Jim Bob yelled. "Let's get everything loaded up first. We need podiums, sheet music, everything for the gig, or at least rehearsal. You can leave your clothes on the bus."

"We're going nude?" one of the girls asked.

"Uniforms, costumes, wardrobe. You know what I mean. You don't need those until tomorrow."

"Does everyone have their swimsuits?" Frankie asked.

One of the girls lifted her T-shirt and showed Frankie her bikini top.

"Okay, nice. You can set up and rehearse or whatever, then hit the pool."

"Great," Ricky said.

Jim Bob and the boys set about rounding up gear. "Let's get this show on the road," Jim Bob said.

"I'll get the kids on the bus and do a head count," Zoe said.

As the kids piled on the bus, Christine found Frankie. "I'm going to ride the bus."

"Tell Zoe I'm riding with Frankie in the truck," Jim Bob said.

"Okay," Christine said as she and Sue ran to the bus.

THE KIDS CARRIED their instruments into the ballroom at the ranch.

"There's the stage," Christine said.

"Is it big enough for us?" one of the dancers asked.

"No, but you have all this," Christine said, waving her hand across the dance floor.

"Wow. We have some choreography to work on."

"Then let's get busy," Ricky said.

The pianist sat down at the grand piano and tried it out.

Christine opened a French door and stepped onto the porch. "This will be backstage. They'll put up some curtains."

One of the boys wandered down the porch and quickly came rushing back. "Wow! Check this out!" Nearly everyone followed as he ran around the corner.

"Come on guys," Jim Bob said. "I'm not unloading all that stuff by myself."

Christine followed the group to see what was going on. She pushed her way through the crowd of kids.

"Oh no!" Christine said. She darted across the pool deck toward Connie, who lay sunning on one of the lounges, topless. Everyone, especially the boys, stared.

"Sweet," a boy said.

"Connie!" Christine said as she approached. "Put on your top."

"Why?" Connie asked.

"You have an audience."

"So?" Connie waved at the kids.

"This is the north of New Mexico, not the south of France," Christine said.

"Don't freak out," Connie said as she slowly retrieved her top.

The kids waved back. Jim Bob stepped up.

"If I see a cell phone pointed in her direction, I will stomp it flat."

Jim Bob pushed his way to the front of the group and held out his arms. "Enough with the peep show. Get your butts back in the ballroom, and out to the truck. Get that gear unloaded."

He herded them toward the ballroom.

"Can the girls go topless?" one of the boys asked.

"You wish," one of the girls said.

"Hell, no," Jim Bob said, "no topless swimming, no topless anything. How did I get roped into this?"

"What's going on?" Zoe asked as the group of kids swarmed past.

"Christine's friend from Saint-Tropez is out at the pool, without no top on."

"Connie?"

"Yeah, that one. How old is she?"

"Sixteen, I think."

"Lord, take me now."

Connie's bare breasts were frequent objects of conversation as the kids set up podiums, instruments, microphones, and went to work. They ran through their entire repertoire from the concert while Franklin and Johnston watched and listened. The dancers choreographed their routines to take advantage of the entire dance floor.

They were an eclectic group, wearing silly hats, oversized sunglasses, and all manner of outlandish clothing. All the female dancers decided to shed their shirts. Luckily, they were wearing bikinis.

"Oh my," Franklin said when Christine finished her first song, "she's really something. Where have you been keeping her?"

"At school," Johnston said.

"I certainly don't know as much about music as you, but young girls aren't supposed to sound like that, are they?"

"No, they aren't. She was remarkable when she was twelve and from what I hear it she was even more astonishing at ten. She's growing into her voice now, and in the right clothes and makeup she looks like an adult, so the effect is less startling."

"With your connections in the music business she should have a record deal by now, shouldn't she?"

"We're taking it slowly. She lost both parents before she was thirteen and was living on the streets with her father not long before she came to the conservatory. She's well cared for now by Professor and Mrs. Valerius. Her late father was insistent that she get a solid foundation in music. But yes, she will be a star."

"A superstar," Franklin added. "It doesn't hurt that she's beautiful as well."

"No, it doesn't."

"She is going to break some hearts."

"Yes, she is, and soon."

The girl group approached Johnston. "Since this isn't the school auditorium," one of them said, "can we do 'Rum and Coca Cola'?"

"I don't see why not," Johnston said.

"Please do," Franklin said. "I love that song. So did my dad, and Daniel Senior, or so I'm told."

"Do you have sheet music?"

"Yes, and we've already memorized the lyrics."

"Tell Ricky to add it to the set list."

25

LOS SEDUCTORES

THE POOL DECK was soaked from all the cannonballs, splashing, and shrieking girls being thrown in. They may have been music nerds, but they were teenagers and hormones were raging. Tomorrow night they would be expected to perform in front of rich and powerful people. Today they were just kids having fun and doing a very good job of it.

Christine had never seen most of her friends from school in swimsuits and found it a bit awkward, sort of like on the beach at Saint-Tropez, but at least here she could keep her top on. She also found it odd that bodily contact that would have never been permitted while fully clothed, especially at school, was somehow quite acceptable when kids were half-naked and wet in a pool. She found more than a few hands on her bare skin during the festivities, reminding her of being in the pool with Raoul at Saint-Tropez. Connie, under almost constant surveillance from the boys, managed to keep her top on.

Christine found Alfonso and they sat down on the lounge next to Connie.

"This is Alfonso," Christine said. "Alfonso, Connie."

"Pleased to meet you, Connie," Alfonso said.

"He's the guy I sing with at school, who all the girls want to do," Christine said. "You said you wanted to meet him."

"Ah, yes. Very pleased to meet you, Alfonso. You're French, right?"

"Italian," he said.

"That works."

"I'm going to help Juanita in the kitchen," Christine said as she stood.

"I told you, they have people for that," Connie said.

"Oh, and Sue wants me to spend the night with her on the train." Christine said.

"On the train?" Connie asked.

"We're staying on the train," Alfonso said.

"Frankie's dad chartered some train cars," Christine said. "Two of them are sleepers."

Connie looked unconvinced.

"It's pretty cool, actually," Alfonso said, "and more fun than a motel."

"Is that okay with you if I spend the night with Sue on the train?"

"Sure, I don't care."

In the kitchen, Christine, now a pro, finished grilling tortillas and put them on the pile. Juanita and the chef dispatched workers with serving pans full of Mexican food. Jim Bob, Erik, and Carlos entered from the ballroom. Erik reached for a piece of fajita meat. Juanita slapped his hand away.

"Where have you been?" Christine asked.

"Rehearsing," Erik said.

"For what?"

"We put a little act together."

"We who?"

"*Los Seductores*," Carlos said.

"What does that mean?" Christine asked.

"The heartbreakers," Jim Bob said, "more or less."

"Are you taking your act on the road?" Christine asked.

"We're taking it out to the pool. We're going to sing for our supper."

"This should be interesting. You do realize everybody out there is something of a musical prodigy."

"Yeah, so?" Erik said. "We'll kick their ass."

"We can hold our own," Jim Bob said, "and they're welcome to join in if they like."

Christine and the boys followed their noses out to the pool, where the kids were already piling paper plates full of food. Juanita watched over the serving line like a mother hen.

"Juanita, if this tastes as good as it smells I'm asking for your hand in marriage," Jim Bob said.

"I'm already married," Juanita said, "but you can come over for dinner anytime."

"Count on it."

"She's really good," Christine said.

"We eat first, then we sing," Jim Bob said, picking up two plates.

"I made the tortillas," Christine said.

"Thanks for the warning."

Christine and Sue sat together for dinner by the pool as the shadows lengthened.

"What's up with your friend Connie?" Sue asked.

"Can you be more specific?"

"She was lying out topless."

"It's a private pool. She wasn't expecting a bunch of people."

"She wasn't in any hurry to cover up when she discovered it wasn't so private anymore."

"That's Connie. Actually, that's everybody on the beach at Saint-Tropez." Christine realized too late what she had just said.

"Everybody?"

"Well, not everybody."

"What about you?"

"What about me?"

"It's like interrogating a murder suspect," Sue said, exasperated. "Did you take your top off in Saint-Tropez or not?"

"I'll never tell."

"Girl, you so did!"

"It's no big deal, and don't tell anybody. I don't want the horndogs at school all up in my business."

"I don't know if I could go topless. My parents would go ballistic."

"It's different on the beach where everybody is doing it. Plus, most of the people you don't even know and will never see again anyway."

"What about Raoul, was he there?"

Christine's face flushed. She nodded.

"Did he freak out? Did you freak out?"

"Nobody freaked out. I was a little nervous, but he had seen topless girls on the beach for years. He definitely looked, who wouldn't, but he tried to not be a jerk about it."

Sue covered her breasts. "A boy you like is looking at your boobs and you're not even making out. That's got to be like, weird."

"It was kind of weird at first, but you get used to it."

"Who else saw your boobs?"

"Good grief, Sue."

"Come on girl, spill."

"Frankie, Erik, a bunch of other people."

"Wow. Was that like worse than Raoul?"

"I don't know. It was different, I guess. Raoul's dad being there was kind of weird, but he didn't even really look."

"His dad? Ew! How gross is that?"

"They go there every year, so I'm sure he's seen plenty of boobs. Can we change the subject?"

"Okay, one more. What about the headmaster?"

"What about him?"

"Did he see your tits?"

Christine felt it run up her spine and hoped that her face wasn't turning bright red. She had only a split second to formulate a response. "We made a pact," Christine said while Sue waited breathlessly.

"A pact?"

"To never be on the beach at the same time," Christine said. It wasn't a lie at all, she reasoned, just an incomplete truth, and after all, they did make a pact.

"I would have been mortified. Can you imagine how embarrassing that would be?"

"Oh yes, I can imagine." She grinned and her face flushed.

"Why is your face red?"

Christine lowered her head and covered her face with both hands.

"The headmaster of our school saw your tits! Isn't that like illegal, or something?"

"You *cannot* tell anybody!"

Sue shook her head. "A whole other life."

While kids went back for seconds and thirds, *Los Seductores*, Jim Bob and Erik on guitar and Carlos on guitarrón, opened with "Cielito Lindo." The kids from school, and the help, joined in enthusiastically.

Franklin and his wife came out onto a balcony overlooking the pool and settled in with wine, listening to the music down below.

The boys played, and sang, "La Bamba." The dancers immediately jumped to their feet and began dancing, and everyone joined in the chorus, even if they couldn't sing.

When the song was over, the exhausted dancers headed for their chairs. "Where are you going?" Jim Bob asked. "Get back out there."

The dancers cautiously returned.

"Sue, you're up!"

Sue stood up. "BRB. I'm going to blow with the boys."

"You're going to what?" Christine was alarmed.

"With, with the boys," Sue called out as she dashed away.

"We don't have any sombreros," Jim Bob said, "so you'll just have to fake it."

Sue picked up her trumpet from a table beside the guys and they played "Jarabe Tapatío," better known as "The Mexican Hat Dance." The dancers tossed down imaginary sombreros and went at it, to the delight of the audience.

Christine watched the dancers as Alfonso and Connie joined in the dancing.

"That was fun," Sue said as she sat down beside Christine. "We really need to start a mariachi group at school."

"Yeah, like we need to take on any more projects."

"Hey, I could play violin and trumpet in the same group."

"Probably at the same time."

Sue laughed.

The dancers were finally allowed to take their seats as Erik began playing "La Malagueña Salerosa," soon joined by Carlos and Jim Bob.

"Christine," Jim Bob called out. "I am given to understand that you have learned the lyrics to this beautiful song from south of the border."

"That's okay," Christine said. "Let Erik sing it."

"Get on up here, young lady. You do not want to mess with the redneck."

Encouraged by the audience, Christine stepped up and sang. *Gritos* rang out from the balcony where Franklin, Johnston, and their wives watched. There was loud applause as Christine took a little bow and sat down.

Jim Bob checked his watch and said, "If you guys want to make the movie on time, this will have to be the last song."

The guitars started playing "Bésame Mucho" and Erik sang.

"He's looking right at you," Sue said.

"Who?"

"Erik."

"How do you know he's not looking at you?"

"No, you. The boy definitely has eyes for you, and he wants to kissa you *mucho*."

Christine didn't respond. She just looked at Erik, looking at her.

"He's seen your tits, so maybe he's just reminiscing."

Christine laughed. "Yeah, that's it."

When the song was over there was a standing ovation, or maybe the kids were just getting up to go to the bus.

"Are you going to the movie?" Sue asked.

"No, I have some things to do first," Christine said.

"But you are sleeping over."

"Yeah, I'll be there."

CHRISTINE WATCHED FROM the porch as the kids boarded the bus and drove away. Erik startled her as she turned to go into the house.

"You didn't want to see the movie?" he asked.

"Not really. I'm spending the night with Sue on the train, so I want to take a shower and wash my hair."

Erik smiled. "Yeah, you don't want to run out of water with that beautiful mane all lathered up." He ran his fingers through her hair.

"Stop it," she said. "My hair is gross. I need to wash out the chlorine."

"I could do that for you."

"Yeah, right."

"I'm serious."

"You are so not taking a shower with me." She was incredulous.

"Oh, I hadn't thought about that, but now that you mention it."

"Do you ever stop working it?"

"Working what? I just offered to wash your hair. That's all," he said. "Then you can take a shower."

"Alone."

"If you insist."

"This is such a bad idea."

"But don't you love it when someone washes your hair for you?"

"My daddy used to wash my hair."

"Oh, sorry. I didn't know."

"I did love it. It was nice."

"Let's just forget it."

She thought it over, changed her mind a few times, and finally said, "No, that's okay. Let's do it."

He followed her up the stairs and into the bedroom where she had stashed her stuff. She dug through a duffel bag and produced a bottle of shampoo.

"So, how do we do this?" she asked.

"What do you mean?"

"I always used to bend over the sink when my daddy washed it."

"They have those detachable wands in the showers," he said.

"I told you I'm not taking a shower with you."

"You're wearing a bikini, and we won't actually be taking a shower. I'll just be washing your hair but getting in the shower will be easier than bending over and trying to not get anything wet."

He was right and she knew it.

"What are you going to wear?" she asked.

"What I've got on." It was knee-length shorts and a T-shirt. "I'll take off my shirt if that's okay."

"You'll get your shorts wet."

"I can take those off too."

She tried to push past him and leave the bathroom, but he grabbed her arm. She glared at him. He released her.

"I'm sorry. I'll keep everything on."

"You'll get everything wet."

"My room is just down the hall. I can dry off and change clothes there."

She hesitated and then peeled off her T-shirt. He took his shirt off. She dropped her shorts. He didn't.

She suddenly felt uneasy as they stepped into the shower. Connie had gone with the band, probably not so much for the movie as trying her charms on Alfonso. Christine hadn't seen Frankie since the bus left and she had no idea who else was in the house, if anyone. Hopefully Juanita and some of the crew were still there cleaning up and making final preparations, and surely they would come running if she screamed.

She wouldn't have worried at all if it was Raoul in the shower with her, but then Raoul had never offered. No, it was Erik. She wasn't just alone with him, and not just alone in a bedroom, but in the shower, and that tiny bikini didn't cover much. Hopefully he wouldn't try anything, she thought, or at least not too much.

"Keep your hands to yourself," she said as he turned on the water.

"Yes ma'am. I'll be just like the wash girl at the beauty shop."

"I never used those," she said. "I always wash my hair myself before I go, to save money."

He took her hand. She looked up, wondering why. He sprayed her hand with the shower wand.

"Too hot?" he asked.

"It's fine."

"Turn around."

She turned around. He sprayed water on her hair. Normally she would have doused herself all over as soon as she stepped into the shower, so it felt weird to have water trickling down her back.

The cascade of water on her head stopped and she felt water on her ankles. She glanced down. The wand was hanging down and the wand was still spraying.

She heard the shampoo squirt out of the bottle and then she felt his hands, starting on her head and slathering shampoo all the way down. Her head bobbed as he tugged at her hair, working in the shampoo. She reached up to wipe away a trickle of shampoo before it could reach her eye. He rinsed and repeated more than once, and she didn't mind a bit. It felt wonderful. He sprayed her back and butt and legs to rinse off the shampoo. He turned off the water and squeezed her hair until it stopped dripping.

"It's just going to get wet again," she said.

"Huh?"

"I still need to take a shower."

"Oh, yeah. I forgot about that."

She turned to face him. "Thank you. That was nice."

She kissed him on the cheek.

"Any time," he said. "I'm equally as good at applying soap as shampoo."

"Good to know. Now clear out."

She had a lot more hair to dry after showering, so Erik was waiting for her in a chair on the front porch.

"You look nice," he said.

"Thanks." She was wearing tight jeans and an unbuttoned shirt tied around her midriff, with a bikini top underneath. She carried a small duffel bag.

"But you're going to get cold."

She set the bag on a chair, opened it, pulled out a denim jacket and slipped it on.

He stood, stepped over, and leaned in close. "You smell nice too."

"It must be the shampoo."

"How are you going to get to the train?"

"I don't know. I can't find Frankie. I guess I'll call your dad to come pick me up." She knew full well he would take her, but she liked sparring with him.

"I can give you a ride."

"A ride?"

"Yes, a ride."

Christine looked at him for a moment, then turned her palms up and said, "This is me, waiting for you to make some vulgar remark about giving me the ride of my life, or whatever."

"Just a ride."

She put a hand on his forehead. "Are you okay, running a fever?"

"Now who's being a smartass?"

"You're right. I apologize."

"Look, I'm trying to stop being such a jerk, because that clearly pisses you off."

"You got that right."

"I'll give you a ride to the train, and you can have a sleepover with your friends."

"They won't be there for another hour or so."

"I'm sure we can find something to pass the time."

"Sunsets are so beautiful in Santa Fe," she said as she turned to watch the sun set over the mountain.

Erik stepped up behind her and put his arms around her waist. He pulled her close. She put her hands on his. She wasn't sure what was going on with him today, but she liked it.

She thought about Raoul, half a world away. She had been warned repeatedly about Erik and had more than enough reason to push him away and run. But she could not. She felt his breath on the side of her face.

"Wait here," he whispered.

She waited. He reappeared on a dirt bike. She got on behind him and held on as they rode away, much faster than on the scooters in Saint-Tropez. Her long, luxurious, freshly washed hair trailed behind.

"Where are we going?" she asked as they headed toward Santa Fe, not that she cared. At this moment she would go anywhere with him.

"You'll see."

ERIK PARKED THE dirt bike close to the *Estelline*. They dismounted and he unlocked the door to the railcar.

"You have a key?" Christine asked.

"Yes."

"Is this where you bring all your girls?"

"No, just the ones that matter."

"How many is that?"

They stepped aboard.

"One."

He turned on the lights.

"Where's Abby?" Christine asked.

"She flew back to LA."

"I thought they were going back after the gala."

"Just the kids from your school. The *Estelline* will be parked at Lamy for a few more days."

"It's warm in here." She pulled off her jacket and tossed it onto a chair.

"The heat's on."

"I shouldn't be here," Christine said.

"Do you want me to take you to my dad's house?"

"No."

"Do you want some wine?" he asked.

"Are you trying to get me drunk so you can take advantage of me?"

"No."

"Okay, just one glass."

"Red or white?"

"It doesn't matter."

He opened a bottle and poured two glasses of white wine.

She took a sip. "It's sweet."

"It's a Napa Chenin Blanc."

"And just one for you too."

"Why?"

"I don't want you to get drunk either."

"Why not?"

"Because I'm afraid of you, that's why."

"Don't be afraid."

"And you have to get back to the ranch. You shouldn't drive drunk, especially on a motorcycle."

He dumped his wine in the sink.

"I'll just taste yours," he said, and then thought about it. "Shit!"

"What's wrong?"

"I was trying so hard to not say stuff like that."

"Like what?" She laughed. "Oh, okay, I get it."

She took a sip of wine. "That's okay." She put the glass down and turned to face him. "Have a taste."

He had a taste, from her lips, not the wine glass.

Decision time had come, and she knew it. They were alone in a private railcar. There was no one in the rest of the train, as far as she knew; they were all at the movies. She hadn't flirted with him, not really, but she had occasionally succumbed briefly to his charms.

Maybe he was just trying for another score, typical boy. Then again, he seemed to be trying, at least today, to not be such a jerk.

The kiss went on forever, increasing in intensity, tongues darting in and out. This was, Christine knew, the longest she had kissed anyone in her life. And this was just the beginning. She thought about Raoul, but not for long. All she wanted right this instant was Erik, and she was afraid she could not resist.

"Stop," she said, pushing him away.

"What's wrong? Did I do something wrong? Whatever I did, I'm sorry."

"No, it's not that." She turned, stepped away and sat on the sofa.

"Then what is it?"

"I don't know if I'm ready for this."

"Ready for what?"

"What we're doing."

"We're just kissing, that's all."

"You didn't bring me here to just kiss."

He sat down beside her.

"If that's all you want to do, then that's all we'll do."

He was really making it difficult.

"For real?" she asked.

"For real."

He put his arm around her. She rested her head on his shoulder.

"We can stop whenever you say."

"Okay." She looked up and he kissed her, this time with more passion, more intensity, and more tongue. She had never experienced anything like this. Thoughts flooded her mind, but she blocked them all out. All she wanted to think about was the moment.

She thought the bikini top with jeans looked cute, but as his hand started to roam across her bare back, she questioned her wardrobe choice. One tug and her shirt would fall open. One more and the bikini top would come loose. One gentle caress and what little protection the top offered would be gone. It was so easy she didn't even realize it had happened until she felt his hand on her breast.

She made no effort to stop him. She wondered if maybe she shouldn't do something as well, but her inexperience betrayed her and she kept her hands on his back, his shoulders, his hair. She was quite content to let him take the lead, and he seemed to be pretty good at it.

She felt one hand slip under her legs, another around her back. He scooped her up and carried her toward the bedrooms. She wanted to tell him to stop, to put her down, but she couldn't. It felt so right.

He pushed open the door to one of the bedrooms and deposited her gently on the bed. He peeled off his shirt.

He lay down beside her. She quickly rolled over into his arms.

The kissing resumed, with enthusiasm, and the hands roamed, all of them. Christine was in way over her head, and she knew it.

"Is this the room?" she asked.

"What room?"

"The room where your great-great-grandfather, you know."

"Did the opera singer?"

"Yeah, that."

He looked around. "Probably."

"What about the bed?"

"Same bed probably, but I'm sure the mattress is new. I can't imagine the step-monster would sleep on an old mattress, especially one with a history."

He went back to work. She pushed him away, but he didn't stop. She knew she should be afraid—boys don't like it when you go this far and then say no—or so she had heard. And this was no ordinary boy. She had been repeatedly cautioned to stay away from him. And yet here she was, with his hands all over her. She felt his fingers inside the waistband of her jeans. The button popped open. She heard the zipper.

"Stop." She pushed him away, harder this time. He got the message. She rolled over, her back to him, and covered her breasts with her arms and hands, clutching tightly.

"This is you saying no, isn't it?" he said.

"It's not that I don't want to, or maybe it is. Maybe I'm just too young. Maybe this is happening too fast. We've only known each other for a few weeks. I'm confused."

"That's okay."

"Not that I don't like what we've been doing tonight. It was fun, and exciting, and mostly new to me, some parts of it were way new."

He smiled.

"Who loses their virginity on a private train car anyway?" she asked.

"I did."

"No way. Seriously?"

He nodded.

"With who?"

"A gentleman never tells."

"Good."

"Frankie did too. He has a key, and nobody ever suspects you're going to use a private railcar as a make-out place. You have to admit, it's a good way to impress girls."

"I'm impressed."

"We won't do anything you don't want to do."

They lay there for a moment and then she turned to face him. The kissing resumed, with renewed interest, and so did the hands. She had given this plenty of thought—what teenager hadn't? She had not expected this moment to come so soon and so quickly. Weren't there supposed to be more steps involved? Weren't things supposed to progress from one date, or even one boy, to the next? She had no experience at all in these matters, and yet here she was in bed, and not with the boy she had expected to have her first experience with.

She wasn't sure when it happened, but the gentleness was gone. His hands no longer softly caressed, but grabbed and poked.

"Stop it!" she said.

"Stop what?"

She pulled at one of his hands. "Stop that."

But he didn't stop and suddenly it was no longer a game, no longer fun, no longer exciting. She was frightened. He was just getting started.

"Stop it!" she screamed. She slapped his face, pounded on his chest with her fists, kicked and wiggled free, rolling off the bed and onto the floor. She quickly got to her feet and backed away.

He sat up on the edge of the bed and looked at her as she covered her breasts. "I thought you wanted to."

"Maybe I did, but not now."

"You're not going to leave me like this are you?"

"Like what?"

"Unfulfilled."

"Handle it yourself."

He stood and reached out, placing a hand on her shoulder. She pushed him away.

"No. Don't. I can't do this. I'm not doing this. This was a mistake."

"You know you want it."

"Where's my shirt?"

"I don't know."

She darted through the door, zipping up her jeans. He followed her into the parlor. She found her shirt on the floor, grabbed it, put it on and buttoned it. Only did then did she remember her bikini top, which we quickly snatched up and shoved into the pocket of her jeans.

"Oh no!" she said, her eyes drawn to a bright light through the windows. "Is that the bus?"

He stepped over and pulled back the curtain slightly. "Yes."

"What are we going to do? We can't let them catch us in here."

"Why not? You're not on the school trip, so you aren't the chaperones' responsibility."

"I don't want anyone to know." She pulled on her jacket.

"That you were with me?"

"That I was with a boy, about to do it."

She pulled on her jacket and fluffed her hair.

"Hurry. Go put on your shirt."

She peeked out through the curtain while he retrieved his shirt and put it on.

"We could ride around the block," he said, "and then show up like we just got here, and I was dropping you off."

"Won't they hear the bike when you start it, and see us ride away?"

"Good point." He looked around. "Let's go."

"Where?"

"Trust me." He took her by the hand and headed toward the door at the end of the train, switching off the light. He locked the door. They hopped off and met the crowd getting off the bus.

Jim Bob looked at them suspiciously. "What's going on?"

"Uncle Franklin wanted me to check the *Estelline*," Erik said. "Make sure everything was locked up, especially the liquor, with teenagers in the next car and all."

Jim Bob nodded, unconvinced.

"We just got here," Christine lied. "I'm spending the night with Sue, on the train."

"And I'm headed back to the ranch," Erik said.

Jim Bob looked around. "Is that your bike?"

Erik nodded.

"Where's your helmet?" Jim Bob asked.

"I don't wear one."

"Not you, her."

"Oh, sorry," Erik said. "I won't let it happen again."

"Damn straight you won't."

"Well, see you guys tomorrow," Erik said. He backed away and waved.

"Be careful with that boy," Jim Bob said.

Sue grabbed Christine by the hand and rushed toward the train.

"Well?" Sue said.

"Well what?" Christine asked.

"Duh, Erik."

"He just gave me a ride."

"You were in the private car with him."

"We were just making sure everything was locked up."

"Who sends a teenager to make sure the liquor is locked up?"

"Uncle Franklin?"

"Come on. Do you think I'm stupid? That boy's all up in you, love songs, googly eyes. I see the way he looks at you."

"We were just hanging out, waiting for you guys to get back from the movie, that's all."

"Hanging out? Is that what the kids are calling it these days?"

26

THE GALA

SUE, HAIR IN A ponytail, wearing a blazer and waving a black necktie, rushed through the other kids hanging out backstage, or rather back-porch, at the ranch.

"Christine!" Sue shouted. "Do you know how to tie a tie?"

"Not even," Christine said. "How did you tie it for the concert?"

"My dad tied it."

"I got it," Jim Bob said. Sue handed him the tie. "Take off your jacket and turn around."

"Huh?"

"I can't tie it backwards."

Sue stripped off her blazer and handed it to Christine. She turned around and pulled up her ponytail. Jim Bob folded up her shirt collar, wrapped the tie around her neck, and began tying it.

"This is weird," Sue said. "Don't you need a mirror?"

"No, I do it by feel." He finished the job. "There, how's that?"

"Looks good," Christine said, handing Sue the blazer.

"Thanks. Gotta go." She turned and went.

"You look nice in a tux," Christine said.

"I didn't bring a suit with me to Los Angeles, so I had to rent something."

"Are you going to the gala?" Christine said. "I mean, actually going, like out there at a table?"

"No, I'm just the band wrangler. I was going to wear jeans and a T-shirt and hide out backstage, but I wanted to dance with my best girl."

"Zoe?"

"Her too," he said as he hugged her.

"Where is she?"

"Upstairs, downloading sheet music. They want her to play piano during the arrivals, so they can save the band for a big intro." He checked his watch. "Speaking of arrivals, you might want to change."

"I guess so. Later."

Christine stopped at the makeup table, where a makeup artist worked on one of the girl singers. "Are you nearly ready for me?"

"Just about. I have one more Andrews Sister."

"Be right back," Christine said.

Christine walked briskly through the ballroom, waving at Carlos, who was dressed in starched waiters' whites, as he and the other workers put the finishing touches on the tables.

She stopped cold in the great room, shocked to see Raoul, carrying a leather suitcase and matching hanging bag.

"What are you doing here?" Christine asked, hoping the look on her face didn't betray her.

"Aren't you happy to see me?"

"Of course I am."

"Well, do I get a hug, or what?" He dropped the suitcase and put his arm around her as she hugged him.

Erik watched from a nearby doorway as Christine and Raoul kissed.

"I didn't know you were coming," Christine said.

"It was kind of last minute. We wanted to support the opera, so here I am."

"Great," she said, smiling and nodding.

"I think it's sold out. I hope they can find a seat for me somewhere."

"You can have mine. I'm part of the entertainment and I never eat before a performance."

"Entertainment?"

"The band got like, stranded on a cruise ship or something, so the Beats are filling in?"

"The Beats?"

"A big band group from school. We did a concert a couple of months ago. I thought I told you."

"Oh yeah, that. So, you're singing?"

"No, I'm playing drums. Of course I'm singing."

"Wearing that?"

"No, silly, I was just on my way to change. Come with me. I guess you need to change too. I don't think jeans and a polo shirt will work."

"I have my tux right here."

Erik stepped back into the doorway as Christine and Raoul went upstairs, and then he followed them, watching as they stepped into a bedroom.

"This is my dressing room," Christine said.

"Where's the boys' dressing room?"

"Backstage."

"Backstage?"

"The porch, outside the ballroom. But you can change in here."

He put down his suitcase and hanging bag on the bed beside her long dress. "Is this your dress?"

"Yeah. Do you like it?"

"Sure."

"It looks better on."

She peeled the T-shirt over her head and tossed it at a chair. He hesitated a moment and then pulled off his shirt.

"I also need to shower and shave. I just got off the plane in Albuquerque. Long day."

"There's a bathroom right through there." She pointed at the bathroom door as she pulled off her shorts.

He pulled off his pants and started toward the bathroom.

"No, wait," she said. "We can talk while I change and then you can shower."

"Okay."

She turned her back and removed her bra.

"Oh shit!" Sue said, shocked as she swept through the door. Christine instinctively covered her breasts.

Sue's eyes darted back and forth between Christine and Raoul. "Shit!" She covered her eyes.

"It's okay," Christine said.

Sue spread her fingers and peeked out. "Are you sure?"

"Yes, I'm sure. We were just changing. It's not like we were making out or anything."

"I am so sorry. I came to get a black scrunchie. Do you have one? Pink just didn't work, too girlie." She reached for a bag.

"Hand me my bra," Christine said. "It's on the bed."

Sue took a step toward the bed, but Raoul had already picked up the strapless bra and handed it to Christine.

"Oh, sorry," Christine said. "Sue, this is Raoul. Raoul, Sue."

"We met at your recital," Raoul said.

"Oh, yeah, duh," Christine said. "I was a little stressed out then."

Christine slipped on her bra. "Hook me."

Sue and Raoul both reached at the same time. Sue pulled back. "I'm sure you have more experience at this than I do."

"Not really," Raoul said, hooking Christine's bra. "I don't wear bras."

"Other people's bras, girls' bras, unhooking them. I'll just shut up now."

Christine slipped into the long dress. "Zip me."

"Again," Sue said, "I yield to experience."

Raoul smiled, and zipped Christine's dress.

"Be sure and do the little hook thingy," Sue said, pointing at Christine's back.

Raoul hooked it, and then kissed Christine on her bare shoulder.

Christine whirled around. "What do you think?"

"You're right," Raoul said. "It looks better on."

"I hope I don't pop out," Christine said, pushing up her boobs and then looking for her shoes. She found them, sat down, and put them on.

"Actually, it looks fantastic on," Raoul said.

"Okay," Sue said. "I'll leave you two kids alone."

"No, wait," Christine said. "Can you stay here while Raoul takes a shower? I need to run down to makeup."

Sue looked at her like she was crazy. "You want me to wait here with your boyfriend while he takes a shower?"

"In case somebody else comes in for a scrunchie or something," Christine said. "I don't want him to walk out all naked and like, freak them out."

Sue still couldn't believe it.

"You don't have to get in the shower with him," Christine said. "Just wait here in the bedroom, at least until he gets his pants on."

Sue looked at Raoul. He didn't have his pants on now.

"Okay, sure," Sue said happily. "But he can totally come out naked if he wants. I promise to not freak out."

Raoul smiled.

"Kiss me one more time before I put on lipstick," Christine said as she stood up and held out her arms. Raoul obliged as Sue watched. Christine started toward the door.

"I thought you were putting on lipstick," Raoul said.

"Hair and makeup are downstairs," Christine said as she swooped through the door.

Sue looked at Raoul and grinned.

THE BAND AND SINGERS paced nervously backstage, listening to Zoe playing classical music on the piano. The dancers stretched.

Christine sat at the makeup table as the makeup artist applied finishing touches.

"There, how's that?" the makeup artist asked.

Christine swiveled around and looked in the mirror. "Perfect," she said. "I guess red lipstick was all the rage in olden times."

"It was."

But clearly nothing was perfect tonight. Saint-Tropez felt a million miles away. Everything had been fine until Erik arrived, and then nothing was. She had come to Santa Fe hoping to be free from both boys for a couple of weeks, while she sorted out her feelings, or predicament. Then Erik had arrived, throwing her life into turmoil, and now Raoul. On top of all that she had to perform in front of an audience of very rich and important people, not to mention people she knew and knew well.

And then there was Connie. They hadn't known each other very long, but they had become good friends, or at least Christine thought so. Now Connie was cold and distant, thinking once again that Christine was trying to steal Erik away. Not that Erik was ever really Connie's to be stolen or that she even wanted to steal him. Or maybe she did. Why did all this have to happen tonight?

The piano playing stopped and there was a smattering of applause.

Zoe stepped backstage and air-kissed Christine so as not to smudge her makeup. "Good luck. Tough room."

"Gee, thanks."

The Beats had been briefed, so they waited patiently while Franklin and Johnston took the stage and Franklin droned on endlessly about the arts and the charities and how everyone appreciated everyone showing up and supporting same.

"I'm sure some of you have heard rumors," Franklin said, "so let me confirm that the band we booked for the evening had a bit of misfortune in the Caribbean. They're all right but could not get here in time."

There were a few groans from the audience.

"Don't worry. You are in for a real treat. We found another band, a very special band, at the last minute. My cousin, Johnston Caldwell, will introduce them."

There was another smattering of applause.

"As some of you already know, my great-grandfather," Johnston began, and pointed to Franklin as he walked back to his table, "our great-grandfather, Daniel Titshaw Senior, built and endowed a music school for children in Los Angeles, the Belen Conservatory of Music. I am honored to serve as headmaster of the school, and to work with this great group of kids. They certainly deserve to be here tonight. As one of my students put it, "We are from Daniel Senior's school. This is his house. We are his kids." Without further ado, let me introduce, the Belen Beats!"

The band rushed on stage, waving and smiling, and took their seats.

Johnston made his way backstage through the dancers waiting to sally forth. "Tough room," he said to Christine.

"So I've heard."

"No problem. Just wait till the blonde girl sings." He put his arm around her shoulder.

They listened as the band launched into "In the Mood," bringing immediate applause.

"Go! Go!" Ricky whispered loudly as the dancers swarmed through the doors.

The applause was even louder as the dancers hit the floor.

"Seventy or eighty years ago, that's exactly the kind of music that was played in this ballroom," Johnston said. "I'm nostalgic for a time I never knew."

"I'll bet it was nice," Christine said.

"I'm sure it was, with the ladies dressed just like this," he said, admiring her dress.

"Are my boobs showing?" She was amazed that those words had just come out of her mouth, directed at the headmaster of her school, but then, this had been an amazing summer.

"Not too much."

"Not too much?" She checked herself, now alarmed.

"You look fine," he said, squeezing her shoulder. "You would have fit right in with the big bands back in the day."

He took her hand, put his other hand around her waist, and they danced. Ricky stared in disbelief. Zoe and Jim Bob joined in and danced.

"Did you find a seat for Raoul?" Christine asked.

"He said you told him to take yours," Johnston said. "Aren't you going to eat?"

"I never eat before a performance."

"Erik didn't seem too happy about the seating arrangements. They're sitting together."

Christine grimaced. "If I get a chance to come out for a few minutes maybe we can squeeze in a chair for me."

"Between them?"

"Maybe I'll just hang out backstage," she said as the song ended.

Johnston smiled. "Don't do that. Enjoy yourself. Come out and dance and save one for me."

She followed him to the door. "Wait."

He stopped and turned.

"Did you know Raoul was coming?" she asked.

"No, he just showed up. Is that a problem?"

"No, not really. I can handle it. It just caught me off guard."

"I hope it doesn't affect your performance."

"It won't. You know me."

"Yes, I do."

He glanced around to make sure no one was watching, took both her hands, and kissed her on the forehead. They stepped through the French doors and watched as the band launched into "Boogie Woogie Bugle Boy." Sue was rocking her trumpet on stage with the girl singers.

"Oh no, Carlos!" Christine said.

"What's wrong?" Johnston asked.

"Look at him."

Carlos balanced a large tray of food while dancing across the floor.

"He's going to get fired," Christine said.

Johnston laughed. "Only if he dumps that tray on someone."

Christine waited and watched with Ricky as the program, and loud applause and cheering, continued.

"They certainly seem to like it," Ricky said.

"Good."

The girl group left the stage and Christine peeked out to see the reaction as Alfonso sang "I'll Get By." It was, of course, quite enthusiastic. These were old people after all.

Christine stood up straight, threw her shoulders back and took a deep breath. "Showtime."

There was loud applause as Alfonso left the stage, high-fiving Christine on her way out.

She sang "I'll Be Seeing You" as couples swarmed onto the dance floor. Raoul and Erik sitting shoulder to shoulder certainly made it easier to cast a glance in their direction, but she was a seasoned pro and made a point to make eye contact with as many people as possible, especially the men.

Several limousines were lined up outside. Some of the drivers slept in their cars, others fingered their cell phones. Some leaned against the cars and chatted. One of them, Angel Álvarez, a clean-cut young man wearing a black suit, white shirt, black tie, and black cap, walked up to the porch, and listened intently as Christine sang.

Christine left the stage to loud applause. Alfonso kissed her on the cheek. "You really kill that song."

"Thanks. My great-grandmother recorded it a long time ago."

"Can I listen to it sometime?"

"Sure, if you have a turntable."

"It's on vinyl?"

She nodded.

"I have a turntable," he said, putting his arm around her. "You'll have to come over."

She elbowed him.

They waited backstage while the girl group sang "Rum and Coca Cola," which was a big hit with the audience.

"If you try to kiss me at the end of this song, you'll be singing soprano for the rest of the evening," Christine said.

"Ouch! What brought that on?"

"Boy problems."

"Sounds like there's a boyfriend in the audience."

"You don't know the half of it," she said as she took his hand and they headed onto the stage. She glanced at Erik and Raoul, both glumly staring into space. "On second thought, do kiss me at the end of the song."

"Is this a trap?"

"No," she said, smiling. "And do it like you mean it."

"I'm not getting into the middle of something am I?"

"Not really. I just want to keep them guessing."

"Them?"

"Boys."

Sue stood and blew the intro. Christine and Alfonso sang "At Last" to an appreciative audience and when it was over, he kissed her. He had her bent over backward, making it difficult to gauge the reaction from Erik and Raoul, but she smiled, or would have had her lips not been otherwise engaged, at the thought of them both fuming as Alfonso kissed her like he meant it.

After a few more songs the band took a short break and Christine decided the time had come to face the music. Scores of eyes followed her as she tried to slip unobtrusively through the ballroom. She found Carlos and he fetched a chair and squeezed it in between Raoul and Erik, who had finished their dinner and were having coffee.

Christine waved at the Valeriuses, sitting across the table.

"You were great," Raoul said as she sat down.

"Thanks," she said, and then turned nervously to Erik.

"Yeah, great," Erik said.

Could a teenage girl be any more uncomfortable? Fortunately, Franklin saved her, coming over from his table and putting a hand on the back of her chair. "I'm stunned."

"Sir?" she said, surprised.

"Johnston said you were good, but that was incredible."

"Thank you."

"It gets better," Johnston said.

"No way. It can't."

"Trust me," Erik said. "It can."

Raoul gritted his teeth. Connie, sitting on the other side of Erik, looked the other way.

"Well, I'd better get back to my table," Franklin said. "Again, Miss Daaé, you were incredible. I hate to say it, but I am happy that cruise ship broke down."

27

NONE SHALL SLEEP

AFTER A FEW minutes of small talk, that felt like an eternity to Christine, the band took the stage and played "Sing, Sing, Sing."

The dancers hit the floor, danced together for a few minutes, and then started seeking partners from the audience. It didn't take long until the dance floor was packed.

At least the music was an excuse to not talk, which was a considerable relief to Christine.

The next song was "Moonlight Serenade," which was Christine's cue. Both boys stood as she pushed back her chair. "Time to go to work," she said.

The boys watched as she leaned over and whispered to Johnston. He smiled. "Duty calls. If you'll excuse me," he said to the others at the table.

He stood, extended his arm and Christine took it. They walked to the center of the dance floor, and he took her into his arms. She put her head on his chest and they danced. She hoped neither Raoul nor Erik would try to cut in.

The song ended and the dance floor cleared. Johnston again extended his arm and escorted Christine to the stage as the band began playing the intro to "We'll Meet Again."

Johnston stepped up to the microphone. "Ladies and gentlemen, Miss Christine Daaé."

He bowed. She curtsied. He left the stage. She sang. The audience loved it and applauded loudly when she finished.

Christine waited backstage for her next number, listening to Alfonso's crooning, when Erik appeared out of nowhere, sipping wine.

"Want a taste?" he asked.

"No thanks. I'm working."

"Did you ask Raoul to come?"

"No, actually, I didn't. He just showed up."

"Why is he here?"

"I don't know, to support your family's charities?"

"He doesn't love you like I do."

Ricky hurried over. "Christine, you're up next." She nodded.

"Can we not do this right now?" she said to Erik. "I'm kind of busy and I don't need the drama."

"Drama? This is my life. I love you."

"No you don't. You just want to screw me."

"I've loved you since the first time I laid eyes on you. You were singing 'Calon Lân.'"

She started to walk away as Ricky became increasingly frantic, and then stopped and turned. "When did you hear me sing 'Calon Lân'?"

"At the beach," Erik said.

"I didn't sing 'Calon Lân' in Saint-Tropez."

"In California, two years ago."

"What?" She was stunned, to say the least.

"There was a bonfire, lots of people and music, a few kids, so I just sort of blended in."

Christine gasped.

"Then I heard you singing on the Promenade a couple of times."

"You've been stalking me for two years?"

"No, it's not like that."

"Christine!" Ricky pleaded. "You're on, now!"

Christine took the stage, composed herself, and sang "White Cliffs of Dover." By the time she finished the tears were flowing. Some of these people no doubt remembered the original Vera Lynn version.

After another short break, the band started repeating instrumentals and threw in a few others that had been cut from the Hollywood Canteen concert.

Christine returned to the table. Fortunately, Erik asked Connie to dance, somewhat defusing the situation.

"Is there something I should know?" Raoul asked.

"About what?"

"Erik."

"Not really."

"He seems a little tense."

"That's Erik."

"I didn't know he was going to be here."

"Neither did I."

"And yet here he is."

"Look," she said. "I didn't know you were going to be here either. I thought it would just be me and Connie, no boys, well Frankie, but he doesn't count."

They looked at the dancers, avoiding eye contact for a moment.

"Why *are* you here?" she asked.

"Connie called me."

"Why would she call you?"

"Apparently she thought I needed to be here."

"I don't know why she thought that, but I'm glad you're here." She kissed him on the cheek.

Connie and Erik returned to their seats when the song ended.

"Let's dance," Raoul said, taking Christine's hand.

He led her onto the dance floor as the band played "Smoke Gets in Your Eyes."

Christine was relieved that Raoul didn't speak. They just danced. She made it a point to dance very closely, not knowing whether it pissed off Erik more than it soothed Raoul, and not really caring, at least right now. There was surely an explosion to come. She just wanted to put it off for as long as possible.

Erik was on his feet even before the song ended and headed their way. Christine was certain he was going to make a scene, but he just swept past them and headed for the stage.

Christine looked at Johnston as she and Raoul sat down. He didn't look happy. "What's he doing?" Johnston asked.

"I have no idea," Christine said.

The band had just started the next song as Erik mounted the stage and signaled the bandleader to stop. A hush fell over the room. Those who knew Erik were worried, but everyone else just assumed it was part of the show.

"Should we stop him?" Raoul asked.

"No," Johnston said. "That might make it worse. Maybe people will think it was planned, whatever it is."

The band sat frozen on stage as Erik, ignoring the microphone, sang "Nessun Dorma."

Within a few notes Christine was transported. She had heard it before, this magnificent tenor, singing "Nessun Dorma" a cappella. She looked at Raoul, who had no reaction, but then he had not heard what she had that night in the little cottage. Tears formed in her eyes. She gripped Raoul's hand so tightly he thought he would lose feeling in it.

By the time the song ended Christine was sobbing openly. With a few tears in his own eyes, Johnston stepped over, took Erik's seat, and put his arm around Christine. Connie watched them, bemused.

There was loud applause as Erik left the stage. Those nearby looked at Christine and wondered what was wrong with the girl. It was a beautiful song, wonderfully rendered by Erik, but she seemed overwhelmed.

Christine stared at Erik as he approached the table. He glanced at her momentarily, and then extended his hand to Connie. "Come on, let's get out of here."

Connie leapt to her feet, and they were gone.

Christine dropped Raoul's hand and threw her arm around Johnston's neck and buried her head in his shoulder.

The bandleader quickly ordered "Pennsylvania 6-5000" and the band began playing.

Christine, wiping tears, left the table. Raoul stood, meaning to follow, but Jim Bob beat him to her, putting an arm around her shoulder, taking her hand, and followed her onto the porch.

"I'm not sure what that was all about, but I'm not going to ask if you're okay," he said. "I'm just going to stand here and hold you."

She started crying again. He just stood there and held her.

They first heard, and then saw, Erik's dirt bike come around the corner. Connie rode behind him, dress hiked up to her waist, clinging tightly to him. Erik gunned it and roared down the driveway onto the road.

The noise attracted the attention of Angel, the limo driver. Once the dirt bike had gone, he turned his attention to the couple on the porch.

"Somebody needs to tell that girl she's not properly dressed for riding a dirt bike," Jim Bob said.

Christine chuckled and wiped her tears. "She's probably not even wearing underwear."

"I wonder where they're going."

"Probably the train."

"To check on the liquor?" Jim Bob said. "I thought you did that last night."

"I think you know that's not what we were doing there last night."

"I was afraid of that."

"Nothing happened," she said defensively. "Well, something, but not that."

"Whew! That's a relief. You're too young for that shit."

"Yeah, I know."

"I may be wrong, but it looks like your boy problem may have just worked itself out."

"Looks like. That one turned out to be a stalker."

"A stalker?"

"It's a long story, and really weird."

"I never did like that boy. Now, Raoul might just be a keeper."

"Might be."

"Your Uncle Redneck could get used to riding on that Gulfstream aeroplane."

"Me too."

"But don't let me influence your decision. There's plenty of boys out there. You'll be beating them off with a stick. Just choose wisely. Sometimes you can follow your heart right off a cliff."

"Yeah, I almost found that out the hard way."

Jim Bob looked through the door. "I think they're about to wrap it up. You ready to go back in?"

She nodded. He extended his elbow, she took his arm, and they stepped back into the ballroom, just as the band began playing "I'm Getting Sentimental Over You."

"I thought you were going to dance with me," she said.

"Things got a little hectic, didn't they?"

"Definitely, but I saved the last dance for you, and they're playing our song."

"That's our song?"

"It'll do."

He took her into his arms. They danced. She rested her head on his shoulder and felt so very comfortable. It wasn't quite as comfortable as her daddy, but it was close.

Sound travels easily through the night mountain air, and Christine could hear the faint wail of a siren, and then another. She turned toward the sound, somewhat concerned, and then put her head back on Jim Bob's shoulder.

When the music ended Jim Bob kissed her on the forehead. "I'd better get backstage and start rounding up kids."

As Christine walked toward Raoul's table, she heard more sirens.

"We have to go," she said, grabbing Raoul's hand.

"Where?"

"We need a car."

"I don't have one. I came on a shuttle."

"Where's Frankie?"

"On the porch," Raoul said, leading her through the mass of people moving toward the door. They found Frankie and Meg, shaking hands with people as they left.

"We need a car," Christine said.

"I'm kind of busy," Frankie said. "Why do you need a car?"

"Erik left with Connie."

"So what? Do you want to follow him?"

"Do you hear the sirens?"

"So he gets busted for DUI. It won't be the first time."

"They were on his dirt bike."

"I'll get a car." He rushed away. Meg stepped over to the porch railing and looked toward town.

"How do you know it's Erik?" Raoul asked.

"I have a bad feeling."

"There are a lot of flashing lights," Meg said.

"Oh, no!" Christine said, covering her face.

"What is it?" Raoul asked. "What's wrong?"

Christine didn't answer, but she was clearly upset.

Frankie's truck careened around the corner of the house. The kids rushed to it and piled in, Meg in the front, Raoul and Christine in the back.

"Where are we going?" Frankie asked.

"Down there," Meg said, "where all those lights are."

Meg checked her cell phone. "I don't see any breaking news alerts, but there probably wouldn't be any yet."

Christine squeezed Raoul's hand as Frankie raced down the hill toward the flashing lights.

Christine grew more worried as they got closer. There were police cars, fire trucks, and ambulances. The road was blocked by a stopped train. First responders swarmed about.

Frankie got as close as he could and parked. "Wait here," he said, getting out of the truck. Raoul jumped out and the boys raced toward the scene but were quickly stopped by the police.

Christine opened the door. "No, stay in the truck," Meg said, but it was too late. Christine was in the street. Meg rushed around the truck and stood beside her. "Just wait here for the boys."

Christine stood frozen. There was no fear, just resignation. After an eternity the boys returned.

"It's a dirt bike," Frankie said.

That was like a knife to the heart for Christine.

"They don't know the names, but they said it was a boy in a tuxedo and a girl in a dress," Raoul said, suddenly reaching for Christine, but it was too late. She collapsed, not slowly, reaching out to break her fall, but suddenly, decisively, completely limp, onto the pavement.

28

THE NIGHT TRAIN

THE HALLWAY OF the emergency room was crowded, the Valeriuses, the Caldwells, the Titshaws, Jim Bob and Zoe, Frankie and Meg. Sue sat with Raoul. Everyone else stood, milling around, checking and rechecking cell phones, sending and receiving texts.

A doctor stepped out from behind a curtain concealing one of the beds. Raoul jumped up, expectantly.

"Can we see her?" Valerius asked.

"She asked for someone called the redneck," the doctor said.

"That would be me," Jim Bob said, stepping forward.

"Are you a relative?" the doctor asked.

"No ma'am, but I've known her since before she was born. She's like a daughter to me."

"We're her legal guardians," Valerius said.

"In a moment," the doctor said, and then turned to Jim Bob. "She said you wouldn't lie to her."

"No ma'am, I won't. So if you don't want her to know the truth, don't send me in there."

"Is she going to be okay?" Valerius asked.

"She has a concussion, so we'll keep her overnight for observation. She's awake, and responsive, but she's had quite a shock."

"When can I see her?" Raoul asked.

"We'll take it one step at a time," the doctor said. She turned to Jim Bob. "I'll go in with you, just in case, and then we'll see how it goes."

"Let's do it," Jim Bob said.

Everyone waited impatiently as Jim Bob and the doctor slipped through the curtain. Jim Bob cautiously approached the bed.

"Hey, honey, how are you doing?"

"My head hurts."

"It's not as hard as we thought, huh?"

Christine managed a smile. "What happened?"

"You passed out, or fainted, or something, and cracked your noggin on the street."

"Not me, Connie and Erik."

"They got hit by a train."

Christine started crying.

"Connie's dead," Jim Bob said.

Christine shrieked and wailed. Jim Bob took her hand. "Do you need to give her something?"

"Not right now," the doctor said.

"What about Erik?" Christine asked.

"He's hurt bad, honey, massive head trauma, I think they called it."

The doctor nodded.

"He's in a coma. We don't really know if he's going to make it or not."

Christine cried softly, tears streaming down her face.

"Can I hold her?" Jim Bob asked.

"Yes, just be careful."

"Is anything broken?"

"No," the doctor said, stepping away, "just bruises and abrasions." She pulled back the curtain. "Don't stay too long." She slipped away.

Jim Bob leaned down and scooped Christine into his arms. "Just let it out, honey. Just let it out."

Christine cried for a while, and then lifted the bed sheet. "Where is my dress?"

"They took it off," Jim Bob said. "Probably cut it off, to see how bad you were hurt."

"They cut off my dress?"

"I guess. That's what they do on the doctor shows on TV."

She sat up. "I need some clothes."

"They're going to keep you here tonight."

"Why? I'm fine."

"You have a concussion. They want to make sure you're okay before they let you go."

"Where's Erik?"

"Just down the hall."

"Can I see him?"

"Not right now. They aren't letting anybody see him, not even his daddy."

She started crying again. "Oh, no, Connie."

He took her by the shoulders and pulled her back onto the bed. "Try to sleep, honey. It's been a tough day."

"Somebody needs to call her mom."

"That's been taken care of."

Christine wiped the tears from her cheeks. "Is Raoul here?"

"Yes, of course. Everybody's here."

Christine started crying again.

"Do you want me to get him?" Jim Bob asked.

She shook her head.

"Okay, maybe later," he said. "You need to rest, or at least that's what they always say on TV."

She smiled and choked back a chuckle.

AFTER WHAT SEEMED an eternity, word came down that Christine was to be moved into a private room for the night. It was all a blur to Christine as the orderly pushed the hospital bed through the emergency room doors. It was like a horror movie, she thought, as they all leaned in to look at her, their faces distorted, like in a selfie taken too close to the camera.

Her eyes moved from one face to the next. They were all concerned, but Sue looked horrified. Raoul tried to hold Christine's hand, but the bed was rolling too quickly.

She reached out for Johnston, and he took her hand. "I am so sorry," she said.

"It's not your fault," Johnston said.

People could say that—they might even mean it—but to Christine it was indeed her fault, and she was overwhelmed by guilt, over Erik, over Raoul, and most of all over Connie, who would still be alive if Christine had not flirted with Erik, led him on, made out with him, and then pushed him away.

Everyone followed the gurney, until they were diverted to another elevator, and then reconvened outside Christine's private room. There was considerable discussion over who should stay. The Valeriuses insisted they absolutely must stay—they were her guardians, after all. The Caldwells would be staying outside the emergency room to be near Erik but would be available for Christine if needed.

One person would be allowed to sleep on a rollaway bed in the room, and

Sue declared herself the obvious choice—she was a girl and could help Christine get to the bathroom and attend to her other girl needs. Mrs. Valerius said obviously she would fulfill that duty. Zoe reminded Sue that she needed to return to the train with the other kids from school, as did she and Jim Bob, as they were chaperones, but would certainly be available as soon as Christine returned to Santa Monica, which, they assumed, would be quite soon.

"You can take the *Estelline*, if you like," Franklin said to Valerius, "tomorrow, actually, if they release her in time, or I can arrange for a jet."

"Thank you," Valerius replied. He turned to Johnston. "I hate to leave you here."

"No, go," Johnston said. "I'm sure it's best for Christine to get away from here as soon as possible. There's nothing anyone can do for Erik at this point."

"She probably wants to see him," Raoul said.

"That's not a good idea, for many reasons. She will have enough to deal with, Connie's funeral, for one."

"I can stay with her tonight," Meg said. "I don't know her all that well, but it's the least I can do."

Professor Valerius stepped away to take a phone call.

"That was Connie's dad," he said as he returned, putting a damper on the debate. "I'll pick them up at the airport in Albuquerque in the morning. That's the earliest they can get here from Vancouver."

CHRISTINE WOKE UP, disoriented, in her hospital room. It took her a moment to realize where she was, and then another moment for it all to come flooding back. She cried softly.

"Are you okay?"

She turned toward the sound, startled, and saw Raoul on a rollaway bed. His tuxedo and shirt were draped across a chair.

She fumbled for the remote and flicked on a light.

"Raoul?"

"They said one person could stay in the room."

"And they picked you?"

"No, but I won."

Christine smiled.

"Is that okay?" he asked. "I guess it should have been Sue."

"No, that's okay. Sue would probably freak out."

Raoul sat up on the bed and swung his feet onto the floor.

"Why does my butt hurt?" Christine asked.

"You passed out and fell on the road. I tried to catch you, but I couldn't. Probably a lot of stuff hurts."

She lifted the sheet and looked down at her body.

"Is anything broken?"

"No, I don't think so."

She rolled over away from Raoul. "Is it all bruised?" she asked.

"What?"

"My butt."

"You want me to look?"

"Yeah."

Raoul stepped over to Christine's bed, lifted the sheet, and looked, which wasn't difficult—she was wearing a hospital gown, leaving little to the imagination.

"Yeah, it's bruised pretty bad."

She rubbed her butt. "I'm not wearing any underwear!"

"Yeah, I noticed."

She rolled back over and adjusted her gown.

"Pervert."

"You told me to look."

"I thought I was wearing panties."

He shrugged.

"How's Erik?" she asked.

"I don't know. I've been asleep."

Christine pulled the sheet up around her neck.

"Do you want me to go check?" Raoul asked.

She nodded her head.

A minute later, Jim Bob, Zoe, and Sue rushed into the room, all trying to talk at once. Assured that she would be okay, Jim Bob announced they had to get back to the train, something about moving it to Lamy in time to hook onto the *Southwest Chief*.

"I wanted to stay with you last night, but they wouldn't let me," Sue said.

"That's okay. Raoul was here."

Sue leaned in and whispered, "You've spent the night with him twice now."

Christine tried to laugh but it hurt too much.

THE *Estelline* had been uncoupled from the short train hauling the Beats and parked on its usual siding at Lamy. Christine was given a choice of how she wanted to travel to Los Angeles, private jet, or private railcar. She chose the *Estelline*. She wanted to be in neither Santa Fe nor Santa Monica right now, and a long train ride might give her time to grieve. Johnston had called Connie's parents as soon as possible and offered to charter a jet, but they declined the offer and arrived on the first available commercial flight out of Vancouver.

Although they didn't blame her for Connie's death, it was difficult for Christine to face her parents when they arrived at the hospital. She was overwhelmed with guilt, for reasons that only she knew, and Erik, of course, but he was in a coma. There were lots of tears, but she somehow got through it.

Rather than return to Paris immediately, Raoul elected to take the train back to Los Angeles with Christine and be on hand to accompany her to Connie's funeral. The Valeriuses were not thrilled with the idea of having him on the train overnight, but reluctantly agreed, hoping it would help Christine grieve.

Christine was obviously not in a talkative mood, so Raoul listened to music on headphones while she stared out the window at the passing landscape, remembering the bus trip with her daddy along the same route. What if that trip had been delayed by a day, or hours? She might not have met Raoul on the Santa Monica Pier. She would not have met Zoe, or the Valeriuses, or gotten into the conservatory. She would not have gone to Saint-Tropez or met Erik. Connie would still be alive. She tried to put those things out of her head and think of music, but no melodies came. She flinched as they met a fast freight train on an adjacent track, laden with shipping containers.

The travel arrangements had come together on short notice and there was no time to fly Abby out to be car attendant. Frankie had loaded provisions at the last minute, so if Mrs. Valerius could figure out how to work the kitchen they would not starve.

"I'll take care of it," Raoul declared as he whipped out his cell phone.

"What are you going to do, order take-out?" Christine asked.

"Sure, why not?"

That brought a smile to Christine's face as she wondered what he was up to. Then she remembered the pizza run to meet the train in Albuquerque. Rich people had a way of doing things that ordinary people would never even think about.

Christine watched out the window as the train pulled into Winslow, Arizona. A waiter stood on the platform, holding two large plastic bags.

He climbed aboard the *Estelline* as soon as the train stopped and quickly deposited the bags on the dining room table.

"It should be hot," the waiter said. "We tracked the train and the chef tried to time it just right."

Mrs. Valerius dug into the bags as the professor pulled out his wallet.

"It's taken care of," the waiter said.

Valerius looked at Raoul. "Dinner is on me, or my dad's credit card."

"Thank you," Valerius said.

The waiter handed him a folder with the bill. Raoul looked it over, added a very generous tip, and signed.

"Oh, it is definitely hot," Mrs. Valerius said as she opened one of the containers.

The waiter looked at the bill and smiled. "Thank you, sir." He stepped back. "I trust you have plates, silverware—"

"And wine," Raoul said.

"Do you do this a lot?" Christine asked the waiter.

"Occasionally," he said, smiling. "It's a pretty popular route for private varnish. There's not enough time to come in for dinner, so they just call ahead."

"Come in where?" Christine asked.

"The Turquoise Room," he said, "in La Posada, right out there."

Christine stepped over and looked out the window. "It looks like my school."

"It was the last of the great Santa Fe Railroad hotels," the waiter said. "It was closed for many years and the railroad used it as a computer center. A couple of guys from LA bought it a few years ago and restored it."

"All aboard," the conductor called out from the platform.

"I'd better bounce," the waiter said, heading for the door. "Enjoy your dinner and call again any time."

"It looks and smells delicious," Mrs. Valerius said as she served dinner.

Christine watched curiously as Valerius put out four glasses and poured wine in all of them.

"Somehow I doubt a cop is going to pull over the train and arrest me," Valerius said. "But don't get used to it."

Christine shrugged, swirled the wine around in her glass, sniffed, and took a sip. "Pretty good."

"Where did you learn to do that?" Valerius asked.

"Saint-Tropez," she said.

"We have a winery there," Raoul said.

CHRISTINE HAD GIVEN no thought whatsoever to the sleeping arrangements, but Mrs. Valerius certainly had. They would take the same room they had on the trip out. Raoul would use the kids' room and Christine would take the master bedroom.

"No way," Christine said. "I'll sleep in the kids' room with Raoul."

"You are not sleeping with Raoul," Mrs. Valerius insisted.

"I slept with Frankie on the way out."

"You what?" Raoul asked.

"We all slept in the kids' room, me and Frankie and Connie." She flinched and closed her eyes.

After a moment of awkward silence Mrs. Valerius said, "There were three of you then. Now there's just two, of opposite sex, so it wouldn't be appropriate."

"Yeah, now there's just two," Christine said. "Connie's dead."

"I'm sorry, but you know what I mean."

"There are bunk beds in there, for kids. Do you think we're going to make out, or worse, at a time like this? We're just going to sleep."

"Wouldn't you be more comfortable in the larger bed?" Valerius asked.

"I am not sleeping in that bed."

"Why not?" Valerius asked.

"I'm just not."

"Then Raoul can take that bed and you can sleep in the kids' room," Valerius said.

THE TRAIN ROLLED ON through the night. Christine had obviously won the bedroom argument, and she and Raoul occupied the two lower bunks of the kids' room. Or maybe she had just outlasted the Valeriuses, who were sound asleep in their own room and the *Estelline* was cloaked in darkness other than the soft moonlight through the windows and the jabs of headlights on the Interstate.

Raoul was obviously asleep, but Christine lay on her back, staring at the bunk above her, thinking about Connie, and Erik, and Raoul. She was just fifteen—why was all this happening to her? There would be yet another funeral. Would she be expected to sing? Would Connie's parents even want her there? What if they found out why Connie was even on the dirt bike with Erik in the first place?

She rolled over on her side and stretched, trying to ease the stiffness. More than her butt and her head had apparently hit the pavement. She sat up and swung her legs over the side of the bed. She watched Raoul sleep for a moment. Why had she betrayed him? He was never anything but good to her, and for her. And here he was now. He could easily have caught a flight back to Paris, or just hung out at the ranch with Frankie for a few days, but here he was, sleeping in a kid's bunk on an old train car. Why couldn't she have just rebuffed Erik's advances in Saint-Tropez? Why didn't she take her turn with Raoul in the boat? He hadn't even offered, but if she had said something, surely he would have jumped at the chance. Things would be different now.

She stood and stepped across the room, rubbing her sore butt. She pulled back the sheet on Raoul's bunk and slipped in beside him. It took a moment, a long moment, but he finally woke up with a smile on his face and something warm and soft close to him.

"What are you doing?" he asked.

"Getting in bed with you."

"Why?"

"You want me to leave?"

"No, you're welcome to stay. I was just curious."

"We need to talk."

"Okay."

He put his arm around her, and she snuggled close. He liked it—she could tell. They didn't speak for a few minutes. He kissed her on the neck.

"Just talk," she said, "but not from over there."

"What did you want to talk about?"

"You're probably going to hate me."

"Why would I hate you?"

"Because of Erik."

"Erik?"

"It started in Saint-Tropez."

Raoul didn't speak.

"You must have noticed," she added.

"I noticed he was a little too interested in your nude painting."

"Topless," she corrected.

"Topless then, but who wouldn't be? He's a guy. Guys like boobs, especially bare boobs on hot girls."

"It wasn't just the painting."

"What was it?"

"We kind of kissed a little."

"Yeah, I know, at the concert."

"It wasn't just at the concert."

"I thought he was all up in Connie."

"I tried to push him away, to stay away, but he just kept after me the whole time we were there."

"And then you met him in Santa Fe?"

"No, it wasn't like that at all. I specifically asked if he would be there. I didn't want to see him. The whole idea was to get away from boys."

"But he was there."

"Yeah, he showed up the first day we were there, the first night actually, and climbed in bed with Connie and me. Freaked me out."

"And then you picked up where you left off," Raoul said sarcastically.

"No, not really, well, he did. I kept hoping he would get with Connie again, but he just kept hitting on me."

"That's why Connie called me?"

"I'm sure it was."

"So, if you pushed him away, what's the big deal?"

"I didn't push hard enough."

"You didn't?"

"Well, not until it almost went too far."

"How far did it go?"

"I slept on the train with Sue the night before the gala. They were all at the movies, and Erik gave me a ride to the train. We kind of ended up in bed on the *Estelline* and I almost made a big mistake."

She wished he would say something—his silence spoke louder than any words. She could feel his hot breath on her neck.

"You kind of ended up in bed?"

"We were making out."

"I guess that explains all the drama at the gala?"

"Yeah. He was kind of pissed off at me."

"For what?"

"For not doing it with him."

"That's why he snatched up Connie and they left?"

"Yeah, and that's why she's dead. It's all my fault."

She waited for him to say "No, it's not your fault," but he never did. She noticed that he had relaxed his grip on her.

"Do you hate me?"

She waited for what seemed an eternity, but he didn't answer. She slipped out of his bed and went back to hers. She started crying softly. After a moment she felt him beside her, against her back. She rolled over to face him, wiping tears.

"I could never hate you," he said, and then kissed her gently on the forehead.

The train rolled on through the night.

BOOK 3

SANTA FE

"It is true, Christine. I am not an Angel,
not a genius, nor a ghost."

—GASTON LEROUX, *The Phantom of the Opera*

1

BOLERO

Long blonde hair cascaded over the bare shoulders of the young woman at the piano. She wore a halter dress with a plunging neckline and a bare back down to her waist. She played and sang "Fly Me to the Moon," to a disinterested group of diners in the upscale restaurant in Marina del Rey. Nearly all the diners were older, but four college students sat at a table not far from the piano.

Frankie Titshaw took a sip of wine and said, *"Ten."*

"Ten what?" asked Harper, the attractive young woman sitting next to him.

They were accompanied at the table by fellow college students Finn and Owen.

"Finn called it 'elevator music.' That's where the expression comes from."

"You lost me," Harper said.

"The movie, with that hot chick in it," Owen said.

"What movie?" Harper asked.

"Ten," Frankie said.

"Ah, yes," Harper said. "The frat house standard."

"Bo Derek," Finn added.

"I would so hit that," Owen said.

"She's older than your mother," Harper said.

"So? I'd still hit it," Owen said.

"You would," Harper said.

"She's still hot," Frankie said.

"You know her?" Finn asked, suddenly interested.

"Not really," Frankie said. "We met at some charity thing."

There was a smattering of applause when the song finished. The girl singer quickly launched into "The Girl from Ipanema."

"More elevator music," Finn said. "Kill me now."

"Nineteen seventy-nine," Owen said, staring at his cell phone.

"Huh?" Harper asked.

"Bo Derek," Owen said.

"That's when she was born?" Harper asked.

"That's when the movie came out," Owen said. "I wonder if she has a daughter."

"Or granddaughter," Finn said.

Harper tried to ignore them, looked at the girl singer, and then back at Frankie. "Is she singing in Spanish?"

"Portuguese, I believe," Frankie said.

"She's actually pretty good," Harper said.

"Even if it is elevator music," Finn said, looking at the singer. "Nice rack, though."

"Check out her tits, Tits," Owen said.

"You guys are such pigs," Harper said.

Frankie looked over his shoulder, turned back, smiled, and said, "Yes, very nice."

"You too?" Harper looked at him, rather disgusted.

"But she looks a little young."

"Probably a freshman," Owen said.

"UCLA," Finn added.

"Music major," Harper concluded.

"You guys seem to know a lot about her," Frankie said.

"Oh. My. God." Harper said, covering her face.

"What?" Finn asked.

"She's playing 'Bolero.'"

"She must have heard us talking," Finn said.

"Ya think?" Frankie said.

The group remained silent, trying to avoid glancing in the singer's direction, while the waiter served coffee and dessert.

Frankie scribbled on a piece of paper and handed it to the waiter. "Please give this to the singer."

The waiter glanced at the paper and asked, "What does it say?"

"'La romance de Nadir.' It's French."

"I don't think she speaks French. She's from Santa Monica."

"Try her."

"Is she going to get mad? Are you trying to hit on her?"

"She won't get mad and I'm not going to hit on her. It's the title of a song."

"Oh. She doesn't take requests."

"She'll take this one."

"I don't think so."

"Trust me. Just give it to her. If she refuses, I promise it will not affect your tip."

"Okay, I'll try." The waiter reluctantly took the slip of paper.

"What the hell?" Finn asked.

"You don't like elevator music, so I thought I'd request some opera."

"Opera?" Finn said, frowning. "That's worse than elevator music."

"Are you nuts?" Owen asked.

"Probably," Frankie said.

"Twenty bucks says she doesn't do it," Finn said.

"I'm in," Owen said.

Owen and Finn reached for their wallets, and each plopped a twenty on the table.

"You're covered," Frankie said.

"Show us your money," Finn said.

"I'm good for it. Besides, that's my forty bucks on the table."

"Yeah, right," Finn said. "We'll see about that."

The girl at the piano had just finished "Bolero" when the waiter handed her the slip of paper.

Frankie shifted in his chair and looked at the girl as she read. She looked up and smiled at him. She nodded to the waiter, and he stepped away.

The girl stood and sang "La romance de Nadir" in flawless French. A hush fell over the room, all eyes on her. Harper closed her eyes and relived the opera.

There was thunderous applause when she finished, even from the waiters, especially Frankie's, who now expected an even bigger tip for services rendered.

Harper sighed and said, "Thank you."

"What the hell?" Finn asked as Harper placed her hand on Frankie's and kissed him on the cheek.

"Frankie took us to *The Pearl Fishers* in Santa Fe last year," Harper said. "It was wonderful."

"What's that, a restaurant?" Finn asked.

"Oh no, she's coming over," Owen said, lowering his head.

"It's an opera," Harper said, "but that song is sung by a man."

"She likes to sing boy songs," Frankie said.

"I do indeed," the girl said, slipping her hand over Frankie's shoulder and kissing him on the cheek.

Frankie quickly stood and she threw her arms around his neck. They hugged tightly and kissed on both cheeks. After an eternity, she backed away, wiping tears.

"I'd like you to meet my friend, Christine," Frankie said. "Christine, this is Harper, and who are you guys again?"

"Funny," Finn said. "I'm Finn. This is Owen."

They all nodded and smiled and exchanged pleasantries. The waiter appeared from nowhere with a chair, quickly sized up the situation, and placed it on the corner, putting Frankie between the two ladies. It also placed Christine next to Owen, requiring him to tilt his head to get a good view.

Christine sat down and reached for what she thought was Frankie's wine glass. "Is this yours?"

He nodded.

"You have ID?" she asked.

"Of course I have ID."

She glanced around the room and took a sip. She grimaced. "Wow, that's strong wine."

"It's Cognac, not wine."

"I thought it was wine. Shows you what I know."

"This is a brandy snifter, different shape than a wine glass." Frankie picked it up. "You hold it like this, to warm the brandy before you sip it."

"I thought you said it was Cognac."

"Cognac is a variety of brandy."

"Whatever."

"Where do you go to school, Christine?" Harper asked.

"I guessed UCLA," Finn said.

"The Belen Conservatory," Christine said.

"What's that?" Finn asked.

"A music school," Christine said.

"Is that like a college?" Owen asked.

"It's like a high school."

"You're in high school?"

Christine nodded. "I'm a junior, soon to be a senior."

"You sang that beautifully," Harper said.

"Thanks. I've never played it on piano, so I just sang it a cappella."

"You didn't need music. It was perfect."

"Okay," Finn said. "Since everyone else is avoiding the issue, what the hell, man? You two obviously have a history, and she's jailbait. What's up with that?"

"Or, to put it more politely," Harper said. "How did you two meet?"

"On the beach at Saint-Tropez," Christine said.

"I've been there," Owen said. "The beaches are topless."

Christine smiled and shrugged.

"You dog!" Finn said to Frankie.

"It was no big deal," Frankie said.

Christine slugged him on the arm. "Way to give a girl a compliment."

"Okay, it was a big deal. Well, they weren't that big."

She slugged him again.

"Big enough," Frankie said, "just right."

Finn and Owen stared at the objects of interest. Harper shook her head.

"But not as big as Connie's," Frankie said, and then flinched. "Oh shit, sorry."

"That's okay," Christine said.

"Who's Connie?" Harper asked.

"A girl we used to know," Christine said, reaching for Frankie's hand, "for one brief, glorious, tragic summer."

Frankie took Christine's hand and squeezed it.

"We slept together on a train," Christine said.

"It was a threesome," Frankie added.

"Two guys or two girls?" Finn asked.

"Two girls," Christine said, "me and Connie."

"We didn't actually sleep together, just in the same room," Frankie said, "in bunk beds."

Finn and Owen were clearly disappointed.

"Well, I'd better get back to work," Christine said, pushing back her chair.

"What time do you get off?" Frankie asked.

"In about an hour. I have to catch the last bus."

"I'll drop Harper off, swing back by and give you a ride home. We can catch up." Frankie turned to Harper. "If that's okay."

"It's fine. I have a final to study for. I shouldn't have even come."

"Where do you go to school?" Christine asked.

"USC, along with these guys."

Frankie slid the two twenties over to Christine.

"What's that for?" Christine asked.

"These two mooks bet me twenty bucks each that you wouldn't take my request, so I guess the money is yours."

Christine picked up the money and held a twenty in each hand. "I charge twenty dollars a song, so you get one more."

"'Lili Marlene,'" Frankie said.

"English, French, or German?" Christine asked.

"French."

"Sure. I love that song." She put her arm around Frankie's neck, pulled him closely, and kissed him firmly on the cheek. "Don't be a stranger."

Finn and Owen stared as Christine walked back to the small stage, stood beside the piano, and sang "Lili Marlene" in French.

FRANKIE OPENED THE door to his car in front of the restaurant. Christine hesitated. "How much have you had to drink?"

"A couple of glasses of wine."

"Is that all?"

"That's all."

"What about the Cognac?"

"Oh, yeah, that."

"So, more than you thought," she said.

"It's been over an hour, so I'm probably good."

"Probably?"

"Do you want to drive?"

"Okay, sure."

"Do you have a license?"

"Of course I have a license. I don't have a car, but I have a license."

Christine drove. "What if we get stopped and the cop smells the Cognac on my breath?" she asked.

"Tell him I've been drinking, and I kissed you."

"What if he makes me blow into one of those thingies?"

"You had one sip an hour ago. You'll blow a zero-zero."

"Okay, cool."

They drove in silence for a moment, Christine concentrating on her driving.

"You dumped your date to take me home?" Christine asked.

"She wasn't my date."

"Looked like a date to me."

"What makes you think she was my date?"

"You acted like a couple at the restaurant, and you took her home."

"Okay, you got me."

"So, Meg is history?"

"No, not at all. She's at UNM."

"What's that?"

"University of New Mexico."

"Ah."

"She's studying dance."

"So, why are you out with another girl?"

"Harper and I have known each other since kindergarten."

"And that makes it okay to cheat on Meg?"

"I'm not cheating. Harper's fiancé is at the Naval Academy. Meg is in Albuquerque. Harper and I go to the same school, so we go out occasionally, dinner, dancing, the symphony, the opera, rubber-chicken events. Meg is totally cool with it."

Christine laughed. "What's a rubber-chicken event?"

"Galas, banquets, charity things, like the one in Santa Fe."

"I didn't eat. Did they serve rubber chicken?"

"No, actually, the food was excellent. My mom saw to that."

"Do you go to a lot of galas?"

"Yeah, when my parents are out of town or double-booked, I end up going. Harper's in the same boat, so I go to some of hers too."

"Must be tough."

"What must be tough?"

"Being rich."

"Actually, it is," Frankie said. "It's a lot of work."

"Do you hear from Raoul?"

"We talk."

"Where is he going to college?"

"Cambridge, last I heard, or will be, in the fall."

"Cambridge? Where's that?"

"England."

"So, not France?"

"Not France."

"Does he have a girlfriend?"

"I don't think so. You'd know these things if you returned his calls."

Christine didn't speak. Frankie looked out the window. "You shouldn't be taking the bus through this neighborhood."

"A girl's gotta make a living."

"You're still in high school. Don't you get an allowance?"

"Mrs. Valerius never seems to remember, and I hate to ask."

"You should remind her, put a note on the refrigerator or something."

"That wouldn't work."

"Why not?"

"It just wouldn't. She's been kind of weird since the professor died, even before that, actually."

"Weird how?"

"Well, at first I thought she was just stressed out because of the professor, all the chemo and stuff, but then it got worse."

"What got worse?"

"She did. She can't remember stuff. Sometimes she thinks the professor is still alive and gets pissed when he doesn't come home from work."

"Wow. I had no idea."

"So I work. I don't mind."

"Okay, back to the bus at night. You're a pretty tempting target."

"That's why I'm wearing a jacket, and I have pepper spray in my purse."

"I still don't like it. A jacket doesn't cover your legs, which look pretty good, by the way."

"Pervert."

"You should take some baggy clothes to work, like a sweat suit, and change before you go home."

"Okay, Daddy."

"Hey, I'm just trying to look out for you."

"I know. I was kidding."

"Didn't you used to sing on the Promenade?"

"I did. Still could, I guess. The money would probably be better, and closer to home, but I did it for charity for so long I wouldn't feel right about keeping the money. Kind of dishonest, you know?"

"Yeah, I guess it would be," he said.

"Jim Bob got us the gig at the restaurant. He played piano. I sang. He left to go to Santa Fe with Zoe. I stayed."

Christine parked in front of her house and handed Frankie the keys. "Here we are. Do you want to come in?"

"Sure. I guess I need to sober up before I drive home."

"Sorry, I'm still sensitive about—"

He reached over and touched her shoulder. "I know."

They got out of the car and walked up to the house. Christine unlocked the front door and pushed it open. "I'm home."

Mrs. Valerius sat in a recliner, watching television, but the television was not turned on.

"Where have you been?" Mrs. Valerius asked.

"At work. You remember Frankie."

"Who?" Mrs. Valerius asked.

"Frankie, from Santa Fe."

"Hello, Mrs. Valerius," Frankie said.

"Does he go to school with you?" Mrs. Valerius asked.

"No," Christine said. "He's Raoul's friend. He went to Santa Fe with us, remember? We rode the train."

"Have you seen the professor?" Mrs. Valerius asked. "He didn't come home."

Christine didn't answer.

"It's a long way to Santa Fe. Is that why you're so late?"

"We weren't in Santa Fe tonight. I was at work."

"Oh, okay." Mrs. Valerius went back to not watching television.

Christine took Frankie by the hand and led him away. "Do you want me to make you some coffee?"

"No, I'm okay," he said, looking over his shoulder at Mrs. Valerius.

"That's not good," Frankie said as they entered Christine's room.

"Tell me about it."

Christine closed the door. Frankie looked around for a place to sit.

"Sorry, my room's a mess," she said.

"That's okay. You should see mine."

"Don't you have a maid?"

"No, I have my own place now, with a roommate, close to campus. I'm doing the whole college thing."

She cleared off a place on the bed and he sat down. She turned her back and peeled off her dress. He tried to not look, but he was a guy, and she was hot. She picked up a T-shirt and slipped it on.

"Have you heard from Erik?" she asked as she turned back around.

"Not since he left the hospital."

"How was he?"

"Not good."

"Not good how?" She plopped down on the bed beside him.

"His face was a mess, but he refused plastic surgery. He just took off."

"Where did he go?"

"Nobody knows."

"What does he do for money?"

"We all have a trust fund, walking-around money until we turn eighteen, then it gets bigger, so at least he has enough to live on."

"Johnston's not helping him?"

"He would if he could, but nobody knows where he is."

"Well, that sucks."

"When is your school out?" Frankie asked, trying to change the subject.

"Next week. Thank God."

"I thought you liked school."

"I did, not so much anymore, especially after Johnston left. The new guy's a dick."

"You can tough it out one more year, can't you?"

"I don't know, maybe. I was never any good at music, composing it or even reading it. The only thing I was good at was singing, and I haven't really cared about that since the accident."

"You sounded pretty good tonight."

"Your friend was right. It's elevator music. Anybody can sing that crap."

"The last two you sang for me."

"I can do it when I want to. I just don't want to anymore."

"What are you going to do for the summer?"

"Keep singing at the restaurant until they get tired of me. Then Mickey D's, I guess, or maybe retail."

"You should come to Santa Fe for the summer."

"Yeah, right."

"I'm serious."

"There's no way."

"Why not?" he asked.

"Um, work."

"You could get a job in Santa Fe."

"Sure, like there aren't kids there already looking for summer jobs."

"What about the apprentice program at the opera?"

"Thousands apply. Few are chosen. Besides, it's too late and I'm too young."

"Maybe you could just get a job there, in the ticket office or something. I could ask Meg."

"Like I said, probably lots of local kids are already in line ahead of me."

"I could ask Johnston."

"What does he have to do with it?"

"He's the new manager of the opera."

"For real?"

"For real."

"When did that happen?"

"A few weeks ago."

"Wow. Cool," she said. "How is he?"

"Okay, I guess. He was really torn up about Erik, and Connie, of course. Then there was the divorce."

"Divorce?"

"His wife left him."

"I never liked her anyway."

Frankie chuckled. "Me either."

"It doesn't matter. I couldn't go off and leave Mrs. Valerius."

"Why not?"

"You saw her. She can't even remember to pay the electric bill. Sometimes I'm afraid she'll burn the house down when she tries to cook."

"What's wrong with her?"

"I don't know. I guess she's going crazy. It's worse at night."

"Has she seen a doctor?"

"Nope."

"You should definitely look into that."

"I wouldn't even know where to look."

"You could call Raoul's mom. I'm sure she could tell you exactly where to look."

Christine rolled her eyes at the not-so-subtle reference to Raoul. "I don't think she would go to a doctor. She doesn't know anything is wrong."

"I'll call my dad and see what he thinks."

The thought of getting away for the summer was tempting. Her social life was nonexistent. She didn't mind working—indeed she enjoyed it—but the responsibility of taking care of the mother figure who should be taking care of her was starting to wear her down. She knew other kids had it much worse. She had had it much worse. But at least she wasn't homeless.

"Maybe I could go to Santa Fe for a few days, if I could bring her with me."

"That could work."

"I want to see Zoe's opera. It's premiering there this summer."

"Yeah, I know."

"You heard about it?" she asked.

"We're underwriting it."

"What does that mean?"

"The family foundation paid Zoe a stipend while she finished writing it, and we're guaranteeing the house."

"How do you guarantee a house? Is that like insurance?"

He smiled. "Yes, actually. We guarantee a certain number of tickets sold for the first few performances. After that it sinks or swims on its own."

"So that's good for Zoe, right?"

"Right. Not that it matters. It's selling well. The premiere is sold out, including standing room."

"They sell standing room?"

"They do at the Santa Fe Opera."

"Daddy would have definitely wanted to see Zoe's opera."

She slid off the bed, stepped over to the window and looked out.

"What are you looking at?" Frankie asked.

"Daddy and I lived out there in the little cottage when we first came here."

"What's a little cottage?" Frankie stood and walked over.

"That's what my daddy called it." She pointed. "Out there."

Frankie looked through the window. "It's a mother-in-law house."

Christine laughed. "A mother-in-law house?"

"That's what they call them in LA. You can't rent them out, but you can let a relative live there."

"Whatever. When Daddy died the Valeriuses took me in. I kind of owe them, or her."

"What are you going to do next year, when you graduate?"

"I have no idea. I just take it one day at a time, like when we were homeless, living on the street."

"From what Raoul says, your dad was quite a guy."

"He was. He gave up everything to get me out here so I could go to the conservatory, and now I've let him down." She started to cry.

Frankie had no idea what to say, so he slipped his arm around her and pulled her close. She leaned her head on his shoulder and they just stood there in silence, looking out the window.

2

THE GHOST ON THE TRAIN

Frankie and the Amtrak porter loaded luggage and a large cooler onto the *Estelline*, attached to the end of the *Southwest Chief* at Union Station in downtown Los Angeles. Christine dropped her backpack onto a sofa and looked around.

"Thank you, sir," the porter said, as he pocketed Frankie's generous tip.

"Are you okay?" Frankie asked.

"I will be," Christine said. "It just brings back memories."

"This was a bad idea. We can fly, or road trip. We can drive straight through and eat junk food from convenience stores."

"No, it's okay."

"Or we can leave in the morning and spend the night at La Posada in Winslow. They have great food in the restaurant."

"Yeah, I know."

"When were you there?"

"I wasn't, actually. When we came back from Santa Fe last time Raoul ordered takeout from there."

Frankie laughed. "He learned that from me."

"It was pretty good."

"Maybe we can order breakfast from there, if you're okay with taking the train."

"I'm okay."

"Actually, we go through Winslow pretty early in the morning. I'll call them tonight and have someone come in early."

"Nah. I'm a low-maintenance girl."

"Okay, then."

"Where's Abby?"

"She's working her ass off for an arrogant, obnoxious, douchebag of a chef."

"Why?"

"Because he's the best and she's learning a lot."

"So, she isn't coming with us?"

"Oh, that. No. It's just us, so I didn't think we needed an attendant."

"We don't, low-maintenance, remember?"

"I know how to work all the stuff. Can you cook?"

"I can make tortillas."

"And I can make fajitas, not nearly as good as Juanita's, but we won't starve."

He opened the cooler. "I think I have everything we need."

Christine rummaged through the cooler. "Look's good."

"Or we can go eat in the dining car."

"No way. We'll cook. It will be fun. Did you bring wine?"

"Duh."

"Don't get me drunk and try to take advantage of me."

Frankie laughed as they started to put away the groceries. "I'm pretty sure you're safe."

"Let's get busy. I'm starving."

The *Southwest Chief* had not yet reached the San Bernardino Depot before Frankie and Christine popped the cork on a bottle of wine and started preparing dinner.

"Who needs Abby?" Christine said as she sliced red, yellow, and green peppers. "I've got this."

Frankie dumped strips of beef into a skillet. "I hope I got the spices right. I should have called Juanita."

Christine scraped the sliced peppers into a bowl with the onions. "I'd better get started on the tortillas."

"We need music."

"I guess this rolling palace has a killer sound system."

Frankie started singing "Cielito Lindo."

Christine smiled and joined in, and before long they were feasting on fajitas and wine.

"It's not as good as Juanita's, is it?" Frankie asked.

"I think it tastes great."

"Especially the tortillas."

"Definitely."

"You got them burned just right."

"Thanks, jerk."

"That's a compliment. If there's not a little singed crust you aren't doing it right. Gives it flavor."

"Are you being serious?"

"I'm serious. It's a delicate art. You have to get them just right, singed, not burned."

Christine picked up the bottle of wine. "You brought Chagny wine?"

"For old time's sake."

"Works for me."

"Are we going to talk about Raoul or just keep avoiding the subject?"

"Keep avoiding the subject."

"Okay, what about school?"

"What about it?"

"Your senior year is coming up, prom, all that stuff. Do they have prom at the conservatory?"

"Yeah, but I probably won't go."

"You have to go to your prom."

"No I don't."

"Why not?"

"With who? I don't exactly have a lot of friends. Maybe I'll just go with Sue. She's also boy-challenged."

"What about that guy you sang with at the gala?"

"Alfonso?"

"Yeah, him. Didn't he have the hots for you?"

"Not really. We were just buddies. Anyway, he just graduated. I went with him to his prom. He had a secret girlfriend at the time."

"Great, so he can still go to your prom with you, can't he?"

"Turns out he really was dating a Disney princess."

"Really? Who?"

"Tegan."

"That Australian chick on TV?"

"Yep."

"Wow, she's hot."

"But not anymore."

"She's not hot anymore or they're not dating anymore?"

"No, they're still dating, and she's still smoking hot, but I don't think she's a Disney princess anymore."

"Why not?"

"Her phone got hacked and her nakie selfies turned up on the Internet."

"That's terrible."

"Yeah."

"Do you have a link?"

She slugged him on the arm. "Why are guys so obsessed with boobs?"

"We're wired that way, from birth." Frankie refilled her wine glass. "Plus, they're nice to look at." He poured himself more wine. "And play with."

Christine shook her head. "You are hopeless." She took a sip of wine. "The last two years have been kind of tough at school."

"How so?"

"Well, Johnston left, and I have to admit, he was letting me skate through a lot of stuff. The new guy isn't."

"What stuff?"

"Reading music."

"So, important stuff?"

"I guess. I just wanted to sing. Now I don't even want to do that."

"Why not?"

"Connie's dead. Erik is—who knows?"

They sat in silence for a moment.

"Life goes on," Frankie said.

"I have kind of a reputation at school."

"What kind of reputation?"

"I was the center of a love triangle, or quadrangle, or whatever, and now one girl is dead, one boy messed up for life, and the other boy ran off to France."

"He didn't run off to France. He lives there."

"Oh, and don't forget the kinky sex and stuff."

"Kinky sex?"

"Sex on the beach, sex in the boat, sex in the mountains, sex at the opera, sex at the ranch, sex in the pool, sex, sex, sex."

"Wow. Somehow I missed out on all that, well, some of it anyway."

Christine smiled. "Now all the girls hate me, and all the guys think I put out."

"Then you should have plenty of invitations to the prom."

"Wiseass."

"You could ask a viscount to the prom."

"A what?"

"It's *vicomte* in French."

"Still not getting it."

"The vicomte de Chagny."

"You want me to go to the prom with Raoul's dad?"

"No, he's comte de Chagny. Raoul is the *vicomte*, or viscount."

"Bzzzzz! Try again."

"Come on, Christine. The boy is crazy about you."

"I've seen him like, once since Connie's funeral, and that was the professor's funeral. All we do is go to funerals."

"He invited you to go skiing in Switzerland, didn't he?"

"The professor was sick. I couldn't go."

"He calls, he texts, or at least he says he does."

"He does."

"You two make the perfect couple."

"Yeah, right, a homeless girl from Santa Monica and a rich boy from Paris."

"That doesn't matter to him."

"It matters to his parents."

"It did before, but not now, not after they got to know you and saw how much he loves you."

"What about all those girls in Paris, or Switzerland, or Saint-Tropez? Does he love them too?"

"There aren't really any other girls, not seriously. It's like me and Harper."

"That's a long way to go for a prom."

"They have a private jet."

"Whatever."

"Call him. He misses you."

"How do you know?"

"He's my best friend. We talk."

"Screw the prom. I'm not even sure if I'll still be at the conservatory in the fall."

"Wait, what?"

"I'm flunking some courses, so they may kick me out. They're supposed to decide in a couple of weeks, probably waiting for auditions to be over so they can find a replacement soprano."

"No way. You're their star."

"Not anymore. No big deal. I don't care."

"What are you going to do?"

"I don't know. Go to public school, I guess."

"What about after that? College."

She laughed. "Yeah, right. How can I afford to go to college?"

"Scholarship?"

"For what? They're hardly going to give a scholarship to someone who can't read music and got kicked out of a conservatory."

"Maybe I can help."

"How can you help?"

"I can loan you the money, or give it to you."

"No way."

"We're friends, Christine. Friends help friends."

"Not like that."

"In case you haven't noticed, my family's loaded."

"Don't worry about it. I'll just sing in clubs, or maybe on a cruise ship. Daddy really liked playing in the orchestra on a cruise ship. I don't need a college education for that, and I can see the world. Cruise ships go to Saint-Tropez, right? Maybe I'll see you there."

"Cannes or Nice, actually, but close enough."

"And lots of other cool places."

"What about Johnston?"

"What about him?"

"He has lots of experience in the music business. Maybe he could get you a record deal."

"A record deal? Don't you read the news? The record business is in the crapper. Kids don't buy CDs anymore. They download music, usually without paying for it."

"Some people seem to be doing okay."

"I guess I could get a bunch of tattoos and piercings, dress like a skank, or nearly naked, stick out my tongue, and learn to twerk."

Frankie laughed. "Ah, no. That's not your style."

"Exactly."

"What about a sex tape?"

Christine laughed, almost choking on her wine.

CHRISTINE AND FRANKIE made short work of the dinner dishes. Frankie said it was important to have everything cleaned and stowed on a train—you couldn't just leave it for tomorrow, or it might end up on the floor, broken.

Frankie allowed her to sample some Cognac, instructing her on the proper procedure. She took only a few sips, finding it much too strong for her taste. A novice drinker, she preferred wine, and white over red.

Christine felt entirely at ease, the stress of school, Raoul, Mrs. Valerius, her job, melting away with the miles. Memories of Erik and Connie would haunt Santa Fe, but there were also good memories, and she was looking forward to being there again. They talked and laughed into the night.

Frankie looked at his watch. "I'm beat. Are you ready for bed?"

"Sure, why not? I've already slept with everybody else."

"Funny. You can take the master bedroom."

"No, you take it. I'll take the small one, or the kids' room."

"You're my guest," he insisted. "You get the big room."

"I don't want it."

"Why not?"

Christine paused, not sure whether to tell him the truth or just make something up. She took a deep breath. "The night before the gala, after rehearsal and the pool party, all the kids went to a movie."

"Yeah, okay."

"I didn't really want to go, so I stayed at the ranch and washed my hair."

"Okay?" He had no idea what that had to do with the master bedroom on the *Estelline*, but he was curious.

"Well, actually, Erik washed my hair."

Frankie leaned closer.

"In the shower," she said.

"You took a shower with Erik?" Now he was really interested.

"Not really. I was still wearing my bikini, from the pool party, and he was wearing shorts or whatever, so it's not like we were naked or anything."

"He just washed your hair."

"Right. Then we kissed some."

"In the shower?"

"On the porch."

Frankie smiled and nodded, waiting for more.

"I was supposed to sleep over with Sue on the train, so he gave me a ride. But they weren't back from the movie. Well, actually, we knew they wouldn't be back."

"So you waited in the *Estelline*?"

She nodded.

"He used to bring girls here," Frankie said.

"He said you did too."

"Guilty."

"We made out. A lot. More than I'd ever done with any boy, even Raoul. Well, there never were any other boys, so it was all new to me. It got really hot and heavy, over there, on the couch."

Frankie looked at the couch.

"Then he picked me up and carried me into the bedroom."

"The master bedroom."

"Exactly."

"And that's why you don't want to sleep in there, because you already did."

"Already did what?"

"Did *it*."

"No way! Well, almost, but we didn't. I just couldn't do it."

"That's good, I guess. If you don't want to do it, you shouldn't let a guy push you into it."

"He didn't push me, not at first anyway. He was being relatively nice, or at least he was trying to, mostly."

"Well, that's an improvement for Erik."

She nodded. "The thing is, I wanted to."

"You did?"

"Yeah, I did."

"So, why didn't you?"

"I don't know, inexperience, fear, guilt, being a good girl, Raoul, my daddy, Jim Bob, whatever. Maybe it just wasn't the right time."

"Jim Bob?"

"He kind of reminds me of my daddy. He was always there when I was little, and he always treated me just like I was his daughter, or niece, little sister, or something."

"That's okay. It's your body. You make the rules. Don't do it until it's right for you."

"You'd make good boyfriend material."

"Tell Meg that."

"I will when I see her."

"Thanks."

"But if I had done it, had sex with him, Connie would still be alive. She'd hate me, but she'd still be alive, and Erik wouldn't be all messed up."

"No, no way, no how," Frankie said emphatically. "Don't even think that. Erik was on a collision course with that train, or something else like it, for years. It could have been you on that bike with him. He's my cousin and I love him like a brother, but you can do better. A summer fling might have been okay, but you had no future together. He would have ruined it, with the drinking, or the drugs, or the other girls, or his temper. You did the right thing. Trust me."

"And Raoul would hate me." She started to cry. "Maybe he does anyway."

"He doesn't hate you."

"How do you know?"

"Best friends, remember?"

"He was so good to me, for such a long time, and I hurt him so bad."

"He still cares about you. A lot."

"It will never be the same."

"Nothing will ever be the same."

Frankie slid over beside her and took her into his arms, hugging her tightly while she cried on his shoulder.

"What was that?" Frankie asked, suddenly looking up.

"What?"

"That noise."

"I didn't hear anything," Christine said, wiping tears.

Frankie got up and went quickly to the attendant's room. He tried the doorknob, but it was locked. He knocked on the door. There was no response. "Is anybody in there?" There was no answer. He rushed over to the key box in the kitchen. "The key is missing."

"What key?"

"The key to the attendant's room."

"Do you think there's somebody in there?"

"Something probably just fell, from the vibration of the train. I'll check it out tomorrow. We have spare keys at the ranch."

"Maybe it's a ghost."

3

KISSING COUSINS

JUANITA DROPPED A flour ball on the kitchen counter, wiped her hands on a towel and shouted, "*¡Mi hija!*"

Christine threw her arms around her, and they hugged.

"Are you here for Miss Zoe's opera?" Juanita asked.

"Yes," Christine said. "I wouldn't miss it."

"Will you be staying here at the ranch?"

Christine nodded.

"Wonderful," Juanita said. "I need to fatten you up. You're too skinny."

"I missed your cooking," Christine said.

Frankie pushed his way in and hugged Juanita. "Me too."

"Have you heard from Erik?" Juanita asked.

"Not a word."

"His papa won't talk about it. I worry about him." Juanita turned to Christine. "And you, *mi hija*, are you doing okay?"

"I'm okay. Better when I get to eat some of your cooking."

"What's for dinner?" Frankie asked. "We had fajitas last night. I cooked."

"I made the tortillas."

"On the train?" Juanita asked.

"On the train," Frankie said.

"I'll send somebody down later to clean up."

"I'll go with them. I need to get the spare key and check the attendant's room."

"What's wrong?"

"A ghost," Christine said.

Juanita crossed herself.

"I don't know," Frankie said. "We heard a noise. Something must have fallen. The room is locked, and the key is missing. No big deal."

"What do you want for dinner?"

"Enchiladas," Christine said.

"Works for me," Frankie added.

"*Bien, bien,* Miss Zoe and Jim Bob are coming for dinner. That gringo likes my enchiladas."

Frankie laughed. "So do I, Juanita, so do I. We had a light lunch."

"Do you want a little something now?"

"No, we're saving room for your enchiladas."

"Do you need me to help make the tortillas?" Christine asked.

"No, you are our guest. You just got here. You go get settled in. Maybe tomorrow you can make the tortillas. How long will you be staying?"

"All summer, I guess."

"*Bien, bien.*"

"Let's go find you a room and dump your stuff," Frankie said. "Then I'll run back down to Lamy and catch the ghost."

CHRISTINE LAY FACE DOWN on a lounge chair by the pool, soaking up sun, her bikini top untied. Her eyes were closed, and she was listening to music through her ear buds, so she didn't notice Johnston standing over her. He wore a dress shirt with no tie, and an expensive sport coat.

"We have to stop meeting like this. People will talk."

Startled, Christine opened her eyes, and pulled out the ear buds. "Oh, crap."

She scrambled to her feet, clutching her bikini top, and threw her arms around him. He hugged her tightly, and then he kissed her on top of her head. She pulled away, looked up and stared at him for a moment, and then they exchanged kisses on both cheeks.

"I missed you," he said.

"I missed you too."

"This is where I would normally step back and say, 'let me look at you,' but you should probably fix your top first."

She laughed, broke away, turned her back and said, "Tie my strings."

He tied her strings. "Okay, now you can look."

He took a long look. "You look all grown up and more beautiful than ever. I can say that now that I'm no longer your headmaster, can't I?"

"You can definitely say that." She hugged him again.

"How's school?"

"School sucks. You should know that."

"Sorry I ran out on you and the other kids."

"That's okay. You had a lot to deal with."

"How's the new headmaster?"

"Not you." Christine said as she sat down on the lounge chair.

Johnston smiled, pulled up a chair and took a seat facing her.

"How's your new job?" she asked.

"Hectic right now, but I love it. We're premiering Zoe's opera soon."

"*Sangre de Cristo.*"

"You've heard of it." He smiled.

"Duh. I was kind of there when she wrote it."

"Oh, yes. They're coming over for dinner."

"Are you staying for dinner?"

"Yes, of course." Johnston looked puzzled. "Oh, I guess Frankie didn't tell you. I'm living here, for the time being anyway."

"I'm guessing your ex-wife got the house in Santa Fe."

He laughed. "Yes, actually. It was really hers anyway. She designed it, decorated it, and has her studio there. It made sense for her to take it. We're remodeling the beach house in Malibu. Then we'll sell it and split the money, so I'm homeless for now."

Christine looked around. "Looks like you're doing okay."

"I'll stay here through the season, and then look for a place, maybe a bachelor pad downtown, or I'll build something out near the opera house. I haven't decided."

"Cool."

"I always had wives to take care of the housing situation. I never had to bother with it."

"Don't look at me. I'm homeless too."

He smiled. "I'm not getting any younger, so I should probably be looking for a place to retire."

"Do you still have your house in Saint-Tropez?"

"Oh, yes, I got that. It was pre-marriage."

"There you go."

"It's a thought."

"Have you heard from Erik?" Christine asked.

"No, have you?"

She shook her head, and then started crying. "I'm so sorry."

"For what? It wasn't your fault."

He stepped over, sat beside her, and put his arm around her.

"I know, but I just wish I could have done something, anything."

"There was nothing you could have done."

"That's what Frankie said."

"Frankie was right. Erik had problems, and he acted out on them in dangerous ways. It was a phone call I expected for years. I'm just sorry that it involved you, and Connie."

"What time is it?" she asked, no longer wanting to talk about it.

"Almost seven."

"I guess I'd better take a shower and put on some clothes."

"That's a good idea."

"Are we dressing up? It's just Zoe and Jim Bob, right?"

"And Frankie."

"Oh, yeah, Frankie. Is Meg coming?"

"Not tonight, it's just family."

"Family?"

"We'll talk later, and no, we aren't dressing up. This is what I'm wearing."

Christine stood. "Okay, cool."

She turned to go, and then turned back. "Oh, thanks for taking care of Mrs. Valerius for the summer so I could come here."

"I'm glad we could help."

"And I would have never gotten her to go see a doctor. So, thanks for that too."

JIM BOB PUSHED through the kitchen door. "Juanita! I can smell your enchiladas all the way out on the porch." He scooped her up in a bear hug and reached for a tortilla. She slapped his hand, but he scored the tortilla anyway and shoved it into his mouth.

"You'll spoil your dinner," she said.

"It's just an hors d'oeuvre."

"Do I look French to you?"

"No ma'am."

"Then take these Mexican hors d'oeuvres to the dining room." She handed him a large platter of nachos.

He took the platter and reached for a nacho. She slapped his hand, but it was again ineffective—the nacho was down the hatch.

"We're gonna need some more of these," he said.

"There's more where that came from. Now, shoo."

Jim Bob backed through the swinging door into the dining room. Christine gave him enough time to put down the platter, and then hugged him. "Where's Zoe?"

"She was right behind me."

"Here I am," Zoe said, entering the dining room with Johnston. "We had some business to discuss."

"Opera business?" Christine asked as they hugged.

"Just business."

"We really need to hire some help," Frankie said, as he placed another platter of nachos on the table. "Juanita has us doing all the work."

"She'll probably make us wash the dishes," Jim Bob said.

"You want to eat, you work," Juanita said as she placed bowls of salsa on the table. "Or you can hire me some help."

"Don't listen to those boys, Juanita," Johnston said, opening a bottle of wine. "We're doing just fine."

As expected, Juanita's enchiladas were wonderful, and luckily, she had prepared a lot of them. The mood was somewhat jovial, under the circumstances, which was a relief to Christine. She had dreaded returning to this house and facing Johnston.

"How is rehearsal going?" Christine asked.

"It's going," Zoe said.

"Problems?"

"There are always problems with a new opera," Johnston said, "but Zoe has it well in hand. I think it's going well."

"We've already cleared the guarantee," Frankie said.

"Seriously?" Zoe asked.

"I talked to Meg's mom this afternoon. She thinks sales will pick up even more after the premiere."

"Unless it sucks," Jim Bob said.

"Way to be supportive," Christine said.

"She knows I love her, and her opera. And it's not going to suck. I might have to kick some ass, but it's not going to suck."

"Who's singing Sofia?" Christine asked.

"La Carlotta," Zoe said.

"Who's she?"

"A semi-famous soprano," Johnston said.

"And a world-class diva," Jim Bob said.

"Diva being the politically correct term for bitch," Frankie added.

Frankie and Jim Bob bumped fists.

"Is she Spanish, or Mexican?" Christine asked.

"I-talian," Jim Bob said.

"Does she speak Spanish?" Christine asked.

"I'm not even sure she sings Spanish," Jim Bob said.

"Close enough," Zoe said.

"Not to worry," Frankie said. "They have little screens at each seat to translate into English."

"And Spanish," Jim Bob said.

Johnston choked back a laugh as Frankie and Jim Bob again bumped fists.

"Okay," Johnston said. "Enough shoptalk."

Juanita entered with a tray.

"What's for dessert, Juanita?" Johnston asked.

"Flan, sopapillas," Juanita answered.

"Yes, please," Jim Bob said.

"I'll get the coffee," Frankie said as he pushed back from the table.

"And some Cognac," Jim Bob said. "We might have something to toast."

"What are we toasting?" Christine asked.

"In a minute," Johnston said. "Let's wait for Frankie."

"Okay, what's going on?" Christine asked.

Frankie returned with a pot of coffee and a bottle of Cognac. Juanita took the coffee and started pouring. Jim Bob took the Cognac.

"We heard from the doctor who saw Mrs. Valerius," Johnston said. "Actually, her sister heard from the doctor and called me."

"Her sister?" Christine said, surprised. "I didn't know she had a sister."

"Yes, in Florida. They weren't that close, but she is her only living relative."

"Wow."

"Mrs. Valerius has early-onset Alzheimer's."

"Is that bad?" Christine asked. "It sounds bad."

"It's bad," Johnston said, "and it won't get better."

"That's why she's worse at night," Frankie said. "It's called sundowning."

"What am I going to do?" Christine asked.

"Unfortunately, there's not a lot we can do for her," Johnston said, "other than make her comfortable, and keep her safe."

"Someone will have to be with her twenty-four hours a day," Frankie said.

"I guess I can drop out of school," Christine said.

"You're not dropping out of school," Johnston said. "Her sister is unable to take care of her, physically or financially, so we are arranging to have her placed in an assisted living facility near her sister's home in Florida."

"Will she have to sell her house?" Christine asked.

"Not right away," Johnston said. "Her sister will have to petition the court to take charge of her financial affairs, and her care. We don't even know what her financial position is, but it doesn't matter. We will take care of it. Our lawyers are already working on it."

"Who's we?" Christine asked.

"Me, Franklin, well, Franklin is letting Frankie take the lead on it, but he's on board."

"Wait, I'm confused," Christine said. "Why would you do this for Mrs. Valerius?"

"She and her husband were long-time friends of mine," Johnston said.

"And we aren't doing it just for her," Frankie said. "We're doing it for you."

"So, I can stay in the house?" Christine asked.

Johnston smiled. "No, that's not exactly what we had in mind."

"What exactly do you have in mind?" Christine was becoming concerned.

"Your legal status is rather precarious," Johnston said.

"Now you're scaring me."

"Your father appointed the Valeriuses your legal guardians. When the professor died, Mrs. Valerius became your sole guardian. Now that she's about to have a guardian appointed for her, that leaves you in legal limbo."

"We still don't know about your mama's people, or your daddy's," Jim Bob said, "so we need to find a way to keep you out of foster care."

"Foster care?" Christine was shocked. "No way. I'll get emancipated."

"How do you know about emancipation?" Frankie asked.

"Kid actors at Ogden Hall were doing it so they could work longer hours or do porn or whatever."

"I don't think it works for porn," Frankie said, smiling.

Christine shrugged.

"Emancipation is a possibility," Johnston said. "Our lawyers are considering it, but it might not be the best choice."

"Or you could do what I did when my grandmother died," Zoe said, "and just fly under the radar until you're eighteen."

"I could do that. I guess. I'd need to get a better job."

Johnston chuckled. "You don't need to get a better job, or any job."

"I don't?"

"No, of course not. You have people who care about you, right here in this room."

"Cut to the chase, Johnston," Jim Bob said. "I'm hankering for some of this fancy Cognac."

"I want to adopt you," Johnston said, "if that's okay with you."

Christine took a moment to process this information. "You'd be my daddy?"

"I could never replace your daddy, but legally, yes, I'd be your father."

"And Erik would be my brother?"

Johnston nodded. "Yes."

She opened her mouth to speak but didn't.

"Is that a problem?" Johnston asked.

She glanced at Frankie and then turned back to Johnston.

"No, not really."

"Oh, no, you two didn't—"

"No," Christine said. "Close, but no, we didn't."

Jim Bob winced. Johnston closed his eyes and shook his head.

"Does that still count as, you know?" Christine asked.

"No," Johnston said. "It doesn't count."

Christine looked at Frankie. "So that would make us cousins?"

"Yes. We would be cousins."

"Kissing cousins?" Christine joked.

"Sure, why not?"

"But Johnston is already your cousin, right? Would that even be legal? This is getting complicated."

"It would be quite legal," Johnston said, smiling.

"Would I have to change my last name?"

"No, that won't be necessary, I don't think. I'll have to check with the lawyers, but probably not."

"So, I would live here with you, in Santa Fe? Cool."

"No, not right away. There's still school, and that's in Los Angeles."

"Oh yeah, that," Christine said. "I don't think they want me back at the conservatory."

"Leave that to me," Johnston said. "I still have some pull there, but you have to promise me that you will apply yourself and make me, and your daddy, proud."

"I can do that. Where will I live?"

"With us," Zoe said, "in Los Angeles, after the season."

"You'll stay here at the ranch for the summer," Johnston said.

"We're going to need a bigger place," Jim Bob said.

"I can sleep on the couch," Christine said.

"I'm pregnant," Zoe said.

"And the hits just keep on coming," Christine said. She pushed back her chair, raced around the table, and hugged Zoe. "So, I'm going to be an aunt, a sister, or what?"

"Hell if I know," Zoe said. "But we'll figure it out."

"You will live in the beach house in Malibu," Johnston said.

"I thought you said you were going to sell it," Christine said.

"I am, but it can wait. You'll have to put up with some remodeling."

"*No problemo*," Jim Bob said. "I've worked construction. I'll keep an eye on them and make sure they don't rip you off."

"What about your ex-wife?" Christine said as she took her seat. "Doesn't she own half of the beach house?"

"I'll deal with her."

"Will you come visit?" Christine asked.

"I'll be in Los Angeles from time to time, and of course, you'll come here for holidays, and Zoe and Jim Bob too if they want."

"We want," Zoe said. She looked at Christine. "Christmas in Santa Fe is wonderful."

"Yes, it is," Johnston said. "There's snow on the mountains."

"I'll go anywhere for Christmas," Jim Bob said, "as long as there's turkey and dressing, and eggnog."

"We always cut down a tree," Frankie said.

"Cool," Christine said.

"We should see if the old sleigh still works," Frankie said. "It's been years since we used it."

"Good idea," Johnston said. "I'm sure Christine would like that."

"But she needs somebody to snuggle up with," Frankie said.

"Don't start." Christine turned to Johnston. "Can I go see Mrs. Valerius?"

"Of course, whenever you want."

"I've never been to Florida."

"Maybe we could go for spring break," Frankie said. "Meg and I will go with you. You can bring some friends."

Christine nodded enthusiastically.

"Mrs. Valerius might not even know who you are by spring break," Johnston said.

"Maybe we could bring her here for Christmas," Christine said.

"We could do that, and Thanksgiving."

Christine turned to Zoe. "Is it a boy or a girl?"

"We don't want to know," Zoe said.

"It'll be a surprise," Jim Bob said.

"I'll babysit," Christine said.

"You'll be away at college," Jim Bob said. "Now can we toast?"

"We're waiting for Christine's answer," Johnston said.

"What answer?" Christine asked.

"About letting me adopt you," Johnston said.

"Oh yeah, that." She turned to Jim Bob. "What do you think Daddy would say?"

"I'd think he'd be okay with it," Jim Bob said. "He'll always be your daddy."

"Do you think I should do it?"

"Yes, I think you should," Jim Bob said. "But I'll always be there for you, no matter what."

"We," Zoe added.

Jim Bob smiled. "We will always be there for you."

"Okay, let's do it," Christine said. "I'm not sure exactly what's going on with all the legal stuff, but I'm in."

"I'll handle the legal stuff," Johnston said.

"Can I have some Cognac?" Christine said as she hugged him and kissed him on the cheek.

"You're already getting me in trouble," Johnston said.

Jim Bob poured some Cognac in Christine's glass as she sat down.

"Not too much," Frankie said. "She's not much of a Cognac drinker."

Johnston looked at him curiously.

They all raised their glasses, except Zoe. "I'll drink a toast in about seven months."

"Are you guys getting married?" Christine asked.

"Yeah, I'm going to make an honest woman out of her," Jim Bob said.

"I'll sing at your wedding," Christine said.

"Damn straight you'll sing at our wedding," Jim Bob said.

"I just want to go to the bachelor party," Frankie said.

Christine started crying.

"What?" Frankie asked. "What did I say?"

"Nothing. I'm just so happy."

"We're having male strippers at the bachelorette party," Zoe said.

Christine instantly went from tears to excitement. She picked up her napkin and twirled it above her head. "Woo-hoo!"

IT HAD BEEN a long, full, and potentially life-changing day for Christine, and she collapsed into bed far too late. She slept soundly until she suddenly awoke with a start.

"Who's there?"

There was no answer. She looked around the darkened room.

"Frankie? If that's you, I'll kick your ass."

Still no answer. She sat up in bed and looked around. Silence. Stillness. A shadow. She screamed.

Frankie arrived first, and then Johnston. Frankie pulled back the curtains, checking everything, while Johnston sat on the bed, holding a trembling Christine.

"It was probably the Cognac," Johnston said. "I shouldn't have let you have any."

"No, there was someone in my room," Christine insisted.

"I'll stay with her," Frankie said. "I'll sleep in the chair."

"Are you sure?" Johnston asked.

"Yes, we'll be okay."

Frankie closed the door when Johnston left, turned out the light, and headed toward the chair.

"You don't have to stay," Christine said.

"That's okay."

"Seriously, I'll be all right. It was probably nothing." She slid under the covers. "Besides, I can always scream again, and you can come running."

"Okay, but I'll just sit here until you go to sleep."

"Why aren't you in bed with Meg tonight anyway?"

"She was rehearsing until really late. We booked a hookup for tomorrow night."

"Ew!"

"What?"

"It's a good thing I didn't hook up with Erik."
"We're not related to the Chagnys."
"Give it up, Tits."
"Okay, okay."
Frankie watched her until she drifted off to sleep.

4

HUEVOS RANCHEROS

THE MORNING SUN was streaming through the window when Christine awoke. She rolled over and looked around the room. It wasn't nearly as scary as it had been last night. She was suddenly embarrassed for screaming at a shadow. Nevertheless, she slid out of bed and checked the curtains, the chairs, the bathroom. Nothing. Nobody there.

She had not noticed it before, assuming it was a window, but she pulled back the delicate lace curtain and discovered a French door. She opened it and stepped out onto a balcony. She leaned over the railing and looked out over the grounds. She held her head back and took a deep breath of mountain air. She smiled as a gust of wind tousled her hair. It also caught the door. She reached out, but the door closed before she could stop it. She tried the handle. It was locked.

"Crap." She tried it again.

"She speaks."

Christine whirled around and peered over the railing. "Frankie?"

"O, speak again, bright angel!"

"What are you talking about?"

"Romeo and Juliet. I forget the rest. You're a girl. You should know this stuff."

"I locked myself out."

"Ah, that's a problem."

"Definitely."

"Maybe you could climb down."

"Or maybe you could go in the house and open it from the inside."

"That's a thought, but the other door is probably locked too."

"Are you kidding me?"

"You were afraid of the ghost, so I made sure it was locked when I left."

"Why are you up so early?"

"I had to muck out the stables and take care of the horses. I would have asked you to help me, but you looked so peaceful, asleep."

"Did you sleep in the chair all night?"

"Yes."

"Just let me in."

"I told you. The other door is locked."

"There's got to be a way."

"There's a way, but I just wanted to enjoy the view for a few minutes."

"What view?"

He looked up at her and smiled. She looked down at herself. She was wearing panties and a tiny T-shirt. "Oh, crap!" She glanced around. "Is anybody looking?"

"Just me."

"Then go let me in before somebody else sees me."

He laughed and headed toward the house.

Christine waited patiently on the balcony, trying to cover her butt while looking around to make sure nobody was looking.

"Finally," she said as Frankie opened the French door.

"Always unlock it when you go out on the balcony."

"Now you tell me." She pushed past him into the bedroom. "Wait, how did you get in? I thought you said the other door was locked."

"Spare key." He held up a key. "Daniel Senior used to have lots of guests, so he had locks installed on the bedrooms when he built the house, like a hotel, so we have to have extra keys for maid service."

"Then I guess I need a key."

"I'll get you one. We don't normally even lock the rooms when it's just family."

"Speaking of spare keys, what about Abby's room, on the train?"

"Oh, that. There was a book on the floor, probably fell off the dresser or the bed."

"So, no ghost?"

"No ghost."

"Unless the ghost knocked the book off."

Frankie smiled. "Or that. What do you want for breakfast?"

"What do they have?"

"Juanita can whip up pretty much anything you want."

"What are you having?"

"I already ate, while you were sleeping."

"Oh. Bacon and eggs, I guess. Do they have bacon? Sausage is okay."

"I'm sure she has bacon."

"Okay, shoo, so I can get dressed."

FRANKIE SAT AT the kitchen table, chomping down on a burrito.

"I thought you already ate breakfast," Christine said as she entered the room.

"That was three hours ago."

"The boy likes my burritos," Juanita said.

"No, the boy loves your burritos," Frankie said.

"I think he's turning into a Mexican."

Christine opened the refrigerator. "Do you have any orange juice?" She looked inside. "Oh, here it is." She picked up the jar. "Wow, this looks like the real deal."

"It is," Frankie said. "Do you want coffee too?"

"Of course, but in a cup, not a bowl."

Juanita poured her a cup of coffee. "Why would you put coffee in a bowl?"

"It's a French thing," Christine said.

Juanita put a large plate of food in front of Christine.

"What's that?" Christine asked.

"Huevos rancheros," Frankie said.

Christine eyed the plate curiously.

"Here, slop some of this on it," Frankie said, pushing a bowl of salsa across the table.

Christine dabbed on a bit of salsa and cautiously took a bite. "It's hot!" She chugged some orange juice.

Frankie laughed.

Christine took another bite. "But it's really good."

"I'll turn you into a Mexican too," Juanita said. She lifted some of Christine's hair. "It will take some work. This hair is really blonde."

"What time is it?" Christine asked.

Frankie glanced up at a large clock on the wall. "Around nine. Why?"

"I want to go to the opera house and see about a job."

"Why do you need a job?"

"Duh. To make money."

"Just ask Johnston for an allowance. Get started off on the right foot with this adoption thing."

"I couldn't do that."

"Why not?"

"I just couldn't. Besides, I'd rather work. I'm not going to just sit around all summer."

"Or lay out by the pool, topless."

"Were you spying on me?"

"Hard to miss."

"Which is why I wasn't topless, just untied," Christine said.

"Sure."

"Just ask Johnston. He saw me." She covered her face and then looked up. "Wait, is that worse?"

"Is what worse?"

"He was headmaster of my school when he saw my tits at Saint-Tropez. Now he's my daddy, or going to be, so is that worse?"

"Did your dad ever see your tits?"

Juanita crossed herself. "*Madre de Dios.*"

"Of course, but I didn't have anything to see. Well, there was this one time, when I cut myself shaving."

"You cut yourself shaving?"

"My legs, doofus. I was in the tub. Daddy came in. It was so embarrassing."

"How old were you?"

"Twelve."

"So there was a little something to see?"

"Frankie!" Juanita said. "Mind your manners. Christine is our guest."

"No, she's not. She's family. She's my cousin, my girl cousin, my younger girl cousin. It's my job to tease her."

"Yes, there was a little something," Christine said.

"Now there's a big something."

Juanita slapped Frankie on the head. "*¡Pendejo!*"

Christine laughed. "Not that big."

"How are you going to get to the opera house?" Frankie asked.

"I guess I'll take the bus."

"There's no bus out here."

"Frankie will take you," Juanita said.

"She could drive if she had a car."

"I'm not asking Johnston for a car."

FRANKIE AND CHRISTINE stood near the stables, looking at a battered 1953 Chevrolet pickup, in desperate need of a paint job.

"Erik and I both learned to drive in this truck. That's why it's so beat up. We bounced all over the ranch, and into a few rocks and trees and gullies." He put his foot on the running board. "They had running boards back then."

"What's a running board?"

Frankie pointed at his foot. "You can ride on these things. Apparently, all kids did it back in the day. Not too smart, though. I'm sure a lot of them fell off. I know we sure did."

"Sounds like you guys had a lot of fun."

"We did. I miss him."

"Me too."

He took her into his arms, and they hugged. She broke away and looked inside the truck. "What's that other pedal for?"

Frankie laughed. "That's the clutch."

"What's a clutch?"

"Climb in and I'll teach you to drive a stick."

"What's a stick?"

Christine drove around the house a few times, and then out on to the ranch roads. Frankie cringed every time she shifted gears, but she finally got the hang of it.

"This is fun," Christine said as they left the ranch and headed out onto a paved road.

She stopped for a stop sign, looked both ways, and pressed the accelerator. Nothing happened.

"What's wrong?" she asked.

"It's dead. You killed it."

"I killed what?"

"The truck."

"How did I do that?"

"You forgot the clutch when you stopped."

"Oh, crap. There's a lot to remember with a stick thingy."

"Yes, there is, but you'll get it. If my mom can drive a stick, so can you."

She got the truck started and they were off.

"Railroad crossing," Frankie said.

"Is there a train?"

"No, but you need to slow down and look both ways."

She slowed down and looked.

"Sorry," Frankie said as they crossed the tracks. "I forgot."

"Forgot what? Oh. Is that where—"

"That's where it happened."

"It looks different in the daytime."

"We should have gone another way."

"That's okay. I can't keep avoiding stuff."

"Like Raoul?" Frankie asked. She ignored him.

Traffic increased considerably as they drove on.

"Wow," Christine said. "It looks different when you're driving."

"That's why you're driving. You might as well learn your way around town."

"Can I drive this thing all summer?"

"Well, since you won't ask Johnston for a car, then I guess you can drive this truck all summer."

"Cool." She thought about it for a minute. "Do you think he'd buy me a car?"

"Of course he'd buy you a car. That's what dads do."

"That's okay. I like the truck. It's already beat up, so if I hit something it won't matter."

"As long as it's not another car, or a person. There are also a lot of historic buildings in Santa Fe, some of them hundreds of years old. Try to not hit those, please."

"Okey-dokey."

"Erik and I were going to restore it, but never got around to it."

"Restore what, a historic building?"

Frankie smiled. "This truck."

"Oh. Do you think he minds if I drive it?"

"I don't think he would mind at all, wherever he is."

"Maybe he's in Saint-Tropez. He liked it there."

"He'll turn up someday. I hope."

Christine made it all the way to the opera house without hitting anything. Their first stop was the rehearsal hall, to see Meg. She only had a short break, but it was enough time to hug and kiss, and squeal and make plans for the summer.

"I hope I can get a job here," Christine said. "Do you think I could work for your mom in the ticket office?"

"I'm sure she can find something. I usually help her during the season, but I'm in the show!"

"Which one?"

"*Sangre de Cristo.*"

"Oh, good. What part?"

"One of the dancers, but I might get upgraded to an Indian kid. Oh! Maybe you could get in it too."

"That's okay. The ticket office is good for me. Besides, I'm kind of burned out on it."

"Burned out on what?"

"*Sangre de Cristo.*"

"How could you be burned out on it?" Meg asked. "We haven't even opened."

"I sang all the girl parts, and some of the boys, while Zoe was writing it. Jim Bob sang the tenors. We stared into each other's eyes and pretended to be love-struck teenagers for so long we both wanted to puke. But I am looking forward to seeing it on stage, with all the costumes and the orchestra."

"And the dancers," Meg said.

"And the dancers."

Someone started playing piano.

"Time to get back to work," Meg said. "Can you have dinner with us tonight?"

"Don't you two have some catching up to do?"

"We talk and text all the time," Meg said. "There's not much to catch up on, except sex."

"Sex on Skype isn't very fulfilling," Frankie said.

"Ew!" Christine said.

"So, we'll have dinner," Meg said. "Then I can boff his brains out."

"Works for me," Christine said. "Dinner, not boffing."

CHRISTINE AND FRANKIE waited in the office until Johnston came in. He dropped a large pile of folders on his desk and sat down.

"You'll be working in all the departments, hair, makeup, costumes, props, scenery, everything."

"I thought I was going to work in the ticket office."

"That too, and the gift shop, of course."

"Don't forget usher," Frankie said. "The serapes are cool."

"Everything," Johnston repeated. "You won't be in the apprentice program, but you'll be doing a lot of the same work, except performing. That might be a problem with the singers if I let you in there."

"That's okay," she said. "The other stuff sounds fine. I'm taking a break from singing this summer."

"Great. You'll start tomorrow morning."

"Do I really have a job here, or is this just your way of giving me an allowance?"

Johnston smiled. "You really have a job here. There was some nepotism involved, but you will get an actual paycheck."

"How much do I make?"

"Minimum wage."

"Not enough to buy a car," Frankie said.

"Do you need a car?" Johnston asked.

"She's driving the old truck."

"She is? Wow."

"What's wrong?" Christine asked.

"Nothing. The boys roamed all over town in it, and Albuquerque."

"And Taos, and Los Alamos, and a few other places," Frankie said.

"You didn't drive it to Juarez, did you?" Johnston asked.

"We'll never tell."

"Your dad and I did, more than once."

"How old is that truck?" Christine asked.

"Really old," Frankie said.

"It's a fifty-three," Johnston said. "It was old when I learned to drive in it. Hell, it's older than I am."

"Well, I like it," Christine said.

"Can she drive a stick?" Johnston asked.

"She can now," Frankie said, "more or less."

5

LA PALOMA

THE LARGE MEXICAN RESTAURANT was popular not only with the tourists but locals as well, and although it was packed, Frankie, Meg, and Christine were shown to a table immediately.

"You guys really should have gone without me," Christine said as Frankie pulled out a chair for her.

"Nonsense," Meg said. "It's only been a few weeks since I've seen Frankie. I haven't seen you for two years. We have a lot of catching up to do."

Frankie seated Meg, and then himself.

"Maybe we should fix her up," Meg said to Frankie. "Then we could double date."

"No thanks."

"There's some really hot dancers at the opera. Some of them are even straight."

"I'm not looking for romance. Been there, done that."

"Well, then, some of them are gay. We could still fix you up. Gay guys make great dates, especially if you like to dance, and they won't even try to get in your panties later."

"That's okay. I'm good. I just want to chill this summer."

"And get used to being a member of the family?" Meg asked.

Christine looked at Frankie.

"Frankie told me," Meg said. "I think it's great."

Christine smiled and nodded.

"So, Erik will be your brother?" Meg said.

"I guess."

"Interesting."

"Don't go there," Frankie said.

"Go where?" Meg asked.

"The whole Erik and Christine, brother-sister place,"

"He had a hard-on for you in Saint-Tropez, when he wasn't hitting on Connie."

"Can we not talk about Erik?" Christine said, turning to look at the mariachis. "Let's just listen to the mariachis. They're pretty good." They played and sang "Cielito Lindo," loudly, and with great enthusiasm.

"He might have been screwing Connie in Saint-Tropez, but it was you he wanted," Meg said.

"Meg, cut it out," Frankie said.

Christine ignored Meg and sang along with several others on the chorus. She heard a male voice behind her also singing along and getting closer to her. As she started to turn, a man's hand slipped over her shoulder. Surprised, she quickly turned to look.

It was Alfonso, who immediately planted a kiss on her lips. She scrambled to her feet and threw her arms around his neck. They hugged and kissed again.

"What are you doing here?" Christine asked as she sat down.

"I invited him to have dinner with us," Meg said.

"In Santa Fe," Christine said. "Why are you in Santa Fe?"

"I'm in the apprentice program."

"Why didn't you tell me?"

"It was kind of sudden. I applied months ago but didn't make the cut. Then some guy dropped out at the last minute and apparently, I was next on the list. They called. I came."

"That's great."

"I check out all the boys," Meg said, "and I thought this one looked familiar."

"Oh, yeah," Christine said, "from the gala."

"So I fixed you up."

"How is Tegan?" Christine asked.

"She's great. She's in Vancouver, working. I was up there with her when I got the call. I miss her, but I'd much rather be working myself than hanging around her trailer."

"Who is Tegan?" Meg asked.

"His girlfriend," Christine said.

"His famous girlfriend," Frankie said.

"What's she famous for?" Meg asked.

"She's an actress," Alfonso said. "She's shooting some crappy TV movie for the money, but she's looking forward to her next film. It's a little indie that's really going to let her break away from her Disney image."

"Oh!" Meg said. "That Tegan. Is she Canadian?"

"Australian," Frankie said.

"Wait, if you have a girlfriend, then maybe I shouldn't have tried to hook you two up."

"That's okay," Frankie said. "Christine can be his Harper."

Meg nodded and smiled. "That works."

"What's a Harper?" Alfonso asked.

Christine laughed. "I saw Frankie a couple of weeks ago at a restaurant where I worked in LA. He was with this girl named Harper. I thought he was cheating on Meg, but it turned out they were just friends."

"So, I did good?" Meg asked.

"You did good."

Alfonso picked up Christine's hand and kissed it. "What about you? What are you doing in Santa Fe?"

"Spending the summer at the ranch. Frankie invited me. It's a long story. I'm working at the opera house, or will be, starting tomorrow."

"Working? Doing what?"

"Whatever. Everything, I guess."

"Singing?"

"Nope, not this girl. I'm just one of the guys."

"Alfonso is understudying for Alejandro," Meg said.

"Wow! That's great. You could totally be Alejandro."

"You know the opera?"

"Sure. Zoe and I are kind of tight."

"Oh yeah. I didn't even think about that." He looked at her. "And you could totally be Sofia." He fingered her hair. "Except for the hair."

Christine laughed.

The song ended and one of the mariachis said, "I see a cute young blonde girl out there and I'm going to try and talk her into singing for us."

"Is that Carlos?" Christine asked.

"That's Carlos," Frankie said.

"Is he looking at me?"

"Are there any other cute young blonde girls here who sing like an angel?"

"Crap."

"Oh, Christine," Carlos called out as he approached her chair.

Christine stood and hugged him. He took her by the hand and led her toward the stage.

"You guys are in for a real treat," Carlos said as they stepped onto the stage. He leaned over to Christine and said, "Let's do 'Cielito Lindo.'"

"You just did it," she said.

"Not the way you're going to do it."

"What do you mean?"

"Take it slow, really slow, like a love song."

She watched curiously as he strummed his guitar very slowly. He started singing quietly. She quickly caught on to what he was doing and took it from there. She found the slow pace weird at first, but quickly warmed up to it. So did the audience. There was loud applause when she finished the song.

"Brava! Brava!" Frankie shouted.

Christine quickly headed for her chair.

"*¡Uno más!*" Frankie called out, followed by more applause from the other diners.

Carlos reached out and caught Christine by the hand. She turned.

"Do you know 'La Paloma'?" Christine asked.

"*Por supuesto,*" Carlos said. "Can you sing it in Spanish?"

"*Por supuesto.* Hit it."

Carlos strummed his guitar.

"Wait, hold on," Christine said. "Alfie, come sing 'La Paloma' with me."

Alfonso stood.

"He sings with the Santa Fe Opera," Christine said to the audience. There was a smattering of applause as Alfonso approached.

Carlos began playing the intro. The other mariachis joined in. A hush fell over the room as Christine and Alfonso began to sing.

Christine and Alfonso weren't just singing—they were fully involved, in each other's arms, faces often inches apart.

When the song ended, they kissed. Most of the diners were on their feet, applauding. Christine ducked her head, her face flushing from the kiss, but she recovered quickly and curtsied as Alfonso bowed. Alfonso waited while she kissed Carlos on both cheeks and then took her arm and led her to her seat, much to the disappointment of the other diners.

"That was so much fun," Christine said as she sat down.

"It was great," Frankie said.

"Hold on," Meg said. "Did you two used to be a couple?"

"What?" Christine asked. "No way."

"That was practically sex," Meg said.

"Ew! It was just a song."

"That was a lot more than a song. And that was no stage kiss."

Alfonso laughed. "Sometimes I get carried away, especially in the presence of such beauty." He leaned over and kissed Christine on the cheek.

"It's just a thing we do," Christine said.

"A thing?" Meg asked.

"All the girls at the conservatory were in love with Alfonso, but there was a rumor that he was gay."

"The boy is a snappy dresser," Meg said.

"When I started singing duets with him it made all the other girls jealous."

"And mean," Alfonso added.

"So, he started kissing me when we sang love songs together, just to piss off the bitches." Christine looked at Alfonso, and then at Meg. "The boy can kiss."

"So, you two—"

"No, no way."

"Christine was my prom date, though," Alfonso said.

"Oh, yeah. Alfonso was a man of mystery. In addition to the gay thing, there were rumors he was dating a teacher, and all kinds of other people. One of them was true."

"Which one, a teacher?"

"A Disney princess."

"Tegan," Meg said.

"Exactly. But her publicist wanted everybody to think she was dating a famous young actor on the same network, so he took her to all the fancy events and then she snuck around with Alfonso."

"O-M-G. I know who you're talking about. I think he actually is gay."

"Tegan thinks so, too," Alfonso said.

"Anyway," Christine continued. "Alfonso and Tegan were going to come out and go to prom together, but then she got a movie in Australia, so I went to prom with Alfonso."

"And really set tongues wagging at school," Alfonso said.

"He was all over me at the prom, but we both missed out on the after-prom sex and stuff."

"It's not too late," Alfonso said, putting his arm around Christine.

"You wish."

"You two make a great couple, especially on stage. You should totally be the leads in *Sangre de Cristo*."

"Yeah, right," Christine said.

Their dinner was served, and Carlos and the mariachis came over to serenade them.

"Do you ever get to go out to eat without having to sing?" Frankie asked.

"Sometimes," Christine said. "At the drive-through."

Frankie laughed.

"Did you know Carlos was going to be here?" Christine asked.

"Not really," Frankie said. "I know he plays at different places around town."

"Doesn't he work at the ranch anymore?"

"He works at the ranch sometimes and anywhere else he can find a job. He works catering, plays with mariachis, picks up gigs wherever he can."

"Sounds like my mom and dad in Chicago."

"He works as much as possible in the summer and at Christmas, so he can go to school."

"Where does he go to school?"

"Texas Tech. He transferred there from NMMI."

"What's that?" Christine asked.

"New Mexico Military Institute."

"Like where they tried to send Erik, but they wouldn't take him?"

"Exactly, only Carlos didn't need any straightening out. He just wanted to go there. It's a good school, with a great ROTC program, and you can get commissioned after just two years. He's already a second lieutenant in the Army Reserve, but still has to finish college."

"Have you heard from Raoul?" Meg asked.

"No," Christine said.

"That's not altogether true," Frankie said. "She's heard from him. She just won't return his calls."

"Why not?"

"It just didn't work out, okay?" Christine said.

"Well, now that you can't marry Erik, and Alfonso is banging a hot young Australian actress, you should hang onto Raoul. He's rich, not that it matters, since you're rich too."

"I'm not rich."

"You will be."

"Huh?"

"Meg, drop it," Frankie said.

Christine looked at Frankie. "What does she mean, I'll be rich?"

"Johnston is adopting you," Meg said before Frankie could answer. "Don't you know what that means?"

"It means I won't have to live in a foster home until I turn eighteen."

"Whoa," Alfonso said. "Caldwell's adopting you?"

"Yes," Frankie said.

"It also means you will inherit a piece of the family fortune," Meg said.

"What?" Christine asked.

"You'll be part of the trust fund," Frankie said, "same as me and Erik and the other cousins of our generation."

"No, no way. I couldn't do that. That's not right."

"Johnston already talked it over with my dad, and me, and the rest of the family that matters. Everybody is on board. My dad's crazy about you. He's thrilled. So is my mom."

"What about Erik?" Christine asked. "Is he thrilled?"

"I'm sure he doesn't even know. How could he? Nobody has seen or heard from him for months."

"It's his money, not mine."

"Well, now some of it is yours too, or will be. There's plenty to go around, and not just the trust fund. That's from Daniel Senior. I assume Johnston will take care of you in his own will. He picked up a pile of cash when he sold his label and Dad put him into some primo investments. He's loaded."

"I don't care about any of that stuff. I'm just glad to have a place to live, and something to eat. I'd trade it all to have my mama and daddy back, and our little house in Chicago."

Alfonso took Christine's hand. She looked at him and smiled. Words were not necessary.

Meg for once, had nothing to say.

6

LA CARLOTTA

THE COSTUME SHOP at the opera house was busy and Christine watched intently as a seamstress hemmed a dress. "I wish I could do that," Christine said.

"You want to try it?"

"No way. I don't want to ruin it."

"Can you sew at all?"

"I had just started to learn when my mom got sick. After she died, I never really had a chance to do it."

"I'm so sorry."

"She used to make a lot of my clothes."

The seamstress smiled. "Maybe you could practice on some scraps."

Christine perked up. "I could do that."

"But later, after we get this show opened."

"Definitely later."

"Do you plan to go into costuming?"

"No, this is just a summer job. I'm supposed to work in all the departments. Well, they might not let me build sets, something about OSHA or something."

"OSHA?"

"I'm seventeen, so it's about power tools or climbing on stuff or something like that. Bummer. It looks like fun."

"You're not in the apprentice program?"

"Nope."

"That's odd. I thought the apprentices filled all the summer jobs."

"I guess you haven't heard the gossip," Christine said.

"What gossip?"

"I kind of know the boss."

"Mr. Caldwell?"

"Yeah. He was headmaster at my school in LA."

"What school is that?"

"The Belen Conservatory of Music."

"So you're a musician?"

"I'm a singer."

"Opera?"

"Not really. I sing some arias, and other stuff."

"Well, right now you're a costume assistant, and this dress is ready for La Carlotta to try on."

"Okey-dokey," Christine said, taking the dress from the seamstress. She headed toward the door, carrying the dress.

"Wait!"

"What?"

"Hang it on a rack. Carlotta doesn't like people handling her costumes."

"Are you serious?"

"I'm serious."

Christine was confused. "How am I supposed to get it to her?"

"Put it on the rack and push it."

"How does she think her costumes get made?"

"I don't know. Out of sight, out of mind, but she doesn't want to see you, or anyone else, other than her dresser, with your hands on her costumes."

"Wow, what a diva."

"World-class."

Christine stepped across the room and pulled out racks full of costumes to get to an empty one.

She shrieked and jumped back. "What was that?"

"What was what?"

"There was somebody behind that rack of clothes."

The seamstress stood and looked around. "There's nobody there."

"He took off, through the door."

"It must have been the Ghost," the seamstress said.

BACKSTAGE AT AN opera house can be a dangerous place, with large, heavy things being pushed around, rigging dangling from above, and enormous doors that can open or close at any moment. Christine had been duly warned to not listen to music while she worked, especially using ear buds, so she sang quietly to herself while pushing the rack carrying Carlotta's dress.

Carlotta sat at the makeup table, wearing a robe, staring intently at herself in the mirror.

"Are you making fun of me?" Carlotta asked as Christine entered the dressing room, pulling the rack.

"No ma'am," Christine said hesitantly.

"Then why are you singing my song?"

"Your song?"

"You're singing Sofia, from the opera."

"Oh, sorry."

"Do you think you would be a better Sofia than me?"

"No ma'am."

"How do you even know this song? Have you been spying on me at rehearsal?"

"No ma'am."

"You Tuba? Is it on You Tuba?"

"I have no clue."

"You have no what?"

"I don't know if it's on Youtube. I never looked."

"So how do you learn this song, my song, my aria?"

"I'm a friend of Zoe."

"Humph."

"I was kind of there when she wrote it."

"Humph."

"I sang it for her dozens of times while she worked on it."

"Well now it will be sung right."

"Here's your dress." Christine reached for the dress.

"Don't touch it!"

"Sorry." Christine turned to go.

"You wait. I try it on. You take it back."

Carlotta stood and dropped her robe. Christine tried to not look and tried even harder to not make a face. It was not a pretty sight.

CHRISTINE PUSHED THE rack with Carlotta's dress toward the costume shop, quietly this time. She heard a loud crash, a groan, and then a scream. She abandoned the rack and raced across the stage. On the landing below, stagehands quickly began trying to lift a large piece of scenery off an unfortunate scene shifter.

Christine quickly descended the steps, joining many others converging from all directions.

"Call nine-one-one!" someone shouted, as if a dozen or more cell phones weren't already so engaged.

"What happened?" Christine asked as she approached Meg, who was watching crew people free the young man from the scenery.

"Don't move him!" someone else shouted. People surged forth, unable to help, but not wanting to miss anything.

"Is he okay?"

"What happened?"

"Oh, no."

"Is his leg broken?"

"That thing fell on him," Meg said to Christine.

"That's awful," Christine said as she watched the young man on the concrete grimace with pain.

"It was the Ghost," Meg said.

"What ghost?"

"The Opera Ghost," Meg said as she looked up onto the stage, scrutinizing the rigging. "He's back."

"Back from where?"

"He was here last season. We hadn't seen him this year, so we thought maybe he was gone."

Johnston raced across the concrete and quickly took charge. "Has anyone called an ambulance?"

"Yes."

"Has he been moved?"

"No."

Johnston knelt beside the injured worker. "How are you doing?"

"I'm okay, I think. My leg hurts like hell."

"Don't move. An ambulance is on the way. Are there any other injuries? Did you hit your head on the concrete?"

"No, I broke the fall with my left hand." He held it up. "I may have sprained my wrist."

"Did anyone see what happened?" Johnston asked. No one spoke, but several people shook their heads.

Someone rushed up with a medical pack.

"Check his left leg," Johnston said. "It's probably broken, but let's see if it's a compound fracture."

The young woman with the medical pack whipped it open, grabbed a pair of scissors and cut away the left leg of the worker's jeans.

"All right, everyone but stage crew back to work," Johnston said.

Most people quickly hustled away, glancing over their shoulder.

"Is that what fell on him?" Johnston asked, pointing to the scenery.

"Yes sir," a stagehand answered. "We moved it off him. Was that the right thing to do?"

"It's probably okay, as long as you didn't move him."

"We didn't."

Johnston looked at the injured worker's leg. "There's no blood, and no bone sticking out."

"That's a good thing, right?" the worker said.

"Yes, that's a good thing."

Johnston looked up at Christine. "Are you on stage crew today?"

"No sir, costumes."

"Then what are you doing here?"

"Sorry." She turned to go.

"Wait. Do you have a cell phone?"

"I'm a teenage girl. Of course I have a cell phone."

"Does it have a camera?"

"Yes."

"Take some pictures of—" Johnston looked at the injured man. "What's your name?"

"Jesse."

"Take some pictures of Jesse, right where he is, then of the flat, from several angles."

"Why?"

"There will be an investigation. I want to preserve all the evidence."

"Okay," Christine said as she pulled out her cell phone.

"You guys put up some caution tape around the area."

"Yes sir," one of the crew said as he dashed away.

Christine completed her photography assignment just as a loud shriek rang out from backstage.

"Good grief," Johnston said. He turned toward the sound. "What now?"

Another shriek pierced the stillness. "Christine, go see what that is and call me if it's serious."

Christine raced away toward the sound.

"Go take care of that," Jesse said to Johnston. "I'll be okay."

"No, I'll wait here for the ambulance. One of the dancers probably saw a mouse."

Jesse chuckled.

Johnston checked his watch. "Hopefully they'll be here soon."

"I'm okay," Jesse said.

"Johns Town! Johns Town!"

Johnston closed his eyes, shook his head, and turned reluctantly toward the sound. Carlotta stood at the top of the concrete stairs leading down to the landing below, where Johnston waited with Jesse. She wore painted-on jeans, although she certainly shouldn't have, and a tube top that put her ample assets on display. No one other than a salesperson on commission in an expensive boutique would call her petite.

Christine and Meg were in hot pursuit as Carlotta jiggled down the steps.

"Johns Town! Johns Town!" Carlotta shouted in fractured English. "There was a *man* in my dressing room! Well, in *the* dressing room. This wretchful waterback—"

"Waterback?" Meg asked. "Do you mean backwater?"

"This wretchful backwater of an opera house—"

"Wretched," Meg interrupted.

Carlotta whirled around and stared at Meg. "Dancing girls do not correct La Carlotta."

"Sorry."

"A proper opera house has private dressing rooms for the stars," Carlotta said, throwing her head back.

The Santa Fe Opera had long maintained separate dressing rooms for principals and chorus, separated by gender, but when performers were polled before undertaking a major renovation of the backstage areas, most all were quite happy with the camaraderie provided by the existing configuration, and saw no need for private dressing rooms for the stars.

"What happened?" Johnston asked.

"I don't know," Christine said. "We didn't see anything."

"There was a man in the dressing room," Carlotta repeated.

"What was he doing there?" Johnston asked.

"He almost watched me *nudo!*"

Meg covered her mouth and whispered to Christine, "Who would want to see her nude?"

Christine choked back a laugh.

"I'm sure you would have survived it," Johnston said.

"It wasn't me," Jesse said, trying to avoid laughing.

"Oh!" Carlotta screamed as she turned to go. "Hoodlums, country bumpers!"

"Bumpkins," Meg said quietly.

"Savages!" Carlotta shouted. "Why did I ever agree to come to the middle of a no place, on a mountain, so far from civilization?"

"It was the Ghost," Meg shouted as Carlotta ascended the stairs, and not gracefully.

"Should I go after her?" Christine asked.

Johnston was interrupted by the siren of the ambulance. "No, run out there and show the paramedics how to get here."

Christine didn't get very far before meeting the ambulance coming her way. The crew had already anticipated its arrival and has spotters positioned.

7

O.G.

Sharing the mesa with the Santa Fe Opera House, nestled in a beautiful garden, and unseen to most operagoers, was a group of buildings housing the administrative offices, rehearsal spaces, and a cantina, the Dapples Pavilion. It was covered, but open air, much like the theater, and offered an excellent view of the mountains. It served the staff, which was quite large during the season, and was open to operagoers before each performance. Christine sat at a table for two with Johnston.

"This is pretty cool," Christine said.

"You haven't eaten here before?"

"I've been brown-bagging it. Juanita hooks me up."

"You can eat here if you like. Lots of the company members do."

"I'm okay. I kind of like hanging with the guys backstage."

He smiled and nodded.

"Is that a pool over there?" she asked.

"It is indeed."

"I thought there was like, a water shortage in Santa Fe, which is why you didn't have a pool at your ex-house."

Johnston smiled. "There is, and that was why we didn't have a pool at my ex-house. There aren't many private pools in Santa Fe, actually. Some of the hotels and motels have them."

"There's one at the ranch."

"It was built decades ago, before the water shortage became acute. The population of Santa Fe has tripled since then. Besides, Daniel Senior could have brought in water by rail from the Great Lakes if he wanted."

"Daniel Senior was an interesting guy."

"See that gigantic roof over there?"

She turned and looked at the roof of the opera house.

"Yeah, so?"

"It collects rainwater, thousands of gallons of it, which we store in huge tanks. We use it to water the flowers and fill the pool."

"That's pretty smart."

"The apprentices use the pool, but no topless sunbathing."

"That's okay. I can always go topless at the ranch."

"What am I going to do with you?"

"Keep me, apparently."

Johnston smiled. "How was your first week?"

"Pretty good. I really like doing all the different jobs."

"That's good."

"It's pretty much the same as at the conservatory, but you have a lot cooler stuff here."

"And more dangerous stuff, so be careful."

"Ten four."

"When the stage doors are open there's a drop off."

"Yeah, I noticed. It's hard to miss."

"Just be careful."

She took a sip of her drink. "When do I get paid?"

"To tell you the truth, I don't know."

"Don't you get paid for being the boss?"

"Yes, but it's direct deposit, so I don't really pay any attention to when."

"Must be nice."

"Didn't they ask you about direct deposit when you started?"

"Yeah, but you have to have a bank account."

"Oh, yes, I guess that's right. Don't you have a bank account in Santa Monica?"

"Nope. I never really had enough money to mess with it."

"Then I guess you'll get a check."

"I saw one of those check cashing places on the way to work."

"Oh no, don't go to one of those. They charge an obscene amount of money to cash a check. I'll talk to payroll and see what they can do. Maybe we get you a debit card and have them deposit to that."

"Okey-dokey."

"Do you need money?"

"The truck is nearly out of gas."

"We have a gas pump at the ranch."

"We do?"

"Yes, but don't use the one with the green handle."

"Why not?"

"That's diesel. Just ask Frankie. He'll show you where the pump is and how to work it."

"No green handle, check."

"Why are you driving that old clunker? You can ride to work with me."

"No thanks. I get enough crap for being the boss's daughter."

"People already know about that?"

"Meg likes to run her mouth."

"That she does. Frankly, pardon the pun, I think Frankie could do better."

Christine giggled. "Back to getting paid, I do need some uh, female products."

"Oh, sorry, I didn't even think. I've been so busy. How much do you need?"

"Twenty bucks?"

Johnston pulled out his wallet. "Here's a hundred. Let me know if you need more."

"Wow, thanks," she said, taking the money.

"I've never had a daughter, and Erik got money from the family trust, which I think he used to buy drugs for resale, so I really have no idea how much allowance I should give you."

"I'll be okay, once I get paid."

"Still, if you need money, just ask. I don't want to spoil you, and I don't think that's possible—you seem like a pretty down-to-earth girl—so I'll have to rely on you to clue me in as we go."

"I can do that." She ate a bite. "How's Jesse?"

"Who?"

"The guy who got smooshed."

"Oh, him. He has a broken leg. He'll be in a cast for a while, so we'll probably find him some light duty that he can do sitting down, unless he wants to go home."

"What do you think happened?"

"We don't really know yet, but it was clearly an accident. We need to investigate and find out how it happened, and what we can do to prevent it from happening again. Do we need better training, better equipment, better procedures?"

"Sometimes it sucks being boss, huh?"

"Yes, my dear, sometimes it does. It's times like this that makes me question why I didn't just retire instead of accepting the position. I could be in Saint-Tropez right now."

"On the topless beach, checking out the hot, rich divorcées."

He smiled.

"Do you think it was the Opera Ghost?" she asked.

"The what?"

"Meg says the place is haunted by the Opera Ghost."

"I wouldn't put too much stock in what Meg says. Oh, shit, what about Carlotta?"

"She split. She said the food here sucks, or words to that effect." She took another bite. "She's wrong. This is good."

"Split? Where did she go?"

"Her hotel, I guess, or apartment, or nest, or wherever you're keeping her."

"Don't ever do that."

"Do what?"

"Become a diva, well, that kind of diva."

"*No problemo.*"

"What did she say about the guy in the dressing room?"

"You mean the Ghost?"

"No, the man she said she saw in the dressing room."

"She said he was an African American."

"Really?"

Christine nodded.

"She used those exact words?" he asked.

"No, she said Negro, but who says that anymore?"

"Are you sure she didn't say *nero?*"

"Could be, why?"

"That's Italian for black."

"Oh, yeah, that makes sense."

"I thought you spoke Italian."

Christine shrugged. "A little. I mostly just sing it. She also said something about mascara, but I have no idea what that has to do with the Ghost."

"Was it *maschera nera*, or something like that?"

"Yeah, maybe. What does that mean?"

"Black mask."

"She also said he was wearing a Houdini."

"A Houdini?"

"Like the guy in that movie, with Saoirse Ronan."

Johnston looked puzzled. "Who?"

"Never mind. I think she meant hoodie. She was talking with her hands, like Italians do."

"Do you think there actually was someone in there?"

"Probably was. I saw him too."

"In the dressing room?"

"No, a few minutes earlier, in the costume shop."

"Wearing a mask?"

"Couldn't tell. It happened like, really fast."

"There really was a man? Carlotta wasn't making it up?"

"There really was a man, or someone, in the costume shop. I saw him. That doesn't mean Carlotta wasn't making hers up."

"Is that Meg over there?"

Christine turned to look. "Yep, that's her, with her mom."

"Her mom?"

"Mrs. Giry. She works here."

"She does?"

"She runs the ticket office. You should know this stuff. You're the boss."

"I've only been here a few weeks. Are you finished with your lunch?"

"Pretty much, why?"

"I want to talk to Meg about this ghost person."

Christine chugged her drink and followed Johnston over to Meg's table.

"Hello, I'm Johnston Caldwell."

"Yes, I know who you are," Mrs. Giry said.

"Do you mind if we join you?"

"Not at all."

"I'm sorry I haven't gotten around to meeting everyone. I've been extremely busy, taking over with a new season starting, and premiering a new opera."

"Yes, I understand. I guess you know my daughter, Meg."

"Yes, quite well."

Christine and Johnston sat down.

"Meg, Christine tells me that you seem to know something about an opera ghost?"

"Yes, I do."

"Have you actually seen him?"

"No, but one of the technician guys has."

"Did he describe him?"

"He said he wore jeans, sneakers, a dark hoodie, and a black mask."

"So, it's not really a ghost, but a guy in a mask."

"Maybe, maybe not."

"I don't understand."

"Maybe there's a guy in a mask, and there's also a ghost," Meg said.
Christine nodded in agreement.

"There was a lot of spooky shit last season," Meg said.

"Meg, watch your language," Mrs. Giry said.

"What kind of spooky shit?" Johnston asked.

"Things disappearing, props, hats, wardrobe, shit like that," Meg said.
"Rigging being messed with, doors opening and closing, trap doors left open.
The director got all pissed off because somebody messed with his electronic
gizmos."

"That was last season?" Johnston asked.

Meg nodded. "We thought he was gone, but he showed up again a few
days ago."

"Why didn't you say something?"

"What? Like I'm going to go to the manager and report a ghost? Get real."

"But you're reporting it now."

"You asked. And Jesse got hurt. Nobody's gotten hurt before."

"So you think this 'ghost' had something to do with Jesse's accident?"

"How do you know it was an accident?"

"What else could it have been?"

"The Ghost comes from nowhere and disappears into thin air. Maybe he
pushed the flat, and then vanished."

"And there's the reserved seats," Mrs. Giry said.

"What reserved seats?" Johnston asked.

"Last season he demanded two reserved seats for every performance,
good seats too."

Johnston laughed. "Are you saying he showed up at the box office and
bought tickets?"

"Oh, no, he didn't show up."

"Online reservations, then? How did he pay, with a ghost credit card?"

"He didn't pay. He demanded them for free."

"How did he demand them? Did he call on the phone?"

"He sent texts."

"Texts?"

"Yes sir, texts."

"And you responded?"

"Yes sir."

"So you have his phone number."

"Not really, it changes."

"Burner phone," Christine said.

"What?" Johnston asked.

"Burner phone. You buy a cheap phone at a convenience store, twenty bucks or so, add some minutes, use it for a while, and then dump it. Keeps NASA from tracking you."

"NSA," Meg said.

"Whatever," Christine said.

"How do you know this stuff?" Johnston asked.

"I'm a teenager," Christine said. "We know stuff."

Meg nodded in agreement.

Johnston shook his head and turned to Mrs. Giry. "And you gave him the seats? How did he pick up the tickets?"

"He never picked them up. The seats were always empty."

"Why didn't you sell them to someone else?"

"We tried that, at the beginning of the season, but then the violin went missing. It belonged to one of the musicians and the company had to pay for it. It was very expensive."

"So, you left two prime seats open for the rest of the season?"

"Yes sir."

"Was this your decision?"

"No sir. The previous manager approved it. He was very superstitious."

"Well, I'm not superstitious. Two prime seats for an entire season is a lot of money. We have a payroll, light bill, insurance. It costs a fortune to operate this company and we pride ourselves on operating in the black. If he makes the same demand this season, let me know."

"He already has."

"When?"

"Yesterday."

"And what did you do?"

"I told him no."

"And then this morning Jesse got whacked," Meg said.

"Sounds like the Opera Ghost to me," Christine said.

Johnston's phone buzzed. He checked it, read a text, and looked puzzled.

"What?" Christine asked.

"Carlotta sucks," Johnston said, reading from his phone. "Dump her. O.G." He looked up from his phone. "Who the hell is O.G.?"

"Opera Ghost," Meg said. Both girls looked around. "He must be watching us."

"How did he get my number? This is my personal phone."

"The Opera Ghost knows all," Meg said.

"Are you going to dump her?" Christine asked.

"I can't dump her. She has a contract."

"I don't think Zoe likes her, and I know Jim Bob doesn't."

"Zoe's not too happy with the choice, but it was made before I got here. Besides, she's an international star. She'll draw an audience on her name alone, and a new opera needs all the help it can get."

"Sofia is poor and hungry," Meg said, "like Katniss."

"Who is Katniss?" Johnston asked.

"Katniss Everdeen, in *The Hunger Games*."

Johnston knew no more than he did before.

"It's a movie but I liked the book better."

"Me too," Meg said.

"It doesn't look like Carlotta ever missed a meal."

"Neither did J-Law. That girl is built like a brick shithouse."

"Word."

Johnston grew more confused by the minute. Mrs. Giry shook her head, obviously knowing no more than Johnston.

"Sofia is young, like seventeen," Christine said, "Carlotta, not so much."

"Yes, but she can sing, and she has a following," Johnston said. "And opera casts much older all the time. It's a necessary evil."

"Her understudy is pretty good."

"Hayley," Meg said.

"Yeah," Christine said, "and she looks the part, young, black hair, sunken cheeks, skinny."

"I think she's part Mexican," Meg said, "and totally hot. The guys hit on her all the time."

"The guy who sings Alejandro is pretty hot too," Christine said, "but kind of old."

"Francisco," Johnston said.

"Oh, baby," Meg said. "I would totally hit that."

"Meg!" Mrs. Giry said.

"Well, I would."

Christine nodded and smiled.

"And he speaks fluent Spanish," Meg said, "Castilian, not Mexican."

"How can you tell the difference?" Johnston asked.

"Our family has been in Santa Fe for more than three hundred years," Mrs. Giry said, "since the original Spanish land grants."

"Wow," Christine said, nodding her head. "Can you top that, Johnston?"

Johnston smiled and shook his head.

"Anyway," Meg said, "Cisco is perfect for Alejandro, except for the age thing. Carlotta just sucks as Sofia."

"Carlotta will sing Sofia on opening night," Johnston said. "And that's final, ghost or no ghost."

8

THE GHOST IN THE GARDEN

RAOUL RANG THE doorbell at the Valerius house. He had been here only rarely since the move to Paris, but he had fond memories of this house, from a simpler time, when everything was clear. People often talk about childhood sweethearts, but he and Christine had actually been such. He remembered their first meeting, on the Santa Monica Pier. He was smitten even before she impulsively kissed him on the lips as a reward for rescuing her scarf from the sea. He grimaced as he remembered how utterly stupid that was, to have leapt off the pier, fully clothed, into the Pacific Ocean, in the dead of winter. She was twelve and he was thirteen. They had been inseparable for a few idyllic months until her beloved father died, she was accepted by the conservatory, and he was whisked off to Paris by his parents.

The door finally opened, just a crack.

"Yes?" A young woman peered out cautiously from behind the door.

"Oh, I'm sorry," Raoul said. "I must have the wrong house."

"Who are you looking for?"

"Christine Daaé."

"She's not here."

"Is this the Valerius house?"

"Yes."

Raoul was clearly impatient with the paucity of information coming from this stranger.

"I'm Lupe. I was hired to take care of Mrs. Valerius for the summer."

"Is Mrs. Valerius in?"

"Yes, of course," Lupe said, but the door didn't budge.

"May I see her?"

"Who may I say is calling?"

"Raoul Chagny."

"Wait here. I'll check."

The door closed. Raoul waited.

"Mrs. Valerius doesn't know who you are," Lupe said when she returned.

"Of course she knows me," Raoul said emphatically. "She and the professor knew my parents for years." He paused to calm down. "I'm sorry. I'm just a bit frustrated."

"Mrs. Valerius is ill, in bed, and not receiving visitors."

"Could you please tell her it's the boy who took violin lessons here, from Mr. Daaé, a few years ago."

"Okay, I'll try."

"Thank you."

Again, Raoul waited, and waited. Finally, the door opened fully.

"Come in," Lupe said.

Raoul stepped into the living room. It was mostly as he remembered it. The piano still had a prominent place. He followed Lupe into the master bedroom. The lamp was off, and the room was dimly lit by a shaft of light through the window. Mrs. Valerius lay in bed, wearing a blue nightgown. Her hair, graying when last he saw her, was now snow white. She was pale, but her eyes sparkled when he entered the room. She held out both hands. He moved toward the bed and leaned over. She pulled him close and kissed him on both cheeks. She had that old lady odor, but he smiled and returned her kisses.

"I'll leave you alone," Lupe said, backing away.

"Who is that girl?" Mrs. Valerius whispered as Lupe closed the door.

"She said her name was Lupe," Raoul said, suddenly realizing that Mrs. Valerius's illness was likely of the mind. "She's here to take care of you."

Mrs. Valerius didn't respond.

"Where is Christine?" Raoul asked.

"She is with the Angel."

"What?" He was alarmed.

"The Angel of Music."

Raoul backed up and sat in a chair.

"You must not tell anyone," Mrs. Valerius said. "It's a secret."

"You can trust me."

"I know I can."

Raoul was more confused than ever, and it was becoming obvious that Mrs. Valerius was not going to clear up anything.

"I would bake you some cookies, like I did when you were a boy, but that girl won't let me in the kitchen."

He nodded. "Who is the Angel of Music?"

"Don't you remember the story Christine's father used to tell, about little Charlotte and the Angel of Music?"

"Yes, of course, but it was just a story."

"Come sit here," Mrs. Valerius said, patting the bed.

Raoul reluctantly stepped over and sat on the bed.

"I am very fond of you, Raoul, and so is Christine."

"She won't return my calls or texts."

"She used to speak of you often."

"Really? What did she say about me?"

"She said she hoped that you two might someday marry."

"She said that?"

"Yes, but it can never be."

"Why not?" Raoul stood and stepped back, suddenly alarmed. "Is there someone else? Is that why she's avoiding me?"

"Why, no. Christine can never marry."

Now he was really confused. "Why can she never marry?"

"Because of the Angel of Music, of course."

"There is no Angel of Music," Raoul said. "It was just a story."

"Oh, no. He is quite real, and he forbids Christine to ever marry."

"How do you know that?"

"He told me."

"You spoke to him?"

"Yes, of course, in the garden."

"When?"

"At night. The Angel only comes at night, when Christine goes out."

"Where does she go?"

"I don't know. She comes home late."

"If I come back tonight, can I see the Angel of Music for myself?"

"Oh, no."

"Why not?"

"He vanished when that girl came," she said, gesturing with her hands. "Poof, like a ghost."

Raoul leaned in and kissed her on the cheek. "I'd better go now, and let you rest."

"Oh, yes. Thank you. Please come again and see me."

Raoul left the room and found Lupe in the kitchen.

"What's wrong with her?"

"Early-onset Alzheimer's."

"She was talking about an angel that only comes at night."

Lupe nodded. "It gets worse at night."

"But she remembered some things perfectly well."

"That's how it works."

"Who hired you, if you don't mind my asking?"

"Mr. Caldwell."

"Johnston Caldwell?"

"Yes."

"Is he in Los Angeles?"

"No, I believe he's in Santa Fe."

"Did Christine leave with Mr. Caldwell?"

"No, she left with a boy she called Frankie. She seemed to know him very well, like he was her boyfriend or something."

Raoul's mind raced as he tried to process this avalanche of information, none of which gave him confidence.

"Do you mind if I look in the little cottage?" he asked.

"What's that?"

"The guest house, out back."

Lupe located the key, and they went out to the little cottage.

"It was a mess when I first got here, fast-food wrappers, pizza boxes, empty bottles and cans, so I cleaned it up."

"Was Christine staying out here?"

"I don't think so. I'm staying in her room in the house. That's where all her clothes are, the ones she didn't take. Maybe she used this to party. I asked Mrs. Valerius if anyone was living here, but she put her finger on her lips and shook her head."

He stepped over to the bed, ran his fingers across the covers, and smiled.

"What is it?" Lupe asked.

"Nothing, just reminiscing. I should go," he said, turning away from the bed. He stopped suddenly; his gaze fixed on a painting thumb-tacked to the wall. He took a closer look. It was the painting of Christine and Connie on the beach in Saint-Tropez.

"Is that Christine?" Lupe asked.

"Yes."

"I thought it was odd, but it wasn't my place to say anything. She's just a teenager, isn't she?"

"Yes. She just turned seventeen."

"Pretty nice work, though."

"Yes, it is. I know the artist."

9

THE STORM

A TAXI DROPPED off Raoul at the Titshaw ranch. The front door was open, so he stepped in. "Hello, anyone home?"

Raoul was headed toward the kitchen when he was intercepted by Carlos. "Can I help you?"

"I'm looking for Frankie."

Carlos was cautious. "He's not here."

"Do you know when he'll be back?"

"A few hours. Can I tell him who was looking for him?"

"Raoul." Raoul extended his hand, and they shook. "Raoul Chagny."

"Oh yeah, Christine's friend," Carlos said, finally recognizing him.

"Yes, and I've known Frankie for years."

"You here for the ball?"

"What ball?"

"The masked ball, fund-raiser for the opera. I'll be going as a waiter."

"No, actually. I didn't know anything about it."

"That's where Frankie is, in Albuquerque, getting some stuff for the ball. He's the head honcho for it. You want some lunch?"

"I've crossed so many time zones I don't even know what time it is, but yes, I could eat."

Carlos pushed open the door to the kitchen. "We could go into town and grab something."

"I'll slap your face," Juanita said. "If you want to eat, you put your *culo* in that chair. Hello, Mr. Raoul. It's good to see you again."

"Good to see you, Juanita."

The boys sat at the table.

"What do you want to eat?" Juanita asked.

"Burritos," Carlos said, and looked at Raoul. "Is that okay? You're French, right?"

"Half French, my mom's American. I grew up in LA, so I know my way around a burrito."

"Well, that's what you'll get," Juanita said.

"Yes ma'am. I remember your burritos."

"They're better when Christine makes the tortillas."

"Is she here?"

"She's at work," Carlos said.

"At work?" Raoul was surprised.

"Johnston got her a summer job at the opera house. I tried to tell her she could make more money working catering with me. She said that's what her mom used to do, but she kind of wanted to do the opera thing."

"Do you go to school with Frankie?"

Carlos laughed and shook his head. "No, not hardly."

"He works here," Juanita said, "when I can get him off his lazy *culo*."

"Juanita is *mi tía*, my aunt," Carlos said. Frankie and Erik used to come here every summer. They treated me like a cousin—still do really."

"Have you heard from Erik? I understand he dropped out of sight."

"No, not since anyone else has. Frankie and I check with each other all the time, hoping one of us has heard, but nothing. I'm sure he feels like shit about that girl."

"Connie."

"Yeah, Connie. She was a cool chick."

"Yes, she was."

"I think she had the hots for Erik."

"She did."

"But Erik had the hots for Christine."

Raoul nodded his head.

"Wanted her bad," Carlos said.

"Did he say something to you about it?"

"Not really, but I know the guy. I was really closer with Erik than Frankie, mainly because he kept bouncing back and forth between his mom and dad and sometimes, he would just show up here to get away from them both."

"Come and get it," Juanita said. "It's roll-your-own."

The boys quickly built burritos from the ingredients Juanita had laid out.

"Are you staying at the ranch?" Carlos asked.

"No, I'm downtown."

"Why aren't you staying here? There's plenty of room."

"I'm not sure I'm welcome."

"Why would you say that?"

"Christine won't return my calls, and when I ask Frankie about her, he seems evasive."

"That doesn't sound like Frankie. He's a pretty straight-up guy."

"I went to Christine's house in Santa Monica yesterday. Mrs. Valerius sounded crazy, but the housekeeper, or whatever she was—"

"Lupe. Her mom is a friend of Juanita."

"Yeah, Lupe. She said Christine left with Frankie, and she thought maybe he was her boyfriend."

"Boyfriend?" Carlos laughed.

"What?"

"You think Frankie is hitting on your girl?"

"I don't know what to think."

"Frankie is all up in Meg. That boy is pussy-whipped. If he cheated on her she'd cut off his *cajones*."

"So, there's nothing going on?"

"Hell no. I saw them last week having dinner at a joint where I play with a mariachi group."

"Them who?"

"Frankie, Meg and Christine."

"Did you talk to them?"

"Yeah, sure. Christine came up and sang a couple of songs. That girl can sing."

"Yeah, I know."

"Trust me. There's nothing going on there. Frankie treats her like a sister, or a cousin, which makes sense, because—"

"*¡Cállate!*" Juanita bonked Carlos on the back of the head.

"Oh yeah, sorry."

"What?" Raoul asked.

"You'd better let Christine tell you, or Frankie."

"Tell me what?"

"It's none of my business. Forget I said anything. Oh, there was another dude there too, Alfonso. He sang a duet with Christine. He's the one I'd be worried about if I were you. They were all kissy-kissy."

———

RAOUL, LOOKING EVERY bit the young, wealthy Euro, nervously paced the lobby of the inn in downtown Santa Fe, just off the plaza. He perked up as Christine entered. He wanted badly to sweep her into his arms and kiss her passionately but counted himself fortunate that she showed up. As she approached, his eyes darted from top to bottom. Her hair fell loosely over her bare shoulders. The hem of her dress danced seductively over her legs, well above the knee. She carried a light jacket. He was immediately reminded of their summer in Saint-Tropez. Christine noticed him looking and was immediately happy that she had been getting some sun at the pool.

The moment had come. They were face to face. Shaking hands seemed too formal, a kiss on the lips seemed too familiar. Finally, he made his decision and they kissed on both cheeks.

"I'm glad you came."

"Well, you're in town, and I can't avoid you forever." She had initially intended to invite him to the ranch for dinner but decided it would be better to meet him alone at a neutral site and avoid all the awkward dinner conversation with Frankie and Johnston present, and maybe Meg, which would have been a disaster.

"So, is this where we're eating, or do you just want to go up to your room and hop in bed?"

"What?" He was stunned.

"Just kidding. You are so easy, but you did invite me to your motel. That might give some girls the wrong idea."

He smiled. It was an upscale inn, hardly a motel, but he saw no reason to correct her. He didn't want anything to ruin the evening.

"We're eating around the corner," he said, relieved.

"Well, check your watch, because I parked on the street. I couldn't figure out that meter thingy. I don't know if I have to feed it in an hour, or what."

"I could have sent a car."

"That's okay. I'm trying to become more self-sufficient."

"Give me the keys."

She pulled the keys out of her small purse.

He took her by the arm and stepped over to the concierge desk.

"Where are you parked?" Raoul asked her.

"I don't know, about a block or two that way." She pointed.

He handed the keys to the concierge. "Could you valet the lady's car?"

"Of course." The man knew a good tip when he saw one. "What kind of car is it?"

"It's a really old pickup truck," Christine said. "It's pretty beat up. I think it used to be red."

The concierge looked at the keys. "We'll find it."

"I guess I should have just pulled up out front and left it."

"You could have," Raoul said as he put his arm around her waist and led her out the door.

"Sorry, I've been living in the real world. I usually take the bus."

"Why are you driving a pickup?"

"It's my work truck. Wow, those are words I never thought I'd hear myself say."

The restaurant really was just around the corner. Christine laughed when she saw the sign as they entered.

"What's funny?" Raoul asked.

"You would find the only French joint in town."

"It's not really French, I don't think. It's just called a bistro. They have quite an eclectic menu, but they do serve our wine, so I thought I'd check it out."

"Works for me. I've been pigging out on Mexican food since I got here. Does this dress make me look fat?"

Raoul froze.

"What?" she asked.

"I was taught that a gentleman never answers that question."

"You were taught well."

"You're not fat. You look quite beautiful in that dress."

"When you said 'inn' I thought it was a motel, so I was going to wear jeans and a T-shirt, but Frankie said I should definitely throw on a dress. You look nice too."

"Thank you."

They were quickly seated, although there were people waiting, a point not lost on Christine. Raoul was his father's son.

"I understand the seafood is flown in daily," Raoul said as they were seated.

"Great. I like fish."

Raoul was thrilled that it seemed to be going so well. Christine seemed in a good mood, but he decided not to push his luck and resolved to continue the small talk until an opportunity presented itself.

The waiter brought the menus.

"May I see the wine list?" Raoul asked.

The waiter leaned down and whispered. "I'm sorry sir, but I'll have to see ID, for yourself and the young lady."

Raoul smiled. "We're not ordering wine. I just wanted to see what you have."

The waiter looked puzzled.

"My family is in the wine business," Raoul said.

"They have their own winery in France," Christine said.

"Yes sir, of course." The waiter turned to go.

"What's good?" Christine asked, looking at her menu.

"I don't know. It's my first time here."

"How do you know the fish flies in daily?"

"The concierge at the hotel told me."

She closed her menu and put it on the table. "You can order for me."

Memories from Saint-Tropez flooded over Raoul. He wanted so badly to lean over and kiss her, but restrained himself, settling for a smile. "Of course, but I thought you wanted to become more self-sufficient."

"You aren't you going to make me split the check, are you?"

He laughed. "No, definitely not. I'm old school when it comes to such things."

Within seconds the owner arrived and handed Raoul a wine list. "Mr. Chagny?" Obviously, he had checked the reservation list.

"Yes."

"We have several of your wines on our list."

"How do they sell?"

"Quite well, especially the whites. We have a lot of European visitors."

"So, let's say we were having the seared tuna. Which wine would you recommend?"

"I'm sorry, sir, but the young lady is obviously not of age."

"I'm not either. I don't want you to lose your license. I'm just interested in what you would recommend."

The owner smiled. "In that case, your Select Chardonnay, of course."

Raoul turned to Christine. "We had that at Rémy's in Saint-Tropez, remember?"

"Sure," Christine said. She had no idea what wine they had at Rémy's.

Raoul handed the wine list to the owner. "Thank you. What would you recommend for an entrée?"

The owner smiled. "The seared tuna, of course."

"Is that okay with the young lady?" Raoul asked Christine.

"Sure. I like tuna fish."

Raoul and the owner both smiled.

"I'll send your waiter to take your order," the owner said as he turned to leave.

"They aren't going to ask me to sing, are they?" Christine asked.

"I don't think they know who you are."

"Good."

"I could always ask."

"Noooo. I just want to eat. And talk. We need to talk."

Raoul felt an enormous weight lift from his body.

"Yes, we do."

But the small talk continued, neither willing to risk ruining such a lovely dinner by mentioning the elephant in the room.

Christine really enjoyed her dinner, although it was unlike any tuna fish she had ever eaten.

The owner returned with a list of dessert wines the kids would not drink, but played the game with Raoul, who made the perfect choice, from his family's vineyards.

"I notice you have a good selection of Appellation High Plains."

"Yes. We get a *lot* of Texans in Santa Fe. There are some up-and-coming wineries on the Texas High Plains, not that far away."

"We're thinking of getting into that market, either buying an existing winery or starting one. California is saturated, and the land is expensive. Texas looks like the future."

"I look forward to it."

RAOUL HAD THOUGHT nothing of putting his hand on Christine's waist as they left the restaurant—that came utterly naturally to them both—and he didn't remember whether it was intentional, or if it just happened, that their fingers brushed together and then joined as they strolled around the plaza. She pulled her jacket closed.

"Are you cold?" he asked.

"No, I'm okay, but it does get chilly here at night."

"It smells like rain."

"Johnston said it doesn't rain here much but there's more in the summer."

"We won't get too far from the inn, then."

Christine chuckled. "Inn, then. You made a little rhyme."

"I could be a rapper."

She laughed out loud. "Yeah, right, Raoul the rapper."

They approached a bench. "Let's sit down," she said, rubbing her shoulders from the chill, giving Raoul an excuse to put his arm around her.

"I'm sorry I haven't returned your calls," she said.

He wanted to say, "or texts, or emails," but held his tongue. She was opening up and he dared not interfere.

She didn't speak again, so he summoned the courage. "Why didn't you?"

"It's complicated."

"We have plenty of time, unless you have a curfew."

"Or it rains."

And rain it did, accompanied by thunder and lightning. They jumped up and raced for cover, first on the sidewalk at the Palace of the Governors, and then finally began working their way back to the inn, darting across streets and under the porches of the buildings around the plaza when it became clear it wasn't going to stop soon.

They were drenched, but laughing, as they swept into the lobby of the inn. No one brought it up, but the obvious move was to go upstairs to Raoul's room.

"Where's the bed?" Christine asked as they entered his room.

"You mean you really did want to hop in bed?"

The look on her face clearly said otherwise.

"It's a suite," he said. "The bedroom's in there. This is the living room."

"Oh, okay."

"You're soaked," he said, stating the obvious—they were both dripping on the floor.

"You are too."

She looked around the room.

"What are you looking for?" he asked.

"Are we in a romantic comedy? Did your family go into the movie business? I hear they do a lot of that stuff in New Mexico."

"No, my family's not in the movie business and we're not in a movie."

"This is the part where you say, 'You need to get out of those wet clothes.'"

"You need to get out of those wet clothes."

She turned her back. "Unzip me."

He unzipped her. She disappeared into the bathroom. He was also drenched, but she was in the bathroom with all the towels. He thought about asking for one, but decided she probably needed more than one, so he quickly stripped off and put on a thick, fluffy, cotton robe from the closet.

Christine soon came out, wearing one towel and drying her hair with the other. He watched with interest.

"What?" she asked.

"Maybe this *is* a movie."

She laughed. "Told you."

She looked at his dripping hair. "Do you need a towel?"

"Yes, please."

"Which one?"

"Whichever one you prefer."

With a sly grin on her face, she reached for the towel she was wearing, but instead tossed him the one on her head. "Nice try, pervert."

He caught the towel and dabbed at his hair.

"Does this look familiar?" she asked.

"I don't know, Saint-Tropez, maybe?"

"The motel in Santa Monica, when we first met, or when you first stalked me."

"Oh yeah, I remember that."

"Zoe called you a pervert."

"Sorry. I tried to look."

"Did you see anything?"

"Not really. Zoe caught me."

"Good."

"There's another robe in the closet, his and hers."

"Why didn't you tell me?"

He cocked his head and smiled. "I was enjoying the view."

She moved toward the closet, but he quickly fetched the robe for her. She held out her hand to take it, but he spread it open so she could put it on.

"Avert your eyes, pervert," she said, turning around and tossing the towel at the same time. He slipped the robe around her shoulders, and she pushed her arms through the sleeves. She pulled it around and tied the belt.

"Do you want me to call room service and have them light the fire?" he asked.

"No, that's okay," she said as she sat down on the sofa.

He sat down beside her. "May I put my arm around you?"

"Sure," she said, snuggling close. "Why did you ask?"

"Ask what?"

"If you could put your arm around me. You didn't ask a few minutes ago, on the bench."

"We were outside, in public. Now we're in a hotel room, and you're kind of naked, well, under the robe."

She laughed. "You are such a gentleman."

"I try."

They sat in silence for a moment.

"You were saying," he said.

"I was saying what?"

"You said 'it's complicated,' before it started raining."

"Oh yeah, that."

"What's complicated?"

"You, me, Erik."

"We don't have to talk about it right now."

"Yeah, I should probably get home."

"Do you want me to take you home?"

"What about my truck?"

"You can get it later. Or we can just stay here and make out."

"Screw you."

"I'm sorry. I was just making a little joke."

"I know," she said. "I'm just messing with you. That's the problem. We're always so comfortable together. Any other guy takes you to his motel room and next thing you know he's in your panties."

"You aren't wearing panties."

"You looked!"

"Just a little. I couldn't help myself."

"Not that it matters. I was nearly naked all over the place in Saint-Tropez."

"Okay, no making out."

He pulled her even more closely and kissed her on the forehead.

"You were always so good to me," she said. "Right from the very beginning, when you jumped off that stupid pier."

"I was smitten."

"You were an idiot."

She pulled her feet up under the robe. "Can you call the guy about the fire?"

"Of course." He reached for the phone.

"There's a hair dryer in the bathroom. I should dry my hair while we're waiting for the fire."

"Good idea."

Room service arrived, with hot chocolate. The waiter quickly lit the fire and disappeared.

"Oh, cool," Christine said as she came out with dry hair and discovered the hot chocolate. "Ooh, little marshmallows."

They sat down and sipped hot chocolate.

"I wasn't trying to avoid the subject," she said. "I was just stalling."

"Take your time."

"I'm so sorry."

"For what?"

"For treating you like I did."

"I just didn't know why."

"Because of Erik, that's why."

"You have feelings for Erik?"

"I did, actually, well not like my feelings for you, but, crap, I don't know how to explain it."

"Any way you like."

"You always treated me so good. Any non-idiot girl would have jumped at a relationship like that. But I'm not that girl. I'm an idiot. It's the old good-girl-bad-boy thingy."

"I understand."

"No, you don't. Remember that night at the cove, my last night in Saint-Tropez?"

"How could I forget?"

"Erik and Connie, and Frankie and Meg were screwing their brains out in the boat, and we just sat there on the beach, like a couple of kids at church camp."

"I thought that's what you wanted."

"It kind of was."

"Would you rather have taken a turn in the boat?"

"I kind of wanted to, but kind of didn't."

"That's okay."

"You loved me, or at least I think you did, and you didn't push me."

"Yes, I did. I still do."

"You do?"

"Of course. I've always loved you, since that day on the pier. We were too young to do anything about it. Well, you were anyway."

"You were too."

"Yes, really, I was."

She laughed.

"What?" he asked.

"Remember when we went to the Renaissance Faire, and Zoe was trying to push up my boobs and you came out carrying that codpiece thingy and didn't know what to do with it?"

"Yes, how could I forget?"

"We were definitely too young," she said. "And then in Saint-Tropez, after all that time, we just naturally fell back into it, like a pair of old shoes."

"Ugh. Was I that boring?"

"No, just comfortable."

"And Erik wasn't comfortable?"

"Hell, no! He was exciting, and dangerous."

"He was definitely dangerous."

"Yeah, look what happened to Connie."

"That could have been you."

"You think I don't know that?"

"Of course you do."

"I was on that dirt bike with him before."

"You were?"

He could feel her breathing. Finally, she spoke. "Do you remember when we were on the train back to LA?"

"Yes."

"There's something I didn't tell you."

"You almost had sex with Erik, but you didn't. I don't need details."

"I wanted to."

"You wanted to what?"

"I wanted to have sex with Erik."

Now it was Raoul who was breathing heavily and not speaking.

"We almost did," she said. "I mean we really almost did. About as-close-as-you-can-get almost did."

Raoul still didn't speak.

"But it just wasn't right," she said. "He didn't love me. He didn't even care about me. It was just sex for him, or would have been. Then I said no, and he just kept on."

"Wait, I thought you said you didn't do it. Are you saying he raped you?"

"Huh? No. We just didn't do it."

"So, what happened?"

"It was a bit tense. He was a lot bigger and stronger than I was, and I was half-naked, but then the bus showed up, with the kids on it."

"What bus? What kids?"

"The Belen Beats, the band, the night before the gala. We were in the private train car. I thought I told you. We started making out at the ranch, and then he took me to the train on his dirt bike. He knew exactly what he wanted. I wanted it too, kind of, maybe, but I backed out, put my clothes on, and we made some lame excuse to Jim Bob."

"Jim Bob? What was he doing there?"

"He was chaperoning the Beats."

"And you were naked?"

"Half-naked. I thought you didn't want the details."

"Sorry."

"I'm sure it pissed him off."

"Who? Jim Bob?"

"No, Erik. Try to keep up."

"Okay, sorry."

He took a moment to process this new information. "So, that's why you haven't returned my calls, not because you had sex with Erik, but because you wanted to?"

"Yeah, that's about it. If you sin in your heart, it's just as bad as actually doing the sin, or whatever. Isn't that what the preachers say? I hurt you bad enough. I was afraid that telling you the truth would hurt you even more."

"I'll admit I was hurt but I had no right to be. We weren't officially together, but yeah, it hurt."

"Then when you said you might be coming to LA, I kind of panicked and stopped returning your calls and texts."

"I thought it was something I said or did."

"It wasn't you. It was me. You invited me to Saint-Tropez. I was staying in your house. I should have pushed Erik away right from the start and never let it go any further."

"But he was new and exciting."

"Yes, and it was Saint-Tropez. Topless beaches, beautiful people, hot clubs with nearly naked people on the dance floor, wine, scooters, yachts. The place practically drips casual sex."

He laughed. "It does, doesn't it?"

"I was just this young, stupid American girl dumped right in the middle of it."

"And Erik thought you were a tasty treat when he first laid eyes on you."

"About that."

"What?"

"The first time he laid eyes on me was at the beach party for Zoe's school."

"He was there?"

"He was there, lurking in the shadows. He stalked me all over Santa Monica."

"When did you find this out?"

"At the gala. He told me."

"There was a lot of tension that night, but I had no idea."

"Enough about Erik. What about us?"

"I thought we were making progress, until the last few days, anyway."

"Making progress? The only time we've seen each other is at the professor's funeral."

"I tried. I invited you places. I tried to come to Santa Monica to see you."

"I don't know. It was just everything, the professor, and Mrs. Valerius, and school, and the kids, and all the drama."

"I could have helped with all that if you had just let me."

"I know, and that's what I love about you."

His heart jumped. She didn't exactly say, "I love you," but it was close enough and he would take what he could get.

"You have no idea how hard it was for me to come here tonight," she said.

"You seemed pretty relaxed to me."

"I guess I'm good at faking it."

"Apparently."

"Crap, what am I saying? I'm terrible at faking it, that's the point. You put me immediately at ease, just like you did in Saint-Tropez, at the pool, when you first got there."

"I remember it well."

She smirked. "I could tell you were glad to see me."

He laughed.

"Why aren't you mad at me?" she asked.

"Why should I be mad at you?"

"Any normal guy would have gotten pissed off at me for making out with another guy, in bed, with my top off. Erik would have gone ballistic."

"I'm not Erik."

"No, you're not." She kissed him on the cheek. "What time is it?"

He checked his watch. "After midnight."

"Crap! I have to go to work in the morning."

"Take the day off."

"I'm not that girl."

"What girl?"

"The boss's daughter."

"Huh?"

"Oh, yeah, there's a lot more we need to talk about."

She snuggled. He waited, but she never said anything more. He sat in silence for a few minutes and then realized she was sound asleep.

10

THE PLAZA

THERE WAS A LOUD knock at the door of Raoul's suite. He tried to gently separate from Christine, but she awoke with a start.

"Who's that?" she asked.

"I don't know. Did you order room service?"

She whirled her head around and looked at the window. It was clearly daylight.

"Oh no!" she said, leaping to her feet.

Raoul opened the door.

"Don't let him in!" she said in a loud whisper, checking to make sure her robe was secure.

"Good morning, Sunshine," Frankie said as he entered. Raoul closed the door behind him.

"What are you doing here?" Christine asked. "What time is it?"

Frankie checked his watch. "Seven-thirty."

"I'm going to be late for work!" She looked around frantically. "Where are my clothes?"

"Don't look at me," Raoul said. "I didn't take them."

Frankie grinned at Christine.

"What?" Christine asked.

"And a good time was had by all."

"Nuh-uh."

Frankie shrugged. "Whatever you say."

"Go look at the bed if you don't believe me."

"That's okay."

Raoul just stood there, enjoying it.

"Oh no. I was wearing a dress. I can't wear a dress to work."

"*Was* wearing a dress?" Frankie continued to tease her.

"It rained. We got wet."

"Okay. I know how it goes. I've seen that movie."

"We must have fallen asleep on the couch."

"I believe you. I brought you some work clothes." He handed her a grocery bag.

"Oh, good," she said, reaching for the bag. She looked inside. "Did you bring me a bra? I wasn't wearing one last night."

"Uh, no, I try to avoid digging in a woman's underwear drawer. I hope you were wearing panties."

Raoul laughed.

"You guys are mean," she said.

"Juanita packed you a lunch." Frankie handed her a brown bag. "Get dressed and we'll grab some breakfast."

"I don't have time for breakfast."

"That's what I thought. Juanita sent you a breakfast burrito. Do you have a microwave?" He pulled a burrito out of the bag and handed it to Raoul.

"Go look at the bed," she said.

"I was just teasing," Frankie said.

"Go look!" She pointed at the bedroom door.

Frankie went into the bedroom.

"How did he know I was here?" Christine asked.

"I texted him when I realized you were asleep. He was about to send out a search party."

"Why didn't you wake me up?"

"You looked so peaceful, asleep on my shoulder, and beautiful in that fluffy robe."

Frankie came out of the bedroom with the chocolates from the pillow. "Okay, I believe you. Have a chocolate, or two."

"Oh, goody," she said, taking both chocolates and dropping them into her lunch bag.

She grabbed the bag of clothes and rushed into the bathroom. She didn't have a hairbrush, so she ran her fingers through her hair. She reached for Raoul's toothbrush, but saw two in wrappers, so she ripped one open and brushed her teeth. She heard the phone ring as she threw on the jeans and

T-shirt that Frankie brought, and then breathed a sigh of relief when she saw sneakers at the bottom of the bag.

The boys waited for her to get dressed.

"So, how did it go last night?" Frankie asked.

"Pretty good."

"Well, the bed was still turned down, so apparently not as good as it could have been."

Raoul smiled and shook his head. "I don't want to push her."

"Good idea. Slow and steady wins the race."

"I'm just glad she's here and talking."

"Me too."

Christine burst forth from the bathroom, dressed for work. "Bye, guys."

"Whoa, hold on," Frankie said.

"What? Oh, where's my burrito?"

"Right here," Raoul said, punching buttons on the microwave, "but your truck won't start."

"I'm already late. Wait. How do you know it won't start?"

"I told them to bring it down when I got here," Frankie said. "They just called and said it wouldn't start."

There was a knock at the door. Frankie answered it. The room service waiter had a pot of coffee and three foam cups on a tray, which he placed on a table. Frankie signed the bill.

Raoul carried the burrito from the microwave, tossing it back and forth between his hands. "Hot! Hot! Hot!" He dropped it into Christine's lunch bag.

"Can I get a ride to work?" Christine asked.

Frankie picked up two foam cups and handed her one. He poured coffee into both. "Let's roll." He turned to Raoul. "Later."

Christine moved toward the door, then turned and kissed Raoul on the cheek. "Sorry, gotta run."

"I guess you already had breakfast, when you mucked the horses," she said as they climbed into Frankie's truck.

"Just a burrito. I'll swing back by and have a leisurely breakfast with Raoul."

She chomped down on her burrito. "So you guys can talk about me."

"Of course."

"We didn't do anything."

"It's none of my business."

"I don't know why I'm telling you. Raoul wouldn't lie and say we did, would he?"

"No, he wouldn't."

"Good. What about my truck?"

"We'll get it started, or have it towed."

"Don't forget me after work. I could ride home with Johnston, but he always works late."

"Don't worry. We'll pick you up."

RAOUL WAS DRESSED and ready when Frankie returned to the hotel.

"Let's get some breakfast and then get you checked out of this dump." Frankie said.

"Dump? I thought it was a pretty nice place."

"It is, one of the best in town. Lots of celebrities stay here, but your place is at the ranch."

"Is that okay with Christine?"

"She's cool."

"Are you sure? I don't want to do anything to mess it up. I can stay here."

"She just spent the night with you. You think she doesn't want you at the ranch?"

"That was an accident. We just fell asleep."

"You're not staying here, Shaggy."

"Okay, fine. I'm starving. The coffee just made it worse."

"And Christine took the chocolates."

"Oh, yeah, she did."

"Well, let's eat."

"I'll call room service."

"Room service is for pussies."

"Then we can go down to the restaurant."

"Nah, I know a place."

They headed out onto the street.

"What's up with Alfonso?" Raoul asked.

"Huh?"

"Carlos said he had dinner with Christine last week."

"Oh, that. He's an apprentice singer at the opera, got in when somebody else dropped out. Meg remembered him from the gala, so she invited him to dinner with us. He and Christine have something of a history."

"A history?"

"It's nothing, apparently. He's hooked up with some hot actress. He and Christine are just friends. They happened to be in the same town, so they had dinner, with Meg and me. No big deal."

They walked around the corner and into the Plaza Café.

"This place looks pretty cool," Raoul said, looking up from the menu.

"Everybody eats here, and I do mean everybody. Johnston and my dad used to come here with Daniel Senior when they were kids. The governor eats here, movie stars, opera stars, everybody. It's the oldest restaurant in Santa Fe, been here for a hundred years."

"So, what's good?"

"I'm sure they can find you a croissant and a bowl of coffee."

"Up yours."

"The huevos rancheros are pretty damned good, but don't tell Juanita you ate them, or she'll kick your ass."

"Huevos divorciados." Raoul read from the menu. "Is that what it sounds like?"

"Divorced eggs."

Raoul laughed. "Okay. What are you having?"

"Chicken fried steak and eggs."

"Works for me."

"Christine thinks we're talking about her so we might as well."

"She what?"

"I told her we were going to have breakfast, and she said, 'so you can talk about me.'"

Raoul smiled and nodded.

"We don't want to disappoint her, so spill," Frankie said.

"Nothing happened."

Frankie laughed. "She said that's what you'd say."

"I'm serious. Nothing happened."

"I know, but that's not what I'm talking about."

"So, what exactly are you talking about?"

"She stopped returning your calls. What's up with that?"

"Oh, that."

"Yeah, that."

"She felt guilty about Erik and said she couldn't face me."

"That's it?"

"She said she had a lot going on, with the professor and all."

"And school. She said she took a lot of shit about what happened in Santa Fe after the gala."

"Yeah, but I thought she was dealing with it, and then she just stopped returning my calls and texts."

"Chicks, man. They're weird. But hey, she's here, you're here. If she didn't care about you, she wouldn't have fallen asleep on your shoulder. She would have split. Hell, she wouldn't even have shown up in the first place."

"I guess you're right."

"Of course I'm right."

"What did she mean about being the boss's daughter?"

"She didn't tell you?"

"She was going to, but she fell asleep."

"I should probably let her tell you, but it's not exactly a secret. Meg already blabbed it all over the opera company."

"So tell me."

"Johnston is going to adopt her."

"He's what?" Raoul was stunned. "When did this happen?"

"A few days ago."

"Wow."

"You saw Mrs. Valerius. We had to get Christine out of there, so we brought her here for the summer. We hired Lupe to look after Mrs. Valerius until we can get all the legal work done."

"What legal work?"

"Mrs. Valerius has a sister in Florida, who will be appointed her guardian, or conservator, or whatever. Then we'll get her into an assisted living facility near her sister. That leaves Christine without a guardian, or a place to live, so Johnston is going to adopt her."

"She'll live with Johnston?"

"He's now the manager of the opera, so he'll be in Santa Fe for the foreseeable future. After the summer she'll live with Zoe and Jim Bob in Johnston's beach house in Malibu."

"Why didn't you call me? We could have adopted her."

"Yeah, right."

"Why not?"

"She would be your sister, you moron."

"Oh, yeah."

"This way she'll be Erik's sister. Two birds with one stone."

Raoul nodded. "That works."

"And Johnston really wants to do it. He's always had a thing for her."

"A thing?"

"He's always kind of looked at her like a daughter."

"Yeah, I guess so."

"Our lawyers are all over it. I was taking care of your lady even if she wasn't speaking to you."

"Thanks. I owe you."

"You don't owe me shit. I care about her too, and now we're going to be cousins. I just feel like an asshole for not keeping up with her since the professor's funeral, especially since I was right there at USC."

"You *are* an asshole."

"Takes one to know one."

CHRISTINE FOUND HERSELF not only smiling, but singing quietly to herself, happier than she had been for a long time. She wasn't sure if things were going to work out with Raoul, but the conversation she had dreaded seemed to have gone well, maybe too well. She expected him to be angry—Erik certainly would have been. Judging from her friends, what few there were, most boys would get angry if you made such an admission. But this was Raoul. She smiled again as she made her way through the backstage area at the opera house.

"You're early," Christine said, surprised as Frankie and Raoul approached. "I don't get off until five."

"We're taking the tour," Raoul said. He badly wanted to lean in and kiss her, maybe a brief peck on the lips, or at least on the cheek, but restrained himself. There was no reason to mess things up. She seemed happy and that was enough.

"The tour was this morning," she said.

"Private tour," Frankie said. "We go to all the cool places where the tourists aren't allowed."

"Yeah, right."

Frankie held up a set of keys. "And we brought your truck."

"Oh, good." She grabbed and pocketed the keys. "What was wrong with it?"

"It was flooded," Frankie said.

"Flooded?" she said. "How much did it rain last night?"

Frankie laughed. "No, the carburetor."

"What's a carburetor?" she asked.

"Never mind."

Christine shrugged. "Okay, thanks. I'd better get back to work." She turned to go.

"Wait," Raoul said. "I need to ask you something."

Christine froze, and then slowly turned. "What is it?"

"Would you like to go on a date with me?"

"A date?"

"Yes, a date."

"What do you call last night?"

"That was a meeting. I'm asking you to go out on a date with me."

"Okay, sure."

"Great. Dinner and a movie?"

"No fancy restaurants," she said. "Just a normal date."

"Just a normal date. Got it. What movie do you want to see?"

"Surprise me."

"Okay, I'll see what's on." He turned to Frankie. "Do they have a movie theater in Santa Fe, or do we have to go to Albuquerque?"

"They have a movie theater in Santa Fe. That will give you more time to make out."

"What time?" Christine asked, ignoring Frankie's comment about making out.

"I'll let you know when you get home. I'm staying at the ranch. Is that okay?"

"Sure. I thought you were at the hotel."

"Seemed stupid for him to stay in a hotel when we have all those empty rooms," Frankie said.

"Works for me. Now I've really got to get back to work before Carlotta has me fired."

"Who is Carlotta?" Raoul asked.

"Her," Frankie said, pointing.

"Oh no," Christine said. "Is she being arrested?"

They all stared as La Carlotta, escorted by two sheriff's deputies, walked swiftly through the corridor and down the stairs.

"That's La Carlotta," Frankie said. "She's singing the lead in Zoe's opera."

"So, what's up with the cops?" Raoul asked.

"Maybe she flipped out, and they're taking her to the loony bin," Christine said.

"Good riddance," Frankie said.

"Doesn't Zoe's opera premiere in just a few days?" Raoul asked.

"Yes, but Carlotta sucks," Christine said. "She's all wrong for the role. Her understudy is a lot better."

"But La Carlotta is a major international star, so we're stuck with her." Frankie said.

11

THE GHOST ON THE MOUNTAIN

CHRISTINE HAD WORKED late and was rushing to get ready for her date. It was her idea to keep it casual, but now she had to decide just how casual that would be. A dress seemed so not casual, so she laid out a skirt and blouse on the bed. She made a face—still not right—and decided on jeans and a T-shirt. She checked herself in the mirror. "Crap," she said to herself. It was the same thing she had worn to work, just a different T-shirt. She peeled off the T-shirt and replaced it with a button-up flannel shirt. She checked the mirror again and was about to strip off the shirt and change when there was a knock at the door. "Screw it," she said, and then answered the door.

"Is this casual enough?" Raoul asked.

Christine inspected his wardrobe, jeans and a pullover shirt, both undoubtedly expensive. "It's okay. You look nice."

"You do too."

She closed the door behind her, and they walked down the hallway. Their fingers did not repeat last night's unexpected action, but Raoul wasn't worried. They were going on a date. There would be plenty of opportunity to hold hands in the movie theater.

"I was going to ask Johnston if you have a curfew, but he isn't home."

"Yeah, he's working late. I'm dying to find out what happened with Carlotta. I asked everybody and nobody knew anything."

"So, do you have a curfew?"

"Well, I spent the night at your motel, so I guess not."

"I'm just asking because I want this to be a real date."

"Just don't keep me out too late. I have to work tomorrow."

"No problem."

Christine laughed as they stepped off the front porch. "Are we going in my truck?"

"Yes. Frankie said it was tradition or something. Is that okay?"

"Sure. Can you drive a stick?"

"I can now. Frankie taught me after we got it started this morning. I drove it out to the opera house."

Raoul opened the door and Christine hopped in.

She laughed and made fun of him as he tried to get the truck in first gear, but they were finally on their way down the mountain.

Raoul checked his phone.

"You shouldn't text and drive," Christine said.

"I'm not texting. I'm using GPS."

"Isn't it supposed to talk?"

"It's supposed to, but it doesn't seem to be working."

"Give it to me."

He handed her the cell phone. "Ooh, pizza!" she said.

"Is that okay?"

"Of course. It's pizza. Turn right at the next light."

It wasn't a chain pizza place, or anything Christine had ever heard of. It was a hole-in-the-wall with a huge adobe pizza oven.

"I'm starving," Christine said. "How long does it take to cook a pizza?"

"Quite a while if you want it done right. I don't think they have a conveyor belt oven."

"Oh, here it comes." Christine leaned back as the enormous, and steaming, pizza was placed on the table. "It smells wonderful."

They each grabbed a piece and chomped down. "Ouch!" Christine said. "Hot!"

"I tried to warn you. This is the real deal."

She blew on her slice and took another bite. "Yes, it is."

"Frankie recommended it. The boy knows his pizza, or food for that matter. He's never steered me wrong."

"When the Beats came in for the gala, we met them in Albuquerque and Frankie had a mobile pizza truck thingy at the station to make custom pizzas for everybody."

"I never heard of a mobile pizza truck."

"Me either."

"But it sounds like a good idea, especially for a party or something. Delivery pizza is always cold."

Christine nodded while she ate.

"Was it as good as this?" Raoul asked.

Christine shook her head, unable to speak with a mouthful of pizza. Slices disappeared while they talked and laughed, just like they did when they were kids.

"Thanks," she said.

Raoul was puzzled. "For what?"

"This."

"Pizza?"

"For normal stuff. Fancy restaurants are fun sometimes, but I'm just a regular girl. This is great."

Raoul smiled. She was anything but regular.

"I'm kind of lost in the rich-people world," she said.

"Well, you'd better get used to it."

"Being lost?"

"No, being in the rich-people world."

"What do you mean?" she asked.

"Frankie told me about the adoption."

"He did?"

Raoul nodded.

"I was going to tell you last night, but I kind of went to sleep on your shoulder," she said.

"I think you'll do fine in the rich-people world. Just stay yourself. Let them adjust."

"I can do that. I really don't think there will be any difference, other than having a place to live and stuff."

"Important stuff."

"And I guess I can go to college now."

"Is that what you want?"

She shrugged. "Not really."

"It's probably a good idea. A college education is a nice thing to have. Expand your horizons, meet some new people."

"You want me to meet new people?"

"Of course."

"What if I meet a hot guy?"

"If he makes you happy, that's okay with me."

Christine laughed. "I thought this was a date."

"It is."

"You seem to be confused about the rules of dating. You probably shouldn't tell your date to find another guy."

"That's not what I meant. I was trying to say I just want you to be happy. I prefer if you could be happy with me, but if it's with someone else, then that's better than not being happy at all."

"Good save."

"Thanks."

"So, you think we should be a couple?"

"Yes."

"You live in Paris. I live in Santa Monica."

"We can work it out."

"And you're going to school in England this fall, right?"

"Right, but just in case you haven't heard, there is this fantastic new invention called a jet airplane."

"And you just happen to have one."

"Well, it's my dad's, or his company's. I can be in Santa Monica, or wherever you're going to college, in a few hours. I might have to fly commercial if the Gulfstream is otherwise engaged, but I can do that."

"What if I want to come to Paris, or England, or Saint-Tropez?"

"I'll send you a ticket."

"So, I'd be like your mistress?"

"No, not like that."

She laughed. "I'm just messing with you."

"If Johnston adopts you, he can buy your ticket."

She nodded. "He could do that. I hear he's loaded."

"He is."

"Does he have a jet?"

"I don't think so, but he seems to have one available whenever he needs it."

"Back to the rules of dating. This sounds more like a negotiation than a date. Shouldn't you be whispering sweet nothings in my ear?"

Raoul leaned over and whispered into her ear. "You look very beautiful tonight. Want to make out?"

She laughed so loudly that people turned and stared.

RAOUL HAD DONE considerable research in picking just the right movie, a chick flick, luckily one she hadn't already seen. He had no way of knowing that with her limited financial situation and all the turmoil in her life she had seen very few movies in theaters lately. She certainly seemed to be enjoying this one, and there was hand holding. It felt like a real date.

The hand holding continued as they walked to the truck after the movie. Raoul tried to guide her to the passenger's side, but she nudged him toward the driver's side.

"Do you want to drive?" he asked.

"No."

He was confused.

"Open the door," she said.

He opened the door. Christine climbed in and sat in the middle. Raoul hesitated a moment, and then slid in beside her, still confused.

"I saw this in a movie," she said. "Back in olden times, before cars had bucket seats, they had seats like this."

"Bench seats."

"Yeah, that, and girls sat in the middle, right next to their date. It looks kind of funny now, but apparently everybody used to do it."

"Works for me."

"Feels weird," she said as they drove away.

"Do you want to move over?"

"No, I'm good." She was very good. Thoughts of Erik had faded away. Santa Monica, the kids at school, Mrs. Valerius, were all a million miles away.

He was good too. The stick shift was right next to her legs, giving him an opportunity to brush his hand across her knee, and to leave it there as he drove with his left hand. She glanced down and smiled. Kids in olden times weren't stupid.

She put her knees together and shifted in the seat, alternately pointing her knees both ways.

He put his right hand back on the wheel. "What are you doing?"

"Girls back then always wore dresses, or skirts, on dates, and to school and everywhere, so I'm wondering how this would work if I was wearing a tight skirt."

"You would want to point your knees this way."

"Why?"

"If you point them away from your date it sends the wrong message, like you are avoiding him, or don't like him."

She pointed her knees away from him and turned her shoulders slightly. "Like this?"

"Like that. It's kind of rude."

She pointed her knees toward him and leaned slightly closer to him. "Better?"

"Definitely better."

"But this is like an invitation, right?"

He chuckled. "Don't get all Freudian on me."

She put her head on his shoulder. "You can put your hand back where it was."

He put his hand back on her knee. They both wished she was wearing a skirt as they headed out of town and toward the mountain.

He stopped at a fork in the road and checked his cell phone. He put it on the seat between his legs and turned left.

"The ranch is that way," she said.

"I know."

"Where are we going?"

"You'll see."

She reached for the cell phone. "I'll navigate." She looked at the phone. "There's nothing out there."

"Frankie gave me the GPS coordinates."

"He's probably jerking you around."

They drove on through the darkness, on dirt roads, sometimes nothing more than trails.

"We're here," she said, looking at the phone. "I have no idea where, but here we are."

Raoul stopped and looked around.

"You must have gotten the coordinates wrong," she said.

"No, I think this is it."

"It what?"

"A place to park."

"You're taking me parking?"

He smiled.

She laughed. "If you just wanted to make out, we could do that back at the ranch."

"We're on a real date, a normal date. This is what kids do, at least country kids, or they used to, like in the movies."

"I love it. Parking. What a concept."

"It's a lover's lane kind of deal."

"Exactly."

He shifted gears and started driving slowly.

"Where are we going?" she asked. "I thought we were parking."

"You'll see." He positioned the truck pointed at the mountain.

"Nice view."

They got out of the truck and walked toward the back.

Christine looked around. "I hope this isn't a horror movie."

"Huh?"

"The slasher always goes after the kids on lover's lane."

"I'm pretty sure we're the only ones here."

Raoul lowered the tailgate and they both sat down.

The lights of Santa Fe shimmered down below. "Oh, okay, I see," she said. "It's beautiful."

He reached for a rolled-up foam mattress and spread it out.

"You thought of everything," she said.

"Frankie thought of everything."

He untied the mattress and spread it out. "Apparently he has experience along these lines, and the proper gear."

"Erik too." She flinched, wishing she hadn't said that.

"Erik?"

"Frankie said he and Erik learned to drive in this truck and went all over the place. Stands to reason they both used it to come up here and make out."

"I'm sure they did."

"Do you think Frankie and Meg used to do it right here?"

"Probably," he said as he sat down beside her.

"We're not doing it tonight."

"I didn't really expect us to. Frankie provided all this stuff, so I thought we could just sit back here and enjoy the view."

"Sit? Then what's the mattress for?"

"We can lie back and look at the stars."

She fell backwards onto the mattress and looked up at the stars. He followed suit. She turned to him and smiled.

"What?" he asked.

"This is fun."

"It is?"

"Yes, it is. I kind of missed out on all this stuff."

"What stuff?"

"Dating and stuff."

"You haven't been dating?"

"Not really. Not at all, actually."

"I'd think guys would be lined up to ask you out."

"I have kind of a reputation at school."

"What kind of reputation?"

"It's complicated."

"Okay."

"I thought I had a boyfriend once, but he dumped me."

Raoul's mind raced. Who was this interloper? Was that why she had been avoiding him? Was it that Alfonso guy?

"Who?" he asked.

"It was you, silly."

"Oh, sorry."

"That's okay. We were just kids."

"We're not kids anymore," he said.

"No, we're not. I thought we were going to make out."

"Ever the romantic."

"That's why we came up here, right? And it's not like we haven't made out before."

"Right. I just didn't want to be too pushy."

"Are you going to kiss me, or what?"

He leaned over and kissed her.

"That wasn't so bad, was it?" she asked.

"Not at all. It was quite nice. I waited a long time for that."

"Me too."

The kissing continued, now accompanied by heavy breathing. They disengaged long enough to scoot up into the bed of the truck, so their legs weren't hanging over the tailgate, and then resumed kissing.

"Sorry," he said.

"For what?"

"I kind of brushed up against your boob."

"That's okay."

Encouraged, he brushed up against it again, or rather intentionally felt her up. She didn't stop him. His hands continued to roam. He began to unbutton her shirt.

"Wait," she said.

He froze, suddenly deflated, and worried. "Sorry, again."

"No, it's just—"

"Just what? Do you want to go back to the ranch, or just stop making out?"

"No. It's kind of fun. It's what teenagers do, right? Except me. I haven't really had much experience in such matters."

"So, we're still making out?"

"Yes, but we're not going all the way, even if I don't tell you to stop."

"Okay." He thought about what she said. "Is this like a test or something?"

"No. I don't know. Maybe it is, but I don't mean for it to be. I just need to know I can trust you."

"You can trust me. I promise."

"I like making out with you, but I don't want to get carried away and go too far."

"Like with Erik on the train?"

She covered her face with her hands, and then nodded her head.

"I understand."

"I'm just not ready for sex, and I don't really want my first time to be in the back of a pickup."

"We can go back to the ranch and do it in your bed."

She laughed loudly.

"I think I know what you mean," he said. "You'll tell me to stop, but even if you don't tell me to stop, I have to stop before we go too far."

"Exactly." She kissed him. "Okay, you can go back to what you were doing."

He went back to kissing her lips while simultaneously unbuttoning her shirt. It wasn't long before her shirt was wide open. He glanced down from kissing to admire the view. His hand was on her ribcage, her white bra shimmering in the moonlight. The way he saw it, she had just given him permission to do nearly anything short of actual sex. He slipped his hand down over her abdomen and felt the waistband of her jeans. It was right there for the taking. He slid his hand over her waist and up her back. She turned slightly towards him. His hand continued up her back until he felt the clasp of her bra. She didn't speak. She didn't stop him. His heart pounded. It was there for the taking, but he couldn't do it. He pulled her closer and kissed her more deeply.

They both heard a muted "whoosh."

She flinched. "What was that?"

"I don't know." He sat up and looked over the side of the truck.

She sat up and looked the other way. "There's somebody out there."

Raoul quickly turned. "Where?"

"Over there." She pointed.

"I don't see anything." He slid off the tailgate. "Wait here."

She buttoned her shirt, which seemed appropriate in such a situation, and waited. He stepped a few feet away from the truck, in the direction of the unseen interloper. He saw nothing, so he pulled out his cell phone, turned on the light, and inspected the truck's tires. "We have a flat tire."

She leaned over the side of the truck as Raoul knelt and looked closely at the tire.

"It just suddenly went flat?" she asked.

"Yes."

"How did that happen?"

"It looks like a sidewall blowout."

"What's that?"

"If a tire rubs up against a curb enough times, or if it just gets old, the sidewall blows out and it goes flat."

"I haven't been rubbing up against any curbs. I just go from the ranch to the opera house. There aren't any curbs."

"It's not you. It happens over time."

He walked around to the back of the truck and raised the tailgate. He crouched down and looked up under the truck. "We don't have a spare."

"What are we going to do?" she asked, peering over the tailgate.

"I'll call Frankie."

She laughed.

"What's so funny?" Raoul asked.

"He knows exactly where to find us."

$$12$$

THE FAIR MAIDEN

Frankie and Raoul dropped Christine off at work the next morning and headed up the mountain.

"Looks different in daylight," Raoul said as they climbed out of Frankie's truck.

"Yes, it does."

Frankie squatted and looked at the tire. "That's no blowout."

"I know."

"Somebody knifed it."

"We heard the 'whoosh.' We sat up and looked."

"Sat up?" Frankie grinned.

"Up yours. She said she saw someone running away."

"So, did you get lucky?"

"Huh?"

"Last night, before the tire blew."

"A gentleman never tells."

"Whatever."

"But lucky enough, I guess," Raoul said. "Lucky we were together after all this time."

"You should probably make out at the ranch. We have beds and stuff, and privacy."

"I thought we had privacy here."

"Apparently not."

"We're going to need a new tire." Frankie stepped back and looked at another tire. "We might as well get a whole new set. No telling how long these have been on here."

"Who do you think did it?"

"Probably just some kids."

"I thought we were on the ranch."

"We are, but it's not fenced off. Kids from town use it for parking. Nobody cares."

"But why us?"

"Did you see anybody else parking?"

"No."

"Did you see anybody following you on the way up here?"

"No, but I didn't really look. I was kind of paying attention to what was in the headlights."

"And the hot babe sitting beside you."

"And that," Raoul said, smiling.

"Some kids were probably making out, or drinking beer, just around the hill, and heard you having too much fun."

"We weren't making any noise. Well, Christine laughed a few times."

"I'll bet she did. If you need some help wooing women, I'm available for lessons."

"Wooing women?"

Frankie smiled and pulled a jack out of his truck.

FRANKIE AND RAOUL sat at a table at the Dapples Pavilion, checking out the scenery—there were several young female apprentices having lunch.

"See that chick with dark hair over there?" Frankie asked, pointing with his head.

Raoul turned and looked. "Yeah."

"That's Hayley. She's Carlotta's understudy."

"She's hot."

"Definitely."

"And Carlotta's not?"

"You saw her."

"Not hot," Raoul said. "Does it matter, for the opera?"

"It should matter, especially for Zoe's opera. Sofia should be young and beautiful."

"Who is Sofia?"

"She's the lead."

"I thought you said it was Carlotta."

Frankie laughed. "Sofia is the character Carlotta plays."

"Sorry I'm late," Johnston said, taking a seat. "Have you eaten?"

"No, we were waiting for you," Frankie said.

"It's been hectic."

"What's up with Carlotta? We saw her leaving yesterday with two cops."

"Off-duty sheriff's deputies. We hired them as extra security. They were taking her to her apartment."

"Why does she need security?"

"There were some threats."

"What kind of threats?" Raoul asked.

"It started a few days ago. I received a text message saying 'Carlotta sucks. Dump her.'"

"She does suck, and you should dump her," Frankie said. "Who sent the text?"

"You, apparently," Johnston said.

Frankie laughed.

"O.G.," Johnston said.

"Who is O.G.?" Raoul asked.

"The girls said it's the Opera Ghost."

Raoul laughed. "Opera Ghost?"

"Yeah," Frankie said. "Meg is constantly going on about some ghost that haunts the opera house. She said he was here last summer, and just came back a couple of weeks ago."

"You're kidding, right?"

"Not entirely," Johnston said. "There was an accident last week. A stage-hand was injured when a flat fell on him. Broke his leg."

"If it was an accident, what does that have to do with a ghost?" Raoul said.

"It looked like an accident and that's what the investigation will probably conclude, but according to scuttlebutt amongst the crew, the Opera Ghost caused it."

"He's also been seen around the opera house," Frankie said. "Carlotta insists she saw him. Christine even says she saw him."

"And now he has threatened Carlotta directly," Johnston said.

"What kind of threat?" Raoul asked.

"Nothing specific, just that she must not be allowed to sing Sofia or something very bad will happen. We're taking it seriously. So is the sheriff."

"You don't actually think it's a ghost, do you?" Raoul asked.

"No, of course not. It's clearly a man, or at least a person."

"I'm trying to think of a *Ghostbusters* joke," Frankie said, "but I got nothing."

"There's more," Johnston said. "He demands that Christine sing Sofia at the premiere."

"Wow," Frankie said.

"Can she even do that?" Raoul asked. "Wouldn't she need to rehearse?"

"She knows the songs but yes, she would have to rehearse, so it's a non-starter."

"If he sent you a text, can't you trace it or something?" Raoul asked.

"Burner phone," Frankie said.

"What are you going to do?" Raoul asked.

"We're having a board meeting, tonight at the ranch, or at least as many as we can round up on short notice. This O.G. person demands that they hear Christine sing an aria from Zoe's opera."

"So, you're giving him what he wants?" Frankie asked.

"Just this. It will buy us some time, and maybe make him think we're giving in."

"You're calling a board meeting so they can hear Christine sing?" Frankie asked.

"Not just that. There are a lot of things to consider, and I want the board to be fully involved, even if I have the authority to act alone. We can't just cancel a performance because of a threat, but we definitely can't risk people being hurt."

"Has he actually threatened to hurt anyone?" Raoul asked.

"Just Carlotta, but there is something of an implied threat if Christine doesn't sing."

"What does Carlotta think about all this?" Frankie asked.

"She's upset of course, but she's also stubborn, and what a temper. So far, she insists she will not be intimidated and will sing Sofia at the premiere."

"What about Christine?" Raoul asked.

"She doesn't know. Well, she was there when I received the first text, and she's heard all the rumors backstage about the Ghost, but she doesn't know he has demanded that she sing Sofia. That came later."

"Meg is right in the middle of it, so I'm sure Christine is fully up to date on the rumors," Frankie said.

"Only a handful of people know about his demand, so whatever you do, don't tell Meg."

Frankie nodded.

"Is Christine in danger?" Raoul asked.

"I don't think so," Johnston said. "Clearly, he wants her to sing, so why would he want to hurt her?"

"I don't know, but something happened last night."

"What happened?" Johnston said, suddenly alarmed.

"Someone slashed a tire on the old truck."

"The one Christine has been driving?"

The boys nodded.

"Where did this happen?"

The boys looked at each other.

"Out where we always used to park," Frankie said. "I'm sure you know the place."

Johnston smiled. The place was well known by generations of cousins.

"Christine and I were kind of making out," Raoul said.

"If I'm going to be a father figure to Christine, I need to start paying attention more. I didn't even know you were out together last night."

"That's okay," Frankie said. "I knew and I trust my boy with her."

Frankie and Raoul bumped fists.

"Good to know," Johnston said.

"I would never do anything to hurt her," Raoul said.

"Just try to not get her pregnant," Johnston said.

"Don't worry. She already laid down the law."

"Good. Not only is she too young, but it could make the adoption process much more difficult."

Frankie laughed. "You'd get a daughter and a grandkid at the same time. Maybe we could get our own trash TV show."

"Okay, back to last night," Johnston said.

"You want details?" Raoul asked nervously.

"No, not about that, about the tire. Any idea who did it? Did you see anything?"

"Christine said she saw something, a guy, but it was dark. I didn't see anything. I just heard it."

"Heard what?" Johnston asked.

"Whoosh."

"I thought it was just kids," Frankie said, "but now, maybe not."

"It probably was kids, but we don't want to take any chances, not with Christine," Johnston said.

"We could send her back to Santa Monica, but she'd pitch a fit," Frankie said.

"She seems to really like her job here. I offered to give her an allowance, but she wanted to work at the opera house."

"Do you think she's safe at work?" Raoul asked.

"I thought so, but now I'm not so sure."

"Okay," Frankie said. "We have sightings at the opera house that may or may not be true, and if true, may or may not be the same person as O.G. It's someone with access to the opera house, and who knows their way around. So cast, crew, staff, apprentices."

"Can't be apprentices and probably not cast," Johnston said.

"Why not?"

"Apprentices are only here for one season. There may be a few cast members who were here last season, but not many. And permanent staff, of course."

"That narrows it down," Raoul said.

"You said you got a text from O.G.," Frankie said. "Was it on a company phone or your personal phone?"

"My personal phone."

"Who has your phone number?"

"Lots of people."

"You've only been boss for a few weeks, so probably not a lot of crew or staff."

"No, probably not."

"Erik has it."

"You think it's Erik?" Johnston asked.

"He knows his way around the opera house."

"He has a thing for Christine," Raoul said.

"Big time," Frankie added.

"He's been stalking her for years," Raoul said.

"He what?" Johnston asked.

"Not long before Christine's audition at the conservatory we went to a party on the beach for faculty and students at the UCLA music department," Raoul said. "A few days ago, Christine said Erik told her he was there, lurking in the shadows."

Johnston nodded. "He was staying with me at the time."

"And it sounds like something he would do," Frankie said.

"Then there's Saint-Tropez," Raoul said. "I don't know how he could have known Christine would be there, but it's suspicious."

"I didn't even know she would be there," Johnston said.

Raoul shrugged. "Maybe he just got lucky."

"And then he shows up in Santa Fe, the first night we're there," Frankie said.

"It was a surprise to me, but he's been known to show up unannounced at all hours," Johnston said.

"I think he was living in the little cottage," Raoul said.

"The little cottage?" Johnston said.

"The Valerius's guest house."

"What makes you think that?" Frankie asked.

"I asked Lupe if I could see the little cottage," Raoul said. "She said it was a mess when she first got there, fast-food wrappers, bottles, and cans. She thought somebody had been living there."

"Christine?" Johnston asked.

"No, she lived in the main house," Frankie said.

"Mrs. Valerius was back and forth between crazy talk and reality, but now that I think about it, she may have seen, and talked to, Erik in the back yard," Raoul said.

"Wow," Frankie said.

"Then there was the painting on the wall in the little cottage."

"What painting?" Johnston asked.

"The one that Connie's mom did in Saint-Tropez."

"What about it?"

"It was of Christine."

"So?"

"We stopped by their house in Saint-Tropez to pick up Connie. The painting was covered, and Connie's mom didn't want anyone to see it."

"Erik, of course, lifted the cover, and Connie's mom kind of freaked out," Frankie said.

"Why?" Johnston asked.

"Christine was topless, with Connie, on the beach," Raoul said.

Johnston sighed.

"Connie's mom didn't know what to do with it," Frankie said. "She was afraid Christine would be pissed, but she said it was beautiful. She couldn't bring it home because, well, boobs."

"Connie's mom was afraid it was child porn and offered to destroy it," Raoul said. "Erik said he'd take it. I told him like hell he would. A few weeks later, Connie called me and said it disappeared. She thought maybe I took it. I told her no way I would do that."

"Erik probably jacked it," Frankie said. "It wouldn't be the first thing he stole."

"Tell me about it," Johnston said.

"But why would he leave it behind?" Raoul asked. "He couldn't very well go back there with Lupe in the house."

"He probably left in a hurry when I took Christine," Frankie said. "Oh, shit."

"What?" Raoul asked.

"Christine and I heard a noise in the attendant's room on the *Estelline*. The door was locked and the key was missing. That asshole probably hitched a ride with us."

"It all fits," Raoul said. "He's crazy about Christine. He's been stalking her. He's heard her sing."

"But hurting people, and threatening them?" Johnston said.

"The boy is certifiable," Frankie said. "He's done some serious shit, most of which you probably don't even know about."

Johnston nodded. "But would he hurt Christine?"

"Maybe not, but we can't be sure, and I'm not willing to let Christine take the risk," Raoul said.

"Nor am I," Johnston added.

"In a fit of jealousy, he might," Frankie said. "Or lust. Guys our age are always horny. Some of us can't control ourselves. Erik's always been a loner. Now, with his face, he's isolated. Lots of time to think about Christine. He might not beat her up, or slap her around, but he thinks with his dick, not his head."

Johnston exhaled and shook his head. "I can't believe I'm saying this, but we have to protect my future daughter from my own son."

"I could take her out of town for a couple of days until you catch him," Raoul said.

"A little romantic getaway?" Frankie asked, smiling.

"I don't know how romantic it would be. I'm not even sure where I stand right now."

"And she really wants to be here for the premiere," Johnston said.

"And the masked ball," Frankie said.

"But getting her out of town might not be a bad idea," Johnston said.

"You would send your daughter, your new virgin daughter, out of town with a horny Frenchman?" Frankie asked.

"Desperate times call for desperate measures," Johnston said, smiling.

"Actually, I do have some business in Texas," Raoul said. "Dad is looking into buying or building a winery there. To convince him to let me make this trip I told him I'd scout some wineries." He looked at Frankie. "You can go with us. Then she wouldn't think I was just trying to get in her panties."

"So, you are trying to get in her panties?" Frankie asked.

"Enough about her underwear," Johnston said. "Where in Texas?"

"Lubbock. It's kind of ground zero for Texas wines."

"Cool," Frankie said. "Carlos can come with us."

"Carlos?" Raoul asked.

"He goes to school in Lubbock. He'll know all the best places to go."

"Wineries?"

"Wineries, clubs, restaurants, whatever."

Raoul shrugged. "Works for me."

"What about the masked ball?" Johnston asked. "Isn't Carlos working it, and aren't you bird-dogging it?"

"It's under control," Frankie said. "Mom and dad are due in at Lamy about now. Angel's picking them up. She'll take over when she gets here anyway."

"We'll have to be back in time for the ball or Christine will get suspicious," Raoul said.

The boys pushed away from the table.

"We'll swing back by and pick up Christine," Frankie said.

"She can ride with me. I need to get home early tonight for the board meeting."

"Oh yeah, that." Frankie turned to Raoul. "Let's roll. We have a fair maiden to save."

13

MARIA

Christine helped Carlos set the dining room table, carefully following his instructions on lining up the silverware just right. Frankie and Raoul were of no help at all but had stayed close since she returned from work.

"Why can't Carlotta sing?" Christine asked.

"She's the star," Frankie said. "They didn't want to bother her."

"So, they decided to bother me instead?"

"That's about the size of it," Frankie said.

"Why can't they just wait for the premiere?"

"It's the board. They're special."

"Then why don't they just go to rehearsal?" Christine asked.

"You know how rehearsal goes," Raoul said. "Would you want people watching?"

"Okay, but I don't know why they want *me* to sing. Why not Hayley. That's kind of her job."

"Maybe they're going to promote you to apprentice singer," Frankie said.

"Can they do that?" Christine asked.

"They're the board of directors. They can do anything they want."

"I don't want to be an apprentice singer. I like working backstage. I'm going to be a floor runner next week, during the performances."

"They should promote Hayley to Sofia and let you understudy her," Carlos said, suddenly drawing everyone's attention. Frankie tried to emphatically shake his head while not letting Christine see him.

"What?" Carlos asked. "Carlotta sucks. Hayley kills that part."

"How do you know?" Christine was curious.

"I get around."

"You've been to rehearsal?"

"Once or twice. Frankie and Erik aren't the only ones who know their way around the opera house."

"Impressive."

"And I jam with some of the apprentice singers in a club downtown," Carlos said.

"Cool."

"It doesn't matter," Frankie said. "Carlotta will sing Sofia."

"Do I have to dress up?" Christine asked.

"A dress would probably be nice," Raoul said.

"What are you wearing?"

"What I have on," Raoul said.

"We're not invited to the meeting," Frankie said. "Just you."

"Do I have to have dinner with them?"

"No, you'll eat with us," Frankie said. "We're grilling burgers out by the pool."

"Good."

CARLOS TENDED BAR in the great room and business was good. Christine had long ago noticed that rich people drink a lot. It was so busy that Jim Bob had stepped in to help. He clearly had experience as a bartender.

Everyone was well-dressed. Christine, innocently stunning in a little black dress, felt out of place as the youngest person in the room, so she gravitated to the bar so she could at least be near friends. Carlos smiled. He understood. He quickly slid a glass of clear liquid toward her.

"What is it?" she asked.

"Tequila."

She made a face.

"It's sparkling water," Carlos said.

She smiled and took a sip.

Frankie and Raoul hovered in a doorway as Zoe sat down at the piano. It suddenly became quiet as she started playing, and the guests drifted toward seats. It was nowhere near cold, but there was a small fire in the enormous fireplace. "Ambiance," Frankie had said as he lit it earlier in the evening.

Christine took a big swig of her drink and slammed the glass on the bar, wondering if these rich people thought she was drinking actual booze.

"Showtime," she said quietly.

She walked over to the piano and turned to face the board, not an easy task as they were scattered around the room. She had previously done a sound check with Carlos at the piano and she anticipated no problem being heard anywhere in the room. She smiled and nodded at Zoe, who immediately launched into one of Sofia's most important arias.

Christine sang it beautifully and the guests were impressed. Her voice did indeed fill the room, and exquisitely so.

Carlos and Jim Bob, standing quietly at the bar, fist bumped, and then both turned to Raoul and Frankie, still lurking in the doorway, and they all air-fist-bumped.

There was polite applause when the aria was over and Christine suddenly wondered whether she should curtsy and wait, or just leave. A rehearsal would have been nice, but here she was, so she just stood, smiling nervously.

"Thank you, *mi hija*. That was lovely."

Christine turned to the woman speaking, Maria Josefina Álvarez de Garcia. She was in her late fifties and made no attempt to hide the flashes of silver in her black hair. Christine assumed she was someone of importance.

Christine stood frozen, not knowing what to do next. Johnston sensed her indecision and stood. "Thank you, Christine." He nodded his head toward the door.

Christine curtsied, wished she hadn't, and then turned and made a bee line for the boys in the doorway.

"That was beautiful," Raoul said. "I can't imagine this Carlotta person doing it any better."

"Let's go eat," Christine said. "I'm starving." They headed for the kitchen. "Oh wait," she said, stopping suddenly. "I need to change."

"So, go change," Frankie said.

"I'll go with you," Raoul said.

"You want to watch me change?" Christine asked.

Raoul shrugged.

"That's a good idea," Frankie said.

"What's going on?" Christine asked.

"Nothing," Raoul said. "I just thought I'd keep you company."

MARIA WAITED UNTIL Christine disappeared with the boys. "It was quite lovely, remarkable, actually," Maria said. "But it was just an aria. She's a child. Do you think she could sing an entire opera?"

"I don't really know," Johnston said.

"And what do you think, Zoe? It's your opera, after all."

"She definitely knows the songs, but she's never sung an entire opera, and hasn't rehearsed this one. I love her dearly, and she has the voice of an angel, but we need a seasoned professional."

"So, why are we here? Not that I'm not looking forward to dinner." She smiled and a few others chuckled.

"To humor the Ghost," Johnston said.

"What ghost? When I got the message from my office, I thought they were playing some sort of prank."

"The person who made the threats against the opera, and specifically La Carlotta, calls himself O.G. The kids backstage call him the Opera Ghost. He was apparently around last season, pulling pranks, stealing things, and just returned a few days ago."

Maria laughed. "You cannot be serious."

"I'm quite serious."

"Why wasn't I informed?" Maria turned to Franklin. "Did you know about this?"

"I heard the rumors, mainly second-hand through Frankie's girlfriend. I assumed you knew."

"And he calls himself O.G.?" Maria said, shaking her head. "That sounds rather silly."

"It doesn't matter what he calls himself," Johnston said. "The threats are very real. We believe he may be responsible for the accident a few days ago, where the stagehand was injured. These threats escalate it to an entirely new level."

"Oh, dear."

"How, exactly, are we humoring him?" Mona asked.

"He demanded that the board hear Christine sing Sofia," Johnston said. "Somehow, in his twisted mind, he believes that we will be persuaded to replace La Carlotta and allow Christine to sing Sofia at the premiere."

"Well, we certainly can't allow this O.G. person to intimidate us now, can we?" Maria said.

"No ma'am," Johnston said. "We cannot."

"But we also can't endanger our employees, or our guests," Franklin said.

"No, of course not," Maria said.

"How would he know that we heard Christine sing tonight?" Mona asked.

"Frankie will tell Meg," Johnston said, and then turned to Maria. "Meg Giry. She's one of the dancers."

"Oh, yes. Mrs. Giry's daughter."

"Yes, and Meg will tell everyone," Johnston said, smiling. "I understand she's good at that."

Franklin laughed. "Yes, I believe you are correct on that."

"Why couldn't you just have Meg spread the rumor?" Maria asked. "Why go to all the trouble to convene this meeting?"

"It's possible that he's watching the house," Johnston said somberly.

Maria looked around the room and at the windows. "Well that certainly complicates things."

"We have off-duty deputies outside," Franklin said.

"We're just buying time here tonight," Johnston said. "We hope to catch him soon and put a stop to this nonsense."

"You say he has threatened La Carlotta," Maria said.

"Yes," Johnston said.

"With bodily harm?"

"With death, actually."

"Oh, my. Have you notified the authorities?"

"Yes, of course. We have also hired security to stay with her at all times."

"And does she plan to sing at the premiere?" Maria asked.

"So far, yes," Johnston said. "If she changes her mind, we certainly won't force her. We'll use her understudy."

"That could jeopardize the success of the opera. I hear she's something of a diva, but La Carlotta is also a big draw. Having her miss the premiere could have repercussions."

"I'm aware of that and I'm considering all options, but safety must come first."

"Of course," Maria said.

CARLOS LOOKED OVER Christine's shoulder as she stood at the cook stove in the kitchen. "We're grilling out by the pool. What are you doing in here?"

"If you want real hamburgers you have to get the buns all hot and greasy and toasty," Christine said. "That's what Jim Bob says."

"Hot buns are my favorite kind. Why don't you fix me one to go? I'll come out and grab it in a couple of minutes."

"*No problemo.* Do you want everything on your buns?" Christine grinned.

"Eighty-six the onions. I don't want to stink up the dining room."

"How's it going in there?"

"A waiter never tells."

"*Pendejo.*"

"*Puta.*"

"Later."

Carlos backed through the swinging doors.

Christine loaded up her buns and headed out onto the pool deck where Frankie was busy grilling burgers.

"Carlos wants one to go," Christine said.

"How's it going in the dining room?" Raoul asked.

"He said a waiter never tells." Christine began spreading mustard on the buns.

"THEN WE ARE IN AGREEMENT," Maria said. "We will continue as planned. If La Carlotta drops out, the understudy will go on in her place. If people demand a refund, we will promptly provide it."

The board members agreed.

"Until then, we will make every attempt to apprehend this 'ghost' person. We will hire additional security and coordinate with the sheriff. We will reconvene before the premiere and make a final decision over whether to proceed, postpone, or cancel."

Again, there was agreement all around.

"We certainly can't be intimidated. Otherwise, we would be cancelling performances right and left, every time someone made a prank call, but as Franklin said, we certainly cannot risk the safety of our employees or guests." She turned to Franklin. "You are underwriting the opera, Franklin. Are you prepared to take such a large loss if we have to cancel?"

"We can't let money have any bearing on our decision. Safety has to be our primary consideration."

"And what about you, Zoe? I'm sorry your first opera had to be caught up in all this."

"If we have to cancel, we have to cancel. I'll survive."

"I certainly do not want to cancel. This opera is extremely important for Santa Fe, for our Native American friends and neighbors, and for New Mexico. That reminds me, the governor plans to attend, and she shares my enthusiasm for the opera. I'll call her office tomorrow and get them up to speed. Perhaps she can provide some help from the State Police."

"Good idea," Johnston said. "We can use all the help we can get."

"Carlos, could you ask Juanita to step in for a moment?" Maria said.

"Yes ma'am." Carlos backed away quickly and through the door.

"That young girl, what was her name?" Maria said.

"Christine," Johnston said.

"Yes, Christine. She has a beautiful voice, and she's a lovely girl, but she's a teenager. This is the Santa Fe Opera. We cannot be intimidated by a ghost."

"Of course."

Juanita cautiously approached, followed by Carlos.

"Juanita," Maria said. "Dinner was delicious. I would try to steal you away from Franklin, but I always know I can come here for a wonderful meal. Thank you."

"Thank you, ma'am," Juanita said.

"And Carlos, how are you doing in school?" Maria asked.

"It's going well, ma'am."

"You will be a senior in the fall?"

"Yes ma'am."

"You are in ROTC?"

"Yes ma'am. Well, actually, I'm working with ROTC. I was commissioned early through NMMI."

"Oh yes, of course. I had forgotten. It's an excellent program. We are fortunate to have it in our state."

"I'm in a reserve unit in Lubbock and I'll go on active duty when I graduate."

"And what about law school? Is that still on the agenda?"

"Yes ma'am, when my active-duty commitment is up. I plan to use the GI Bill for law school."

"Excellent. We need more bilingual lawyers, especially good ones."

Carlos followed Juanita into the kitchen and then dashed out to the grill and Christine handed him a burger wrapped in paper.

"They're about to have coffee and dessert," Carlos said as he turned to go, chomping down on the burger.

Christine looked over her shoulder.

"What are you looking for?" Raoul asked.

"Who are all those guys hanging around?" Christine asked.

"Security," Frankie said. "There are a lot of rich, important people in there."

Christine nodded and went back to her burger. They sat by the pool and ate, but Christine occasionally glanced into the darkness.

14

THE GHOST IN THE ROOM

CHRISTINE PULLED BACK the lace curtain on the balcony door and peered out into the night. She saw no movement—apparently the security guys had gone home. All was quiet. She opened the door and stepped out onto the balcony, met first by a cool breeze and then by a few drops of rain. She flinched as a bolt of lightning cut through the blackness in the distance, followed by the crack of thunder. She held her head up and let the breeze blow her hair until the rain became more than a sprinkle. She stepped back into her room, closing the door behind her. She went into the bathroom, toweled off her face, and then slipped into bed, pulling the sheet up to her chest. She drifted off to sleep as the rain became a torrent, occasionally punctuated by thunder and lightning.

The rain came down in sheets, first trickling down the mountains and then gushing, pushing dirt, rocks, and downed branches ahead of it, rushing toward a reservoir down below, where it would be captured to provide water for Santa Fe in the coming months.

The rain was soon mixed with hail, the blobs of ice exploding as they crashed onto the tile roof of the ranch house. The previously calm surface of the swimming pool danced with miniature geysers as it was pummeled by hailstones.

In the stables, the horses were uneasy, frightened by the thunder and lightning and now hail. Puddles of water soon spread out on the ground around the house and stables.

Thousands of tons of ice falling from the sky can drop the ambient temperature quickly, and Christine felt a sudden chill as a gust of wind blew in through the balcony door. She pulled the blanket up around her neck, but the cold breeze continued. She rolled over and saw the door, standing partially open. "Crap," she said softly as she pulled the covers back and got out of bed. She felt the cold breeze on her bare arms and legs as she stepped briskly across the room.

She brushed aside the billowing lace curtains and reached for the door. She felt something on her cheek. Before she could react, a hand covered her mouth, preventing her from screaming. She tried to turn her head to see the source of the attack, but the intruder held her head firmly in place. The damp curtains licked at her legs. His left hand slipped around her ribcage, pulling her tightly against him. She tugged against his arms, causing him to tighten his grip. She felt his left hand and arm just under her breasts. Thoughts of terror rushed through her mind.

And then she fainted straight away. She didn't sigh and swoon and put the back of her hand on her forehead like in the movies. She dropped straight down; her descent halted by the intruder's firm grip. He scooped her up and carried her to the bed.

When she came to, she was lying in bed, on her back, uncovered. The balcony door was closed. The intruder sat on the bed beside her. He was dripping wet, dressed in black denim jeans and a black hoodie zipped up tightly around his neck. The drawstrings pulled the hood around his face, which was obscured in the darkness. There was only a glint of light in his eyes.

She was afraid but dared not move. She glanced down quickly and determined she was still dressed, as it were. She wore what she normally wore to bed, but her T-shirt was hiked up above her panties. She instinctively tugged at the shirt, covering herself somewhat.

She parted her lips to scream, but the intruder put a finger on them, his threat implied. Her eyes were drawn to his finger as he drew it away. She stared at him for a moment. Her heart began to race. She wondered if he could hear her breathing, her heart racing.

All the blackness of his clothing blended together, but she could now tell that he was wearing a black mask which covered his entire face, with only slits and holes for his eyes, nose, and mouth.

"Is this a dream?" she asked.

He shook his head. "No, it is very real."

She recognized his voice. She gasped and covered her mouth. "Erik?"

She reached for the mask, but he grabbed her hand and pushed it away forcefully.

"Why are you here?" she asked.

"To help you."

"To help me what?"

"La Carlotta will be unable to sing at the premiere. You will take her place."

"If Carlotta can't go on, Hayley will sing Sofia, not me."

"You will sing Sofia at the premiere."

"I can't sing Sofia."

"Of course you can. No one knows it better than you."

"How do you know that?"

"I heard you."

"When?"

"In Santa Monica."

She was stunned.

"In your room," he said.

"You were in my room?"

"I was outside, but I could hear you through the open window."

She was aghast but decided to change the subject rather than pursue it.

"Carlotta's a big star. People are paying money to see her, not me."

"Don't worry about other people. I'll handle it."

"Handle what?"

"Why do you think you sang for the board tonight?"

"You did that?"

He nodded. "You will sing Sofia. Everyone will see what you can do."

"I haven't rehearsed."

"And then we will go away together, and you will be my wife."

"Your what?"

"My wife."

"Uh, no."

"Why not?"

"It doesn't work like that."

"But I love you, and you love me."

"I don't love you."

"Do you love him?"

"Who?"

"Raoul."

"I don't know."

"Does he love you?"

"I don't know! We just got back together. We're not even back together, really. I don't know what we are. I don't know where it's going."

"It's going nowhere. I forbid it."

"You can't forbid it. You don't own me."

"We'll go away together, and no one will find us. We can live in a little cottage in Saint-Tropez."

"People know you there."

"Then somewhere else." He became agitated. "But you will marry me, not Raoul, not anyone else. Do you understand?"

He put his hand on her thigh.

"Now you're scaring me," Christine said.

He lifted his hand, and she pulled the sheet up over her bare legs, or as much as she could with him sitting on the bed.

"How are you going to stop Carlotta from singing at the premiere?"

"Leave that to me."

"She's pretty stubborn."

"She won't sing."

Christine covered her mouth, eyes widening. "That was you in the dressing room?"

He shrugged. "Can't you see that I love you more than anything?"

"Can't you see that I don't love you?"

"Of course you do. Don't you remember Saint-Tropez?"

"How could I forget?"

"And here, when I washed your hair, and on the *Estelline*?"

"Where you almost raped me?"

"Rape? You know you wanted it."

"I told you no. I pushed you away. I didn't want it."

"You didn't push *him* away."

"Raoul? How do you know I didn't?"

"I saw him undressing you." He seethed. "Pawing you, his filthy hands on your delicate young flesh, his horrible mouth on your sweet lips."

She was shocked. "You were spying on us?"

"I was watching over you."

"I can't believe you would do that."

"If I hadn't slashed the tire, he would have ravaged you. I should have killed him then and taken you away."

She turned away from him and covered her face.

"I had to save you from him," he said.

"And what if I don't want to be saved from him? What if I want him to ravage me? At least I would be a willing participant. What if I want to marry him?"

"You will not marry Raoul."

"How are you going to stop me?"

"I'll kill him."

She gasped.

He took her hand and slipped a plain, gold wedding ring on her finger.

"I'll give you some time to think it over. We will meet again at the masked ball, and you will give me your decision. No one will be hurt until then."

"So, I'm supposed to just go to work tomorrow, like nothing happened?"

"Yes."

"I'll call the police."

"No you won't."

"I'll tell your dad."

"Then I'll kill Raoul."

"You wouldn't do that."

"I have nothing to lose. Look at me." He ripped away his mask. His face was horrible, like hamburger meat that had dried up. There were two ugly holes where his nose should be.

RAOUL AWOKE WITH a start. It was not thunder, but a sudden shriek from next door. He leapt out of bed and raced out into the hallway. He tried to open Christine's door, but it was locked. He knocked. No answer. He knocked again, more forcefully.

"Christine." He listened again but heard nothing. He raised his fist to knock again when he heard Christine say, "Who is it?"

"It's me, Raoul."

"What do you want?"

"Can I come in?"

She opened the door. "It's the middle of the night."

He stepped into the room, closing the door behind him. "I thought I heard you scream."

"It was probably thunder," she said, turning away from him.

He flipped on the light. She covered her eyes. He glanced around the room but saw no one. The balcony door was closed, as was the bathroom door.

She suddenly rushed toward the bed and adjusted the sheet, but not before Raoul saw the large wet spot where Erik had been sitting. He said nothing. She sat down on the bed, felt the wet spot, and covered it with a sheet.

Raoul stepped into the bathroom and checked behind the shower curtain. There was no one there. When he returned to the bedroom Christine was in bed with both the sheet and a quilt pulled up to her waist.

He pulled back the lace curtains and checked the door to the balcony. "Why are the curtains wet?"

"The door blew open. I guess I did scream."

She watched as he sat on the edge of the bed, right where Erik had been just moments before.

"Are you sure you're okay?" he asked.

As soon as he saw it, he looked away, but there it was, a gold wedding band on her left hand. He wanted to ask her about it but decided to keep his own counsel for the time being.

"I'm sure. Go back to bed."

He leaned forward and kissed her on the forehead. "See you in the morning."

She watched closely as he stood to go.

"Turn out the light," she said.

He turned out the light and closed the door. She immediately slipped out of bed and double-checked the balcony door. It was locked. She crawled back into bed.

15

THE SKULL

Sunshine streamed through the lace curtains of the balcony door as Christine awoke. She glanced at the door and then sat up and put her feet on the floor. She looked at the bed. The wet spot was gone, but the memory of last night was not. She briefly considered the possibility that it was all a dream but knew otherwise. She put her left hand on her thigh, where he had touched her. The gold wedding band dashed any notion that it was but a dream. She gasped. *What if Raoul had seen it?*

She removed the ring as she stepped over to the dresser. There was no way she would be able to explain it to everyone who would ask, especially Raoul, assuming he had not already seen it, so she dropped it into a drawer. Erik would be none the wiser.

She opened the door and stepped out onto the balcony. She took a deep breath. The air was always cleaner after a thunderstorm. The ground below was rain soaked, and her first thought was how would she get to the pickup without getting her shoes muddy, but she knew that was silly compared to the recent revelations. She wanted to run and tell Raoul and wished she had told him last night when he came to her room. He was right to be worried about her, but she had dismissed him. She knew he was suspicious—not only had he searched her room, and bathroom, but he had kissed her on her forehead. It wasn't like they were lovers, although they had shared a very romantic, or at least sexy, encounter in the pickup. However, Raoul's kiss last night on the forehead instead of the lips, or even the cheek, was designed to send a message. She suddenly dreaded facing him at breakfast.

Then there was Johnston. She knew he was devastated by Erik's disappearance. She had to tell him and Frankie as well, but she could not, at least not yet.

Carlotta was hardly her favorite person, but she worried about what Erik might do to her to keep her from performing. Then there was Raoul. While Erik might have been kidding about Carlotta, Christine feared what he might do to Raoul. Connie was dead because of Erik's insane jealousy. Raoul was certainly in jeopardy.

Yes, she had to speak up.

But Erik had given her a reprieve, at least for a couple of days. He had promised to take no action, or at least to not hurt anyone, until the masked ball. She was to meet him there to give him her answer. Would she go away with him to prevent harm to others? She couldn't imagine herself doing so, but at least she had time to think it through and maybe come up with an alternative that left no one hurt or killed.

Her course was clear. She would go to work as if nothing had happened. She would watch and listen and try to extract information wherever she could. She would even be nice to Carlotta, in hopes she would reveal some tidbit of information that might help her with her decision. Maybe Carlotta would just have a diva moment and go back to Italy. That would solve everything. Hayley would sing Sofia and she would be perfect for it. Even Erik had to see that.

Christine showered, dressed, dashed downstairs and burst into the kitchen. "I'm late for work, Juanita. Can I get a burrito to go?"

She stopped suddenly and watched as Juanita picked up the plates in front of Johnston, Frankie, and Raoul.

"Oh, I thought you would already be gone," Christine said.

"I was waiting for you," Johnston said.

"Do you want me to ride in with you?"

"No, you won't be going in to work today."

All eyes were on Christine.

"What's going on? Is this an intervention or something? I promise I'll give up the drugs."

She waited for a laugh that never came, but at least Johnston smiled.

"Sit down."

Christine slowly took a seat. Juanita put a burrito on a plate in front of her, along with a cup of coffee.

"Am I in trouble?" Christine asked.

"No. As I'm sure you're aware, there are some things going on at the opera house."

"What things?"

"Things with Carlotta, Jesse, others."

"What does that have to do with me? I didn't do anything."

"If there's another accident, I don't want you to be there."

"Lots of other people are there. I can't let them down."

"They are adults. They can make their own decision."

"I can make my own decision. I want to go to work."

"I'm afraid it's not up to you. I can't allow it."

"You aren't my daddy yet."

"No, but I am your boss."

"Great. What am I supposed to do, sit around the house? Maybe I could lay out by the pool topless."

"You can go to Lubbock with me," Raoul said.

"Lubbock?" Christine said. "Why in the world would I want to go to Lubbock? I don't even know where that is."

"I'm looking at some wineries and vineyards for my dad."

"For how long?"

"A couple of days."

"I'll miss dress rehearsal and the ball."

"You'll be back in time for the premiere," Johnston said. "And you just saw a full rehearsal yesterday."

"So, we would stay in a motel?" Christine asked.

"A hotel, a nice one," Raoul said. "I assume they have nice hotels there."

Christine looked at Johnston. "Okay, Johnston, switch from boss mode to dad mode. This boy just asked me to go shack up with him in a hotel for a couple of days. I realize you guys are all rich and sophisticated and stuff, but seriously?"

"It's not like that," Raoul said. "Frankie is going with us."

"What? Why?" Christine asked, and then put her hand on Frankie's arm. "No offense."

"None taken," Frankie said.

"Chaperone," Johnston said, bringing a smile from Christine.

"If the Chagnys are buying into west Texas wine properties, we might want in on the action," Frankie said. "Dad is getting fed up with doing business in California, taxes, regulations, outright hostility. Texas is starting to look pretty good."

"Whatever," Christine said. "I guess if I can't go to work then a road trip beats hanging around the ranch by myself. It could be fun, if we're back in time for the masked ball. I am so going to that. I already have my costume picked out."

There was no sense fighting it. The decision had been made. It obviously had something to do with Erik, or at least the Opera Ghost, but they weren't showing their hand and she certainly didn't intend to show hers. Erik had given her until the masked ball to make her decision. He had promised to harm no one until then. What would it matter if she went to work, hung around the ranch, or went on a trip? She would be going with Raoul, but how could Erik possibly know that? What Erik didn't know couldn't piss him off.

"Well, I have to get to work and see if the opera house is still standing," Johnston said as he stood. He leaned over and kissed Christine on the head. "And you need to pack a bag, young lady."

"I call shotgun." Christine said.

FRANKIE OPENED THE back door of a large Chevy Suburban and Christine tossed in her duffel bag. "Why aren't we going in your truck?"

"This is better for a road trip," Frankie said.

"Whose is it?"

"Ours. The ranch."

They stepped back as Raoul and Carlos tossed in bags.

"You mean you've had this all along?" Christine asked.

"Sure. We have several vehicles at the ranch. This one is good for picking up guests at the airport and running them out to the opera and around town."

"Then why have I been driving that beat-up old truck?"

Carlos laughed.

"It's like initiation," Frankie said. "All the cousins had to drive it, even the girls. Most of us learned to drive in it."

"Wait. There are girl cousins?"

"Sure, from the east coast branch of the family. They may be here for Christmas."

"Cool." She looked at Raoul. "Did you know about the girl cousins?"

"Absolutely," Raoul said, smiling. "They've been to Saint-Tropez a few times."

Christine rolled her eyes as she walked around the Suburban, shaking her head. "So, not only did you know about the girl cousins and didn't tell me, but you've seen their boobs? Great."

"It never came up," Raoul pleaded.

"How old are these girl cousins?"

"About your age," Frankie said.

Christine slid into the front passenger seat. Carlos got behind the wheel. "Are you going with us?" Christine asked.

"I'll be your driver," Carlos said.

"Expedition guide," Frankie corrected as he and Raoul got in the back.

"Or, we could ditch the rich boys and have some real fun," Carlos said.

"That's okay," Christine said. "We need them to pay for gas and stuff."

RAOUL KNEW NONE of the words of "Cielito Lindo," so he was left out while the rest of the crew sang loudly as they rolled eastward on I-40. Even Frankie had to drop out when Carlos and Christine started singing "Naranjitay."

After the second or third time through the song Raoul asked, "What in the world are you singing?"

"'Naranjitay,'" Carlos said.

"It's a love song," Christine added.

"A love song?" Raoul asked, unconvinced.

"About a guy who's in love with a little orange," Christine said, bumping fists with Carlos.

Raoul looked at Frankie, who just shrugged.

Christine looked out the window. "Where are the trains?"

"What trains?" Raoul asked.

"My daddy and I saw lots of trains when we came out on the bus."

"Not around here," Frankie said.

"Isn't this Route 66?"

"It was. Now it's I-40. You probably saw the trains west of Albuquerque."

"I guess. I wasn't really paying attention to where we were."

"Are we going through Clovis?" Frankie asked.

"Yeah," Carlos said. "We'll cut off the Interstate at Santa Rosa and go through Fort Sumner and then Clovis."

"The BNSF Southern Transcon runs through Clovis. You'll see plenty of trains."

"I have no idea what you said, but, cool," Christine said. "Oh, look!" She pointed at a large green road sign up ahead, "Tucumcari."

"We aren't going through Tucumcari," Carlos said.

"Why not? There's the sign, right there."

"Who goes to Tucumcari on purpose?"

"I do."

"I'm sure we could go through there if you like," Raoul said. "How far out of the way is it?"

"I don't know," Carlos said, "thirty, forty miles, no big deal."

"But no trains," Frankie said.

"That's okay," Christine said. "We can see the trains on the way back, right?"

"Right. Set your course for Tucumcari, mate."

"Aye aye, captain," Carlos said.

"Great," Christine said.

"Why do you want to go to Tucumcari?" Raoul asked.

Christine began singing "Two-Gun Harry from Tucumcari."

Christine had finally stopped singing and drifted off to sleep when Carlos pulled off the Interstate at Tucumcari.

Frankie poked Christine over the seat. "Wake up, sleepyhead. You're missing it."

Christine stirred and sat up. "Missing what?"

"Tucumcari. We're on Route 66."

"Goody," she said, looking in all directions. Unfortunately, there wasn't much to see.

"Where to?" Carlos asked.

"The train station," Christine said.

"I don't think there is one."

"There used to be. Let's find it."

"Maybe we should stop and ask someone," Raoul said.

Frankie laughed. "Just follow the railroad tracks."

"Or that," Raoul said.

"Hang a left," Frankie said.

Carlos took a left and then a right on Railroad Avenue, and after a few blocks, there it was. Carlos pulled over and parked. Christine jumped out and ran toward the station. The boys quickly followed.

"It's a pretty big station for such a small town, isn't it?" Raoul asked.

"There used to be lots of passenger trains through here back in the day," Frankie said. "This was a major stopover between Chicago and El Paso, and on to the west coast, but there hasn't been any passenger service here for at least fifty years."

Carlos looked at the building. "Looks pretty good for something that hasn't been used for that long."

"They remodeled it not long ago," Frankie said.

"Could your train come here?" Christine asked.

"It did, actually."

"Huh? When?"

"Come inside and I'll show you."

They followed Frankie inside. "It's a railroad museum now," he said. "They have events and stuff here and set up some huge model train layouts. Kids love it."

"How do you know all this?" Christine asked.

"If it's about trains, Frankie knows it," Carlos said. "The boy would rather ride the rails than screw."

"Ew!" Christine said.

"Come to think of it, he'd rather ride the rails *and* screw. The *Estelline* is an old-school pussy wagon."

Christine shrieked and covered her face.

"Sorry," Carlos said. "But did I lie?"

"You didn't lie," Frankie said, grinning.

"Boys," Christine said, shaking her head.

Frankie walked along a wall of photos and the others followed.

"My dad made a big donation when they were raising money for the restoration. And we gave them some memorabilia."

"Cool," Christine said.

"Union Pacific sent a special train around the state for the Centennial. Dad made some calls and got us hooked up. If a steam locomotive is pulling a passenger train, my dad will find a way to be on it."

"A steam locomotive?" Raoul asked.

"UP 844," Frankie said, talking as he walked, searching photos on the wall. "Union Pacific operates a couple of steam locomotives for public relations."

Frankie pointed at a photo. "Here she is, UP 844, when they were kicking off remodeling of the depot. The *Estelline* is on the end of the train."

He pointed at another photo. "And here is the *Estelline* back in the forties or fifties. That's Daniel Senior. He owned oil properties in the state and came through here occasionally."

He looked around a bit and pointed out another photo. "He always stopped for lunch at Harry's Café. That's the song you were singing, Christine. Two-Gun Harry owned the café."

Christine leaned in, read the caption, gasped, and covered her mouth.

"What's wrong?" Raoul asked, putting his hand on her shoulder.

Christine pointed at the photo. Harry, wearing a white apron and chef's hat, stood in front of the café. Standing beside him was a smiling young waitress. "That's my great-grandmother," Christine said.

"Your great-grandmother?" Frankie asked as he examined the photo. "She worked at Harry's?"

Christine nodded. "She left home in Oklahoma, I think, to become a singer. She got as far as Tucumcari before she ran out of money, so she got a job as a waitress. She planned to save up and keep heading west until she made it to Los Angeles."

"Did she make it?" Raoul asked.

Christine nodded again. "She made it. She became a lounge singer and made a few records." She looked around. "She met my great-grandfather here. He was a Marine, on a train headed to California. The train stopped here, and he came into the café to eat along with lots of other guys."

"World War II?" Raoul asked.

"There were lots of passenger trains through here during the war," Frankie said.

"It was Korea, I think," Christine said. "My mom told me the story," Christine said. "She taught me the song. She always said we were going to take a road trip along Route 66, and stop here, but she died before we could do it. When my daddy and I came through here we were on a bus, so we couldn't come see it."

She looked at the picture for another moment. "Thanks for bringing me, guys."

"No problem," Carlos said. "Glad I thought of it."

Christine grinned, and then sang a few bars of "Two-Gun Harry from Tucumcari" and danced as if she were in a musical.

"Did your great-grandmother record that song that you were just singing?" Raoul asked.

"No. It was some famous singer. I guess she came through here on the train."

"Lots of famous people came through here on the train back in the day," Frankie said.

"Dorothy Shay," Carlos said, looking at his cell phone, "She was apparently a pretty big deal back in the fifties."

They walked out of the depot onto the platform.

"This way," Frankie said, walking east. The others followed.

They stopped a few yards away. Frankie pointed at a strip of old buildings. "I'm not sure which one, but Harry's Café was one of these."

Christine took a step forward and looked.

"Looks like it's a thrift store now," Carlos said.

"Yeah, that was a long time ago," Frankie said. "It was a busy place back then. The train would stop for a few minutes to refuel and change crews, and the passengers would swarm into the café and eat. It's sad."

"What's sad?" Christine asked.

"Everybody's in their cars, or on airplanes. They don't know what they're missing, the romance of the rails."

Raoul turned toward the rumbling sound of a motorcycle, creeping along the dirt and gravel road between the depot and the old buildings. The motorcyclist, wearing black jeans and a black hoodie, looked right at him. It wasn't the clothing that caught Raoul's attention, but the skull mask covering the rider's entire face. There were openings for the eyes, which locked with Raoul's for a moment before the motorcyclist turned, accelerated, and rode away.

Raoul said nothing, and no one else noticed.

16

APPELLATION HIGH PLAINS

Frankie was at the wheel, with Christine still riding shotgun. Carlos, thumbing his cell phone, sat in the back with Raoul. There was nothing much to see outside—everything had looked pretty much the same for the last couple of hours, flat and featureless.

"The Overton is one of the nicest hotels in Lubbock," Carlos said. "I work catering gigs there quite a bit. It's near the campus."

"Works for me," Raoul said. "Do they have suites?"

"Oh, yeah. I worked private parties in some of those."

"I thought this was a road trip," Christine said. "We need a cheap motel."

Carlos looked at Raoul, who shrugged.

"How cheap?" Carlos asked.

"Not a fleabag," Frankie said. "Look, a train!"

Frankie pointed and Christine looked. It was a long BNSF freight train carrying double-stacked containers.

"It's coming from Lubbock, on the Coleman Cutoff, headed for Belen," Frankie said.

"Are we nearly there?" Christine asked.

"Another hour or so."

"How about this one?" Carlos asked, showing Raoul his cell phone.

"Works for me."

"How many rooms?"

"Two, connecting, with two beds each."

"Roger that." Carlos punched the screen of his cell phone. "But the Overton is really nice, and the neighborhood is crawling with cute co-eds, even in the summer."

"That's okay. If Christine wants a cheap motel, that's where we'll stay, although my dad's accountant might wonder why."

"So, this really is a business trip?" Carlos whispered.

"Yes. And you're the only one of legal age, so you'll be our designated wine taster."

Carlos smiled. "I'm your man."

"But you have to spit it out," Christine said.

"Seriously?" Carlos asked.

"You can swallow," Raoul said.

"As long as you aren't driving," Christine added.

"Hey, I have ID," Frankie said. "I can taste the wine."

"This is corporate espionage," Raoul said. "Don't get us all arrested."

THE MOTEL CARLOS SELECTED was not just cheap, but funky as well, decades old and not part of any chain.

"Are you sure you want to stay here?" Raoul asked as they entered one of the rooms.

"This is great," Christine said.

She hadn't even questioned the sleeping arrangements, but Raoul made a point of opening the door to the connecting room, just as Frankie opened the other. Christine immediately stepped through to inspect the other room. Each room had two beds.

"Cool," she said, nonchalantly, as if it were an everyday thing to be in a strange town in a cheap motel with three guys.

"You're the expedition guide," Frankie said. "Suggestions?"

Carlos checked his watch. "Most of the wineries are outside of the city, so we won't be able to get many of them in today. I'd say let's hit McPherson Cellars downtown. It's in the old Coca-Cola bottling plant."

"I want to see Lubbock High School," Christine said.

"Why would you want to see a high school?" Raoul asked.

"It's where Buddy Holley went to school, and Zoe's grandmother."

"We can do that," Carlos said. "Hell, we can take the Buddy Holley tour if you want."

"I want," Christine said.

On this trip, if Christine wanted, Christine got.

They dumped their luggage, climbed into the Suburban and headed out.

"It's probably closed for the summer," Frankie said as they drove past Lubbock High School.

"That's okay," Christine said. "I just wanted to see it. It's really pretty. It kind of reminds me of the conservatory."

"It is the same style, with the sand-colored brick and red tile roof."

"Are you a Buddy Holley fan?" Carlos asked.

"Yeah, I guess," Christine said. "Zoe is really into him. So is Jim Bob. We should have brought them along."

"I think they're kind of busy, with the opera and all," Frankie said.

"Oh, yeah, that."

Carlos was about to turn off 19th Street onto Texas Avenue when Christine pointed. "Oh look," Christine said, "Buddy Holly Avenue."

"Well, as long as we're here," Carlos said, and continued east.

"Why did they misspell his name?" Christine asked.

"That's the way everybody spells it," Carlos said.

"Not Zoe," Christine said. "She said her grandmother insisted it should always be spelled right, not the way it ended up on some record."

"But this is what you're really looking for," Carlos said as he turned left onto Crickets Avenue.

"The Buddy Holly Center," Christine said. "They misspelled that one too. Can we go in?"

"Of course. But we have to hurry if we are going to hit the winery before they close."

Carlos parked the Suburban.

"You'd think they would spell his name right in his own hometown," Christine said before opening the door and flying out. The boys raced to catch up as she entered the center.

"Zoe is going to be so pissed that she missed this," Christine said as she reveled in the exhibits.

"Maybe we can bring her back later," Raoul said, "when she isn't so busy with her opera and stuff."

"Okay, sure."

"This is an old Fort Worth and Denver depot," Frankie said as they headed to the Suburban.

"How do you know?" Christine asked.

"I read the historical marker while you were taking a picture with Buddy's statue," Frankie said.

"I guess that's why they call it the depot district," Carlos said.

"Where's the winery?" Raoul asked, checking his watch as they climbed into the Suburban.

"Just a couple of blocks," Carlos said.

They toured McPherson Cellars and Carlos sampled lots of wine, letting Raoul sniff it, under the watchful eye of staff.

"An urban winery," Raoul said as they got into the Suburban. "I would have never thought of that."

"Why not?" Christine asked.

"Wineries are usually in the country, surrounded by their own vineyards. That's kind of hard to do in an urban setting."

"I think most of the wine grapes around here come from Terry County, just south of here," Carlos said.

"But I like it," Raoul said. "It's definitely something to think about."

Carlos navigated from the back seat as Frankie drove through downtown Lubbock.

"The locals say downtown was a busy place back in Buddy's day," Carlos said.

"Looks kind of dead now," Christine said.

CHRISTINE SAT ON THE bed in the motel and looked around. The TV was positively ancient. It wasn't even a flatscreen. "This place is kind of a dump, isn't it?"

"I tried to get us a suite at a nice hotel," Raoul said.

"That's okay. I like dumps. It reminds me of the one in Santa Monica where I lived with Daddy for a few days."

"Where I saw you naked?" he asked, smiling.

"Don't get any ideas, pervert."

"I won't."

"You'll be in the boys' room anyway."

"I will?"

"You got two rooms, one for the boys and one for the girls."

"There's only one girl."

"And I have an extra bed, so I guess you can sleep in my room."

"Thanks."

"But if you don't behave, I'll go sleep in the other room."

"And let Carlos and Frankie see you naked?"

"I'll change in the bathroom."

"Have you seen the bathroom?"

"Why? What's wrong with it?"

"Nothing, I guess."

She rushed over and opened the bathroom door. "Ew."

He followed her and looked over her shoulder. "It's not that bad."

"Maybe we should have stayed at that other place, the one Carlos said," she said.

"The Overton?"

"Yeah, that."

"It's not too late," he said. "We can move."

"But you already paid for this one."

"That's okay, we'll move if it makes you happy."

She pushed him back through the door. "Nah, this will do. It's only two nights, right?"

"Right."

She plopped onto the bed and fell over onto her back. "I'm starving. Where are they?"

"They'll be here soon, unless they met a couple of hot babes."

He sat down beside her on the bed. "Are you okay?"

"Sure, why?" she asked. "The boss gave me two days off. I'm on vacation. Why wouldn't I be okay?"

"For the last couple of days you've seemed, I don't know, kind of distant."

"Distant? I'm right here with you, on a bed, in a motel, alone."

"It's just that things seemed to be going so well, in the pickup."

"So, do you want to make out while we wait for the guys?"

He smiled. "No, that's okay."

She spread her arms. "Here it is. Help yourself."

"Don't do that."

"I was just kidding." She sat up and grinned. "But it was fun in the pickup, until the tire got slashed."

"How do you know the tire got slashed?"

She held her breath while trying to quickly formulate an answer.

"I didn't buy that whole rubbed-against-the-curb thingy. I'm a good driver. And I know I saw somebody out there. I just figured you didn't want to tell me what really happened."

"The tire was slashed."

"Who did it?"

"That's a good question, probably some kids."

"Or the Opera Ghost."

"Could be. Johnston thought it was a good idea to get you out of town for a couple of days while they try to catch the guy."

"And Frankie and Carlos are like, bodyguards?"

He smiled. "Something like that."

"And the whole winery thing was just made up?"

"No, not at all. We really are considering it."

"Yeah, right."

"Really. Don't you remember when we had dinner at the bistro in Santa Fe? I talked to the guy about it."

She shrugged.

"We could have gone anywhere to get you out of town," he said, "but I thought this would be the easiest."

"Or the least likely to make me suspicious."

"That too. But hey, we went to Tucumcari, and you found your grand-mother's picture, so that's a good thing, right?"

"Great-grandmother, but yeah, that's a good thing." She kissed him on the cheek. "Thanks again for taking me."

"You're welcome, but I can't take credit for it. It just happened."

"Why are you telling me all this now?"

"All what?"

"About the tire being slashed and getting me out of town while they try to catch the Opera Ghost."

"I don't want there to be any secrets between us."

He put his arm around her shoulder. She quickly leaned in closer.

"Get dressed, grub's here," Frankie shouted from the connecting room.

"Don't come in!" Christine shouted, "We're naked."

Frankie, carrying a double armload of paper sacks, leaned through the door for a look.

"Made you look," Christine said as she slid off the bed, fully dressed.

Raoul followed her into the other room.

"I hope you like barbecue," Carlos said. "We have brisket, turkey, and Ger-man sausage, along with all the trimmings." He handed the receipt to Raoul. "I work catering for them sometimes, so I got you a discount."

"And wine," Frankie said. "We loaded up on Texas wine. The guy at the liquor store thought we were pulling something."

"He checked my ID really close," Carlos said.

"And he really looked at your credit card," Frankie said to Raoul. "He probably thought it was stolen."

Carlos handed Raoul the card. "I told him I worked for your dad's company, and we were picking up wine for a company party. He ran it and it worked, and here we are."

Raoul inspected a bottle of wine.

"We got all the best ones, or at least all the most expensive ones," Carlos said. "Is that what you need?"

"Yeah. This is great. Now I can taste some."

"Taste, hell," Frankie said. "We're drinking these suckers."

They drug in two chairs from the other room and squeezed around the small table. Along with the meat there was plenty of fried okra, pinto beans, and potato salad. Carlos also laid out a spread of pickles, onions, and jalapeño peppers.

"If everybody eats onions it will cancel each other out."

"In case there's any kissing later," Frankie said.

"Are you guys planning on making out?" Christine asked.

"That's cold," Carlos said.

They ate barbecue and drank Texas wine. When they had finished it all off Frankie pulled a large foam container out of a paper bag and put it in the middle of the table.

"There's more?" Christine asked. "I'm stuffed."

"You can't have barbecue without peach cobbler."

Carlos placed a white towel over his arm and held out a bottle of wine for Raoul's inspection. "For dessert, monsieur. Does this meet with your approval?"

"Definitely. I love a good Gewürztraminer."

"I like it really cold," Frankie said, "so we iced down a few bottles at the liquor store."

Christine was seeing spots in front of her eyes when they finished the cobbler and wine, but she insisted on helping Carlos clean up and bag the mess.

Frankie dried off the table with a towel and placed a deck of cards on it.

"What's that for?" Christine asked. "Bridge?"

"Poker. It's not a road trip without poker."

"I don't have enough money to play poker with rich kids."

"Me either," Carlos said. "That's why we're playing strip poker."

"Nuh-uh."

"Just kidding. I brought poker chips; no money involved."

"Works for me."

"Do you know how to play poker?"

She nodded and smiled. "Jim Bob taught me."

"Uh-oh," Frankie said. "We're toast."

And toast they were. After a couple of hours of wine and poker, Christine had all the chips. "Okay, strip."

"Huh?" Frankie asked.

"You guys wanted to play strip poker. I won, so strip."

"You're kidding, right?"

"Of course I'm kidding. Do you really think I want to see your ugly asses naked?"

She stood up, or tried to, but was quite wobbly. Raoul and Carlos both stood and reached out. She teetered for a moment and fell into Raoul's arms. He scooped her up and carried her into the other room. Carlos and Frankie followed. Raoul spread her out on a bed, and they all stared at her for a moment.

"Do you think she'll be okay?" Raoul asked.

"How much wine did she drink?" Carlos asked.

"Not that much. She's just not used to it."

"We should check her, just in case."

"Check what?" Raoul asked.

"I have a breathalyzer app on my phone."

"Seriously?"

"Yeah, but she has to blow into it. See if you can wake her up."

Raoul went into the bathroom.

"Maybe we should put her in the shower," Frankie said.

"Nah, that's for drugs, not booze," Carlos said.

Raoul returned with a wet washcloth as they sat her up. He wiped her face. She opened her eyes and looked at the three guys staring at her. Her head reeled. She grabbed the washcloth from Raoul and covered her mouth.

"She's gonna blow," Carlos said, backing away.

Christine leapt off the bed and ran to the bathroom.

"Go with her," Carlos said to Raoul.

"Why?"

"To hold her hair back, dude."

Raoul rushed after her but was too late. She was already on her knees, hurling into the toilet. He pulled her hair back anyway. Frankie and Carlos watched from the doorway as she threw up repeatedly.

"That should help," Carlos said. "Upchuck the alcohol before it gets into the blood. Waste of good peach cobbler, though."

Christine pushed away from the toilet and sat back against the wall. Raoul knelt beside her. She looked down at her shirt. "I threw up on my shirt."

"And your hair. Sorry I didn't get here in time."

She peeled her shirt over her head. "I need a shower."

"And that's our cue to leave," Frankie said as he and Carlos backed away.

Raoul helped her to her feet. She unbuttoned her jeans.

"What are you doing?" he asked.

"I'm taking a shower."

She tried to wiggle out of her jeans but couldn't maintain her balance. Raoul grabbed her and she managed to step out of her jeans.

"You're too drunk to take a shower," he said. "You'll fall and hurt yourself."

She looked at the shower and then at him. He was right.

"You can get in with me and hold me up."

He smiled. "That's okay."

He closed the lid on the toilet and sat her down on it. "Hold on." He watched to make sure she wouldn't fall over while he wet another washcloth.

"What are you doing?"

"Washing your hair."

"With that?"

"There's not that much puke. This will do for tonight. You can take a shower in the morning when you're sober."

"Okay."

She watched, their faces only inches away, as he dabbed at her hair with the washcloth and then dried it, as much as possible, with a towel.

"Wait here," he said.

"Where are you going?"

"To get your toothbrush."

He dug through her duffel bag and returned with her toothbrush and toothpaste. He helped her up and held her by the waist in front of the lavatory while she brushed and rinsed. She dabbed at her mouth with a towel and then looked at herself in the mirror.

"Can you get me a clean T-shirt?"

"Sure."

He stepped out of the bathroom and pulled a T-shirt out of her bag. Her bra was off when he returned to the bathroom. He thought briefly about turning away, but just handed her the shirt.

She leaned against the lavatory to steady herself while she pulled on the T-shirt.

"Are you ready to go to bed?" he asked.

She nodded and then moved toward the door. The room was still spinning, so he scooped her up into his arms, squeezed through the door, and carried her to bed.

He lowered her to the floor and held her up with one hand while pulling back the covers with the other as she climbed into the bed. She lay back on the pillow.

"You could have totally taken advantage of me."

"No, I couldn't."

She smiled.

"Are you going to be okay?" he asked.

She nodded.

He stepped away and returned with an ice bucket and a towel, which he placed on the nightstand. "Just in case."

"Why are you so good to me?"

"Because I love you."

He leaned down and kissed her.

"You smell like onions," she said.

"I'll be in the next room if you need anything."

"You're sleeping in there? I was just kidding about the rooms."

"No, I'll sleep in here, in the other bed."

"Okay."

"I just need to talk to the guys about something," he said, turning out the lamp beside the bed. "Good night."

"Good night."

He went into the other room, closing the door behind him.

Frankie was on the phone.

"Is she okay?" Carlos asked.

"Seems to be," Raoul said.

"We didn't hear the shower."

"I just washed the puke out of her hair. She couldn't even stand up by herself. I wasn't going to let her get in the shower."

"Dude, get in there with her."

"That's okay, not like that."

"Yeah, you're probably right, diminished capacity and all that."

"We got her drunk and put her to bed," Frankie said on his cell phone.

"You what?" Johnston asked, alarmed.

"Don't worry. She's a cheap drunk. She didn't have that much wine, although it was very good wine."

"Well, be careful. I don't need you guys getting in trouble with the cops."

"We're careful. We're using designated drivers. The fair maiden is safe."

They spoke a bit longer and Frankie hung up. "No word from the Ghost. No sightings. No nothing."

"Any of that Gewürz left?" Raoul asked.

"Sure, boss," Carlos said, reaching into the cooler. He poured a glass for Raoul, and then filled his and Frankie's.

Raoul took a sip of wine. "I saw something when we were about to leave Tucumcari. I didn't think much about it at the time."

"What was it?" Frankie asked.

"A guy in a black hoodie on a crotch rocket. He looked right at me, then split."

"I always thought you might be a little gay."

Carlos laughed.

"He was wearing a skull mask, like Halloween."

"Biker," Carlos said. "Typical."

"So?" Frankie said.

"It was weird," Raoul said. "Maybe it's nothing."

17

TRUE LOVE WAYS

Carlos made a good case for a local diner, where all the first responders ate, so it had to be good, but Christine insisted on having breakfast at McDonald's.

"Well, Christine, what do you think?" Carlos asked.

"About what?"

"About seeing us all naked last night."

"Huh?"

"Strip poker. Don't you remember? You won."

"We didn't play strip poker. I wasn't that drunk. But I did win, didn't I?"

"Yes, you did," Raoul said.

"Was that the best water you ever tasted?" Frankie asked.

"What are you talking about?" Christine asked.

"At the motel this morning, when you first got up."

"Now that you mention it, it was pretty good."

The boys all laughed.

"What's so funny?"

"Any water tastes good when you have a hangover," Carlos said.

"Good to know." She looked at Raoul and grinned. "The coffee was pretty good too."

"Coffee?" Frankie asked.

"Somebody left a cup of coffee in the bathroom while I was in the shower."

"It wasn't me," Frankie said.

"It damned sure wasn't me," Carlos said.

Raoul smiled.

They finished their McStuff.

"Let's roll," Frankie said. "We have a lot of wineries to hit."

"I don't have to drink any wine, do I?" Christine asked.

"No, not today," Raoul said. "Carlos will taste the wine."

"And I'll drive," Frankie said.

FRANKIE DROVE AND Carlos rode shotgun, leaving Raoul and Christine in the back seat.

"What exactly are we looking for?" Christine asked as they approached the first winery on the itinerary.

"The general layout," Raoul said. "Do they have a tasting room? Well, they kind of have to have a tasting room, but how is it set up? Do they have a barrel room for public display? Do they have a place for weddings and events?"

"That's a lot to look for."

"Do they sell wine at the winery?"

"Duh, of course they do, right?"

"They probably do, but that's one thing to check on. What are the local laws? Can they ship wine to consumers?"

"You guys check on all that. I'll just look around."

"We need to decide whether to buy an existing winery or build our own. Are any of them in financial trouble? Can they be snatched up cheap?"

"You should definitely build your own," Christine said.

"What style?" Raoul asked.

"Like the one in Saint-Tropez. It's pretty cool."

"But it's so French. How would that fit in on the Texas plains?"

"You ask too many questions."

"Maybe a French château would work, but maybe it would just be out of place."

"Good point," Frankie said. "This is kind of Mexican, or Spaniard, and Indian territory."

"Mexican?" Christine asked.

"This used to be part of Mexico before Santa Ana got his ass kicked by the Texians," Carlos said.

Christine laughed. "Texians?"

"That's what Texans were called back then. Mexicans who lived in Texas were called Tejanos."

"So, Tejano music is music by Mexicans who live in Texas?"

"Selena. Exactly."

AFTER A DAY OF touring wineries, a brief Buddy Holley tour, and a fast-food lunch—Carlos knew all the best places—they were on their way to the Depot District. They found a parking spot and strolled along Buddy Holly Avenue.

"There's the Cactus Theater," Carlos said. "It used to be a movie theater way back when. Now they have live music events. It's pretty cool."

"Is that where we're going?" Christine asked.

"No, I don't think they have anything tonight. We're going out to dinner." They walked a short distance. "This is where we're going."

"It looks fancy. I thought we were road tripping."

"It's not that fancy."

They went inside. Christine noticed musical instruments on a stage. "They aren't going to make me sing, are they?"

Carlos laughed. "No, they're going to make me sing."

"They are?"

"I play here sometimes during the school year. I know these guys."

"What guys?"

"The band." Carlos checked his watch. "They'll be here soon."

"Where's your guitar?"

"In the car. I'll get it after we eat."

They ordered food but didn't even attempt to order wine. Carlos had his fill tasting at the wineries and was planning to play later. Frankie and Raoul didn't want to risk getting carded and busted in unfamiliar territory, and Christine was reconsidering her relationship with alcohol.

After dinner, Carlos retrieved his guitar and took the stage. Christine was happy to see that they played a lot of Buddy Holley songs, and that Carlos did a pretty good impression.

"'Blue Days, Black Nights,'" Zoe said over the phone. "It's one of his early works."

"Cool," Christine said.

"Tell Carlos I'm going to kick his ass."

"Why?"

"Because he never told me he could sing Buddy Holley songs."

"He sounds pretty good, huh?"

"Yes, he does."

Christine held the phone so Zoe could listen.

"'Girl on My Mind,'" Zoe said.

"Another early one?"

"Pretty much."

"Words of Love" was next. "Jim Bob sang this one for me," Christine said.

"Damn straight I did," Jim Bob said, "and I meant it."

"Are you listening too?" Christine asked.

"Hell, yes. I wish I was there. We could burn that place down."

Christine laughed.

"I'm starting to detect a pattern," Zoe said as Carlos started singing "Not Fade Away."

"What's that?" Christine asked.

"Love songs."

"Yeah, I noticed."

"I'll bet that boy gets laid a lot," Jim Bob said.

Christine laughed again.

"Oh crap," Christine said as the song ended.

"What?" Zoe asked.

"Carlos is looking right at me."

"He probably wants you to sing."

"No way. I told him I wouldn't."

When the applause died down Carlos said, "Thank you ladies and gentlemen. I'd like to dedicate this next song to that cute little blonde girl right over there." He pointed at Christine. Everyone turned to look. "Her name's Christine. But it's not what you think. She's not my girl. I'm not that lucky. That's Raoul with her. He's French. Raoul. Don't you just love the way that rolls off the tongue? Raoul."

Christine covered her face. Raoul smiled as people stared.

"Okay, here it is, for Christine and Raoul," Carlos said.

He sang "Oh, Boy!"

Just as the song was over Raoul turned toward the sound of two young women snickering. Outside on the sidewalk, looking in through the plate glass window, was the guy in the skull mask.

Raoul had started to push back from the table when Christine handed him her phone. "Hold my phone so Zoe can hear." She pushed away from the table and stood up.

"Where are you going?" Raoul asked.

She didn't answer.

Raoul tried to watch both Christine and the guy in the mask. He punched Frankie and pointed. "It's the guy in the mask, from Tucumcari."

Frankie turned to look just as the guy walked briskly away. Frankie leapt up and went after him.

"Uh-oh," Carlos said. "Here she comes. She's probably going to kick my ass."

The audience loved it. Christine stepped onto the stage. She covered Carlos's microphone. "Do you guys know 'True Love Ways'?"

"Yes ma'am," one of the guys said. "We don't have all the right instruments, but we can fake it."

"Are you going to sing it?" Carlos asked.

"I'm going to show you how it's done," she said.

They played. She sang.

There was enthusiastic applause when the song ended. Despite attempts to get her to continue, Christine returned to her table.

"Where did Frankie go?" she asked as she sat down.

"He thought he saw someone he knew," Raoul said.

"Did you hang up the phone?"

"Yeah, Jim Bob was crying."

Christine smiled.

It was late when they got back to the motel.

"You guys play strip poker," Christine said. "Raoul and I need to talk."

"You want some wine?" Carlos asked.

"Not tonight."

Carlos looked at Raoul, who shook his head.

"You kids have fun," Carlos said as Raoul closed the connecting door behind them.

"So, what's with the guy in the mask?" Carlos asked.

"He got away on a crotch rocket," Frankie said.

"Do you think it was Erik?"

"I don't know, could be. But how could he know where we are? Nobody but Johnston knew where we were going. I didn't see anybody following us, did you?"

"Nope, and I kept checking, just in case."

"So how did he know?"

"Christine?"

"No way," Frankie said. "She doesn't know he's back. Hell, we don't even know for sure it's him."

"Chicks, man. They can do some stupid shit when they're in love."

"She's not in love with Erik. Not even close. You have no idea."

"GPS."

"Huh?"

"Maybe he slipped a tracker on the Suburban."

"Nah, he couldn't have known we were leaving, and even if he did, he couldn't have known which vehicle we would take."

"Maybe he put a tracking app on her phone."

"How could he do that, and when?"

"Hell if I know. I'm just spitballing."

Frankie thought about it. "He had plenty of opportunity two years ago in Saint-Tropez, and then Santa Fe. Maybe he put it on in Saint-Tropez and that's how he knew she was in Santa Fe, both times."

"Makes sense, and he's a sneaky SOB."

"Oh, shit."

"What?"

"We think he may have been crashing in the guest house where Christine was staying in Santa Monica."

Carlos shrugged.

"Can you find it and disable it?" Frankie asked.

"Yeah, probably, if I had the phone and plenty of time, but it would be easier to just take out the battery."

"Then he'll know we're on to him."

Carlos nodded.

"He obviously knows where we are now," Frankie said. "We're going back to Santa Fe in the morning. Let's just leave it until we get back and then talk to Johnston."

Christine and Raoul sat on the bed.

"Thanks for last night," she said.

"You're welcome, I guess. What did I do?"

"That thing about the shower, that was the booze talking, not me. I don't want you to think I'm a slut."

"I would never think that."

"Why didn't you do it?"

"Do what?"

"Take a shower with me."

"Like you said, it was the booze talking. I would never take advantage of you like that."

"Now I see how girls end up doing stuff they never wanted to do."

He nodded.

"I guess I'm lucky," she said.

"You just need to be careful who you trust."

"Exactly."

"Not that I wasn't tempted."

She smiled.

"If you hadn't been so drunk, I might have done it."

"But you didn't want me to wake up and wonder where my clothes went?"

"That was definitely a concern. You do remember taking off your bra yourself, right?"

"Yes. That I remember."

"So, do you want to take a shower now?"

"Together?"

He smiled. "You're sober, right?"

"I'm definitely sober, but maybe after."

"After what?"

She took a deep breath. "Do you have a condom?"

"Whoa! Where did that come from?"

"I'm ready to do it."

"Are you serious?"

"Yes. I'm serious. I'm ready."

"Just like that?"

"Well, it's not exactly just like that. You were my first kiss, my first date, the first guy who saw me naked, before there was much to see, the first guy I slept with." She put finger quotes around "slept."

He smiled.

"Let's see, what else? You were the first guy to see me naked after it mattered."

"I was?"

"On the beach, remember?"

"Oh yeah, but my dad was there too."

"Ew!"

"And you weren't completely naked, just topless. What about the painting?"

"That was just Connie and her mom, unless some guys were lurking in the bushes or something, so that doesn't count."

"I was the first guy who groped your butt, or at least I hope I was."

"Huh? Oh, yeah, in the pool. You were the first, and the first guy I made out with in the pool, and on the beach, and on a boat. Wow, we have a lot of history."

She wanted there to be more firsts, but unfortunately Erik had claimed some of those, so she cut it short. "Now I want you to be my first time."

"That's a lot to think about," he said, clearly pondering the ramifications.

"Come on, lover boy, a girl is offering herself to you. What is there to think about?"

"Is this another one of those yes-means-no deals?"

"No, this is the real deal."

"You don't want to make out first, fool around?"

"Duh. Of course. I want to do all that. But I don't want to do all that and then say, 'okay, now do me,' and you'd be all, 'does yes mean no?' and we never do it."

Raoul spun his head around.

"What's wrong?" she asked.

"I'm trying to get my head around all that."

She laughed. "I just want it to be a conscious decision, made in advance, and not in the heat of the moment. I tried that. It didn't work."

"Okay, that makes sense, and it's very grown up. That's probably the way it should be."

"So, do you have a condom or not?"

"No, actually. I wasn't exactly expecting this incredible offer."

"I thought all guys carried an emergency condom in their wallet."

"Not this guy, and especially not with this girl."

"This is a limited time offer."

"I could ask Frankie."

"Meg's on the pill, so he probably doesn't have any, unless he's cheating on her, but then she'd kick his ass."

"Then I'll ask Carlos, unless you don't want him to know. I guess I could go to a convenience store, but the guys would want to know why."

"Just ask him. He probably already thinks we're doing it."

Raoul opened the connecting door

"Sup?" Carlos asked.

Raoul stepped into the room. He could hear the shower running. Luckily, he wouldn't have to deal with Frankie as well.

"Do you have a spare condom?" Raoul asked.

Carlos grinned. "Sure." He reached for his wallet. "You think you'll get lucky tonight?"

"I don't know, maybe."

"Here you go." Carlos handed him a condom. "Heavy duty, for a real man."

"Thanks," Raoul said as he slipped back through the door and closed it behind him.

Christine smiled as he held up his prize. "You go first," she said.

"Go where?"

"To the bathroom, to do whatever guys do before they do it."

Raoul went into the bathroom and brushed his teeth. Christine waited nervously on the bed. She could hear him taking a piss, and the flush was even louder. Her heart started racing. This was becoming real.

"Your turn," he said as he stepped out.

She slid off the bed and headed into the bathroom.

He undressed and tossed his clothes onto a chair. He debated over which bed to use and decided on hers. He climbed into bed and pulled the covers up to his waist.

Christine brushed her teeth and washed her face. She looked at herself in the mirror for a moment. She stepped over to the door and leaned out.

"I'm kind of new at this. Do I take off my clothes in here and just come out naked, or what?"

"Whatever you want."

She decided on a compromise. She stripped and wrapped herself in a towel. She turned off the light as she left the bathroom.

"I thought about letting you rip my clothes off but that seemed kind of high school."

"This is fine."

She sat on the bed. He watched with interest as she slipped off the towel and tossed it at the foot of the bed. She lay back and covered herself with the sheet in one fluid motion. He rolled over almost on top of her.

"Boy, you get right to it, don't you?" she said.

"Huh?" he asked as he reached for the lamp switch.

"Oh, the light."

He turned out the light and laughed. "Did you think I was just going to jump right on?"

"Like I said, I'm new at this, so I don't really know what to expect."

"How do you want to start?"

"You could kiss me."

She rolled over toward him. He pulled her close. She flinched at the bare-skin contact.

"What's wrong?" he asked.

"Nothing. That was just a totally new experience."

"Oh, sorry."

"Don't be. It feels kind of weird, but nice."

They made out for what seemed forever, and Christine felt completely comfortable and at ease. She couldn't help comparing it to the night on the *Estelline* with Erik. She liked this much better. It felt completely right.

Their eyes had adjusted to the darkness, aided by the soft glow of light creeping in around the curtains. Raoul reached for the condom, which he had carefully positioned on the nightstand. She watched with anticipation, her heart pounding. She was ready.

"I can't do this," he said, putting the condom back on the nightstand and turning on the light.

"What?"

"I can't do it."

"Are you crazy? I'm ready. Just do it."

"I can't." He lay back on the pillow. "It's just not right."

"How could it not be right? How could it possibly be more right?"

"I don't think you're ready."

"Are you kidding me? I'm lying here in bed, naked, all worked up. We already talked about it. I already said yes, so do me."

"There's something that's upsetting you. I don't know exactly what it is, and you won't tell me, but I don't think we should take such a big step right now."

She considered, for a fleeting moment, telling him everything, but she could not.

"You got drunk last night," he said. "That's not like you."

"Wow. I offered you my virginity and you turned me down. Way to make a girl feel good about herself."

She pulled the covers up to her neck, suddenly feeling exposed.

"Come on, Christine. You know I want to. You have no idea how much I want to. The horndog in me will regret this tomorrow, but remember when you said you could trust me?"

"Yeah."

"Well, trust me now. This isn't right."

She started crying.

"Don't cry. When the time is right, I want to be your first. I really, really want to be your first, and only, I hope."

She wiped her tears. He slipped his arm under her shoulders, pulled her close and kissed her.

"You know I'm right, don't you?"

She nodded.

"We can still cuddle."

"Okay. Can we fool around?"

"Absolutely."

"Good, because that was fun."

He turned off the light and they fooled around.

18

THE MASKED BALL

Carlos was somewhat concerned when Raoul slipped him the unopened condom the next morning but didn't ask any questions. Raoul just shrugged and shook his head. They loaded up and headed out, stopping only once, at Fort Sumner, for food, drinks, and restrooms.

As soon as they had unloaded the Suburban at the ranch Carlos immediately went to work helping with final preparations for the masked ball.

In an upstairs bedroom, Christine watched as Raoul, already shirtless, stripped off his jeans and tossed them on the bed.

"Where's my costume?"

"Over there," she said, pointing at a chair.

"I thought that was the dirty laundry."

"Put this on." She handed him a skull cap.

"What is it?"

"It's a skull cap."

He shrugged and put it on.

"Duh, tuck in your hair."

He tucked in his hair.

"Sit on the bed," she said.

"Why?"

"I have to do your face."

"You have to what?"

"I'm going to paint your face."

"Why can't I just wear a mask? It's a masked ball, right?"

"Don't give me any crap. Sit on the bed."

He sat on the bed. She retrieved a tray of paints, brushes, and a box of tissue.

"Why did I have to strip for you to paint my face?"

"I don't want to get paint on your costume."

"I could have worn a T-shirt and washed it later."

"This is more fun." She pointed. "Stretch your legs out that way."

He stretched out his legs.

"What about you?"

"What about me?" She put the tray on the bed.

"Aren't you going to strip?"

"You wish." She climbed on his lap, facing him.

"Uh, I'm not complaining, but what are you doing?"

"I need to get up close."

"Is this the way professional makeup artists do it?"

"Probably not."

She wrapped her legs around him and scooted up close.

"This could get interesting," he said.

"Try to control yourself."

"Yes ma'am."

She started smearing white grease paint on his forehead.

"Wait," he said.

"What's wrong?"

"Can I at least have a kiss first, before you paint me?"

She smiled and then kissed him. She pulled back and looked into his eyes. She moved in and kissed him again, this time passionately, wrapping her arms around his neck and squeezing tightly, while trying to avoid smearing the grease paint.

"Wow," he said. "What brought that on?"

"Life is uncertain. Find happiness when you can."

She went to work on his face, leaving him to ponder what she had just said. He was rather distracted, however, by a hot girl sitting in his lap, face to face.

It was unlikely Christine would soon find work as a makeup artist, but she did a serviceable job. His face was white with black eyebrows and eyeliner, with small butterfly lips drawn in the center of his own. She finished the job with a single black tear drop beneath one eye.

She held up a mirror. "What do you think?"

"Dudes will probably hit on me."

She laughed. "Just don't kiss any of them. It will mess up your lips."

"It might be worth it to not look like this anymore."

"Come on, man up."

"Man up? I look like a geisha girl."

She crawled off him and picked up his costume.

"Here, put this on."

She handed it to him. He held it up and looked.

"Seriously?"

"It's a Pierrot. It's French for domino."

"Domino is French for domino."

"It is?"

"Yes. I speak French, remember?"

"Whatever. That's what they called it when I picked it up at the opera house."

"What are you wearing?"

"It's a secret."

"I really need to know what you're wearing."

"Why?"

"So I can keep an eye on you. The Ghost, remember?"

"There will be people everywhere. I'll be okay."

"Yes, but everyone will be wearing a mask, right? You won't know who to trust."

"You worry too much."

He held out the costume and examined it. "Why do I have to wear this? I have time to go pick up something less dorky."

"Nobody will know it's you. Besides, I already did your face. Just disguise your voice if you talk to anybody."

"Do I have to disguise my voice to talk to you?"

"No, silly, but you have to find me first."

"The things I do for love."

"It'll be fun. Put it on."

He put it on, and she zipped up the back. He turned around and modeled it for her. She laughed. "Perfect."

"I look like a snowman with black buttons."

"Put on the beret. That's French for hat, right?"

He smiled. "Beret is English for *béret*, but okay, it's a hat."

He put on the beret.

"That works," she said, picking up the collar. "Turn around." He turned around. She attached the collar, which fanned out eighteen inches all around his neck.

"How am I supposed to eat, or drink, or dance?"

"Very carefully."

"This is so embarrassing."

"Hey, look on the bright side. You don't have to wear a codpiece."

He looked down at the baggy costume. No codpiece required.

"Now scoot, so I can change."

He reached for the doorknob. "Be sure and lock the door."

"Yes, Daddy."

A flash of red caught Raoul's eye as he left Christine's room. He turned to look just as billowing red fabric disappeared around the corner at the end of the hallway.

BOTH THE BALLROOM and great room were filled with opera stars, patrons, and supporters, and various others willing to donate to charity in order to rub shoulders with the rich and famous. The costumes and masks were part of the fun and made it easy to engage in conduct one might not otherwise dare.

Raoul made his way through the crush of people in the ballroom, searching everywhere for Christine, looking at everyone who was the right size and shape. He glanced down at his own costume and decided shape would not be a good indicator.

"Carlos," Raoul said, tapping him on the shoulder.

Carlos spun around, balancing a tray of drinks. He was dressed in starched waiter whites and a white eye mask.

"Drink, sir?"

"It's me, Raoul."

Carlos stared and shook his head. "Oh, man, and my phone's in the kitchen. I have got to have a picture. This is so going on the Internet."

"Up yours."

"Does this mean Christine is available?"

"Huh?"

"Well, you've obviously switched sides."

"Very funny. Have you seen her?"

"I don't know. What's she going as?"

"She wouldn't tell me."

"Well, good luck. I've got to get back to work. Do you want a drink or not?"

Raoul fingered the collar. "How the hell am I supposed to drink wearing this thing?"

Carlos laughed, turned, and walked away.

Raoul continued searching, to no avail. He was, however, drawn to a most unusual sight, a man dressed in a flowing red gown with an enormous red hat, complete with red feathers. Even his shoes were red. The man turned before Raoul could get a good look at his face, or at least his mask. Raoul shook his head and muttered to himself, "What a freak show."

"Hey, gay snowman."

Raoul turned. Frankie wore a train conductor's uniform, and a black mask. He snapped a picture with his cell phone.

"For Carlos. Do you two have something going on?"

"Christine made me wear it."

Frankie laughed.

"Have you seen her?" Raoul asked.

"No. I don't know what she's wearing."

"Me either."

"We'll find her."

"Where's Johnston?" Raoul asked.

"Around here somewhere. He's dressed as Faust."

"I'm worried about Christine."

"We all are."

"I think something is going on."

"Like what?" Frankie asked.

"When she was painting my face she kissed me, almost knocked my teeth out, tongue down my throat, the whole nine yards."

"That's a good thing, right?"

"Yeah, but it was something she said."

"Okay, I give. What did she say?"

"Life is uncertain. Find happiness when you can."

"Whoa. What the hell does that mean?"

"I don't know, but last night she wanted to do it, have sex."

"No shit?" Frankie asked.

"No shit."

"So, you scored?"

"No, we didn't do it. I wouldn't."

"You turned down sex with a hot girl, with Christine?" Frankie asked, surprised.

"Yes. Something was wrong. Why did she get drunk and then suddenly want to have sex the next night, in a motel?"

"With you, of all people."

"I think it has to do with Erik. I'm not sure she's being straight with me, with us."

"Surely he won't try anything here, with all these people around."

"Do we have enough security?"

"They're swarming around outside, and there are a couple of undercover guys inside."

"Undercover?"

"They're dressed as SWAT team, with black hoods over their face and everything."

Raoul nodded. "Clever."

"I thought so. Their guns are real, of course."

"Of course."

"Let's split up and see if we can find her."

They split up. Raoul soon encountered the man in red again, turning toward him. He wore the same skull mask Raoul had seen in Tucumcari and Lubbock.

Raoul rushed forward but was caught up in the crush of costumed merrymakers and the man in red slipped away. Raoul scanned the crowd, but there was no sign of him. He felt a touch on his arm and turned. It was a girl with short black hair dressed as a black domino. She wore a black beret and a black eye mask. The costume itself was Spandex and looked like a second skin. It left little to the imagination.

The girl took his hand and led him away. He willingly followed, certain it was Christine, and he frequently turned to look for the man in red, now lost in the crowd. They hurried into the great room and up the stairs. He glanced over his shoulder and saw the man in red in pursuit.

"Wait," he said.

"No," she whispered. "We have to hurry."

They rushed down the hallway and into Frankie's room. Raoul tried to get another look at the man in red, but she closed the door and stood against it.

"It's him," Raoul said.

"Him who?" Christine asked.

"He was following us, in Tucumcari and Lubbock."

"You're imagining things."

"No, I have to stop him."

"Stop him from what?" she asked

"From hurting you."

"Why would he want to hurt me?"

"It's Erik."

"What?" She was stunned. "What makes you think it's Erik?"

"The painting."

"What painting?"

"Of you and Connie on the beach in Saint-Tropez."

"It disappeared," she said. "Nobody knows what happened to it."

"I saw it."

"Where?"

"In the little cottage."

"When?"

"When I went to Santa Monica, right after you left for Santa Fe."

"I don't know what you're talking about."

"And the ring," he said.

"What ring?"

"The wedding ring. You were wearing it, the night I heard you scream and came to your room."

"It was my mother's. I wear it sometimes."

"Your dad pawned their wedding rings for the money to get you to Los Angeles."

"Who told you that?"

"You did, when we were kids."

She didn't speak.

"Are you married to him?" he asked.

"No, of course not."

"Engaged?"

"No."

"Then what?"

"I can't tell you."

"How long have you been seeing him?"

"I haven't."

"Christine, stop lying."

"I'm not lying."

"Mrs. Valerius said she saw the Angel of Music in the garden. I think she was talking about Erik."

"She has Alzheimer's. Some days she didn't even know who I was."

"You never saw him in Santa Monica?"

"No. I swear. He just showed up here the night before we went to Lubbock."

"That's why you screamed?"

"Yes."

"Why didn't you tell me it was him?"

She didn't answer.

"What does he want?"

"I can't tell you."

"This is insane. I'm going after him." He tried to push her aside, but she wouldn't budge.

He reached for the doorknob, but she blocked him.

"Please, Raoul. Don't go after him."

"Why? Are you in love with him?"

She slapped him, stunning him long enough for her to slip through the door. He tried to chase her down the hallway, but unlike his, her costume offered no impediment to rapid movement. By the time he reached the stairway she had disappeared.

Raoul pushed his way through the crowd until he found Carlos.

"Erik is here. He's wearing all red, with a hat, cape, feathers, and a skull mask."

"Red Death. I saw that dude."

"I think Christine is with him. She's wearing a skin-tight black body suit, like Catwoman, with white spots on the front. Black wig."

"Yeah. I saw her earlier, smoking hot. I didn't realize it was her."

"Find Frankie."

"What about security?"

"Them too."

Carlos dumped his tray of drinks on a table, stood on a chair and scanned the room. Raoul set off in search of Christine.

Carlos couldn't find Red Death, but he spotted Frankie and waved to get his attention.

"Call security," Carlos said as soon as he hooked up with Frankie.

Frankie dialed his phone.

"Erik is Red Death," Carlos said. "Raoul thinks Christine is with him."

"How is she dressed?"

"The Black Domino, skin-tight body suit."

"Wow. That's Christine?"

"Yeah, you can feel guilty later for ogling her. Let's roll."

19

RED DEATH

RED DEATH WAITED until a security guard turned and trudged off in the other direction, and then scurried across the yard to the stables, his cape billowing up as he ran. He checked to make sure he had not been seen, and then reached for the door to the stable.

But he had been seen, by Raoul, searching around the pool. Raoul quickly whipped out his phone and dialed.

Red Death stepped through the stable door and closed it behind him. He looked around.

"It's not a trap," Christine said.

Erik's eyes quickly turned in the direction of her voice. She moved slightly, and the white spots caught a sliver of light.

"Did you have to wear that?" Erik asked.

She stepped out of the shadows. "You didn't give me any instructions on what to wear. I had already picked this out. Don't you like it?"

"All the men were watching your every move. You may as well have been wearing body paint."

"I could take it off. Is that what you want?"

"Did you take it off for Raoul?"

"Yes."

"Did you fuck him in that cheap motel?"

"Yes, and it was wonderful."

He slapped her. She screamed.

Raoul, searching outside, heard the scream. "Christine!" he shouted.

Carlos arrived first, leaping over a short fence around the pool. Frankie rushed out the back door of the main house.

"Christine!" Raoul shouted again, as Erik, with a death grip on Christine's arm, dragged her, stumbling, from the stable.

Raoul rushed forward and stopped cold.

Erik had a knife at Christine's throat.

"Christine! Are you okay?" Raoul asked calmly.

Christine nodded weakly.

Carlos and Frankie closed in, now joined by several security guards, uniformed deputies, and two SWAT guys.

Erik backed away, turning his head frequently to track his opponents.

"Back off! Or she dies."

"No! Let her go."

"Erik!" Johnston shouted, "Is that you?"

"Go away. Everyone, go away."

The circle tightened. The deputies and SWAT team, guns drawn, motioned for everyone else to back away as they inched closer.

"We have snipers on the balcony," the chief deputy said. "Let the girl go."

"No. She's mine. If I can't have her, no one will."

Erik spun Christine around so everyone could see the knife.

"Erik, no!" Johnston said. "We can work this out. I know you care about her. We all do. Don't hurt her."

Raoul continued to slowly approach. Erik backed away at the same speed, dragging Christine.

"Erik, please," Raoul said. "Take me and let her go."

"I'll deal with you later," Erik said, as he continued to back away.

The beam of one of the many flashlights on the scene crossed from Christine's face to Erik's, catching the blade of Erik's knife in the process.

Jim Bob, dressed as Don Quixote, surged forward with his lance. Erik, startled, backed away to avoid the tip of the lance. Jim Bob watched as Zoe, dressed in a vintage baseball uniform with letters spelling LUBBOCK HUBBERS sewn on the shirt, came up slowly behind Erik.

Jim Bob nodded. Zoe swung an aluminum baseball bat, whacking Erik on the side of his knee.

Erik screamed in pain, instinctively turning toward the source of the attack, jerking the knife away from Christine's throat.

Jim Bob poked Erik in the chest with his lance. It was plastic and did no damage, but it did distract him as Raoul rushed forward and tackled Christine, breaking Erik's death grip on her arm, taking her to the ground, shielding her with his body.

Now separated from his hostage, Erik turned to run.

Deputies took aim.

"No, don't shoot!" Johnston said. "He's my son."

"Hold your fire!" Carlos shouted as he and Frankie raced after Erik, who quickly disappeared into the night, favoring his injured leg, deputies and the SWAT team in hot pursuit.

A moment later, Erik, leaning forward, almost one with his roaring motorcycle, blasted through the yard in a blaze of red robes, scattering everyone.

Deputies raced for their cars.

Raoul rolled off Christine and pulled her up to a sitting position. "Are you okay?"

She nodded, crying.

Raoul turned to Jim Bob. "Are you insane? He could have cut her throat."

Jim Bob picked up Erik's knife from the ground and stabbed the palm of his hand. The tip of the blade curled up. "Aluminum bat beats rubber knife."

Zoe raised her bat. "Do not mess with a Texas girl."

"How did you know it was rubber?" Raoul asked.

"The flashlights," Jim Bob said. "Rubber doesn't reflect as much light as steel."

Raoul stood and helped Christine to her feet. "Are you sure you're okay?"

She nodded and threw her arms around his neck.

With the immediate threat abated, costumed guests streamed out into the yard, chatting excitedly, not wanting to miss anything else.

Franklin, dressed as a train engineer, and his wife, dressed as a Harvey Girl, broke through the pack.

Maria, dressed as a medieval noblewoman, took Johnston's arm. "So, it was Erik?"

Johnston nodded. "Yes, I'm afraid so."

"If there is anything I can do, just say the word."

"Christine!" Johnston suddenly turned and raced toward Christine. Maria followed.

"Christine, are you okay?" Johnston asked.

"I'm okay," Christine said, breaking away from Raoul to hug Johnston. "I'm so sorry."

"For what?"

"For not telling you."

"That's okay, honey. That's okay."

"We're going to need to take her statement," the chief deputy said.

"Can't it wait?" Johnston asked.

"Assault with a deadly weapon, kidnapping. Those are some serious charges. We need to get right on it."

"Here's the deadly weapon," Jim Bob said, handing him the knife. "It's rubber. I don't think he really wanted to hurt her."

Raoul put his arm around Christine. "Is there anything you could tell them tonight that might help find Erik?"

Christine shook her head.

"Do you know where he's staying?" Raoul asked.

Christine shook her head.

"Why don't you just let me talk to her tonight?" Johnston said. "You can take her statement tomorrow, if necessary. In the meantime, just try to find Erik."

"Deputy, I'll call the sheriff in the morning," Maria said. "I'm sure we can work everything out. For tonight, let's just call it a family matter. Erik is Mr. Caldwell's son."

"Do you have reason to believe anyone is in danger tonight?" the deputy asked Johnston.

"No, I don't think so. We have private security here, and you can leave a couple of deputies if you like, but I don't think he will come back tonight."

"What about you, Mr. Titshaw?" the deputy asked. "I understand this is your ranch."

"The ranch is owned by the family trust, and I agree, let us handle it as a family matter tonight, and reevaluate in the morning. Unless you can find Erik tonight, the far more pressing matter is the opera."

"The opera?"

"We are premiering a new opera soon at the opera house and threats have been made."

"You think it's the same guy?"

"I believe so, yes."

"Well, I'll call the sheriff at home and see what he wants to do."

"I'll send everyone home," Franklin said.

"No," Johnston said. "Go on with the party."

"Are you sure?" Maria asked.

"Yes. People will be gossiping anyway. We may as well let them do it here while they're all in one place. That way you and Franklin will be available to try to keep it under control."

Johnston turned to the deputy. "I'll talk to Christine. If anything comes up that I think you should know, I'll call."

JOHNSTON, JIM BOB, Zoe, Frankie, and Christine gathered around the kitchen table.

Raoul searched the cabinets.

"What do you need, Mr. Raoul?" Juanita asked.

"Paper towels. I want to get this crap off my face."

Juanita handed him a roll of paper towels and he started wiping his face.

"Well, I'd better get back to work," Carlos said. "Everybody is going to need a drink."

"No," Johnston said. "Stay here. They can get their own drinks."

"Yes sir," Carlos said, taking a seat.

Raoul sat beside Christine, and she took over the makeup removal.

She finished wiping Raoul's face after getting off most of the makeup and dropped the paper towel onto the table.

"Did he hurt you?" Johnston asked. "Are you okay?"

"My butt hurts."

"Sorry," Raoul said.

"That's okay."

Johnston looked confused.

"I kind of tackled her," Raoul said.

"Ah, yes. Did Erik do anything? Did he harm you in any way?"

"He slapped me. Is my face red?"

Raoul checked, touching her cheek with his fingers. "A little."

"He slapped you?" Johnston was angry. "Why?"

"I kind of pissed him off."

"How?"

"It's not important."

Carlos stood, retrieved a glass and a bottle of wine, and poured some for Christine, which brought a stern look from Johnston.

"She looks like she needs a drink," Carlos said. "Anybody else?"

Everybody but Zoe nodded their head. Carlos poured a round and opened another bottle.

Juanita moistened a dish towel and handed it to Christine, which she used on Raoul's face.

"Erik said he was in Santa Monica," Christine said. "He heard me singing songs from *Sangre de Cristo* and decided I should sing the opera instead of Carlotta."

"He showed up in Lubbock, while you were on the phone with Christine at the club," Frankie said to Zoe.

"How did he know you were in Lubbock?" Zoe asked.

"We think he put a GPS tracking app on Christine's phone," Frankie said.

"How could he do that?" Christine asked.

"He had lots of opportunity in Saint-Tropez, or Santa Fe, or even Santa Monica. He could have slipped into your room when you were asleep, or in the shower."

"Ew."

"Can you get rid of it, the tracking app?" Johnston asked.

"Probably," Frankie said, "or we could just take out the battery, but we decided to leave it on there for the time being, so he wouldn't know we're on to him."

"Good idea," Johnston said.

"I'll take your phone home with me tonight," Carlos said. "That should throw him for a loop. If he shows up, I'll kick his ass and then call the cops. Otherwise, I'll just try to locate the app and wait until we decide what to do."

Christine nodded. "Okay."

Carlos held out his hand.

"Duh. I don't have it on me." She held up her hands. "Look at me. Where would I put it?"

A round of laughter lightened the mood.

"Yeah, that's some costume," Carlos said. "I definitely noticed you."

"I do like the beret," Zoe said, "and the black hair."

"My phone's in my room," Christine said. "I'll get it before you go home."

"There aren't any naked selfies are there?" Carlos asked.

"Ew!" Christine said. "No."

"That's her friend, Tegan," Frankie said.

"Tegan, the Disney chick?" Carlos asked.

"That's the one," Frankie said and then leaned over and whispered. "I'll get you the link."

"Who is Tegan?" Johnston asked, now feeling even more left out.

"It's not important," Frankie said.

"Boys," Christine said, shaking her head.

"We should leave her phone here tonight," Jim Bob said.

"Why?" Carlos asked.

"Same as before. As long as Erik doesn't know we know about the tracking app, then we might be able to use it against him," Jim Bob said.

"How?" Christine asked.

"Well, for example, Frankie and Carlos could drive your phone to Los Angeles while you and Raoul go the other way."

"Erik follows the phone, and we catch him," Frankie said. "Works for me."

"Better still, I take the phone, let him follow me, and I become his worst nightmare," Jim Bob said.

"I kind of need my phone," Christine said.

"I'll get you a new one," Johnston said. "You should be on my plan anyway, if I have a plan. I don't really know. I'll call my accountant."

"Mine has a broken glass," Christine said. "It got smooshed."

"Okay," Johnston said. "Let's focus. I told the deputy I would call if there was anything I thought he should know. Christine, is there anything you can tell us that might help us find Erik?"

Christine looked at Raoul and then Johnston. "Not really."

"Why were you with him outside? Did he pull you out there?"

Christine paused, not wanting to admit what she was about to say. "I told him to meet me in the stable."

Zoe gasped.

"Why?" Johnston asked. "Why would you do that?"

"He came into my room a few nights ago, during the storm."

There was stunned silence.

"He said I was going to marry him," Christine continued. "He put a wedding ring on my finger."

"What?" Raoul said, surprised. "Surely you weren't going to, were you?"

"No. I don't know," she said, starting to cry again. "I don't know what I was going to do. I just didn't want him to hurt you."

"Hurt me?" Raoul asked.

"He said he would kill you if I didn't go away with him."

Everyone was stunned. She turned to Raoul. "I'm sorry I lied when you came to my room. I didn't want to marry him or go away with him, but I didn't know what to do. He said he would give me until the masked ball to decide. He found me in the ballroom, I don't know how, nobody else recognized me, and I told him I'd meet him in the stable. That was probably a stupid thing to do, but I thought I could reason with him."

"You can't reason with Erik," Frankie said.

Christine shrugged. "I didn't want to go away with him and didn't think he would kidnap me with all those people around, but I couldn't let him hurt you." She turned to Raoul.

"So, last night?"

Christine nodded. "I thought I would never see you again."

"What happened last night?" Johnston asked.

"It's nothing," Raoul said, trying to divert attention, and then turned to Christine. "You should have said something. I won't live in fear of Erik, and neither should you. I'll take you away, to Paris."

"I'm so sorry," Christine said, tears running down her face. "I didn't know what to do. I tried to fix it."

"That's okay," Raoul said. "It's not your fault. We'll handle it."

"Yes, definitely," Johnston said. "We can get you out of here tomorrow."

"No, no way. I am not leaving before Zoe's opera. You can hire bodyguards if you want, but I am not going to miss the premiere."

"Yes, of course, but Erik clearly knows which room you are in, so we'll need to move you to another room."

"She can stay with me," Raoul said.

"No, he might know where you are as well. We'll move you both to a new room."

"One room?" Christine asked.

"Yes. We'll have off-duty deputies available, but I want at least one of the boys with you twenty-four-seven. I guess it makes sense for Raoul to take the night shift, if that's okay with you."

"That's okay with me." She turned to Raoul. "But don't think you're getting lucky. You had your chance last night and you blew it."

20

NIGHT SHIFT

BEDROOMS WERE REASSIGNED. Carlos insisted on staying the night, just in case. He and Frankie decided to take Christine's old room. They were unwilling to share the bed, so they tossed a coin. Carlos lost and slept on the floor. There were rollaway beds available, but he didn't bother. Christine's phone, fully charged, lay in wait on the nightstand in case Erik decided to make another attempt. Both boys hoped he would, and they were prepared. Cowbells had been attached to both doors and they slept lightly, ready to pound him if he dared enter in search of Christine.

Private security officers and off-duty deputies patrolled outside the house and retreated to the porch when a light rain began falling.

Christine once again sat in Raoul's lap on the bed, facing him, and once again, he thoroughly enjoyed it.

"I feel like such an idiot," she said as she wiped the remaining grease paint from his face.

"Why?"

"Erik was outside my window in Santa Monica when I was singing songs from Zoe's opera. I sensed someone was out there, and, like an idiot, thought it was the Angel of Music."

"Your daddy told you the story all those years and you wanted to believe it."

She nodded. "Close your eyes." He closed his eyes and she smeared on cold cream.

"Kids believe what their parents tell them," he said. "Santa Claus, religion, politics, whatever."

"I guess." She wiped off the cold cream. "You can open your eyes."

He opened his eyes and they looked at each other for a moment.

"And then when he came into my room a couple of days ago, I first thought it was the Angel of Music."

"You were asleep. He woke you up. Maybe you thought you were dreaming."

"I did, for a minute. I should have known that it was somebody there, an actual person, not an angel. That's why I'm in idiot."

"You're not an idiot."

She wiped away the last of the cold cream. "You need some lip gloss."

"Guys don't wear lip gloss."

He watched as she smeared lip gloss onto her little finger and then pulled back as she held it up and showed it to him. He watched cautiously as she applied it liberally to her own lips. She grinned and then kissed him.

Teeth were brushed, faces washed, and they prepared for bed much the same as they had the previous night. Raoul was first into bed, wearing briefs, his normal sleep attire. He thought she had made it clear there would be no sex tonight and he certainly did not want to appear to be expecting it. His decision was confirmed when Christine came out of the bathroom wearing a T-shirt.

He watched as she stepped over to the balcony door and checked to be sure it was locked.

"I already checked it," Raoul said.

"Just double checking."

"Plus, he doesn't know which room we're in."

She pulled back the lace curtain on the door and peered outside. "I like the rain."

"Me too."

"It doesn't rain much in LA."

"I know."

"Only in the winter. Here it only rains in the summer."

She turned toward him. The lamp beside the bed was still on, casting a warm glow on her. He smiled.

"What?" she asked.

"You look beautiful."

"I'm wearing a T-shirt."

"I can see that. You still look beautiful."

She turned out the lamp, slid under the sheet and snuggled up close to him.

"About last night," she said.

"What about it?"

"Now I understand why we didn't do it."

"You do?" he asked.

"Yeah, I do, I think."

"Good, because I really wanted to."

"I know. You were right. There *was* something bothering me, obviously."

"Obviously. And I didn't want to take advantage."

"But you could have, easily, and you didn't, so that's good."

They cuddled for a moment.

"On the train, with Erik," she said.

"You already told me."

"I know, but I've been thinking about it."

"You have?"

"Yes, I have. I've been thinking about what kids are thinking about when they have sex for the first time."

"A lot of them probably aren't thinking."

"I know, right? They're just doing it. But if they do think about it, they're probably trying to be all rebellious, or curious, or everybody-else-is-doing-it, or whatever."

"True, for girls anyway. Boys just want to get laid."

She laughed. "Exactly. And that's probably okay, I guess. I mean everybody has to have a first time, so maybe everybody's first time should be all about the mechanics of it all, just get it over with, and then move on."

"So, is that what you want to do?"

"What?"

"Just do it and then move on?"

"No, of course not," she said. "Well, I mean I don't want to move on."

"You don't?"

"No, you might be a keeper."

"So, you want to do it?"

"Maybe, but not tonight."

"Good. I don't want to ask Carlos for another condom."

She laughed out loud. "Kiss me."

He kissed her.

"You can do better than that," she said.

He did better than that.

"You can use your hands," she said.

He used his hands. It went on for a couple of minutes and then she broke away.

"And that's the difference," she said.

"Okay, now I'm confused. What's the difference?"

"Erik only stopped when I slapped him and hit him and kicked him. You stop whenever I want."

"Isn't that the way it's supposed to be?"

"Yes, it is, for me anyway."

He leaned in for a kiss and then stopped millimeters short.

"What's wrong?" she asked.

"I don't want to push." He grinned.

She put her hand on his neck, pulled him in, and kissed him. They made out for a long time before coming up for air. Then they lay in each other's arms, both breathing heavily.

"Wow, it's really coming down," she said, looking at the balcony door.

"I like making out while it rains."

"Me too."

They cuddled and watched the rain pelting the balcony door and sliding down the glass.

"There's something I need to tell you," she said.

"What?"

"I haven't told you before because of all the crap that's been going on."

"What is it?" He was alarmed.

"*Je t'aime.*"

    21

JE T'AIME

Christine was asleep in Raoul's arms. He tilted his head so he could see her face, and then held his breath so he could hear her breathe. He watched as her chest rose and fell with each breath. The moment was shattered by a loud knock at the door.

"Yo, Romeo," Frankie shouted. "Rise and shine. Johnston wants to see Juliet before he leaves for work."

Christine awoke with a start, looking around the room before realizing she was safe, and in Raoul's arms.

"Give us a minute," Raoul said loudly. "We need to shower and stuff."

"Okay, but hurry."

Raoul started to roll over, but Christine put her hand on his chest. "Wait."

"What?"

"I could get used to this."

They kissed, for too long, before she finally broke away. "We'd better go see what Johnston wants."

Johnston and Frankie had already finished their breakfast and were having coffee when Christine and Raoul rushed into the dining room. Christine headed toward the kitchen. Carlos stopped her. "Sit down, I'll get it. What do you want to eat?"

"Whatever," Christine said.

Carlos pushed through the swinging door to the kitchen.

Frankie looked at her, grinning.

"What?" she asked.

"You look happy this morning."

She shrugged.

"Actually, you have a certain glow, and Raoul looks like the cat that ate the canary," Frankie said.

Christine looked at Raoul.

"I'm just in a good mood," he said.

Christine looked at Frankie. "*Cabrón.*"

Carlos laughed as he reentered the room bearing coffee.

"Why is everybody so interested in my sex life?" Christine asked.

"We're not," Johnston said. "Just be careful."

"Or non-sex life, actually."

"Whatever you say," Frankie said.

"We didn't do anything!" She looked at Raoul. "Back me up here, lover boy."

"We didn't do anything. Much."

She punched him on the arm.

"Cousins," Frankie said. "Remember? It's my job to tease you."

"Oh, yeah. I never had any cousins that I know about, but I'm a fast learner and I'll get you back."

"I can help you with that," Carlos said, pouring coffee.

"Okay, to the business at hand," Johnston said. "We made it through the night, and we have one more night before the premiere. After that, I agree with Raoul. We should get you out of town while we deal with Erik. I don't think it will be Paris, however."

"Why not?" Raoul asked.

"She's a minor. We'd have to get Mrs. Valerius to sign off on her leaving the country, and then persuade a notary that she was of sound mind."

"Oh, yeah. What about New York? We have an apartment there," Raoul said, looking at Christine. "Have you ever been to New York?"

She shook her head, clearly excited at the prospect.

"We could see some shows. You'll love it." He looked at Johnston. "If that's okay with you."

Johnston smiled and nodded.

Carlos served breakfast for Christine and Raoul and then took a seat at the table.

"It looks good," Christine said, eyeing her plate.

"Erik knows his way around New York," Frankie said. "His mom lives there. Better to not stay put. We'll ride the rails."

"We'll what?" Raoul asked.

"Ride the rails, like hobos. Well, actually we'll be on the *Estelline*, so we'll be riding in style."

"I like it," Johnston said. "Stay on the move."

"Sounds like fun," Christine said. "Can Carlos come?"

"I don't see why not," Johnston said.

"I have to work for a living," Carlos said.

"You can be our Abby," Christine said, "and Johnston can pay you."

"Your what?"

"Car attendant," Frankie said. "Cooking and cleaning and stuff."

"So, the same thing I do here, only on wheels?"

"Pretty much."

"I'm in," Carlos quickly said.

"Hold on," Johnston said. "I know you have to make a living, so we'll keep you on the payroll at the ranch, but you will be going as a friend, not an employee. Everyone can cook and clean, and they don't need a waiter."

"Works for me," Frankie said. "I know how to operate everything, and Christine can make tortillas. I don't know about Shaggy, though." He turned to Raoul, "What can you do?"

"Dishwasher," Carlos said. "I can teach you."

Christine laughed.

"We'll figure it out," Frankie said.

"Can we go to Florida?" Christine asked. "I'd like to see where Mrs. Valerius will be living and meet her sister."

"You can go anywhere Amtrak goes," Johnston said, "Florida, New York, Seattle. The *Coast Starlight* is a pretty impressive run."

"Party train!" Frankie said.

"Okay," Johnston said, pushing back from the table. "I'd better get to work. There is a lot going on today."

"Wait," Christine said between bites. "I'll go with you."

"Why?" Johnston asked.

"I want to see my friends and catch up on all the gossip."

"I don't think that's a good idea," Johnston said. "You need to stay here with the boys."

"We'll bring her out later," Frankie said.

"All right," Johnston said. "But be careful."

"You take care of La Carlotta. We'll take care of Cousin Christine."

———

RAOUL ANSWERED HIS phone while Christine, under the watchful eyes of Frankie and Carlos, chatted up her friends at the opera house. A deputy sheriff hovered nearby, scanning the area.

"My parents are at the airport," Raoul said when he hung up.

"Do you need to go get them?" Christine asked.

"No, I'm staying with you."

"I can go with you."

Raoul smiled. "That's okay. Frankie's dad is picking them up. You'll see them at the ranch later. You can't leave now anyway."

"Why not?"

Raoul pointed over her shoulder. Christine turned and saw Sue racing toward her, screaming. Christine immediately joined in the screaming and they happy danced, drawing the attention of everyone within earshot.

"I didn't know you were coming," Christine said.

"I'm here for Zoe's premiere," Sue said.

"Why didn't you call me?" Christine asked. She looked at Carlos. "Did Sue call me?"

Carlos shrugged. "You didn't have any messages. I checked."

"Why does he have your phone?"

"It's a long story. I'll tell you later."

"I didn't call. I wanted to surprise you. I came with Teegs. It was hell convincing my parents to let me come."

"Do you have tickets? It's sold out."

"Alfonso scored some tickets."

Christine turned and saw Tegan and Alfonso approaching, holding hands. Tegan broke away from Alfonso and hugged Christine.

"I thought you were in Vancouver," Christine said.

"We just wrapped. I hauled ass to LA, picked up my girl, who just got in from Seoul, and here we are."

"We're jetsetters," Sue said.

"Oh, sorry, guys, this is Tegan," Christine said. "Tegan, Raoul."

"The Frenchman?" Tegan asked.

Christine smiled and nodded. Tegan kissed Raoul on both cheeks. "That's how the French do it, right?"

"Works for me," Raoul said.

"Carlos," Christine said.

"Up here, mate," Tegan said as Carlos stared at her chest—she wore a small, low-cut, form-fitting T-shirt that emphasized her ample assets. "This one's not French."

"Mexican," Carlos said.

"Ooh, I'm surrounded by Latin lovers."

"And my cousin, Frankie."

"Cousin?" Sue said, startled.

"We have a lot to talk about," Christine said. "Where are you staying?"

"On Alfonso's couch."

"You should stay at the ranch," Christine said, turning to Frankie. "Is that okay?"

"Sure."

"Great," Sue said. "I won't have to listen to them going at it all night."

"You might as well get used to it," Alfonso said. "There'll be plenty of that in college."

"You guys can stay at the ranch too," Christine said, and again turned to Frankie. "Do we have enough room?"

"We may have to double up a few people, and get creative, but we have room."

Alfonso grinned. "That's okay. My roommate found a better place to stay for a couple of days."

"All I need is a bed and a bloke," Tegan said.

RAOUL AND FRANKIE floated on separate rafts in the pool at the ranch.

Christine snapped her fingers in front of Carlos. "Earth to Carlos."

"What?"

"You're staring."

"Oh, sorry. Do you want something to drink?"

"Uh, yeah, and you're sitting on the cooler."

He was indeed staring. Tegan lay face down on a lounge chair. Her bikini top was undone. Sue, in a far less revealing bikini, occupied the adjacent lounge chair.

Carlos stood and opened the cooler. Christine retrieved three diet sodas. "You were waiting for her to turn over, weren't you?"

"You got me."

"I thought Frankie gave you a link."

"He did, but pics on the net can't compare to a live look."

"Well, if she does turn over, *do not* take a picture with your cell phone, or my cell phone, especially mine."

"Don't worry. I know the drill, but I can still look." He put his finger against his temple. "Click. Click. And remember it forever."

"You should go to Saint-Tropez with Frankie. There are topless *chicas* all over the place."

"You went there, didn't you?"

Christine smiled and nodded.

Carlos looked at her chest.

Christine laughed. "Boys and boobs." She turned to go and rejoined Sue and Tegan, glancing over at Carlos who was still enraptured by the nearly naked Australian lass.

"Is Alfonso coming?" Christine asked.

"He's coming later," Tegan said. "He wanted to run through the opera again with that girl—"

"Hayley," Christine said.

"Yeah, her." Tegan sat up, barely holding on to her top. "I think I'll take a dip. Can I go topless?"

"I guess, but we might have to give Carlos CPR."

Tegan laughed. "Americans are so uptight." She glanced at Carlos, who quickly turned away. "Is there anyone else around, like old people that might be all offended?"

"Raoul's parents are taking a nap, jet lag and all, but they definitely wouldn't be offended. They have a house in Saint-Tropez."

"What about the copper? It's not like, illegal or something is it?"

"Nah, it's private property. You might as well give the cop a thrill. I'm sure it's been a pretty boring day for him."

"Right, then," Tegan said, whipping off her top. She stood, took a few steps, and dived in. The waves rocked the rafts, drawing the attention of Raoul and Frankie. Carlos stared, spellbound.

"Are you taking off your top?" Sue asked, clearly concerned.

"Not today," Christine said.

"Good. I am so not ready for that."

Christine laughed. "It's no big deal. Besides, we don't want to give the boys whiplash."

"Huh?" Sue asked and then thought about it. "Oh! I get it."

They both laughed and then watched the boys watching Tegan for a moment.

"Speaking of the cop," Sue said. "Wasn't there something you wanted to tell me?"

"Oh, yeah, that. Let's see. Erik has been stalking me for years. He came into my room at the ranch and told me I was going to marry him. He threatened to kill Raoul. He tried to kidnap me last night at the masked ball. He's trying to shut down Zoe's premiere tonight. Johnston's adopting me, so Frankie will be my cousin and Erik will be my brother."

Sue's mouth hung open, unable to form words.

"We went on a road trip to Lubbock, took the Buddy Holley tour, and I got drunk on expensive wine in a cheap motel and barfed. Raoul washed it out of my hair. Oh, and I slept with him last night, and the night before. We didn't do it. We just slept together. Well, we almost did it. I was willing, but he wasn't, which is a good thing. More about that later. We did a lot of other stuff, though, and it was really fun."

Sue stared, shell-shocked.

"Did you bring your violin?"

Sue nodded.

"I need to talk to Carlos. Make a list of questions and I'll be right back."

THERE WAS NO RAIN in the forecast for another twenty-four hours, so Frankie's mom decided a casual buffet by the pool would be better than something more formal in the dining room. The weather was beautiful as the sun dipped toward the Jemez Mountains. The air was still fresh from last night's rain.

Johnston arrived late, having spent a hectic day at the office, and went directly to the pool, where Juanita and Carlos were putting the finishing touches on the buffet.

"I invited Maria to join us," Johnston said, "but she was having dinner with the governor."

"Maria?" Christine asked. "Is there something going on there I should know about? Am I getting a new mom also?"

Johnston laughed. "No, I doubt it. But she is a wealthy widow and an excellent dinner date, or any kind of date, I suppose."

"You should invite her to Saint-Tropez."

"Maybe I will," Johnston said, smiling. He looked around at the guests, the Titshaws, the Chagnys, Jim Bob and Zoe, Raoul and Christine, Frankie and Meg, Alfonso and Tegan. "Boy, girl, boy, girl. Well, Sue, I guess you'll be my date tonight."

"Woo-hoo," Sue said, falling in with him at the buffet. "I guess it's okay now that you're not the headmaster."

The guests filled their plates and took their seats.

"How did you talk your parents into letting you come?" Johnston asked Sue. "As I recall from the conservatory, they were pretty strict."

"I threatened to give up the violin," Sue said.

"Seriously?" Johnston asked.

"I seriously told them that, but I would never give up the violin, or my horn."

"Do you plan to continue with music in college?"

"I'll always be involved with music, but I'm going to major in something that pays." She looked around. "I could get used to this."

Johnston smiled. "I have no doubt you will excel in whatever field you choose."

"How is your opera?" Christine asked Zoe.

"It's looking good."

Jim Bob rapped his knuckles on the table. "Knock on wood."

"Any word from the Ghost, or I guess I should say Erik?" Christine asked.

"Not a peep," Johnston said. "What about here?"

"*Nada*," Christine said. "I hope it stays that way."

Dinner conversation turned to more pleasant subjects and laughter abounded. Christine was happy and content, and Raoul was quite attentive. Alfonso and Tegan were like teenagers in love. Frankie and Meg were more like an old married couple.

After dinner Christine insisted on helping Carlos bus the table and then she sent him for his guitar. He began playing while Christine and Juanita finished clearing dishes.

"Will you be singing for us this evening?" Franklin asked as Christine picked up his plate.

"Yes sir. I believe I will."

"Excellent."

Carlos strummed his guitar, doing instrumentals, until Christine returned and joined him. Everyone waited in anticipation.

"I'd like to sing a song for you."

There was loud applause.

"Just one, but it's a pretty special song, or at least I think it is."

She looked directly at Raoul for a moment.

"There are a lot of couples here." Christine looked at Sue. "Sorry, Sue, someday soon you'll find a boy."

"That's okay," Sue said, grabbing Johnston's arm. "I've recently become interested in older men."

Johnston feigned embarrassment while the others laughed.

"What about me?" Carlos asked, still strumming.

"I'm guessing you get plenty," Christine said.

The dinner guests roared with laughter. Carlos smiled and nodded.

Christine kissed Carlos on the cheek and whispered, "Hit it, lover boy."

He began playing. She sang "Je t'aime" as she had never sung it before, filled with passion, her French perfect, looking mostly at Raoul, but glancing around to see lots of kissing and more than a few tears. Sue swooned as Johnston planted a kiss on her cheek. It bothered Raoul not at all that everyone else was kissing. He knew his would come later.

At the end of the song everyone jumped to their feet, applauding loudly. There were several shouts of "Brava! Brava!"

Christine curtsied and then rushed into Raoul's arms, kissing him passionately, tears streaming down her face. *"Je t'aime,"* she said between kisses.

"Je t'aime," Raoul responded.

"Wow," Tegan said. "The girl can sing."

"Do you sing?" Johnston asked.

"I thought I did until I heard her sing."

22

TAILGATING

Christine and Sue scrambled off the porch as Alfonso and Tegan pulled up in front of the ranch house. The girls were dressed almost identically, bikini tops and cutoffs, as if there were some sort of unspoken dress code. Alfonso glanced up at the sky as he stepped out of his car. "I don't think you're going to get much sun today."

"That's okay," Christine said. "The boys are putting us to work."

"Doing what?" Tegan asked.

"Helping set up the tailgate party."

"Tailgate party?" Tegan asked. "Like at American football games?"

"Exactly. Only at the opera it's gourmet food and fine wine instead of burgers and beer."

"Works for me." Tegan turned to Alfonso. "Can we go?"

"The cast and crew will have our own tailgate party out behind the opera house. Then we'll do a run-through and kick back for a while before show-time. You can probably make them both."

"Great."

"I wish I could go to the crew party," Christine said.

"Why can't you?" Alfonso said. "You're crew."

"Well, according to Cousin Frankie, I now have family responsibilities. That includes being hostess at the tailgate party, although his mom will prob-ably handle most of it."

"Well, I'd better get out to the opera house," Alfonso said.

Everyone turned toward the rumbling sound of a large diesel engine. A huge RV, the size of a bus, driven by Frankie, crawled around the corner of the house as Carlos spotted for him.

"What's that for?" Christine asked as Frankie stepped off the RV.

"The tailgate party."

"It wasn't there when we went to the opera last time."

"Dad just got it when I started to USC. He had his eye on one for a few years, so tailgating at the football games was his excuse."

"Nice ride," Alfonso said.

"Dad likes to go first class."

"Prevost," Alfonso said, reading the name from the front of the RV. "That's what the rock stars use for tour buses."

Frankie grinned and nodded. The girls piled on, followed by the boys.

"Wow," Christine said. "This is Uncle Franklin's?"

"Yes," Frankie said.

"Party bus!" the girls shouted in unison.

"That's actually what it is," Frankie said. "Dad prefers the *Estelline* for road trips. This is set up for partying instead of sleeping. It's in LA most of the time, but we bring it up here for the season."

"Party later," Carlos said. "We've got shit to haul. Let's get a move on."

"Okay, I'm out," Alfonso said, stepping off the bus. "See you guys later. Maybe I can slip out and make an appearance at your tailgate party." He stepped back and looked at the RV. "You won't be hard to spot."

Alfonso left and the others began loading up, under the watchful eyes of two uniformed deputies and one mysterious young woman with long blonde hair dressed in jeans and a windbreaker. They were aided by Julio, an occasional employee at the ranch. There were lots of folding tables and chairs, coolers, and boxes and boxes of things that seemed very important to Juanita as she fretted over placement of everything.

They filled Frankie's pickup, the back of the Suburban, and the jockey boxes on the Prevost. Carlos fetched the old pickup and they filled it as well.

"We'll get the food and booze later," Carlos said.

"There's more?" Christine asked.

"Oh, yeah. Madama is sending over her cook to help Juanita rustle up the grub."

"Madama?" Christine asked.

"Maria Josefina Álvarez de Garcia. You met her at the dinner for the board the other night. She's kind of the queen bee around Santa Fe, and chairman of the board of the opera."

"Doesn't she have her own tailgate party?"

"She used to," Frankie said, "but not so much since her husband died. She's throwing in with us on this one. It will be sort of the official tailgate party, lots of VIPs and celebrities."

"And Tegan," Sue said. "We're bringing our own celebrity."

"Hey, I'm just an Aussie girl from the Blue Mountains," Tegan said. "And I helped load all this crap."

"Let's roll," Franklin said. "We have to get everything set up and get back in time for the girls to get ready, which will probably take what, three, four hours?"

"I don't even take that long for a film," Tegan said. "Look at us. Do we look like we need a lot of prep work?"

The boys looked, and then shook their heads.

Tegan looked up at the parting clouds. "We may even have time for a dip, if you blokes will get your arses in gear."

Christine moved toward the old pickup and motioned to Sue and Tegan. "Come on. You guys can ride with me."

"Whoa," Raoul said. "You ladies should probably ride on the bus."

"Why? I know how to drive. We're not children."

"Erik," Raoul said.

"You think he's going to snatch me out of the pickup on the way to the opera house?"

"We just want you to be safe," Frankie said.

"So, who's going to drive my truck?" Christine asked.

"This is your truck?" Sue asked.

"My work truck," Christine said. Sue was still confused.

"I'll drive it," Carlos said. "Julio can drive the other truck and Raoul can drive the Suburban."

All three girls stood shoulder to shoulder, arms crossed, giving them that look.

"I'm driving my truck," Christine said firmly.

"I'll ride with the *chicas*," Julio said, climbing into the back of the old pickup.

"Okay," Frankie said. "We'll convoy. Christine, you follow me in the Prevost, then Carlos and a deputy in my truck, and then Raoul in the Suburban. Everybody stays together. If you get cut off at a light, I'll pull over and wait for you."

As the convoy pulled slowly out of the ranch Christine noticed that the young blonde woman was riding with Carlos and the deputy was nowhere to be seen.

"You can drive a stick?" Sue asked, moving her knee so Christine could shift gears.

"I can now. Frankie taught me."

"I drive a stick back home," Tegan said, "but it would be really weird shifting with my right hand."

Sue looked confused.

"They drive on the wrong side of the road," Christine said.

"It's not the wrong side," Tegan said. "It's the other side."

Tegan shifted Sue's right knee. Sue squealed and pushed her hand away. Christine grabbed Sue's left knee and she squealed again.

"This is great for dates. You can sit in the middle, right next to your boy-thing."

"Oh, cool," Sue said as she moved closer to Christine. "Or it will be, if I ever get a boy-thing."

"It's definitely cool. I went on a date in it with Raoul."

"Yeah, trucks are great for dates," Tegan said, looking over her shoulder, "especially if you bring along a mattress."

Christine blushed and covered her face.

"Oh, no you didn't," Sue said.

Christine nodded.

"You are so bad," Sue said.

"We didn't really do anything. We just parked on a dirt road and made out."

"We always did things when we parked," Tegan said, grinning. She leaned out the window. "You okay back there, Julio?"

Julio waved.

Christine was too busy laughing and giggling with the girls to notice the motorcycle coming up on the left.

Carlos noticed, tracking it in his mirror. "Heads up," he said. "This may be him. Motorcycle coming up on the left."

The young blonde woman in the passenger seat ducked her head. The deputy, lying down in the back seat, reached for his walkie-talkie, but remained hunkered down.

Erik, on the motorcycle, quickly passed the truck. His head was down. He didn't look at Carlos, but Carlos looked at him. Erik wore the skull mask and a hoodie.

"That's him," Carlos said.

"Get the license number," the deputy said, sitting up and pushing the transmit button on his walkie-talkie.

Erik pulled alongside Christine's truck and looked at her. She saw him, screamed, and instinctively hit the brakes just as Carlos swerved around her and punched it.

Erik did a wheelie and blasted off through traffic, Carlos in hot pursuit. Frankie immediately pulled over and the rest of the convoy slowed to a halt. Within seconds sirens could be heard from multiple directions.

Julio leapt out of the truck and positioned himself beside the driver's door, eyes sweeping the scene, spoiling for a fight. Christine opened the door and stepped out, still shaken. Raoul rushed forward and swept her into his arms. Frankie and another deputy came running from the Prevost.

"Are you okay?" Raoul asked.

Christine nodded.

A sheriff's car pulled up behind the Suburban and a deputy jumped out.

"What is going on?" Sue asked.

"Erik put a GPS app on Christine's phone so he could track her," Frankie said. "We found it and left it there to see if he would follow us."

"So, this was a trap?"

"I guess you could say that."

"You used Christine as bait?"

"Not really," Frankie said. "Carlos has Christine's phone. We used that blonde girl riding with him as bait. She's a deputy sheriff."

"I wondered who she was," Christine said.

"I tried to get you ladies to ride with me in the Prevost."

The deputy listened to his walkie-talkie. "They lost him," he said.

"Shit," Frankie said.

"It's hard to follow a motorcycle through narrow streets and alleys," the deputy said, "especially in the summer when the town's crawling with tourists."

"Well, let's go set up the tailgate party," Christine said. "I'm not going to let Erik run my life."

"Will you at least ride in the RV with Frankie?" Raoul asked. "Julio can drive your truck."

Christine nodded.

"I'll follow you," the deputy said.

"What about Carlos?" Christine asked.

"He'll catch up," Frankie said.

Johnston was waiting as the convoy pulled into the parking lot at the opera house and he climbed aboard the Prevost as soon as Frankie opened the door.

"Are you all right?" Johnston asked, hugging Christine tightly.

"I'm fine. He just drove by. He didn't do anything."

"Yes, but he got too close."

"That's okay. I had my posse with me."

"Good." He hugged her again. "You should probably go back to the ranch. Take the guys with you. I'll get someone else to set up."

"No way. We're already here, and there's cops everywhere."

The entire mesa had been swarming with police and private security all morning. State troopers brought in K9s to sniff every nook and cranny. Since Erik knew about it and might have access, even the Prevost had been thoroughly searched before leaving the ranch.

A mobile command post had been set up in the staff parking lot. Once it was determined that the facility itself was secure attention would shift to observing everyone who entered. It had been decided that TSA-style searches would be a bit much, but everyone who entered would be under the watchful eyes of security.

"I guess you're right," Johnston said. "Just be careful."

"Okay, okay," Christine said. "Now get back to work. You have an opera to premiere."

"Yes ma'am." He kissed her on the forehead and headed for the opera house.

The Erik scare was soon forgotten as the kids went to work, while doing a lot of group singing, mostly in Spanish.

In addition to the large awning on the Prevost there was a tent covering the folding tables. The linen tablecloths would remain in the Prevost until just before the guests started arriving.

"Is this your good stuff?" Carlos asked as he and Raoul unpacked wine bottles.

"Yes, of course. Zoe was part of our family for years, so my dad insisted on bringing the very best."

"Well, then, I guess I won't pinch a bottle."

"At least you get to drink some," Frankie said. "My dad already laid down the law—no minors get any booze tonight. He said it's one thing at home, or the ranch, but not here."

"That's okay," Raoul said. "I already swiped a few bottles and stashed them in my room for later." He bumped fists with Frankie and looked at Carlos. "Stop by if you get a chance."

Christine tugged at a very heavy box. "Whoa," Carlos said. "Let me get that."

"What is it?"

"China. And we have to be very careful with it." He put the box on a table and opened it. Christine picked up a plate, looked at it, shrugged and handed it to Tegan.

"It's kind of plain," Tegan said, unimpressed.

"It's kind of rare," Frankie said. "It's Santa Fe Railway china."

"Is that good?" Tegan asked.

"Definitely. My great-great-grandfather started buying it up when passenger service on all the railroads began to decline. I don't know if he thought it would be worth something someday or if he was just sentimental about it."

"The plates don't match," Tegan said, picking up another.

"It's all Santa Fe, but different patterns, different trains, different times."

"It's pretty," Christine said.

"My mom found the stash in a barn on the ranch years ago and about had a heart attack."

"Why?"

"It's the real deal, not reproduction. She called an expert in New York, and he caught the next plane to Albuquerque. They spent several days cataloging it. He said it's the largest collection of Santa Fe Railway china in existence. It's worth a fortune."

"And they use it for tailgating?" Tegan asked. "What if one gets dropped?"

"Shit happens. My mom said we should use it so people could appreciate it rather than just keeping it in a box or a china cabinet. It's a big hit with the opera crowd, and they handle it with care. Everyone knows the story."

Carlos looked up at the gathering clouds. "Looks like another thunder boomer blowing in. Julio, you good?"

"I'm good," Julio said, checking one of the uprights on the tent. "If the wind gets too high, I'll strike the tent and wait it out."

"Well, we need to bounce and get these ladies cleaned up and looking respectable for the bigwigs."

Julio laughed. They looked pretty good to him, but he didn't dare say anything. Carlos was practically a member of the family, so he could get away with it.

"I'll come back with Juanita," Carlos said.

Frankie pulled a quarter out of his pocket. "Call it." He tossed the coin.

"Tails," Carlos said. "What are we flipping for?"

Frankie caught the coin and put it on the back of his hand. "Heads," he said, although he was the only one who saw it. "I'll take Sue. You get stuck with the Australian movie star."

"What the hell?" Tegan said.

"Alfonso and Meg are working tonight, so I'll escort Sue and Carlos will take you." Frankie said, and then looked at Christine. "Unless you want to upgrade."

"No, I'm good," Christine said, taking Raoul's arm. "This one will do."

"You want me to go to the opera?" Carlos asked.

"Johnston said you're supposed to stick with Christine," Frankie said. "You can't do that if she's in there and you're out here."

"I have to help Juanita."

"She's got it covered."

"I don't know, man."

"Hey, mate," Tegan said. "Plenty of blokes would give their left nut for a date with me."

Carlos laughed. "Well, if you put it that way. Do you think there will be paparazzi? That would be good for my street cred."

"I haven't seen any since I've been here, but you never know. If they don't show, we can take a selfie and I'll upload it to Instagram."

Carlos nodded. "That works."

"Do you have a tux?"

"I'm a waiter. Of course I have a tux. Are we going formal?"

"Pretty much," Frankie said. "We're sort of Zoe's official party for the premiere, so we thought we'd go all out." He looked at the girls. "You did bring fancy dresses, didn't you?"

"Yeah, we got the memo," Sue said.

"We'll be so hot nobody will be looking at the stage," Tegan said.

"I can't wait," Carlos said.

"Okay," Frankie said. "Christine and Raoul can ride with me and the deputy in the Suburban. Carlos will drive my truck. I guess you two girls can ride with him."

"What about my truck?" Christine asked.

"It stays here."

"Why?"

"We've used it for tailgating here as long as I can remember. It provides the titular tailgate."

"Oh, yeah. It was here the last time. I thought it looked familiar."

Lying prone in the scrub brush on a hill above, Erik watched through binoculars as the kids loaded up and headed down the narrow road toward the highway. When they were out of sight, he turned his attention to the opera house.

23

PRELUDE

THE FLOWERS AND PLANTS on the mesa glimmered with raindrops. The clouds had parted, and shafts of late afternoon sun raked the roof of The Santa Fe Opera House. Groundskeepers used brooms and squeegees to spread out rainwater standing in low spots on the concrete and pavement. Cars, shuttles, and charter buses streamed off the highway onto Opera Drive. There was tangible excitement in the air.

Although the K9s had finished their work and the uniformed police presence had mostly been withdrawn from public view, there was still a considerable amount of apprehension. Rumors of the Opera Ghost, even sightings, abounded. While people-watching was de rigueur, tonight it took on an entirely new dimension—nearly everyone was suspect. Few people knew that the Ghost was Johnston Caldwell's own son.

None of this had a negative effect on attendance, however. Santa Feans took fierce pride in their opera and Mrs. Giry was at wit's end trying to accommodate all the VIPs requesting, even demanding, tickets to a sold-out premiere of the new opera.

The parking lot was alive with tailgate parties of all sizes, from couples sitting in lawn chairs behind their small cars, to lavish spreads under tents. Gallons of wine, much of it quite expensive, would be consumed before the opera began. None of the spreads was more impressive than the Titshaw's. Daniel Senior had been one of the original patrons of the fledgling Santa Fe Opera and his progeny continued the tradition. They were particularly pleased to be serving exquisite wines from the Chagny vineyards in France, personally selected by the count and flown in for the occasion on his Gulfstream jet.

Hannah was no stranger to hosting the rich and famous, and Mona was happy to have her help. They kept a close eye on everything, although Juanita and crew clearly had the food under control, and the men were handling the wine.

After working the crowd, the young people had spontaneously congregated.

"O-M-G," Tegan said. She turned and surreptitiously pointed. "Is that who I think it is?"

"Yeah, probably so," Frankie said. "He lives in Santa Fe. His wife has a shop on the square."

"Do you know him?"

"I see him around town. He's been out to the ranch a time or two."

"Who is he?" Sue asked. "Somebody famous?"

"He is an acting god. I would kill to be in a film with him."

"I think he's retired."

"So, you'd play, like, his granddaughter or something?"

"I'd play his mistress," Tegan said, smiling.

Christine laughed. "You would."

"Okay, guys," Franklin said as he approached. "I've been in negotiations with Mrs. Giry. A lot of VIPs have been calling and just showing up, so we're swapping a lot of seats."

"Do we still get to go?" Sue asked.

"Oh, yes, definitely. But we'll be sitting on folding chairs on the concourse."

"Folding chairs?" Sue asked, not impressed.

"Actually, they're the best seats in the house," Frankie said. "We do it often when it's sold out." He glanced at Tegan's abundance of bare skin. "I hope you brought a jacket or sweater."

"Sure. Christine said it gets kind of chilly here at night."

Frankie looked up at the skies. "Looks like another thunderstorm is blowing in. That's okay, we have plenty of blankets in the Prevost."

"Blankets?" Tegan asked.

"You'll see," Christine said.

"The governor is here," Franklin said. "Excuse me."

The girls turned to look as Maria arrived at the party, accompanied by the governor and her husband. The state troopers escorting her joined the sheriff's deputies at the perimeter.

"Don't forget to eat something," Frankie said. "It's a party."

"I'm too nervous to eat," Christine said.

"You're not performing," Sue said. "Pig out."

"I know, but I'm nervous for Zoe."

"I'll go rustle up some grub for the cops," Carlos said.

"I guess they don't want any wine," Raoul said.

Carlos laughed. "Probably coffee."

It was perfect timing. A light rain started falling just as the operagoers began filing into the theater to the sounds of the orchestra tuning up.

The girls felt the cool breeze on their bare shoulders as Frankie led them to their seats. Tegan noticed that many of the well-dressed attendees not only had winter coats, but blankets. Apparently, Frankie knew the drill.

"These *are* good seats," Sue said as she picked up a blanket from her chair and sat down.

"Yes, they are," Frankie said. "It's hard to explain to someone who has never been here before—they think folding chairs mean a bad deal, so we give them our seats and take these."

"The only problem is there are no subtitles in the folding chairs," Carlos said. "But I speak Spanish, so I can hook you up."

"Good to know," Tegan said, taking her seat beside Carlos. "Okay, translate the title for me."

"*Sangre de Cristo*, literally translated is 'Blood of Christ.'"

"So there's blood? Good show."

"Actually, there is blood," Christine said, "and lots of flashes of red in the costumes."

"But the title of the opera comes from the name of the mountain range behind us," Carlos said, pointing over his shoulder. "In the winter, when the mountains are covered with snow, they have a red tinge to them."

"The blood of Christ," Tegan said.

"Exactly."

"Wow," Sue said. "There's no back wall on the stage."

"And no curtain," Christine said. "Pretty cool, huh?"

"Pretty cool."

"Especially for this opera," Christine said.

"Why is that?" Tegan asked.

"You'll see," Christine said, taking Raoul's hand. He leaned over and kissed her.

"The landscape is part of the opera," Carlos whispered to Tegan.

"Well, this is it," Raoul said.

"What?" Christine said.

"Zoe's big moment."

"Oh, yeah."

"I hope it goes well. She deserves it."

"I'd text her, but I don't want to get arrested," Christine said, glancing around at all the law enforcement.

"Arrested?" Tegan asked.

"No photos in the theater," Christine said.

"Where is Zoe?" Raoul asked.

"Down front I think," Christine said. "Or maybe backstage."

The stragglers took their seats. It was sold out, including the standing room at the back.

Christine leaned over to Raoul. "Thank you."

"For what?"

"Everything. I'm so happy."

The conductor raised his baton.

A hush fell over the theater.

The orchestra began playing the prelude. The stage was empty, the Jemez Mountains shrouded by clouds in the background.

Christine stared in awe, caught up in the music.

La Carlotta took the stage to thunderous applause. She wore a simple, bare-shouldered, off-white peasant dress, with a white sash around her waist. She raised her head and basked in the adulation.

And then she barfed.

The audience gasped.

"Oh, no!" Christine said.

La Carlotta threw up again, splattering all over the stage, even onto some of the musicians in the pit below.

The music stopped. Francisco rushed onto the stage, took Carlotta by the arm, and led her offstage.

The audience immediately began chattering. There was some scattered laughter.

"This is where a curtain would be a good thing," Sue said.

But there was none, so stagehands dressed as Indians bearing mops and buckets rushed onto the stage.

"What the hell?" Sue asked.

"Since there's no curtain, the stagehands dress in costume," Christine said, "so they can blend in."

Sue laughed. "Blend in? There's nobody else on stage."

"And they're mopping up puke," Tegan said. "This rocks."

Johnston stepped onto the stage, wearing a tuxedo, clearly not in costume. The audience fell silent.

"Ladies and gentlemen, as you can obviously see, we've had a bit of misfortune. Please remain in your seats and we will begin again in just a few moments."

"Hayley is going on," Christine said.

"The understudy?" Tegan asked.

"Yes. She's also a lot better for the role."

"So that's a good thing, right?"

"Yes, it is, but it's kind of a bad start for Zoe's opera. People paid money to see Carlotta, not the understudy."

"It happens," Frankie said. "They'll understand."

"Do you think your mom should go backstage?" Christine asked.

"Why?" Raoul asked.

"She's a doctor."

"She's a trauma surgeon. Carlotta just threw up. It's not like she got hit by a truck."

THE DIRECTOR STOPPED Johnston as he stepped off the stage. "We have a more serious problem."

"What could possibly be more serious than this?"

"Come with me."

Johnston followed the director into the women's dressing room. Hayley was bent over the toilet, throwing up. Alfonso held her hair back.

"What the hell?" Johnston said.

"Looks like food poisoning," the director said. "Paramedics are on the way."

"Is anyone else sick?"

"Not so far."

"Great."

"We'll have to cancel the show."

"Not yet," Johnston said, pulling out his cell phone and dialing.

"We don't have anyone to sing Sofia. There's no way we can go on without her. What do you suggest?"

Johnston hung up his phone. "No answer, obviously."

He walked briskly away with the director in pursuit. The director stopped as Johnston stepped out onto the stage. Once again, the chatter quickly ceased.

"Is Christine Daaé in the audience?" Johnston asked.

Christine stood up. "Present."

There was some laughter.

"Would you please come backstage?" Johnston said.

"Yes sir."

Raoul stood. "Do you want me to go with you?"

"No, that's okay," Christine said. "I'll just see what he wants and be right back."

Four thousand eyes watched as Christine headed backstage, followed by a deputy sheriff.

"What's going on?" Tegan asked.

"Erik may be pulling it off," Carlos said.

"Pulling what off?"

"Ladies and gentlemen," Johnston said loudly from the stage, regaining the audience's attention. "We are having some difficulties." He looked at his watch. "We will take a thirty-minute break and then I'll let you know if we will be able to go on with the show. The bars are open, and drinks are on the house."

There was a round of loud applause and then people jumped to their feet and headed for the bar.

Franklin, his wife, and the Chagnys stood. "Do you kids want to go to the club with us?" Franklin asked.

"No, we'll hang here," Frankie said.

"What club?" Tegan asked.

"There's a private club for donors. It's mostly old people. I want to stay here and see what happens."

"Cool."

"Is there anything we should do?" Raoul asked.

"Not really," Frankie said. "Mom and Dad will work the donors. Everyone else is hitting the bar." He looked at his phone. "Johnston's not answering his phone."

"What do you think they wanted with Christine?" Sue asked.

"Could be good, could be bad." Frankie looked around at the now mostly empty theater. "Do you guys want to go get a soda or something? We can't really go to the bar."

"Too crowded," Carlos said.

"What about the RV?" Tegan said. "We could pinch some wine, and it has its own loo."

"Nah, it was buttoned up before the opera started."

"Frankie."

Frankie turned around. It was Mrs. Giry, accompanied by a rather unassuming man in his forties. He had a small moustache and carried a fedora in his hand, with a Burberry trench coat draped over his arm.

"I need one of your seats," Mrs. Giry said.

"I'm afraid we don't have any extras."

"Actually, you do. Mr. Caldwell informs me that Christine will be remaining backstage."

"Wow. Why?"

"I'm not supposed to say."

"Okay. Well, then I guess we have an extra seat."

"This is Cedric Highsmith, from London," Mrs. Giry said.

Frankie shook hands with Cedric. "This is Raoul, Sue, Tegan, Carlos, and I'm Frankie."

"I'm sorry to intrude," Cedric said. "I wasn't planning on coming, but I just couldn't resist a new opera, and in one of my favorite houses, so I hopped on a plane. I was quite willing to stand in the back, but Madam Giry insisted on upgrading me. These are excellent seats."

"Well, I guess this will be your seat," Frankie said, pointing to Christine's empty chair.

Cedric sat first, and then the others joined him. "It's quite exciting, isn't it?"

"Yes, quite," Tegan said.

"Australian?" Cedric asked.

"You got that from two words? You must have quite an ear for accents."

"I do, actually, but my daughter watches you on the telly. It's such a lovely name, Tegan."

"Thank you. I like it."

"Quite common in Australia." Cedric pulled out a notebook, filled with notes. "So, what do we know about the understudy?"

"Hayley," Frankie said. "She's pretty good, actually. Physically she's better suited for the role, but the board thought La Carlotta would be a bigger draw."

"Yes, of course. That's opera—cast a middle-aged cow to play an ingénue."

Tegan stifled a giggle.

"You don't like Carlotta?" Frankie asked.

"On the contrary, she's superb," Cedric said. "I've attended many of her performances."

Frankie nodded, somewhat confused.

24

THE GHOST ON THE STAGE

A FEW OF THE cast and crew scurried about, trying to help, as paramedics attended to Carlotta and Hayley, but most just stood and waited, unsure of what to do in such a situation. Zoe and Jim Bob, clearly worried, stood beside Johnston and the director. Christine stared at Johnston, her mouth hanging open.

"You want me to what?" Christine asked.

"We want you to sing Sofia."

Christine looked around. "Am I being punked? Where's Frankie?"

"You are not being punked, whatever that is. Hayley is also sick."

"Oh, crap."

"She's lying down," Alfonso said as he stepped up. "Meg's with her, but she's definitely not going to be able to go on."

"Erik," Christine said.

"Almost certainly," Johnston said. "But we have two thousand people out there who paid good money to see this opera. Do we cancel it to spite him, and ruin Zoe's big night, or give him what he wants?"

"Don't ask me," Christine said. "You're the boss."

"But it's your decision. I can't force you to do it."

Christine looked at Zoe. "What do you think? It's your opera."

"I know you can sing it, but frankly I'm worried about the staging."

"Duh. I've seen like, one full rehearsal. I'd be bumping into the scenery."

"Obviously," the director said, clearly not fond of Johnston's plan. "We have to cancel."

"I can help you backstage when you're not on," Alfonso said, "and I can give you the cues."

"No, I'll do that," Francisco said, stepping forward.

"But you'll be on stage," Alfonso said.

"No, you will."

"Whoa," Johnston said. "Now I'm confused."

"I'm old enough to be her father. When it was Carlotta and me, it was no big deal. We're both old farts and people accept that, but there's just too big an age difference between me and this beautiful child. It would be cringe, as the kids would say."

"He's right," Jim Bob said. "I sang with her while Zoe was writing, and it was definitely cringe. There's some serious passion between those two, or there should be."

"You want Alfonso to go on in your place?" Johnston asked.

"Yes," Francisco said. "Think about it. Carlotta is a bigger star than I am. If people are already pissed off because she can't go on, then they won't even care if I go on or not. Let the kids do it. They are almost exactly the correct age for the roles, right Zoe?"

Zoe nodded. "Yes, they are."

Francisco looked at Christine. "What do you think, Christine? Would you rather kiss this old fossil or Alfonso?"

"Well, I've kissed him on stage before and it wasn't too cringe," Christine said.

Alfonso laughed. "I promise to not stick my tongue down your throat."

"And I promise to not kick you in the *cajones*," Christine said, bringing a bit of levity to the moment.

Christine looked around at everyone, gritted her teeth and nodded. "Okay, let's do this."

"You're the director," Johnston said. "What do you think?"

"Wardrobe!" the director shouted.

The wardrobe mistress stepped up.

"Can you make it work?" the director asked.

"Definitely not with Carlotta's wardrobe, but maybe with Hayley's. There may be a lot of safety pins. Hopefully there won't be any wardrobe malfunctions."

"Wardrobe malfunctions?" Christine said, now somewhat terrified.

Alfonso fingered Christine's hair.

"Where's hair?" the director asked.

"Right here," the hairdresser said.

"Can you make her hair dark?"

"It will take some time."

"We don't have any time."

"What about a wig?" Alfonso asked.

"Screw it," Johnston said. "She goes on blonde."

"She's supposed to be Mexican," the director said.

"Trust me," Johnston said, taking Christine into his arms and hugging her tightly. "Let the blonde girl sing."

FRANKIE CHECKED HIS cell phone. "Dad says they're taking bets in the club on whether the show will go on."

People began drifting back to their seats, many standing, talking, waiting, checking their watches.

Frankie's cell phone vibrated. He checked it again. "Son of a bitch!"

"What?" Raoul asked.

"Hayley is sick too."

"So, they're canceling?" Raoul asked, clearly disappointed.

"Christine is singing Sofia," Frankie said.

Sue screamed, attracting a lot of attention.

Cedric scanned his notes. "Who is Christine?"

"My BFF," Sue said.

"BFF?" Cedric asked.

"Best Friends Forever. We go to school together."

"University?"

"High school. Well, the Belen Conservatory of Music."

"A schoolgirl is singing the lead?"

"Looks like it," Frankie said.

"Can she do it?" Cedric asked. "Has she understudied the role?"

"She hasn't understudied, but she can do it," Frankie said. "She knows the composer and she sang all the songs while it was being written. I'm not so sure about the staging and blocking, though."

"How exciting," Cedric said, writing furiously. "What is Christine's last name?"

"Daaé," Raoul said. "D-A-A-E with an acute on the E."

Cedric wrote in his notebook. "And she knows the composer?" He flipped through pages.

"Zoe Hathaway," Raoul said. "She used to be my nanny, although I never liked calling her that. I always thought I was too old for a nanny."

"And you are?" Cedric asked.

"Raoul Chagny."

"Christine's boyfriend," Sue said.

"Chagny?" Cedric said. "You sound American."

"My mom's American. My dad's French."

"Comte de Chagny?"

"Yes."

"Oh, my," Cedric said as he wrote in his notebook.

"What?" Raoul asked.

"This is too good," Cedric said, writing furiously.

"What are you writing?" Raoul asked.

"Cedric?" Franklin asked as his group stepped up.

"Franklin," Cedric said. The men shook hands.

"I didn't know you were going to be here. I would have invited you to our tailgate party."

"I just got in. There was a problem with the shuttle. I grabbed a sandwich at the airport. But here I am. I made it just in time for the hilarious opening scene, and then Mrs. Giry found me a seat here. Is this your group?"

"Yes. You know my wife. This is Alain and Hannah Chagny."

"Comte," Cedric said, nodding his head as they shook hands. "I've just met your son. He tells me your nanny composed the opera."

"Yes," Hannah said, laughing. "But we never called her a nanny."

"So I'm told."

"This is my son, Franklin Junior," Franklin said.

"I seem to have stumbled into the best seat in the house."

"Cedric is an opera critic from London," Franklin said. "And a rather noted one at that."

"Oh, cool," Sue said. "In that case, you need to know how Christine and Raoul met, which kind of started this whole dealie."

Raoul tried to shush her, but Sue pressed on. "Raoul and his nanny, Zoe, were on the Santa Monica Pier one day after school. He was wearing his school uniform. He heard the most beautiful voice he had ever heard, singing, what was the song?"

"'Suo Gân,'" Raoul said.

"In Welsh?" Cedric asked.

"Of course," Raoul said.

"Anyway, it was Christine, who was homeless and busking with her dad," Sue said. "Her scarf blew away into the ocean and Raoul jumped off the pier to get it."

"Is this true?"

Raoul nodded.

"But can the girl sing opera?"

"She sings arias," Sue said. "We're about to find out if she can sing an entire opera."

"She sang 'Nessun Dorma' for her audition to the conservatory," Raoul said. "She was twelve at the time. I accompanied her on violin."

"'Nessun Dorma'?" Cedric was skeptical. "A twelve-year-old girl?"

"Grown men wept," Raoul said. "Including the headmaster of the conservatory at the time, Johnston Caldwell, now the manager of the Santa Fe Opera, who you just saw on stage."

"It got her into the conservatory," Sue said.

"She has the voice of an angel," Franklin said. "You will not be disappointed."

"That's an understatement," Carlos said. "She also sings in Spanish, which will come in handy tonight."

"Well, this promises to be a most interesting evening," Cedric said. "I cannot wait."

The theater filled rapidly as the final gong sounded and the orchestra tuned up again, not that they really needed it, but it seemed like the thing to do under the circumstances.

"Oh, Tegan," Franklin said. "I almost forgot. Alfonso is singing Alejandro."

Tegan and Sue covered their mouths, shrieked, and hugged.

"Who is Alfonso?" Cedric asked.

"Francisco's understudy," Franklin said.

"My guy," Tegan added.

"Christine and I went to school with him at the conservatory," Sue said.

"Is Francisco sick too?" Frankie asked.

"No," Franklin said. "But he said he was old enough to be Christine's father and thought Alfonso would be a better match. Actually, I think he was just covering his ass in case this whole thing is a disaster."

"A disaster?" Cedric asked.

"Just kidding," Franklin said. "It's going to be fantastic. And please don't write down what I just said."

"I'll hold it in abeyance until I see the opera," Cedric said, grinning.

Johnston once again stepped onto the stage. First the orchestra, then the audience fell silent.

"Thank you for bearing with us, ladies and gentlemen. Both La Carlotta and her understudy have fallen ill, leaving us, as you might imagine, in somewhat of a pickle." He waited for the murmuring to die down. "The Santa Fe Opera has a proud tradition of going on with the show."

It did indeed. When the original structure burned to the ground the show went on in a local gymnasium.

"Fortunately," Johnston continued, "we have with us today an extraordinary young lady, who is very near and dear to both me and the composer, and who is prepared to go on as Sofia. She knows the songs, but she has not had the benefit of rehearsal, so we ask you to bear with us."

There was more murmuring in the audience.

Johnston continued. "Francisco is also a bit under the weather—we suspect food poisoning—and his understudy will be going on as well." He waited for the audience to consider the latest bombshell. "I realize that many of you bought tickets expecting to hear both La Carlotta and Francisco tonight. The box office is open and fully staffed, ready to provide you with a full refund if you like, or to exchange your tickets for a future performance."

A few people stood to go.

"Personally, I believe that would be a mistake," Johnston said. "I have heard the girl sing. She is my former student at the Belen Conservatory of Music in Los Angeles."

The would-be deserters hesitated, and then took their seats.

Frankie leaned forward, looked both ways and then at his dad. "No one is leaving."

"Ladies and gentlemen, it is my great pleasure to introduce to the opera world, Miss Christine Daaé." Johnston nodded to the orchestra. "Maestro." He stepped off the stage.

The conductor raised his baton, but held it for a moment, waiting for the thunder after a bolt of lightning bisected the stage from the heavens into the Jemez Mountains.

The orchestra began playing the prelude, and all eyes were on the stage as Christine, wearing a simple, bare-shouldered, off-white peasant dress, with a white sash around her waist, appeared. Naturally, she wore it much better than did La Carlotta.

"You go girl!" Sue shouted, far too loudly, and then slapped her hand over her mouth.

Christine, obviously hearing Sue's shout, smiled and took a deep breath.

"Oh, my," Cedric said. "She's blonde, so very blonde."

"Just wait until the blonde girl sings," Sue said.

The blonde girl sang, and Cedric leaned forward, mesmerized.

Rain began falling, but no one noticed. All eyes were on Christine, in command of the stage. Her soaring highs were crystal clear. The audience was entranced. All eyes followed as she turned her head slowly toward a magnificent tenor voice.

Cedric was momentarily distracted by Sue and Tegan grabbing each other and silently screaming as Alfonso took the stage and then swept Christine into his arms.

As the opera continued it was clear that Christine had not rehearsed the staging, but Alfonso easily covered her mistakes, making it all look good. No one seemed to mind, however. It was a thing of beauty.

There was a thunderous standing ovation at intermission. People hesitated to leave lest they miss even a note. Finally, the call of nature won out and they flooded to the exits to dehydrate and rehydrate.

"We're going to run out to the club," Franklin said.

"To collect your bets?" Frankie asked.

Franklin laughed. "No, since I had inside knowledge it would not have been right to take bets, but I will not hesitate to poke fun at those who did and lost. Cedric, will you join us in the club?"

"No thanks. I'll be busy expanding my notes."

An usher, wearing the Santa Fe Opera's iconic serape, pushed through the crowd, scanning faces. All the young men in tuxedos looked very much the same to her.

"Are you Raoul?" the usher asked.

"No, I'm Frankie. This is Raoul."

"Could you come with me?" the usher asked.

"Where are we going?" Raoul asked.

"Backstage."

"Can we come?" Sue asked excitedly.

"I'm afraid not. It's pandemonium back there, but Christine asked for Raoul and Mr. Caldwell said it would be okay."

Raoul followed the usher as the other kids milled around, stretching their legs, and chatting.

Cedric kept his seat and put pen to paper.

"Does anyone need to pee?" Frankie asked. "You'd better go now, or you won't make it back in time. The lines will be long."

———

THE USHER STOPPED at the open dressing room door and held up her hand to Raoul. "Just a minute. She's changing."

"Raoul!" Christine shouted.

Raoul pushed past the usher and Christine leapt into his arms.

"Kiss me now before I go back into makeup."

He obliged, with vigor, as all the attendants stood and waited.

"Did I suck?" she asked.

"Suck? Hell, no."

"I couldn't really read the audience. I was too busy trying to not trip over my own feet. Alfie really saved my butt out there."

"You're killing it."

"Seriously?"

"Seriously. They love it. They love you. You're amazing. Sue about crapped her pants."

"I nearly lost it when she gave me a shout-out. That's so Sue."

"Tick-tock," the wardrobe mistress said, holding up an outfit.

Raoul stepped back as Christine slipped into the costume.

"I'm wearing Hayley's clothes. I hope I don't pop out."

"Yeah, me too."

"How's my Spanish? How would you know? You're French." She was clearly high on adrenalin.

"I need to touch you up," the makeup artist said, putting a bib around Christine's neck as the wardrobe mistress zipped up her back.

"One more kiss first," Christine said, putting her hand around Raoul's neck, pulling him in and planting a wet, sloppy one on him.

"Okay, scoot. Kiss Sue for me, and Tegan. Tell her Alfie is making me hot."

"He's what?"

"Just kidding." Christine plopped down at the makeup table. "Not really." The makeup artist started work.

Christine looked in the mirror. Raoul had not moved. "Bounce!" Christine commanded.

Raoul turned to go.

"Oh, wait!" Christine said.

Raoul stopped and turned.

"*Je t'aime.*" she said.

"*Je t'aime.*"

———

THERE WAS NO PROBLEM, other than the long lines at the restrooms, in getting people back into their seats after intermission. On a night of surprises no one wanted to miss anything.

The other kids were standing at their seats when Raoul returned.

"How is she?" Sue asked.

"She's great." Raoul quickly kissed her. "That's from Christine," he said. "She heard your shout-out."

Sue covered her face. "I'm so embarrassed."

Then he kissed Tegan, full on the lips.

"Whoa, mate."

"That's also from Christine. She said your boy is making her hot."

"Yeah, they looked pretty cozy to me."

Cedric looked up from his notebook.

"So, how's it going so far?" Raoul asked.

"Quite nicely. The young girl is amazing."

"Yes, she is," Raoul said, smiling. "Amazing."

While the days are warm in Santa Fe during the summer, the evenings are cool, especially when a thunderstorm blows in and drops the temperature even more. The rain came hard and fast, whipped by the wind through the open sides of the opera house. It was all quite disconcerting to the uninitiated, but the regulars simply buttoned up their winter jackets, wrapped themselves in blankets, and hunkered down. This was not their first rodeo.

"Time to break out the blankets," Frankie said.

"Oh, good," Tegan said, picking up her blanket from under the chair. "Now I see what Christine meant."

Clearly aware of the protocol at the Santa Fe Opera, Cedric stood, put on his trench coat and hat, sat back down, and picked up his notebook.

Both the drama and tension were ratcheted up for the second half. Christine continued with the performance of a lifetime, and Alfonso held up his end, making everyone believe they were impoverished young lovers from northern New Mexico.

Raoul and Tegan, although fully aware that it was only acting, still flinched as Sofia and Alejandro kissed passionately.

Tears flowed as the finale approached and Alejandro died in Sofia's arms. Her white sash was now red with his blood.

As Sofia stood, holding the bloody sash toward the heavens, and began to sing the signature piece of the opera, Cedric was a blubbering mess, choking back tears.

Others had similar reactions, not only those in the audience, but cast and crew backstage, and the police on the perimeter. They might have known nothing about opera, but they knew this was something extraordinary.

The audience held their collective breath as Christine sang as if possessed. When she finished, she bowed her head, and waited for the applause that did not come.

Instead, there was a bolt of lightning behind the stage, far too close, brilliantly illuminating the stage and flooding Christine in backlight. The audience stared in awe as a black figure descended from above the stage. Since this was the first public performance of a new opera, most everyone assumed it was part of the show.

The Opera Ghost, wearing black jeans, a black hoodie, and a skull mask, swept down by rope from the rafters, dropping behind Christine.

The audience burst into applause, and then rose to their feet, cheering and clapping. "Brava! Brava!"

Unaware of the Ghost's presence behind her, Christine basked in the adulation, but only for an instant.

"Is that part of the opera?" Raoul asked.

"It's Erik!" Frankie said, surging out of the chair.

Christine screamed as the Ghost swept her into his arms and turned to run. Alfonso scrambled to his feet and gave chase. Jim Bob was next to act. From near the front of the theater, he leapt out of his seat, crawling and climbing over the orchestra to get onto the stage.

Raoul, Frankie, and Carlos immediately followed, but by the time they got onto the stage Christine was gone, swallowed up by the darkness.

The audience realized something was wrong, and the applause quickly died down, replaced by murmuring, as the boys, Jim Bob, Johnston, and much of the cast and crew, along with law enforcement officers, lined up at the back of the stage and stared helplessly into the black abyss.

25

THE LINE SHACK

While thunderstorms are common in northern New Mexico during the summer, they are usually brief, although sometimes intense. After the initial sound and fury, this one settled into a steady, sometimes driving rain that went on for hours. A scientists would say "water seeks its own level," but to most people water just runs downhill. That was exactly what it was doing tonight, and dragging mud, rocks, and vegetation along with it, seeking its own level in the gullies, smaller streams turning into larger ones, crashing down onto a small terrace on the side of a mountain in the Sangre de Cristo range. There it rose and pooled until it found a way to continue its journey down the mountain toward the reservoir below.

Sharing the terrace with the pooling rainwater was an old line shack, thoroughly soaked in the downpour. It was constructed with upright planks and wood shingles on the roof. Much of the wood was weathered by decades of sun, wind, rain, heat, and freezing temperatures, but some was relatively new.

There were two small windows, one on either side of a wooden door centered on the front side of the building. There was a pile of firewood next to the door, mostly fallen deadwood and kindling. Rough cedar posts held up the extended roof, creating a small porch. A horizontal crosspiece provided a hitching post. The windows were covered on the inside by fabric of some kind, but a hint of light crept through the windows and door as well as cracks between the planks. Smoke drifted through a stovepipe protruding from the roof.

Inside the shack, Erik, still wearing the skull mask and hoodie, pushed a small piece of wood into the potbellied stove. A hurricane lamp illuminated the small room. A large, lazy Labrador warmed himself on the floor by the stove.

Christine sat on a steel bed, much like an army bunk, single width, with a thin, bare mattress. Her dress, the same one she was wearing when snatched from the stage, was torn, wet and muddy. Her legs and bare feet were covered with mud and a bit of blood, some caked, some wet and dripping.

"I need to pee," Christine said.

Erik pointed at a bucket in the corner.

"You'll have to untie me," she said.

"I can't do that."

"How am I supposed to get my underwear down?"

"I can help you with that."

She glared at him. "That's okay. I'll hold it." Having just finished a grueling performance she was somewhat dehydrated but didn't want to admit it was just a ruse to get him to untie her.

"Suit yourself."

"I'm cold."

He pulled off his hoodie and put it around her bare shoulders.

"Are you going to take off your mask or does that make it easier to hide your cowardice?"

He stared at her for a moment and then slowly pulled off the mask. She gasped. When she had seen his face before it was mostly in darkness, but even the dim glow from the hurricane lamp was sufficient to reveal the full horridness of what had once been a very handsome young man.

"Does my face offend you?"

"You offend me."

"How do I offend you?"

"You kidnapped me."

"I arranged for you to sing Sofia at the premiere of Zoe's opera. You should thank me."

"Thank you? You poisoned Carlotta and Hayley."

"I did it for you."

"They could die."

"A small price to pay for your love."

"For my love? Are you insane?"

"I am insanely in love with you. In time, you will return that love."

"Not going to happen."

"Where is your ring?"

"What ring?"

"The wedding ring I gave you and told you to wear."

"Not on my finger, obviously."

"Why not?"

"Because I'm not your wife."

"You will be."

Christine opened her mouth to speak, but decided it was like arguing with a child.

She watched as he stepped over to the stove, picked up a kettle of water, poured it into a small pail and tested the temperature. He returned with the pail, a washcloth and towel.

Her mind flashed back to the night he washed her hair in the shower and wondered what he now had in mind. He dropped to his knees and began washing her feet.

"Your feet are bleeding."

"You dragged me through all kinds of crap to get here."

"Why weren't you wearing shoes?"

"Sofia was barefoot in the final scene, and somehow I just couldn't find the time to change *before you kidnapped me.*"

"I'm afraid the cuts will get infected. I don't have any peroxide."

"No problem. Just drop me off at the emergency room on your way out of town."

He continued washing her feet and legs but to her relief, never got above her knees.

"Where exactly are we?" she asked.

"In the mountains, the Sangre de Cristo Mountains, rather fittingly."

"Well, it's been great, but I think I'll go back to the ranch now."

"Oh, no, not on our wedding night."

She felt the fear shoot up her spine, but she dared not panic. She had been snatched off the stage in front of over two thousand people, including everyone she knew and loved, so someone had to be looking for her.

He had bound and blindfolded her for the trip, so she had no idea where they were, somewhere in the Sangre de Cristo Mountains, apparently. She thought the trip had not taken long, but she couldn't be sure—she was confused and frightened, perhaps even in shock.

That she knew her kidnapper did not lessen the severity of her predicament—indeed, knowing what she did only made it worse. He had frightened her during their encounter on the *Estelline*, and again in her room at the ranch, but now, tied up with little chance of escape, and no reason for him to restrain himself, she was terrified. She needed time.

"How was my performance?"

"Outstanding, of course."

"I thought it was better with Alfonso."

"How did that happen?"

"Don't you know? You poisoned Francisco too." She immediately wished she hadn't said that. She needed to carefully choose her words to keep his mind off their wedding night while not pissing him off.

"No, I didn't."

"It was Francisco's idea," she admitted. "He thought he was too old for me, and it would be creepy."

"He was probably right. Alfonso was better, but I didn't like the way he kissed you."

"It was just acting." She wasn't going to tell him about the other times she and Alfonso had kissed on stage, and she certainly wasn't going to admit that tonight she was particularly swept up in the passion.

Pretty much everyone gathered in the great room at the ranch, including Cedric, caught up in the confusion and bused home with the family. He had slept rather fitfully on the flight from London and had gone straight to the opera house with his luggage, so he craved sleep, but the journalist in him relished the opportunity to be at the center of activity. He sat quietly in the corner, watched, and listened.

Carlos quickly opened the bar.

"I should have been quicker," Alfonso said. "If only I could have grabbed his ankle or something."

"You were dead," Frankie said. "You couldn't have known. Hell, I saw dress rehearsal and it still took me by surprise. There's nothing you could have done."

"How did he get over the ledge?" Carlos said, fixing himself a drink. "That's a steep drop."

"Who knows?" Johnston said. "It all happened so fast."

Raoul paced, powerless.

Sue and Tegan huddled together in one large chair in front of the fireplace. Meg sat nearby.

Franklin tossed a log on the fire and then turned. "Oh, Cedric. I'm so sorry. We were supposed to drop you off at your hotel."

"That's quite all right. I didn't realize where we were going until we arrived."

"I'll get someone to drive you."

"I had just as soon stay awhile, if you don't mind. I feel like an interloper, but I am genuinely concerned about the girl."

"Of course. Actually, you might as well spend the night here."

"I don't want to impose."

"You wouldn't be imposing. We have plenty of room."

"In that case." Cedric shrugged.

"Come on. I'll buy you a drink."

They headed toward the bar.

"The girl's performance was astonishing," Cedric said as he bellied up to the bar alongside Franklin. "I've never seen anything like it."

"Yes, it was."

"I need to separate the events after and concentrate on my review of the opera and her performance, but the journalist in me cannot ignore the other."

Franklin nodded, not smiling.

"Word will spread quickly," Cedric said, "and others will be on the story soon."

"I understand."

"My review will be untouchable—I am a critic, after all—but I think you will be quite pleased. My paper, however, would be livid if I ignored the rest of the story and allowed them to be scooped by the competition."

"Do what you have to do."

Cedric checked his watch. "It's morning in London."

"I assume you are aware," Johnston said as he stepped up, "that the kidnapper is almost certainly my son."

"Yes, so I've heard, hence my quandary," Cedric said.

"Our most immediate concern is Christine's rapid and safe return," Johnston said.

"Hear, hear," Franklin said, raising his glass. The men, now joined by Jim Bob and Chagny, toasted.

Alfonso stepped up beside Raoul. "Shouldn't we be out looking for her or something?"

"We don't know where to look," Raoul said. "They could be anywhere."

"The cops searched the opera house grounds," Frankie said. "And they still have a lot of guys out there, in case they're hiding out somewhere, maybe in one of the buildings. Erik could very well have keys."

"Maybe we should go out there," Raoul said.

"No, we just need to put our heads together and figure out where he would go. We know him better than anybody."

"What about your train car?"

"Erik wouldn't take her there. He's not that crazy."

"Well, he kidnapped her in front of hundreds of people and lots of cops. He's definitely crazy."

"Let's roll."

CHRISTINE LAY ON her side, her shoulders in pain. Erik was engrossed in his cell phone. She wondered if he was demanding ransom or something even more diabolical.

"I can't feel my hands. Can't you at least untie me?"

"No." He didn't even look up from his phone.

"Are you afraid I'll beat you up?"

He chuckled. "You might try to run away."

"Where would I go? I wouldn't even know which way to run, and I don't have any shoes."

She knew the Sangre de Cristo Mountains were east of Santa Fe, the same side as the ranch. Unfortunately, it was dark, and she didn't know which side of the mountain they were on. She might be able to walk down the mountain right into Santa Fe, but what if they were on the other side? She had no idea what was there, if anything, or how far it might be to a town. Either way, he was bigger and stronger, and knew exactly where they were. She knew her chance of running away and escaping were almost nonexistent. Except for the scratches and bruises she was unhurt—hopefully the numbness in her hands was temporary—and people were certainly looking for her, so she put aside thoughts of running.

He stood, pocketed his cell phone, and pulled a large hunting knife from a scabbard on his belt. She had not noticed it before and resolved to take more notice of her surroundings. Anything could be important. He stepped over to the bed, but she felt no fear. Surely, he hadn't gone to such great lengths to just stab her to death in this shack. If he wanted her dead, he could have already accomplished it with much less trouble.

She rolled over and then felt the back of his fist against her bottom. He took her wrist in his other hand and cut the cable tie. She quickly rolled over on her back as he pulled away his hands. He tossed the cable tie onto the floor. She began rubbing her wrists and hands. The cable tie had cut deep, red grooves into her wrists.

He holstered the knife and pulled a chair up beside the bed. He took one of her hands and began massaging it, digging his thumb deeply into the inside of her wrist and lower arm, running it almost to her elbow. At first it felt strange as there was no sensation in her wrists and hands, but then wonderful as the feeling returned.

"Thank you," she said as he went to work on her other hand.

She watched as he worked. Under different circumstances it would have been a loving thing to do, enjoyable, even sensuous.

"Do you have any water?"

He nodded but didn't get out of the chair. He continued to hold her hand.

"Could I have some, please?"

He finally stood and stepped over to a crude cabinet. She glanced over at the bucket. She would eventually have to answer the call of nature and could not imagine anything more awkward. She thought about people trapped in small spaces. What did they do?

Erik returned and handed her a bottle of water. She opened it and took a sip.

"I thought you needed to pee," he said.

"Do you really expect me to pee in that bucket?"

"You could go outside."

"It's raining."

"Or pee your pants."

THE TRIP TO THE *Estelline* came up empty and when Raoul and Frankie returned to the ranch, they found the girls asleep on a sofa by the fireplace and most of the adults in the kitchen raiding the refrigerator and drinking coffee, spiked with brandy, no doubt.

Carlos, Alfonso, and Jim Bob stumbled into the kitchen, drenched, dirty and muddy.

"Where have you guys been?" Frankie asked.

"We decided to check the barns, stables, and outbuildings," Carlos said. "He was here before. We thought he might be right under our noses."

"Good idea," Frankie said.

"Obviously he wasn't on the *Estelline*," Jim Bob said.

Frankie shook his head.

"Any word from the cops?" Raoul asked.

"Nothing," Johnston said. "They really don't know where to look. They can't exactly search every building in Santa Fe."

"And they could be anywhere," Jim Bob said. "The opera house is right on the highway. They could be halfway to Mexico."

"So, they should be looking for two kids on a motorbike," Raoul said.

"I don't think so," Frankie said.

"Why not?" Raoul asked.

"It's kind of hard to carry a hostage on a bike."

"I guess you're right."

"What about the opera house?" Alfonso asked.

"The cops already searched it," Frankie said.

"They searched it thoroughly before the opera, with dogs and stuff, and Erik still managed to get in and hide," Alfonso said. "Maybe they never left. They just disappeared. Maybe they're still there. There are lots of places to hide."

"And Erik knows all of them," Frankie said, "but so do I. Let's do it."

"Beats sitting around here, waiting," Raoul said.

"I'll go with you," Johnston said. "I think I have enough keys, at least enough to get us into the key box."

CHRISTINE CHUGGED THE bottle of water. If she had to pee later, she would just have to deal with it, however creepy. Right now, she was dry as a bone. She put the cap on the empty bottle and handed it to Erik. He tossed it across the room.

"You should invest in a trash can," she said.

He sat beside her on the bed. "You know I love you."

She started breathing heavily as she weighed all possible responses before deciding silence would be best.

"I've always loved you." He lifted her left hand and rubbed his thumb over her ring finger. "You should be wearing your ring."

She didn't answer.

"I'll get you another one." He leaned over to kiss her, but she pushed him away.

"I'm not your wife. I will never be your wife."

She turned her head as he tried again to kiss her. He grabbed her by the chin and pulled her head. She resisted until she thought she would sprain her neck. Determined to not give him even the slightest satisfaction, she gritted her teeth and clinched her lips as he kissed her. He held his hand behind her neck, pulling her to him, but she continuously jerked her head around as much as possible, presenting him with a moving target.

He was too strong to push away using her hands, so she crossed them tightly at her chest to keep his roaming hand off her breasts.

She closed her eyes and tried to think of Raoul, and his gentle caresses, but could not. All she could think about was Erik's crude, repulsive groping. She knew he had the capacity to be gentle—he once was—but this was not the Erik she had known before. This was a monster.

She was momentarily relieved when he abandoned his attempt to grope her breasts, but she soon felt the same hand on her knee and then her thigh. She tried again to push it away, but he was much too strong. She thought of screaming, of crying, of pleading, but knew it would do no good. Then she thought of death, of how people talk about going toward the light. Her entire body went numb and there was a ringing in her ears. What she had been saving for her true love, Raoul, was about to be taken, stolen, ripped away by this beast.

His hand continued moving up her leg. She screamed. The dog leapt to his feet and barked, circled nervously, but did nothing to aid her. He finally lay back on the floor and watched as Erik continued with his conquest.

She leaned forward and tried to get off the bed, to run, but he grabbed her hair and pulled her onto her back. She fought her away into a sitting position, but he slapped her hard and pushed her back down. She put her hand on her stinging face, stunned.

She felt both his hands under her dress, ripping away her panties, tossing them across the room. He loomed over her, eyes wide, panting. She knew this was the end. She thought of Raoul. She could see his face, smiling, and saying, *"Je t'aime."*

He lifted her dress, leaving her utterly exposed. He unzipped his jeans.

"I'd rather die," she said as he stood over her, pulling his pants down.

She rolled over and kneed him in the groin. He hunched over in pain. She planted her feet on the floor and put her shoulder into him. He went down, unable to maintain his balance with his pants around his knees.

She bolted toward the door. She had no idea where she would go, or how long she would live, but she was truly ready to die rather than be raped by him.

She reached for the door, but he grabbed her ankle and pulled her onto the floor. The dog yelped and ran for cover.

She kicked furiously, but he dragged her across the floor and held her down until he was able to pull up his pants and get onto his feet. He stood, jerked her to her feet, dragged her across the room and pushed her face down onto the bed. He put his knee into the small of her back to hold her down while he picked up her sash, now red with fake blood. She had been holding it in the final scene of the opera and had clung to it all the way to the shack without even thinking about it. He used it to tie her hands behind her back.

Once again, she resigned herself to a fate worse than death. But he didn't touch her. He just sat in the chair and watched her as she lay there, helpless, and exposed.

After what seemed forever, he got out of the chair, put out the hurricane lamps and crawled onto the bed beside her. She felt the denim of his jeans against her bare skin.

"You'll come around," he said as he pulled a blanket up over them.

She was relieved. At least he had his pants on. Maybe he would sleep for a few hours, giving the cops a chance to find her before hell on earth started once again. Her thoughts raced as she lay there waiting for him to go to sleep. She was trapped between him and the wall, no way to get out of bed without waking him. Even if she could she knew she wouldn't be able to get far in the mountains at night, barefoot, with her hands tied behind her back. She finally drifted off to sleep.

26

GHOST RIDERS

THE TITSHAWS AND CHAGNYS finally retired to their bedrooms, along with Zoe, at Jim Bob's insistence. She was, after all, pregnant, and there was nothing she could do that he couldn't. He had promised to wake her up the instant they heard anything. Juanita had refused to leave. She insisted on staying at her post—people would have to eat—but Johnston persuaded her to find an empty bedroom and get some rest before breakfast. It was an odd sight, Johnston thought as he settled into a chair in the great room with Jim Bob and the kids, already asleep. While Alfonso and Meg had changed out of costume and into street clothes before leaving the opera house, all the others were still dressed to the nines, the boys in tuxedos and the girls in formal dresses. It looked like the aftermath of a wild prom. Some of the tuxedos were dirty and muddy, making it even more surreal. He had tried to get them to go upstairs but was touched that they preferred to stay together. He settled into a chair and quickly dozed off.

Johnston awoke with a start, having set his cell phone to the loudest possible ring. Most everyone else heard it as well, and quickly shook awake those who didn't. They gathered around Johnston, trying to interpret his brief responses to something of obvious import.

Johnston pocketed his phone. "There was a Jeep stolen from the Walmart parking lot last night."

"So?" Frankie asked.

"It belonged to one of the night shift stockers, so it wasn't discovered for several hours."

Frankie held his hands palms up, wondering what this had to do with anything.

"They found a motorcycle nearby, probably Erik's," Johnston said.

"That's how he took her away," Raoul said.

"They put out an alert, but he could be hundreds of miles way by now, in any direction."

"Or holed up nearby," Frankie said. "Was it four-wheel drive?"

"What difference does it make?" Johnston asked.

"He's going cross country," Carlos said.

"There are a few line shacks on the ranch from back when Daniel Senior ran cattle," Frankie said.

"What's a line shack?" Alfonso asked.

"Where cowboys eat and sleep when they're tending cattle out in the boondocks."

"What does this have to do with Christine?" Raoul asked.

"Most of the shacks have fallen down over the years, but there is one that Erik and I fixed up," Frankie said. "We used to ride out there and spend the night, like camping, but with a roof."

"Can you get there in a Jeep?" Jim Bob asked.

"You can get close," Frankie said. "You'd have to hike in the rest of the way. We used to go up there in the pickup, hauling lumber and stuff."

"Let's go," Raoul said.

"It's been raining all night," Frankie said. "I doubt we'd make it, even with four-wheel drive."

"Then how could Erik make it?"

"It's rained a lot more since he snatched her."

"Well, we have to do something," Raoul said. "How far is it? Can we walk?"

"We can ride," Frankie said.

"Let's saddle up," Jim Bob said.

"Can you ride?" Frankie asked Alfonso.

Alfonso nodded.

"I've been riding since I could walk," Tegan said.

"In that?" Frankie asked, looking at her designer dress.

"I'll throw on some jeans."

"That's okay. I think we've got enough guys. You can be the dispatcher."

"What's that?"

"Walkie-talkies."

"Oh, yeah, like on a film set."

"Exactly."

"I'll get the radios while you guys saddle up," Carlos said.

"Can't we just use cell phones?" Alfonso asked.

"Service is spotty on the back side of the mountain," Frankie said.

"Shouldn't we call the cops?" Sue asked.

"I'll call them," Johnston said, "but the boys will be out there before the deputies even get here, and like Frankie said, the roads will probably be useless."

"Do they have a helicopter?" Alfonso asked.

"I'll check," Johnston said, whipping out his phone.

"Let's ride," Frankie said.

Juanita and the girls rushed out to the stables carrying burritos and coffee, which the boys swallowed while saddling their horses. Jim Bob lashed a lariat to his saddle.

Tegan handed Alfonso a garbage bag.

"What's this?"

"Clothes for Christine. She was hardly dressed for traveling."

He tied the bag to the saddle horn.

"Bring back my girl!" Sue shouted as the boys rode away.

The rain continued to fall, not as much as overnight, but more than a drizzle. The sun rising on the other side of the mountain, even though masked by the clouds, provided enough light for the horses to slog through the mud.

They were an odd sight, five young men, four wearing tuxedos, riding horseback along a ridgeline, silhouetted by the morning light.

"They're bringing up a helicopter from Albuquerque," Tegan said on the radio. "It will be about an hour. They want GPS coordinates."

"I have no idea what the coordinates are," Frankie said. "Just tell them to look for five horsemen. We're north of the ranch, headed north by northeast."

"Ten four."

The boys rode on, Frankie in the lead, until he slowed, raising his hand, and stopped. They quickly dismounted and led their horses a few more yards.

There was a Jeep, driver's side window smashed out, parked at the end of what served as a road.

"You should call it in," Raoul whispered.

"Can't take the chance on him hearing the radio squawk," Frankie said, as he turned down the volume on his walkie-talkie.

"Where is the shack?" Jim Bob asked as they crouched down.

"Just down there." Frankie pointed.

"Can we get there on horseback?"

"We can, but it's probably better to leave the horses here and walk in. Less chance of being seen or heard."

They tied their horses to nearby bushes and crept up on the ridge line. Down below was the line shack, a trickle of smoke wafting from the stovepipe.

"Is there a back door?" Jim Bob asked.

"No," Frankie said. "One door, two windows, right there."

"So, what's the plan?" Raoul asked.

"Sneak down there, kick the door in, and rescue the fair maiden," Frankie said.

"What if he's armed?" Jim Bob asked.

"It's a chance we'll have to take," Raoul said. "I'll go first."

"I should go first," Carlos said. "I'm in the Army. I've at least had some training."

"No," Jim Bob said. "It's me and Raoul. She's ours. I'll put my shoulder in the door and go for Erik." He looked at Carlos. "If I go down, you climb over and me and take out Erik. Raoul will grab Christine and get her out of there."

"Or we could wait for the helicopter," Alfonso said.

"What are they going to do?" Carlos said. "There's no place to land, and I seriously doubt they have Rangers or SEALs on board. All they'll do is alert him. Those suckers are loud."

"Good point," Frankie said.

"Let's go get our girl," Jim Bob said.

They started downhill along the trail, crouching down to avoid being seen.

In the shack, the Labrador's ears perked up. He scrambled to his feet and started barking.

"Shit," Frankie said. "He has a dog."

The boys froze.

The door to the shack burst open and Erik stepped out, pointing a rifle in their direction.

"Come on down boys. I'll have the little wife put on a pot of coffee."

The boys slowly approached.

"Keep your hands where I can see them."

The boys obliged. There was nothing else they could do.

"That's close enough," Erik said when they were just a few feet away.

"Christine!" Raoul shouted.

Erik didn't budge, thinking Raoul was merely calling out to her in the cabin. But he did notice Raoul's eyes, tracking left to right, with his head slightly following, giving him away.

Erik turned quickly to see Christine, hands still tied behind her back, running, not toward the boys, but around the corner of the shack.

Before Erik could turn back, Carlos surged forward, his right hand sweeping upwards, grabbing the rifle, pointing the barrel toward the sky. Erik fired one shot before Carlos snatched the rifle from his hands and smashed him in the chest with the butt. Erik staggered backward from the impact, then turned and ran around the cabin.

"Christine! Wait!" Raoul shouted as he raced after her.

But he was too late. Christine slipped and slid, screaming, down the bank. He scrambled down the hill after her, Alfonso close behind.

Carlos handed Jim Bob the rifle and, along with Frankie, chased Erik. They followed him to a point overlooking the swollen stream below.

Raoul went prone and extended his hand as Christine slid into the stream, but she couldn't reach out with her hands tied behind her back.

Erik jumped into the stream ahead of Christine.

Raoul barreled into the water and half swam, half floated, yards behind Christine and now Erik. Alfonso continued along the bank, trying to get ahead of them.

Christine's peasant dress billowed up in the water, which was fortunate, because that's what Erik latched onto. He grabbed a tree stump and clung to Christine's dress until Raoul arrived, fighting the water himself. He floated a few yards downstream before finding a mooring. He looked up, exhausted and choking on muddy water.

Erik struggled to maintain his grip on Christine's dress, but it finally ripped, and she slipped away. Erik released the tree stump and swam after her.

Raoul reached out and grabbed Christine, her tied-up hands providing an excellent grip. She was limp in his arms, but he managed to hang on, pulling her too him and getting her head out of the water.

But Erik was gone, swept away by the raging water.

Frankie and Carlos scrambled down the bank to the edge of the water just as Alfonso arrived.

"Are you okay?" Frankie shouted.

"I am, but Christine's not moving."

Frankie inched carefully forward.

"Don't come in!" Raoul shouted. "Erik already washed away."

Frankie glanced downstream, but Erik wasn't really a concern. He turned, looking for something, anything that might help. Carlos was already trying desperately to uproot a small tree. A shank of rope landed at his feet. He grabbed it and looked up. Jim Bob was coming down the bank. Carlos wrapped the rope around his waist and tied it off.

"What are you doing?" Frankie asked.

"You guys hang on to the rope. I'll go in and get Christine, then go back for Raoul."

Jim Bob tied the other end of the rope to a sturdy tree. "Just in case," he said as he and Frankie took up positions on the rope.

Carlos plowed into the water, fought his way across, and took Christine from Raoul. She was limp, so Carlos squatted down, and Raoul helped get her over his shoulder in a fireman's carry.

Jim Bob and Frankie reeled them in. Alfonso grabbed Christine as soon as they were out of the water and lowered her onto the ground. Jim Bob fell on her, administering CPR.

Carlos turned back to the water.

"Take care of her," Raoul shouted. "I'm okay."

"Jim Bob's got her. I'm coming."

Carlos went back into the water. Raoul grabbed on and Frankie and Alfonso struggled to pull them in, but it was too much.

"Just hang on," Carlos said. "Let us go downstream and we'll swing over to the bank."

Frankie and Alfonso struggled to hold onto the rope as Carlos and Raoul fought their way to the bank and climbed to safety. Carlos untied the rope, and they ran toward Christine, arriving just as she spit water in Jim Bob's face. Jim Bob pulled her upright, bent her over, and pounded on her back as she choked and coughed up water.

She was stunned for a moment, unsure of what had happened, but obviously alive. Her blurry vision cleared long enough to see Raoul moving toward her. He kissed her briefly, afraid to cut off her air supply, and then hugged her tightly. She cried and choked and laughed and then kissed Raoul some more.

"Are you okay?" Raoul asked.

Christine looked down at her bare legs. "My dress is kind of ripped."

"That's okay. Did he hurt you?"

She started crying. He hugged her.

Frankie and Carlos looked downstream.

Jim Bob untied Christine's hands and then stood. "Why don't you guys look for Erik? We'll take Christine back to the ranch."

"Can you find it?" Frankie asked.

"I figure we'll just give the horses their head and they'll go to the barn."

Raoul scooped up Christine.

"I can walk," she said.

"I like this better."

With Jim Bob's help he managed to get her up the stream bank and into the line shack.

"I'll go help Alfonso bring down the horses," Jim Bob said as they got to the cabin. "Keep a close eye on her. She may be in shock."

"Can you ride?" Raoul asked Christine.

"I guess. But I'm not wearing any underwear."

"We'll find something."

She clung tightly to him, shivering, hyperventilating, her head buried in his shoulder. He could feel her back press against his hands as she breathed. After a moment, her breathing became normal. She kissed him on the neck and whispered in his ear, "This is the part where you say, 'You need to get out of those wet clothes.'"

"You need to get out of those wet clothes," he said.

She dropped the dress to the floor and backed up to the wood stove. Raoul found a towel and dried her. She held him close as he dried her hair. The dog lay on the floor beside the remains of her wet dress and watched.

"Sorry," Alfonso said as he stepped into the cabin. He turned away.

"It's nothing you haven't already seen," Christine said.

Raoul looked at Alfonso, who shrugged.

"See if you can find me something to wear," Christine said.

"You're in luck," Alfonso said. "Tegan sent you a bag of clothes." He handed her the garbage bag.

Christine released Raoul, turned her back to Alfonso, and dumped the bag of clothes on the bed. "Thank you, Teegs." She pulled on the T-shirt first, mostly covering herself, just as Jim Bob came through the door.

"Where are the clothes she was wearing?" Jim Bob asked.

"Her dress is right here," Raoul said, pointing at the floor.

"We should bag it and take it back for evidence."

"We know who it was."

"Doesn't matter. Cops have a procedure."

"He ripped off my panties," Christine said. "I don't know what happened to them."

Alfonso bent over and carefully picked up the panties and dress and placed them in the garbage bag.

Christine dressed quickly in jeans, T-shirt, and sneakers. She pulled on a jacket, zipped it, and pulled the hood over her head. "I'm ready. Let's get out of here."

Jim Bob watered the horses and left two of them securely tied to the hitching post. He tried to get the dog to go with them, but he refused, curling up on the porch near the horses.

"Christine can take my horse and I'll wait here for the cops," Alfonso said.

"She can ride with me," Raoul said.

Alfonso smiled and nodded.

"We don't know how long it will be before the cops get here," Jim Bob said. "Just ride out with Frankie and Carlos."

Raoul shook hands with Alfonso. "Thanks, man."

Raoul mounted first and Alfonso helped Christine on behind him. Jim Bob tried the dog once more and then set off in the lead, with Raoul and Christine close behind.

The rain had stopped, the clouds parted, and Christine felt the warmth of the sun on her face as they approached the ranch where several deputies, paramedics, and an ambulance awaited.

Raoul lowered Christine into the arms of a paramedic as everyone raced forward. The deputies were able to restrain all but Sue, who practically knocked Christine to the ground. They hugged and cried and squealed until Hannah separated them.

"Get her on the gurney," Hannah commanded.

Raoul led Christine the few steps to the gurney. She sat down, then lay back and the paramedics strapped her in. Johnston took her hand and kissed her on the forehead.

Christine tried to hold Raoul's hand, but he was pushed aside as the paramedics went to work.

Hannah quickly examined her while the paramedics took her vital signs and covered her with a blanket. She noticed a bruise on Christine's forehead. "Did you hit your head, honey?"

"I don't remember, maybe."

"She fell into the stream," Raoul said. "She might have hit her head on the rocks. She was limp when I grabbed her, so yeah, probably."

"Do you know who I am?" Hannah asked.

Christine smiled. "You're Raoul's mom."

The paramedics loaded Christine into the ambulance and Hannah climbed aboard. Raoul tried to follow, but Hannah stopped him. "No," Hannah said. "You can follow us to the hospital but get someone else to drive."

Raoul handed her the garbage bag. "This is what she was wearing."

"Which hospital?" Jim Bob shouted.

"St. Vincent," a paramedic said as he closed the back door of the ambulance.

"I know where it is," Johnston said.

JOHNSTON PACED THE floor outside the emergency room while the others waited in chairs, quite a sight, Jim Bob and Raoul in mud-encrusted tuxedos, Tegan, and Sue in evening gowns, the Titshaws, Chagny, Zoe, Alfonso and Meg casually dressed.

A doctor, wearing scrubs, accompanied by Hannah, approached.

"Mr. Caldwell?"

Johnston rushed forward expectantly. "Yes."

"Are you a relative?"

Johnston hesitated only briefly. "Yes."

The doctor looked as everyone gathered around.

"Family," Johnston said.

"Very well. Other than scratches and bruises, she appears to be physically unharmed."

"Was she—" Raoul asked.

"There is no evidence of sexual assault," the doctor said.

Raoul was visibly relieved.

"She said she fought him off, and you guys got there before he could try again," Hannah said.

"That's one tough little lady," the doctor said. "She suffered a mild concussion, so we'll keep her overnight, but it looks like she'll be just fine. She has some cuts and scrapes. She's going to be sore for a while and there are a lot of bruises. Whoever did the CPR got a little carried away."

"Sorry," Jim Bob said. "I didn't want to lose her."

"That's okay," Hannah said. "Every second counts when someone's not breathing. The bruises will go away."

"When can we see her?" Raoul asked.

"She wants to see you now," Hannah said.

Raoul looked at Johnston.

"You go," Johnston said. "I'll see her later. Tell her I love her."

27

NOTICES

ONCE AGAIN, RAOUL refused to leave Christine's side during the night. She was placed in a room with its own shower, so Hannah brought him a change of clothes. She also brought Sue, who quickly changed clothes herself and selected Christine's outfit for the next morning. A rollaway bed was brought in, and Raoul and Sue agreed to take turns sleeping while the other kept an eye on Christine, but they were both exhausted and at some point during the night they ended up in bed together.

The next morning a nurse nudged Sue, who reluctantly opened her eyes. The nurse pointed to Christine, awake in the hospital bed, with a look of disapproval on her face.

"What?" Sue asked.

"You're sleeping with my boyfriend," Christine said.

The nurse laughed.

Sue shrieked as she scrambled off the rollaway bed, waking Raoul. She covered her face and backed away.

"What's wrong?" Raoul asked. "Are you okay?"

"I'm fine," Christine said.

Raoul pointed at Sue. "What's wrong with her?"

"Never mind," Christine said, holding out her arms. "Do I get a good morning kiss, or what?"

Raoul stepped over and kissed her.

"If you're going to make out you should brush your teeth first," Sue said, retrieving a bag. "I brought stuff."

"That's okay," Raoul said. "She tastes just fine."

Christine put her arms around his neck, and they hugged.

"Smells pretty good too," Raoul said.

"I need a shower," Christine said.

"You had a sponge bath last night while I was in the shower."

"Yeah, and you probably peeked."

"No, I didn't. Did you?"

Christine laughed and then frowned. "Ow! My chest hurts."

"Jim Bob did CPR."

She lifted her hospital gown and looked. "I'm all bruised."

"Is it bad?"

"Do you want to look?"

"Sure."

"Pervert," she said, pulling the sheet up to her neck.

Raoul grinned.

"What?" Christine asked.

"Mom says you're going to be okay."

"When can I go home?"

"Probably this morning, when the doctor makes his rounds," the nurse said. "Do you want breakfast?"

"I guess. I'm kind of hungry."

"Hospital food?" Sue asked.

"Can I have a burrito?"

"Actually, they have burritos in the cafeteria downstairs," the nurse said. "They're pretty good too. This is Santa Fe, after all."

"I'll go," Sue said.

Raoul patted his pockets. "Where's my tux?"

"Johnston gave me some money," Sue said, following the nurse to the door.

"What about Erik?" Christine asked.

"They hadn't found him when Frankie was here last night," Raoul said. "I guess they'll start looking again this morning."

"Frankie was here?"

"Yeah, and Carlos. They searched until dark and then came to see you."

"They did?"

"You were asleep, and they didn't want to wake you up."

"So, Erik got away?"

Raoul didn't answer.

"Tell me," she demanded.

"He's probably dead."

"Probably?"

"Frankie thinks so. He said that river we were in is usually dry, so when the rain stops, they might find his body in it, or in the reservoir down below."

"I didn't want him to die. I just wanted him to stop."

"Stop what?" Raoul caught himself. "Oh, sorry."

"That's okay. No secrets, remember?"

"No secrets."

"I fought him off, but if you hadn't come to rescue me—"

"You were very brave." He kissed her lightly on the lips. "It's over now. You're safe."

AFTER ARRIVING AT THE ranch Christine had a never-ending stream of people fussing over her. She was at least allowed to shower alone, but Sue and Tegan insisted on washing, drying, and styling her hair. Hannah changed the dressing on the scrapes and cuts.

Raoul had been banished, along with the other boys. He didn't really mind—Christine was safe and in good hands—and it gave him a chance to sink into a much-needed slumber for a couple of hours.

There was much selecting, trying on, pressing, styling, and accessorizing, but Christine, accompanied by Sue and Tegan, finally made an appearance for dinner by the pool.

It was a rather large group, the Titshaws, Chagnys, Zoe and Jim Bob, Meg and Frankie, Tegan and Alfonso, Christine, and Raoul. Sue remained dateless, as did Carlos, currently tending bar while Juanita and Julio set up the buffet. Christine was somewhat surprised to see Maria in attendance.

Johnston stood and clinked on his drink glass. "I realize that Juanita's cooking smells wonderful, but I refuse to wait until after dinner. The reviews are in."

Everyone gathered around and took seats.

"What reviews?" Christine asked, and then realized what he meant. "Oh! I forgot all about the opera." She looked at Zoe. "Sorry." She turned back to Johnston. "I've been a little preoccupied with other stuff."

"Of course. We all have. We are all under a lot of stress and this is probably not the best time to be having a celebration, hopefully, depending on the reviews." He was quite experienced at public speaking, so he paused for the laughter. "But Christine is back with us, safe and sound, a little banged up, and Doctor Chagny assures me that she will be fine." He paused again for the applause.

Johnston picked up a tablet computer from a nearby table and looked at Christine. "We all agreed to not peek until you were here."

"So, peek!" Christine said.

Johnston poked at the screen for a few seconds and then handed the tablet to Tegan. "Here, Tegan. You're a professional actress. You can do a dramatic reading."

"I'd be honored," Tegan said, stepping up and taking the tablet.

Johnston took a seat beside Maria. Carlos brought them drinks and then sat on the arm of a nearby chair.

Tegan read from the tablet for a moment. "Oh, this is the bloke who sat with us."

"Cedric Highsmith," Frankie said.

"Yeah," Tegan said.

"Are you going to read the review, or what?" Alfonso teased.

Tegan scanned. "I'll just hit the high points." She read. "It is a promising, self-assured debut by composer Zoe Hathaway."

There was loud applause.

"Due to Miss Hathaway's connections with the family that underwrote the production, I was at first concerned that this would turn out to be some sort of vanity production." She looked up. People groaned. She smiled and continued reading. "I was wrong. It is a stunning work and will be forever tied to the magnificent house in which it was first performed. The opera is woven so tightly into the northern New Mexico culture and landscape that the Santa Fe Opera may be the only venue in which it can be properly presented, but that's not a bad thing. It belongs to Santa Fe."

There were nods of agreement.

"The arias soar. The music seems to reverberate off the surrounding mountains, or does it come organically from the mountains?" Tegan paused. "I have no idea what that means, but it sounds pretty cool."

There were chuckles.

"There's more about the music and the opera and stuff," Tegan said, scanning the tablet. "Oh, here's the good part."

Everyone leaned forward in anticipation.

"Unfortunately, the opera got off to a bad start. After a thrilling prelude

by the orchestra, the renowned diva La Carlotta was suddenly, and spectacularly, taken ill on stage in front of a sold-out house before singing a single
note. What happened next is destined to become opera legend. With the
understudy also quite ill, reportedly food poisoning, seventeen-year-old
California schoolgirl Christine Daaé was plucked from the audience to step
in and introduce the role of Sofia. A confidante of the composer, she had
sung the songs as they were being written, and so knew them by heart, but
had never rehearsed the opera."

Tegan took a dramatic pause and then smiled.

"It was reported that Francisco Florencio, who was to sing Alejandro, had
also been taken ill, but I have it on good authority that, fearing the age difference was far too great, stepped aside in favor of his own understudy, opera
newcomer Alfonso Bellini, one of the singers in the apprentice program at
the Santa Fe Opera. Perhaps he was just trying to avoid being part of an impending disaster."

"Oh, no," Christine said.

"Shush, girlfriend," Tegan said, and then continued reading. "The result
was a match made in heaven. On any other night, singing with any other
soprano, Bellini would have been the big news. Indeed, he acquitted himself
admirably and has a bright future on the opera stage."

Tegan stepped over and kissed Alfonso. "Well done, you."

She continued reading. "But the star of the evening was the young schoolgirl soprano, Christine Daaé, singing Sofia. The lighting was obviously
designed for a dark-haired Sofia, resulting in an angelic halo surrounding
the fair-skinned, blonde-haired, Daaé. Beautiful as the visuals were, however,
it was her voice that left the audience breathless. Daaé sang with a voice so
clear, so pure, so assured, so passionate, that one might assume there was
someone behind the curtain doing the actual singing. But of course, the
Santa Fe Opera has no curtain, and such subterfuge would never be allowed
in any event. It was the young blonde girl center stage, singing as if possessed
by the music. A star is born."

Tegan looked up. "Well done, Christine."

Christine covered her face, somewhat embarrassed, while everyone else
applauded.

Tegan scanned the tablet. "Oh, wait, more Alfie."

She continued reading. "Due to Daaé's unfamiliarity with the staging of
the opera, Bellini had his work cut out for him. More than once he literally

swept his co-star off her feet and planted her on her mark, their bodies intertwined, eyes locked, looking for all the world like young lovers, especially when they kissed."

"We are so not lovers," Christine said.

Alfonso picked up her hand and kissed it. "We are, just not with each other."

Christine kissed Raoul.

"Is there more?" Sue asked.

"More kissing?" Tegan said.

"More review."

Tegan read. "Tears flowed, including those of this reviewer, as Daaé, standing over the dead body of her lover, sang her final, most powerful aria. The magnificence of the opera was overshadowed, or perhaps enhanced, by what came next. A dark, masked form descended by rope from above, landing directly behind Daaé. As the audience, on our feet, roared approval, she was swept up and whisked away into the darkness. There was at first confusion—was this just a part of the opera? That question was quickly answered as Bellini arose from the dead and gave chase. In a heartbeat, other young men swarmed the stage, but Daaé was gone, kidnapped and carried away into the darkness by the mysterious Opera Ghost."

"Wow," Sue said as everyone else sat in silence for a moment.

Tegan continued. "There is, of course, much more to the story, but for now, the important thing is that Miss Daaé is safe at home, rescued, in the true tradition of the American Southwest, by a posse of horsemen riding through the rain, fittingly, in the Sangre de Cristo Mountains. The group included the fiancé of the opera's composer; the son of the family that underwrote the opera; an Army lieutenant; Daaé's co-star Bellini; and her real-life beau, a French viscount."

Tegan put down the tablet. "Okay, I am totally playing Christine in the TV movie." She turned to Christine. "But you'll have to dub the singing."

"Okay, sure," Christine said.

"No mention of Erik?" Johnston asked.

"No," Tegan said. "That's about it."

"How did Cedric know so much about the boys and the Opera Ghost?" Johnston asked.

Meg ducked her head. "Sorry. I have a big mouth."

Sue picked up the tablet. "But wait. There's more." Sue poked the screen.

"I thought we said no peeking," Alfonso said.

"That was just the reviews," Sue said. "Not this." She handed the tablet to Tegan as others tried to catch a glimpse. It was a photo of Tegan, standing beside the ambulance, doors open, holding a walkie-talkie, with Sue standing nearby.

"What is it?" Johnston asked.

"TMZ."

"What's that?"

"A celebrity gossip website. Tegan's a hero. According to *TMZ* she ramrodded the entire rescue with her walkie-talkie."

"I do look pretty hot, especially the boobage. Maybe I'll get some work out of it."

"Read the comments," Sue said.

"I'd totally hit that," Tegan read, and then looked up. "Of course you would, nerd boy, in your dreams."

"Read the next one," Sue said.

"I'd totally hit that hot Asian chick." Tegan laughed. "You go girl!"

"Meg, do you know something about this?" Johnston asked.

"What can I say? I'm an Internet news junkie. And Tegan might get some work out of it, so that's a good thing, right?"

"I might get a date out of it," Sue said. "That's an even better thing."

"Okay, enough!" Christine suddenly shouted.

Everyone froze.

"I'm starving. Are we going to eat, or what?"

"Absolutely," Johnston said as he stood, taking charge. "Juanita has prepared all your favorites."

"And I have brought our finest Champagne," Chagny said, "not that cheap California swill."

Champagne was poured, but Christine refused to allow the toasts to begin until they were joined by Juanita, Carlos, and Julio.

Under the circumstances, a toast to Christine was first, of course, and then Zoe. Since Zoe couldn't drink, Jim Bob insisted on having two glasses himself. There were various other toasts, to Alfonso, Johnston, Maria, the Titshaws, Hannah, and everyone else present who had anything to do with the opera or Christine's rescue.

They finally ran out of toasts, if not Champagne, and lined up for the buffet. Juanita took up her position behind the serving line, but Johnston insisted she get in line along with everyone else and enjoy the evening.

The mood was relaxed, almost jovial, during dinner, but Christine found herself occasionally looking toward the stables, the barn, the mountains, ever so slightly on edge.

After dinner Christine finally found an opportunity to get Johnston alone. "I'm so sorry," she said.

"For what?" Johnston asked.

"Everyone is celebrating and congratulating me."

"As well they should. You gave a magnificent performance."

"But everybody seems to be forgetting about Erik. It must be awful for you."

"It is awful, but no one is forgetting about him, especially me."

"Me, either."

"He did a terrible thing, but he's still my son. I don't know if he's even alive. The sheriff says probably not, so we're all in limbo. There will be time for grieving later, but this is your moment. Enjoy it. They come all too seldom in life."

He pulled her close and kissed her on the forehead.

"I want to remember the good things about him," she said. "Is that wrong?"

"No, of course not. That's what I'm doing, and there are plenty of good things to remember about him."

"Yes, there are."

28

RATON

Christine was eager to return to the opera house. She had become friends with many on the crew, genuinely enjoyed working backstage, and was eager to return to her former position, although it might be a few days before she fully recovered from her ordeal. She was also concerned that the crew might treat her differently after being thrust into the starring role of the opera.

None of that mattered, because there she was backstage, accompanied by Raoul, Frankie, Carlos, Sue, and Tegan. Alfonso and Meg were back at work, although somewhat in limbo until the fate of *Sangre de Cristo* was officially determined.

Christine heard loud cheering from the landing outside, below the stage, where the stagehands often worked on sets.

"What's that all about?" Christine asked.

"La Carlotta is wheels up," Carlos said.

Christine scrunched her nose. "What does that mean?"

"Her airplane just left the runway at Albuquerque," Frankie said. "She's headed home to Italy. Johnston graciously let her out of her contract."

"So, Hayley will sing Sofia?" Christine asked.

"I guess," Frankie said.

"Good. What about Alfonso?"

"We don't even know if the show is still going on. Johnston's still in meetings. Hopefully, we'll find out soon."

"Let's go see if we won," Carlos said, scampering down the stairway to the landing.

"Won what?" Christine asked.

"There's a pool to see exactly what time Carlotta's plane took off," Frankie said. "The crew sent someone to the airport to watch the takeoff and report back."

Jesse, the stagehand who had been injured by the falling flat, won the pool and despite the good-natured jeering and ribbing, all agreed he deserved it.

Everyone wanted to hug Christine, congratulate her, and ask if she was all right. Some even wanted to see the cuts and scratches on her legs. Luckily, she was wearing shorts.

Tegan, wearing short shorts, and a very small, very tight T-shirt, diverted much of the attention, at least from the guys, for which Christine was grateful.

Hayley was still recuperating at her apartment, which was a relief to Christine. She really wasn't looking forward to seeing her, afraid of what her reaction would be.

Christine and her posse made their way through all departments until the hugging, congratulations and well-wishing finally came to an end. Alfonso and Meg soon joined the group, and they made their way to the cantina and made small talk while they waited for Johnston to join them.

The cantina was almost empty as they took their seats.

"Isn't it a little early for lunch?" Christine asked.

"Or late for breakfast," Frankie said. "Johnston wanted to see us all, and this is better than his office."

"What does he want to see us about?"

"Don't know."

"Do you think it's about Erik?"

Frankie shrugged.

Christine gave up on that line of questioning and changed the subject, turning to Sue. "When do you have to go back to LA?"

"Whenever."

"Your parents are letting you stay?" Christine asked, surprised.

"My mom said family comes first and you're family."

"Cool. We'll have so much fun, and maybe even find you a boy."

"I told her to send me some clothes, but she just loaded up my debit card and told me to go shopping."

"Wow. When are we going?"

"We went to Walmart early this morning," Tegan said, "while you were canoodling with Raoul."

"Canoodling?"

"Making out."

"We were not making out. I just didn't want to get out of bed."

"Uh huh."

"It's been a tough couple of days. I was exhausted."

"Yeah, that's it, exhausted. Me too."

Alfonso laughed.

"What about everyone else?" Christine asked. "Is everyone going to hang around for a while? It could be fun."

"I have a film in Louisiana, but I'm waiting on a start date," Tegan said. "I think they're still looking for money."

"Louisiana," Carlos said. "Ugh."

"What's wrong with Louisiana?"

"Have you ever been to Louisiana in the summer?"

"No, actually, I haven't. I hear it's hot, but then it's hot in the Valley."

"Louisiana is hot and humid," Frankie said. "It makes the Valley look like Palm Springs in the winter." He looked at Carlos. "Are you going to Fort Polk for summer camp?"

"Nah, Fort Hood, not that much better though."

Christine laughed. "Summer camp?"

"Army Reserve," Carlos said.

"Oh, yeah. You're an Army guy."

"In my other life."

"I just want to go back to my job and drive my truck to work," Christine said. "And hang out with Sue, of course. Maybe you could get a job here too."

"Sounds good to me."

"I know the boss. I'll put in a good word for you."

Johnston hung up his cell phone and took a seat at the head of the table.

"What about Zoe's opera?" Christine immediately asked.

"Still undecided. It's on hold for now, but we'll have to make a decision soon."

"I'm taking a short trip," Raoul announced, diverting Christine's attention away from Johnston.

"You are?" Christine asked, surprised. "Where?"

"Chicago."

"Why are you going to Chicago?"

"I have some business there; someone I need to talk to. I thought maybe you could go with me."

"Sure."

Raoul looked at Johnston. "If that's okay with you, sir."

"It's fine with me, but I think you should be chaperoned."

"Chaperoned?" Christine asked, incredulous. "After all we've been through?"

"Well, yes. You don't think I'd let you go off with a boy alone, do you?" He looked at Christine very sternly and waited as she tried to formulate a response.

"Why don't you all go?" Johnston suggested.

"All who?" Christine asked.

"Everyone here, except me, of course. I'm old and I have lots of work to do. It's quite busy here."

Christine looked around. Everyone seemed to know something she didn't.

"Take the train," Johnston said. "Isn't that what you and the boys were going to do anyway? It'll be fun."

"It won't exactly be a party train, like we talked about," Frankie said, "not with all that's happened, but it will be good to get away for a couple of days. Carlos will bring his guitar. We'll sing. Well, those who can, will sing. I'll listen."

"I have my violin," Sue said.

"Is there enough room for everybody?" Christine asked.

"Girls in the bedrooms and boys in the bunks," Frankie said.

Christine thought about it for a moment. "Or you and Meg in one bedroom, Teegs and Alfie in the other, and the rest of us in the bunk beds." She turned to Sue. "Is that okay with you?"

"It's fine with me. I'm told that Carlos is an officer and a gentleman, so I guess I'll be safe."

Christine looked at Raoul, who smiled and nodded. She turned to Frankie. "When do we leave?"

Frankie checked his watch. "Right now. We have about two hours to pack and get to Lamy, so throw some chonies in a bag and let's bounce."

JUANITA HAD PREPARED sandwiches for lunch, along with fruit and cheese, which they ate onboard the *Estelline* while waiting for the train. The passengers aboard Amtrak's eastbound *Southwest Chief*, stopped briefly at Lamy, probably didn't even notice the gentle thud as a Santa Fe Southern locomotive nudged the private varnish onto the end of the train.

"I'm glad we're doing this," Frankie said as the train pulled out of Lamy. "This may be my last trip over the Raton Pass by train."

"Why is that?" Raoul asked.

"BNSF upgraded the Belen Cutoff, double track all the way, and routed all their freight traffic through there. Amtrak had to take over maintenance if they want to keep using the Raton line. Unless they cough up about a hundred million, they'll have to reroute the *Southwest Chief* through Belen, Clovis, and Amarillo. The scenery's not nearly as good, but time marches on."

"Belen?" Christine asked, suddenly interested. "Are we going through there?"

Frankie chuckled. "No, it's the other direction from here."

"Bummer. I kind of wanted to see it."

"What's so special about Belen?" Tegan asked.

"It's a long story," Frankie said, "but it figures prominently in Christine's life, all of ours, actually."

"You can say that again," Christine said.

"I'll take you to Belen someday," Frankie said.

"Great, thanks."

FRANKIE WAS RIGHT about the scenery. The Sangre de Cristo Mountains were beautiful. The kids settled in and enjoyed the view.

"I wish we'd had time to borrow a dome car," Frankie said. "Those are really nice in this part of the country."

"This is fine," Sue said. "This is great, actually. It beats the shit out of working in my parents' store for the summer."

"I could get used to this," Tegan said.

"I thought people rode trains all the time in Australia," Carlos said.

"Not like this, mate," Tegan said.

Even spectacular scenery eventually gets boring, and Christine soon nodded off—it had been a rather exhausting couple of days. She awoke and looked out the window when the train stopped at Raton.

"Look at all the Boy Scouts," Christine said.

"Boys!" Sue shouted. "Let me off the train!"

"I think they're a little young for you, girl," Tegan said.

"Oh, yeah, but they're so cute in their short pants."

"Philmont Scout Ranch is just a few miles from here," Frankie said. "Boy Scouts have been coming here by train for decades."

"What happens when the train stops coming here?" Christine asked.

"I guess they'll have to take the bus," Frankie said.

"Well, that sucks," Christine said.

"Let 'em hike in," Carlos said.

Frankie laughed. "Like we did when we were Boy Scouts?"

"Hell yeah. Remember the time Erik decided we'd hike from Philmont to Glorieta so we could pick up girls at the church camp?"

"That boy never was very good with geography," Frankie said, laughing.

"What's so funny?" Christine asked.

"It's like a hundred and fifty miles."

"Less if you go cross-country over the mountain," Carlos said.

"Which is what Erik would have done if we hadn't stopped him."

Tegan blew a kiss at one of the Boy Scouts, just as he snapped a photo with his phone. He smiled and waved as the train pulled out of the station.

"That one's definitely old enough for you, Sue," Tegan said.

"Yeah, but it was you he took a picture of."

"How do you know he wasn't taking a picture of you?"

"It'll be on his Instagram within ten seconds, and it won't be hashtag hot Asian chick on a train."

Tegan laughed.

The Southwest Chief crawled uphill.

Christine tried to look out every window at once. "Is this it?" she asked.

"Almost," Frankie said.

"Is this what?" Tegan asked, confused.

"The Raton Pass," Frankie said.

"What's the big deal?" Tegan asked.

Frankie smiled. "It's a big deal to Christine."

"Why?" Tegan asked.

"To make a long story short, the Belen Conservatory of Music came into being because a long time ago a major winter storm dumped several feet of snow right out there and the Santa Fe *Super Chief* couldn't get through the pass."

"Don't forget the opera singer," Christine said.

"Ah, yes, Estelline."

"Estelline?" Tegan said. "Isn't that the name of this wagon?"

"Wagon?" Carlos said, confused.

"Estelline was also the name of an opera singer," Christine said, "and she was something of a ho."

"You'll be sleeping in her room tonight," Frankie added.

"Are you trying to tell me something?" Tegan asked.

Alfonso laughed.

Raoul made his way next to Christine as the train entered the tunnel. "Aren't lovers supposed to kiss when going through a tunnel?"

"Is that a thing?" Christine asked.

"It is now," Raoul said as he kissed her.

PREPARATION OF DINNER was a group effort. Christine and Meg made the tortillas while Carlos manned the grill. Frankie chopped onions and peppers. Raoul assumed the role of sommelier.

"Okay, am I the only one who finds this weird?" Alfonso asked as they ate dinner.

"What's weird?" Raoul asked.

"We're eating homemade burritos and drinking expensive French wine, while rolling along in a luxurious private railcar that's probably a hundred years old."

Frankie shrugged. "Seems normal to me."

Carlos laughed.

"It sounds more upscale if you call them fajitas," Meg said.

"I guess we could have brought an attendant and had a fancy dinner," Frankie said.

"I like this better," Christine said, chomping down on her burrito.

"We can have a fancy dinner in Chicago if you want," Raoul said. "My treat."

"Or we can have Chicago dogs," Christine said.

"That works," Raoul said.

"What's a Chicago dog?" Tegan asked.

"Hot dogs, Chicago style," Christine said. "Jim Bob's a connoisseur, so don't tell him, or he'll be mad he didn't come along."

Since she had been of little help cooking, Tegan insisted on doing the dishes, and didn't object as Meg snapped a photo with her cell phone. It would be all over social media in minutes.

Carlos pulled out his guitar, Sue her violin, and a jam session began as the train rolled into the night. Those who could, sang.

"Erik taught me that song," Christine said as she and Carlos finished "Malagueña Salerosa."

"There's something I have to say," Raoul said, "and I guess this is as good a time as any. I already told Johnston."

Carlos stopped playing.

"What?" Christine asked, suddenly concerned.

"Erik and I certainly had our differences. I guess that's what happens when a girl comes between two guys."

"Raoul, don't."

"There's something you should know, something everybody should know." He paused, carefully choosing his words, and then looked at Christine. "Erik did a horrible thing, but he died saving your life."

"He did?"

"Yes, he did. That's why he was in the river. He wasn't running away. He was running to save you. He got to you before I did and held on until your dress ripped. Then I caught you and he washed away."

Raoul kissed Christine.

"I am forever in his debt." Raoul raised his glass, and others followed.

"Hear, hear," Frankie said.

Christine smiled and leaned her head on Raoul's shoulder.

CHRISTINE WAS AWESTRUCK by the Great Hall in Chicago's Union Station. "Wow. This is beautiful."

"You've never been here?" Frankie asked. "I thought you were from Chicago."

"I am, but we never came here."

"It's definitely impressive."

"O-M-G!" Tegan said.

"What?" Alfonso asked.

"The staircase," Tegan said, pointing.

"So?" Sue asked. "It's a staircase."

"The baby carriage," Tegan said.

Sue shrugged.

"Kevin Costner," Tegan said.

Sue shrugged again.

"Brian De Palma, *The Untouchables*. It's a movie."

"Oh, yeah," Frankie said. "*That* staircase."

"Great movie," Carlos said.

"Where's Raoul?" Christine asked, looking around.

"Over there," Sue said, "talking French with some dude."

Christine turned to look as Raoul took a Zero Halliburton briefcase from a man in a suit. They shook hands and the man walked away.

"What was that about?" Christine asked when Raoul returned.

"He's one of our company executives. He just got in from Paris."

"On the train?"

Raoul smiled. "No, on a plane. This was just a convenient place to meet up."

"What's in the briefcase?"

"It's a family thing."

After finishing off a large quantity of Chicago dogs from a street vendor, the kids piled into a shuttle bus and drove to the cemetery.

"This is as close as we can get," Frankie said as the bus stopped. He checked his cell phone. "Does this look familiar, Christine?"

"Not really. It was a long time ago."

"That's okay," Raoul said. "We'll find it."

"Wait for us," Frankie said to the bus driver. "Keep the meter running." There was no meter, of course, but the driver knew what he meant.

They found the gravesite and Christine burst into tears. As promised, Count Chagny had purchased a tombstone for Christine's parents. Sue stepped up and handed Christine a bouquet of flowers, which she placed at the base of the tombstone.

"I did it, Daddy. I sang an opera, just for you. I wish you and Mom could have been there."

Sue started blubbering and Frankie pushed everyone back while Christine and Raoul stood in silence at the grave for a few moments.

Christine took Raoul's arm and squeezed it. "Thank you so much for bringing me."

"You're quite welcome."

"We should probably go. Don't you have someone to see in Chicago?"

"Yes. He's right here."

"Huh?"

Raoul broke away from Christine's grip and took a step forward. "Mr. Daaé, I want to thank you for allowing me into your daughter's life. I know she loves you very much, and you loved her more than anything, so I don't know exactly how to say this, but I promise to treat her with respect, and love her, and protect her, and do everything I can to make her happy, just like you wanted."

Sue gasped.

"Mr. Daaé," Raoul continued. "I have come all this way and brought Christine's friends to bear witness."

Christine started trembling as tears rolled down her cheeks.

"Mr. Daaé, I am here to ask for your precious daughter's hand in marriage."

Sue screamed.

Christine gasped.

"Onya mate," Tegan said.

"What did he say?" Christine asked as Raoul turned to face her.

"He said it would be okay with him."

Frankie stepped forward and held open the briefcase. Raoul removed a small box.

Christine was half laughing, half crying as Raoul dropped to one knee. He opened the box, revealing a stunning engagement ring, and took Christine's hand.

"Christine Daaé, will you marry me?"

BOOK 4

SANGRE DE CRISTO

"Did your father tell you that I love you, Christine
and that I cannot live without you?

—GASTON LEROUX, *The Phantom of the Opera*

1

THE TUB-THUMPER

With the high elevation and steep grades, the westbound *Southwest Chief* crawled over the Raton Pass. The tunnel was more than a half mile long, which suited Christine just fine, as it allowed more time to remain lip-locked with Raoul. Sue, on violin, and Carlos on guitar, provided romantic music.

"Okay, guys, we're out of the tunnel," Sue said. "You can come up for air."

Tegan and Alfonso, who had also transited the tunnel while engaged in deep kissing, did as requested.

Christine and Raoul took considerably longer to disengage, and even longer for the smile to disappear from their faces.

"We need more tunnels," Christine said.

"Just close your eyes," Raoul said. "It will be a virtual tunnel."

"Works for me."

They were still kissing when the train pulled into Raton.

Frankie opened the door and Johnston, accompanied by a young woman carrying a designer briefcase, stepped aboard. Carlos stepped off.

Christine hugged Johnston. "Are we in Lamy?"

"No, Raton," Johnston said.

"They've been smooching," Sue said. "She hasn't looked out the window for miles."

"What's wrong?" Christine asked.

"Nothing," Johnston said, smiling. "Nothing at all."

"Where's Carlos going?"

"Juanita sent lunch," Johnston said. He turned and nodded as Carlos and Julio lugged a cooler aboard. "We'll have to cook it, but that shouldn't be a problem."

Frankie and Carlos carried the cooler into the kitchen. Julio took off in the Suburban.

Christine was confused as she shifted her attention from Johnston to the cooler and then to the young woman.

"Hi. I'm Sharon." The young woman extended her hand to Christine.

"She's your tub-thumper," Tegan said.

"My what?" Christine asked, shaking hands with Sharon.

"Your publicist," Sharon said.

"Okay. I'm confused," Christine said, looking around. "First, what's a tub-thumper?"

"*Variety*-speak," Tegan said, "for publicist."

Sharon laughed.

"Huh?" Christine asked.

"I'll explain it later," Tegan said.

"And why do I need a publicist?" Christine asked.

"Nobody told her?" Johnston asked.

"Told me what?"

"We thought we'd let you tell her," Raoul said.

Christine was now more confused than ever. "So, tell me, whatever it is."

"Tell her," Frankie said. "I'll start lunch."

Meg followed Frankie to the kitchen.

Johnston kissed Christine on the forehead and shook hands with Raoul. "Well, first, congratulations on your engagement."

"You knew already?" Christine asked, flustered. "I was going to tell you when we got back."

"Raoul talked to me before you left for Chicago," Johnston said.

"He did?"

"Yes."

"Did he ask you for my hand in marriage?"

"Yes, actually, he did."

"He asked Daddy too."

"I like to cover all my bases," Raoul said.

"Good idea." She kissed him. "Now, someone please tell me why I need a publicist, or a tub-thumper, or whatever."

Johnston smiled. "Mrs. Giry has been swamped with phone calls. The website also went down from the load."

"So, people want their money back?"

"No, not at all, quite the opposite in fact. We had to cancel the next couple of performances of course, but we'll reschedule those, swap dates with other shows. We are almost sold out through the end of the season."

"I'm confused again. I thought Carlotta went back to Italy."

"She did."

"So, Hayley will take over?"

Everyone waited in anticipation, all eyes on Christine.

"What?" Christine asked, looking around, wondering what everyone seemed to know that she didn't.

"Mrs. Giry said the callers all asked the same question." Johnston took a dramatic pause, enjoying toying with Christine, who threw up her hands and shrugged her shoulders.

"Will the blonde girl be singing Sofia?" Johnston said.

Sue screamed.

"You want me to sing Sofia?" Christine asked.

"If you want the job."

"Do I get a raise?"

Johnston laughed. "I'm sure we can work something out. I'm already talking to your attorney."

"I have an attorney?"

"Several, actually, but this is your entertainment attorney. She will handle all your contracts related to the entertainment industry. Since you are still a minor, and Mrs. Valerius is unable to sign for you, it's a bit tricky, but I think we have it worked out."

"Cool," Christine said, nodding, trying to process everything. "What about Alfonso?"

"He gets a raise too."

"Alejandro?"

"Alejandro."

"Yes!" Tegan said.

Christine smiled at Alfonso.

"What about Francisco?" Christine asked, turning back to Johnston.

"Well, at the moment, he's fly fishing with Franklin in Colorado," Johnston said.

"So, he's cool with it?"

"Of course. If you recall, he's the one who said he was far too old for you and insisted Alfonso take the stage."

"Oh, yeah. And Hayley?"

"She will continue to understudy Sofia. She's a trouper. She completely understands."

Christine turned to Raoul. "I'll be kissing Alfonso all summer. Is that okay with you?"

Raoul smiled. "I'm engaged to a world-class opera diva, so I'll have to get used to it."

"Good, because I'm doing it anyway."

"I wouldn't have it any other way. But the kissing stops when you step offstage. Then it's my turn."

"Sorry, dude," Alfonso said. "I don't like you in that way."

There was a round of laughter.

"Can I have Christine's old job?" Sue asked.

"Sure, I guess," Johnston said. "Are you staying for the summer?"

"If that's okay with you, and my girl," Sue said. "My parents will only let me stay if I have a job."

"It's definitely okay with me," Christine said. "Raoul is going to Russia or somewhere with his dad, playing junior businessman, so yeah, you should totally stay."

"Okay, back to the business at hand," Johnston said. "We have a lot to talk about before the train gets to Lamy."

"Like what?" Christine asked.

"The most immediate need is a crash course in dealing with the press, and the paparazzi," Sharon said.

"I can help with that," Tegan said. "I deal with those buggers all the time."

"Do you two know each other?" Christine asked.

"Our firm also handles Tegan," Sharon said. "She's quite a handful."

"I am not!"

"Just kidding. Well, there was that whole naked selfie thing."

"Oh, yeah, that."

"Indeed," Sharon said, smiling. Her smile quickly disappeared as she turned to Christine. "Please tell me you don't have any naked selfies on your phone."

"As if!"

"Good. Keep it that way. In fact, don't keep any personal pictures at all on your phone. I'll set up a meeting with our tech guy as soon as things settle down. Until then, be very careful with your phone. Don't leave it where just anybody can pick it up. Don't download anything. Don't post anything to social media without talking to me first."

"Ten four," Christine said, not happy.

"Just until we get everything under control. Then we will work with you to get your life back."

Christine nodded.

"It's not that bad, once you get used to it," Tegan said. "And the perks are worth it."

"Perks?"

"You get free stuff, and the best tables at restaurants."

"We can expect paparazzi when we get to Santa Fe," Sharon said.

"Why would the paparazzi be interested in little old me?" Christine asked.

"Seriously?" Sharon asked.

"Seriously."

"You were kidnapped off the stage at the Santa Fe Opera before an audience of two thousand. The press tends to notice things like that."

"Yeah, I guess."

"Then you were rescued by your boyfriend, now fiancé, who happens to be a French count," Sue said.

"Viscount," Sharon corrected.

"How did you know that?" Christine asked.

"Our firm is already interfacing with the Chagny PR team in Paris," Sharon said.

"Cool, I guess." She looked at Raoul. "You have a PR team?"

"The company does. They also handle our personal stuff."

Christine pointed at Sharon. "My tub-thumper handles my personal stuff."

Raoul smiled.

"Which brings up the other matter," Johnston said.

"What other matter?" Christine asked.

"The engagement."

"We need to get ahead of it, but the entertainment press has already descended on Santa Fe," Sharon said.

"And Lamy," Frankie said. "I just got a text from the stationmaster. Apparently, someone tipped them that Christine is on the train."

All eyes turned to Meg.

"It wasn't me!" Meg insisted. "I swear."

"How would anybody know I'm on the train?" Christine asked.

"It's no big secret that the *Estelline* is on the *Southwest Chief*," Frankie said. "Railfans keep up with things like that. They post it on websites, but they wouldn't really know who is on board nor the purpose of the trip."

"Railfans?" Sharon said.

"Guys who like trains," Frankie said.

"That's a thing?"

"That's definitely a thing."

"Maybe that explains it. The firm sent me this on the drive up."

She pulled a tablet out of her bag, punched the screen, and extended it toward Christine. Everyone gathered around to look. It was a photo of the *Estelline* at Raton, taken from the platform.

"We just picked this up from social media," Sharon said.

"Boy Scouts," Tegan said, laughing.

"Boy Scouts?" Johnston asked.

"There were Boy Scouts on the platform at Raton, on the way up. One of them was staring at me, so I blew him a kiss. He snapped a pic with his phone. It happens all the time."

"There, mystery solved," Christine said. "All the hoopla is about Tegan. When we get to Lamy she can work the crowd and I'll slip out the back while they're ogling her boobs."

Tegan leaned in for a closer look and pointed at the tablet. "And there's you, Christine. And Raoul."

"Oh, and me!" Sue said. "And my Latin lover."

"Latin lover?" Johnston asked.

"Carlos. Just kidding."

"Okay, so there's a picture of me on the train with Raoul," Christine said. "What's the big deal? We're engaged. Why does it have to be a secret?"

"It doesn't," Sharon said. "But there is the matter of protocol. The Chagnys are a very well-known family in France, with extensive business and social connections. We don't want people to find out from some blog that Raoul is engaged. We much prefer a formal announcement."

"That makes sense," Christine said.

"And we have to determine how to word the announcement," Johnston said. "Normally the parents of the bride would make the announcement. In this case, Mrs. Valerius is your legal guardian, so it should be her, but of course—"

"Oh, yeah," Christine said, turning to Raoul. "Maybe we should just elope."

"Works for me, but my family would probably disown me."

"Does that mean we couldn't use the beach house, or the jet?"

"I'm afraid so."

"Then we're kicking it old school, baby."

There was laughter all around.

"Plus, you're under eighteen," Sue said. "That's a problem, right?"

"That's a problem, a small one, for the wedding, not the announcement." Johnston said. "Have you set a date?"

"Not really. Next summer, I guess," Christine said, looking at Raoul. "I'll be eighteen then." She turned to Johnston. "Or whenever my lawyers and tub-thumpers decide to let me get married."

"Come and get it!" Carlos shouted. "I cook it. I don't serve it."

"Smells wonderful," Christine said as she stood.

Large platters were quickly filled with food and strategically positioned around the dining table. Everyone took a seat and dug in.

"What about wine?" Frankie asked, holding up an unopened bottle.

"Definitely not for Christine, or anyone else under twenty-one for that matter," Johnston said. "If the media is at Lamy we'll all be in close proximity, so no booze for anyone."

"Bummer," Christine said, and then quickly added, "Just kidding."

Johnston, sitting directly across from Christine, suddenly reached out and took her left hand, turning up the engagement ring. "Wow, it's beautiful," he said.

"Yes, it is."

"That's one hell of a rock," Tegan said.

"It was my great-grandmother's," Raoul said.

"So, it's a family heirloom?" Johnston asked.

"Yes. My grandmother insisted it should be Christine's."

Johnston released Christine's hand.

"Oh, crap," Christine said, looking at the ring.

"What?" Johnston asked.

"I guess I should take it off before we get there, since it's like a secret and stuff."

"I don't know," Sue said. "Maybe people will just think it's a promise ring or something."

"No way," Meg said. "That's definitely an engagement ring."

"Yes, you should take it off," Sharon said. "We do not want this to get out before everybody is ready."

"Remind me when we get there," Christine said to Raoul, "and you can put it in your pocket."

Raoul nodded.

"Is that okay?" Christine asked.

"Sure."

"I mean is it okay if I don't wear it?"

"Of course. We know we're engaged. I don't really care what anyone else thinks."

"Great. I probably shouldn't wear it on stage either, right?"

"Probably not," Johnston said.

"You definitely don't want to leave it in the dressing room," Tegan said.

"Why not?"

"It looks rather expensive."

"We have a safe at the ranch," Johnston said.

"Problem solved," Christine said.

"What about wardrobe?" Tegan asked.

"Wardrobe?" Johnston said.

"We're all kind of casual. Way casual. Shouldn't Christine throw something on?"

"No," Sharon said. "We aren't supposed to be expecting the press at the station. We'll act all surprised that they're there. The press conference isn't until tomorrow morning."

"Press conference?" Christine said with a pained expression on her face.

"At one of Maria's hotels," Johnston said.

"What do I wear for the press conference?"

"A dress, of course," Tegan said. "You have great legs. Just be sure you don't flash the press when you sit down."

"Like you," Sue said.

"Like me," Tegan said, smiling.

"I didn't bring many dresses to Santa Fe," Christine said.

"I have a stylist pulling some things, along with shoes and accessories," Sharon said. "She'll bring them to the ranch tonight and we'll try them on."

"Cool," Christine said.

"What about hair and makeup?" Tegan asked.

"Handled," Sharon said.

"Wow," Christine said. "I could get used to this."

"You will, trust me," Tegan said.

"What will I say?" Christine asked.

"Don't worry," Johnston said. "It's officially about *Sangre de Cristo*, so we'll all be there fielding questions."

"Zoe?" Christine asked.

"Of course," Johnston said.

"Okay," Sharon said, checking her watch. "Let's get started. Christine, like Johnston said, the press conference is officially about the opera, but you are the media darling of the moment, so we expect most of the questions to be directed at you. Whenever possible, feel free to pass it off to someone else, Zoe, Johnston, Maria. I'll be nearby, on my feet, ready to jump in if things get out of hand."

"Out of hand?" Christine asked, concerned.

"Although I'll brief the reporters with the parameters of the press conference, they are reporters and there will almost certainly be questions about Erik, the kidnapping."

"Which we will answer carefully, or not at all," Johnston said, firmly.

Christine nodded.

"You are young and beautiful, and so there will be questions about your personal life, your love life, whatever," Sharon continued. "If there has been any leak about the engagement, we will soon know."

"And if there is, it wasn't me," Meg said. "Frankie threatened to strangle me."

Christine nodded.

"Which is why I'm loaning you my boyfriend getting off the train," Tegan said. "Keep those wankers guessing."

"You're loaning me your boyfriend?" Christine asked.

"You and Alfonso will get off the train together, so that the photos and video will be of the two of you," Sharon said.

Christine looked at Alfonso. "Do we have to hold hands and act all lovey-dovey and stuff?"

Tegan laughed.

"No," Sharon said. "You two are the stars of the opera. Remember, we want to direct the narrative towards the opera, not your personal life, and definitely not your engagement, until such time as we are ready to make the announcement."

"But holding hands is fine," Tegan said. "I do it with co-stars all the time at press events. It's expected. Some of the rags will try to turn it into something else, but that just gets you more exposure."

"Got it," Christine said nodding. She turned to Alfonso. "Just like old times, huh?"

"Just like old times."

"And I'll take care of your boy," Tegan said, glancing at Raoul.

"Wait a minute," Christine said, turning to Sharon. "If you're Tegan's publicist, then it was you who wouldn't let her be seen with Alfonso."

"Guilty. But it wasn't my idea. That was all the studio's doing. They wanted to hype the young actors on their own shows, not some unknown tenor from the conservatory. We could have just as easily made Tegan and Alfonso the 'it' couple of the decade."

"And I got a date to the prom with a hot guy," Christine said.

"We have file photos of you two at the prom."

"You have what?"

"We sent a photographer, discreetly, of course. We were going to leak them to social media, but then—"

"Then what?"

"My phone got hacked," Tegan said, using air quotes. "My show was cancelled, the studio dropped me, and I got my man back."

"And a lot of new fans," Sue said.

"It worked. You can only play fourteen for so long anyway. And those frumpy clothes they made me wear!"

"Can I get copies of the prom pics?" Christine asked.

"Of course," Sharon said. "We work for you now, but don't post them on social media just yet. They are part of our overall strategy for the opera promotion."

"How?"

"Schoolmates and prom dates from the prestigious Belen Conservatory of Music. This story writes itself."

"Good thing the photographers didn't follow us into the hotel for afterprom sex," Christine said.

"Say what?" Tegan said.

"Just kidding. Your man is safe with me, as long as he behaves himself."

Tegan looked at Alfonso.

"We were joking about it a few weeks ago," he said.

"They were," Meg said. "Frankie and I were there."

Christine's crash course in dealing with the press and paparazzi began even before she had finished her fajitas. Sharon talked fast but had an uncanny ability to know when Christine didn't understand something, and she went over it again. It was overwhelming, but Christine was a quick study. After all, she had taken the stage without rehearsal on opening night of a new opera. How hard could it be?

2

THE PAPARAZZI

Sharon was right—the sleepy little Amtrak station at Lamy was crawling with press, and paparazzi, along with lots of others, drawn by social media. The few Amtrak passengers waiting to board, and people there to pick up arriving passengers, positioned themselves along the platform, expecting the train to stop where it always did. The press, paparazzi and the merely curious milled around the station itself, not knowing how things worked. A handful of railfans, cameras ready, were some distance up the track, where they could photograph the *Southwest Chief* as it arrived, and the *Estelline*, which they knew would be at the end of the train.

"Wow," Christine said, looking out the window as the train slowed to a stop. "There sure are a lot of people."

One of the paparazzi noticed the small group of railfans and their expensive camera gear. He quietly slipped away from the pack and walked slowly toward the railfans as the *Southwest Chief* pulled in. The group at the station watched as the locomotives continued past them. They scanned the passenger cars and then noticed the one odd car, completely unlike the others, at the end of the train. They had no way of knowing that the engineer would stop the train at the same spot where it always stopped, positioning the cars where they always were, without regard to the private varnish at the end.

As soon as the train stopped, the conductor opened the door of one of the passenger cars and stepped off, only momentarily drawing the attention of the paparazzi. The real action was obviously at the end of the train and the herd instinct quickly took over. They sprinted down the platform, pushing aside passengers disembarking and those waiting to board, in a headlong rush to the *Estelline*.

"Here they come," Sharon said.

Raoul flinched. "What are you doing?"

"Putting my ring in your pocket," Christine said.

"I thought you were feeling me up." Raoul patted his pocket to make sure the ring was secure.

"That too. I would kiss you, but they could probably see through the windows."

"Positions," Tegan said, grabbing Raoul's arm and pushing Christine aside.

Christine took Alfonso's arm.

"Oh, look, there's Julio and Jim Bob," Christine said.

"How did Julio get here before we did?" Sue asked.

"He drives like a bat out of hell," Carlos said. "You go with Johnston. I'll help Julio with the bags."

"Is everybody lined up?" Sharon asked. "I'll go first. That way I can keep things moving on the ground."

Jim Bob offered his hand to Sharon as she stepped off the train and went immediately to work. The actual press recognized her and knew the action would follow her.

Other than that, Sue was first, holding hands with Johnston, basking in the glow of celebrity, however temporary, waving at the cameras and having a good laugh.

Frankie and Meg were next, clearly accustomed to making an entrance, but aware they were not the main attraction. Still the video cameras continued to roll—footage was footage, even if it would be merely filed for future use.

Standing in the doorway, Tegan turned and hugged Christine. "I'll warm them up and then you'll knock them out."

"You go, girl," Christine said.

"Tits out," Tegan said, straightening her back and smiling broadly.

Christine laughed, and clinched Alfonso's hand.

The paparazzi surged forward as Tegan and Raoul stepped off the train, looking very much like a young couple in love. Raoul just smiled and waved, but Tegan clung to his arm and made plenty of contact, acting the part, giving the press plenty to gossip about, deflecting attention from Christine's hopefully still-secret engagement.

"They look good together," Christine said as Tegan kissed Raoul on the cheek while doing what appeared to be a Marilyn Monroe impersonation.

"So do we, babe, so do we," Alfonso said. "It's showtime."

Alfonso stepped off the train and held out his hand for Christine. She paused a moment, instinctively raising her head and smiling while the cameras rolled, and the flashes popped. She took Alfonso's hand and stepped down onto the platform. The protocol was to take his arm and follow Tegan and Raoul, but she suddenly rushed into Jim Bob's arms, burying her face in his chest, and hugging him tightly as Alfonso waited patiently.

Sharon cringed. This was not planned. The press converged. Who was this guy? Christine pulled away. Jim Bob kissed her on the forehead, and she patted him on the chest.

Christine took Alfonso's hand, and then his arm and sallied forth into the frenzy.

A reporter shoved a microphone in Jim Bob's face. "Who are you?"

"Baggage handler," Jim Bob said, turning away. "Let's load 'em up, Carlos, and move 'em out."

The reporter turned her attention to Christine.

"Julio and I will get the bags," Carlos said. "You keep an eye on Christine."

"*No problemo, compadre,*" Jim Bob said. "I don't trust those assholes."

"Alfonso?" Carlos asked, grinning.

"The paparazzi."

Jim Bob quickly caught up with the procession, positioning himself close enough to Christine to jump in, if necessary, but far enough away to remain unobtrusive. She noticed and smiled.

Paparazzi pushed for position. Reporters shoved microphones in Christine's face and peppered her with questions. Christine, as instructed by Sharon, just smiled and waved. Sharon wanted her well-prepared, and rehearsed, before meeting the press.

"It was just a little train trip with friends," Tegan said in answer to one of the questions. "What's the biggie?"

"Who are you wearing?"

"Oh, this little thing?" Tegan said, looking down at her form-fitting, low-cut, designer T-shirt. "I picked it up at a little shop on the plaza. The shopping there is fantastic. Downtown Santa Fe, if you've never been. You should check it out."

Sharon lowered her head and smiled. Not only was Tegan deflecting attention from Christine as planned, but if that sound bite made the news, or went viral on social media, she would be offered a considerable amount of free clothing from the merchants on the plaza. The girl knew how to work it.

With the *Estelline* at the end of the train it was a considerable distance along the platform to the station, and the pack of press and paparazzi was in pursuit all the way. Frankie and Meg broke away and rushed ahead, leaving Sharon to keep the procession moving.

Frankie found their ride, parked as close to the station as possible, a black "limo bus," a term that both Frankie and the driver detested, but it did serve their purpose well—there were too many for a standard limousine and Frankie refused to ride in an outrageously stretched Hummer, or "prom bus," as the driver called them, although the company did have a couple available for just such occasions.

There was a sign on the front door: ANGEL'S LIMOS. A young man in his early thirties, dressed in a black suit, black tie, black hat, and white shirt, stood by the door, hands crossed at his waist, the standard pose for a limo driver.

Frankie and Meg stepped up quickly and Frankie bumped fists with the driver. "Angel, my man." Frankie looked around. "Perfect."

"I got here early," Angel said. "No extra charge."

Frankie smiled.

"Good thing too," Angel said. "I've never seen this many people at Lamy. They have remote trucks and everything."

"It kind of hit social media."

"My wife saw it on the Internet and told me to get my ass over here early."

Angel held out his hand and helped Meg board the bus. Frankie waited outside, watching as the procession neared.

"Carlos is getting the bags?" Angel asked.

Frankie nodded. "He's in the Suburban with Julio. He'll be along later. We'll just load up and go."

The reporters continued shouting questions as the group boarded the bus. As soon as Christine was aboard Jim Bob said to Frankie, "I'll ride with Carlos and Julio."

With Angel already in the driver's seat, Frankie took up position at the door. Sharon turned to face the crowd. "I'm sorry you all came all the way out here for nothing, but the press conference is tomorrow at ten and we will be happy to take all your questions at that time. See you there. At least you got some good B-roll of the train."

The video cameramen knew she was right about that. You don't see beautiful young celebrities stepping off vintage private railcars every day.

Sharon boarded the bus with Frankie right behind her. Jim Bob stood guard as Angel closed the doors.

"Party bus!" Christine said as she took a seat beside Raoul.

"Angel prefers to call it 'executive transport,'" Frankie said.

"Oh, wait, can they see in?" Christine asked.

"I don't think so," Raoul said. "Tinted windows."

Alfonso sat down, sandwiching Christine between him and Raoul. "Just in case," Alfonso said.

Tegan took a seat beside Sue. "I went to an awards show in one of these things. They're great. Some of them have a loo and you can fix your makeup and hair."

"And the ladies can step off standing up and not have to worry about a paparazzi's camera between their legs," Frankie said.

"Unless that's what you're going for," Sue said, looking at Tegan.

"Be a bitch, why don't you?" Tegan said and then quickly hugged Sue as everyone laughed.

Christine leaned over and whispered to Raoul. "That guy is staring at me in the mirror."

"What guy?" Raoul asked.

"The driver."

Raoul turned and looked. Angel's eyes were on the road ahead.

"Maybe he thinks you're hot," Raoul said. "Or maybe he's looking at Tegan."

"Thanks, jerk," Christine said. She glanced up at the mirror and then back at Raoul. "He's definitely watching me. It's kind of creepy."

"Ask Frankie," Raoul said. "I think he knows the guy."

"Okay, I will." Christine started to stand, but Raoul grabbed her hand.

"Wait until we get to the ranch."

"Oh, yeah, good idea."

It was a half-hour drive into Santa Fe, and a bit longer up the mountain, but the paparazzi followed closely all the way, nearly all of them driving the default paparazzi vehicle—black SUVs, making the convoy look like a motorcade of feds. The actual press, who knew better than to follow, took their time loading up at Lamy, picked up some more B-roll around the station, and then leisurely drove into Santa Fe, checking their smartphones for recommendations on the best places to eat and drink.

Outside of Santa Fe, Angel slowed and turned off the pavement onto a dirt road. Julio, standing next to the old pickup, waved as the limo bus passed by and then stepped into the road behind it, holding up his hand and stopping the convoy of paparazzi.

One of the paparazzi leaned out the window and yelled, "Get out of the way, asshole!"

"Private road, *pendejo*," Julio replied, pointing to a large sign: PRIVATE ROAD / CALLE PRIVADA.

The ranch house was far beyond the range of even the most powerful telephoto lens, not to mention obscured by topography and foliage, so the paparazzi pulled off the pavement and took up positions along the road. Christine had to come out eventually. She was still an unknown quantity, and apparently an opera singer at that, not exactly prime paparazzi material, but there was buzz surrounding her, not to mention being in the company of extreme wealth, and it didn't hurt that she was a young, stunning, fresh-faced, blonde beauty. Then there was Tegan, well-known to them all, who never missed an opportunity to give them what they wanted.

Thanks to modern technology, their first photos of Christine at Lamy were already being shopped worldwide, and there was plenty of interest from buyers. These paparazzi knew instinctively that there was money to be made on this one, and so they waited. The Tegan shots were also selling well, with Alfonso doing okay in Los Angeles and Raoul trending in Paris.

ZOE WAS WAITING in the driveway at the ranch. Christine rushed off first, and into Zoe's arms, laughing and crying and hugging and kissing. Raoul was close behind and joined in as the others stepped off the bus and gathered around.

"Where's the ring?" Zoe asked, lifting Christine's left hand.

"Oh, crap! I forgot."

Raoul pulled the ring from his pocket and slipped it onto Christine's finger, which she immediately presented for Zoe's inspection.

"Wow," Zoe said, and then looked at Raoul. "*Grand-mère?*"

Raoul nodded.

"I had to take it off when we got off the train," Christine said. "My tub-thumper wants to wait until everybody is ready to make a formal announce-ment."

Zoe laughed. "Your tub-thumper?"

"Publicist. I have a publicist."

"I know. We've been preparing for the press conference."

"Oh, yeah, duh," Christine said.

"¡Mi hija!" Juanita shouted as she raced through the great room and swept Christine into her arms. "I'm so happy for you." She looked at Raoul. "You treat her good or I poison your food."

"I promise I will treat her well. I don't want to get poisoned."

Christine confronted Frankie as soon as possible. "The driver was watching me."

"He was checking on his passengers. It's his job."

"Do you know him?"

"Yeah, sure. We do a lot of business with him. Carlos knows him better than I do."

"So, he's okay, not like a stalker or something?"

"I seriously doubt it. He's good people. He has a wife and a little girl. He's not just a driver. He owns the company, started out with one limo, and built it up into a pretty good business. He likes to drive his best customers himself. Maria thinks he's her personal chauffeur. Her hotels have their own shuttle buses and vans, but Angel handles her special guests, especially the ones who come in by private jet, or private railcar."

"His name is Angel?"

"Yeah."

"Weird, huh?"

"Now that you mention it."

"Sorry. I guess I'm just paranoid."

"That's okay. You're in the public eye now. You have to be careful."

"Did Erik know him?"

Frankie nodded.

WHILE SHARON HUDDLED with the adults to discuss the upcoming press conference the kids hit the pool.

"I'm so happy," Christine said as she snuggled with Raoul on a lounge chair. The sun was not yet down, but there was already a chill in the air. He pulled her close.

"I wish you could stay," she said.

"I am staying."

"For the summer?"

"Oh, no. I thought you meant tonight."

"When do you have to go?"

"I'll talk to dad late tonight—it will be morning there—and try to stay a few more days, at least until the next performance."

"And you'll be back for closing night?"

"I'm sure we'll all be back for closing night, and we'll bring champagne."

"Great. Feel free to pop on over before then if you get a chance. You do have your own jet and all."

"I'm sure I can make that happen, at least for a couple of days."

"Sue's great, and we're going to have a blast this summer, but she's not you."

"I know."

"But the good news is that you will be really busy with your dad, so you won't have time to chase girls."

"My girl-chasing days are over. I caught the one I always wanted."

"You just remember that when you're on the—what's the name of the beach in Saint-Tropez?"

"Pampelonne?"

"Yeah, that one, while you're ogling all the beautiful bare boobies on the beach."

"I'll be thinking only of your boobies."

She laughed. "My lolos." She grimaced. "Oh, sorry."

"For what?"

"I learned that word from Erik."

"That's okay. It's common slang in French."

"I'm going to have to learn French."

"Well, you don't *have* to, but it would probably be nice."

"Are we going to live in France?"

"We can live wherever you like. First there's the matter of school. I have to go, and that's in England. Have you decided what you are going to do about college?"

"Not really."

"You have time to decide."

"I guess we could get an apartment near your school, and I could just hang out."

"You don't have to do that if you don't want to. You could live in Paris, or LA, or New York, or Santa Fe, wherever you want."

"I want to spend lots and lots of time in bed with my new husband, and I don't care where the bed is."

"That can be arranged."

"Maybe I should go to college in England or France, so we could see each other on weekends, and shag—that's British for, you know, right?"

"Right, and I'm definitely looking forward to it."

"Me too."

They kissed.

"This is a lot to handle," she said. "It's kind of overwhelming."

"Kissing?"

"No, silly, everything that's happened so far, and now I'm going to be singing the lead in Zoe's opera, and then I have to bust my ass to graduate from the conservatory, and then I'm getting married, to a French dude."

"One step at a time. First, Zoe's opera, but we already know you can do it."

"Yeah, I guess you're right."

They snuggled.

"Actually, you may be spending a lot of time in hotels after we're married," Raoul said.

"Huh? Why?"

"You may be touring with *Sangre de Cristo*."

"You think?"

"Could be. We'll soon know."

"Nah, it's a Santa Fe opera. It should only be done here, at the opera house."

"There are other operas. I predict I will soon be engaged to a major new opera star."

"You're dumping me for an opera star?"

He smiled.

SOME OF THE paparazzi sat in their vehicles, but most lounged in lawn chairs at the intersection of the private road—you come prepared when your job is to wait hours for a few seconds of opportunity. There was a variety of smartphones, tablets, and laptops, as they conducted business, selling photos, sniffing out the next job.

As soon as the first one took notice and sat up, they all reached for their cameras. The old pickup bounced along the dirt road, headed their way. Christine drove, with Sue, Tegan and Meg squeezed in beside her. Carlos and Raoul rode in the back. Frankie and Alfonso followed in Frankie's truck.

Hundreds of photos had already been snapped by the time the trucks stopped and the girls hopped out, all wearing short shorts and bikini tops.

That's when the real action began. The paparazzi surged forward, not believing their sudden good fortune. The old pickup was a nice touch.

"Back off, wankers," Tegan shouted. "We brought security."

Carlos and Raoul quickly appeared, followed by Frankie and Alfonso.

"And fajitas," Christine said. "Who's hungry?"

"You brought food?" one of the paparazzi asked, suspiciously.

"Sure, why not?" Christine said. "You have to eat."

"Did you bring beer?" another asked.

"No way," Tegan said. "You lot drive like maniacs anyway. We are so not giving you alcohol."

Frankie and Carlos quickly set up a grill and hooked up the propane tank.

Cameras continued to click—there was simply too much bare skin on display to ignore.

"Okay," Tegan said. "You have your shots. Cameras down if you want to eat. And another thing, my girl Christine is new to all this, so be nice."

"We're always nice," one of the paparazzi said as the cameras were quickly put away.

In short order Frankie was grilling beef, onions, and peppers while the girls laid out the folding table.

Carlos produced his guitar and took a seat. "A little dinner music," he said as he began to play.

"If you blokes behave, Christine might even sing," Tegan said.

The paparazzi lined up to fill their paper plates.

"I made the tortillas," Christine said.

Cameras were completely forgotten as the paparazzi chowed down on fajitas, while Carlos strummed his guitar.

"Aren't you eating?" one of the paparazzi asked Tegan.

"Nah, we'll eat later, up at the house," Tegan said, "but Christine wanted to feed you wankers."

The paparazzi nodded his head, mouth full.

Juanita darted around the kitchen, preparing dinner for a large group.

Sharon pushed opened the door. "Have you seen Christine?"

"She went to feed the papa-what-you-call-its," Juanita said.

"The paparazzi?" Sharon asked, suddenly concerned.

"*Sí.*"

"She went alone?"

"No, with the girls. They made fajitas."

"Oh no. Where are the boys?"

"They went with the girls."

"Johnston!" Sharon called out.

THE PAPARAZZI PAID no attention as the Suburban slid to a stop in a cloud of dust. Johnston, Sharon, Jim Bob, and Zoe quickly jumped out and approached the group. Sharon immediately stepped forward. Johnston took her arm and pulled her back.

"Wait," Johnston said.

Jim Bob quickly assessed the situation.

Carlos sat on a stool playing guitar. Sue stood beside him, on violin. Christine and Alfonso sang a song from *Sangre de Cristo*. The paparazzi watched and listened in rapt silence. More than one wiped a tear. When the song was over, Alfonso took Christine into his arms and kissed her, duly recorded for posterity in both stills and video.

"That's the money shot," Tegan said quietly to Raoul. "It'll be all over the net in minutes."

"That's opera?" one of the paparazzi asked.

"That's opera, done right," Frankie said.

"I thought opera singers were fat and ugly," another said.

"Not this one," Alfonso said, putting his arm around Christine. "You can see her on stage at the opera house."

"Along with him," Christine said, nodding toward Alfonso, "my co-star."

"Unfortunately, the show is almost sold out for the rest of the season, so be thankful you got a free preview," Meg said.

"Encore!" someone shouted.

"She owns the paparazzi," Tegan whispered to Sharon.

"I guess this was your idea."

"No way. It was Christine all the way. I just gave her some pointers."

"Did she answer any questions?"

"They're paps, not reporters. They just want pics, preferably with skin."

"Which they got plenty of," Sharon said, looking at Tegan's chest.

"Don't worry. Nothing popped out." She looked down. "Well, not too much, anyway."

"Let's shut it down while we're ahead," Johnston said. "Dinner is ready at the house."

"In a minute. Sue is about to burn the place down."

"She's what?" Sharon said, alarmed.

"Wait for it."

"Jim Bob, get in here," Sue shouted.

Jim Bob cautiously stepped forward. "For what? I didn't bring my guitar or fiddle."

"Vocals."

"You want me to sing?"

"More or less. I think you know this one."

"Alfonso is right here. He's the real deal."

"I need a real redneck."

Alfonso used a cooler for a drum. Carlos played guitar. Sue played violin, or in this case, fiddle, with Jim Bob on vocals, as they enthusiastically launched into "The Devil Went Down to Georgia." Tegan and Meg danced and sang backup.

The paparazzi loved it.

Frankie and Raoul loaded gear into the trucks.

Johnston put his arm around Christine and pulled her close.

"Did I mess up?" Christine asked.

"No, you did good."

"You introduced opera to a whole new audience," Zoe said, laughing.

"Just be careful," Sharon said. "The paparazzi are not your friends."

THE STYLIST ARRIVED shortly after dinner and the boys were drafted to help unload a large collection of dresses, shoes, and accessories. The girls immediately tore into the stash, but the boys were somewhat less enthusiastic.

Raoul turned to Frankie. "Poker?"

"I'll get the chips," Frankie said.

It didn't really matter to Christine what she wore to the press conference—she would look good in just about anything, including jeans and T-shirt—but with three other young women helping, along with Sharon and the stylist, the selection of outfit took some time.

The poker game was still going strong, loud, and lively, when Christine and Sue went upstairs.

"Why don't you sleep in my room tonight?" Christine said.

"Uh, okay," Sue responded, confused.

"With me."

"What about Raoul?"

"What about him?"

"I assumed you would be sleeping with him, literally or figuratively."

"It just doesn't feel right."

"You're engaged, girl. It better feel right."

"No, I mean, Johnston is going to be my adoptive daddy, and this is his house."

"Oh, that. But rich people are different. He probably wouldn't care."

"What if my daddy was still alive?"

Sue laughed.

"What's so funny?" Christine was more than a little miffed.

"Sorry. I was just thinking what would happen if I brought a boy home to spend the night. My dad would go ballistic."

"Exactly."

"Let's get my stuff. Did you tell Raoul?"

"He's a smart boy. He'll figure it out. Besides, they'll probably be playing poker all night."

Sue slept soundly as Christine slipped out of bed, stepped over to the French doors, pulled back the lace curtains, and peered out. There was enough moonlight to illuminate the grounds around the ranch house, and the mountains in the distance. She checked the lock, for the third time, and went back to bed. Sue never stirred.

The search for Erik had been suspended. Even Johnston seemed to accept that his son was dead. But there was still no body. The sheriff said it would probably eventually turn up, most likely in the reservoir. It wasn't meant for her ears, but she heard them talking in whispers, something about decomposition producing gas that caused a corpse to float to the surface.

She shuddered at the thought, pulled the covers up to her neck and tried to sleep. Tomorrow would be a big day.

3

THE PRESS CONFERENCE

WHILE THE OTHER kids slept in and had a leisurely breakfast, Christine was up early and had breakfast in the dining room with Johnston, Maria, Zoe, Jim Bob, and Sharon. The table had just been cleared when a young woman entered the room and hurried to the table.

"Sorry I'm late." She extended her hand to Christine. "Hi, I'm Aubrey."

"Christine."

"I'm the publicist for the Santa Fe Opera."

"Did you have breakfast?" Johnston asked.

"I grabbed a bite on the way. Where are we?"

"We were just about to begin," Sharon said.

"Why are there two tub-thumpers?" Christine asked.

"I'm sorry. We've all been working on this for days and I have not done a good job of keeping you in the loop. Aubrey is the publicist for the Santa Fe Opera. I am your publicist. We are working together on this press conference. Her job is to promote the opera house, and this opera. My job is to promote you. You don't really need promotion right now; you need protection from the vultures. So that's what I'll be concentrating on, while Aubrey handles the opera."

"Okey-dokey."

"Have you held a press conference before, Christine?" Aubrey asked.

"Not really, just school stuff at the conservatory."

"This might be a bit more intimidating."

"Why?"

"Under other circumstances, it wouldn't. Had both Carlotta and Hayley simply become unable to perform, and you were snatched from the audience to sing Sofia, that would be an easy press conference. There would be lots of nonthreatening questions like, 'Were you nervous? Were you scared? Were you afraid you'd mess up, forget the lyrics, not hit your marks?'"

Christine nodded. "Yes, to all those."

"But you were kidnapped off the stage," Sharon said. "That's a huge story on its own. Everything else pales in comparison. Aubrey and I have been making lists of who's here. There's local news, entertainment news, the trades, broadcast, newspapers, magazines, and lots and lots of bloggers. Only a handful of them care anything about opera."

"Cedric Highsmith is here," Aubrey said. "We'll be sure to call on him."

"He gave us a fantastic review of the premiere, and he was right in the middle of everything that happened," Johnston said.

"Good, and there are a couple of opera bloggers," Sharon said. "But *TMZ* is here, *Inside Edition*, and the tabloids, print and broadcast."

"Wow," Christine said. "So, this is a pretty big deal."

"A very big deal," Aubrey said.

"Unfortunately, all they care about is you," Sharon said. "We expect them to hammer you for all the juicy details about the kidnapping."

"And we want to avoid that," Johnston said. "It's not that we don't want you to be the center of attention. You earned it. You deserve it. But we would much prefer that you are feted for your extraordinary accomplishment on stage, and not for what happened after you sang the last note."

"Okay, now I get it."

"My job is to draw attention to the opera and sell as many tickets as possible," Aubrey said.

"And to promote the Santa Fe Opera in general," Maria said. "Most of those reporters who will be there have never even heard of the Santa Fe Opera."

"So, plug the opera, not the kidnapping," Christine said.

"Yes," Aubrey said.

"And there's another angle," Sharon said. "You are young and beautiful, and extremely desirable, as are Tegan, Raoul, and Alfonso. And Raoul is rich, French, and has a title. That's chum for sharks. They are no doubt scouring the Internet for photos of you, preferably showing skin, or in a compromising position."

"Oh, crap," Christine said.

"What's wrong?"

"Saint-Tropez."

"What about it?" Sharon asked.

"The beaches are topless," Christine said.

"Were you?"

Christine made a face and nodded.

"Anybody take photos?"

Christine shrugged. "Could be. There were lots of people around. If any did turn up on the Internet, I'm sure the boys at school would have found them by now."

"Oh, well, Tegan's tits are all over the Internet and it hasn't hurt her career," Sharon said.

"Christine is a minor," Johnston said, turning to Christine. "You were what, fifteen that summer?"

Christine nodded.

"Hopefully the press will take that into account if they happen to find any photos," Sharon said.

"I'll call our lawyers," Maria said. "Just in case."

"Do I have lawyers for that?" Christine asked.

Johnston smiled and nodded.

"Problem solved," Christine said.

"It's not that big a deal in Europe," Johnston said. "The press and paparazzi didn't know who she was at the time. Just another young, beautiful, topless blonde on the beach."

Christine lowered her head and covered her face.

"What's wrong?" Sharon asked.

"Nothing." Christine removed her hands from her face and looked up at Johnston.

"Am I missing something important?" Sharon asked.

"Not at all," Johnston said, smiling.

"They will go after your friends," Sharon said.

"I don't have that many friends, and most of them are upstairs." She pointed up.

"We will get them all together later today. Tegan already knows the drill. Dating her, Alfonso has had a taste. Raoul's PR people assure me he is accustomed to dealing with the press. That leaves Sue."

Christine laughed. "Don't worry about Sue. She has my back. She can be a hoot, but she's usually the smartest person in the room."

"She is," Johnston said.

"Good, we can use that," Sharon said. "I'll still need to meet with her."

"Don't forget Meg," Christine said.

"We have already met with Meg," Aubrey said. "If we need something planted in the press, she's our go-to girl."

"Okay, Christine," Sharon said. "When they come at you with questions about Erik, the kidnapping, Raoul, the engagement, anything other than the opera, try to steer them back to the subject at hand—*Sangre de Cristo*, and the Santa Fe Opera."

"Got it."

"Once we get past the kidnapping, that will just be filed and brought up in passing down the road. When the new wears off the opera story, we will start promoting you rather than protecting you. The announcement of your engagement will be comparatively easy work. After that it's up to you, whether you pursue opera, other musical genres, maybe movies?"

Christine laughed. "I'm just a teenage girl trying to graduate from high school and marry my guy. I'm not looking that far into the future."

SHORTLY BEFORE TEN, Angel's limo bus pulled up to an elegant hotel in downtown Santa Fe, the paparazzi lying in wait. Hundreds of photos were snapped as the group stepped off the bus, the order carefully arranged by Sharon. Christine, as expected, was their target, but shots of Tegan were always good for a payday.

Christine had learned her lesson well. This was a scheduled event, the paparazzi were expected to be there, so she dutifully stopped, smiled, and posed for the cameras.

"Christine! Over here!"

Christine turned toward the sound and smiled.

"Tegan!"

One of the paparazzi motioned for Tegan to stand next to Christine. She obliged. Hands found waists and the girls worked it.

One of the paparazzi shouted, "Where's Sue?"

Christine pointed. "Back there, with the boys."

"Get in there, Sue," the paparazzi said.

Both Christine and Tegan encouraged Sue to join them and she reluctantly obliged. The paparazzi converged and fired off dozens of shots, Sue laughing all the time.

Audrey quickly took charge and ushered everyone inside, except the paparazzi, who were turned away by security. No matter, they had their shots, which would be on offer as soon as they could get online.

Christine was surprised by the number of video cameras set up, as well as all the lights. There were reporters, not only from the entertainment television shows from Los Angeles, but also the network stations from northern New Mexico, for whom this was local news. There were also freelancers, who, like the paparazzi, would be offering up their footage, and hopefully an interview, on the open market.

Christine was escorted to a table set up on risers. From the back, Christine could see that it was just two folding tables, covered with a linen tablecloth. There was an empty glass and a bottle of fancy sparkling water at each position, along with a microphone. Names were printed on cards that stood in front of each microphone.

Sharon and Audrey had carefully positioned Johnston, Maria, Christine, Alfonso, and Zoe, so that the two attractive young stars of the opera were in the middle, with the older representatives of the Santa Fe Opera on either end.

Christine took her seat, remembering Tegan's advice, and carefully positioning her legs so the reporters, seated in rows of chairs facing the table, couldn't see up her skirt. She smiled and choked back a laugh thinking that Tegan herself would have probably taken the opportunity to flash the audience.

Christine was accustomed to stage lights in her face, preventing her from seeing the audience, and this was much the same, although as her eyes adjusted to the lights, she spotted Raoul and the others taking seats behind the reporters.

Audrey, standing beside the table, laid down the ground rules, and the press conference got underway. Both Johnston and Maria made opening remarks, but the reporters were impatiently waiting for questions to begin.

Ignoring Audrey's rules, reporters immediately began peppering Christine with questions.

"Who was the boy you were with on the train?"

Christine paused only briefly before answering. "I was with several boys, young men actually, all close friends."

"What were you doing in Chicago?"

"I'm originally from Chicago. I was visiting family and eating Chicago dogs. That's the only place you can get the real deal. That's what Jim Bob says."

"Who is Jim Bob?"

"He is a very important man in my life," Christine answered.

"Is he your boyfriend?"

Christine laughed. "He was a friend of my parents. He used to change my diapers. He's Zoe's boyfriend, fiancé, actually."

"Zoe?"

Johnston leaned forward to his microphone and gestured toward Zoe. "Zoe Hathaway is the composer of *Sangre de Cristo*, the opera, which is why we are here, is it not?"

Apparently not. "So, who is your boyfriend?"

Christine glanced at Raoul. "I have several friends who are boys. What does that have to do with the opera?"

"What about Alfonso?"

"He's a boy, and he's my friend." Christine smiled and put her hand on Alfonso's.

"You two are a couple?"

Christine laughed again. "We go way back. We went to school together, appeared in a lot of productions together, sang a lot of love songs, so I guess you could say we're a couple, but probably not like you think. Maybe duet would be a better word."

Tegan leaned over to Raoul and whispered, "She's good."

"I'm looking forward to appearing with him again in *Sangre de Cristo*," Christine said. "He makes me very comfortable on stage, in his arms. He's also a pretty good kisser."

The reporters laughed.

"Is that true?" Raoul quietly asked Tegan.

"Damn straight, and that's not all he's good at."

"Should I be worried?" Raoul asked, smiling.

"Hell no. He's mine. She's yours."

"Who is Raoul Chagny?" a reporter shouted.

Christine held her breath for a moment, smiled, and looked at Raoul. "He's a friend, a very close friend."

"Is that all he is?" the reporter asked.

"Let's get back to the reason we're here. I am honored to be asked to sing the female lead in my friend Zoe's opera, *Sangre de Cristo*. It is underwritten by Mr. Caldwell and his cousin Franklin Titshaw, and their family foundation, who are long-time patrons of the Santa Fe Opera." She paused and smiled. "But since you only seem to care about boys, here we go, so try to keep up."

There was some laughter from the audience. Johnston grimaced, expecting the worst. Sharon stepped out in front of the table, off to the side, waving, trying to get Christine's attention, shaking her head furiously. It didn't work.

Christine continued. "Johnston, Mr. Caldwell, was the headmaster of the Belen Conservatory of Music in Los Angeles, where I went to school. I still go there. I'm a senior. That's where I met Alfonso." She put her hand on Alfonso's arm. "This boy. He graduated this year. The conservatory was founded by Johnston's great-grandfather?" She turned to Johnston, who smiled and nodded. "Daniel Titshaw Senior. Daniel's great, great, some number of greats, grandson, is Frankie, another boy, who is out there somewhere." Christine pointed toward the audience. "I can't really see him because of the lights. Frankie has been friends with Raoul since forever. Zoe was Raoul's nanny, but he didn't like that word since he thought he was too old for a nanny."

Zoe smiled. Some of the reporters laughed.

"Raoul was thirteen, I think, when we first met, so maybe he was too old for a nanny. I was twelve. He rescued me from the streets. Those are the boys in my life. Oh, wait, I almost forgot Carlos. He works at the ranch, and I think he's in the Army now. He's a good guy to know. I would trust all of them with my life. I have, actually."

"What about Erik?" a reporter asked calmly.

Johnston started to answer, but Christine put out her hand and stopped him.

"Erik is Johnston's son. He is something of a musical genius, but he never really pursued it."

"Is that all he was?" the reporter asked.

"He was a friend, a very close friend at one time. We spent a wonderful summer together, along with Frankie, Meg, Raoul, and my friend Connie, in Saint-Tropez."

"Is Connie the girl Erik killed?" a reporter asked.

"There was an accident, a terrible accident. Connie was killed. Erik was badly injured."

"He kidnapped you off the stage while you were performing an opera," another reporter said. "What was that like?"

"Okay," Johnston said, interrupting. "I think that's enough of this line of questioning."

"No," Christine said. "I'd like to answer."

"You don't have to," Johnston said. "We can end this right here."

Christine smiled and patted him on the arm.

"It was otherworldly, terrifying, confusing."

"What happened at the cabin?" a reporter asked.

Christine looked at Johnston, who clearly wanted to put a stop to it, and smiled. She turned back to the audience.

"I was rescued," she said calmly. She fought back tears as she looked at Raoul. "My boys, men actually, Raoul, Alfonso, Frankie, Carlos, and Jim Bob, on horseback, rescued me from the cabin, from a raging river, to be precise." She wiped tears. "Erik was washed away by the flood, trying to save me. I wish it could have ended differently. I want to remember him in better times, and there were better times, much better."

The reporters were silent. Christine contemplated what to say next. "And now, Alfonso and I have to go to rehearsal. We have a show to put on. Tickets are available at the box office, I guess?" She looked at Johnston.

"Reopening night, as Christine calls it, is sold out, but tickets for subsequent performances are available at the box office and online," Johnston said.

"Oh, okay, good. If you guys have any questions about the opera, Johnston and Maria can hook you up. They're the boss anyway. I'm just the girl singer. Oh, and Zoe wrote the thing. Ask her."

Christine pushed back her chair and stood. Alfonso quickly stood and hugged her and kissed her on the head. Raoul started it, but soon nearly everyone in the room was standing and clapping.

"And that, boys and girls, is how you handle the press," Tegan said to Raoul. "You will soon be sleeping with a superstar."

4

REOPENING NIGHT

THERE WAS NOT a single complaint from any of the cast and crew on *Sangre de Cristo* about the accelerated and exhaustive rehearsals so that Christine could properly take over the role of Sofia. They had all been there opening night and witnessed for themselves a star being born. They had also witnessed the shocking kidnapping and were glad that it had ended well, if not for Johnston's son, at least for Christine. Everyone tried to handle her with kid gloves, but she quickly put a stop to that, and rehearsal was soon running smoothly, with Christine working harder than anyone. They had only days to fully integrate Christine into the opera, all while other shows were going on nightly.

"I'm so sorry," Christine said as she hugged Hayley. "You should have gone on in Carlotta's place."

"It was obviously not to be," Hayley said. "O.G. wanted you and he got what he wanted."

"Are you okay?"

"I threw up for two days. The good news is I lost five pounds. The bad news is it will come back now that I'm eating again, and holding it in."

"Are you okay with being my understudy?"

"Of course. That's what I was hired to do, and I'm still doing it."

"But I'm just a kid. This is your career."

"Never apologize for catching a break. Make the most of it."

"Thanks."

"I'm really looking forward to seeing your performance. I left early for the last one, in the back of an ambulance."

"Yeah, I kind of had an unexpected departure myself, at the end."

Hayley laughed loudly and then apologized. "Sorry. Gallows humor."

"That's okay. Sometimes it helps to joke about bad things. Did you really puke up your guts?"

"You have no idea, but you should have seen Carlotta. That bitch can barf."

Both girls laughed.

WHILE SUE HAD officially taken over Christine's old job and was quite willing to be a slave in every department, Johnston insisted that she stay as close to Christine as possible, something of a personal assistant.

"Sure," Sue said, "no problem."

"Are you sure you don't mind being your best friend's assistant?" Johnston asked.

"She'd do the same for me."

"The departments can get by without another pair of hands, but I want Christine to be worry-free, concentrating on her performance, and not the details."

"I'm a detail girl. Besides, I'm getting paid. You are paying me, right?"

"Yes, we are paying you."

"Plus, free room and board, and pool, at your rancho, a fabulous old truck to haul around town in, and all this," Sue said as she waved a hand toward the mountains. "What's not to like?"

"Speaking of rooms. You can have your own room. We have plenty."

"That's okay. You don't want Christine to worry, right? I need to be close by."

"I understand. But we have bigger rooms, with two beds."

"We're good. One bed is fine."

Johnston nodded.

"Wait, it's not like we're lesbians or something," Sue said.

Johnston laughed. "I think that's pretty obvious."

"But a bigger room with two beds would be nice."

"I'm just surprised she isn't sharing a room with Raoul."

"We talked about that. I guess she didn't want to say anything to you."

Johnston was suddenly worried. "What?"

"Since you're going to be her new dad and all, she thought it wouldn't be right, sharing a room with Raoul in your house."

Johnston smiled and nodded.

"She said she thought about what she would do if her dad was still alive, and thought you deserved the same respect, or words to that effect."

"I never had a daughter, so this stuff is all new to me. I realize it's no longer politically correct to say it, but it is definitely different for boys."

"You can say that again. My parents are old school, old country, old everything."

"Have I told you how happy I am to have you here this summer?" Johnston asked, putting his arm around her, and hugging her.

REOPENING NIGHT CAME all too quickly, but Christine was confident she was up to the task—she had, after all, sung the opera on a moment's notice just days before. Now, after hours of rehearsal with the full cast, and more hours alone with Alfonso, and Sue watching from the wings, she was ready for her official debut.

Security was tight. Johnston held out little hope that Erik was still alive, but there was no body, and he was not taking any chances with his cast and crew, his audience, and most of all, Christine.

Mrs. Giry was under enormous stress, fielding phone calls from the rich, the famous, the powerful, the well-connected, all wanting tickets. Standing room had long since been sold out and folding chairs squeezed into every available space under the watchful eye of the fire marshal.

Season ticket holders were unwilling to give up their seats. Although they had seen the previous performance, with its exciting and unbelievable conclusion, they did not want to miss reopening night. Maria made the first move, giving up her two prime seats next to the governor's, whose office was besieged with requests for tickets. Some of the patrons followed suit, offering their own tickets directly to friends and business associates from out of town, although it did little to help Mrs. Giry deal with her own long list.

Franklin came up with a rather bizarre plan to position portable bleachers just outside the theater. Owing to the unique open-air construction of the opera house, they could still see, and hear, the opera, from the bleachers. It quickly became a badge of honor for the well-heeled donors to sit on aluminum bleachers after giving up their seats inside the theater. If it rained, it rained. They came prepared, as always. It helped that the Opera Club was just a few steps away.

Zoe and Jim Bob immediately gave up their seats—they would be backstage anyway, Jim Bob pacing in the wings while a comfortable chair was quickly positioned for the very pregnant Zoe. Johnston would also be backstage and hadn't even thought about his own seats until Mrs. Giry reminded him and quickly took possession.

The stage crew wasn't normally happy to have the diva's entourage getting in the way backstage, but this was different. There was never any question that Sue would be at Christine's side every moment she was not actually on the stage, but no one complained when Frankie, Raoul and Tegan also arrived, their seats offered up to Mrs. Giry. Meg was a dancer in the show anyway, and after quickly hugging Christine before the show, remained with the dancers and out of the way.

While the boys were casually, though elegantly dressed, Tegan showed up in jeans and a T-shirt, declaring herself to be Sue's assistant, and Sue didn't hesitate to put her to work. If Christine sneezed, two tissues would instantly appear.

Alfonso got just one brief kiss from Tegan and then he was on his own. He didn't mind. He was pumped. Rehearsal had gone well, and he was more than eager to take the stage with Christine. He was also relieved to see that she would be well taken care of offstage.

Raoul and Christine had locked lips in the dressing room before going to makeup. In order to not distract Christine with his presence, Raoul had intended to then position himself on the opposite side of the stage, along with Jim Bob, to keep an eye out for the unspoken threat that Erik might decide to arise from the dead and reappear on reopening night. Security professionals had also raised the possibility of a copycat seeking his fifteen minutes of fame on the Internet—no doubt hundreds of cell phones would record the incident. Frankie would be on the dressing room side, along with Johnston.

"No," Christine said. "I want you close by. You won't be a distraction, but don't expect a lot of kissy face as I whizz by. If I ignore you, it's not you—I'll be running on adrenaline."

"Got it," Raoul said.

"Frankie can take the other side, with Jim Bob. He knows every nook and cranny in the opera house. On this side it will be you and Johnston, unless he's out in the theater, directing traffic." She smiled.

"It's pretty hectic out there," Raoul said. "Have you looked?"

"No. I just hope everything goes well."

"Tailgating was epic. I wish you could have been there."

"Me too, but I like this better," she said as she pulled her T-shirt over her head.

Raoul was startled, but he couldn't not look.

"Hair and makeup," Christine said as a makeup cape was quickly draped around her bare shoulders.

"I guess that's my cue," Raoul said.

"Wait. One more kiss before I put on lipstick."

They kissed once more, and Raoul departed.

Johnston was indeed directing traffic in the theater, shaking hands, welcoming VIPs who had never been to the Santa Fe Opera, encouraging them to come again soon. Franklin and Maria were doing the same, working the crowd, scanning for empty seats that might be available.

Mona took charge of the bleachers, pressing ushers into service to assist the ladies on the precarious climb. Everyone took it in good spirits, along with actual spirits from the nearby Opera Club.

In addition to security provided by the opera house, several private bodyguards flanked the bleachers—billions of dollars of net worth was perched on those aluminum seats.

There was nothing for a publicist to do during an actual performance, so Johnston suggested that Sharon sit in the bleachers and enjoy the opera. The real action, for her, would come later.

"Wow. This is a big deal," Sharon said as she squeezed in beside Franklin and his wife.

"Yes, it is," Franklin said.

"This place is amazing. I had heard of the Santa Fe Opera, but always thought it was an old building downtown."

"We're quite proud of it."

"And who would have imagined people in tuxedos and evening gowns tailgating in the parking lot? I didn't even know that was a thing at a place like this."

"It's a thing, a big thing."

"So I noticed," Sharon said as she looked around at all the people eagerly awaiting the start of the opera. "Christine is our first opera singer. I have a lot to learn."

Franklin laughed.

"What?" Sharon asked.

"Christine is not your average opera singer. I suspect most others would be much more trouble. Christine is a real gem."

———

Johnston checked his watch and hustled backstage, just as Christine stepped out of the dressing room.

"Sorry, I wanted to get here before you were in makeup, so I could hug you, but it got kind of busy out there."

Christine threw herself into his arms, planted her face on his chest, and hugged him tightly.

"Makeup!" Sue called.

"Thank you so much," Christine said as she pulled away.

"For what?"

"Everything, absolutely everything."

Johnston smiled, pulled her back into his chest, patted her on the back and kissed her on the head. "Break a leg."

"Is the house full?" Christine asked as she pulled away and turned toward the makeup artist, while at the same time reaching out for Raoul's hand.

"It's full and overflowing. Franklin and Maria, along with a lot of the patrons, are sitting on bleachers."

"Really?"

Johnston nodded. "It's a big night, a huge night. No pressure."

Christine laughed. "No pressure." She turned and looked around. "Where's Alfie?"

"Probably being serviced by Teegs," Sue said.

"Is not," Tegan said, indignantly. "I'm right here, for my girl. I'll do him later." She put her arm around Christine and hugged her sideways, holding her head to the side so as to not disturb Christine's freshly fixed face.

Alfonso suddenly appeared from nowhere, took Christine's hands and stood facing her. "It's showtime," he said. They air kissed on both cheeks.

Christine looked at Raoul and blew him a kiss. She and Alfonso turned and stood, side by side, holding hands, facing the stage as the orchestra played the prelude.

Raoul stood in awe as the show progressed. He had seen Christine sing many times, including this very opera just days ago, but he knew he was witnessing something extraordinary. Christine *was* Sofia, and threw herself into the role, oblivious to the audience, all those in the wings, the weather, thoughts of Erik, everything. She and Alfonso were the very essence of tragic young lovers.

"We should make out," Tegan whispered to Raoul as they watched from the wings.

"Huh?"

"To offset that."

"Offset what?"

"That is pure sex, with their clothes on."

Raoul chuckled. "Yeah, it is kind of hot, even if it is my own girlfriend, and your boyfriend."

"I don't know about you, but that boy is so getting laid tonight. Good thing he's off tomorrow."

Raoul smiled.

The weather cooperated, or not, depending on one's point of view, and there was no rain, but also no thunder and lightning, which had become part of the spreading legend of opening night for *Sangre de Cristo*. It mattered little, as the audience was so swept up in the performance that by the time Alejandro died in Sofia's arms there was not a dry eye in the house.

Backstage, Sue and Tegan watched Christine intently while Johnston, Jim Bob and the boys continuously scanned the stage, the rafters, the rigging, the scenery, the wings, but there was no sign of the Opera Ghost, or Erik.

Christine stood, clutching the bloody sash. The audience held its collective breath as she sang, a voice so pure, so clear, so angelic, so possessed, so filled with emotion that there was no doubt the previous performance was no fluke.

Lying dead on the floor, Alfonso was glad the audience could not see his face. The big smile might have given him away. He didn't have to see the audience to know that Christine was taking their breath away. He always knew she was good, but this topped it all. He couldn't wait to leap up from the stage floor, sweep her into his arms, and take their bows.

The audience rose to their feet, the applause and cheers almost deafening. Christine trembled and gasped for breath. She had missed this moment previously, and she now basked in the glow. She reached out for Alfonso and immediately felt his hand in hers. Her chest was heaving as she turned to look at him. He smiled. She turned back to the audience as the applause continued.

"Wow," Tegan said.

"Yeah," Raoul said. "She nailed it."

"Did she ever."

"You go girl!" Sue shouted, certain she could not be heard over the roar of the crowd, but not really caring.

Christine turned and looked at her friends, gritting her teeth and making a face like the excited teenage girl she was, knowing that she had done well.

———

BOTH JOHNSTON AND Franklin assumed the main after-party would be at the ranch. It had been handling large crowds for decades. But Maria insisted the party be at her flagship hotel in downtown Santa Fe. There were a lot of out-of-towners new to the opera, and the area, and a downtown location would be much easier to find, she argued, not to mention a shorter drive, and most of the out-of-town guests would be staying at hotels near the plaza anyway. Johnston was far more concerned with making sure the performance itself went off without a hitch, and Franklin agreed that his wife certainly would not mind turning over the planning of the party to Maria. That turned out to not be the case however, as Mona soon received a phone call from Maria asking her to co-host. She laughed, agreed immediately, and the two were soon having lunch at the hotel and laying plans for what was sure to become a legendary after-party.

The party was well underway in the hotel ballroom, spilling out into the lobby and onto the veranda when Angel's limo bus pulled up. A bellman quickly opened the door and the paparazzi swarmed.

Sue, having ditched her work clothes for a dress, stepped off first, alone, and mugged for the cameras as flashes fired. "Hi, guys!"

The paparazzi greeted her, but were waiting for the main event, the money shots. Sharon followed, avoiding the cameras, back in tub-thumper mode. Frankie and Meg were next, pushing through the paparazzi. They stopped and turned so Frankie could keep an eye on Christine when she stepped into the fray.

After a quick conference with Sharon on the bus, it was decided that, once again, Raoul and Tegan would walk the line together, and then Alfonso and Christine. Sharon's firm hadn't picked up on any hard information that anyone suspected Christine and Raoul were engaged, and tonight was all about the two young stars of the opera anyway, so it was an easy decision.

Before leaving the opera house, Tegan traded her jeans and T-shirt for a stunning cocktail dress showing plenty of legs and cleavage as she stepped off, holding hands with Raoul. The paparazzi ate it up.

Finally, the stars appeared. Alfonso stepped off and held out his hand for Christine. She smiled, looked up for the cameras, took his hand, and stepped off, walking arm in arm with Alfonso, looking side to side for the photographers, but making frequent eye contact with Raoul, now standing beside Frankie.

Applause broke out when Christine and Alfonso entered the ballroom, somewhat embarrassing Christine. She was accustomed to applause for a successful performance, not for merely entering a room.

Under Sharon's watchful eye, and on Alfonso's arm, Christine worked the room like a pro, shaking hundreds of hands, making small talk with big VIPs. Sharon kept her moving and she soon made her way to Johnston and Maria.

Christine immediately hugged Johnston and kissed him on the cheek. "Thank you. This is amazing."

Christine extended her hand to Maria but was quickly swept up in a hug. "You must be exhausted. It's been a big day."

"Yes ma'am."

"You don't have to stay. I'm sure you would prefer to be with your friends, not us old folks."

"Are you sure?"

"I'm sure."

Christine looked at Johnston, who nodded in agreement. Christine smiled. "We'll stay a little while longer. I don't want to seem rude."

"And now you know why I insisted on having the after-party here," Maria said.

Johnston was confused.

"I'm guessing that instead of going out to a club, Christine and her friends are headed to the ranch."

"Good thinking," Johnston said.

"That's why you have me."

After a reasonable time, the kids made their way to the door, Frankie on his cell phone, calling Angel to bring up the bus.

CHRISTINE, WHO NEVER ate before a performance, was famished, and Juanita immediately sprang into action. The kids gathered around the pool to eat, talk, and laugh. With some food in her belly, Christine finally came down from her opera high and collapsed into Raoul's arms.

"Do you mind if we stay here tonight?" Tegan asked.

"Not at all," Frankie said. "We have plenty of rooms."

"Good. That performance made me so hot I can't wait to ravish this boy."

Christine laughed. "Really? We were just playing our roles."

"I know. I am an actress, remember? I know how to work it, but what you two did on that stage tonight was a whole other dimension."

"Thanks?" Christine said, making a face.

"I was thinking of you all the time," Alfonso said to Tegan.

"Yeah, right. Whatever. Just keep it up. You guys killed it. Seriously. I'm not joking. That was amazing. If they gave Oscars for opera, you two just took home the little gold guys."

"Do they have awards for opera?" Sue asked.

"Yes, actually they do," Frankie said. "I'll check into it, but I see some nominations in our future."

"Well, I'm going to bed," Sue said as she stood. "I'm exhausted. You love birds can make out by the pool."

Christine looked at Raoul. "I should go with her."

"I think she'll understand," Raoul said.

Christine smiled. They kissed, not even noticing that Tegan and Alfonso had also departed.

Frankie and Meg hung around a bit longer, but eventually went inside, leaving Christine and Raoul seriously making out by the pool.

5

THE DIVA WRANGLER

THE REVIEWS FOR reopening night of *Sangre de Cristo* were even better than before, and there were more of them. It helped that the star had rehearsed this time. The previous performance had been the premiere for just another new opera, but after Christine was spectacularly kidnapped off the stage in front of the audience, everyone took notice, and the media converged on Santa Fe.

Sharon had gathered the best reviews and loaded them onto a tablet for Christine to read at breakfast, or brunch, as she had slept in, exhausted after the previous night's performance.

Raoul sipped coffee, having eaten breakfast hours earlier, fiddled with his phone, and then looked at Christine, not smiling.

"What's wrong?" Christine asked.

"The jet will be returning to Paris from Los Angeles this afternoon with some company executives. Dad said it will stop in Santa Fe and pick me up."

"Well, crap."

Raoul smiled. "I'll text him back and tell him I'll stay another night and fly commercial tomorrow."

"Oh, how sweet. You'd do that for me?"

"Of course."

Christine laughed. "That's okay. Take the jet. I have to go to the opera house later anyway. The director wants to do a—what did they call it?"

"Postmortem," Sue said, between bites.

"Tell me where I messed up."

"See if anything needs fixing before the next performance. Not just you."

"So, you're saying I did mess up?"

"You know what I mean."

"It looked perfect to me," Raoul said.

"Thanks, but you have to say that."

Raoul nodded. "Yeah, but it still looked perfect."

"Look. I wish you could stay another night, another week, or all summer, but I knew what I was getting into when I put the ring on my finger. You're going to be a big-shot international businessman, jetting off all over the world. I get it. We might as well start now."

"And you're going to be a big-time opera diva, jetting off all over the world."

"We'll see about that."

"So, you're okay with me catching the jet today?"

"I'm cool. I've got my girl Sue, and we're going to be plenty busy for the next few weeks."

"Frankie will probably be here all summer. And Carlos will be back from summer camp in a couple of weeks. He'll hang out until he has to go back to school."

"Are you saying I need guys to protect me?"

"Just being careful."

"Like at Ogden Hall when you had your buddies bodyguard me after you got suspended for punching out that guy?"

"Oh, that was so romantic," Sue said.

"You told Sue about that?" Raoul asked.

"I tell Sue everything."

"Good to know."

"Don't forget Alfie. He can keep an eye on me, when we're not making out on stage."

"How could I forget?"

"And Tegan has to go shoot a movie, so Alfie has more time for me."

"Maybe I should stay."

At any other airport it might have been an unusual sight—a battered old pickup slowly approaching the sleek Gulfstream jet waiting on the tarmac. The pilot smiled. Sue drove the pickup, with Christine in the middle, pointing out how to shift gears. Raoul rode shotgun.

Raoul insisted that he could walk the few yards through the private terminal and onto the tarmac, but Sue thought it would be cool to drive right up to the jet. "I've seen it in movies," she said, "but who really gets to do that?"

An employee of the fixed-base operator handling ground services for the jet rode in the bed of the pickup, along with Raoul's luggage, shouting directions to Sue, keeping a careful eye on the Gulfstream's wingtip, and banging on the roof when necessary.

There was kissing and tears, and more kissing, but Christine finally let go of Raoul and he bounded up the stairs to the jet.

Sue dropped off their escort, who closed and locked the gate behind them, and then found a spot to park where she and Christine hopped into the bed of the truck and watched and waved as the Gulfstream roared down the runway and into the sky.

ONCE INITIAL REHEARSALS were over, and they settled into the routine, there was more downtime for Christine and Sue, and Johnston told them to take advantage of it.

"You're going to pay me to goof off?" Sue said.

"Don't worry about it," Johnston replied. "*Sangre de Cristo* is selling like crazy and is generating plenty of revenue. It's well worth it to keep our star happy."

"Are you sure?" Sue's parents had worked hard after coming to the United States and she was expected to do the same. Taking money for hanging out with her best friend seemed somehow wrong.

"Trust me. Compared to the demands of some divas, the cost of Christine's entourage is nothing. Besides, you're both staying at the ranch, and driving the old truck, so the opera is saving thousands on room and board and transportation."

"Okay, then. It sure beats working in my parents' store for the summer."

"By the way, you do realize that you can drive the Suburban, or I can rent a car for the summer, something more suitable for teenage girls. You don't have to drive that old truck."

"We love the truck. It's a total blast to drive, and people stare."

ANGEL'S LIMO BUS dropped off a load of tourists at Palace of the Governors. Angel rolled down the window and looked across the street where Christine sang, with Sue on violin, Jim Bob on guitar and Carlos on guitarrón. After a moment Angel drove away.

Maria stood a few yards away. "Did you know about this?" Maria asked Johnston on the phone.

"It's news to me. Are you sure?"

"I'm standing on the plaza watching it right now."

"I'll be right there."

By the time Johnston a large crowd had gathered around as Christine sang "Cielito Lindo."

Johnston and Maria stood silently as Christine sang.

"I'm impressed," Maria said. "I've never heard 'Cielito Lindo' done that way. The girl is remarkable, but then we already knew that."

"Yes, she is. But what's going on here?"

There was loud applause as Christine finished the song.

Jim Bob checked his watch. "Sorry, folks, time's up. We have to go."

The crowd expressed their disappointment.

As the musicians packed their instruments, Christine spotted Johnston and Maria and rushed over.

"Am I in trouble?" Christine asked.

"I don't know," Johnston said. "What exactly are you doing?"

"Busking. Like on the Promenade in Santa Monica."

"Do you have a permit?" Maria asked.

"Of course. I'm licensed to busk in two states. So are Sue and Jim Bob. I think Carlos is just good in Santa Fe."

"Are you collecting money?" Johnston asked, watching as Sue gathered up money from her violin case.

Christine laughed. "Oh, that. It's for charity."

"Charity?"

"The homeless shelter. There are homeless everywhere, even Santa Fe. We have a sign and everything." She looked around and pointed. "Look, Carlos has it."

"Well, that's a relief."

"I guess I should have asked first, since I sing at the opera house and all."

"It would have been nice. But since it's for a good cause." He pulled a wad of bills bound by a silver money clip from his pocket, peeled off a hundred, and handed it to Christine.

"I'll send a check," Maria said.

"Thanks," Christine said. "Oh, by the way, while we're on the subject—Carlos jams with the apprentices at a joint over there somewhere." She pointed toward a wide swath of downtown Santa Fe.

"I know it well," Johnston said.

"Is it okay if Sue and I sit in tonight?"

Johnston smiled. "Yes, of course. We'll be there." He turned to Maria. "Unless you have other plans."

"I'm looking forward to it."

"Cool," Christine said.

THE JOINT OVER THERE somewhere was a very popular restaurant. The owner hit on the secret to success in the restaurant business: good food, good service, reasonable prices, and live entertainment. Anyone could sing for their supper, and during opera season, the place was frequented by apprentice singers from the Santa Fe Opera. Tonight was no exception. Zoe sat at the piano. Jim Bob and Carlos nearby with guitar and guitarrón, accompanying Hayley as she sang "Dormite."

Christine, Sue, and Alfonso sat at a nearby table, along with other apprentices.

Johnston and Maria joined in the applause as they were shown to their table.

"Her Spanish is perfect," Maria said as they were seated.

"She sings beautifully," Johnston said.

"Is she okay with Christine taking over Sofia?"

"She seems to be. We should invite her back next year and put her in something."

"Definitely."

Sue took the stage and played "Petite Fleur" on trumpet.

Johnston took Maria's hand and they stepped onto the dance floor.

After enthusiastic applause, Sue put down the trumpet and picked up her violin. She stepped up to the microphone. "And now, straight from the Santa Fe Opera, the young stars of *Sangre de Cristo*, Alfonso Bellini and Christine Daaé."

Christine and Alfonso stepped onto the stage amid loud applause. Sue began "The Prayer" on violin, then Zoe on piano. Christine began singing in English, soon joined by Alfonso in Italian.

"They look wonderful together," Maria said. "Are you sure Christine is engaged to someone else?"

Johnston smiled. "Positive. Alfonso's duet partner graduated the year before Christine started at the conservatory. He staked her out immediately, and the results have been spectacular."

When the song ended, and the applause died down, Christine and Sue joined Johnston and Maria at their table.

"That was extraordinary," Maria said.

"Thanks," Christine responded.

"And Sue, a double threat. That was wonderful."

"Thanks," Sue said.

"She also plays piano," Christine said.

"Who doesn't play piano?" Sue said.

"Are you joining us for dinner?" Johnston asked.

"We already ate with the gang," Christine said. "We sang for our supper. We just stopped to say 'hi' before going back up there. This is fun."

Christine and Sue became a familiar sight all over Santa Fe in the old truck. Johnston insisted they take a vehicle less likely to break down for their out-of-town trips, along with one of the boys, just in case. They spent a day in Albuquerque, at Old Town, and rode the tramway up to Sandia Peak. They roamed all over northern New Mexico, including Taos and Los Alamos.

"Los Alamos?" Frankie asked, somewhat surprised. "Why do you want to go there?"

"Have you ever heard of the White Train?" Christine asked.

"Of course."

"What's a white train?" Sue asked.

"It was a special government train that delivered nuclear bombs from Amarillo all over the country," Frankie said. "Now they just use trucks."

"My grandfather was a guard on the train," Christine said.

"No shit?" Frankie asked.

"Really."

Frankie pulled out his cell phone. "I have to text my dad. He'll crap his pants."

"I'm confused," Sue said. "What's the big deal?"

Christine shrugged.

"It's a big deal to railroad nuts, like my dad," Frankie said. "He's going to have a lot of questions for you."

"I don't really know anything about it. I never even met my mom's parents. I just remember she mentioned it a couple of times and I looked it up online."

"Who knew?" Sue said. "I never even thought about how nuclear bombs got delivered."

"They're built just outside Amarillo, and they have to get to their destinations somehow," Frankie said. "It's not exactly something you just ship by UPS. They need guards to keep them from getting hijacked."

———

THE SUMMER FLEW past all too quickly and as it wound down Christine and Sue went out for pizza on a night off from the opera.

"This is where Raoul brought me," Christine said as they waited in line for a table.

"Cool," Sue said. "Is the pizza any good?"

"I don't remember," Christine said, covering her face to hide her embarrassment.

"You slut," Sue teased. "Uh-oh, nine o'clock."

"Is it that late?" Christine asked, confused.

"No, over there," Sue said, tilting her head. "Boys."

Two teenage boys approached. "They're giving us a table for four," one of them said. "There's a long line. Would you like to join us?"

Sue looked at Christine for approval, who grinned and said, "Sure, why not?"

Sue laughed.

"Tourists?" one of the boys asked after they were seated and had ordered.

"Not really," Christine said. The girls giggled.

"I win," the other boy said.

"Win what?" Sue asked.

"We had a little bet over whether you were locals."

"You aren't mad, are you, that we made a bet about you?" the other asked.

"Briefs," Christine said, looking sternly at the boy.

Christine and Sue looked at the other and said in unison, "boxers."

The boys were puzzled.

"We're not mad," Sue said.

"So, do you just hit on the tourists, or also the townies?" Christine asked.

"Uh—which is the right answer?"

"It doesn't matter. We were just hungry and didn't want to wait."

"What school do you go to?" one of the boys asked.

"It's not around here," Christine said.

"I thought you weren't tourists."

"We're not," Sue said. "But we are here for the summer. We work at the opera house."

"Box office or gift shop?"

"How do you know we aren't in the apprentice program?" Sue asked.

"You look like high school girls."

"We are, kind of," Christine said.

"Kind of?"

"We go to the Belen Conservatory of Music."

"In Belen?"

"Los Angeles," Christine said.

"What about you guys?" Sue asked.

"St. Michaels."

"Catholic school."

"How do you know about the opera house?" Christine asked.

"We live in Santa Fe. You can't not know something about the opera house."

"Should we tell them what we do?" Sue asked Christine.

"Sure. They look like nice guys."

"I'm the diva wrangler," Sue said

"What's that?"

"I make sure the diva is well taken care of," Sue said.

"And what do you do?" one of the boys said, turning to Christine.

"She's the diva," Sue said.

"You're an opera singer?"

Christine shrugged.

"No way," one of the boys said.

"Yes way," Sue said. "She is."

"You're that girl!"

"What girl?" Christine asked.

"That got snatched off the stage. You're Sofia."

"Were you there?" Christine asked.

He nodded. "My parents are season ticket holders."

"Wow," the other said. "We're having pizza with a celebrity."

"I CAN'T BELIEVE you gave him your number," Christine said as she and Sue walked down the sidewalk after leaving the pizza place.

"He seemed harmless enough. I'm almost eighteen. I need some experience in the department of romantic arts and sciences before college."

Christine laughed, and then stopped. "Where's the truck?"

They looked around.

"We parked it right here, didn't we?" Christine said.

"Yeah, I'm pretty sure we did."

Christine pulled out her phone.

"What are you doing?" Sue asked.

"I'm calling Frankie. Somebody stole the truck."

Sue scanned the street. "No, wait! There it is."

"Where?"

"Over there." Sue pointed.

The girls quickly crossed the street to the truck. Christine whipped her head back and forth.

"There's no way we parked here," Christine said.

"Yeah, I know. Somebody moved it."

"Frankie?"

They drove to the ranch and confronted Frankie.

"It wasn't me," Frankie said. "Are you sure you turned the key all the way? You do know you can start it without a key."

"Of course we know," Christine said. "You told me and I told Sue. We always lock the ignition. We're not stupid."

"That's not what I'm saying. Maybe you just forgot. I forget sometimes."

"We didn't forget. Somebody has a key."

"Who?"

"What about Carlos?" Sue asked. "Maybe he punked us."

"I'm sure he could get a key if he wanted, but he would never do something like that," Frankie said. "Besides, he left for Lubbock yesterday."

"Erik," Christine said grimly.

"No way. Erik's dead."

"Have you seen the body?" Christine asked. "Has Johnston?"

"Okay, let's say Erik's alive, just for the sake of argument. Why in the world would he move the truck across the street?"

"Why do you think? He's jacking with me."

"No money has been withdrawn from his bank account. He hasn't used his debit card. What's he doing for money? How is he living? It may be a few years before a judge can declare him legally dead, but he's gone. It's time to move on. I have. Johnston has. His mother has."

"Maybe it was some of the guys from the opera house," Sue said. "They all know we drive the truck, and they like to pull pranks."

"There you go," Frankie said. "Or maybe it was just some local teenagers."

"You're probably right," Christine said. "Let's not say anything to Johnston. No sense in worrying him."

They all agreed.

While Sue was in the shower, Christine locked the door to their room, stepped out onto the balcony, and stared into the darkness at the Sangre de Cristos Mountains. She pushed aside the billowing sheer curtains, locked the balcony door, and then checked it.

RAOUL STEPPED OFF the Gulfstream, smiling and waving as a Suburban approached, driven by Julio, with an FBO employee in the passenger seat. Following closely was the old pickup with Christine and Sue. Christine opened the door before the pickup stopped and rushed into Raoul's arms.

"I missed you," Christine managed to say between kisses.

"Me too."

Sue helped Julio load luggage, and cases of wine, into the back of the pickup. Christine hugged Raoul's parents.

"I suppose you will be riding with the girls," Chagny said.

Raoul smiled and nodded.

Chagny laughed, took his wife by the hand, and headed toward the Suburban. While Christine and Raoul made out like crazy, Sue followed Julio off the tarmac and through the gate. Eventually the lovebirds settled for holding hands.

"Is it sold out?" Raoul asked.

"It has been, all season," Christine said.

"And there's a lot of media in town," Sue added.

"But our little secret didn't leak?" Raoul asked.

"Nope," Christine said. "The reporters are just here for closing night, and there's not that many of them."

"Did Tegan make it in?" Raoul asked.

"She'll be here tomorrow morning to reclaim her man," Sue said. "Frankie got her a seat on somebody's private jet to Albuquerque. That boy knows how to get stuff done."

"Did you find an apartment in Cambridge?" Christine asked.

"Not yet. I'm going back next week to look at a few possibilities. I'll probably just get a small place for this year, and then when you come over, we can find something bigger."

"I don't take up much space," Christine said.

He smiled. "Dad may want to buy a townhouse. He said it looks like a good investment, especially if I stay on for an advanced degree."

"Oh, good. Then Sue can come visit," Christine said.

"Visit?" Sue said. "Maybe I'll go to school there."

"Really?" Christine asked.

"Nah, I'll probably stay closer to home."

"Oh, look, I'm wearing my ring," Christine said.

"I noticed," Raoul said.

"We came straight from the ranch, so nobody saw us."

"Just one more day."

"Remind me to put it back in the safe when we get there. We have your room all ready."

"My room?"

"Your room."

"Unless you want to sleep in our room," Sue said. "Could be fun."

"I don't know if I can handle two hot young babes at the same time."

Christine shrieked.

"You probably need a nap first," Sue said.

"Actually, I do. I'm jet lagged."

"You can take a nap while Sue and I run out to the opera house," Christine said. "Then we can go out tonight."

"Threesome?"

"I have a hot date with Travis, so you'll have her all to yourself," Sue said.

"Who is Travis?" Raoul asked.

"We went to that pizza place you took me to," Christine said. "There was a long line, so two cute guys asked us to join them at their table."

"Cute guys? I don't like where this is going," Raoul said.

"Confucius say, 'Just because you already ordered doesn't mean you can't read menu,'" Sue said.

Raoul laughed.

"Sue gave one of them her number."

"He called," Sue said. "He's coming over for dinner, and then we're going to a movie while you two make out."

"Works for me," Raoul said.

THE OLD PICKUP bounced along on its way up the mountain. Raoul drove while Christine worked the GPS app on her phone.

"Are you sure you want to do this?" he asked.

"You don't want to park and make out?"

"Sure I do, but why here? Why not at the ranch, or somewhere else?"

"I want to exorcise my demons."

"Your what?"

"Demons, spirits, ghosts." She took a deep breath. "Erik." She checked her phone. "We're nearly there."

They found the place, and Raoul maneuvered the pickup into position. They unrolled the foam mattress, climbed in, leaned against the cab, and watched silently as the sun dipped below the Jemez Mountains.

"It's taken a while to get comfortable at the opera house. I still flinch when I see a shadow, a sudden movement. It helps that Sue is always with me, ready to kick somebody's ass, and I know all the guys would pile on."

He put his arm around her.

"When we're driving, I always check the mirror, looking for a motorcycle, listening. I double check the locks in my room at the ranch. Frankie says Erik is dead, but his body has never been found, so I worry."

"I understand."

"By coming here, where he spied on us, listened to us, and slashed the tire, I'm reclaiming my territory, piece by piece."

"Happy to help, ma'am."

They kissed, for a long time.

"When he snatched me off the stage, I was scared, terrified. I didn't know what was going to happen."

"We don't have to talk about this."

"Yes, we do. No secrets, remember?"

He nodded.

"I talk to Sue, but it's not the same. I can't really talk to Johnston. He's not my dad yet, which makes it kind of awkward, but he is Erik's dad, so that makes it even harder."

They cuddled for a moment.

"It's not like being kidnapped by a stranger. I knew him. I cared about him, or did once, but no matter what happened, it was going to be bad. He tied my hands behind my back. In the cabin, he kept telling me he loved me, that it was our wedding night. He asked why I wasn't wearing his ring. Then he washed my feet and legs and tried to be all tender. I tried talking to him, hoping it would stall him until help arrived."

"We were looking everywhere, cops, stage crew, everybody."

"Or until—"

He hugged her tightly and kissed her on the head.

"I finally got him to untie my hands. Then he started pawing, groping, trying to kiss me. He ripped off my panties and then I heard a zipper. I knew what was coming, so I told him I'd rather die."

She looked at him and smiled.

"Funny how your mind works at times like that. I thought about something Sue used to say."

"Sue?"

"Confucius say, 'Girl with skirt up run faster than boy with pants down.'"

Raoul laughed, and then said, "Sorry."

"That's okay. Gallows humor."

He watched as she hiked up her already short skirt and said, "Want to pull down your pants and try it?"

"Maybe later."

She laughed, and then there was silence for a moment.

"I had no idea where I was or where I was going, and I was barefoot, but anything was better than what was about to happen in that cabin, so I kicked him in the *cojones* and ran. I almost made it to the door when he lunged at me and grabbed my ankle. It hurt like hell when I hit the floor. He picked me up and dumped me on the bed. He tied my hands behind my back again. I closed my eyes and tried to think about you instead of what was coming."

She stared at the lights in the valley below as he held her.

"Then he pulled up his pants and just sat in a chair and stared at me. I rolled over so I wouldn't have to look at him. After a long time, he got on the bed beside me and said, 'You'll come around.' Then I dozed off and nothing happened until the cavalry arrived."

"You were very brave."

"Thanks. Enough talk. Let's make out."

They made out enthusiastically for a few minutes and then she said, "Confucius say, 'Girl like frying pan—must get hot before putting meat in.'"

6

THE ANNOUNCEMENT

The publicists, lawyers, families, everyone with a vested interest, finally agreed on the wording and it was decided to make the formal announcement while the Chagnys were in Santa Fe for closing night.

"It sounds so Dickensian," Christine said.

"What does?" Sharon asked.

"Ward," Christine said.

"Dickensian?" Johnston said, smiling. "You *were* paying attention in school?"

"Yeah, I'm not dumb. I just kind of lost interest in school."

"But that will be corrected in your senior year."

Christine nodded and read the announcement again.

"Everybody's 'late,' and your name isn't even there. You're going to be my father."

"I certainly wish the adoption procedure was moving along more quickly. It would have simplified things, but an engagement announcement isn't really a legal document. It doesn't matter if my name is there. We all know."

Christine smiled and nodded.

"And you do want your parents mentioned, right?" Sharon said.

"Of course. And you're right. My daddy made the Valeriuses my guardians, so I guess that makes me their ward, or hers, since he's 'late.'"

"It has been vetted by experts. Trust me. It is absolutely the correct wording."

"Shouldn't it be *comte* and *vicomte* instead of count and viscount?" Christine asked.

"It will be in the French version."

"Oh yeah, duh. Okay, let's do it."

———

CLOSING NIGHT WAS sold out, including standing room. The parking lot was packed with tailgaters. The tailgate party hosted by Johnston and Maria, along with Franklin and his wife, was the largest by far. The Prevost coach and the battered pickup were in their regular position. Juanita, Julio, and additional staff prepared and served hors d'oeuvres in large quantities. Bottles of the finest Chagny wines graced the bar table.

Christine insisted that Sue see the opera on closing night from the audience, elegantly dressed, and not from backstage, wearing jeans and T-shirt. Having no such wardrobe with her in Santa Fe, Sue grudgingly agreed to allow Johnston to buy her a new dress, along with all the accessories. He insisted it was a well-deserved bonus for being the diva wrangler. Travis, her date for the evening, wore a rented tuxedo.

Tegan, dressed to thrill, approached Sue and Travis. "You must be Travis," she said, before kissing him on the cheek.

Travis, momentarily stunned, watched as Tegan hugged Sue. "You're that actress," he said.

"In the flesh," Tegan said. There was plenty of flesh on display and it was admired by Travis. She turned to Sue. "He's cute."

Travis glanced back and forth between Sue and Tegan. "How do you two—"

"Know each other?" Tegan said. "We're besties."

Tegan felt hands slip around her waist from both sides. She swung around and kissed both Frankie and Raoul on the cheek.

"How was your flight?" Frankie asked.

"Fantastic. It was a G650, but you probably already knew that."

"Yeah, I thought you might like it. I've never been on one."

"Dad has his eye on the G650ER, or the Global 7500," Raoul said.

"I can't believe they stopped in Albuquerque just to drop off little old me," Tegan said.

"Did you sign any autographs?" Frankie asked.

"They apparently never heard of me, so I mostly hung out with the flight attendant."

Everyone turned toward the sound of applause as Christine and Alfonso approached, holding hands, waving, closely followed by Sharon and Audrey.

"There's press and paparazzi around," Sharon said as Christine kissed Raoul briefly on the lips, and Tegan planted a big one on Alfonso.

"We're being good," Christine said as she hugged Tegan and then Sue.

"Your friends are a kissy bunch," Travis whispered to Sue.

"Yes, we are," she said, and then kissed him.

CHRISTINE AND ALFONSO were in top form as they performed *Sangre de Cristo* for the final time. The applause was loud and long at intermission. Some patrons headed for the bar, others to the restrooms.

"That was incredible," Travis said.

"You like it?" Sue said.

He nodded. "I can't believe that's the same girl we had pizza with."

"Same girl. Regular girl, most of the time. But when she sings, she becomes someone completely different."

"I'll say. Does she speak Spanish?"

"A little. She sings in several languages."

"Her pronunciation is excellent, very Santa Fe."

"It's different than LA, right?"

"Yes."

As patrons began returning to their seats, Tegan and Raoul made their way backstage, where they found Christine and Alfonso clinched tightly.

"Leggo my man," Tegan teased.

Christine broke away from Alfonso, wiping tears.

"What's wrong?" Raoul asked.

"Sorry, it's just a little emotional, last performance."

"And what a run," Alfonso said.

"Are you kids ready?" Johnston asked as he approached.

Christine smiled and nodded. "It's showtime."

There was considerable murmuring from the audience as Johnston stepped onto the stage, followed by silence. The last time he made such an appearance was on opening night, and the subsequent performance, and aftermath, had been the stuff of legend.

"Good evening, ladies and gentlemen. I hope you are enjoying the opera."

He waited during the applause and whispers. Christine and Alfonso, in costume, walked briskly onto the stage, holding hands, to even more applause. A moment later, Tegan and Raoul followed them, also holding hands.

"We have an announcement to make, and tonight, here at the opera house, seemed like a good time and place to make it." More murmurs. "My soon-to-be adoptive daughter, Christine Daaé, star of our opera, is engaged to be married."

There was wild applause.

"She's marrying her co-star?" Travis asked.

"Wait for it," Sue said.

Raoul and Alfonso traded places.

"To Viscount Raoul Chagny, son of Count and Doctor Chagny of Paris."

Christine and Raoul kissed.

A lone designated photographer, under the watchful eye of Sharon and Audrey, rapidly snapped photos. There was thunderous applause as the audience stood.

CHRISTINE HAD NO family, and most of the Chagny friends and business associates were in Paris, so the engagement party was combined with an already scheduled after-party for the opera and held at Maria's stately home in Santa Fe. A small combo provided the music. Chagny provided the wine. Christine and Alfonso had to change after their performance, and were the last to arrive, along with Tegan and Raoul, Sue and Travis, who had rushed backstage immediately following the finale.

Audrey was already working the room, and Sharon arrived with the guests of honor in Angel's limo bus. Sharon worked her phone. She began receiving calls, texts, and emails within minutes after Johnston made the announcement on stage at the opera house. Local media had already arrived and staked out the entrance to Maria's house. The arrival was largely a repeat performance of the *Estelline* a few weeks earlier, only now Christine and Tegan were arm in arm with their own men, and Sue had a new man on her arm.

Sue and Travis were first off the bus. One of the paparazzi shouted "Sue!" Sue laughed, smiled, waved, and clung to Travis, who was much impressed. Tegan and Alfonso were next, followed by Christine and Raoul. All posed for photos until Sharon herded them inside.

The engagement ring had been removed from the safe at the ranch and Christine wore it in public for the first time at Maria's party. It quickly became an object of interest for every female there, all of whom seemed quite impressed. Christine glowed, rarely letting go of Raoul's hand all evening. She had never been happier.

Hardly anyone noticed when Alfonso slipped away from the table. Moments later Zoe began playing piano and Alfonso sang "There, I've Said It Again." He strolled across the floor and serenaded Christine.

During the applause when the song ended, Travis whispered to Sue, "She's marrying Raoul, but Alfonso is singing love songs to her?"

Sue nodded. "We're an incestuous bunch."

Alfonso followed with "Take Good Care of My Baby."

The string of guests arriving at their table with best wishes for the newly engaged couple finally slowed, allowing Raoul an opportunity to dance with his fiancée. Christine rested her head on his shoulder, happy, content, smiling, as she watched the diamonds in her ring glimmering as she and Raoul moved as one.

CHRISTINE'S LAST FEW DAYS in Santa Fe had been a whirlwind of activity. She and Raoul said their long goodbyes and he boarded the Chagny Gulfstream for Paris.

Frankie, Christine, Sue, Zoe, and Jim Bob boarded a Cessna Citation bound for Los Angeles. The kids had to get back to school, something of a letdown after the eventful summer. Franklin and his wife would follow later in the *Estelline*.

"This is not as big as Raoul's jet," Christine said as they took off from the Santa Fe Airport.

Frankie laughed.

"Sorry, I didn't mean to insult your airplane," Christine said.

"It's not our airplane. We don't actually own a plane."

"You don't? I thought all rich people had their own jets."

"We own fractional shares in several jets. Dad says if it's good enough for Warren, it's good enough for us."

"I don't understand."

"It's like a time-share condo. We have a plane when we need it but the rest of the time, instead of being parked, it gets chartered out and earns some income. If our plane is busy, we get another one. All be benefits of a private jet with none of the hassle. If we need a different size plane, it's available. This one is ideal for this trip, but if we want to go to Europe, Saint-Tropez, for example, we would pick a bigger plane with longer legs."

"Airplanes have legs?" Christine asked, bemused.

"Longer range. like the Chagny Gulfstream. Raoul's dad owns and runs companies all over the world, so they need a long-range jet, and it's in the air a lot. The family isn't even on board most of the time, just company executives."

He could tell it was all flying over Christine's head. "If you need to fly somewhere, just let me know, or Johnston. He doesn't fly nearly enough to own a jet either, so Dad convinced him to buy into the same deal, but he rarely uses all his time."

"Great," Christine said, and then turned to Sue. "Party plane!"

The girls high fived.

"Just kidding," Christine said. "The train is fine."

Frankie laughed.

"But I do want to go to Florida to see Mrs. Valerius before she gets any worse."

"No problem. Johnston will probably want to go along. He's known her for years."

7

THE WEDDING CHAPEL

Christine and Sue emptied the closet and dresser drawers onto the bed as Frankie watched. Packing her things at the Valerius house was bittersweet for Christine. So much had happened there, so many memories. It was eerily quiet without Mrs. Valerius, who had already been spirited away to an assisted living facility near her sister in Florida.

"Why don't we just live here?" Christine asked.

"Who?" Frankie asked.

"Me, Zoe, Jim Bob."

"I thought you were going to live in the beach house."

Christine shrugged.

"It's a beach house, in Malibu," Frankie said. "Most people would kill to live there."

"I'm a low-maintenance girl, remember? So is Zoe, and Jim Bob's used to crashing on couches."

"Works for me," Jim Bob said, leaning through the door. "What about you, babe?"

"What about me?" Zoe asked, coming down the hallway.

"Why don't we live here instead of the beach house?"

"It's fine with me."

"Are you sure?" Frankie asked.

"It's perfect," Christine said. "I can take the same bus to school."

"Johnston said he'll buy you a car," Frankie said.

"He can buy me a car if he wants to, but I don't want to fight traffic downtown and find a place to park. I like the bus for school."

"This way Christine won't have to move, just us," Jim Bob said. "I like it."

"Is there enough room?" Frankie asked.

"We were in a tiny one-bedroom before we went to Santa Fe for the season," Jim Bob said. "Yeah, I'd say there's plenty of room."

"I'm moving too," Christine said.

"Wait. What?" Frankie said, confused.

"To the little cottage, out back," Christine said, pointing. "That's where I lived with Daddy, until he died and then they made me move in here. I wanted to move back out there anyway, but when the professor died, and Mrs. Valerius went—you know—I thought I should stay in here with her."

"That was going to be my man cave," Jim Bob said.

"Oh, sorry," Christine said.

"I'm just pulling your chain, honey. Are you sure you'll be okay out there?"

"I'll be okay. I'm not a little girl anymore. I'm seventeen and engaged to be married. It's not like I'm going to be sneaking boys in, just Sue."

Christine and Sue looked at each other and said in unison, "Sleepover!"

"Besides, we're going to need this room for the nursery, right?" Christine said.

"After the first few weeks, yes," Zoe said. "That would be helpful."

"We'll redecorate, put up baby stuff. It'll be fun."

"I was kind of looking forward to the beach house, but this makes more sense, and it's a lot shorter bus ride," Sue said.

"It's furnished, and has a good piano," Zoe said. "What's not to like?"

"Why were we going to live in the beach house anyway?" Christine asked.

"Johnston owns it, and it was available," Frankie said. "At the time, we didn't know how long it would take to relocate Mrs. Valerius, or what her sister wanted to do with the house."

"What does she want to do with it?" Christine asked.

"It would take a lot of legal work to sell it, so she told Dad to rent it out to someone he can trust."

"If he can't trust his cousin, who can he trust?" Christine asked. "Wait. Will he be my cousin or uncle?"

"Second cousin, I think. He's Johnston's first cousin. I'll have to check with Mom. Just call him Uncle Franklin."

"I've been living here for years, and I haven't burned it down yet."

"I'll call Johnston, but I'm sure it will be okay with him. The beach house is being remodeled anyway. If they don't have to work around people living in it, they can finish early, and it can go on the market. His ex should like that."

"Tell him I'll go out there occasionally and keep an eye on the contractors," Jim Bob said.

"Let's go look at the little cottage," Christine said, grabbing Sue by the hand and bolting for the door.

Frankie fumbled with the ring of keys and unlocked the door. Since Christine moved into the main house the little cottage had once again become the repository for boxes, furniture, appliances, and other detritus.

"We should probably change the locks," Frankie said.

"Definitely," Christine said.

Frankie stepped in and flipped on the lights. "A lot of memories here, from what I understand."

"A lot of memories," Christine said.

"Is that the bed?" Sue asked.

Christine smiled and nodded. "Yeah. That's where I first slept with Raoul." She turned quickly to Frankie. "Not really, well, yes really, but we just slept. We didn't do anything."

"So I heard," Frankie said.

"This is where you first heard it?" Sue asked.

"Heard what?" Christine said.

"The Angel of Music," Sue said.

Christine nodded. "It was Erik, but yeah, this is the place. I can't believe I sang 'Nessun Dorma' for my audition."

"It worked," Sue said, "so I'm glad you did."

"Me too," Christine said, wiping tears and hugging Sue tightly.

"Ah, the infamous purloined nude," Frankie said, pointing at the topless painting of Christine and Connie on the wall.

"I was so not nude, just topless."

Sue looked at the painting. "You slut! Your tub-thumper will probably blow a gasket if she sees it."

"It's not like it's a naked selfie. It's art," Frankie said. "Pretty nice rack, though."

Christine slugged him.

"We should probably burn it," Christine said.

"Don't burn it," Sue said. "You look totally hot, girl. Send it to Raoul. The boy will need something to get him through those long, cold English nights."

CHRISTINE, ZOE, AND Jim Bob quickly settled into the Valerius house. Christine slept in her old room for a few nights while Jim Bob did a quick refurbish on the little cottage. He fixed the plumbing, aired it out, checked all the window latches, and gave it a fresh coat of paint. Sue helped Christine decorate and they announced their first sleepover, just the two of them, of course.

Despite their reservations, Christine and Sue were soon back in the swing of things at school. They had never given it much thought, but soon discovered a curious dynamic at work. After Connie's death Christine had practically been a pariah, the girl who was involved in a love triangle resulting in her best friend being killed. Sue, being Christine's actual best friend, stood by her and tore into anyone who dissed her, hardly elevating herself in the school's social hierarchy, not that she cared.

When school started this year, however, Christine was suddenly nothing short of a celebrity. Not only had she been called up from the audience to sing the lead at a new opera, at none other than the world-renowned Santa Fe Opera, but she had been kidnapped off the stage by the very boy, the son of their former headmaster, who had caused the death of her friend just two years ago. And if that wasn't enough, she was rescued by the hottest group of heroes they could imagine, including not only the conservatory's very own dreamboat, Alfonso, but a French viscount, to whom she was now engaged to be married. Christine was suddenly big girl on campus, and everybody wanted to be her friend.

"I don't need any new friends," Christine said to Sue.

"Me either. Screw 'em."

And so it was. Christine and Sue laughed a lot that school year. Their few old friends became even closer, and they got a kick out of watching the suck-ups suck up.

Now THAT HER engagement was officially announced, Christine wore the ring to school. Everyone seemed to notice, and more than a few were quite impressed.

"It's cubic zirconium," one snotty girl was overheard to say.

"What's that?" Christine asked.

"Fake diamonds," Sue said.

"Raoul wouldn't give me a fake diamond."

"Of course he wouldn't. Ignore her."

"You should have my dad check it out," Benjamin, one of the old friends, and viola virtuoso, said casually.

"Huh?"

"He works in the diamond district," Benjamin said.

"He does?" Christine said.

"He cuts diamonds. Real diamonds."

Christine texted Zoe that she would be home late, hanging out with Sue. After school they took the bus to the diamond district, which was not that far from the conservatory.

"Exquisite," Benjamin's dad said. "The main diamond is superb. The cutter knew his business."

"So, it's not fake?" Christine asked.

The diamond cutter chuckled. "No, not fake. Seven figures, easily."

"What does that mean?"

"It's worth more than a million dollars," Sue said.

Christine was stunned, her eyes widening. "A million dollars, for a ring?"

"I could live forever on a million dollars," Sue said.

"Or feed a lot of homeless people," Christine said.

"The boy did not buy it at the mall. It's probably a family heirloom; late nineteenth century would be my guess."

"A million dollars?" Christine repeated, still not believing.

"More, probably. I'm going by the diamonds, and those really need to be graded by an expert. I'm just a cutter. You should get an appraisal." He took one last look at the ring and handed it back to Christine. "Very nice work. A young lady should be so lucky to have such a ring."

He turned to Benjamin. "You're keeping up with your lessons?"

"Yes sir."

"He's our best viola," Sue said.

"Good. Good. Now I get back to work. Does your mother know where you are?"

"Yes sir," Benjamin said.

Christine refused to leave the diamond dealer's place of business, with an armed guard and bulletproof glass, until she called Jim Bob.

"Say again?" Jim Bob said. He listened intently, and then said calmly. "I'll be right there."

Christine kept the ring on her finger—the kids all agreed that was safer than her pocket—but she checked it repeatedly while they waited for Jim Bob to arrive.

"I called Johnston," Jim Bob said as he hustled the kids into the car under the watchful eye of the security guard. "He said we can take the ring to Franklin's house and put it in the safe with his wife's jewelry. They're already set up for this kind of deal."

Christine went to school bare fingered until Saturday, when Frankie arrived to take her shopping for a much more modest engagement ring to wear to school while the outrageously expensive heirloom remained in Franklin's safe.

It was clear to the jeweler that Christine was the bride, as she was the one trying on the rings, while Sue gave her opinion and sorted the candidates.

"I think it's good to allow the bride to select her own engagement ring," the jeweler said.

"Yeah, she didn't like the one I gave her," Frankie said. "Too cheap."

Sue laughed.

"He is not my fiancé," Christine said, poking Frankie with her elbow. "He's my cousin, or will be, and the ring Raoul gave me was definitely not cheap. That's the problem."

"That one is in my mom's safe," Frankie said. "Christine was afraid she'd lose it on the bus, or at school. Her fiancé is at university in the UK, so I'm acting as his proxy to buy her a substitute ring that she can wear to school."

"I understand," the jeweler said, suddenly becoming much more attentive. "I'm sure we can find something suitable for your situation."

"I'm not really into bling, but I am engaged, so I do want to wear a ring, just not one that costs more than a house."

"To keep the horndogs away," Sue said, browsing jewelry in the case. "Do you have anything that says, 'I'm available'?"

Christine laughed. "Your boy is out there, Sue, probably waiting for you at college. He just doesn't know it yet."

THE BRIDE WAS PREGNANT, so the decision was made to have an intimate ceremony with just family and close friends at a small wedding chapel in Santa Monica. The Chagnys flew in from Paris on their Gulfstream. Christine was in Raoul's arms before he stepped onto the tarmac. Kissing ensued.

A few hours later the gang was back at Van Nuys Airport. A Cessna Citation, in which Johnston owned a fractional share, was dispatched from Dallas, touched down briefly in Lubbock to pick up Carlos, then Santa Fe for Johnston, Maria, and Meg. Christine, prodded by Sue, had developed an interest in private jets. She found the Citation "cute," but preferred the Gulfstream.

"Wait until you ride on a BBJ," Frankie said.

"A what?" Christine asked.

"You'll see."

Tegan and Alfonso flew commercial from Atlanta, the film industry's current darling for shoveling taxpayer money at multinational conglomerates to persuade them to make films and television shows in their state.

"I'm playing a crack whore," Tegan said, "so we'll take the red-eye back and I'll show up on set hung over and beat."

"Method acting," Alfonso said.

The bachelor party was held in a country and western bar where Jim Bob knew some of the musicians. Minors were allowed in, but not allowed to consume alcohol. Johnston, Franklin, and Alain, all dressed in designer denim jeans and custom-made western shirts, sipped their cheap beer, and watched the younger men dance with the cowgirls. Jim Bob and Carlos joined the musicians on stage.

Jim Bob played "Last Date" on piano, and then called Alfonso up to sing "Your Cheatin' Heart."

The bachelorette party, held at the Titshaw estate in Beverly Hills, was somewhat more subdued, until the police arrived. It was actually a male stripper dressed as a policeman—cliché but de rigueur. No one complained. Sharon was present, but hardly needed to remind this group of the dangers of photos finding their way onto the Internet, where they would forever remain. Christine obliged, but Tegan said it would only enhance her reputation—besides, it wasn't her wedding. Nevertheless, she yielded shot selection to Sharon, who then arranged to have the selected photos leaked.

All agreed that the video of Sue riding on the stripper's bare shoulders, swinging his shirt over her head, was an instant classic, one that her parents would never, ever, see. Unlike their male counterparts at the bachelor party, the older ladies let down their hair, sipped expensive Chagny wine, and joined in the fun—no photos, of course—they too, had a reputation to maintain.

As the party raged on, Christine and Zoe slipped outside.

"Is it just me, or are Johnston and Maria becoming an item?" Christine asked Zoe.

"It's not just you," Zoe said.

"So I'm going to have a—what exactly will she be—a stepmother?"

Zoe laughed. "No, I don't think she'd be that, would she? Maybe she would if Johnston adopts you and then marries her."

"I don't know. It doesn't matter," Christine said. "I like her, and she's been really good to me. If they want to get married, it's fine with me."

A SONG WAS COMMISSIONED for the occasion, music by Zoe, lyrics by Jim Bob. Putting together a few strings and a piano player was no problem, finding room for them in such a small chapel was a bit more challenging.

Johnston gave away the bride and, as promised, Christine sang at Zoe and Jim Bob's wedding.

8

SOFIA

JOHNSTON PACED NERVOUSLY in the hospital waiting room. Frankie, Christine, and Sue sat in the uncomfortable chairs, fingering their phones. The doors opened suddenly, and Jim Bob burst through.

"It's a girl!"

"Woo-hoo!" Sue shouted, leaping to her feet.

"Can we see her, and Zoe?" Christine asked as she rushed Jim Bob and then hugged him.

"In a few minutes. They have to hose her down. I need to get back in there."

Jim Bob disappeared, and everyone went to work on their phones.

The wait seemed interminable, but the newborn baby girl was soon bathed, oiled, and dressed to receive company.

Johnston and Frankie hung back with Jim Bob while Christine and Sue crowded in for a closer look.

"She's so cute," Christine said.

"She takes after me," Jim Bob said.

"You probably wanted a boy."

"Hey, I like girls, but a little brother would be nice. There's more where this one came from."

"Easy for you to say," Zoe said.

"What are you going to name her?" Christine asked.

"We were thinking Sofia Christine," Zoe said.

Christine burst into tears.

"What's wrong, honey?" Jim Bob asked, stepping forward and slipping his arm around Christine.

"It's perfect."

"We'll call her Sofia," Zoe said. "We already have a Christine."

"SCB," Sue said, "The monogram works. Good thing her middle name isn't Olivia."

Christine laughed.

"Can I hold her?" Christine asked.

"Sure," Zoe said.

Zoe handed Sofia to Christine, who handled her like the delicate little package she was.

"Hold her up a little higher," Frankie said. "I'll send a pic to Raoul, so he can see what he's in for."

Christine raised Sofia up near her face and smiled while Frankie snapped a photo with his phone.

"THAT'S YOUR FIANCÉE?" Raoul's classmate asked as they looked at the photo of Christine and Sofia on Raoul's phone.

"That's her," Raoul said.

"She's a stone fox."

"Yeah, I guess she is."

"Shouldn't you be there?"

"Where?"

"With your kid."

Raoul laughed. "The kid's not ours. She's my nanny's."

"Your nanny?"

"It's a long story."

The classmate took another look at the photo.

"You are one lucky asshole."

"Yes. I am."

To SAY THAT Baby Sofia was spoiled would be an understatement. Jim Bob started playing his guitar and softly singing love songs to her as soon as they got home, something he had been doing for months before she was born.

There was a definite musical theme to the nursery, which Jim Bob had remodeled as soon as he finished work on the little cottage. Sue did some research, ran it by a tech nerd friend, and Zoe ordered a baby monitor with two parent units, one for their bedroom and one in the little cottage. Christine doted on Sofia, as did Sue whenever she was around, which was often.

"You might as well get used to changing diapers," Jim Bob told her. "It won't be long until you have one of your own."

"That's okay," Christine said. "I'm in no hurry. I'll just borrow yours."

Christine had never given much thought to having children and hadn't even gotten around to discussing it with Raoul. She made a mental note to bring it up the next time Raoul visited.

SOFIA LAY IN her crib in the living room, curiously eyeing first Christine and then Jim Bob, both wearing headphones, staring at their tablets, speaking in French, repeating the same phrases, over and over.

Zoe and Jim Bob had agreed that Sofia would be bilingual before she started school, multilingual if she picked up a little Spanish from Jim Bob along the way, with a redneck accent. Jim Bob had immediately joined Christine in learning French, and frequently practiced in front of Sofia on the theory that children can easily learn multiple languages if they start early.

Jim Bob turned toward the sound of keys in the front door.

"*Entrez, s'il-vous-plaît,*" Jim Bob called out, butchering the pronunciation.

"Pretty good," Christine said.

Zoe stepped through the door and went immediately to the crib, showering Sofia with kisses.

"Well?" Jim Bob asked.

"I got the gig," Zoe said.

"What gig?" Christine asked.

"Scoring a film. It's another low-budget indie, but work is work."

"That's great," Christine said.

"It sure is," Jim Bob said. "I can continue being a kept man."

"Nuh-uh. We could go back to playing at the restaurant in the marina."

"No way. You need to study. You promised Johnston. And you need to learn French. Don't worry about me. Zoe will be working mostly at home, so I can pick up some session work."

"And guitar lessons," Zoe said.

"I'll have to use your little cottage," Jim Bob said to Christine. "I don't want to melt Sofia's face just yet."

"Or damage her hearing," Zoe said.

Christine laughed. "Sure, any time." She watched Sofia watching her for a moment. "It's nice to have music in the house again. I'm going to miss it."

"Miss it?" Jim Bob asked.

"I'm getting married, remember?"

"Oh, yeah. You two can always come visit and stay in the little cottage."

"No way," Zoe said. "I'm turning that into a music studio as soon as Christine clears out."

Jim Bob gave Zoe a stern look. Christine laughed.

"The Chagnys bought an apartment in Westwood when they sold the house," Zoe said. "Christine and Raoul might want to get their own place, for when they're in town, which I hope is often."

"So, we're staying here after Christine starts shacking up with that French dude?" Jim Bob asked.

"I don't see why not," Zoe said. "We'll have to take over the rent payments from Johnston of course, and maybe even try to buy it when they decide to sell. What do you think?"

"Works for me. Great location, but we might need more room."

"Room for what?" Christine asked.

"Little ones."

"Oh no," Christine said, stunned. "Are you pregnant again already?"

Zoe laughed. "No, not right now. I need a break, and we're losing our live-in babysitter in a few months. But yes, we do anticipate the pitter-patter of little feet again in the future."

"Oh, that kind of reminds me," Christine said. "There's something I need to talk to you about."

"What is it?" Zoe asked, concerned.

"I'm going to ask Sue to be my maid of honor."

"Of course. She's your best friend."

"I thought about asking you, well, I guess you'd be the matron of honor, since you're like married and all."

Zoe smiled. "Yes, that would be the proper term, but Sue is the obvious choice."

"Besides, you have another job."

"I do?"

"I want you to be MOB."

Zoe was taken aback. "Me?"

Christine nodded. "It probably should be Mrs. Valerius, since she's still my legal guardian, but her doctors say she's getting worse and probably won't even know who I am by then."

"MOB?" Jim Bob asked.

"Mother of the bride," Zoe said. "Weddings have their own language."

"I'm the FW," Christine said.

Jim Bob threw up his hands, clueless.

"Future wife."

"Shouldn't you be the B?" Jim Bob said.

"Raoul is the FH. Oh, Frankie's is my favorite. He's the BM."

Jim Bob laughed. "That one I get."

"You'll be FOB."

"Whoa, hold on. Is that what I think it is?"

"Father of the bride."

"No way, no how. You can make a good case for Zoe as MOB or whatever, but Johnston will be your adoptive father by then, so that's a no-brainer."

"I want you both."

"Can you do that?"

"It's my wedding. Frankie said I can do anything I want."

"I like it," Zoe said.

"Did you talk to Johnston?" Jim Bob asked.

Christine nodded. "He's cool with it."

"I don't know," Jim Bob said. "Seems odd to me."

"You were there when I was born. You changed my diapers. You knew my mom before she met my daddy."

Jim Bob shrugged.

"You could actually be my daddy," Christine said.

Jim Bob held up his hands. "Uh-uh, no way. Your mom and I were just friends."

Christine laughed. "Yeah, that didn't come out right, did it?"

Jim Bob shook his head.

"You know what I mean," Christine said. "I've known you all my life. Remember when you told me that when Daddy died you would have snatched me up and gone on the lam?"

Jim Bob smiled and nodded.

"You what?" Zoe asked.

"There was no way I was going to let her go into foster care, and definitely not an orphanage. But it didn't matter. Viktor already took care of it before he died. He made the right decision at the time. He had no way of knowing the professor would die and Mrs. Valerius would get sick."

Christine nodded, and then smiled. "You would have probably made a lousy pearl fisher."

Zoe was completely confused.

"So, you are walking me down the aisle, along with Johnston," Christine said. "I'll have to practice holding the bouquet with a dad on each arm."

"What about Maria?" Zoe asked.

"She will be grandmother of the bride," Christine said.

"GOB?" Jim Bob asked.

Christine laughed. "I don't think there is a thingy for that."

"Is she okay with that?" Jim Bob asked. "I mean she's definitely old enough to be your grandmother, but aren't she and Johnston an item?"

"They are, but they aren't married yet, and may never be, so she said it wouldn't be right for her to be MOB."

"You already talked to her?" Zoe asked.

"Yes, when I talked to Johnston about having two FOBs. They are both on board. Maria said she would be honored to be my grandmother. She only had one condition."

"What's that?" Zoe asked, suddenly concerned.

"She wants Carlos to walk her down the aisle."

"Carlos?" Jim Bob asked.

"He's going to be one of the groomsmen. The grandmothers get seated right before the mothers. The MOB is the last to be seated. She's kind of special."

Christine looked at Zoe and smiled.

"Yes, she is," Jim Bob said.

9

THE GIRL COUSINS

Christine and Sue walked down the steps in front of the conservatory, backpacks slung over their shoulders, conversing in French.

"*Dieu merci, c'est vendredi,*" Christine said.

Sue laughed. "TGIF."

They stopped suddenly when they spied a long, black limousine parked directly in front of the school, in a no-parking zone. The driver stood on the sidewalk, with a sign: CHRISTINE DAAÉ. The girls cautiously approached.

"I'm Christine Daaé," Christine said, eyeing the driver suspiciously.

As the driver reached for the back door it suddenly swung open and two teenage girls burst out and onto the sidewalk.

"Surprise!" they said in unison.

Christine and Sue stared nervously.

"We're your cousins," one of the girls said.

"From Boston," the other said.

"We're kidnapping you."

The other one elbowed her, hard.

"What?" the injured party asked.

"Duh."

"Oh shit, bad choice of words. We're here to pick you up."

"Didn't Frankie text you?"

Christine looked at her phone and shook her head.

"Are you twins?" Christine asked.

"No, we just look alike."

"No, we don't."

"Do too."

"Do not."

"I'm the cute one."

"I'm the hot one."

"Okay, you caught us."

"We're twins."

"Identical."

"Frankie never said you were twins," Christine said.

"He doesn't know."

"We never told him."

"I'm Cindy."

"I'm Mindy."

"I thought you were Sandy."

"Then you must be Mandy."

"Mia."

"Nia."

Sue stared in disbelief.

"Hold on," Christine said, looking at her phone. "Frankie just texted me."

"Oh, good," the girls said in unison.

"What did he say?"

"He said our crazy girl cousins are picking me up from school," Christine said.

"Cray."

"Cray."

"Okay, enough of the twin shtick. I'm Addison."

"I'm Kendall."

"We're not really crazy."

"We just like to jack with people."

"Especially cousins."

"New cousins."

"Where are our manners?"

"We don't have any."

"You must be Sue," Addison said, extending her hand to Sue.

Sue nodded and shook hands with both girls.

"Frankie told us about you."

"Told you what?" Sue asked.

"He said you were Christine's BFF."

"So now you're one of us."

"He also said you were scary smart."

"And that you applied to USC."

Sue nodded. "I applied to a lot of schools."

"And they'll probably all accept her," Christine said.

"We're in town for a campus tour."

"USC."

"We're probably going there."

"Legacies and all that."

"Well, I guess I'll head out," Sue said, backing away.

"Where are you going?" Kendall asked.

"To the bus stop."

"Get in. We'll take you."

"It's just a couple of blocks," Sue said.

"Not to the bus stop, to wherever you're going."

"Koreatown," Sue said.

"No problem," the twins said in unison.

Sue hesitated.

"Get in."

"Why take the bus when you can ride in a freaking limo?"

Christine nodded. Reinforcements would be nice. Sue stepped back beside Christine.

"Well," Addison said, "let's go."

The girls piled into the limo, and it pulled away. Sue gave the driver the address.

The nonstop chatter continued until Koreatown.

"Up there, on the corner," Sue said to the driver.

The driver pulled over.

"Cliché, I know," Sue said. "Koreans running a convenience store."

"Nothing wrong with that."

"Entrepreneurs."

"Our kind of people."

Sue opened the door and started to exit the limo.

"Do you have plans tonight?" Addison asked.

"Who, me?" Sue asked.

"Yes, you."

"Let's see, play some violin, study some calculus, and then probably do some French with Christine online, typical Friday night."

"French?"

"I kind of have to learn French," Christine said. "So, my girl is doing it with me. She already speaks Korean and some Chinese."

"That can wait."

"Come to dinner."

"Again, who, me?" Sue asked.

"Again, yes, you."

"And Christine, of course."

"When, where?" Sue asked.

"Seven-ish."

"At Frankie's parents' house."

"They're in Omaha, so we have the run of the place."

"I'll have to ask my parents," Sue said.

"So ask."

"Then get with your girl and let us know."

"We'll drop off Christine."

"See the baby."

"And then go terrorize Frankie."

"We already did that."

"Oh, yeah."

"He's coming to dinner."

"He can swing by and pick you up."

"It's right on the way to BH."

"Or we can send the limo."

Sue stood and stared as the limo pulled away from the curb.

AFTER A BARRAGE of texts, a dress code was established, transport was arranged, and everyone arrived at the Titshaw house in Beverly Hills. Christine and Sue followed Frankie into the kitchen, where the twins were busy chopping and dicing.

"Don't you have people for that?" Sue asked.

"They have a few days off while my parents are out of town," Frankie said.

"And we like to cook," Addison said.

"We may want to open a restaurant," Kendall said.

"I thought we were doing the tech thing."

"Oh, yeah, that too."

"I'll go fire up the grill," Frankie said.

"Works for me," Christine said.

"Do you eat meat?" Addison asked Sue.

"I'm Korean, not vegetarian."

"I thought you were Californian," Kendall said, smiling.

"Ha ha," Sue said. "I get it."

"You should see her wolf down Juanita's fajitas," Christine said.

FRANKIE GRILLED, AND the girls did the rest, not that there was a lot to do as the twins had already handled most of the work before their guests arrived. Christine insisted that the hamburger buns be grilled and greasy. "In honor of the redneck," she said.

"Now I see why sweaters were recommended," Sue said as they sat outside around the fire pit.

"You're lucky," Addison said.

"Try eating outside at night in Boston this time of year."

Frankie poured wine.

"Oh, good, wine," Addison said.

"The good stuff?" Kendall asked.

"Good enough," Frankie said.

Frankie paused before pouring a glass for Sue.

"Hit me," Sue said.

"Are you sure? I don't need an angry Korean dad on my ass."

"He may be old school, but not that old," Sue said. "Besides, I'm not planning on getting wasted, just a glass of wine."

Frankie stoked the fire and took a seat.

"I've been meaning to ask you guys, and now that you're here," Christine began.

"Yes?" Addison said.

"Spit it out," Kendall said.

"Would you be bridesmaids at my wedding?"

"Hell, yes."

"We thought you'd never ask."

"On one condition."

"What's that?" Christine asked, concerned.

"We aren't wearing ugly dresses."

"Why are bridesmaids' dresses always ugly?"

"The bride doesn't want to be upstaged."

"I don't care about that," Christine said. "I'd just as soon elope."

"You can't elope."

"No way."

The twins looked at Frankie. "Tell her, Tits."

"You can't elope," Frankie confirmed.

"Why not?" Christine asked.

"Obligations. Family, social, business, politics."

"Think of it as a performance," Sue said. "You're the star."

"Great," Christine said, unconvinced.

"How many bridesmaids do you have?" Addison asked.

"Counting you?" Christine said.

"Counting us."

"Two."

"Two?"

"What about Sue?"

"She's my maid of honor," Christine said, smiling at Sue.

"Duh."

"Duh."

"You're going to need a lot more bridesmaids."

"Why?" Christine asked.

"Raoul will have a lot of groomsmen."

The twins looked at Frankie.

"Obligations," Frankie said.

"So you need the same number of bridesmaids," Addison said.

"Symmetry, and all that shit."

"For the recessional."

"For the what?" Christine asked.

"When we all walk off arm in arm after you lay a big sloppy wet one on the groom and they play the music."

"I hope I get a good one."

"You don't have to do him, just walk with him."

"Whatever."

"How many groomsmen will Raoul have?" Christine asked.

The twins looked at each other and shrugged. "A dozen?" they said in unison.

"Twelve?" Christine asked, incredulous. "So, I need twelve bridesmaids?"

"I'll hold auditions at school," Sue said. "There are plenty of suck-ups available."

The twins nodded. "Smart."

Christine laughed. "Okay."

"Two down, ten to go," Sue said.

"Oh, crap, Tegan," Christine said.

"No duh," Sue said. "Nine more."

"Tegan?" Addison asked.

"The Australian actress," Frankie said.

"With her tits all over the Internet?" Kendall said.

"The very same," Sue said.

"You know her?"

Christine shrugged. "Yeah, we know her."

Sue laughed. "Do we ever."

"Cool."

"She's our kind of people."

"I'll say," Frankie said.

"What's that supposed to mean?" Kendall asked.

"I've spent time with Tegan. You will definitely hit it off."

"What about Alfonso?" Christine asked. "Do you think Raoul would let him be a groomsman?"

"Let him?" Frankie said. "Raoul insists that both Alfonso and Carlos be groomsmen."

"Alfonso, Carlos," Addison said. "Who are these boys?"

"They sound so exotic," Kendall said.

"Part of the posse that saved Christine from Erik," Sue said.

"Oh yeah, that," Addison said.

"And Alfonso is Tegan's main squeeze," Christine said, "when he isn't squeezing me."

"Huh?" Kendall said.

"He was my co-star in *Sangre de Cristo*, and we went to school together."

"Sorry we didn't make it to the opera," Addison said.

"Oh, Meg," Christine said. "How could I forget Meg? She can walk with Frankie."

"Frankie walks with me," Sue said.

"He does?" Christine asked.

"He's Raoul's best dude, right?"

Frankie nodded. "Best man walks with the maid of honor."

"So, we need how many more bridesmaids?" Christine asked.

"Eight, maybe seven," Sue said. "Does the maid of honor count?"

"No," Frankie said. "There will probably be twelve groomsmen and twelve bridesmaids in addition to us. I won't have a firm count for a few weeks. Line up the girls you really want, and then we'll top it off before the wedding."

"I'll cast some alternates," Sue said. "This is going to be fun."

"What about Harper?" Christine asked. "I liked her."

"Sure," Frankie said. "We have a thing to go to next week. I'll ask her. She's already on the guest list, along with her fiancé."

"Still cheating on Meg?" Christine teased.

The twins looked at Frankie.

"Rubber chicken circuit," Frankie said.

The twins laughed.

"I think Cliffie is going to be an alternate groomsman," Kendall said.

"Depending on what happens after graduation."

"Active duty and all."

"Who is Cliffie?" Christine asked.

"Clifton," Kendall said.

"Harper's guy," Addison said.

"Fiancé," Kendall said.

"You know Harper's fiancé?" Christine asked.

"Yeah, since forever."

"They're getting married when he graduates."

"At Annapolis."

"We're bridesmaids."

"Unless the dresses are ugly."

"We are so glad you are marrying Raoul."

"You are?" Christine asked.

"Definitely."

"Now we don't have to kill each other over him."

Christine's eyes darted back and forth between the twins.

"He is such a hottie."

"We both had a crush on him."

"But it could never be."

"Why not?" Christine asked.

"Duh."

"There's one of him."

"And two of us."

"You could share," Sue said.

The twins burst into laughter.

"That's okay."
"Christine got him."
"So we get to keep him."
"As a cousin-in-law."
"We'll find our own boys later."
"You really had a crush on Raoul?" Christine asked.
"Yeah, we used to go to Saint-Tropez nearly every summer."
"We were just kids."
"Until we weren't."
"Huh?" Christine asked.
"We were what, ten?"
"Ten."
"Flatter than pancakes."
"No tits."
"No asses."
"We had been going topless on Pampelonne for years."
"No big deal."
"Raoul didn't pay any attention."
"And then, when we were eleven."
"Over the winter."
"We developed."
"Developed?" Christine asked.
"Sprouted boobs."
"In a big way."
"Well, not that big."
"Big enough."
"Mine are bigger."
"Mine are cuter."
"Raoul noticed."
"Did he ever."
"At the beach."
"The topless beach."
"Pampelonne."
"He had wood."
"Wood?" Christine asked.
"A boner."
"A hard on."
Christine laughed.

"So did Frankie."

"Ew!" Christine said. "You're cousins."

"It was an involuntary reaction to visual stimuli," Frankie said.

"Well, in that case," Christine said.

"Anyway, we had a major crush on Raoul."

"And we had his attention."

"Bare boobies and all."

"Lolos."

"But he was pining over some California girl."

"Big time."

"So we struck out."

"Good thing too."

"Or we would have killed each other."

The twins looked at Christine.

"That would be you."

"Who?" Christine asked, confused.

"The California girl."

Christine smiled.

"So, tell us about your first time," Addison said.

"My first time?" Christine asked, defensively.

"Isn't that kind of personal?" Sue said.

The twins laughed.

"First time topless."

"On the beach."

"With boys."

"Oh, that. I was fifteen. I didn't grow up doing it like you guys, so I was really nervous. Zoe said I didn't have to do it if I didn't want to."

"But you did, right?"

"Right," Christine said, grinning.

"What about Raoul?"

"How did he react?"

"He acted all nonchalant and stuff," Christine said.

"Yeah, they all do."

"But they look."

"They definitely look."

"He definitely looked but he didn't stare, so it wasn't that bad," Christine said. "The other guys on the beach didn't really pay any attention, just another topless chick. They were everywhere."

The twins laughed.

"What?" Christine asked.

"Frankie told us about how you two met."

"He did?" Christine asked.

"Tits!" the twins shouted in unison.

Christine covered her face. "That was so embarrassing."

"Why?"

"It was just Frankie."

"He's harmless."

"I think she means Johnston," Frankie said.

Sue laughed. "Your headmaster."

"Oh, yes, that!" Addison said.

"That was freaking classic," Kendall said.

"Like in a movie and shit."

"You should totally get one of your film-geek friends at SC to do that," Addison said to Frankie.

Christine kept her face covered.

"At least it was Johnston," Addison said.

"He's seen plenty of teenage titties," Kendall said.

"Including ours."

"Definitely ours."

"But he was your headmaster!"

"Priceless."

"Okay, enough teasing," Frankie said.

"There's never enough teasing," Addison said.

"Especially cousins," Kendall added.

"Erik was there too, wasn't he?" Addison asked.

"Yes, he was there," Christine said.

Kendall elbowed Addison.

"What?" Addison asked.

"She doesn't want to talk about Erik," Kendall said.

"That's okay," Christine said. "Erik was part of my life, an important part of my life. I don't want to erase him, or pretend he never existed, no matter what he did."

"Good."

"Because we liked Erik."

"We loved Erik."

"Erik was always the fun cousin."

"Gee, thanks," Frankie said.

"Frankie was the solid, stable one."

"The one you went to when you were in trouble."

"Erik was the one you went to when you were looking for trouble."

"We had fun with Erik."

"Big fun."

"He taught us everything we know about sex."

"Ew!" Christine said.

"Not like that!"

"We didn't do anything!"

"Much."

"He just told us shit."

"We still love him."

"We don't know for sure he's dead."

"Nobody has seen the body, right?"

Frankie shook his head. "Can we change the subject?"

"Let's get back to the wedding," Sue said. "Where's it going to be?"

"Paris, I guess," Christine said. "Raoul obviously has more people than I do."

"No way," Kendall said.

"No how," Addison added.

"Why not?" Christine asked.

"The bride's people throw the wedding."

"The groom's people show up."

"Los Angeles."

"Santa Monica."

"Beverly Hills."

"Whatever."

"Not Paris."

"Okay," Christine said. "I give up. Frankie, you're in charge of the wedding. Get with Sue. Set stuff up. Just tell me when to go on."

"No problem," Frankie said. "By the way, the wedding will be in Santa Fe."

"Why Santa Fe?" Addison asked.

Frankie smiled. "You'll see."

10

THE DRESS

As soon as the engagement was announced the media went into a feeding frenzy, as did designers on three continents. Christine was almost entirely insulated from it as few people had any idea where to find her. Inquiries to the conservatory were forwarded to Sharon. No one found the Valerius house in Santa Monica. The paparazzi staked out the convenience store, but gave Sue wide berth, no doubt because she threatened them if they dared pursue her BFF.

Although Frankie had been authorized to handle everything, he felt Christine should have approval of the dress. She and Sue, along with Tegan, in town for a few weeks, pored over sketches and pitches. Major fashion houses sent representatives, and PowerPoint presentations. The girls controlled the urge to laugh out loud, and patiently sat through all of them.

Tegan, already a media darling, not to mention a stunning female specimen, and a regular on red carpets, was besieged. She shined them all on, gleefully accepting their offers of clothes for her own use, and then presented their sketches to the committee: Christine, Sue, and herself.

In the end, they all agreed on Christine's favorite, not a major house, not the flavor of the month, not a designer to the royals, or the rich and famous, but a young Korean girl named Nari, who lived and worked in a loft over the cell phone store next door to Sue's parents' store.

Nari was stunned. Like Sue, she was the daughter of Korean immigrants who worked hard and wanted a better future for their daughter. She had worked her way through fashion design school and with a small loan from her parents, hung out her shingle as a designer. Competition was fierce and cutthroat, and she was struggling to stay in business. Sue had encouraged her to submit her designs to Christine mainly for the experience, never dreaming that she would stand a chance against world-famous designers. But Christine loved her sketches. So did Tegan, who was routinely dressed by experts and invited to fashion shows around the world. Sue saw no reason to abstain from voting due to nepotism, so she gladly made it unanimous, and Nari's career was about to be made, provided she could deliver.

Nari was a one-woman operation, so Johnston, on Frankie's recommendation, immediately agreed to pay a large advance to cover fabric, materials, and seamstresses. As the media descended, private security was engaged, at Johnston's expense, twenty-four-seven. Sue's parents happily sold them coffee and snacks and provided them a chair and table in their store.

Sharon insisted that no one see the dress who wasn't directly involved in its creation and that no photos be taken of the dress or any part of it. Thorough background checks were conducted, and seamstresses were required to sign nondisclosure agreements. Bonuses were tied to everyone successfully keeping the dress secret until the wedding. Scraps of fabric were stashed in the loft and would not appear in the dumpster until after the wedding. The fabric itself was purchased by a shell company in another state and delivered to Nari's loft at 3 a.m. in an unmarked van driven by a retired Army Ranger, along with another riding shotgun.

Nari was overwhelmed but went immediately to work.

"Oh, by the way," Sue said, "they want bridesmaids dresses as well, and the choir."

"The choir?" Nari asked.

"Yeah, Frankie's going all out. They'll need choir robes, or whatever. You don't have to worry about the orchestra. They'll just wear black."

"I'm going to need some help, a lot of help, and some sewing machines."

"No problem. I'll call Frankie. But concentrate on the dress. Don't worry about the bridesmaids and the choir for now. We'll figure something out."

11

SANTA FE SUNSET

As the Christmas break rapidly approached Christine was disappointed that her adoption had not become final, preventing her from leaving the country and accepting Raoul's invitation to spend the holidays at his family's chalet at Courchevel. That disappointment was tempered somewhat by the fact that she had never been on skis in her life and was not looking forward to making a fool of herself falling on her ass in the French Alps in front of Raoul's family and friends. Making matters even worse, Sue was obligated to spend the holidays in Seoul. No one had said anything to the contrary, so Christine assumed it would be a quiet Christmas in Santa Monica. At least she would be able to catch up on sleep, and homework.

"We were planning on going to Santa Fe for Christmas," Zoe said.

"Why didn't you tell me?" Christine asked.

"We kept hoping the adoption would come through in time, but it didn't, so we went to Plan B," Jim Bob said.

"Santa Fe is beautiful at Christmas," Zoe said.

"Yeah, I guess."

"Some of the family will be there."

"The twins?"

"I think they are fleeing the cold in Boston and going to the French West Indies."

"Where's that?"

"The Caribbean."

"That's okay. They're exhausting."

Zoe laughed. "They are indeed. Frankie will be there. We're going on the train with him. His parents will be flying in from wherever."

Christine insisted on decorating the *Estelline* for Christmas. Frankie begged off, using studying as an excuse, so he handed over two hundred in cash.

"Is that enough?"

"Sure."

Christine drafted Jim Bob into the enterprise, and they went shopping. Jim Bob laughed as Christine checked the price on a string of tiny Christmas lights.

"What's funny?"

"We're shopping at the dollar store to decorate a private railcar that's probably worth a million bucks."

Christine shrugged and smiled.

IT WAS PROBABLY an unusual sight for a traveler on the highway along the train tracks: a century-old Pullman railcar with twinkling Christmas lights in every window behind a sleek Amtrak passenger train.

Inside the *Estelline* was a fully decorated Christmas tree with presents underneath. Christine went all out.

"Are you bored?" Frankie asked as Christine sat curled up in an overstuffed chair, staring out the window at the desert.

"Not at all, just reflective."

"Reflective on?"

"Life." She sat up straight in the chair. "How's the wedding coming along?"

"It's coming. Not much happening because of the holidays, but I'll get back on it next month."

"Thanks for handling it. I'd have no idea what to do."

"No problem, cousin. Are you happy with the dress?"

"It's beautiful, at least the sketches. I like the bare shoulders."

"Bare shoulders are sexy as hell."

Christine smiled and nodded.

Sofia turned out to be a good traveler and was the center of attention for the entire trip, when she wasn't asleep. Jim Bob played guitar and Christine sang lullabies.

———

MEG TOOK CHRISTINE shopping on the plaza in Santa Fe, with Johnston's credit card, and outfitted her with ski wear.

"Ski clothes are ski clothes. The main thing is to look really hot. But you'll want to rent skis and boots until you get the hang of it, decide which ones work best for you, and then get properly fitted," Meg said.

"No problem. This is all new to me."

Frankie loaded the four-wheel drive pickup with the girls and his parents.

"Are you sure you don't want to come with us?" Frankie asked Jim Bob.

"This redneck does not slide down a mountain on greased sticks. I'll just hang here by the fireplace with a cold brew."

"Isn't Johnston coming?" Christine asked.

"He's having lunch with Maria," Meg said, smiling.

"It's not the French Alps," Frankie said as they headed up the mountain, "but it's pretty decent, and good for a beginner."

Christine fell, a lot, but, along with the help of a very patient, and very cute, ski instructor, made it through her first day on the slopes, battered and bruised, but no bones broken.

THERE WAS A knock at Christine's door as she dressed for dinner.

"Who is it?"

"Johnston."

"It's unlocked. Come on in."

He pushed the door slightly open. "Are you decent?"

"Close enough."

Johnston stepped into the room and flinched as Christine slipped into her dress.

"Zip me."

Christine turned her back and Johnston zipped her.

"I wanted to talk to you about something," Johnston said, "while we're alone."

"We're definitely alone. What's up?"

"I want to keep Erik in my will until I know for sure he's gone."

"Of course."

"I'll divide my estate between the two of you."

"You don't owe me anything. You've done plenty already."

"His share will be held in trust until he's declared dead, which could take several years, then it will go to you, after I'm gone, of course."

"Well, I'm hoping that won't happen for a few more years, a lot more years."

"So do I, but that's the purpose of estate planning. You make sure everything is set up in advance. Life is uncertain, as we have all so recently seen."

"Yeah, I know, but really, I don't need your money. I'm sure Raoul will take care of me."

"That's the other thing. The pre-nup."

"What's that?"

"The pre-nuptial agreement, a legal document outlining who gets what if the marriage breaks up."

Christine started to speak, but he cut her off.

"I know. I know. You two love each other. You're not going to break up. You'll be together forever and ever. But that's what everyone thinks when they get married. That's why you plan ahead, when everyone is calm and reasonable. Trust me. Been there. Done that. Have the scars."

"Raoul hasn't said anything about it."

"And he won't. His father and I have already discussed it."

"You what?" Christine was offended.

"Don't worry. It's what people do, what parents do, when the bride and groom are as young as you are. Raoul is barely an adult himself and doesn't really have many assets of his own. He will inherit, as will you, so we want to work everything out now."

"I guess you're right. I just don't want to think about that stuff."

"Don't worry about it. When there's this much money involved, everyone does it. It's nothing to be ashamed of. It's just common sense."

"What about you and Maria?"

"What about us?"

"You two are spending a lot of time together. Do I hear wedding bells in the future?"

"Could be, but not before the bells toll for you and Raoul. We wouldn't want to upstage you, not that it would even be possible."

"What do you mean?"

"You are having a big wedding, a huge wedding. Lots of people want to come."

"Really?"

"Really. Frankie is working overtime on it. So is his mom, and Maria. Sharon is going nuts. I'm just writing checks."

"Sorry. I don't mean to be so expensive."

Johnston smiled. "That's okay. I never had a daughter, and I always wanted one. A big wedding has always been in the cards."

"Okay, glad I could help."

"Frankie could have a future as an event planner if that's what he wanted to do."

"Is that what he wants to do?"

"No, not at all. He's going into business with the twins."

"Those two are a lot of fun."

"Yes, they are, but also very smart, as is Frankie. The family money has always been in railroads, timber, energy, real estate, but Frankie and the twins are more interested in high-tech, the Internet, entertainment, although I'm trying to steer them away from the music business. They'll do well. Frankie will weigh the risks, watch the bottom line, and the twins will attack like barracuda."

"I can picture that."

"If Maria and I do decide to marry, and that's a big if, because we're happy the way things are now, that pre-nup will be about a paragraph long."

"Why is that?"

"She's loaded. Her late husband was quite well off, and the hotels have always been in her family. She doesn't need my money and I don't need hers. It makes things a lot simpler, like with you and Raoul, now that you are in my will. And of course, once the adoption is final, you will be part of the Titshaw trust, same as the other cousins."

Christine put her arms around Johnston and kissed him on the cheek.

"Have I told you how much I love you?" she said.

"Not as much as I love you." He kissed her on the forehead.

He held out his arm, she took it, and they went down to dinner.

CHRISTINE WAS WORN OUT from a day on the slopes, a leisurely dinner, and lots of talking by the fireplace after dinner. She was awakened by a knock on her bedroom door. She checked the clock on the nightstand, two a.m. Her first thought was that something must be horribly wrong.

She hopped out of bed and raced to the door, opened it, and gasped. Raoul's hands slipped around her waist, but he didn't need to pull. She slammed into him, and they kissed, and kissed, and kissed.

"I thought about sneaking in and slipping into bed with you but decided that wasn't a very good idea."

"Why not?" she asked between kisses. "Oh, yeah, right." She pushed away. "Wait sixty seconds and do it."

"Do what?"

"Sneak in and surprise me."

She closed the door in his face. He stood there, staring at the door, wondering what had just happened. Then he checked his watch and waited.

The room was dark as he entered, but he could make out her shape in the moonlight. He quickly undressed down to his shorts and slipped into the bed beside her. He put his hand around her waist and snuggled up close, her back to him.

She "awoke" with a start. "Oh, what a nice surprise," she said.

He laughed.

"Ow," she said.

"What's wrong?"

"My butt hurts."

"Sorry." He pulled away.

"No, that felt nice, but my butt hurts from skiing all day."

"You went skiing?"

"I went trying to ski. Mostly I went falling on my butt, which is what I was afraid of doing in, where was it?"

"Courchevel."

"Which brings up the obvious question. What are you doing here?"

"We always ski at Courchevel over the Christmas holidays, and I didn't want to disappoint my grandmother. She's quite a handful."

"She is?"

He nodded. "But when I walked in, she said, 'What are you doing here?' along with some choice cuss words, in French. She told me my place was with my fiancée, not my grandmother, and then she threw me out on my ass."

Christine laughed. "And here you are. Good thing your dad has a jet."

"He always sends the Gulfstream in for routine maintenance and gives the flight crew time off when we're at the chalet for Christmas. I tried to book a commercial flight, but there were so many connections, and it's Christmas, so I called Frankie. He somehow managed to get me on a private jet that was deadheading back from Europe."

"Deadheading?"

"No passengers, just crew, going to pick someone up, or bringing the plane back to its base, or whatever. The boy sure knows how to get things done. He even persuaded them to land in Santa Fe before flying on to Los Angeles. I'm sure Dad will get a bill for the extra fuel and landing fees, and I think there were tickets to the opera and a few cases of wine involved, but here I am."

"Thank you, Cousin Frankie," Christine said as she rolled over and kissed Raoul. There was suddenly nothing left to talk about as the kissing and caressing intensified.

"What are you doing?" she asked.

"Massaging your butt. You said it hurt."

She laughed. "Thank you. It feels nice."

They kissed some more.

"What's that?" she asked.

"What?"

"Your stomach is growling."

"Yeah, I'm starved. They had already cleaned out the galley, and the flight crew ate before takeoff, so the only thing they had on board was coffee and water."

Christine sat up. "Come on. I'll make you some breakfast."

"Now? I thought we were going to make out."

"There will be plenty of time for that later. I'm feeding my man, like a good little wife."

Frankie was staring into the refrigerator when Christine and Raoul stepped into the kitchen.

"What are you doing up?" Christine asked.

"I picked up Raoul at the airport. Couldn't sleep so I thought I'd raid the refrigerator."

"Sit down. I'm cooking."

Frankie sat down beside Raoul as Christine went to work making breakfast, which she quickly served.

"I thought you'd be making out," Frankie said as he dug into his eggs.

"Me too," Raoul said, "but I guess she thought I'd need some fuel first."

Christine smiled and sipped coffee.

"Aren't you eating?" Frankie asked.

"I don't need any fuel. I'm good to go."

The boys laughed.

"I'm sorry I missed meeting your grandmother," Christine said. "Maybe she could come to LA, so she can approve me before the wedding."

"She doesn't need to approve you. She said if I'm happy, she's happy."

"And she doesn't fly," Frankie said.

"She doesn't?" Christine asked.

"Never," Raoul said.

"Her son owns his own jet, and she doesn't fly?" Christine said.

Raoul nodded.

"Is she afraid of flying?"

"She's not afraid of anything. She just doesn't fly."

"She says it's bourgeois," Frankie added, "but I think she really is afraid of flying."

"How does she go places?"

"Well, in her opinion, there's nothing much worth seeing or doing outside the Continent," Raoul said. "She gets around by train, mostly, or car. She can even get to London by train through the Chunnel, or ferry."

"What's a Chunnel?"

"A tunnel under the English Channel. Trains go through it."

"Like the subway?"

"Like the subway."

"How is she going to get here for the wedding?" Christine asked.

"We're going to put her in a container and ship her ocean freight," Raoul said.

"Nuh-uh."

"We're working on it," Frankie said, "probably the *QM2*."

"What's that?"

"It's a British ocean liner. The last of the liners still making trans-Atlantic crossings, although she spends most of her time cruising. That's where the money is."

"Don't worry, *grand-mère* will be here for the wedding."

"*Grand-mère*, that's French for grandmother," Christine said to Frankie. "I've been studying." She kissed Raoul.

"WE'RE GOING ON A PICNIC?" Christine asked as Frankie packed the picnic basket in the kitchen.

"Yes."

"It'll be dark soon. Isn't it a little late, and cold, for a picnic?"

"Yes, but it's a special picnic," Frankie said.

"I made sandwiches," Juanita said. "Everything will be fine cold."

"Especially the wine," Raoul said.

"Do you know where we're going?" Christine asked.

"I have no clue, but I was put in charge of the wine." He held up a bottle.

"Just one bottle?" Meg asked.

"There's more in the cooler," Raoul said.

"Who's driving?" Christine asked. "I don't want anybody driving drunk."

"Carlos," Frankie said. "I want to have some wine too."

"Carlos?" Christine said, surprised.

"Yes, *chica*, Carlos," Carlos said, slipping up behind Christine. He put his arms around her waist and kissed her on the cheek.

"I didn't know you were in town."

"Just got in. I had some Christmas gigs in Lubbock."

"You're going with us?"

"I'm driving you out. And then I'll come back and pick you up when you call. I am not hanging around to watch you make out."

"Make out?"

"You think these horndogs are taking you ladies on a romantic picnic at night to watch the stars?"

"Interesting."

"Does anybody need to go to the bathroom?" Frankie asked.

They quickly loaded up and headed out.

Carlos stopped the Suburban at the gate to the parking lot at the opera house. Frankie hopped out, unlocked the gate, and opened it. Julio opened the door of the old pickup and got out as Carlos drove up and parked.

"What's the pickup doing here?" Christine

"For tailgating," Frankie said. "Tradition, remember?"

"Nuh-uh. There's no opera tonight. It's too cold in there."

The opera house was indeed dark in the fading daylight and had been winterized until spring. The parking lot was deserted except for the pickup and the Suburban. The boys unloaded the picnic basket and cooler. Christine looked at the bed of the pickup and smiled. There was an inflatable mattress, blankets, and pillows.

"Are we having an orgy?"

Meg laughed. "We aren't that kinky."

"Okay, later," Carlos said. "You kids have fun."

Carlos and Julio jumped in the Suburban and drove away.

"Get in," Meg said.

"This is weird," Christine said, as she climbed onto the mattress. Meg quickly followed.

The boys placed the picnic basket and cooler on the tailgate and climbed aboard.

"We need to hurry," Frankie said, digging into the picnic basket. "We're losing daylight."

They quickly retrieved sandwiches, Raoul poured wine into plastic cups, and they found positions in the bed of the pickup, plumping pillows behind their backs.

Everyone but Christine seemed to be looking east. "What are we looking at?"

"Wait for it," Frankie said. "It's a perfect night, high thin clouds."

"Perfect night for what?"

"Santa Fe sunset," Meg said. "Wait for it."

They waited, ate, and drank.

"Oh, wow," Christine said, looking up at the mountain.

"*Sangre de Cristo,*" Frankie said.

The rays of the setting sun set the clouds ablaze, in various shades of red, along with the snow atop the Sangre de Cristo Mountains.

"It's beautiful," Raoul said.

"Blood of Christ," Frankie said. "The snow on the mountains is tinged with red. The clouds are just a bonus."

"I ordered them just for you," Raoul said.

Tears formed in Christine's eyes. "It's so amazing."

"Haven't you seen it before?" Raoul asked.

"Sure, but in the summer, never when there was snow on the mountains."

Frankie waved his hand toward the sunset. "This was Zoe's inspiration for the opera."

"It was?" Christine asked.

"Of course. She had specific instructions for wardrobe and set design."

"Your white peasant dress was the color of the snow on the mountains," Meg said.

"The sash, soaked in Alejandro's blood," Frankie added, "was red, maybe a little redder than this."

Christine gasped. "I never even noticed it. I was mainly interested in the songs."

"Zoe did a lot of good work. Great work. That's why we underwrote the opera. It has a special meaning in northern New Mexico."

"Thank you so much," Christine said.

"For what?"

"For bringing me."

"But you'll be making out with me, right?" Raoul asked.

"Definitely. Prepare to be ravished."

Christine looked back up at the mountains and the clouds. "Although this is pretty much like sex already," Christine said. She turned to Raoul. "I guess."

Frankie laughed. "Yes, it is somewhat orgasmic."

ZOE HAD BEEN right about Christmas at Santa Fe—it was an incredible experience and Christine looked forward to many more, although Raoul's description of Courchevel made it sound inviting as well. She added "learn to ski" to her growing list of things to do. School and work beckoned, however, and friends and family began dispersing. Zoe and Jim Bob, along with Sofia, would join Franklin and his wife aboard the *Estelline*, bound for Los Angeles. Frankie elected to stay another night in Santa Fe with Meg before flying home.

Julio drove Christine, Raoul, and Johnston to the Santa Fe Airport where they boarded a Cessna Citation. They were the only passengers on board. After takeoff, Christine and Raoul occupied the sofa, where they could smooch for the too-short flight.

At Dallas Love Field the Cessna was guided to a stop just yards away from a Bombardier Global 7500. Johnston remained in his seat as Christine and Raoul stepped off the plane.

"Wow," Christine said as she looked up at the much larger jet. "Is that your dad's?"

"No, it belongs to a company Dad does business with. It's on its way back to Paris, and I'm hitching a ride."

They clinched and kissed, hard and fast, before Raoul pulled away. "*Je t'aime*," he said and kissed her again.

"*Je t'aime*."

"Gotta go." He bolted and rushed up the stairs, turning at the top to wave. Christine blew a kiss, wiped a tear, and waited until the door was closed before reboarding the Citation.

A BLACK SUBURBAN pulled up next to the Citation at the Fort Lauderdale/ Hollywood International Airport as Johnston and Christine stepped off. Christine stared out the window as they drove to the nursing home, wondering what Mrs. Valerius's condition would be.

At the nursing home, Christine hugged Mrs. Valerius, with no response. She stepped back and took a seat beside Johnston.

"Did you have lunch with the professor?" Mrs. Valerius asked.

"No," Johnston said. "I haven't seen him for a while."

"Some men came and brought me here."

"Yes. We thought it best. They can take care of you here, and your sister is nearby."

"Who?"

"Your sister."

"Oh, yes. She's getting married soon to a wonderful boy. Even our father approves of him." She leaned forward toward Johnston and whispered. "Who is that girl?"

Christine cried softly as they left the room.

Johnston rented a two-bedroom suite for the night in a luxury hotel overlooking the beach. Christine thought it was extravagant, especially compared to the room she shared with her father in the cheap motel in Santa Monica.

They had not brought beachwear, and the weather was cool, but they took off their shoes and strolled along the beach, holding hands.

"Daddy took me to the beach when we first got to LA," she said.

"Santa Monica?"

"Yes, and it worked out well, didn't it?"

"That's where you met Raoul, isn't it?"

"On the pier, second day we were there. Just imagine if we had gone to a different beach instead."

"Was it fate or destiny?"

She hugged him.

"Either way, I'm happy you chose that beach," he said.

"This is my fourth beach. The one in Chicago wasn't all that great, and it's probably frigid there today. Santa Monica is nice, and this one isn't bad, but Saint-Tropez is my favorite."

"So far. I see many more beaches in your future. Tahiti is nice, and Fiji. Good place for a honeymoon."

Johnston ordered room service for dinner, along with wine.

"You could probably be arrested for this," Christine said.

"For what?"

"You're shacked up in a hotel, with a teenage girl, and you gave her wine."

He smiled. "It's a chance I'm willing to take, and you just get one glass of wine."

"That's another thing I need to add to my list of things to learn about."

"Wine?"

She nodded. "The Chagnys are really into wine."

"That's an understatement. They have vineyards in several countries. They are quite big in the wine business."

"Are they really starting a winery in Texas, or was that just an excuse to get me out of town?"

"They really are, although it was a good excuse. We're going in with them. I am apparently investing several million. Franklin is handling the details for the family."

12

THE WEDDING PLANNER

Frankie sipped coffee at the Plaza Café. Mercedes, a woman in her forties, dressed casually elegant, carrying a large bag and a small tablet computer, stepped briskly through the crowded restaurant.

"Mr. Titshaw?" Mercedes asked.

"Frankie." He stood, and they shook hands.

She quickly took a seat. "Mercedes. Sorry I'm late."

"You're right on time. I'm early."

"Have you ordered?"

"No."

A waitress appeared, and they both ordered quickly without looking at the menu.

"I come here often," Mercedes said to Frankie.

"I do to, when I'm in town," Frankie said.

"It's a good place to meet clients. Everybody knows where it is. You never have to give directions."

"My dad has done a lot of deals here."

"How can I help you?"

"I need to plan a wedding."

"That's what I do." She smiled and opened her tablet, ready to take the order. "Who is the bride?"

"Christine Daaé."

"Is she a local girl?"

"Los Angeles, Santa Monica, actually."

"The groom?"

"Raoul Chagny, Paris, currently in school in the UK."

"I see," she said, seeing dollar signs.

"The wedding will be in Santa Fe."

"I'm a bit confused but I like to be direct. What is your role in the wedding?"

"Best man. I'm also the bride's cousin, or will be soon."

"The bride and/or her mother are usually the ones making the arrangements. I don't believe I've ever had the best man planning the wedding."

"I suppose it is a bit unusual. I have no experience planning weddings. But the bride is a senior in high school and is quite busy. Her parents are deceased. She has authorized me to handle all the details."

"Well, that eliminates the bridezilla and momzilla, and I've never encountered a best-man-zilla, so we're off to a good start."

She typed rapidly on her tablet. "Have you set a date?"

"Late June."

"That gives us plenty of time, or enough anyway. What about a venue?"

"The opera house."

"The Santa Fe Opera?"

"Yes."

"They don't do weddings."

"They'll do this one."

"No, I'm quite sure they won't. But I can find something suitable."

Frankie smiled. "I got your name from Maria."

"Maria?"

"Maria Josefina Álvarez de Garcia."

"Well, that certainly sheds a new light on the matter."

"And the bride's father is Johnston Caldwell, manager of the opera."

"I thought you said her parents were deceased."

"He is her adoptive father, or will be, hopefully by the wedding date. In any event, the venue is not a problem."

"Very well. Given the venue, I assume this is a large wedding. Formal?"

"Yes, quite large, formal, and traditional."

"What about music? That's a large room for a piano or organ and I assume a boom box is out of the question."

"We're bringing in the large orchestra from the Belen Conservatory of Music in Los Angeles."

"Orchestras come in sizes?"

"Yes, actually, they do."

"You couldn't find one locally?"

"There's a reason for that particular orchestra. We'll also bring in a composite choir from the conservatory and Ogden Hall, a private school in Santa Monica where the bride and groom once went to school. The orchestra is about a hundred kids and the choir about the same, maybe more, definitely better than a boom box."

"June will be the tourist season. That's a lot of motel rooms. I guess they could stay in Albuquerque and drive up."

"Not a problem. It's already being handled."

"Okay," she said, unconvinced.

"And the bride will sing."

"At the wedding, or the reception?"

"Both."

"Oh, no. Singing at the reception is bad enough, but not at the ceremony, not in a formal wedding. Trust me on this."

Frankie smiled. "No, trust me."

"Okay, moving along," Mercedes said, avoiding the issue. "Is there a budget?"

"Not really. Johnston is willing to spend whatever it takes but let me remind you that our family has auditors that make an abused pit bull look like a lap dog. We don't mind paying for quality and service, but we don't like being ripped off."

"Noted."

"I'll establish individual budgets for all the departments but overall, I just kind of have an idea in my head and Johnston is good with it."

"Departments?"

"Transportation, hospitality, wardrobe, hair and makeup, security, music, production design, interpreters, protocol, publicity."

"Sounds like a movie production."

"Yeah, it kind of does."

"Are you in the movie business?"

"No, but I go to USC and have friends in film school there. The wedding video will be epic."

"You mentioned security. Do you expect problems?"

"Nothing out of the ordinary, but the wedding guests will include politicians, dignitaries, businesspeople, movie stars, rock stars, opera people, music people, probably some royalty, people with titles, and the merely wealthy, so we definitely need security. We will provide umbrella security for the event and coordinate with all the private and government security and bodyguards."

"It sounds like you have already done a lot of the planning."

"I have and will continue to handle much of it myself. I'll also have help from my mom, who loves stuff like this, as well as Maria, who will provide overall concierge service for the entire event in addition to her own hotels. What I need from you is the specifics of the wedding, the girly stuff, no offense, protocol, order of the processional and recessional. Are those the correct terms?"

"Yes."

"Who walks with who. Who gets seated where and when and by who."

"You have come to the right person. How many groomsmen and brides-maids?"

"A dozen of each, along with alternates in case someone doesn't show up and we have to balance the number."

"That's a lot, but for a wedding this size, not really."

"We'll also use ushers from the opera house. They know the house and will probably do most of the actual seating work, while the groomsmen will handle the special cases, like mothers of the bride and groom, along with a lot of smiling and shaking hands as the guests enter."

"That's a good idea." She typed on her tablet and stared at the screen. "Hmm."

"What?"

"I'm looking at a seating chart. The opera house doesn't have a center aisle."

"It has two aisles. But as the tech kids say, that's a feature, not a bug. I have some ideas but would like to get your input."

"I'll work on it." She typed some more on the tablet and leaned in for a closer look. "Can you get to the stage from the floor? I'm thinking of the processional and recessional."

"Not really. But the stage crew will build ramps or stairs over the orchestra pit."

"What about the orchestra? Where will they sit?"

"They'll be on stage, facing the audience, in front of the choir, who will be on risers."

Mercedes nodded. "It also looks like there are steps in the aisles. That could be a problem, especially for the little kids like the ring bearer and flower girl."

"Little kids are cute, but we'll go with a bit older, ten to twelve, for the ring bearers, flower girls and train wranglers. They will also have dance or gymnastic experience, so they'll be more sure-footed than regular kids, and will be wearing the proper shoes."

"Train wranglers?" Mercedes asked, laughing.

"To keep the bride's train from getting snagged."

"It must be some dress."

"It is, or will be. I haven't actually seen it, or the sketches, but the maid of honor tells me it has a really long train and instructed me to have people there to handle it."

"What about the rehearsal dinner?"

"Maria will host the rehearsal dinner at one of her hotels."

"She sounds very involved in all this. Will she be mother of the bride? It's no secret that she and Mr. Caldwell are seeing each other."

"No, she has actually agreed to be grandmother of the bride, as Christine has no living relatives that we know of. The mother of the bride will be Zoe Hathaway. Christine is currently living with her and her husband while she finishes school in Los Angeles."

"The reception?"

"At the ranch. The family has been hosting big events there for decades."

"Do we need to hire a band for the reception?"

"We have one. It's a subset of the orchestra."

"You appear to have put a lot of thought into this."

"I have. We have."

"With all the money being spent and effort going into it, the bride must be a very special girl."

"You mentioned bridezillas. That's not Christine. She is a real sweetheart. This is for the families, who both have wide-ranging business, social, and political obligations. Christine would just as soon have a small ceremony, or elope, but she is being a good sport about it and going along. She does have a wicked sense of humor, however, so she may have some special requests."

"Like singing at her own wedding?"

Frankie smiled. "Do you remember last summer, when the young girl was kidnapped off the stage at the opera house?"

"Who doesn't? It was the talk of the town for weeks."

"The girl was Christine Daaé, our bride, and star of the opera, *Sangre de Cristo*, which was composed by Zoe Hathaway, MOB, and underwritten by my family."

"I thought the name sounded familiar."

"Singing at her own wedding will not be a problem, and I believe she's only singing one song, and maybe a few more at the reception.

13

THE HEIRESS

CHRISTINE WALKED QUICKLY down the deserted hallway at the conservatory. Being called out of class to go to the office was either very good or very bad and this time she had no idea which. As soon as she entered the secretary's office, she saw Frankie. She immediately suspected the worst.

"What's wrong? Is it Johnston? Did something happen?"

Frankie smiled. "Nothing's wrong. Calm down. Today is the day."

"The day for what?"

"We're going to court."

"Why? Am I in trouble?"

"We're going to be cousins, unless you say something stupid to the judge."

"Why would I do that?"

"Just kidding. You'll do fine." He turned to the secretary. "Are we good?"

"Yes. Congratulations, Christine."

"Thank you."

"Let's roll," Frankie said.

They raced from the conservatory and into a waiting taxi, which quickly sped away and only a few blocks later screeched to a halt. Frankie handed cash to the driver.

"Keep the change."

"Wow, thanks."

Frankie took Christine by the hand and rushed toward the entrance to a tall building.

"Wait!" Christine said. "Shouldn't I change?"

"Zoe is bringing you a dress and shoes and stuff."

"Zoe?"

"The lawyers want her and Jim Bob there in case the judge asks questions about your living arrangements."

"Where are we?" Christine asked, quickly looking around. "Is this the courthouse?"

Frankie laughed. "No, we still have a way to go."

The color drained from Christine's face, and she was speechless as Frankie opened a door and led her onto the rooftop where a helicopter waited. They ducked instinctively as they rushed to board.

"Sue will so not believe this," Christine said, thumbing her phone as the helicopter flew above Los Angeles.

The helicopter soon landed at Van Nuys Airport and Frankie and Christine hopped on a golf cart for a short trip across the tarmac to a waiting private jet.

"I thought we were going to court," Christine said as Frankie practically pushed her up the stairs to the jet.

"We are. I guess I forgot to mention the courthouse is in Santa Fe."

"You totally forgot."

Christine noticed two middle-aged men in suits sitting at the front of the plane but paid little attention as Frankie whisked her past them.

Further back, Zoe and Jim Bob were already on board and there were hugs and congratulations all around.

"Sit down and buckle up!" Frankie commanded as the flight attendant closed the door. "We're in kind of a hurry."

"Where's Sofia?" Christine asked.

"We're flying back tonight, so I didn't want to bring her on such a long trip," Zoe said.

"Who's watching her?"

"Frankie's mom."

"Does she have baby monitors and a crib and stuff?"

"She's at our house."

"Oh, okay. That works."

"You're gonna make a great mama," Jim Bob said.

Christine smiled and relaxed. She looked around the interior of the jet.

"I like this one," Christine said. "Kind of big for just us, but it has a flight attendant."

"It's a little bigger than what we needed, but it was available, so we snagged it."

"Who are those guys up there, lawyers?" Christine whispered to Frankie.

"No, the lawyers are already in Santa Fe, or on the way. Those guys are just hitching a ride."

"You can do that?"

"Yes. In this case we might be the ones hitching. The jet will drop us off in Santa Fe, take them to Denver, and then come back and pick us up for the return trip. I'm not sure if it's our charter or theirs. My dad set it up. Either way we all save money over taking two jets to the same part of the country."

"Am I worth it?"

"You are definitely worth it. At least Johnston thinks so. He's the one paying. I'm just along for the ride."

Once the jet was at cruising altitude Frankie went forward to visit with the men in suits. Christine listened to music and dozed off. Somewhere over Arizona the flight attendant nudged her awake.

"Lunch?" the flight attendant asked.

"Oh, sure," Christine said, straightening up in her seat. "It looks good."

"I thought we'd have a light lunch," Frankie said. "Maria has invited us to an early celebration dinner at her house."

After lunch, one of the men approached Christine. She removed her headphones and looked up.

"Miss Daaé?"

"Yes sir."

"I just wanted to say my wife and I absolutely loved your performance last summer at the opera. It was sublime. You have a rare gift."

"Thank you."

He quickly returned to his seat.

Christine looked at Frankie and grinned. "I have a fan."

"He and his wife are friends of Mom and Dad. They'll be on the guest list for the wedding. Oh, by the way, I checked, and this is his charter."

A few minutes later, Frankie checked his watch and leaned over to Christine. "We're almost there. You should probably get changed."

"Where? The bathroom is kind of tiny."

Frankie pointed over his shoulder with his thumb. He stood up and tapped Jim Bob, who quickly joined him in the aisle.

"Ha ha," Christine said. "Instant dressing room."

Zoe unzipped the hanging bag and Christine changed clothes while hiding behind Frankie and Jim Bob.

———

JULIO WAS WAITING with the Suburban as the jet taxied up at the Santa Fe Airport. Frankie raced down the stairs with Christine, Zoe, and Jim Bob in hot pursuit. As Julio roared through the gate, he fell in behind a police car.

"Police escort?" Jim Bob said. "I'm impressed."

"Maria knows everybody," Frankie said. "We'll barely make it in time."

The Suburban chased the police car through Santa Fe.

"Remember, honey, sir or ma'am, as the case may be, or your honor," Jim Bob said.

"Got it, your honor," Christine said.

"Be polite and smile a lot."

Christine nodded, more interested in her phone. "Okay. Sue will go to our house after school and relieve Frankie's mom."

"She doesn't have to do that," Frankie said. "My mom doesn't mind staying."

"Well, if we're having dinner at Maria's, and then flying back, it's going to be late."

"She has a point," Jim Bob said.

"Sue will stop by her house and pack a bag so she can sleep over."

"Works for me," Zoe said.

CHRISTINE AND JOHNSTON sat at a table in the courtroom, along with several lawyers, waiting for the judge to appear.

"Hurry up and wait," Jim Bob said as he sat in the gallery with Zoe and Frankie.

Everyone stood when the judge entered, and then took their seats when instructed after the judge sat down.

The judge glanced over the papers and looked up. "Quite an array of attorneys for one adoption," she said. "We have an orphaned minor child, born in Illinois, currently a resident of California, with a guardian in Florida who herself now has a guardian due to Alzheimer's, being adopted by a divorced man who is a resident of New Mexico, and a family trust in New York to which the minor child will become a beneficiary."

"Yes, your honor," one of Johnston's lawyers said.

"And everyone has a lawyer," the judge said, smiling.

"Yes, your honor. We wanted to make sure that everyone was on the same page."

"Mr. and Mrs. Butrell?"

"Yes ma'am, your honor," Jim Bob answered, quickly standing, followed by Zoe.

"The minor child—Christine," the judge said, looking down at the papers, "is actually living with you, not Mr. Caldwell?"

"Yes ma'am. We moved into the Valerius house, where Christine has been living for the past few years, so there would be minimal disruption to her life and school. Johnston thought it would be better than uprooting her and moving her to Santa Fe with just one year left in school. He comes into town whenever he can, and we come here for holidays." Jim Bob clearly wanted to help Christine's case as much as possible.

"And what is your relationship with Christine?"

"I've known her since she was born. Her parents were good friends of mine, in Chicago."

"And you, Mrs. Butrell?"

"I was her fiancé's nanny. Christine introduced me to my husband."

"Christine is engaged to be married?" the judge asked.

"Yes, your honor," Zoe said.

"Mr. Caldwell, do you approve of her marrying at such a young age?" the judge asked.

"I would prefer she wait until after college, but I have no reservations about the young man she is marrying. Raoul comes from a good family, in Paris, longtime friends of mine, and I firmly believe he will make her happy."

"When is the wedding?" the judge asked.

"June," Johnston answered.

"She's on the guest list," Frankie whispered to Zoe.

"So, Mr. Caldwell. Christine has not been living with you since you initiated adoption proceedings. She will be eighteen in just a few weeks, married in June, and presumably moving away to live with her new husband in Paris."

"Yes, your honor. Although I'm not sure they will be living in Paris. Raoul is attending university in the UK and I'm hoping Christine also goes to college, although she may be performing somewhere."

"Performing?"

"She sings a bit. Opera. Perhaps you saw her last summer in *Sangre de Cristo*."

"Yes, actually, I did," the judge said, turning to Christine. "That was you?"

"Yes ma'am."

"Oh, my. Quite impressive."

Christine modestly bowed her head. The judge turned to Johnston.

"Why didn't you just wait until she was eighteen instead of going to all the trouble to adopt her? You must really want her to be your daughter."

"There were practical considerations at the time, perhaps not so critical at this point. When Mrs. Valerius became ill, we were concerned that Christine would end up in foster care, which we simply could not allow. But yes, I really want her to be my daughter. I know I can never replace her late father, but I will do my utmost."

"Is Mrs. Valerius present?" the judge asked.

"No, your honor," her lawyer answered. "Her doctor thought the trip would be too stressful. We have his affidavit attesting to the fact that she would not even know what today's proceedings are about."

"Christine," the judge said.

Christine immediately stood. "Yes ma'am, your honor."

"What do you think about all this?"

"I think there are a lot of lawyers."

The judge smiled. "Yes, indeed. What about your living arrangements with Mr. and Mrs. Butrell?"

"It's great. Jim Bob helps me with my homework. He used to teach in college. I promised Johnston I would buckle down for my senior year. He was kind of worried about me. I'm doing pretty good and will graduate soon. My friend Sue comes over a lot, and we get to babysit Sofia while we practice French. We want Sofia to speak French too. There's always music in the house, just like before."

"Do you want Mr. Caldwell to adopt you, to be your father, legally and in every other sense of the word?"

Christine choked back tears. "Yes ma'am, I do."

"Does anyone here have any objection?"

No one spoke.

The judge signed the document. "Mr. Caldwell, you may kiss your daughter."

Johnston kissed Christine on the head and then hugged her tightly as she burst into tears.

Christine was relieved that the adoption was final. She had always been confident that things would work out legally, or that she could just fly under the radar until she was eighteen, but in the back of her mind feared that someone would find out about Mrs. Valerius and rat her out to the authorities. As a teenager in southern California, she frequently heard stories of kids being snatched by Child Protective Services and placed in foster care or sent to "juvie." Sue was constantly monitoring the gossip at school for word of just such a rat.

The adults were more concerned about the media. While most reporters, especially the ones who had gone to journalism school, had some remaining shred of ethics in the Internet age, there were too many who lived to dig up dirt. There were innumerable ways for them to discover Christine's situation and pump up a scandal.

Although they would have easily passed a background investigation, and everyone involved trusted them implicitly, both Jim Bob and Zoe were easy targets for today's breed of "journalists." Zoe could only hope that none of them checked her background and discovered the baseball bat incident. Jim Bob made a conscious effort to tone down the redneck act, something that Baby Sofia had already influenced anyway.

Sharon and her team constantly monitored the media, especially social media, and had Johnston's lawyers on speed dial, but somehow, after the initial media blitz with the kidnapping and the successful run of *Sangre de Cristo*, all that faded, and the vultures went after the next big thing, which was fine with Christine.

With a stroke of the judge's pen Christine's biggest worry was over.

SUE WATCHED AS Christine slipped her new debit card from its little envelope, shoved it into the ATM at Sue's parents' store, punched in her PIN and waited for the little slip of paper to appear. Both girls leaned forward to read the numbers.

"O-M-G!" Sue said. "You get that every month?"

"Apparently so. Frankie said it goes up when I'm eighteen."

"Wow!"

Johnston had already been quite generous with her allowance, but Christine hadn't much changed her spending habits and most of her allowance had been accumulating in a savings account. She had everything she needed and only occasionally splurged at the mall. She had no intention of letting her newfound wealth from the Titshaw family trust affect her day-to-day habits. She had already declined Johnston's offer to buy her a car. Parking was a constant hassle in Santa Monica. She didn't really want to drive to school, and park blocks away, so she continued to take the bus. Besides, she was to be married soon and quite likely living in Europe. Owning a car in Santa Monica seemed foolish.

The adoption also solved the problem of leaving the country. Johnston could now take her to the airport, sign the form, and she would be on her way. That had been the plan for Christmas in the Alps, but it was not to be. Now that she could, there was no time—a weekend trip to Paris or London wouldn't leave much time on the ground. Nevertheless, it was nice to know it was possible.

14

THE NIGHT CALLER

CHRISTINE STOOD IN the living room, holding Sofia while Zoe, elegantly dressed, leaned in, and kissed her. Jim Bob, wearing a coat and tie, also kissed Sofia and then opened the front door.

"We won't be too late," Zoe said.

"Don't worry about us," Christine said. "Go. Have fun. Go out for a drink after if you want."

"Okay, we'll call after the symphony and see how it's going."

"It will be going fine. I've got this."

Christine lifted one of Sofia's tiny hands. "Wave bye-bye."

Zoe finally stepped through the door.

"Lock the door," Jim Bob said as he took Zoe's hand and led her away.

"Yes, Daddy," Christine said.

Christine closed the door and locked it. She walked through the house singing with Sofia on her shoulder. She put her in the crib, went into the kitchen, prepared a bottle, came back to the bedroom, and fed her, singing all the while.

Back in the kitchen, Christine made a sandwich, carried it to the table, along with the baby monitor, sat down, and ate.

After she ate, Christine carried the baby monitor into the living room, picked up her laptop and settled into a comfortable chair. After a few keystrokes Sue appeared on the screen.

"*Bon jour*," Sue said.

"*Bon jour.*"

After a few minutes of French exercises Christine switched to English. "Sofia is crying."

She went into the bedroom, put her laptop on a table, picked up Sofia and patted her back.

"*Bon jour*, Sofia," Sue said.

"She says, '*Bon jour*, Sue.'"

Sue watched on the webcam as Christine sang for a moment and then returned Sofia to her crib. Christine sat in a chair beside the crib and the girls continued their French lesson.

"Did you hear that?" Christine asked after a few minutes of French.

"What?"

"BRB."

"Where are you going?"

"Watch Sofia for me."

Halfway across the living room, Christine froze, gasped, and covered her mouth. A man stepped out of the kitchen. He was wearing dirty jeans and a dark hoodie, partially covering his face. Christine was stunned and speechless.

"Aren't you happy to see me?" he said.

Panic gripped Christine's body. Her first instinct was to run, run fast, run far, get away, call 911, pound on a neighbor's door, anything, but she knew she could not abandon Sofia. She just stood there, trembling, chest heaving, mind racing.

"Have a seat." Erik sat down in the recliner that had been Professor Valerius's favorite chair, and now Jim Bob's. Christine hesitated. Her eyes scanned the room. She finally decided it didn't matter where she sat—she wasn't going to run—so she picked a chair and sat down.

"We thought you were dead."

"Sorry to disappoint you."

She didn't respond.

"We have a lot to talk about, sis."

Christine didn't speak.

IN THE BEDROOM, on the laptop screen, Sue's head silently danced to some imaginary music. Sofia wiggled but didn't fuss. After a moment Sue stopped dancing and leaned in, listening. She reached for headphones, put them on, hooked up and listened again. After a moment she reached for her cell phone.

"Yo," Frankie said, answering his phone.

"Somebody is in Christine's house."

"Somebody who?"

"I can't tell. She said 'BRB' and didn't come back."

"Whoa. Back up and start over."

"We were doing French lessons in Sofia's room."

"You're in Sofia's room? Where's Christine?"

"No. I'm at home. Christine is at her house. We were on webcam. She heard something and went to check it out. She never came back, and I can hear people talking."

"How long has it been?"

"I don't know, a couple of minutes, but there's somebody in her house!"

"Where are Zoe and Jim Bob?"

"At the symphony."

"Maybe it's just a friend."

"She doesn't have that many friends. And who would just show up at night? She would have come back and told me. And the doorbell didn't ring. She said she heard something and went to check. Something is wrong, very wrong. We have to do something. Should I call the cops?"

"I doubt the cops would consider it an emergency. I'll head that way. Keep watching the webcam and call me if anything changes before I get there."

"Okay, hurry."

"Do you like your new allowance?" Erik asked.

"What allowance?"

"From the trust fund. Now that you have been adopted by my dad you'll be cut in on the goodies, right?"

"I don't care about the money. He just didn't want me to end up in foster care. It doesn't even matter now. I'll be eighteen soon."

"And I guess he put you in his will and kicked me out."

"No, actually, he didn't kick you out of his will. He's always held out hope that you were alive. He said your share would go into trust unless a judge declares you dead—or this."

"My share?"

"He told me he was dividing his estate between the two of us."

"How generous of him."

"Look, like I said, I don't care about the money. You can have it all if you want it, but then you'd have to—I don't know—call your dad and tell him you're alive."

"I'm guessing you'll tell him."

"Duh."

"I don't really care about the money either. It won't do me much good in prison."

Christine looked around. "You don't look to me like you're in prison."

"Although I could use my monthly allowance. It's hard to be on the run broke."

"Use your debit card. Frankie said the trust is still making deposits."

Erik chuckled. "Yeah, right, and let the cops know where to find me?"

"Call your dad."

"That's okay. I'll get by."

Christine's fear had turned to annoyance. She shrugged. "Whatever."

"By the way, congratulations."

"On what?"

"Your engagement."

Christine gritted her teeth. "How do you know about that?"

"Even the homeless have access to the Internet. It seems you have become quite the celebrity since the kidnapping." He paused. "You're welcome."

She turned her head and tried to ignore him.

"I guess the asshole won," he said.

"What do you mean?"

"Raoul, the asshole. He won."

"He's not an asshole and I'm not a prize to be won," she said, turning to stare him down.

"And yet he ended up with the girl."

"You had your chance. Raoul treats me with respect. He never pushed me. He never tried to go too far. He never kidnapped me. He never tried to rape me."

"I never tried to rape you."

Christine froze. Erik turned his attention to the baby monitor when Sofia cried.

"What's that?"

"The baby." Christine stood.

"Yours?"

"Certainly not yours."

"Raoul's?"

"Actually, it's Zoe's."

Christine headed to the bedroom with Erik close behind. She assessed the situation. Her laptop screen faced away from the door, so she quickly picked up Sofia from the crib and turned, practically pushing Erik out the door before he could see that Sue was on the computer.

"Do whatever you came to do, Erik," Christine said, emphasizing his name, "but please don't hurt the baby."

Sue covered her mouth. She disconnected her microphone and then screamed.

Traffic was mercifully light on the Santa Monica Freeway and Frankie was well on his way when he answered his phone and heard Sue shrieking.

"What?" Frankie said, alarmed.

"It's Erik in the house!"

"Are you sure? Did you see him?"

"I'm sure. I didn't see him, but Christine came in Sofia's room where her laptop is, and she clearly called him Erik."

"Shit."

"She also said, 'don't hurt the baby.'"

"Call nine-one-one."

"I already did. Haul ass."

Christine sat in a rocking chair in the living room and began rocking Sofia, patting her on the back.

Erik paced for a moment and then sat down.

"I never meant to hurt you."

"Which time?"

"At the line shack, after—"

"After you kidnapped me?"

"Yes. I'm sorry."

Christine started singing softly to Sofia.

"I was angry, at Raoul, at you, at myself, at the world."

Christine continued rocking and singing.

"At your dad?"

"My dad?"

"You hurt him, badly. He's still grieving, and it's been even worse because the cops keep telling him you're dead and he doesn't want to believe it."

"There's nothing I can do about it now."

"Sure there is."

"What?"

"Call him."

"And he'll call the cops."

"Maybe not."

"What do you mean?"

"Well, I was the one who was kidnapped and sexually assaulted."

"I did not sexually assault you."

"Not as much as you intended but stop arguing. If I don't press charges, you don't go to jail, or at least that's how it works on the TV cop shows, doesn't it?"

"You'd do that for me?"

"I don't know, maybe. But you can't go on like this."

Erik shrugged. "I did a lot of other shit too."

"Like what?"

"Like the jeep. I stole a jeep. That guy's gotta be pissed."

"That's not so bad, not as bad as kidnapping a girl, so Johnston can probably get you out of it."

"Don't count on it. He got me out of too much shit already. I think he's done."

"He already bought the guy a new jeep."

Eric paced.

"You did a horrible, horrible thing and it will be with me forever, but I don't want to go through life hating you. We were friends once. We might have been more than friends, but that's over. You screwed up, bit time. I'm with Raoul now and that's not going to change. There's nothing you can do to stop it. We're getting married. I'm going to be happy. But I don't want you to go to prison, and I don't want you to be on the sex offender's list or whatever. It's not too late. People love you. Your dad loves you. Addison and Kendall love you, a lot. I'm sure they will help."

"You met the twins?"

"Yeah, we met." Christine smiled. "They're a handful."

Erik chuckled. Christine was relieved. Maybe she and Sofia would be safe.

"Call your dad. He was always there for you, right? No matter how much you messed up, he was there to bail you out, get you into rehab, into a new school, whatever. He never gave up on you. He won't give up on you now. I won't let him, especially now that you are my brother. I kind of have a responsibility."

Erik hung his head and started crying.

FRANKIE CAREENED AROUND the corner in the quiet, residential neighborhood, now just yards from the Valerius house, a police car in hot pursuit, and another one coming the other direction, lights flashing, sirens wailing. Frankie slammed on the brakes, screeched to a halt, left his car in the middle of the street, and sprinted up the sidewalk.

In the house, Christine held her breath and stared at Erik as Frankie pounded on the door shouting, "Christine! Christine!" She hugged Sofia tightly.

Erik leapt to his feet and ran to the kitchen.

Christine quickly opened the front door. Frankie burst through, followed by two cops. Christine pointed toward the kitchen.

Frankie put his hands on her shoulders. "Are you okay?"

She nodded.

Frankie tore out toward the kitchen.

"Wait!" one of the cops said. "He could be armed."

Frankie ignored the cop, dashed into the kitchen and through the open door into the back yard. One of the cops stayed with Christine as the other followed Frankie.

"Sue!" Christine screamed and then headed for the bedroom.

"Is there someone else in the house?" the cop asked, following Christine as she raced into the bedroom and plopped into the chair in front of her laptop.

"Are you okay?" Sue asked.

Christine nodded.

"Sofia?" Sue asked.

Christine wiped tears with one hand while clinging to Sofia. "She's fine. He's gone."

"Was it really Erik?"

"Yes."

"I was scared shitless. I thought he was going to kill you. I called Frankie and then the cops."

"Thank you. You always have my back."

Christine turned toward the sound of a motorcycle.

Frankie and the cop rushed through the house and out the front door as more police cars converged. Frankie watched helplessly as Erik blasted down the sidewalk on his motorcycle, zigzagging to avoid being shot as multiple cops drew aim. No shots were fired, however, in the suddenly crowded neighborhood as neighbors stepped into their yards to rubberneck. Erik got away, although with two police cars in pursuit.

"Christine!" Franklin called from the living room.

"In here," Christine said.

Franklin and his wife swooped into the room. His wife reached for the baby. Christine reluctantly gave up Sofia and fell into Franklin's arms.

Frankie's mom sat in the chair in front of the laptop and rocked back and forth with Sofia on her shoulder. "Thanks for calling us, Sue."

"I called everybody. Johnston and Raoul are on their way."

"Raoul's coming?" Christine asked, wiping tears, and turning toward the laptop.

"Damn straight he's coming. It will be a while. It's what, nine hours from London?"

"Christine!" Jim Bob bellowed. "Sofia!"

The nursery got very crowded very quickly. Zoe took Sofia. Jim Bob took Christine away from Franklin, practically crushing her with one arm while using the other to pull Zoe and Sofia into a group hug.

"Looks like it's getting busy there," Sue said. "Get back at me."

Detectives soon joined the crowd of cops in and around the house and began taking statements. Frankie waved off one of them while he talked to Sue on the phone.

"I'll check the bus schedule," Sue said.

"I'll send an Uber."

Jim Bob sat with Christine at the kitchen table, ready to pounce on anyone who upset her. Zoe rocked Sofia, who was blissfully unaware, until she went to sleep.

"Can we continue this tomorrow?" Franklin asked the lead detective. "The baby is asleep, and Christine needs to get some rest. It doesn't sound like she can tell you anything that would help you find Erik tonight."

"You're probably right. We can leave a unit here tonight, just in case."

"Thank you. That would be very much appreciated. We will arrange private security, or hire off-duty officers going forward, if necessary."

"That is one brave little lady. She did everything right. It could have ended quite differently."

FRANKIE AWOKE FROM A fitful sleep on the sofa in the little cottage. He sat up, stretched, and tried to work out the kinks in his back. Christine and Sue were splayed out on the bed, sound asleep. He checked his watch, pulled on his clothes, and quietly slipped out the door and into the back yard as the first rays of sunlight filtered through the trees.

Frankie and Johnston sat at the kitchen table as Jim Bob cooked and served breakfast, with lots of strong coffee.

"How did he get in?" Johnston asked. "Didn't you change the locks?"

Jim Bob pointed at a window. "We leave the kitchen window cracked open." He shrugged. "It's Santa Monica."

Johnston nodded. While the inland communities often struggled under oppressive heat, air conditioning was free near the beach—just open a window and let in the sea breeze.

"I'll put in some window locks," Jim Bob said. "We can still get some air, but an intruder can't get in without smashing the window."

"Maybe we should just get an apartment in Westwood, with a doorman and security," Johnston said.

"I think the Chagnys already have one there. Zoe said they bought it when they sold their house."

"They do," Frankie said. He glanced up. "You have a visitor."

Johnston quickly turned and leapt to his feet. Christine fell into his arms and started crying.

"She can stay with me," Sue said.

"We wouldn't want to put your parents in that position," Frankie said.

"What position? Everybody in my family knows tae kwon do. We'll kick his ass. Besides, you're already paying for security for the dress, right?"

"She makes a good point," Johnston said, still hugging Christine.

"I'm so sorry," Christine said.

"For what?"

"Sofia could have gotten hurt."

"But she didn't. You saved her. You talked him down."

"I thought about running. He would have chased me. But I couldn't leave Sofia. And he would have probably grabbed me before I got out the door, like he did before."

"You did good, honey," Jim Bob said. "Real good."

"I told him to call you," Christine said to Johnston.

"I hope he does."

"I told him he doesn't have to go to prison."

"I don't know. He's in a lot of trouble. But that's not important right now. You are. Do you want to go back to Santa Fe with me?"

"No, I want to stay here and go to school. I promised you I'd graduate, remember?"

"I remember. But I think you can take the day off, at least."

"Erik is not going to control my life. I'm going to school, with Sue, on the bus."

"You're not taking the bus," Frankie said. "I'll give you a ride, and you're going to be late."

"When did you get here?" Christine asked Johnston.

"Couple of hours ago. Jim Bob said you were asleep, so we caught a few winks in the living room."

"I'm hungry," Christine said, wiping tears and sitting at the table.

"Me too," Sue said. "What's for breakfast?"

"Whatever you want," Jim Bob said. "You name it. I'll cook it, if we have it in stock, so no eggs Benedict."

FRANKIE AND RAOUL waited outside the conservatory for Christine and Sue to come out after school. Christine rushed into Raoul's arms.

"Did you guys figure out what to do?" Sue asked.

"We have a plan," Frankie said.

"What is it?" Christine asked as she released her grip on Raoul and turned.

"I'll let Johnston tell you when you get home."

"In that case, I'm going with you," Sue said.

Johnston, Jim Bob, and Zoe waited in the living room as the kids streamed in.

"BRB," Christine said as she and Sue went immediately to the nursery to check on Sofia.

"You're going to have to get one of those, Raoul," Jim Bob said.

"I don't think we're in any hurry. We plan to practice a long time first."

Raoul took a seat on the sofa and Frankie sat on the piano stool.

"Okay, what's the plan?" Christine asked as she and Sue returned to the living room and plopped down on the sofa.

"As much as I'd like to have you with me in Santa Fe, I agree that you should stay here and graduate from the conservatory," Johnston said. "How's that coming, by the way?"

"I think I'll make it, if I don't get snatched by my brother."

Johnston smiled.

"It seems kind of weird to call him that," Christine said.

"We've considered several options, getting an apartment with a door-man—"

"Or just using our apartment," Raoul said.

"I don't want to move. Remember when I told you I was reclaiming my territory?"

Raoul smiled. "I remember it well."

"It's not just you, honey," Johnston said. "There's Sofia to consider."

Christine gasped. "Do you think he would hurt Sofia?"

"I don't know. I would hope not, but we don't think it's a good idea for you to be here alone with her."

"So, I can stay here?"

"Yes. We're all in this together. We'll make it work."

"There won't be any more date nights until you graduate and fly the coop," Jim Bob said.

"You guys can go out whenever you like," Sue said. "Just load up Sofia and Christine and drop them off at my house. My mom will spoil Sofia rotten. Surely Erik's not stupid enough to mess with a rooftop Korean packing a forty-four magnum."

"That works," Frankie said.

"No offense, Johnston," Sue said.

"None taken. If the boy had any sense he'd be at USC, rooming with Frankie, and we wouldn't be in this mess."

"We'll install an alarm system," Frankie said, "with panic buttons in every room, and wireless ones that you can carry around, like between here and the guest house."

"Can I stay in the little cottage?"

"I would prefer you move into the main house," Johnston said, "but I'll let you and Jim Bob and Zoe decide what's best."

"I'll set up a bed in the nursery," Jim Bob said. "You can hang out in the little cottage until time for bed and then come inside."

Christine smiled and nodded. "That works."

"I'll hire off-duty cops to park in front of the house twenty-four-seven, and do walk-arounds," Johnston said.

"Won't that be kind of expensive?" Christine asked.

"You're worth it," Johnston said.

"We'll notify the neighbors, so they won't be alarmed," Frankie said.

"I'll sleep over a lot, if that's okay," Sue said.

"Definitely," Christine said.

"We'll need bunk beds in the nursery," Jim Bob said to Frankie, who smiled and nodded.

"And you can crash at my place sometimes," Sue said. "Keep him guessing."

Christine nodded in agreement.

"I hired a car service to get you to and from school," Johnston said.

"The bus is fine," Christine said.

"It's not the bus that's a problem," Frankie said. "It's the walk to and from the bus stop."

"Oh, yeah."

"You're right on the way, so the car might as well stop and pick you up," Frankie said to Sue.

"Yeah, baby."

Christine shrugged. "Works for me."

"Besides, it's only a few weeks until the wedding," Johnston said.

"Yes, and less than that until graduation," Frankie said. "You might as well pack your bags and head out to Santa Fe right after that."

"That's where all the pre-wedding action will be anyway, right?" Jim Bob said.

"Right," Sue said. "We'll move our headquarters to Santa Fe right after commencement."

15

COMMENCEMENT

SUE LOOKED UP, pocketed her phone, and waited as the big black Suburban approached. She turned and waved to her mother who watched through the window of the convenience store. The Suburban pulled up to the curb and the driver opened the door to get out, but Sue hopped into the back seat beside Christine before he took even one step.

"You don't need to get out," Sue said. "We're low maintenance girls."

"This is Henry," Christine said.

"Hi, Henry, I'm Sue."

"Pleased to meet you, Sue," Henry said.

"You'll never guess what the name of the limo service is," Christine said.

"Um, Henry's limo?"

"Music Express," Christine said.

"Seriously?"

Christine nodded.

"Do you know Johnston Caldwell?" Sue asked.

"Oh, yes," Henry said. "I drove lots of people from his label for many years. Mr. Caldwell was a very generous tipper, even if his artists weren't."

"His daughter is sitting right behind you," Sue said.

Henry glanced up at the mirror. "I didn't know he had a daughter."

"He didn't, until a few weeks ago," Christine said. "He adopted me."

"How nice."

"Have you driven anybody famous?" Sue asked.

Henry smiled. "Lots of them."

"But I guess you won't name names."

"We pride ourselves on discretion and confidentiality."

"Will you be our regular driver?" Christine asked as the Suburban approached the conservatory.

"Yes, I will. I'm nearing retirement so I switched to days a few months ago. Let the young guys handle the 'artists' and their entourages."

The Suburban slowed and stopped.

"Do we need to tip you?" Christine asked.

Henry smiled. "No. It's taken care of."

"Okay. See you later alligator."

Students stared as the girls hopped out of the Suburban.

"I could get used to this," Sue said.

As she closed the door to the Suburban, Christine slowly turned her head, surveying the area. No sign of Erik.

THE FINAL DAYS OF school raced by, too quickly Christine sometimes thought. But Erik was nowhere to be seen, hopefully no longer even in town. Henry had been told Christine had a stalker, but not that it was her own brother. He constantly checked his rearview mirrors. Even though the girls insisted he did not need to open the door for them, he still got out and looked in all directions, waiting until they were inside the conservatory or their homes.

Christine and Sue quizzed Henry endlessly about Johnston's days in the music business, but in line with his policy of discretion, little was revealed, so they changed tack.

"How long have you been married?"

"Forty years."

"Childhood sweethearts?"

"Yes."

"Any kids?"

"Three."

"Grandkids?"

"Eight so far."

"What are you going to do when you retire?"

"Fish."

"Fish?"

"God does not subtract from one's allotted lifespan time spent fishing."

"Did Confucius say that?" Sue asked.

"Probably."

"Where are you going to fish?" Christine asked.

"Back home. Tenkiller Lake."

"Where's that?"

"Eastern Oklahoma, near Muskogee."

"You're an Okie from Muskogee?"

"I'm a red-blooded Okie."

"You listen to country music?"

"The old stuff. Not a fan of what they're doing now."

"What about rap?"

Henry looked up at the rearview mirror and smiled. "Same as Mr. Caldwell."

The girls laughed.

"Isn't your grandmother from Oklahoma?" Sue asked.

"Great-grandmother," Christine said. "She left in the early fifties to go to California and become singer."

"Did she make it?" Henry asked.

"Yes. She met a Marine in Tucumcari and they got married. He was killed in Korea."

"Sorry." Henry paused a moment. "I was in the Marines. That's what brought us to southern California, and then I guess I got into the music business too."

"Does your wife work?"

"I guess you could say she does."

"What does she do?"

"She's an investor."

"An investor?"

"I drove a cab when I got out of the Marines, and she stayed home and took care of the kids. People would leave magazines and newspapers in the cab, and I'd bring them home. She read the *Wall Street Journal* and business magazines and started investing. It was just a few bucks a week at first, but when the kids started school, she went to work part-time cleaning houses and invested everything she earned."

"Was she good at it?"

"Oh yes. When the kids were old enough, she went to work full-time and put them to work so she'd have more money to invest. A few years back, she told me I could quit work if I wanted."

"But you didn't quit work."

"No. I told her I liked my job and wasn't ready to retire, so I kept driving. She sold her cleaning business so she'd have more time to manage her investments. She's in Oklahoma right now watching the contractors like a hawk while they build our retirement house at the lake."

"She sounds like a keeper," Christine said.

"Can she give me some investment advice?" Sue asked.

PRIVATE JETS CRISSCROSSED the country, and the Atlantic, as graduation season got underway. Carlos was first up, graduating from Texas Tech in early May. Maria insisted on picking up the tab for his entire family and several friends to travel to Lubbock for the occasion. She chartered a large motorcoach, through Angel's company, and she and Johnston came along, although opera season was rapidly approaching, as was the wedding. Juanita packed lunch for the entire group, and they set out on an easy day's drive.

Christine and Sue were in the home stretch at the conservatory and there were papers and musical compositions to be turned in, recitals and performances, and, of course, looming final exams, so they reluctantly agreed to stay in Los Angeles while Frankie flew to Lubbock.

Next was the twins' graduation from their exclusive private school in Boston, where they were the co-valedictorians, confirming Frankie's insistence that although they came off as rather ditzy, they were quite brilliant. The ceremony was on Thursday. Unfortunately for Christine, finals at the conservatory were Wednesday through Friday. She could have probably persuaded Johnston to pull some strings, but reason ruled, and she decided to concentrate on graduating herself. Besides, it wasn't really the twins' graduation she cared about, but the trip to Boston, where she had never been. There would be plenty of time for that later, and she didn't want to fail in her promise to Johnston.

Christine teased Frankie about flying off with Harper, but he informed her Harper was already on the east coast in preparation for her wedding. He would travel with his parents, stopping in Santa Fe to pick up Meg, Johnston, and Maria, and then on to Boston for the twins' graduation. He and Meg, along with the twins, would then swing down to Annapolis for Clifton's graduation from the Naval Academy, the wedding, and associated festivities. Then back to New York to meet up with the old folks and catch a couple of shows before boarding the private jet to Los Angeles for the main event.

———

WHILE THERE WAS always an air of excitement around commencement at the conservatory, this year was rather special. With Christine's triumphant run at the Santa Fe Opera, after being plucked from the audience, the conservatory was suddenly swamped with applications and media inquiries. After a brief flurry of media activity when Christine began her senior year, even the paparazzi soon abandoned their daily stakeouts, which was fine with Christine.

With relatively small graduating classes the conservatory's auditorium had always been adequate for commencement, but this year the Titshaw family, founders of the conservatory and contributors to the scholarship fund on which so many students depended, would be there en masse, along with several friends and business associates. Ticket requests began flooding in as the rumor spread that Christine would sing.

Christine was nervous.

"Relax, girl, you passed," Sue said. "This is just a show. We don't even get real diplomas, just blank paper rolled up."

"They aren't real?"

"No. It's easier to just use blanks than to try to match everybody up to their actual diploma. The real ones come in the mail. We could skip graduation and it wouldn't make any difference."

"That's okay. I came this far. I'm definitely walking across the stage and getting my blank paper."

"Good idea. You have tons of people here."

"Did your grandparents get in yet?"

"Oh, yes. I am rapidly forgetting English."

Christine laughed. "I'm glad they're here. I'm looking forward to meeting them."

"No, you're not," Sue said.

The next few days were a blur to Christine, parties, recitals, dinners, Sue's grandparents, and finally, commencement. Johnston, the proud papa, pulled out all the stops. Christine had her own limousine, driven by Henry, at least until it stopped to pick up Sue, whose parents and grandparents also had their own, compliments of Johnston, as did Jim Bob and Zoe, and Sofia, of course. Small children at commencement were discouraged, but an exception was made for Sofia, who quickly became the center of attention.

The rest of the family arrived in a fleet of limousines, providing ample opportunity for the paparazzi and reporters. Tegan and Alfonso arrived early so as to not draw attention away from Christine and Sue.

Raoul didn't even quibble when Christine asked him to arrive with his parents, and not her. She and Sue had been inseparable at the conservatory for years. Sue always had her back. Christine and Sue would arrive together, arm in arm, no need for escorts.

And so they did, stepping out of the limousine under the watchful eye of Sharon, smiling and waving at the paparazzi, recognizing several from last summer in Santa Fe.

Excitement ran high, even through the boring parts and the speeches, and Sue's valedictory address, until the big moment arrived. Most high school commencement ceremonies are content with a CD in the PA system, or maybe a piano player, but this was the Belen Conservatory of Music. Cheers rang out as the large orchestra, with several conspicuously empty chairs for the seniors, began playing "Pomp and Circumstance," soon joined by the choir, also with empty spaces for the seniors.

As instructed, the audience withheld their cheers and applause as the graduates marched across the stage. Sue graduated with honors. Christine graduated, holding her blank piece of paper high, tears flowing. After crossing the stage, the graduating seniors took their seats in the orchestra or their places in the choir. Christine waited in the wings until the last one crossed the stage. She continued to wait patiently through the thunderous applause and cheering.

The headmaster was finally able to quiet the audience. He turned to Christine and bowed. The maestro tapped his baton on the music stand. The orchestra took up their instruments.

Christine took the stage. The audience held their collective breath. Christine turned and motioned for Sue to join her. Sue and Christine hugged, kissed, and wiped tears. The audience murmured. This was most unusual. Sue took a step back and to the side, turned and nodded to the maestro, who smiled and again tapped his baton.

Zoe reached for Johnston's hand and squeezed it tightly.

Christine sang "Nessun Dorma," accompanied by the orchestra and chorus, with Sue on violin standing beside her.

Students who were not on stage for the ceremony were pressed into service as ushers, ticket takers, and other jobs. Several of them huddled around the entrances to the auditorium, cracking open the door to better hear Christine.

Erik, his face almost completely covered by a dark hoodie, slipped up behind them, watched and listened as Christine sang.

The evening's previous ovations had been merely a warm-up for what followed. Christine brought down the house.

The students quickly swung open the doors and fastened them to the wall as the audience filed out, chattering. Erik wiped a tear from his cheek and blended in with the departing crowd.

16

NARI

Christine and Sue, exhausted, slept in after a night of partying and going to Van Nuys Airport to see Raoul off on the Chagny jet. He had to get back to London for school and wouldn't see Christine again until just before the wedding. The girls finally dragged themselves out of bed, staggered into the kitchen and plundered the refrigerator for orange juice.

"What's for breakfast?" Christine asked.

"Eggs Benedict," Jim Bob said.

"What's the occasion?" Christine asked.

"Duh," Sue said.

Zoe opened a bottle of champagne and poured a little into each girl's glass of orange juice. "Don't tell your parents, Sue."

"My lips are zipped," Sue said.

"What about Johnston?" Christine asked.

"I'm pretty sure he's seen you have a few sips of wine," Zoe said.

"And no driving today," Jim Bob said.

"Not a problem," Christine said. "I guess I should start packing."

"We're going to miss you," Jim Bob said.

"Me too," Christine said. "I can't believe it's time. I was concentrating so hard on graduating I didn't even think about what comes next."

"Well, it's not like we'll never see you again," Zoe said.

"Definitely not. You are coming to Saint-Tropez, aren't you?"

"We'll see. I'll take Sofia to the doctor and make sure she's up to the trip."

"And it's not like we'll be flying coach," Jim Bob said.

"Great," Christine said. "It will be nice having everyone there." She looked at Sue.

"I am definitely there," Sue said. "I am eighteen and a high school graduate. This girl intends to rip shit up and talk dirty to boys in French."

"What about the topless beach?" Christine asked.

"That too."

"Just don't sit next to Tegan."

"Why not?"

"She draws paparazzi like flies. Your parents would have a cow."

"Not a problem. Everybody will be looking at Tegan's boobs, not mine."

"How many people did you invite on your honeymoon?" Jim Bob asked.

"I don't know," Christine said. "Everybody?"

"The twins definitely," Sue said. "But we're not showing up until Christine has Raoul all to herself for a few days." She looked at Zoe. "Unless you need a babysitter, and then I'm like totally there."

"No, I think we're going to wait a few days," Zoe said. "We'll probably all go together. Frankie said something about a BBJ."

"What's that?" Christine asked. "Frankie wouldn't tell me, and it sounded dirty."

"Big Blow Job?" Sue asked.

Jim Bob laughed. "Boeing Business Jet. It's a 737 fitted out for private use. Frankie said it makes that Chagny Gulfstream look like a minivan." He put his hand on Christine's shoulder. "No offense, Mrs. Chagny."

"None taken," the future Mrs. Chagny said.

"It has a bedroom and everything, and we can install a crib for Sofia," Jim Bob said, "with a seatbelt, or a crib-belt."

"On the really fancy private jets, the ones with bedrooms, do people wear seatbelts in bed?" Christine asked.

"You got me," Jim Bob said. "A better question is, how do people 'sleep together' in a bed on a private jet?" He added finger quotes.

"I'll let you know some time," Christine said, blushing.

"You are so bad," Sue said.

"I mean, you're cruising along, making whoopee, hit some serious turbulence, and then *whoopee!*" Jim Bob said.

Christine and Sue both laughed, and blushed.

"Jim Bob, there are children present," Zoe said.

"Not anymore," Jim Bob said.

FRANKIE AND THE GIRLS assembled at Nari's loft so Sue, Tegan, Meg, and the twins could try on their dresses, and the twins could pass judgment.

The models who normally inhabited the loft for such occasions were in the habit of changing in front of whoever happened to be there, so there were no actual changing rooms or even screens. Tegan and the twins certainly didn't mind. Sue was a bit more hesitant, but the rich kids' nonchalance about such things was starting to rub off on her. Frankie suddenly found himself surrounded by beautiful girls in their underwear. He remained stoic.

"What the hell?" Addison said.

"What's wrong?" Nari asked, suddenly alarmed.

Addison moved around in front of the mirror and then said, "Duh!" and looked at Kendall, who modeled for her.

"What?" Christine asked. "Do you hate them?"

"Boobs!" Addison said.

"Cleavage!" Kendall said.

"Skin!"

"Bare shoulders!"

"Is that a problem?" Nari asked.

"Hell no!" Addison said.

"They're spectacular," Kendall said.

"Definitely," Meg said.

Kendall lifted the hem of her dress and examined it.

"What's wrong?" Sue asked.

"What do you think, Tegan?" Addison asked.

Tegan nodded and smiled.

"This is so not polyester," Kendall said.

"We don't do polyester," Addison said.

"Neither do I," Nari said.

"We love them," the twins said in unison.

"Me too," Tegan said. "I'm keeping mine. I can wear this sucker on the red carpet."

"Although it would kind of blend in," Addison said, rubbing her fingers across her dress.

"What do you call this color?" Kendall asked.

"Red?" Sue said.

Tegan stepped in front of a window and moved around in a shaft of sunlight. The fabric glimmered.

"Santa Fe Sunset," Nari said.

"It is. Look." Christine rushed over to Tegan and grabbed her dress. "You can see different shades of red when the light hits it just right."

Christine turned to Nari and hugged her. "Thank you. It's perfect."

"Totally," the twins said.

"How did you know about the Santa Fe sunset?" Christine asked.

"Frankie sent me up there for inspiration," Nari said, "on the train so I could see the country."

"On the *Estelline*?" Christine asked.

"Of course," Frankie said. "She came back on a private jet, taking off just before sunset and circling the mountains until magic hour."

"I spent a day at the Georgia O'Keeffe Museum with Maria, oh, and all the vendors at the Palace of the Governors, and the shops on the plaza," Nari said. "Did I get it right?"

"You totally got it right," Christine said. "I don't know how many wedding guests will notice, but I definitely did."

"Maria will notice," Addison said.

"And Johnston," Kendall said.

"Tons of people will notice."

"Raoul will notice," Frankie said. "Boys will notice."

"Boys don't notice dresses. Boys notice boobs."

"You knocked it out of the park, Nari."

"Are you sure we won't upstage the bride?" Addison asked, brushing her fingers over her cleavage.

"Christine will have to be practically naked," Kendall said.

"You said you wouldn't be bridesmaids if the dresses were ugly," Christine said. "Don't worry about me. I'll be okay."

"Are you planning on scaling up after the wedding?" Addison asked.

"Scaling up?" Nari asked.

"You'll be in demand," Kendall said.

"We're already hearing your name mentioned in Boston," Addison said.

"And New York," Kendall said.

"You are?" Nari said.

"And Hollywood," Tegan said.

"My mom has already offered to bankroll her," Frankie said.

"Oh, good," Addison said. "We love fashion, but we know nothing about the fashion business."

"We're more into tech startups," Kendall said.

"Look at this one," Christine said, holding up a very small dress that matched the bridesmaids' dresses, or at least made from the same fabric.

"O-M-G!" Addison said.

"That's so cute," Kendall said.

"Who's it for?" Addison asked.

"Duh," Sue said, "Sofia."

"She's going to the wedding?" Kendall asked.

"Of course," Christine said, "in her own little bridesmaid dress."

"You aren't afraid she'll cry and fuss."

"No, not at all. Besides, it's my wedding. She can cry if she wants to."

"Isn't that a song from the sixties?" Frankie asked.

"She will look adorable," Addison said, "but we will look totally hot."

"We are so getting laid," Kendall said.

"Like that would be a problem anyway," Frankie said.

"Be a bitch, why don't you?" Addison said.

Nari looked confused.

"We're kidding," Kendall said.

"We're not really sluts," Addison said.

"We just play them on TV," Tegan said.

"Exactly," the twins said.

Christine laughed and hugged Sue. "You look really hot yourself."

"I don't want to get laid, necessarily," Sue said. "I just want to meet a nice boy."

"Well, there should be plenty of eligible bachelors there," Christine said, "and you'll be in a high-visibility role, so shopping should be good."

"Do we get to see it?" Addison asked.

"See what?" Sue asked.

"The dress," Kendall said.

"You're wearing it," Sue said.

"*The* dress," Addison said.

"The one that these little numbers aren't going to upstage," Kendall said.

"It's not finished," Nari said.

"That's okay," Meg said. "We just want a peek."

"Not with him here," Kendall said.

"Who me?" Frankie said.

"You're the only 'him' here," Addison said.

"Bounce," Kendall said.

"I'm not the groom," Frankie protested.

"Close enough," Addison said. "You're a boy."

"Go," Kendall said. "It's a girl thing."

"Okay, I'll be next door," Frankie said, "drinking coffee with Johnston's security guard."

FRANKIE CALLED IN reinforcements and Alfonso met them for lunch. Christine had expected the twins to want to go to some froufrou place in Beverly Hills, but they seemed thrilled when Frankie and his harem pulled into Pink's on La Brea.

"We love this place," Addison said.

"Is your headshot on the wall?" Kendall asked.

"Probably," Tegan said. "My tub-thumper has them up all over town. Some of them even have my actual autograph."

They ordered a pile of hot dogs along with all the extras and gathered around two tables on the patio. Frankie picked up the check. "I'll put it on Johnston's tab for the wedding."

"Is everybody going to Santa Fe together," Christine asked.

"Sure, why not?" Tegan said. "I have some time off and so does Alfie. We're in."

"We're following our girl," Addison said.

"I'm with him," Meg said, nodding toward Frankie.

"Great," Christine said. "Are we taking your train?"

"No, Dad has the *Estelline* booked," Frankie said. "I guess we could take Amtrak."

"Ugh," Kendall said. "Work your magic."

"Get us on somebody's private jet."

"We have a lot of people," Alfonso said.

"So, book one and charge it to Johnston," Kendall said. "He never uses all his hours."

"It's his wedding," Addison said.

"I thought it was my wedding," Christine said.

"He's paying for it," Addison said.

"We could take the Prevost," Frankie said.

"No shit?" Kendall said.

"Is it in town?" Addison asked.

"It's been here since football season," Frankie said. "We were going to fly Julio out to drive it back to Santa Fe for the season."

"Road trip!" the twins said.

"Is that the big-ass bus you had at the premiere last summer?" Alfonso asked.

"Yeah," Frankie said.

"Road trip for sure," Alfonso said. "You'll have to teach me how to drive that big mofo."

"I can do that," Frankie said. "It's pretty easy to handle on the highway, but I'll do all the close-in work. You have to be careful to not hit the curb when you turn, or the fuel pump, or pedestrians."

"Can we all sleep in it?" Christine asked.

"Eight people?" Frankie said. "Not really. It's big, but it's set up for entertaining, not sleeping."

"We'll camp out," Addison said.

"Totally," Kendall said.

"I've never been camping," Christine said.

"It's like the beach at Saint-Tropez," Frankie said, "only all night."

Christine smiled. "Yeah, but we're kind of short on boys."

"We'll share," Addison said.

"In your dreams," Tegan said.

The twins laughed. "Exactly."

Alfonso smiled.

"We could drive straight through," Frankie said. "I've done it before, easy work with two drivers. But there's really no hurry. The wedding's not going to start without us, and Raoul isn't due in for a few days, so we might as well take our time. We can take I-40 all the way, probably stop at Flagstaff. There are lots of campgrounds in the area."

"Do you have camping stuff?" Christine asked.

"We have some. I can scrounge some more."

"It'll be fun," Meg said.

"I'm game," Sue said, "as long as I don't have to pee behind a bush."

"We can pee on the bus," Christine said, and then looked at Frankie. "Right?"

"You can pee on the bus. Unless we find a campground with hookups there won't be enough water for everybody to take a shower, but we'll manage."

"We could always go skinny dipping," Kendall said.

"Like Christine said, not enough boys," Addison said.

"But plenty of girls," Alfonso said. "Sounds like a plan."

Tegan elbowed him.

"What have I gotten myself into?" Sue asked.

"Think of it as a warm-up for Saint-Tropez," Christine said.

17

ROAD TRIP

The huge Prevost coach stood idling, double parked, blocking the narrow street in front of the Valerius house. Frankie and Alfonso loaded Christine's baggage.

"Are you sure you don't want to come with us?" Christine asked as Frankie closed the baggage doors.

"I think all those hyper kids might be a little much for Sofia," Zoe said.

"And I'm sure you don't want a couple of old fogies along," Jim Bob said. "I know what happens on road trips."

"We might need chaperones," Sue said.

Jim Bob hugged Christine. "And, truth be told, we want a few days without you before we leave for Santa Fe."

"You do?" Christine asked.

"That way when we get back it won't be as much of a shock having an empty house," Jim Bob said.

"It won't be empty," Christine said, taking Sofia from Zoe and hugging her. "You'll be plenty busy."

"You know what I mean," Jim Bob said.

"I know what you mean. It's all happening so fast."

They walked with her to the coach, reluctant to let her go, but finally, after all the hugs and kisses, Christine climbed aboard and waved.

"Drive safe!" Jim Bob called out as the door closed. "See you in a few days."

He put his arm around Zoe. "Well, Mama, the next one will be even harder."

"I know," Zoe said, wiping tears. "But we'll have a few more years."

Some of the neighbors stood in their yards and watched as the Prevost coach pulled away.

Not long after Frankie turned east onto I-10 the gang had come to hate "The Wheels on the Bus." No one knew all the lyrics of course, so someone came up with the bright idea of finding them on the Internet and downloading them to everyone's phone.

By the time they reached the high desert the fun had worn off. As they headed east out of Barstow, with seemingly endless stretches of empty desert and light traffic, Alfonso took his first turn at the wheel. While the girls dozed off, Frankie sat up front to keep Alfonso awake. As they approached the Arizona state line Frankie leaned over Alfonso's shoulder and checked the fuel level.

"We'll make it," Frankie said.

"Make what?" Alfonso asked.

"I just put in a few gallons before we left so we could fill up in Arizona," Frankie said. "Diesel is a lot cheaper once you get out of California."

Alfonso laughed.

"What?" Frankie said.

"Rich people don't stay rich by throwing away money," Alfonso said.

"True," Frankie said, smiling.

As the bus rolled on Alfonso reached over and punched Frankie on the shoulder.

"Wake up, asshole," Alfonso said. "You're supposed to be keeping me awake."

"Where are we?"

"Coming up on Needles."

"How's your fuel?"

"Looks like we still have some."

"Stay on the interstate and blow past Needles," Frankie said. "There's a truck stop on the right just a couple miles after you cross the river."

"I thought the girls were asleep," Alfonso said, glancing over his shoulder.

Frankie turned to look. The girls' giggling turned to loud laughter as they hunched over someone's tablet. Frankie unbuckled his seat belt and headed down the aisle.

"Telling dirty jokes?" Frankie asked as he approached the girls.

"We found a place to camp," Kendall said.

"I already have a place," Frankie said.

"Not like this one," Addison said.

"What's so special about it?"

"We can go skinny dipping," Tegan said.

Frankie smiled. "Yeah, right."

"What's the matter cousin, chicken?" Kendall said.

"You guys are serious?"

"Totally serious," Sue said.

"You want to go skinny dipping?"

"Sure, why not?" Sue said. "I'm going topless in Saint-Tropez in a few weeks, so I might as well get the hang of it before I go."

"It's no big deal, really," Addison said.

"After the initial, you know, reveal," Kendall said.

"Are you sure you're not letting these party girls talk you into it?" Frankie asked.

"I'm an adult," Sue said. "I make my own decisions."

"What about me, Tits?" Christine asked. "Aren't you concerned about me?"

"I've already seen your tits," Frankie said.

The twins laughed.

"So have I," Alfonso shouted from up front.

Christine covered her face.

"When was that?" Frankie asked.

"Dressing room," Christine said. "It's a theater thing."

The girls laughed. Frankie looked at Meg, who shrugged.

"Big places, like the opera house, have separate dressing rooms, but in small theaters, it's just one big, happy family," Meg said. "Nobody really pays any attention. It's just stuff."

Frankie shook his head. "Okay, back to skinny dipping. Are we talking topless, or what?"

"Or what," Addison said.

"Boys swim topless anyway," Kendall said.

"Everybody has to have some skin in the game," Meg said.

"We're talking the full monty," Tegan said.

"We're all friends here, right?" Sue said.

Frankie nodded.

"And half of us are cousins," Addison said.

Frankie turned toward the front of the bus. "What do you think, Alfonso?"

"Two dudes and six hot girls," Alfonso said. "What's not to like?"

Frankie turned back to the girls. "Okay, somebody give me the coordinates to Sodom and Gomorrah."

Frankie gave Alfonso his first lesson in off-freeway driving when they pulled into a truck stop just inside Arizona and parked at the fuel pump without hitting anything. The girls swarmed into the building and returned with large bags of junk food.

"We have food and drink on board," Frankie said. "I stocked up before we left."

"We need junk food," Addison said.

"And souvenirs," Meg said.

"And postcards," Sue said.

"It's a road trip," Christine said.

"Be sure to pull over if you see a snake farm," Kendall said.

"What's a snake farm?" Tegan asked.

"It's an American thing," Kendall said.

"In Australia it would probably be a crocodile farm," Addison said.

Tegan still didn't get it.

"If you ladies are serious about skinny dipping then we probably won't be making any more stops until we get there," Frankie said.

"Why not?" Christine asked.

"Flagstaff is almost as high up as Santa Fe," Frankie said. "It gets cold at night, so we need to hurry."

"We swim at the ranch," Christine said.

"The pool at the ranch is heated," Frankie said. "Swimming holes around Flagstaff, not so much."

"Oh, no," Sue said. "I didn't think about that."

"Come on, Sue," Tegan said. "Pull on your big girl panties."

"Or pull them off, as the case may be," Christine said.

Everyone laughed.

"All aboard!" Sue shouted before climbing on the bus.

As the bus approached Flagstaff the girls disappeared into the bedroom two at a time and came out wearing nothing but shorts, T-shirts and flip-flops.

"What are they doing back there?" Alfonso asked.

"I have no idea," Frankie said.

"We're changing," Meg said as she approached, and then kissed Frankie on the cheek.

"Into what?" Frankie asked.

"Into as little as possible, so we can strip off in a hurry when we get there."

"You can go ahead and strip off right now if you like and then just dash off the bus naked," Alfonso said. "Save a lot of time."

"You wish," Meg said.

The girls might have picked a place more accessible to the behemoth, but Frankie, with Alfonso outside guiding him, managed to get the Prevost relatively close to their assigned campsite.

"We don't have much daylight left," Frankie said as he turned off the bus and turned on the generator. "Are we still doing this?"

"We're still doing this," Sue said, taking a deep breath. "Open the door."

Frankie opened the door and the girls rushed off the bus, leaving a trail of clothes along the way. Frankie and Alfonso watched appreciatively as the naked girls disappeared over a small hill.

"We could just go watch, or steal their clothes," Frankie said.

"That would be mean," Alfonso said.

"Yeah, but a lot of fun," Frankie said.

"Do you want to get laid tonight, or sleep in the tent with me?"

"You're right. Let's man up and do this."

They stepped off the bus and immediately heard shrieks as the girls hit the water.

"I tried to tell them," Frankie said.

"Hold on. They forgot towels. We could score points by bringing some."

The boys climbed aboard the bus and loaded up a stack of towels.

They walked to the top of the hill and slowly stripped while the girls watched and cheered. They paused for effect, and one last round of cheers, and then dove in. It was definitely cold. They swam, splashed, played grab-ass, and laughed.

"Remember that time at coding camp?" Addison asked.

Kendall laughed. "Oh, yeah."

"Coding camp?" Christine said.

"Summer camp for kids who want to learn to program computers," Addison said.

"During the day," Kendall said, "and go skinny dipping at night."

"Sounds like fun," Christine said, sarcastically.

"Except all the guys were nerds," Addison said.

"So were the girls."

"Except us, of course."

"And there weren't that many girls."

"So we were in charge of fun."

"Were we ever!"

"Nerds really like to party."

"They just need guidance."

"Oh, shit!" Sue said. "There are people over there."

"Don't worry," Tegan said. "They don't look like paparazzi."

"They look like skinny dippers," Frankie said as the strangers stripped. "Are you okay?"

"I'm fine," Sue said. "When everybody's naked it's no big deal. It's kind of liberating."

"It is," Christine said.

"My parents would freak out," Sue said.

"So, no posting pics?" Tegan said.

"Hell, no," Sue said. "Except you, of course. Your fanboys are probably jonesing for some more nakie selfies."

"Oh, shit!" Christine said. "Our phones!"

"I locked the bus," Frankie said. "You never know who's out there."

The couples coupled, and the singles frolicked. Christine soon drifted away from Sue and the twins and floated on her back.

"Go see about Christine," Tegan whispered to Alfonso.

"What's wrong?" Alfonso asked, turning to look.

"She seems a little melancholy," Tegan said.

"Melancholy?" Alfonso repeated, smiling.

"Just go."

Alfonso swam over and slipped a hand over Christine's waist. She flinched, and then treaded water. She smiled.

"Are you okay?" Alfonso asked.

"Sure," she said. "Why wouldn't I be?"

"You seemed a little sad," he said, pulling her to him.

"Whoa!" she said.

"Sorry."

"That's okay." She put her arms around his neck, and they hugged. "We've done this a lot, just never naked."

"True. It does add a whole new dimension."

Christine laughed. "It certainly does."

"Do you miss Raoul?"

"Not at the moment," she said, grinning.

He raised his eyebrows.

"Just kidding," she said. "Yes, I miss him, but it's not that." She looked around at the others. "So much has happened. I was homeless. My dad died. The professor and his wife took me in. Then he died. Then she went crazy or whatever. Then Johnston adopted me and now I guess I'm rich, but I don't feel any different. This is what's important, friends and family."

He hugged her tightly and then she pulled away so she could see his face.

"Then there was Erik, and Connie, and Raoul, and Saint-Tropez," she said. "And now there's this huge wedding and I only know a few people who are on the guest list. And Sue's going off to college and you and Teegs are going off to make movies and sing opera and stuff. And I just met the twins and now they're moving to LA just as I'm leaving."

She grinned. "So, yeah, I guess that's sad, or the next best thing."

He laughed.

"Did Tegan send you over here?" she asked.

"Yes," he said, "but only because she noticed before I did. I'll always be there for you. You know that, right?"

"Yes. I know that." She kissed him on the lips.

Christine flinched again as Tegan swam up behind her and pulled close.

"Who's that?" Christine asked.

"If you're going to mack on my man we might as well make it a three-some," Tegan said.

Christine laughed out loud, attracting everyone's attention.

"Christine sandwich!" Addison said.

"Orgy!" Kendall shouted.

They all swam in, surrounding Christine, creating a floating huddle of naked bodies.

"Okay, this is weird," Sue said, "but kind of fun."

"Who's hungry?" Frankie called out after a few moments of embarrassed giggling.

The pack broke up and everyone swam for shore.

"Oh, good, towels!" Meg said.

"Told you," Alfonso said to Frankie.

Everyone wrapped themselves in a towel and headed for the bus, gathering clothes along the way. It didn't really matter whose clothes they picked up. Once aboard the bus towels flew, and they swapped clothes.

"Is this what it's like backstage?" Frankie asked.

"Pretty much," Christine said.

"I should have majored in theater."

The girls had a lot more hair to dry, so Frankie and Alfonso pulled on jeans and T-shirts and went to work. They built a fire and pitched four tents around it.

Meg had some experience with the Prevost and managed to get the grill pulled out and fired up. By the time the boys finished pitching camp the girls were streaming out, bearing food and drinks.

"Where's the wine?" Kendall asked.

"Everybody here is a minor," Frankie said, "and we're crossing two state lines in a million-dollar RV that looks like a tour bus to a state trooper. Too big a risk, especially right before Christine's wedding."

"Bummer," Addison said.

"What about beer?" Tegan asked.

"No beer," Frankie said.

"Just kidding," Tegan said.

"We'll survive," Christine said.

Everyone pitched in and dinner was soon served under the stars. The mood was jovial.

"We have some news," Tegan said.

"You're pregnant," Sue said.

"You're getting married," Christine said.

"Geez," Tegan said. "Alfie got cast in a film."

"Congratulations," Christine said.

"When did you become an actor?" Sue asked.

"Thanks for the vote of confidence," Alfonso said.

Sue laughed. "You know what I mean."

"It's tough to make a living in opera, or even musical theater, so I thought I'd better enlarge the target," Alfonso said.

"My agent started sending him on auditions," Tegan said, "little things at first, and he started getting callbacks."

"I signed up for acting classes," Alfonso said. "And I liked it."

"What's the movie?" Frankie asked.

"It's just a little indie, but it's SAG, so I'll get my card."

"It might be a little indie," Tegan said, "but he's the male lead."

"Are you in it?" Christine asked Tegan.

"I wish. It's a great role, but the female lead was already cast. She's good. I think they'll be great together, kind of like—what was that little opera you did, honey, with that blonde chick?"

Christine laughed.

"When does it shoot?" Frankie asked.

"October, in Louisiana, or Oklahoma, depending on who gives the producers the most taxpayer money," Alfonso said. "Tegan doesn't have anything booked right now, so hopefully she can come along, for moral support."

"And to keep that bitch's claws off my man," Tegan said.

"Well, congratulations," Frankie said, followed by the same from the others.

"Since you brought it up, we may as well tell you," Tegan said.

"Tell us what?" Sue asked.

"We are delaying the official announcement until after Christine's wedding," Tegan said.

"O-M-G," Sue said. "You *are* pregnant!"

"We're getting married," Tegan said.

After the cheering and congratulations died down, Frankie asked, "When?"

"Probably January or February," Tegan said.

"In LA?" Frankie asked.

"Australia," Tegan said. "I have a big family."

"Won't it be kind of cold?" Meg asked. "Or is that summer down under?"

"It's summer. We can hit the beach."

"Topless?" Sue asked.

"Topless," Tegan said. "Some of them are full nude if you're feeling really adventurous. You're all invited, of course."

"Can we go?" Christine asked Frankie.

Frankie laughed. "You don't have to ask my permission."

"Duh. You're my travel agent."

"Oh, yeah," Frankie said. "I guess I'd better get to work. Get a head count and I'll see what's available."

"Maybe we can take the Big Blow Job," Sue said.

"The what?"

"The Boeing BBJ."

Frankie smiled. "Oh yeah, that. It's a definite possibility." He turned to Christine. "Where will you be in January?"

"I have no idea," Christine said. "We still haven't decided. If I go to college, I'll take a year off to get used to being married and all, so probably in the UK with Raoul."

"We'll be in LA at SC," Addison said to Frankie, "so we'll just ride with you."

"Bondi!" Kendall said.

"Surfer dudes!" Addison said.

They ate and talked and laughed and lounged around the fire.

"This is fun," Christine said. "I am so happy we decided to road trip."

"Me too," Sue said. "Private jets and trains are cool and all, but this rocks. We should do this more often, but then Christine is abandoning us, marrying a Frenchman, and changing hemispheres."

Christine hugged Sue. "I'll see everybody in just a few weeks," Christine said. "Everybody is coming, right?"

"Absolutely," Tegan said.

"Wouldn't miss it," Sue said, "now that I'm an experienced skinny dipper. Look out, French boys."

"It's times like this that I miss Erik," Addison said.

"Shush," Kendall said.

"That's okay," Christine said. "I miss him too."

"The boy likes to skinny dip?" Tegan asked.

"The boy likes to do anything that's fun," Addison said.

"This reminds me of that night on the beach in Saint-Tropez," Christine said. "Erik played his guitar, and we sang."

"I could go get my violin," Sue said.

"That's okay," Christine said. "I like the quiet." She looked up at the stars. "It's a beautiful night."

"Speaking of Erik," Frankie said. "I didn't say anything earlier because everyone was looking forward to the trip."

"What about Erik?" Christine asked, suddenly concerned.

"I saw him last night," Frankie said.

Christine sat up straight. "What? You saw Erik?"

"Yes," Frankie said. "And talked to him."

No one spoke for a moment.

"Well, spill!" Addison finally broke the silence.

"I went to the storage facility to check on the Prevost, make sure it would start, charge the battery, whatever, so it would be ready this morning. Erik was there."

"What was he doing there?" Kendall asked.

"He had been living in it," Frankie said, "or at least crashing. Fortunately, he had the good sense to use the bathroom somewhere else. Otherwise, the stench would have been awful when the tank filled up."

"Ew!" Addison said.

"It was in storage," Frankie said, "not exactly hooked up to water and sewer."

"How did he know it was in LA?" Kendall asked.

"He knew Dad always brought it back after opera season, for football, and he knew where we parked it, so he just checked. We changed the locks on the *Estelline*, but nobody suspected he would try the Prevost, or even knew he had a key."

"Okay, enough chitchat about the effing bus," Christine said. "What did he say?"

"He apologized for what he did to you, and his dad, and the family," Frankie said. "He actually seemed remorseful, no more of the swagger and screw-it-all attitude of his."

Christine nodded.

"But when I told him to call his dad, or turn himself in, he got pissed and started to leave," Frankie said. "I asked him where he was going, and he said he was going to hitchhike cross-country and try to get a fake passport, so he could go to Europe."

"Can you do that, get a fake passport?" Christine asked. "Or is that just in the movies?"

"Oh, yes, you can do it, if you have the money and know where to look."

"Does he have money? He said if he used his debit cards the cops could find him."

"He started using it again after he paid you a visit. He's probably been taking out the daily maximum for the last few days, so he won't have to use it after he leaves LA."

"Did you tell Johnston?"

"Of course. As soon as Erik took off, I called him and asked him what he wanted me to do, call the cops or what."

"Did you call the cops?"

"No. Johnston said he would call the sheriff in Santa Fe. I'm not sure if there were any charges filed in California, or even New Mexico for that matter, so it wasn't like I was aiding a fugitive by not trying to hold him down and call the cops."

Christine nodded. "That's okay."

"The cops got the license plate number on his bike the night he came to your house, so they were on the lookout. He got chased a couple of days later and ditched the bike, so now he's on foot, unless he found another ride."

"Do you think he will show up at the wedding?" Sue asked.

"I don't know," Frankie said. "If you're going to hitchhike cross-country from LA you're going to take either I-10 or I-40. This time of year, I-10 is hotter than hell, and I-40 goes right through Albuquerque. Johnston said we would beef up security, just in case."

"Do you think he followed us?" Addison asked.

"I don't think so," Frankie said. "I told him Julio was flying in to drive the Prevost back to Santa Fe. He joked that he would be happy to drive it to Santa Fe. I doubt he suspected we were all road tripping in it. Even if he did, there's really no way he could be following us. But I checked the rearview mirrors along the way, just in case, especially after pit stops."

Frankie watched Christine for a moment as she processed everything.

"You and Sue can sleep in the RV tonight if you want," Frankie said.

"Nah," Christine said. "Like you said, there's no way he could be following us. I'll be fine. Sue has my back."

"Or Sue could share a tent with Teegs and I'll sleep with Christine," Alfonso said.

Christine burst out laughing. "Nice try, Don Juan."

"Or," Tegan said when the laughter died down, "I'll sleep with Christine, and you can sleep with Sue."

"And I'll kick *your* ass," Sue said.

"Ouch," Alfonso said.

"Okay," Christine said as she stood up. "I'm going to bed. If anyone wants to sleep with me, you know where to find me." She looked at Sue. "Which tent are we in?"

18

THE WAR ROOM

As the oldest state capital in the United States, the streets of Santa Fe, especially downtown, were ill suited to normal RVs, let alone the beast Frankie was driving. Nevertheless, he pulled up in front of a seemingly vacant storefront near the plaza.

"Come on, guys," Frankie said. "I have something to show you."

Everyone piled off the bus and Julio, appearing suddenly from nowhere, climbed on.

"You can valet a bus?" Alfonso asked as the bus drove away.

"That's Julio. He works at the ranch." Frankie said. "He'll go find a place to park and then swing back by and pick us up when I call."

Frankie pushed open the door and they followed him in. The building was identical to hundreds of thousands of others in towns and cities, large and small, across the country, long and narrow, with a suspended ceiling that long ago, to save on energy, covered what was above it.

There were two rows of folding tables facing a center aisle, covered with computers, printers, phones, and other electronic gear. Nearly all tables were occupied by people on the phone or computer.

"What is this place?" Christine asked.

"It looks like a political campaign office," Addison said as they stepped inside. "Folding-table chic."

"Totally temporary," Kendall said.

"This is the war room," Frankie said nonchalantly.

"The war room?" Christine said.

"This is where we are managing your wedding," Frankie said.

"All this for my wedding?" Christine asked, incredulous.

"And the collateral events."

"Okay, I'm lost."

"There are about two thousand people coming to your wedding, from all over the world," Frankie said.

"I don't even know that many people."

"Most of them are family, friends and business associates from both sides of the aisle. There are a lot of private railcar owners, friends of Mom and Dad, coming by train. Lots of people are coming from France. We have several events planned, dances, dinners, excursion trains around the area."

Addison laughed. "This is so Frankie."

"This is the concierge desk, graciously provided by Maria," Frankie said. "She loaned us a couple of her best people. No matter where they are staying, wedding guests can call the concierge here for dinner reservations, galleries, shows, nightclubs, tours, whatever they want."

"Wow," Christine said. "Pretty cool."

"Maria's staff block-booked advance reservations at all the best restaurants and clubs around town, and she says they're going fast."

"The local businesses are going to make out like a bandit," Alfonso said.

"This is the protocol desk," Frankie said as they walked. "We have people with titles, politicians, royalty, so these guys will handle all that. Some of the Chagny people are helping out here."

"Just tell me when to curtsy," Christine said.

"Publicity," Frankie said as he continued down the line. "You know Sharon, of course."

"Hi, Sharon," Christine said. She waved at Aubrey, two chairs down, immersed in her phone.

"Sharon is monitoring the media and the Internet," Frankie said, "and trying to quash rumors."

"What rumors?" Christine asked.

"Well, my favorite is that Sofia is yours," Frankie said.

Christine laughed. "Who's the baby daddy?"

"Raoul and Alfonso were running neck and neck, but Alfonso has pulled ahead," Frankie said.

"Probably because he's now a movie star," Sue said.

"But the odds-on favorite is Erik," Frankie said.

"I'm marrying the guy in third place?" Christine asked.

"Erik sells more tabloids," Frankie said.

"And more page views," Sharon said.

Sharon showed Christine a photo of her carrying Sofia, strolling along the Promenade with Sue.

"Wow," Christine said.

"It wasn't even paparazzi, just some jerk with a cell phone," Sharon said.

"What else?" Christine asked.

"The press has been sniffing around in Florida," Frankie said, "trying to get to Mrs. Valerius."

"That's just mean," Christine said.

"We sent someone to the assisted living facility to brief the staff and give them tips on how to handle it," Sharon said.

"And Johnston beefed up security," Frankie said.

"It will all die down after the wedding," Sharon said.

"Why do they care about Mrs. Valerius?" Christine asked.

"They want to know who will be mother of the bride," Frankie said.

"Why is that any of their business?" Christine asked.

"It's not," Sue said. "Screw 'em."

"One of the tabloids picked up on the fact that Johnston and Maria have been seeing each other and twisted into a story that Maria is outraged because you snubbed her as mother of the bride," Frankie said.

Christine was stunned. "That is so not true!"

"They make shit up and find a photo that fits the narrative," Tegan said. "You just have to roll with it. We'll be lesbian lovers before you know it."

Christine looked at Tegan, grinned, and then put a finger on her lips. Sue laughed.

"You'll notice that this is the biggest table," Tegan said to Christine, changing the subject.

And it was indeed. Several people handled the phones and computers at the publicity table.

"This has become quite the media event," Sharon said.

"I promise to behave myself," Tegan said.

"That's good," Sharon said. "I hope the rock stars do as well."

"Rock stars?" Christine asked.

"Oh, yes," Frankie said. "Johnston knows a lot of people from his days in the music business. People who aren't even attending the wedding are flooding into Santa Fe, passing around tips on where the best jam sessions might be held. Since all the local hotels are fully booked, Angel is running charter buses to and from hotels in Albuquerque."

"We expect inside information," Kendall said.

"Our cousins, Addison and Kendall," Frankie said to Sharon.

"Stay in touch," Sharon said. "I'll hook you up, if I have the information. There's no telling where some of these guys might turn up."

"We are so partying with the rock stars," Kendall said.

"Security," Frankie said, moving along to a table with people in both civilian clothes and police uniforms. "We don't want cops and bodyguards attacking each other, so everything clears through this desk."

"Don't forget about Erik," Sue said.

"Already handled," Frankie said, pointing at the next table. "This is the wedding planner's desk, but Mercedes prefers to do business on her phone and tablet, and she's probably out at the opera house, terrorizing the staff."

"Where's the fashion desk?" Addison asked.

"Nari will be set up at Maria's hotel," Frankie said. "They have better bathrooms and it's a lot nicer place for the ladies to try on their dresses and get final adjustments."

"Works for me," Addison said.

"The fashion press will go through Sharon," Frankie said. "She brought an associate just to handle them."

"When is Nari coming?" Christine asked.

"A couple of days before the wedding," Frankie said. "She wants to get everything finished before she leaves LA, so all that's left is fittings and final adjustments. She's bringing a small crew with her, and we will hire some locals, all fully vetted by Maria, of course."

"This is Alicia," Frankie said as Alicia hung up the phone. "She runs the transportation desk. Christine, you remember her husband, Angel. He picked us up at Lamy last summer when we got back from Chicago."

"I remember," Christine said. "Hi."

"Hi," Alicia said, and then turned to Frankie. "I've called our competitors and lined up all the cars I can find," she said. "We have just about all the cars in Albuquerque committed. I have limos coming in from El Paso, Denver, Amarillo, and Lubbock. I might be able to get a few funeral cars, but they don't like to let those go, in case somebody, you know, dies."

"Plus, they look like funeral cars," Frankie said.

"Exactly," Alicia said. "Most of the guests are looking for limos, but we may have to use shuttle buses."

"Just make sure there aren't any prom buses, or pimp-mobiles," Frankie said. "None of those forty-foot Hummers that hit high center trying to get into a parking lot."

"I'll do what I can," Alicia said.

Frankie started to walk away and then turned back. "Call rental car companies and reserve town cars, Suburbans, Explorers, big stuff, just in case."

"Where are we going to get drivers?" Alicia asked.

"School bus drivers," Frankie said. "It's summer, so most of them are off. They're licensed to drive commercial vehicles and carry passengers. Offer them a good hourly wage plus tips. They drive whining brats around all day. This should be like a vacation."

"Then again, a lot of rich people are whiny brats," Addison said.

"But they tip better," Alicia said, smiling.

EVEN BEFORE THE bride's arrival the ranch house was already a beehive of activity. Carlos was sorely missed as they staffed up for the coming events and guests. Frankie had intended to house both families at the ranch, but Mercedes persuaded him otherwise.

"With the size of the wedding, the importance of the families, and the expected media coverage, it would be inappropriate," Mercedes said. "Remember when you said you wanted me to handle the girly stuff? This is the girly stuff."

"I don't want Raoul's family to think we're pushing them aside," Frankie said. "They always stay at the ranch when they're in town."

"Don't worry," Mercedes said. "I've already talked to their people. They know the drill. They can spend as much time as they like at the ranch, but they will sleep elsewhere."

Maria was also well aware of protocol and offered to host Raoul's family in her own home, and their special guests in her hotels.

Juanita was accustomed to feeding a large number of guests, but the ranch hadn't seen anything this big since Daniel Senior's heyday. Delivery trucks arrived frequently, and Julio carefully checked every load against the invoices.

19

GRAND-MÈRE

While Raoul wrapped up his school year in the UK, his parents and grand-mother, Chantal de Chagny, arrived in New York, took in a couple of shows on Broadway, did some shopping, and visited friends. They then set out from Penn Station aboard the *Lake Shore Limited* in a private railcar borrowed by Franklin from friends on the east coast. Raoul had flown in from London the night before and was waiting when they arrived at Union Station in Chicago. While their railcar was serviced and transferred to the *Southwest Chief*, Raoul took them to lunch.

"What did you call this?" Chantal asked as they stood on the sidewalk near a street vendor.

"A Chicago dog," Raoul replied.

"And how is that different from a hot dog?" she asked.

"Ask Christine when you meet her," Raoul said.

"I intend to," Chantal said, and then took a bite. "It's good."

Christine and Sue fussed over every detail as they got dressed.

"Is that what you're wearing?" Addison asked.

"I guess. Why?" Christine responded.

"I don't know. I suppose it's okay."

"What's wrong with it?"

"It's not the dress," Kendall said. "It's *grand-mère.*"

"Huh?"

"She's kind of—what's the word—stuffy," Addison said.

"Stuffy?"

"Dowdy, maybe?" Kendall said.

"Like the Queen."

"Yeah, like the Queen."

"Conservative."

"That's it, conservative."

"What should I wear?" Christine asked, alarmed.

"This is okay, really," Addison said.

"She's not marrying you," Kendall said. "Raoul is."

"And he likes you to show a little skin," Addison said.

"Oh, no, Sue, help me find something," Christine said, now seriously flustered.

"I have no clue," Sue said. "Do we have time to go shopping?"

"No!"

"Okay, okay," Addison said.

"We're just teasing," Kendall said.

"What?"

"She's not that bad," Addison said.

"What you have on will be fine," Kendall said.

"Are you sure?"

"Close enough," Addison said. "We haven't seen her for a few years, so maybe she's mellowed."

"Mellowed?"

"She was a holy terror," Kendall said.

"Why don't you come with me, for moral support," Christine said.

"Oh, no, we can't do that," Addison said.

"Why not?"

"She hates us," Kendall said.

"She does?"

"Since that time in Courchevel," Addison said.

"Yeah, that," Kendall said, nodding and then rolling her eyes.

"She called us tramps."

"She's a real bitch."

"And not in a good way."

CHRISTINE WAS HYPERVENTILATING and squeezing Sue's hand tightly as they stood on the platform at Lamy and watched the *Southwest Chief* approach.

"What's wrong, honey?" Johnston asked.

"I'm afraid Raoul's grandmother is going to hate me," Christine said.

"Why would she hate you?" Johnston asked.

"The twins warned me about her," Christine said.

Frankie laughed.

"What's so funny?" Christine asked.

"The twins," Frankie said.

No explanation was forthcoming, so Christine turned her attention to the private railcar stopped directly in front of them. The car attendant hopped off and positioned a stepstool. Raoul's father stepped off next and held out his hand to assist Hannah. Raoul came next, smiling quickly at Christine, and then assisted his grandmother onto the platform.

She was nothing like what Christine had imagined, nor what the twins had described. She was tall, thin, wearing designer jeans and a silk shirt unbuttoned halfway to her waist. She wore a small fortune in jewelry. Her hair, once brown, was streaked with silver.

Johnston and Maria stepped forward. Chantal and Johnston exchanged kisses on both cheeks, while Raoul waited patiently.

"Chantal, this is my friend, Maria," Johnston said. "She will be your host while you are in town."

The two regal ladies exchanged cheek kisses.

"I've been looking forward to meeting you," Chantal said. "I've heard so much about you."

"And you as well," Maria said.

"Are you coming to Saint-Tropez with Johnston?" Chantal asked.

"Yes, for a short time," Maria said. "Our season is about to get underway."

Chantal turned to Sue, swept her into her arms and hugged her. "And you must be Christine," she said.

"No ma'am. I'm Sue."

Chantal roared with laughter. "I know. I'm just kidding. You don't have blonde hair. You're Christine's, what do you call it, dear?" She turned to Raoul.

"BFF," Raoul said.

"And maid of honor," Chantal said. "Are you taking good care of our girl?"

"Yes ma'am," Sue said.

Chantal turned to Christine and held out her arms. Christine cautiously stepped forward and was quickly pulled in. They hugged and kissed.

Chantal stepped back. "Let me look at you, *mon cheri*. Just as Raoul described you."

"I sent you pictures," Raoul said.

"I know, dear," Chantal said. "I was being dramatic. Humor an old lady."

She took Christine's hand and looked at the engagement ring. "I heard you kept this in the safe."

"I wore it today, for you," Christine said. "Raoul said it was yours."

"Oh, no, I still have mine. This belonged to Raoul's great-grandmother, and now it is yours. Cherish it, my dear, and my grandson."

Christine started to choke up. "Yes ma'am. I will."

"Are you just going to stand there, Raoul, or are you going to kiss the girl?"

Raoul pulled Christine into his arms and kissed her.

THE TWINS WERE waiting when Angel's limo bus pulled up in front of Maria's house.

"Oh, no," Christine said quietly.

"What?" Sue asked.

"The twins," Christine said.

As they stepped off the bus Chantal held out her arms. "Come here, you little tramps."

"Chantal!" the twins shouted as they rushed in for a hug.

"How was the road trip?" Chantal asked.

"It was a blast," Addison said.

"We went skinny dipping in the mountains," Kendall said.

"Skinny dipping?"

The twins were stumped.

"*Baigner nu*," Raoul said, and then looked at Christine, who grinned sheepishly and shrugged.

Chantal laughed. "Have you already located the hottest clubs in town?"

"Of course," Addison said.

"And we've been checking the guest list for eligible bachelors of a certain age."

"Rich, eligible bachelors."

"I'm rich enough, and not looking for a husband," Chantal said, "just a good time."

"You came to the right place," Addison said.

"We can hook you up," Kendall said.

"I thought she hated them," Christine whispered to Frankie.

"You got punked," Frankie said. "She loves them like granddaughters. They fly over to Paris on weekends just to hang out with her. They go shopping, have lunch at those little sidewalk cafés, go to the opera or symphony, whatever girls do in Paris."

"Those bitches," Christine said.

"Twitches," Frankie said.

"I'll get them back," Christine said.

"Count me in on that," Frankie said.

CHRISTINE DARTED AROUND the kitchen, checking everything.

"Go, get dressed," Juanita said.

"Everything has to be perfect," Christine said.

"When have I ever let you down, *mi hija?*"

"Um, let's see. Never?"

Juanita shrugged.

"But Raoul's grandmother is so French," Christine said.

"So is his papa, but he always cleans his plate at my table."

"Yeah, you're right. I'm just a little nervous, and Raoul's other grandmother will be here too. She's from California."

"Everybody checked the menu, Frankie, his mama, Maria, the wedding planner lady, the twins," Juanita said. "It's not even Mexican. It's Southwestern cuisine."

"Southwestern cuisine? What's that?"

"Mexican, Spanish, Native American. I've been cooking it for years and didn't even know it had a name until Maria told me. All the rich people think it's a big deal."

"Well, it smells amazing."

"I should open a restaurant on the plaza."

"No! What would we do without you?"

"That's what I always tell Mr. Johnston when I want a raise," Juanita said, smiling. "But I'm not going anywhere."

"Damn straight, you're not," Jim Bob said as he burst into the kitchen and hugged Juanita.

"When did you get in?" Christine asked, getting her hug.

"Right now. We were going to take the train, but Zoe wanted to get here early to make sure Sue was taking good care of you, so I called Frankie and he got us on somebody's private jet that was headed this way. That boy sure knows how to get shit done."

"Yes, he does," Christine said.

"Damn, this smells good, Juanita," Jim Bob said. "And I'm starving."

"Where are you staying?" Christine asked.

"Here, I guess. We may have to sleep in the barn. This place is filling up."

"Sue and I have a room with two beds, so we can move the twins in with us," Christine said. "It'll be like a sleepover."

THE YOUNGER SET planned to go dancing after dinner and dressed accordingly. The boys didn't have a lot of decisions to make, but the girls, after a conference, had decided on short skirts or dresses.

"We all have killer legs," Addison offered.

Tegan nodded in agreement.

"You three are taken," Kendall said, "but the rest of us are still shopping."

"And boys like bare legs," Addison said.

"So, we're all wearing skirts?" Christine asked, unsure.

"Hell, yes," Tegan said. "When you got it, flaunt it. Besides, the paps might be there."

"Does that mean you already tipped them off?" Alfonso asked.

"Uh, no," Tegan said indignantly. "That's Sharon's job."

Christine laughed.

Dinner, in the tradition of the ranch, was casually elegant. The tablecloths were linen, the silver real, the china vintage Santa Fe Railway. The speechifying was thankfully limited—there would be plenty of opportunity at the later events—this was just immediate family and close friends. There were a few toasts, however.

Chantal sniffed and then took a sip of Chardonnay. "Not bad," she said. "This is Texas wine?"

"Yes," Chagny said. "Appellation High Plains."

"You can do better, of course," Chantal said.

"Yes, Mother, of course," Chagny said. "The soil and climate are ideal for a number of varietals in which we specialize."

"Frankie, you and your parents are on board?" Chantal asked.

"Yes ma'am," Frankie said. "We know very little about wine, and defer to your family on that, but we know plenty about business, and this looks to be a good investment."

"And a lot of fun," Raoul said.

"Fun?" Chantal asked.

"Frankie, this is your department," Raoul said.

"There's a short-line railroad that runs from Lubbock to Brownfield, which is in the largest wine-grape growing county in the state," Frankie said. "We're planning our own version of the wine train, like they have in Napa. Dad and I are already shopping for rolling stock, and a locomotive."

Chantal smiled. "I like it." She raised her glass of Texas Chardonnay in a toast. "To our new venture."

Chantal turned to Christine. "And you, *mon cheri*, what do you think of this?"

"I don't know much about wine, just what Raoul has taught me, but I want to learn more, and I loved your winery in Saint-Tropez. It was so beautiful."

"You will help design our new winery in Texas?" Chantal asked.

"I don't know, ma'am," Christine said, hesitantly. "Aren't there people who do that?"

"Of course, but it will have your mark on it."

"It will?"

"The boys have discussed a French chateau, Southwestern adobe, Spanish mission, various styles. This venture is for a new generation, your generation. You will be part of that discussion."

"Yes ma'am. I'll do my best."

"You will select the art for display in the winery."

"I don't know much about art, either."

"When you come to Paris, I will take you to the great art museums, galleries, and some friends' houses, and my own, of course. I will teach you about art. If you decide on a Southwestern theme, then you will want to consult with Maria. Her Southwestern collection is superb, and her O'Keeffes are nothing short of exquisite."

"Yes ma'am."

"This is a fairly quick trip, but I'll be back next year. I'll probably stay all summer, see some operas with Maria, spend some time with her art collection, and you and I will go to Texas, have a look around and discuss your ideas."

"Will we be here?" Christine asked Raoul.

"Well, of course you will, my dear," Chantal said. "Oh, no, have I spoken out of turn?"

Christine was curious.

"We haven't said anything to you," Johnston said, "because it wasn't definite, and we didn't want to distract you from finishing school."

"What is it?" Christine asked, now concerned.

"It appears *Sangre de Cristo* will be back next summer, by popular demand," Maria said. "Mrs. Giry said everyone keeps asking for it, and indeed, all my friends keep demanding it."

"If you are available to sing Sofia," Zoe said.

Christine turned to Raoul.

"It's your decision. I will support whatever you decide."

Christine nodded. "Yes, yes."

"It's official, then," Johnston said. "I will start making the arrangements."

"What about Alfonso?" Christine asked.

"We are hoping he is available as well," Zoe said, turning to Alfonso.

"He is so available," Tegan said.

Alfonso smiled.

"To *Sangre de Cristo*," Johnston said, raising his glass.

DESPITE THE TWINS' pleading, Chantal declined to go dancing after dinner. "We have grownup things to talk about, especially with my new BFF, Maria."

Zoe and Jim Bob, however, decided to go along, "as chaperones," Jim Bob joked.

"Yeah, right," Christine said. "You just want to rock out."

"You got me," Jim Bob said.

"What about Sofia?" Christine asked.

"I can babysit," Sue said.

"No way," Christine said. "You're going dancing."

"We have a babysitter," Zoe said.

"Who?" Christine asked.

"Cynthia," Zoe said. "She's on the list of approved babysitters at Maria's hotels, who are all thoroughly checked out. She's also the daughter of friends of Maria's, home for the summer. She's working on her master's in early childhood development."

"Well, in that case, she has the job," Sue said. "I'm going dancing."

The paparazzi were out in force as the kids, along with Zoe and Jim Bob, stepped off Angel's limo bus at the nightclub. The killer legs were on full display. Jim Bob rocked out. So did the kids. Tegan and the twins were the center of attention on the dance floor, while Christine and Raoul spent more time holding hands at the table than dancing.

Addison suddenly stopped dancing, threw up her hands and screamed. She rushed toward Chantal, who pushed her way through the throng onto the dance floor. Chantal danced with the twins, and the young crowd went wild over the silver-haired cougar. Chantal quickly replaced the twins with two hot young men and showed them how it was done.

Chantal finally fell into a chair at the kids' table and shouted, "A Sidecar, *s'il vous plait.*"

"I'll get it," Raoul said.

"Where are your drinks?" Chantal asked.

"It's America," Frankie said. "We're minors."

"How bourgeois," Chantal said.

"Did you come alone?" Kendall asked.

"No, a nice young man brought me," Chantal said. "I believe his name was Angel."

20

ROLLING STONE

A CONSIDERABLE AMOUNT of thought had gone into it, polls had been taken, the choices narrowed, and a meeting held to make a final determination. Many of the suggestions were stupid, vulgar, or simply boring, and an argument ensued over those remaining, none of which seemed likely to survive a vote.

"We can't insult Christine," one said. "Whether you like her or not she's one of us and she has been great for the conservatory."

The *Belen Baller* was an early favorite, but since half the choir would be from Ogden Hall, it was rejected. The *Rock-and-Roll Express* remained a possibility, but although they all listened to rock, these were almost all classical musicians.

"We also listen to rap," one said. "We could really riff on some raunchy rhymes."

"No way," another said. "Mr. Caldwell hates rap with a passion."

"And he is paying for this gig, right?"

"Exactly."

The kids weren't being paid, but a sizeable donation was being made to the activity fund of both the conservatory and Ogden Hall, and all expenses were being covered. Being paid was not even a consideration—nobody turned down this gig. The trip had already achieved legendary status, and they hadn't even left Los Angeles.

"Don't forget that we'll be live tweeting, live Instagramming, live Facebooking, live Youtubing, live blogging, live TikTokking, and live whatever else there is. Everybody will see it."

"You guys are idiots," a moody, black-haired Goth girl finally said.

She was weird, but she was also the resident music historian. If you had a question about music history, from Paleolithic flutes to Beethoven to big bands to Buddy Holley, she was the go-to girl.

Goth Girl had everyone's attention. "You want a cool name, but you don't want to piss off the old people, especially Mr. Caldwell," she said. "And, by the way, those old people lived through the fifties and sixties, when there was real music, so you numbnuts don't know shit."

"Do you have something better?" someone asked.

"Of course," Goth Girl said.

"Lay it on us."

IN ADDITION TO the normal assortment of Amtrak passengers, mostly older people in no hurry, pulling their roll-aboard bags, and Metrolink commuters sprinting to catch their trains, Los Angeles Union Station was bustling with parents dropping off their kids from the Belen Conservatory and Ogden Hall, and then waiting to see them off.

There was also a steady stream of limousines, black town cars, Suburbans, and an assortment of extremely expensive automobiles.

As word spread, compliments of modern technology, various others made their way to the station. For many of them it was the first time they had ever been in the historic railway station. There was a noticeable uptick in riders on all inbound Metro lines at a time when most people were headed the other way.

Security had been beefed up and additional baggage handlers were on hand. Food and drink vendors had been given advance notice to stock up and were happy to see brisk business on an otherwise routine day.

Film students from USC, wearing jeans, T-shirts and sneakers, the uniform on film sets everywhere, scurried about as quietly and unobtrusively as possible, capturing it all on film, or rather digital video.

All available seats in the station were occupied and hundreds of people milled about while dozens danced to the big band sound of the Belen Beats, in full regalia, behind podiums atop a stage, temporary but hardly makeshift, as they played "In the Mood."

Replacing Christine as the girl singer for the Beats had been no easy task, but after rounds of auditions, one was selected. Christine had fully approved and freely offered advice on singing the old songs. The successful candidate now held the audience entranced, singing "Sentimental Journey," as dancers danced, casual observers swayed in time to the music, expensive movie cameras whirred, and television reporters whispered into their microphones.

Few noticed as scores of teenagers in jeans and T-shirts emblazoned with either BELEN or OGDEN HALL wandered into the room and mixed in with the audience. Half of them carried musical instruments, drawing the attention of those nearby.

When the song ended, the girl singer, talking over the thunderous applause, announced, "Thank you. We have a train to catch, but we have time for an encore. As you can see, we are bringing in reinforcements."

Dancers dispersed as roadies carrying folding chairs hustled onto the dance floor, followed by the T-shirted teenagers.

The band members dismounted the stage and took up positions in the orchestra. The girl singer found her way into the choir where her 1940s hair style and slinky, bare-shouldered dress stood out among the more casually dressed choir members.

There were murmurs of anticipation from the audience as they raised their cell phones when the maestro raised his baton. While the big band music that had been played for the past hour had been unusual, it was nothing compared to the explosion that followed. All other activity in the station ceased. Everyone stopped. Everyone watched. Everyone listened in rapt silence as the large orchestra and composite choir performed "Ode to Joy" with unbridled enthusiasm.

When the thunderous ovation finally came to an end, the orchestra and choir had taken their bows, and there was at least a semblance of silence, a voice came over the PA system, "The Amtrak *Rolling Stone* is now ready for departure on track three. All aboard."

The teenagers cheered, and then thundered into the tunnel, waving last goodbyes to family, carrying and dragging their instruments, followed by the roadies, hauling the rest.

Much longer than the *Southwest Chief*, consisting of several sleepers, dining cars, baggage cars, dome cars and lounge cars, loaded with more than two hundred rowdy teenagers and several chaperones, who were already reconsidering their commitment to this enterprise, the *Rolling Stone* pulled out of Union Station and rolled eastward.

At the end of the train, separated from the raucous teenagers by the chaperone's car, were cars for Nari, her staff, roadies, security, the film crew, and baggage car, loaded with road cases, locked, lashed, and secured together by cables. Inside were the dresses, choir robes, and in an unmarked case, The Dress.

The *Southwest Chief* had departed an hour earlier, but since the *Rolling Stone* would not have to stop to pick up or drop off passengers along the way, it would easily overtake the regularly scheduled Amtrak train not long after negotiating the Cajon Pass and would then highball it across the desert.

The following private train was on a more leisurely schedule.

Even before the wedding date was locked in, Franklin and his wife began making travel plans. They had often joined private excursion trains and had long discussed with other private railcar owners a private train running coast to coast. With many of their friends who owned private railcars already on the guest list, Christine's wedding provided them with a perfect opportunity. The coast-to-coast private train would depart Los Angeles, stop in Santa Fe for the wedding and festivities, and then resume its journey over the Raton Pass to Chicago. After an overnight stay in Chicago for dinner and dancing, it would follow the route of the *Lake Shore Limited* into New York.

As word spread among private railcar owners the special train quickly achieved critical mass. The excitement began to build, and weeks before the event private railcars began migrating to Los Angeles, most attached to Amtrak passenger trains but some an unusual sight at the end of freight trains. Many private cars in the charter business also signed on, including Pullman sleepers, diners, lounge cars, dome cars, and various other types of equipment, offering accommodations to additional passengers looking for the journey of a lifetime. It didn't hurt that among the passengers would be celebrities from movies, television, and music.

As the *Rolling Stone* rolled out of Union Station, what was, by all accounts, the longest string of private varnish ever assembled, stood ready for passenger boarding on the adjacent track. A small army of baggage handlers scurried up and down the platform.

Top chefs and their crews worked at full throttle aboard the train. Before-dinner drinks would keep passengers occupied for a time, but dinner would soon follow, in private cars and luxurious dining cars, each chef vying to outdo the others. The train had been provisioned with cases of fine wine, champagne, and top-shelf liquor. These were not budget travelers.

Spirits were high, and flowing, as Franklin's private train pulled out of the station and began to pick up speed.

Railroad police at stations all along the route added extra help to deal with the expected crowds of railfans as the long private train rolled through.

Many passengers would walk several miles during the trip as they strolled from car to car, having drinks, hors d'oeuvres and dessert along the way.

Passenger trains, by law, had track priority over freight trains. In practice, however, it didn't always work that way, especially on a major east-west rail corridor carrying more than one hundred trains daily. Dispatchers were under strict orders to clear the right of way for the *Rolling Stone* so that it would complete the trip from Los Angeles to Albuquerque in just over twelve hours, several hours faster than the *Southwest Chief*. They found it odd that a trainload of teenagers would receive such preferential treatment, when passengers on the following private train collectively owned a significant portion of the holding company that owned the railroad that owned the tracks. The private train also carried a few high-level Amtrak and BNSF executives and their guests in the company's own business cars. Nevertheless, the *Rolling Stone* was cleared to run while Franklin's train cruised leisurely through the night, occasionally pulling onto a siding to clear the way for critical freight traffic. None of the passengers paid any attention.

Franklin and his wife stayed up until the wee hours of the morning, in their element, entertaining wealthy friends and business associates aboard thousands of tons of luxurious big iron.

The departure time of Franklin's train had been carefully scheduled, to allow guests to dance to the big band music of the Belen Beats in Union Station before boarding, and so that gourmet dinners would be served shortly after departure. In order to receive the full experience of Franklin's elaborate plan his private train would arrive in Albuquerque four hours after the *Rolling Stone*.

21

3751

It was an age when Americans built things, big things, magnificent things. In 1927, a new, but hardly shiny, steam locomotive rolled out of the Baldwin Locomotive Works in Pennsylvania. Built for the Atchison, Topeka, and Santa Fe, it was the railroad's first 4-8-4 Northern-type locomotive. Santa Fe 3751 went to work immediately, pulling fast passenger trains, a task for which it was ideally suited.

On May 7, 1939, Santa Fe 3751 pulled the first passenger train into the newly opened Los Angeles Union Station, the last of the great American railway stations to be built before the decline of passenger rail. The train was the *Scout*, from Chicago.

"Wakie, wakie," Frankie said as he opened the door to the girls' room and stepped in, followed by Raoul.

"What's this, a panty raid?" Kendall said, sitting up.

"I'm not wearing panties, are you?" Addison said.

"What time is it?" Christine asked.

"Early," Frankie said, "damned early."

"Throw on some clothes," Raoul said.

"We have a train to catch," Frankie said.

The girls slowly swung their legs over the side of the beds. None of them wore much in the way of nightwear, nor did they seem to care there were two young men in the room.

"Where are we going?" Sue asked.

"Albuquerque," Frankie said.

"What the hell is in Albuquerque?" Addison asked.

"You'll see," Frankie said.

"Do we have time to eat breakfast?" Kendall asked.

"We have burritos and coffee," Raoul said. "We'll eat on the road."

"Where's Juanita?" Christine asked.

"In Albuquerque," Raoul said. "Get your asses in gear."

"And nice asses they are, by the way," Frankie said as the twins headed for the bathroom.

"Get out!" Christine said. "We have to do girl stuff." She pushed past Raoul and headed out into the hallway, followed closely by Sue.

"Where are you going?" Raoul asked.

"Four girls, one bathroom," Christine said. "We're using yours."

"Here, Christine, put this on," Frankie said, holding up a small pair of striped overalls, tailored, with the legs cut off and hemmed.

Christine turned and took the overalls. "Kind of cute, but what the heck?"

"Photo op," Frankie said. "And by the way, Nari did the alterations, so they should fit. She said something about your dress dummy."

The girls, now joined by Tegan and Alfonso, were still clueless as to the purpose of the trip when they stepped off Angel's limo bus at the station in Albuquerque. Knowing Frankie's love for trains, however, the enormous steam locomotive, facing north on the adjacent track, belching steam, likely had something to do with it. It was surrounded by a throng of curious on-lookers, as well as dedicated railfans, snapping photos and shooting video. Frankie's film crew, far better equipped, and prepared, focused their attention further down the tracks.

Retired from service in 1953, after far more efficient diesel-electric loco-motives took over, Santa Fe 3751 was on static display in southern California for many years until it was restored by a group of dedicated volunteers and generous donors. It had since been seen occasionally pulling excursion trains.

"Is this yours?" Christine asked as she approached the steam locomotive.

"No," Frankie said. "It's owned by a nonprofit in San Bernardino. Dad made a rather large donation, pulled some strings at the railroad, and per-suaded them to bring it to New Mexico for a few days."

"For what?" Christine asked.

"Dad likes to arrive in style," Frankie said. "His train is about four hours out."

"Then why isn't this pulling his train?" Raoul asked.

"Even in the heyday of steam, a locomotive only went about a hundred and fifty miles before it had to stop for fuel, water, and to be greased and inspected. To avoid delaying the train they would just swap out the locomotive for a fresh one. The run from Los Angeles to Chicago required about a dozen locomotives, strategically placed along the way."

"Makes sense," Raoul said.

Frankie looked up at the locomotive. "She left San Bernadoo last week, pulled the *Southwest Chief* on some segments, a BNSF freight on others, and made a few overnight stops along the way, for maintenance, and to visit old friends."

"Old friends?" Christine asked.

"At the Grand Canyon Railway in Williams, Arizona," Frankie said. "The kids will stop there on the way back and take an excursion train up to the canyon rim."

"I smell coffee," Kendall said as she noticed a large tent nearby, where Juanita and several other women were busy making tortillas and cooking on grills.

"What's all this?" Christine asked as they walked toward the tent.

"Breakfast for the kids on the train," Frankie said.

Christine hugged Juanita and immediately started making tortillas.

A small group of film crew members approached Frankie and one said, "ETA seven minutes, chief."

"Did you guys eat already?" Frankie asked.

"Oh, yes," the film crew member said, smiling.

Frankie checked his cell phone. "What about Dad's train?"

A man wearing an orange safety vest and a hard hat said, "They made good time last night so they're on a siding at Gallup while the passengers tour the depot. Traffic is running smoothly on the Transcon and we should time out just about right. We'll detach 3751 in Santa Fe as soon as the cameras stop rolling, pull her back here, top off the tanks and be ready when your dad's train arrives."

"Sounds good," Frankie said. "There may be a delay anyway. Dad has some friends coming into ABQ by air who want to ride the last leg into Santa Fe."

By the time the *Rolling Stone* arrived Christine had taught the other girls how to make tortillas. Fortunately, more experienced hands had already produced an adequate supply.

Folding tables and chairs had been set up, but most of the burritos were wolfed down on the go, as the teenagers lined up for photo ops with 3751 after it had been attached to the front of their train.

"All aboard," Frankie called out.

A hair stylist pulled Christine's hair into a ponytail and carefully positioned an engineer's cap at just the right angle to satisfy the film director. A makeup artist quickly applied finishing touches.

Christine climbed the ladder onto the locomotive and posed for photos as the teenagers scrambled aboard the train, cleaning out the last of the breakfast burritos and coffee along the way.

The Amtrak conductor checked the train and platform and signaled the engineer on 3751.

Christine blew the whistle, leaned out the window and checked both ways. She flinched as the big drive wheels engaged and started to turn. She wasn't actually driving the train—that was done by a real engineer on the other side of the cab—but it certainly looked that way to the movie cameras while passing muster with all the authorities.

The train only went a few yards before stopping. Christine clambered down the ladder.

"That was fun!" she said, "But we didn't go very far."

"Movie magic," Frankie said. "When they edit the wedding video it will look like you drove it all the way."

"I didn't think it could pull the whole train," Christine said as they headed down the platform to board the train.

"Easy work," Frankie said. "She can pull this train and a whole lot more." He pointed up at the Amtrak diesel locomotives as they walked by. "We'll just use these as generators to run the lights and air conditioning."

With Christine safely aboard, chattering with friends, the *Rolling Stone*, led by Santa Fe 3751, pulled out of the station for real and headed north to Santa Fe as a convoy of railfans gave chase.

It was an impressive sight, with the old steam locomotive blowing and going, pulling a modern passenger train across northern New Mexico, along the same tracks where it was in revenue service more than a half century earlier.

Railfans chased the train, in cars, pickups, and buses, hanging out the window, shooting photographs and video, wherever a road ran parallel to the tracks. Once sufficiently out of Albuquerque, drones swarmed overhead, shooting additional footage for the wedding video.

The train slowed to a stop just outside Santa Fe and Frankie and Christine ran to the locomotive and climbed aboard.

Mercedes, curious as to how Frankie would handle the logistics of the orchestra and choir, was on hand along with Sharon when the *Rolling Stone* arrived in Santa Fe.

"Oh my," Mercedes said. "Is that the bride driving the train?"

"Apparently so," Sharon said.

The paparazzi swarmed. Christine blew the whistle.

Mercedes watched in awe as teenagers piled off the train, carrying their instruments, and raced for school buses parked in the street, chaperones trying to keep up.

"Why are they in such a hurry?" Mercedes asked as Frankie and Christine climbed off the locomotive.

"It's a long train, and police have closed off streets for us," Frankie said. "And we have to clear the tracks before the *Rail Runner* gets in."

"You came in on the train?" Mercedes asked Christine.

"Yeah," Christine said. "I like trains, and they let me drive it."

"I didn't know you had left town," Sharon said.

"Quick trip," Christine said.

"What's with the outfit?" Sharon asked.

"Pretty cute, huh?" Christine said.

"You can see the video later," Frankie said.

Mercedes watched as the kids boarded the buses.

"Where are they going?" Mercedes asked.

"The opera house, to rehearse," Frankie said.

"Rehearsal is tonight," Mercedes said.

"The wedding rehearsal is tonight," Frankie said. "These guys will check out the stage and facilities, run through the music, then hang out and goof off until rehearsal."

"What did you do about a place to stay?" Mercedes asked.

Frankie pointed at the train.

"They're sleeping on the train?" Mercedes asked, surprised.

Frankie laughed. "It's not like sleeping on a bus. These are Superliners. They have beds and bathrooms."

Mercedes took another look at the train, unconvinced.

"We did it before, on a much smaller scale, a couple of years ago for an event at the ranch," Frankie said. "The kids loved it. They called it summer camp on wheels. These guys have been on their best behavior for weeks so they wouldn't miss this trip."

"I'm impressed," Mercedes said.

"This is nothing," Frankie said, checking his watch. "Wait until you see my dad's train."

For the railfans, this run was just a warmup. They had all been fully briefed. They watched as the train backed out of the depot and parked out of the way, clearing the tracks for the *Rail Runner*. They continued photographing and filming as 3751 was detached and hooked onto a diesel-electric locomotive. They followed as the diesel pulled 3751 backwards all the way to Albuquerque. They snapped a few photos of the *Southwest Chief* as they waited for the main event, the crowd swelling as locals arrived. Word spread quickly as the special train approached, confirmed by the announcement, "The *Amtrak America* is now arriving."

The railfans were in awe as three Amtrak locomotives pulled in, followed by private railcars as far as the eye could see. It was an explosion of color with cars painted in the livery of historic railroads, some long forgotten. Included were a string of shiny silver BNSF business cars, along with a few yellow cars of their competitor, Union Pacific, whose senior executives weren't about to miss out on the train of a lifetime. A few well-heeled passengers climbed aboard under the watchful eyes of railroad and local police. Still and video cameras recorded every detail as 3751, now fueled and watered, backed up and hitched onto the train.

This was certainly a media event, and local media were out in force. The engineer of 3751 blew the whistle, perhaps a bit longer than necessary, and the long private train pulled out of Albuquerque, headed north. As soon as the last railcar had passed, railfans piled into cars, trucks, buses, motorcycles, and RVs, and the chase was on.

22

TDY

CARLOS WAITED PATIENTLY at Fort Hood until the company clerk sent him into the company commander's office. Carlos snapped to attention and saluted. The captain returned his salute.

"At ease, lieutenant," the captain said. "Do you have friends in high places?"

"No sir, not that I know of," Carlos said.

"What about the governor of New Mexico?"

"We've met when I worked catering gigs, but I wouldn't say we're friends."

"Well, the governor has requested your presence this weekend," the captain said. "Orders came down from the Pentagon. Do you have any idea what this is about?"

"No sir. I was asked to be a groomsman in a wedding there this weekend, but I've only been on active duty for a few weeks, so I didn't want to ask for leave."

"That's smart, and you're not getting leave."

"Yes sir."

"You're getting TDY."

"TDY?"

"Temporary duty."

"Yes sir. I know what it means. I just don't understand."

The captain held up a sheet of paper. "You have orders for temporary duty attached to the governor's office in Santa Fe, New Mexico, for three days."

"Yes sir. Do I need to go over to transportation, drive, or what?"

"That won't be necessary. You are to be at the airfield at fourteen hundred hours." The captain pointed at the paper. "Call this number. They'll tell you where to go."

"Yes sir."

"Do you have pinks and greens?"

"Yes sir."

"Good, wear those and look sharp. I hate those damned blue bell boy suits."

"I'm still confused, sir. What do I do when I get to Santa Fe? What kind of duty?"

"How should I know? Report to the governor's office, I guess. Just don't embarrass the Army, the First Cav, and especially me."

"Yes sir."

"That's all."

"Sir, I assure you I didn't call anybody. I don't want to make any trouble."

"Don't worry about it. It happens. Usually it's some asshole using connections, but you seem as surprised about this as I am. Fortunately we're not on maneuvers or being deployed. It's summer and a lot of guys are taking leave, so it's a good time. Just don't make a habit of it."

"Yes sir."

Carlos snapped to attention and saluted.

"Dismissed," the captain said.

As soon as he was out of the captain's office, Carlos dialed the number on his orders for instructions. It wasn't an airline, but an FBO, a fixed-base operator. Having picked up and dropped off ranch guests at the airport in Santa Fe a few times he knew exactly what that meant. He quickly packed, put on his dress uniform, and set out for the airport, on the civilian side.

Carlos looked up at the tail of the private jet as it taxied up. There was a yellow and black First Cavalry insignia and crossed sabers, with a "9" above and a "1" below. The FBO crew loaded his bags and Carlos took the stairs to the private jet two at a time. A smiling flight attendant took his hat and jacket, and the only passenger, a man in his early seventies, wearing a western shirt and cowboy boots rushed down the aisle, extending his hand.

"Bill Burlington," the man said.

"Carlos Navarro, sir."

They shook hands.

"Don't call me sir, I work for a living," Bill said.

Carlos smiled and nodded. It was an Army thing.

"Is this an Army plane?" Carlos asked.

"Hell, no. This is my little plaything, compliments of the good Lord up above and hydraulic fracturing down below."

Carlos laughed.

"You must have seen my tail feathers," Bill said. "First Cav, Viet Nam, sixty-nine seventy, first of the ninth, Hueys."

"Pilot?"

"Door gunner. Buck sergeant. Like I said, I work for a living."

The flight attendant closed the door and approached the men.

"Come on, son, have a seat and buckle up. The lady wants to launch this sucker."

The flight attendant served drinks as soon as they were airborne. Bill leaned forward and looked at the brass on Carlos's collar.

"Infantry. What outfit?"

"First of the Seventh."

"Custer's old outfit."

Carlos grinned and nodded.

"See any action?"

"No sir. I've only been on active duty a few weeks. I just graduated from Texas Tech."

"I guess you're going to the wedding."

"I guess so. I was supposed to be a groomsman but didn't want to ask for leave. Apparently, somebody pulled some strings."

Bill laughed. "Sounds like it. Franklin Titshaw's boy called me last night and asked for a favor. When I found out what it was, I said, 'favor, hell, it's my pleasure.'"

"Thanks for the ride."

"Do you have a place to stay in Santa Fe?"

"Yes sir. That's where I'm from."

"I have a little hacienda up Santa Fe way. It's hotter than hell in San Antonio in the summer, so we like to get up there whenever we can. My wife's already there, getting ready for the wedding and opry season."

"It's that time of year."

"I don't care much for opry, but I go to keep my wife happy. She was all excited about that new one last summer, *Sangre de Cristo*."

Carlos smiled.

"It was pretty damned good," Bill said. "That little blonde girl sang like an angel. And it was in Spanish, so I didn't have to use that little screen. I came up in south Texas, so I speak the lingo. It's a little crude, but I get by."

"I need to refine my Spanish. I plan to go to law school when my active-duty commitment is up and get into international law."

"No shit? That sounds like a good plan, but you should probably learn Chinese."

Carlos laughed. "I'll stick with what I know."

The flight attendant refilled their drinks.

"Were you there for opening night?" Carlos asked.

"Where?"

"The opera, *Sangre de Cristo*."

"Yes, I was," Bill said. "Wasn't that something? That boy snatched that little girl right off the stage. We all thought it was part of the opry, and then those boys jumped up on the stage and gave chase."

Bill studied Carlos.

"Wait a minute," Bill said, pointing his finger at Carlos. "I know you. You were one of the boys who rescued that girl."

"Yes sir."

"Son-of-a-bitch!" Bill said, leaning forward and vigorously shaking hands with Carlos. "And that little girl's the bride. Now I see why Franklin's boy wanted you up there for the wedding. Hell, he should have called me first. I play golf with the First Cav CG."

They laughed and told war stories for the rest of the flight.

Julio was waiting when the private jet landed in Santa Fe.

"Do you have a ride back to Hood?" Bill asked as they entered the FBO's lobby.

"Not that I know of. I'm sure Frankie has something in mind. Doesn't matter to me as long as I get back in time."

"Well, if you can't find something, call me. I'll be up here for a few days, but I'll send you back on my plane."

Carlos was astonished. "You'd do that?"

"Hell yes, son. You're my kind of people." He pulled a business card out of his pocket and handed it to Carlos. "Stay in touch."

"Private jets and shit," Julio said as they walked toward the pickup. "You big time *pendejo* now, homes."

"Up yours, *cabrón*," Carlos said as they shadow boxed.

23

REHEARSAL

THE OPERA HOUSE was buzzing with activity, not only in preparation for Christine's wedding tomorrow, but also for the opera season starting just days later. Fortunately for the ladies, the dressing rooms were on the bride's side of the venue, and curtains were installed so Christine would be concealed before making her entrance. The men would use the men's dressing room and then hike around to the groom's side where trailers and tents were set up as a waiting area and for last minute adjustments.

Two hundred musicians and singers, dozens of members of the wedding party, several reporters, Frankie's film crew, stage crew, and various hangers-on, a large group in an ordinary wedding venue, occupied only a small portion of the seats in the opera house. Folding chairs were set up on stage, facing the audience, for the orchestra, and behind that, custom-built risers for the choir. Ramps had been constructed leading from the two aisles onto the stage. Frankie stood on the stage, along with Mercedes, Bob, and Kacie.

"We have a lot of work to do today, and a short time to do it, so let's get underway," Frankie said. "This is Bob. He is the floor director, in charge of the stage and the house. He and his crew will work with Mercedes, our wedding planner, to make sure everything goes smoothly. We have a large wedding party, an enormous room, an unusual setup, and a somewhat non-traditional processional, so timing is important. Bob and his crew will work with you to use musical and visual cues so that you stay on time during the processional. We have a lot of people to get down the aisle, and I understand the bride's dress has its own entourage." That drew a few laughs.

Frankie motioned to Kacie. "This is Kacie, our film director, who is shooting the mother of all wedding videos." He paused for laughter. "I am a student at USC—go Trojans—and we have a film school of some repute, so I recruited some of my friends there and they put together a crew. I told them they would sleep four to a room in cheap motels, eat fast food and be paid minimum wage. They said, 'Wait, we get paid?'" There was loud laughter and applause from the film crew. "Apparently I have ruined them for the real film business."

There was more laughter and then Frankie continued. "This will be dress rehearsal for the orchestra and choir, so the film crew will be concentrating on them. Tomorrow, when the rest of you are all dressed up, and the house is filled with guests, they will be pointing their cameras in the other direction." He swept his hand across the audience. "And, of course, the wedding party on stage. Hopefully the weather will cooperate. It seems the rain is passing us by this year."

He pointed at the two ramps below the stage. "You have probably already noticed that we have two aisles, not one. The bride and her posse will enter through this aisle." He pointed to the aisle on his right. "And the groom and his crew on this one." He pointed to the other aisle. "When we all leave together, it will be on this aisle." He again pointed to his left. "Don't read anything into that." He waited for a few chuckles, mostly from the older folks. "It gives guests on this side of the house a chance to get a better look at our lovely bride."

"And bridesmaids," Addison shouted from the audience.

"Yes, and bridesmaids, and the kids. Nobody cares about looking at me or the groomsmen."

There was more laughter.

"Okay, the media. There may be some surprises revealed at rehearsal, so before we begin, you will be ushered into a room where Sharon will take your questions, pass out your packets, and get you set up for tomorrow, and yes, we will provide B-roll footage from the rehearsal today."

Frankie paused and chose his words. "All the family, and close friends already know this, but rumors are already starting to spread, so, for the benefit of the media, I want to say that this huge, elaborate, spectacular wedding, was not Christine's idea. She would have been happy to elope, but she's a trouper and no stranger to the stage, so she is gamely going along with it."

"It's not too late," Raoul shouted from the audience.

Christine, sitting next to him, covered her face.

"I'm in," Frankie said. "Let's load up the Prevost and head to Vegas." He started walking offstage, to loud applause, and then stopped and turned.

"Actually, it is too late," Frankie continued. "My dad just brought in a trainload of wedding guests. Private jets are stacking up at the airport here and in Albuquerque. The hotels are full. The restaurants and nightclubs are staffed and ready. We have this wonderful orchestra and choir, so unless Christine gets cold feet tonight, the show will go on."

"I'll be here," Christine shouted.

"Okay, getting serious again," Frankie said. "I don't want to see any more stories in the press about Christine the bridezilla. Blame me, and my dad, and my cousin, Johnston, for all this. Maybe we went a little overboard, but Christine is very special to all of us, not just to Raoul. Theirs is a love story for the ages, far better than anything the press could make up. So please join us in this wonderful, magical moment as these two families, friends for many years, are now to be joined in matrimony."

There was loud applause.

"Let's get this show on the road," Frankie said. "Orchestra and choir, please take the stage. Media, get out, and follow Sharon. And yes, security will be checking everyone to make sure they are authorized to be here."

The orchestra and choir surged out of their seats and scrambled up the ramps and onto the stage.

A girl walked quickly down the aisle toward Christine.

"Christine," the girl said. "Do you remember me?"

Christine looked at her and shook her head. "Not really."

"We were in choir together at Ogden Hall."

Christine still didn't recognize her.

"We were singing 'Suo Gân' and I said you were singing the wrong words," the girl said.

"Oh, yeah," Christine said, remembering.

"Well, I just wanted to say you were right. It is so much more beautiful in Welsh."

Christine smiled. "Yes, it is."

The girl turned to go, and then turned back. "And thank you so much for letting us come. The train is so much fun. We are having a blast." She turned and dashed onto the stage.

Raoul kissed Christine. "I guess I'd better go rehearse kissing the bride."

"You have plenty of practice. You don't need to rehearse that part."

"Are you going to rehearse your song?" Raoul asked.

"No, my stand-in will do it."

"Can she sing?"

"I guess. She's one of the apprentice singers. They picked her because we're the same height, and she's blonde. I've never heard her sing."

"You're saving yourself for tomorrow?"

Christine grinned. "Definitely."

He kissed her again and then rushed off.

Mercedes watched as the orchestra, wearing black pants and red shirts, took the stage. "I thought they were wearing all black," she said.

"We had to have a special run of fabric for the bridesmaids' dresses, so we ordered enough for shirts for the orchestra," Frankie said.

"Very colorful."

Mercedes and Frankie continued on through the sea of teenagers.

"One," a choir member shouted as she started a line beside the wardrobe cases.

"Two," the next one said, lining up.

"Three."

Silence.

"I'm five," someone said, looking around.

"Where's four?" an assistant asked.

"Four! Four!" a girl shouted, rushing forward. "I'm an alternate."

"How tall are you?" the assistant asked, looking at a clipboard.

"Five-two, but I have a quarter apple," she said, holding up a wooden box, exactly two inches thick.

Mercedes watched curiously as the teenagers were issued serapes.

"Those are the choir robes?" Mercedes asked.

"Nari got all caught up in the Santa Fe thing and decided to go with serapes, like the ushers at the opera house," Frankie said.

The choir members, wearing black pants and long-sleeved black shirts, donned their serapes.

Christine settled in and watched as Arnaud, now first violin after Sue graduated, warmed up the orchestra.

As the choir milled around, their serapes just seemed a random explosion of color, but as they mounted the risers and took their positions, something entirely different emerged.

Christine screamed.

Arnaud spun around, and the orchestra stopped playing as everyone in the house turned toward Christine.

Christine stood and stared.

"What's wrong?" Arnaud asked.

"Where's Nari?" Christine asked loudly.

Nari stepped warily onto the stage.

"It's Santa Fe Sunset," Christine said.

"Yes, it is," Nari said.

As the choir stood shoulder to shoulder, carefully arranged by height, and positioned on the risers, the combined serapes revealed a spectacular sunset over the snow-capped Sangre de Cristo Mountains.

"Brava! Brava!" Christine shouted. "Take a bow."

There was loud applause as Nari curtsied and then hurried off the stage.

Carlos slipped into a seat beside Christine. She put her head on his shoulder and he hugged her and kissed her on the head.

"I'm so glad you made it," she said.

"I'm not sure what happened, but here I am."

She pulled back and looked at him.

"You look nice in your uniform."

"I didn't have time to change. Julio brought me straight here. What's going on?"

"Rehearsal."

"Why aren't you rehearsing?"

"I'm the bride. Brides don't rehearse. They watch. It's tradition or something. But if Raoul kisses my stand-in, I'll kick him in the *cajones*."

"Ouch." Carlos looked at the orchestra and choir on the stage, who were currently rehearsing. "You think you got enough guys for the band?"

Christine laughed. "Frankie went all out."

"Damn. I've been to weddings before, but nothing like this."

"Yeah, it is kind of overwhelming."

"Wow. Check out the choir."

"Pretty cool, huh? It's Santa Fe Sunset."

"It sure is. Am I supposed to be doing something? I just got orders to come to Santa Fe. Julio said Johnston told him to bring me straight here."

"You're a groomsman. You'll be walking with Addison."

"Addison?"

"One of the twins, from Boston."

"She's just a kid."

"Not anymore. Let's go find her."

She took his hand and they rushed outside.

"Whoa!" Addison said as they approached. "Soldier boy."

Carlos eyed her.

"Don't you remember me?" Addison asked.

"You look kind of familiar."

"Addison. I've filled out."

"You certainly have."

"Me too," Kendall said.

"Wow, you were scrawny little girls the last time I saw you," Carlos said as he hugged them both.

"We tossed a coin and I won," Addison said. "You walk with me."

"Walk where?" Carlos asked.

"Down the aisle," Addison said.

"Okay, no problem," Carlos said. "Just tell me what to do."

Frankie and Raoul rushed up and shook hands with Carlos.

"Glad you could grace us with your presence, lieutenant," Frankie said.

"Glad to be here. Beats the shit out of Fort Hood."

"Are you Carlos?" Mercedes asked.

"Yes ma'am."

"I'm Mercedes, the wedding planner. We've been working around you, but now we need to rehearse your most important job."

"Kissing the bride?" Carlos asked.

Christine laughed.

"A comedian," Mercedes said. "You're walking Maria down the aisle."

"I thought I was walking Addison."

"That's later. Maria is first. She was quite insistent that it be you. Let's go."

"Later," Carlos said as he rushed to keep up with Mercedes. They located Maria, Chantal, Hannah's mother, Clifton, and a young Frenchman who appeared to speak no English. Introductions were quickly made.

Frankie introduced Clifton to Carlos. "He just graduated from Annapolis."

"ROTC," Carlos said.

"I'm Bob, the floor manager," Bob said.

An interpreter translated everything into French in almost real time.

"The groom has two grandmothers," Mercedes said to the Frenchman, as the interpreter translated. "You will walk with his maternal grandmother."

She took him by the arm and pushed him toward Hannah's mother.

"I'll take the sailor," Chantal said, taking Clifton by the arm. "My father was an officer in the French Navy during the war."

"Actually, the paternal grandmother of the groom goes first," Mercedes said, "and then the maternal grandmother."

Raoul's grandmothers and their escorts switched places.

"Maria will be standing in as Christine's grandmother," Mercedes said to Carlos.

"This one is mine," Maria said, taking Carlos by the arm. "You didn't think I'd let anyone else walk me down the aisle at Christine's wedding, did you?"

"Ah, the governor," Carlos said.

"I pulled a few strings. I hope it didn't get you in trouble with the Army."

"I'm good."

"They tell me 'Here Comes the Bride' will last over nine minutes, so we will be making some changes in the traditional processional," Mercedes said.

"Here comes the bride?" Chantal whispered to Maria.

"*Lohengrin*," Maria said. "'The Bridal Chorus.'"

"Ah, yes," Chantal said, nodding.

"We have just over three minutes to seat the grandmothers and mothers," Bob said. "I'll be down front during rehearsal with a stopwatch, telling you to speed up or slow down. We will be using two aisles, so that will make it easier."

"Wow," Carlos said. "What did I get myself into?"

"It's just like marching," Clifton said. "You ground-pounders should know how to do that."

"I suppose you'll just sail down the aisle."

Clifton laughed.

Considering the size of the wedding, with all the planning by Mercedes and Frankie, rehearsal went off remarkably well.

24

THE SPEC SCRIPT

Rehearsal wrapped early enough so that all in attendance could move on to other events. The crews had a cookout on the opera house grounds while the wedding party went to the rehearsal dinner at Maria's hotel. The orchestra and choir were treated to a pizza party, a movie, and then dancing at one of the hottest clubs in town, with the liquor locked up of course, all rented by Frankie and paid for by Johnston.

After the rehearsal dinner, the older members of the wedding party joined many of the wedding guests in a dance already underway in Maria's largest ballroom, with music provided by the Belen Beats.

Neither Christine nor Raoul were much interested in drunk, raunchy bachelor and bachelorette parties, replete with strippers and naughty gag gifts. Many of the bridesmaids and groomsmen were minors and couldn't legally drink anyway, and Johnston didn't want anyone busted the night before the wedding, so the younger members of the wedding party hit the dance club.

While the orchestra and choir had boundless energy to burn and danced until the club shut down, the bride and groom, along with most of the groomsmen and bridesmaids, stayed and danced for a couple of hours and then returned to the ranch for a quiet party by the pool.

Sue's recruited bridesmaids from the conservatory found the party by the pool boring and took the shuttle bus back to the dance, leaving only the bride and groom and their closest friends and family, which was just fine with Christine.

When the younger bridesmaids left, Frankie looked around and said, "I don't think Johnston would mind if we had a little wine."

"Works for me," Raoul said.

Christine smiled and nodded.

"I'll get it," Carlos said.

"I like this," Addison said.

"What?" Christine asked.

"This little party," Addison said. "Bachelorette parties are so passé."

"Yeah," Kendall said. "Everybody gets shit-faced and then has a hangover for the wedding."

"Bummer," Addison said.

"And the strippers," Kendall said.

"Boring," Addison said.

Sue snorted. Christine grinned.

"There was this bachelorette party in Boston last year where the bride caught the clap from the stripper," Kendall said.

"Ew!" Christine said.

"In her mouth," Addison said.

"Double ew!" Christine said.

"What did I miss?" Carlos asked as he returned with two bottles of wine and a stack of plastic cups.

"I need some wine to wash the bad taste out of my mouth," Christine said.

The twins laughed. Carlos opened a bottle of wine and poured a round.

"I met a friend of yours, Carlos," Christine said. "Yolanda. She said you went to school together."

"Yeah," Carlos said. "We went to middle school together, then I went to NMMI."

"Who is Yolanda?" Raoul asked.

"She goes to USC," Christine said. "Sue and I have been hanging out with the film crew."

"She's in the screenwriting program there, but I think she's working as a grip on this show," Frankie said.

"We were talking," Christine said.

"About?" Frankie asked.

"*Sangre de Cristo*," Christine said, and then took a sip of wine. "We think it could be a movie."

"Whoa. A movie?"

"Sure, why not?"

"Filmed operas aren't exactly box-office gold."

"We aren't talking about a filmed opera."

"What then?"

"There's a lot of backstory in Zoe's opera, the families, the Spanish land grants, the territorial government, the railroads, the wars, native Americans, the cavalry, it's friggin' epic. We think it could be made as a drama, with plenty of music, but no sung dialog."

"We?"

"Me, Sue, and Yolanda. She saw the opera when she was home from school last summer."

Frankie smiled. "I'm guessing she has a pitch and wants to write the screenplay."

"She has a screenplay. She wrote it on spec."

"Have you read it?"

"Yes."

"Is it any good?"

"I think so. I don't really know anything about screenwriting, but I liked it."

"Me too," Sue said. "It was very well-structured, with great character arcs, and she really nailed the motif of blood and red and the sunset, although that's really the director's purview, right?"

Frankie looked at Sue.

"What?" Sue said. "I was born in LA. Everybody in town has a headshot and a screenplay."

"Exactly," Frankie said. "She's just using you to try to get to the family money."

"So?" Christine said. "Isn't that how it works in Hollywood?"

"Checkmate," Raoul said.

"Okay, I'll read it," Frankie said.

Christine picked up her phone and started thumbing.

"Me too," Tegan said. "I've read plenty of screenplays. Most of them suck. Send it to Alfie too."

"Us too," Addison said.

"Do you want to read it?" Christine asked Raoul.

"Sure, but if you like it, I like it," Raoul said.

"We think it can be made for a price," Sue said. "It's a period piece, but so is Santa Fe."

"And the state gives you taxpayer money to shoot here, right?" Christine said.

"Yes," Frankie said. "Some of the other states are currently offering better deals, but I can't really see shooting *Sangre de Cristo* in Louisiana or Georgia."

"So, you're starting to see it?" Sue said.

Frankie smiled and nodded.

"And Maria could get us all kinds of cool locations, like the Palace of the Governors," Christine said.

"I assume you would play Sofia," Frankie said.

"No way. I'm a singer, not an actor. We need some T and A."

"You want nudity in it?" Frankie asked, surprised.

"Well, Yolanda did sex it up a little," Christine said.

"And it totally works," Sue said.

"But 'T and A' means Teegs and Alfie," Christine said. "Alfie will be Alejandro, of course." She turned to Tegan. "And you will be Sofia."

Tegan was stunned. "You want me to play Sofia?"

"Sure, why not? You're an actress. I'm not. You said you were tired of crap roles, so here it is."

"O-M-G!" Tegan said. "Are you serious?"

"I'm serious."

"You might want to read it first," Sue said.

"I don't have to read it. Who do I have to screw to get the part?"

Christine laughed. "Alfie."

Tegan fell into Alfonso's arms.

"And you get to show your tits in a quality piece of work," Sue said. "We'll sell a million tickets to your fanboys who don't even care what the movie's about."

"Whoa," Frankie said. "Hold on. It's a long way from a movie. You need a producer, a director, and most importantly, financing."

"You'll be the producer," Christine said.

"I'm not a producer."

"You're producing my wedding, and the video. Same thing."

"She's right," Addison said.

"You live for this shit, Tits," Kendall said.

"And Sue," Christine said. "She'll produce, but only part-time. She has to stay in school."

"We'll need a producer with experience, and credits," Sue said, "but we can hire him, or her, preferably her."

"What about a director?" Frankie asked.

"If we have the script and the money, directors are a dime a dozen," Sue said. "We can take our pick."

Frankie stared at her, amazed.

"Zoe will score, of course," Christine said.

"Of course," Raoul said.

"I'll sing on the soundtrack," Christine said.

"Where are you going to get the money?" Frankie asked.

"Duh," Christine said.

"We're in," Addison said.

"We'll talk to Dad," Kendall said.

"Of course I'm in, or Mom and Dad are," Raoul said.

"I don't see how Johnston can resist," Frankie said, warming up to the idea. "Maria will probably want to invest. We should make them executive producers, anyway."

"Definitely," Christine said. "Your mom and dad should also be executive producers. If it weren't for them, and Johnston and Maria, the opera would have never been produced."

"I'll talk to Dad, after I read the screenplay," Frankie said. "They already underwrote the opera, so it should be a slam dunk, provided the screenplay is as good as you say it is."

"You'll love it," Sue said. "It rocks."

"We'll also have to talk to Zoe," Frankie said. "It is her opera. She created it from nothing."

Christine laughed out loud. "You really think she's going to say no?"

"Good point," Frankie said.

"She wants to score films," Christine said. "This is kind of a no-brainer."

"Are you sure you don't want to play Sofia?" Tegan asked.

"I'm sure," Christine said. "Acting is your thing. Singing is mine." She leaned into Raoul's arms. "Besides, I'm going to be busy."

"When do you want to do this?" Frankie asked.

"Not until after next summer," Christine said, "when we do the opera again. If it's another sold-out season, that will be the right time. We'll shoot it the following winter, when there's snow on the mountains."

Christine noticed Raoul staring at her. "What?" she said.

"I'm impressed," Raoul said.

"You didn't think I was just going to be your little housewife, did you?"

"No ma'am," Raoul said. "I never thought that."

———

THOSE WHO WEREN'T staying at the ranch left on the shuttle bus, except for Raoul and Christine, who hung on as long as possible, sitting in one large, leather chair in the great room, making out.

"Are you sure you can't stay?" Christine asked.

"Julio is standing guard at the gate, and the media and paparazzi have Maria's house staked out, so I kind of have to show up there tonight," Raoul said.

"The shuttle bus already left," Christine said.

"Frankie said there are some late arrivals coming in a limo," Raoul said. "I'll catch a ride back into town."

They continued kissing until the front door opened and an elegant, well-dressed, older couple stepped in.

Christine sat upright.

"You must be Christine," the woman said as she approached.

"Yes ma'am," Christine said, jumping to her feet.

"Then I must be your grandmother," the woman said.

25

MARJORIE

Since the wedding wasn't until late afternoon, the orchestra and choir had been assured they could sleep in after a very late night of dancing. They discovered such was not the case when people started pounding on their doors.

"Rise and shine. Rehearsal!"

"We already rehearsed."

"Twice."

"They added a song."

"Who added a song?"

"Doesn't matter, we have to rehearse it."

"What is it?"

"Don't know. Something from *La Traviata*."

"Do we have sheet music for that?"

"It's the Santa Fe Opera. They have sheet music for everything."

"Do we get breakfast?" was asked by more than one as they boarded school buses.

"At the opera house."

"They serve breakfast there?"

"Apparently."

"Does *La Traviata* have a chorus?" asked one of the choir members.

"I don't know, but everybody's going."

"The wedding is in a few hours," Mercedes said on the phone. "You can't just add a song."

"Sure we can," Frankie said. "We have an orchestra and choir and everything."

"The ceremony is too long already."

"Trust me. Nobody is going to ask for their money back."

Frankie was waiting as Mercedes drove into the parking lot, where workers were setting up tents, tables, and chairs. Several RVs, including the Prevost, were parked around the perimeter.

"I can't believe you're actually doing this," Mercedes said as she stepped out of her car.

"Doing what?" Frankie said.

"Tailgating."

"We do it at the opera all the time."

"But this is a wedding. We'll have food at the reception."

"People will have a bite here, and then a little more, and cake, at the reception."

Mercedes was not convinced.

"The bride and groom each have their own tailgate party, side by side," Frankie said. "All the top hotels in town are hosting wedding guests, so they're set up here as well. Some of the locals may set up their own, but all guests will be encouraged to browse different parties, graze, and drink wine along the way. The Chagnys brought in a truckload of their best wine."

"But it's a wedding, a formal wedding!"

"A most unusual wedding. There are lots of people here from all over the world who have never been to the Santa Fe Opera. The place is crawling with celebrities. Think of the publicity for the opera, and Santa Fe."

As Frankie and Mercedes walked toward the opera house the orchestra and choir were lined up for breakfast burritos, coffee, and juice.

CHRISTINE HOVERED BEHIND Juanita in the kitchen at the ranch.

"They'll be down any minute," Juanita said.

"Do you need me to set the table?" Christine asked, looking at the empty kitchen table.

"Julio already did. You'll be eating in the dining room."

"Should I go change clothes?" Christine asked, suddenly concerned.

Juanita laughed. "No, *mi hija*. It's not formal or anything. There's just too many people for the kitchen table. We weren't expecting the late arrivals last night."

"Do you know her?"

"A little bit. She used to come here a long time ago. Now she lives in Switzerland or Italy or someplace."

"Thanks for helping out on such short notice," Frankie said to a young man and woman, both apprentice singers, as the orchestra took their seats on stage.

"No problem," the woman said. "We're happy to have the opportunity."

"And hopefully meet them," the man said.

"I'm sure that can be arranged," Frankie said. "Are you familiar with the piece?"

"Of course," the woman said.

"This is rehearsal for the orchestra and choir, but the maestro thought it would be good to have singers stand in, for timing or whatever."

"We understand," the man said.

Johnston pushed through the swinging doors into the kitchen, hugged and kissed Christine.

"Good morning, Sunshine," he said. "I understand you met my mother last night."

"Yes, I did," Christine said. "You could have warned me. I was making out with Raoul when they came in."

"It was a complete surprise to me. She had a hip replacement recently and didn't think she would be able to make the trip, but she decided she just couldn't miss it. Frankie made the arrangements but didn't bother to tell me."

"Or me."

"Shall we go in?" He offered Christine his arm.

Most of the Titshaw family was in the dining room, along with others staying at the ranch.

"Where's Maria?" Christine whispered.

"Since she's hosting the groom's family at her home, she thought it best that she be there," Johnston said.

Christine nodded.

It was obvious during breakfast conversation that Marjorie had not been around much for the past several years. She commented on how much the twins had grown. Not much was said about the mysterious Italian gentleman accompanying her, introduced only as "my friend, Rinaldo," and Christine didn't dare ask. She could always corner Frankie later, although he was conspicuously absent.

"Christine, my dear," Marjorie said. "I believe I met your grandmother once."

Silence fell over the table and all eyes were on Marjorie.

"Or perhaps it was your great-grandmother," Marjorie said, "Stella Williams."

Christine gasped.

"Wasn't that her name, dear?" Marjorie asked.

"Yes," Johnston said.

"I was in New York, at the Met," Marjorie continued. "I went out with friends to a nightclub. It was the sixties, and those places were a dying breed, actual nightclubs, where ladies wore dresses and gentlemen wore coats and ties. Stella was singing with a big band. Oh, how I miss that style of music."

"You should have arrived a few hours earlier last night, Mother," Johnston said. "We danced the night away to just such music."

"Yes, so I heard," Marjorie said, and then turned her attention back to Christine.

"She had a magnificent voice," Marjorie said, and then launched into few bars of "I'll Be Seeing You."

Christine burst into tears.

Marjorie suddenly stopped singing. "Oh, no, my dear. I've upset you."

Christine shook her head, wiped her tears, and smiled. "Johnston gave me one of her vinyl records. That song was on it."

Marjorie smiled. "Just about every girl singer of the era recorded it. Hell, so did some of the boys."

Some of the older folks chuckled.

"I always thought Jo Stafford's was the definitive version, until I heard Stella sing it that night."

Christine smiled. "Thank you."

"You should hear Christine sing it," Sue said, and then looked around as all eyes fell on her. "What? She totally kills it."

Johnston smiled and nodded. "She does."

"I look forward to hearing it," Marjorie said.

"Did you talk to her?" Christine asked.

"Yes, I did. She came over to our table for a few minutes. She knew one of our party. She was quite charming but seemed troubled somehow."

"My mom said she had a hard life," Christine said.

"Isn't it amazing?"

"What is?"

"How in such fleeting moments, seemingly unconnected dots coalesce. My grandfather couldn't keep it in his pants, which led to his interest in music, especially opera, and then to the conservatory, my alma mater, our alma mater, and here we are."

"Here we are indeed," Johnston said.

THE PAPARAZZI, CONFINED to an area just outside the gate at the opera house, snapped thousands of photos as the wedding guests arrived in a continuous parade of limos and anything else Alicia could muster. Some guests rolled down windows, waved and smiled, but others only rolled down the windows opposite the paparazzi, where security, carrying photos of Erik, looked inside every vehicle. A state police helicopter circled overhead.

Angel's limo bus stopped at the gate and the door opened. The paparazzi waited, and then went quickly to work as beautiful young women began piling off the bus. Christine was last, waving and smiling, holding hands with Sue.

"Thanks for the potty, Christine," one of the paparazzi said.

Christine laughed. "You're welcome."

"What's a potty?" Tegan asked.

"Loo," Sue said. "Christine had Frankie bring in a trailer, so they would have a bathroom. She also had it stocked with Juanita's burritos and plenty of coffee." She pointed at a large fifth-wheel trailer, with its awning deployed over tables of food and drink.

The girls posed for pictures, made small talk with the paparazzi, and then reboarded the bus for the short trip into the parking lot.

The tailgate parties were in full swing, and those who found tailgating at a wedding rather odd were quickly convinced otherwise as they feasted on world-class cuisine and fine wine.

Rock stars and movie stars mingled with politicians and billionaires, with bodyguards, publicists, and assistants not far away.

Journalists were restricted to their own tent, and not allowed amongst the guests enjoying the tailgate party. Those willing to be interviewed would be brought to the media tent by their publicists. A platform was set up outside the tent for the interviews, providing a background of not only the wedding guests at the tailgate party, but also the opera house and the mountains.

"I should have dressed up," Christine said as she walked through the tailgaters, hand-in-hand with Raoul.

"You look beautiful," he said.

She wore a flowery, summer dress, suitably short. Raoul wore a blazer and an open-collared shirt.

"Everybody is dressed up," she said.

"Nobody expects you to wear your wedding dress for tailgating," he said. "You could have worn shorts and a T-shirt and you'd still be the most beautiful girl here."

Christine and Raoul stopped to watch and listen as Mariachi Belen, a small group of orchestra members from the conservatory, strolled and played "El Jarabe Tapatio," complete with dancers, and then followed them to the groom's tailgate party.

Christine shrieked. "Rémy!" She rushed forward into his arms. They hugged and kissed on both cheeks. "I didn't know you were coming," she said.

"How could I miss your wedding?" Rémy said. "How proud your father would have been today."

"I'm so glad you're here," Christine said.

"I brought my chef," Rémy said, "to cook for Alain's—how do you say?"

"Tailgate party," Raoul said.

"Yes, that," Rémy said. "Have you eaten?"

"I never eat before a performance," Christine said.

"Excuse me for a moment. Don't go away," Rémy said and then stepped away.

"It's our wedding," Raoul said. "I hope it's not just a performance."

Christine laughed. "You know what I mean, but it does seem like opening night, doesn't it?"

"Yes, actually, it does," Raoul said.

"And you'd better perform tonight, or I'm recasting the role."

"I'll do my best," Raoul said as Rémy returned, accompanied by Marcel.

"You remember Marcel," Rémy said.

Marcel stepped forward, kissed Christine's hand, and spoke rapidly in French. He was impressed when Christine responded, albeit haltingly, in French.

"His nephew, Arnaud, is now first violin of the orchestra at the conservatory," Rémy said.

"Yes, I know," Christine said. "He earned it. He's very good."

Rémy translated and Marcel nodded. "*Oui, oui.*"

"We'd better go," Raoul said. "We have a lot more tailgates to hit and not much time."

They stepped next door to the bride's tailgate party. Christine was quickly occupied exchanging air kisses and a few real ones. Raoul leaned over and whispered, "You may not be eating, but I'm not going to pass this up."

"Go ahead," Christine said. "You'll need fuel for later."

He put his arm on her shoulder and pulled her around.

"Abby!" Christine said as she hugged Abby, who wore a chef's hat and a spotless white apron.

"How are you?" Abby asked.

"Great. Did you ever open your restaurant?"

"I think we finally found a location in Los Angeles, on the west side. We'll probably open this fall. I'm still catering until then."

Christine looked for Raoul, who stepped up, carrying a plate of food.

"Are you sure you aren't hungry?" he asked.

"Okay, just a bite," Christine said as she reached for a piece of finger food.

"Isn't it bad luck for the groom to see the bride before the wedding?" Abby asked.

"That's just in the wedding dress," Christine said, "I think. Right?" She took a bite.

Raoul shrugged. "I have no idea. I just stand where they tell me."

"Whatever," Christine said. "It's too late now." She took another bite. "This is delicious. Be sure and let me know when you open your restaurant."

"There you are," Sharon said, approaching rapidly. "You're on."

"On what?" Christine asked.

"Media tent."

"Where's Sue?" Christine asked. "And Tegan?"

"Right here, girlfriend," Sue said, wolfing down finger food. "Teegs is already over there, warming them up."

26

ODE TO JOY

The wedding party was backstage getting dressed and ready for the cere-mony. Shortly after the mariachis disappeared the orchestra began warming up. With no walls, and excellent acoustics, they could easily be heard at the tailgate parties, which were already winding down as the appointed hour drew near.

The groomsmen were first up, so they could greet guests as they entered, and escort special guests to their seats. They milled around as Mercedes approached and counted heads.

"Are you a groomsman?" Mercedes asked Carlos, who wore an Army mess blue uniform.

"Yes," Carlos said. "I was here yesterday, remember?"

"Don't you have a tuxedo?"

"Yes, actually, I do."

"Why aren't you wearing it?"

"Orders."

"Orders from who, the general?" she asked sarcastically.

"The bride," he said, smiling.

"She told you to wear this?"

"Yes. I didn't even own a set of mess blues. Never thought I'd need them, but as soon as I arrived, we were rushed off for a fitting. Frankie flew some-body in from Kansas with a pile of uniforms and a tailor."

"We who?" Mercedes asked.

"Me," Clifford said.

"Oh, no," Mercedes said. "There's another one." She looked at Clifford. "You don't even match."

"Well, I'm in the Navy," Clifford said. "He's in the Army."

"IS EVERYBODY DECENT?" Sue asked as she stepped into the women's dressing room, followed by two twelve-year-old boys in tuxedos.

"No, but come on in," Tegan said.

The girls all stopped and stared at the boys, who were identical twins.

"Carlos got called back to the Army," Sue said to Addison, "so we had to find a replacement."

"Who?" Addison asked, looking over the heads of the boys.

"Right here," Sue said.

"I'm Javier," one boy said as he bowed and kissed Addison's hand.

"And I'm Joaquin," the other said, kissing Kendall's hand.

"We got you one too, so you'd match," Sue said.

"What the hell?" Addison asked, clearly upset.

"Are you twins?" Kendall asked.

"Takes one to know one," Javier said.

"They're so short," Addison said.

The boys put their arms around the girls' waists and buried their faces in their breasts.

"Just right," Javier said.

"Ew!" Kendall said as both girls pushed both boys away.

"You little perverts," Addison said.

"How old are you?" Kendall asked.

"Twelve," Joaquin said.

"We like older women," Javier said.

"Is this a joke?" Addison asked.

"No way. Short notice. Pardon the pun," Sue said.

Kendall looked around and spotted a young woman with a small video camera, trying to be discreet.

"We're being punked," Kendall said.

"Christine!" Addison said.

Christine, wearing a short dressing gown, stepped out from her hiding place, laughing hysterically.

"So, the old bitch hates you?" Christine said.

"Okay, you got us back," Kendall said.

"Who are you guys?" Addison asked.

"Actors," Javier said, "from Albuquerque."

"Sorry about the face plant in the chest," Joaquin said.

"She made us do it," Javier said, pointing to Christine.

"That's okay," Addison said, pulling Javier's head into her chest and hugging him. "You did a good job. Here, cop another feel for your effort."

Kendall did the same with Joaquin. The boys clearly enjoyed their rewards.

"That's our mom over there," Javier said, motioning toward their mother, who tried to remain unobtrusively in the background.

"She said she'd bust our butts if we ever did that for real," Joaquin said.

"She's right," Addison said.

"You're lucky we didn't whack you," Kendall said.

"We were ready for it," Javier said. "We've had stage combat training."

"And we worked with a stuntwoman yesterday to learn how to take a punch to the face," Joaquin said.

"Frankie set it up," Sue said. "He rented the tuxes and everything."

"That boy will go to any length for a good practical joke," Addison said.

"Well played," Kendall said.

"Where is Frankie?" Addison asked.

"Doing groom stuff," Christine said. "But the video will live forever."

"Have you blokes been in anything I might have seen?" Tegan asked.

The boys stared, dumbstruck.

"I'm Tegan."

"We know," Javier said, continuing to stare.

"Frankie said we could meet you," Joaquin said.

"Hey, what about us?" Addison asked.

The boys ignored her.

"Just a few little things, a couple of commercials," Javier said.

"But we're up for a three-episode arc on *Better Call Saul*," Joaquin said.

"Our agent said we'll probably get it since we're the only twelve-year-old identical twin Mexican boys in the business," Javier said.

"In New Mexico anyway," Joaquin said. "It's local casting."

"Can we get a selfie?" Javier asked.

"I can do better than that," Tegan said. She stood between them, and they grinned ear to ear as they put their arms around her waist and one of the staff photographers snapped away.

"That's my cue," Christine said as the orchestra began playing "Ode to Joy." She turned to the boys. "You are coming to the reception, right?"

"Yes ma'am," Javier said. "Frankie said he would introduce us to the train wranglers."

"They're really cute," Sue said.

"Okay, a quick pic," Christine said, "and then another tonight when I'm dressed better."

The wedding photographer snapped a few quick shots of Christine and the boys and then Christine hustled off with Sue.

"Get over here, you little perverts," Addison said. "We get pictures too."

The boys eagerly posed with the twins.

WORD OF THE program had spread quickly among the wedding guests, and most were seated when "Ode to Joy" began, while the ushers rushed to seat those remaining. The audience quickly rose to their feet in a standing ovation when the piece ended. When the applause finally died down Alfonso stepped onto the stage.

"I'll bet you weren't expecting that when you received your wedding invitations," Alfonso said.

There was laughter and applause from the audience.

"I doubt there are a lot of standing ovations at weddings, especially before the bride even makes an appearance," he continued, and then looked over at Christine, waiting offstage in her wedding dress. She smiled.

"She's standing over there, and wow, she looks stunning. Raoul is a lucky man."

The audience applauded.

"Christine asked me to sing today, a very special song, not only to her, but to both families. Although it was written for a tenor, she sang this song as her audition piece for acceptance to the Belen Conservatory of Music. It worked. She was accepted. She was accompanied by a single violin, played by our groom, Raoul."

There was murmuring among those who were not already aware of the story.

"In attendance was Johnston Caldwell, then headmaster at the conservatory, now manager of the Santa Fe Opera, and now Christine's adoptive father." Alfonso waited for the applause. "I am told there were tears in his eyes when he first heard her sing. There definitely were, not only in his, but mine, and others as well, when she sang it again at her graduation ceremony just a few days ago."

There was scattered applause.

"I tried to beg off singing it today, because Christine sings it so much better than I ever could, but who can refuse a bride on her wedding day?"

Alfonso looked over at Christine.

"With the arrival last night of some unexpected guests, there has been a slight change of program." He grinned and paused while the audience murmured. He gestured toward the orchestra. "Our orchestra today is from the Belen Conservatory of Music in Los Angeles. The conservatory was founded by Daniel Titshaw Senior, Johnston Caldwell's great-grandfather. Daniel Senior asked that when he died this song, his favorite, be sung at his funeral by the best available tenor. Johnston was a student at the conservatory at the time and accompanied the tenor to Los Angeles where the song was performed by the tenor and a previous incarnation of this very orchestra."

He gestured again toward the orchestra.

"The young tenor was already making a name for himself and is now a living legend in the opera and classical music community. When he arrived last night, I immediately offered to step aside, of course, but he insisted we do it as a duet." The murmurs from the audience grew louder. Alfonso turned to the choir. "Boys and girls, what you are about to see is a master class in singing. I will be the student, schooled by the master."

There was laughter from the choir, the orchestra, and the audience.

"He needs no further introduction. Ladies and gentlemen, the legendary Rinaldo."

The audience gasped, and then rose to their feet and applauded loudly as Rinaldo stepped onto the stage and took a bow.

When the applause died down and the audience took their seats, Alfonso turned to the maestro and nodded.

The orchestra played, and Alfonso and Rinaldo sang "Nessun Dorma," accompanied by the choir. Alfonso more than held his own alongside the master.

Tears flowed down Christine's face as she and the bridesmaids watched and listened in stunned silence.

When the singers finished and took their bows to thunderous applause, Tegan said, "I am so hitting that tonight."

"Which one?" Christine asked, laughing as she wiped tears.

"I haven't decided," Tegan said. She looked at Christine. "Oh, shit. Makeup!"

"Flying in," the makeup artist said, approaching rapidly.

When the ovation finally subsided, Alfonso said, "But wait; there's more."

The audience was excited. What could possibly top that?

Alfonso and Rinaldo took a step back and looked offstage as Johnston, with Marjorie on his arm, walked onto the stage. Some in the audience recognized her immediately, gasped and began applauding, but quickly stopped as Johnston spoke. "I believe some of you know my mother, Marjorie Caldwell."

The audience again rose to their feet, applauding and cheering. Marjorie took a bow.

"I tried to argue that this next song wasn't really appropriate for a wedding, but Christine said she loved it and insisted we do it," Johnston said. "Well, not we—I certainly don't sing."

The audience laughed.

"I'm just going to wait over there and listen," Johnston said.

Johnston kissed his mother and withdrew from the stage, along with Alfonso.

The orchestra began playing and after only a few notes the audience burst into applause and then quickly went silent as Rinaldo and Marjorie, backed by the choir, sang "Libiamo," from *La Traviata*. The young choir members went overboard on the drunk improv, much to the chagrin of their chaperones, standing just offstage.

There was another thunderous ovation when the song ended, and the performers took their bows. Both Rinaldo and Marjorie bowed to the conductor, orchestra, and choir.

When they were finally allowed to leave the stage, Alfonso stepped back on. He looked offstage. "Christine, that's going to be a tough act to follow." He turned to the audience. "She says she's up to the challenge."

The audience roared.

"Since that song was added at the last minute, I'm going to do a little standup while everyone gets into position for the main event." He looked offstage again. "I see paramedics giving oxygen to Mercedes, the wedding planner."

The audience laughed.

"Both Johnston Caldwell and his mother graduated from the conservatory, as did Christine and her maid of honor, Sue, along with yours truly," Alfonso said.

He gestured toward the orchestra. "Our orchestra today is from the conservatory, along with part of the choir."

He gestured toward the choir. "The rest of the choir is from Ogden Hall, a private school in Santa Monica, attended by Raoul for several years, and briefly by Christine before she was accepted by the conservatory. Let's hear a big round of applause for these kids."

As the applause died down Alfonso looked out over the audience and received a signal from the floor director.

"Okay, the bride's posse is lined up and ready, so I'm going to break protocol and run down that aisle right there and take my position with the groom's crew."

27

TREULICH GEFÜHRT

With the addition of Marjorie, the bride now had two grandmothers, which matched the groom's count, but unfortunately added minutes to the procession. Mercedes was skeptical, but the floor director and groomsmen insisted they could handle it.

As if that weren't enough, Mercedes suddenly had a new problem to deal with.

"Who are you?" Mercedes asked, curiously eyeing a young woman wearing a black Victorian dress with full skirts and topped with an enormous hat.

"Cynthia."

"Are you a bridesmaid?"

"I'm the nanny," Cynthia said.

"Shouldn't you already be seated?" Mercedes asked.

"No," Tegan said. "Sofia is a bridesmaid. She can't walk, so Cynthia will push her in the perambulator."

"The what?" Mercedes asked.

"The baby carriage," Tegan said, pointing at a vintage black perambulator, flown in from London, festooned with red ribbons.

"In the processional?" Mercedes asked.

"Of course," Tegan said.

"Why wasn't I told about this?" Mercedes asked.

"Christine wanted it to be a surprise," Tegan said.

"A surprise for who?" Mercedes asked.

"Zoe," Sue said. "It's something of an inside joke."

"Your parasol," a crew member said, opening a parasol and handing it to Cynthia.

"Thank you," Cynthia said.

"I give up," Mercedes said. "Do whatever you want."

"Chill," Tegan said. "If the boys can get an extra granny down the aisle in time, we can handle one baby and a nanny."

The boys did indeed get the grannies down the aisle with time to spare. Alfonso escorted Marjorie; Carlos, Maria; Clifton, Chantal; and the Frenchman escorted Hannah's mother.

Frankie escorted Hannah. Alfonso escorted Zoe to her seat, the last to be seated before the actual processional began.

CHRISTINE WAITED IN position, just out of sight of everyone, especially the groom.

"Okay, final checklist," Mercedes said. "Something old."

"My engagement ring," Christine said, holding up her hand.

"Something new."

"Pretty much everything else, but I'll go with shoes."

"Something borrowed."

"Sue's ankle bracelet."

Christine started to hike up her dress but stopped. "You'll just have to trust me on that one."

"Something blue."

"My panties."

"We'll have to trust you on that one too," Jim Bob said.

Nari tied a red scarf loosely around Christine's neck.

"What is this?" Mercedes asked.

Nari took a step back and waved her hands dramatically. "It is a slashing streak of blood red against the pure white innocence of the dress," Nari said.

Christine laughed. Mercedes was speechless.

"It's her scarf," Nari said.

"It's *the* scarf," Christine said.

"I don't understand," Mercedes said.

"Same deal as the nanny and the perambulator," Sue said.

"Just go with it," Nari said. "I did."

Nari pulled the veil over Christine's head and fiddled with it until it was just right.

As the time grew near Jim Bob and Johnston took up positions beside Christine, waiting to go on.

"We're thinking of J. Viktor Alain if it's a boy," Christine said casually. "J. is for both Johnston and Jim Bob."

"Oh, no," Johnston said. "Are you pregnant?"

"Ew! No. I'm talking later, way later."

"Well, that's a relief," Jim Bob said.

"I can say with absolute certainty that I am not pregnant."

Johnston and Jim Bob looked at her suspiciously.

"What? I am wearing white to my wedding."

"Lots of brides wear white," Johnston said.

"Well, this bride wears white honestly."

"You haven't—I mean—not that it's any of my business—our business—but you and Raoul never—" Johnston said.

"Nope. There were some close calls, and it's not like we didn't do some serious making out, but we never did the deed."

"Wow," Jim Bob said.

"I like totally offered, but he turned me down."

"He did?" Johnston asked.

"Well, the first time, I was drunk, and he could have taken advantage of me, but he didn't. Any gentleman would have done the same, right?"

"I certainly hope so," Jim Bob said.

"But the next night I was sober, and ready, and willing. That was in Lubbock, when I thought Erik might do something terrible and I would never see Raoul again. He sensed that something was wrong and said the time wasn't right. I mean we were already naked and stuff, so that was like a big deal, right?"

"That was a big deal," Jim Bob said. "Not many young guys would pass that up."

"That's when I knew he was the right guy for me. After that I decided to wait for my wedding night. My daddy was pretty cool, and he and mom were probably going at it in Chicago before they got married."

"I plead the fifth," Jim Bob said.

"Still, he would have probably liked it if I waited, so it was kind of for him, but mostly for me."

"That's good, old school, but good," Johnston said.

"But tonight, I'm going to have my way with him."

Johnston and Jim Bob laughed.

———

THE MINISTER STEPPED onto the stage from the wings. The groomsmen led off on the groom's side, followed by Frankie and Raoul, who stopped briefly to kiss his mother.

There was a bit of chuckling when Sofia was pushed down the bride's aisle by Cynthia, and Raoul laughed and applauded loudly.

The ambulatory bridesmaids followed, and then Sue.

The fire marshal wouldn't allow the perambulator to remain in the aisle; Cynthia's dress would have occupied more than one seat; and her hat would have obstructed the view of guests behind her, so she stopped long enough to transfer Sofia to Zoe and then quickly pushed the perambulator into the wings.

The orchestra played "Treulich geführt."

Stopwatch in hand, the floor director dispatched the two ring bearers, a girl on the bride's side, carrying a plain gold wedding band, and a boy on the groom's side, carrying an extraordinarily valuable stunner of a diamond ring, dispatched by a security guard in a tuxedo. Another guard stood at the front of the theater to watch the boy, and ring, every step of the way down the aisle. The ring had been firmly planted in the pillow and Frankie had repeatedly practiced excising it from its bonds.

Mercedes was relieved when the wedding party had taken up their positions on stage long before those who recognized the music turned to watch as four flower girls spread flower petals on the bride's aisle.

Christine listened quietly along with "Treulich geführt" for a few seconds and then said, "We're up, guys."

More people turned to look when the horns joined in. All eyes were on Christine as she stepped out from behind a screen, with Johnston on one arm and Jim Bob on the other.

The media, restricted to an area on the bride's side, and just outside the theater, swarmed, cameras snapping and recording. The fashion press immediately began rating and reviewing the dress while uploading photos and video to the Internet.

Christine and her escorts rounded the corner and entered the theater. People, mostly the ladies, gasped. The dress, which fit like a second skin above the waist, with bare shoulders, now covered by the veil, was to die for and Christine wore it well. The two young wranglers deftly handled the extremely long train as Christine and her two daddies walked down the aisle.

"Wow," Raoul whispered to Frankie. "That's one hell of a dress."

"Yes, it is." Frankie said. "And that's one hell of a girl wearing it you lucky SOB."

Guests whispered about the flash of red beneath Christine's veil.

Christine stopped briefly, and Jim Bob lifted her veil just enough to kiss both Zoe and Sofia.

28

VICOMTESSE

There had been considerable discussion on the entire matter of giving away the bride and the exact wording to accompany it. Having handled a great many weddings, Mercedes had experience with one or both of the bride's parents being deceased, as well as brides with adoptive parents. Those had usually been adopted quite young, and the adoptive parents were handled the same as birth parents. In Christine's case, however, her adoption was more a formality and had occurred only weeks before the wedding.

Frankie knew Christine to be a strong and independent young woman who might object to the concept of being "given away," and he had broached the subject as delicately as possible.

Christine laughed. "Yeah, that's kind of weird, but it's like centuries-old tradition and stuff and this is a really formal wedding, right?"

Frankie nodded.

"Daddy took care of me all by himself after Mom died," she said. "It was just me and him. So, if he was alive, he would totally give me away." She scrunched up her face. "That does sound weird, doesn't it?"

"I think the actual words used are 'Who gives this woman to be married?'" Frankie said.

"That's definitely better," she said.

"Mercedes said there are other options, and I googled it," Frankie said. "We might be able to come up with something else if you want."

"No, I like that fine." She shrugged. "Johnston just got me and he's already giving me away."

The minister was aware that with all the music and singing, the ceremony was already quite long, and kept his part mercifully brief.

Mercedes was no fan of two men giving away the bride, but Christine had insisted, and it had gone well enough during rehearsal when Johnston had simply answered, "We do," to the question.

Mercedes could not see the grin on Christine's face when the minister asked, "Who gives this woman to be married?"

"Her late daddy," Jim Bob answered with authority.

"Her adoptive daddy," Johnston said.

"And the redneck," Jim Bob said. "That's me."

Raoul choked back a laugh as some guests gasped and others chuckled. Mercedes cringed.

Johnston lifted Christine's veil and kissed her on both cheeks, as did Jim Bob, and then both men walked quickly down the ramp and took their seats.

With her veil pulled back, as Christine turned toward the audience the red scarf caught everyone's attention. She smiled.

Frankie stepped forward and faced the audience. "The first song a couple hears together is forever known as 'their song.' Some of us get lucky, while some others undoubtedly pick a new 'our song,' thinking no one will notice." He waited for the laughter. "In this case, however, there was a witness, Zoe Hathaway, who identified the song to a young Raoul." He motioned toward Zoe. "Zoe, now Butrell, is standing in today as mother of the bride. For bonus points, Christine, who was twelve at the time, was singing the song on the Santa Monica Pier, in Welsh, I might add, accompanied by her father on violin, when Raoul first saw her, so this is and will forever be, without question, 'their song.'"

Frankie stepped back and stood beside Raoul as the orchestra began playing and the choir sang "Suo Gân."

It was too late for makeup to fly in as tears streamed down Christine's face. She was not alone. When the song was over, Christine wiped tears with a handkerchief she had pulled from Jim Bob's pocket, where it had been carefully pre-positioned.

The minister moved the ceremony along quickly and there was loud applause as the groom kissed the bride.

Raoul and Christine, holding hands, turned to face the audience. Raoul looked at the audience, smiled, and began to speak.

"Frankie said Mercedes, the wedding planner, strongly advised against the bride singing at her own wedding, especially a traditional and formal one, like this. I believe words like "tacky," and "karaoke" were used."

Mercedes ducked her head and covered her face as the audience laughed.

"Let's hope that's not the case today." He paused. "The song you are about to hear was her father's favorite song," Raoul said. "From today, it will be her husband's favorite song." He looked at Christine and smiled, and then turned back to the audience. "Ladies and gentlemen, may I present my beautiful bride, the vicomtesse Christine Daaé de Chagny." He kissed her briefly, released her hand, bowed, and took a step back.

Christine turned to the maestro and nodded.

Tears streamed down Christine's face as she sang "Con te partirò," followed by an extended standing ovation.

Raoul stepped up and took Christine's hand as six herald trumpeters entered from each side of the stage. Banners dropped as they raised their trumpets for an extended fanfare before the orchestra played Mendelssohn's "Wedding March."

"Frankie may have gone overboard with the herald trumpets," Raoul whispered to Christine.

"Ya think? But I do like the flag thingies."

"That's our coat of arms," he said.

"You have a coat of arms?" she asked.

"*We* have a coat of arms, Mrs. Chagny," he said as he kissed her. "Is that your mom's scarf?"

"Yes," she said, grinning.

"Nice touch," he said.

"Is that my daddy's aftershave?"

"Yes. I saved it for just this occasion."

He extended his elbow. She took his arm and they stepped off the stage, leading the parade.

As THE WHITE stretch limo, freshly washed and polished, pulled onto the highway from Opera Drive, Angel glanced into the mirror and smiled as Christine and Raoul kissed, lost in their own world. Looking back to the road, Angel didn't pay any attention to the scruffy hitchhiker with a hoodie pulled over his face, holding a cardboard sign: I-40 EAST.

The hitchhiker looked up and watched as the long white limo accelerated and headed toward Santa Fe. He couldn't see through the tinted windows but knew who was inside. He also knew that there would soon be a stream of vehicles containing people who might recognize him, so he tucked away the cardboard sign and ducked behind the brush.

ANGEL OPENED THE back door of the limo at the ranch. He smiled, noticing the lipstick on Raoul's face.

"What?" Raoul asked.

"You have lipstick on your face," Angel said.

Raoul laughed. "That's okay. We're married."

Angel looked away briefly as Christine, now wearing a much shorter dress, swung her legs out of the limo and took Raoul's hand.

"Thanks for the ride," Christine said.

"Any time," Angel said. "Congratulations, and best wishes."

Christine rushed up the steps onto the porch. Raoul followed her as she made her way to the kitchen, where Juanita swept her into her arms.

"¡Mi hija!" Juanita said.

"I wish you could have been there," Christine said.

"My place is here, making sure everything is ready. I'll watch the video later."

"I think they're on their way I'm going to run upstairs and fix my makeup."

They hugged once more and then Christine released her and turned to go, taking Raoul by the hand.

"What's the hurry?" Raoul asked as Christine practically dragged him up the stairs.

"You'll see."

They raced down the hallway and into Christine's room.

"Unzip me," she said, turning her back and lifting her hair.

"I thought this was the dress you were wearing to the reception," he said, unzipping it.

"It is, but I don't want to get it messed up."

She turned to face him as she wiggled out of the dress.

"Are we going to do it?" he asked.

"No," she said, unhooking her bra. "That's tonight."

He watched with interest as she slipped off her bra. "Okay, I'm confused."

"Foreplay, before everybody gets here."

He whipped off his jacket in a flash. "I've never made out with a vicomtesse before," he said as he continued to strip.

"I made out with a vicomte a few times," she said, shrugging her shoulders. "It's no biggie."

A LONG LINE OF CARS, SUVs, limos, and shuttle buses crawled up the road to the ranch, stopping long enough to disembark passengers and then followed the directions of young people wearing reflective orange vests, pointing them to the parking area. For those driving themselves, valets immediately hopped in their cars and whisked them away.

Frankie arrived in one of the first vehicles, along with Meg, Sue, Tegan, and Alfonso. Frankie immediately raced to the kitchen to check with Juanita, who, as usual, had everything under control.

"It's not my first rodeo," Juanita said. "Besides, Miss Abby and that Frenchman are doing most of the cooking."

"What about the cakes?" Frankie asked.

"Delivered about four hours ago," she said. "They're in the walk-in cooler, but we should probably take them out and let them warm up now that everybody is showing up."

"I'll check the ballroom," Frankie said, turning to go.

"It's perfect," his mother said as she entered the kitchen.

She hugged Juanita. "Thank you so much, Juanita. What would we do without you?"

"Only the best for *mi hija*," Juanita said.

"Where is she?" Frankie asked.

"Upstairs," Juanita said.

Sue, Tegan, and Meg headed down the hallway toward Christine's room. Sue grabbed the doorknob and started to open it, but then put her ear to the door and listened.

"Christine, is that you?"

"Yeah, it's me," Christine said, giggling.

"What are you doing?" Sue asked.

"Making out, with Alfie."

"I'll claw your eyes out, bitch," Tegan said.

Christine laughed as Raoul, wearing nothing but briefs, suddenly opened the door. All the girls immediately glanced down as he tried to cover his obvious erection, and then pushed inside.

Christine, wearing nothing but panties, sat up in bed.

"Nice try, but Alfie rode with us," Tegan said.

"Where is he?" Christine asked.

"Looking for the band. Why, do you need some pointers?"

Christine laughed. "No, I think I have the hang of it."

"You couldn't wait?" Meg asked.

"We were just fooling around before everybody got here."

"Well, they're here, and more coming," Sue said. "Do you need hair and makeup?"

"I guess so. Raoul is wearing my lipstick."

Tegan licked her thumb and tried to wipe some of it off Raoul's face.

"Ew!" he said.

Tegan laughed. "Just like your mom, right?"

Raoul nodded.

"I'll go try to find the makeup and hair people," Sue said. "They might be stuck in traffic. There's a *lot* of cars out there." She headed for the door. Meg followed.

"You have time for a quickie," Tegan said, but didn't budge.

"Do you want to watch?" Raoul asked, sitting on the bed.

"Sure," Tegan said.

Christine laughed.

"Get out," Raoul said.

Tegan leaned over him and kissed Christine on the cheek.

"You do have time to make out, or whatever," Tegan said. "There's plenty of booze, so nobody will even notice you aren't there."

"That's okay," Christine said. "I had my appetizer. I'm saving the main course for later."

"Threesome!" Addison said as she stepped into the bedroom.

"If we had more boys we could have an orgy," Kendall said.

"What are you doing here?" Raoul asked.

"This is our room," Addison said.

"I would ask what you're doing here, but it's kind of obvious," Kendall said.

"They were making out," Tegan said. "I was just leaving so they can get back to it."

"We brought hair and makeup," Addison said, "which you obviously need."

"Or they brought us," Kendall said. "Frankie had a car waiting and we slipped out the back way to beat the rush."

She pointed at two women standing in the hall, carrying tackle boxes.

"We can come back later," one of the women said.

"That's okay," Christine said. "The show must go on."

Addison picked up Raoul's clothes.

"We'll go dress Raoul while you work on Christine," Addison said.

Kendall took Raoul's hand and pulled him off the bed.

"I'll stay with Christine," Tegan said.

Tegan picked up Christine's dress and brushed it with her hand as the two women stepped in.

Christine climbed out of bed just as Alfonso entered.

"Oh, sorry," Alfonso said, trying not to look.

Raoul turned, looked at Christine, almost naked, shook his head and followed the twins out the door as Christine stepped into the bathroom.

"Sue is going to sit in with the Beats," Alfonso said. "They want to know if you are going to sing."

"Are you?" Christine said, wrapping herself in a towel and stepping back into the room.

"Maybe one or two, but it's their gig. I don't want to take it over."

"Yeah, I know what you mean. Maybe we'll do a duet, for old times' sake."

Alfonso nodded and smiled. "Sounds good to me."

Christine put her arms around his neck and hugged him. "Thanks, for everything."

She looked at him for a moment and then kissed him on the lips. "You're the first one to kiss the bride, except for the groom, of course."

"I'm honored," he said.

"And I'm naked, so get out. And close the door."

29

I'LL BE SEEING YOU

THE TWINS, ALONG with Raoul, waited in the hallway near the landing on the staircase as Christine, now fully dressed, coiffed, and made up approached, accompanied by Tegan.

"He cleans up really nice, doesn't he?" Addison asked.

"Yes, he does." Christine looked at Raoul. "I'd kiss you, but I have fresh makeup."

"That's okay," Raoul said. "I'll just look." He leaned in and air-kissed both cheeks. On the second one he whispered in her ear.

She shrieked and blushed, covering her face.

"Easy there, tiger," Kendall said.

"We'll go down first," Addison said.

"And check out the boys," Kendall said.

"Doesn't Carlos look smoking hot?" Addison asked.

"Yes, he does," Christine said. "I'm glad he came."

"Men always look better in uniform," Kendall said.

"Come on," Addison said. "Let's go shopping."

They headed down the stairs.

Christine and Raoul waited a moment, holding hands, and then followed. The twins had obviously tipped everyone off, as there was a drum roll when the bride and groom entered the ballroom, followed by loud applause.

The Belen Beats played, and Sue sat in on trumpet, looking rather out of place in her maid of honor dress, but nobody complained. The guests were mostly older, who loved the music and danced to it.

So did the younger ones, including Javier and Joaquin, who were putting serious moves on the train wranglers. They were quite happy that their agent had insisted on dance lessons among all the other training, although this probably wasn't what she had in mind.

The cakes were cut, photos were taken, and Christine even managed to dance with her husband, along with Johnston, Jim Bob, and a seemingly endless stream of others. Christine insisted that Sue step off stage and dance with some of the eligible bachelors.

"I'm married," Christine said. "Your MOH duty is done. Have some fun. Dance. Meet some boys. Maybe get lucky."

Sue laughed, but the point was well taken. She danced with some of the young Frenchmen, who were quite impressed by her French.

Christine kissed a lot of people. Fortunately, it was air kisses or cheek kisses for most and there were no sloppy drunks. Carlos got a real kiss, however, and then he took her by the hand.

"There's someone who wants to meet you."

He led her through the crowd and found Bill Burlington and his wife. Introductions were made.

"He gave me a ride on his jet from Fort Hood," Carlos said.

"Did you get a ride back?" Bill asked.

"Yes sir," Carlos said. "Frankie said an entire fleet is taking off in the morning, with several headed that way, so he fixed me up."

Bill turned to Christine. "We were at the opera last summer," he said, "for opening night."

"*Sangre de Cristo*," Carlos said.

Christine smiled and nodded. "Did you enjoy it?"

"Hell, yes, we did," Bill said. "Young lady, you sing like an angel."

"Thank you," Christine said.

"We hear you're making a movie version," Mrs. Burlington said.

Christine was surprised. "Where did you hear that?"

"Word gets around," Bill said.

"We want in," Mrs. Burlington said.

"You want to be in the movie?" Christine asked, confused.

"We want to invest," Mrs. Burlington said.

"Invest?" Christine asked.

"In your movie," Bill said. "We get hit up all the time to invest in movies, but most of them are crap."

"We want to put our money in something good," Mrs. Burlington said.

"Wow," Christine said. "I guess we should talk to Frankie."

"Already did," Bill said. "He still needs to do his due diligence and put a deal together, but I told him to call us first. We put Franklin into some pretty sweet oil and gas plays, so he owes us."

"Well, okay," Christine said.

"Are you sure you won't play Sofia?" Mrs. Burlington asked.

"Yes ma'am. I'm sure," Christine said. "I'm a singer, not an actress, but I'll sing on the soundtrack. I want my friend Tegan to play Sofia. She's really good."

"Well, we won't keep you any longer," Bill said. "You have a big room to work."

ANGEL AND HIS WIFE, Alicia, sat in lawn chairs beside the white limo, listening to the music, and Christine singing, "I'll Be Seeing You."

Angel jumped up as Carlos came down the steps from the house, balancing a tray with one hand, carrying two bottles of wine in the other.

"What's this?" Angel asked.

"Old times, homes, old times. Juanita was going to make you some burritos, but I told her I'd just scavenge some fancy grub from the ballroom."

"It looks good," Alicia said.

"Do you remember Abby?" Carlos asked. "She used to be the attendant on the *Estelline*."

"I remember her."

"She's catering this gig. The Southwestern cuisine is hers."

"Southwestern cuisine?" Alicia asked.

"Mexican food," Carlos said, "for rich people."

Angel and Alicia laughed.

"And there's a lot of French stuff too," Carlos said. "The Chagnys brought some restaurant owner from Saint-Tropez and his chef. Check it out. It's pretty good."

He handed Alicia the wine. "Slip this in the trunk for later, compliments of the groom."

Alicia read the label. "French?" she asked.

"Yeah, from the Chagny vineyards. This is some good shit."

"Is that the same band that was here a couple of years ago for some charity thing?" Angel asked.

Carlos nodded. "The night Erik got messed up."

"Who is the girl that was just singing?"

"That's Christine, the bride."

"Was she singing that night, with the band?"

"Yeah," Carlos said. "She was their main singer then, but she just graduated from the conservatory. I think she's just doing a couple of songs tonight."

Angel looked at Alicia. "It's her."

THE BAND PLAYED ON, and the guests ate, drank, and danced.

Alfonso stepped onto the stage. "I tried to get the bride to do a duet with me, but she seems preoccupied with her new husband." He waited for the laughter. "I guess it's you and me, Sue."

Sue stepped forward and began playing "It's Been a Long, Long Time" on her trumpet. The band quickly joined in and the guests, including Christine and Raoul, swarmed onto the dance floor. Alfonso sang.

When the song was over Alfonso looked over the ballroom and said, "Where's my man, Carlos?"

"Right here," Carlos said, stepping forward.

"Are you ready?"

"I'm always ready," Carlos said, taking Addison's hand.

"We actually rehearsed this, but feel free to join in if the spirit moves you," Alfonso said. He stepped off the stage and took Tegan's hand as the drummer launched into "Sing, Sing, Sing."

Javier, Joaquin, and the train wranglers led off, to enthusiastic applause. The kids could dance.

The groomsmen and bridesmaids joined in.

Frankie tried to beg off, claiming two left feet, and Meg was already paired up with her groomsman, but he gamely did his duty and danced with Sue and her trumpet.

The dancers stepped aside to clear the center floor for Christine and Raoul, who gave it their best shot, but were soon overshadowed as Chantal and Rémy showed the youngsters how it was done. Others joined in when it became obvious the band was playing the long version.

Everyone had a chance to catch their breath with "Moonlight Serenade." Christine and Raoul seemed glued together and lost in their own world as they danced, along with nearly everyone else.

When the song was over, Christine stepped onto the stage.

"I want to do one more song, but I don't think it's in the band's repertoire, so Sue and Zoe will accompany me."

Sue swapped her horn for violin. Zoe sat at the piano.

Christine sang "Your Love," looking mostly at Raoul.

When the applause finally died down, she smiled and said, "Thank you all for coming tonight. Feel free to stay and dance, but right now, I'm going upstairs with my husband."

"You go girl!" Sue shouted, followed by laughter, cheers, and applause.

As Christine stepped off the stage and took Raoul's waiting hand, Sue played "Charge" on her trumpet. Christine covered her face and raced away with Raoul. She headed for the stairway, but Raoul pulled her back.

"You aren't backing out, are you?" Christine asked.

"No way, but I think Frankie has other plans."

"Frankie?" Christine asked, confused, just as Frankie entered from the ballroom, followed closely by Sue.

"Right this way, ladies and gentlemen," Frankie said, gesturing toward the front door.

"Where are we going?" Christine asked.

"It's a wedding night surprise," Frankie said.

"Well, make it quick. I have somebody to do."

Raoul smiled. Sue laughed.

"One step ahead of you," Frankie said.

Frankie pushed open the front door and the foursome stepped onto the porch. The white limo was running, the back door open, and Angel in his waiting pose. Alicia stood nearby.

"Hold up," Carlos said, coming out of the house as they started down the stairs.

"What's wrong?" Frankie asked.

"Nothing," Carlos said. "Angel would like to speak to Christine, if that's okay with you." He looked at Raoul.

"It's not up to me," Raoul said.

"What is it?" Christine asked as she stepped off the stairs.

"I think I've heard you sing before," Angel said.

"I've sung around town with Carlos, and the opera, of course. Oh, and at the gala, three years ago."

"Yes, I was here for that, driving Maria, actually." Angel said. "I heard you sing and thought it might be the same girl, but I wasn't sure until tonight."

Christine smiled but didn't know what to say.

"It was about six years ago," Angel said.

"Santa Monica?" Christine asked, now curious.

"Amarillo," Angel said.

Christine gasped and covered her mouth. She surged forward and hugged him as Raoul and Frankie stared.

30

THE BRIDAL TRAIN

SLIVERS OF SUNLIGHT streamed through small gaps in the curtains of the master bedroom of the *Estelline*. Christine lay in Raoul's arms, watching him sleep, listening to him breathe. She ran her fingers lightly over his chest and glanced down at the rumpled sheet over his waist. She smiled. She suddenly turned and looked in the direction of a small noise. She waited. Silence. She turned back to Raoul and kissed him softly on the lips. He stirred, and she kissed him again. He awoke and smiled, then flinched as her hand slid under the sheet.

"What a nice surprise," he said.

"Do you smell coffee?" she asked.

"Actually, smell wasn't the first sensation that came to mind."

She ran her hand up over his chest.

"Don't stop," he said.

"Didn't you get enough last night?"

"No, not really. I'm ready for an encore."

"There's somebody here."

"Frankie probably set the timer on the coffee pot. What time is it?"

"Daytime."

There was a knock at the door.

"Room service," Sue said.

"It's open," Raoul said.

"Is everybody naked?" Frankie asked.

"Yes, but covered," Raoul said.

Frankie opened the door and stepped in, followed by Sue, carrying two cups of coffee.

Christine and Raoul sat up in bed. Christine covered herself with the sheet.

"Sorry to interrupt your wedded bliss, but your public awaits," Frankie said.

Christine gulped coffee. "What public?"

Frankie pointed at the window. Christine looked at him curiously, put her coffee on the nightstand, and slid out of bed while covering herself with a pillow. She stepped over to the window, pulled a curtain back slightly, and peeked out.

"The press?" Christine asked.

"Press, paparazzi, along with the wedding video crew and a few onlookers," Frankie said.

"Uh, girlfriend," Sue said.

Christine looked at Sue.

"You're like, naked," Sue said.

Frankie laughed.

"You've already seen everything anyway," Christine said as she crawled back into bed and pulled up the sheet.

"Yes, but you do need to get dressed," Frankie said. "There's a mile-long train backing into Santa Fe as we speak, so we need to get a move on."

"Okay, boys out," Sue said.

"Why?" Raoul asked.

"Duh, girl talk," Sue said as she picked up Raoul's briefs from the floor and handed them to him.

Frankie and Raoul headed to the kitchen. They sat at the table, sipping coffee, as Sue and Christine laughed loudly.

"I don't think you did it right," Frankie said.

"What do you mean?" Raoul asked.

"They're laughing."

"Nobody was laughing last night."

Sue screamed.

"Now that sounds more like it," Raoul said.

THE SMALL DEPOT at Santa Fe was hardly equipped to handle such a long train, so it had been split up at various locations over Santa Fe and Lamy, wherever there was available track space. Santa Fe Southern Railway had been busy overnight reassembling the train which now crept slowly backwards toward the *Estelline* and an attached lounge car, parked at the depot, surrounded by a crowd of press, paparazzi, railfans, and onlookers.

Carlos climbed aboard the *Estelline*. "Here she comes."

"Are you ladies ready?" Frankie called out.

"We're always ready," Christine said, now fully dressed, as she stepped into the parlor, followed by Sue.

"I'm shutting off the generator so they can hook us up," Frankie said. "The lights will be out for a couple of minutes."

"I thought you were going back to the Army," Christine said as she hugged Carlos.

"In a couple of hours," Carlos said. "I came to see you off, and to help Julio with the barrels."

"Barrels?" Christine asked.

"Hang on," Frankie said.

Christine hung onto Raoul. There was a thud and a clank as the *Estelline* moved slightly.

"What was that?" Christine asked.

"The train," Frankie said.

The lights came back on, and the conductor entered. "I hope you're ready. We have a lot of streets blocked."

"We're ready," Frankie said. "Let's roll." He raced through the *Estelline* and into the lounge car, followed by everybody else.

"What's this?" Christine asked as she looked through the windows at all the people outside.

"It's a lounge car. Dad calls it a 'whistle-stop car.' It has a back porch so politicians can make speeches, or brides can wave." He opened the rear door. "I need the bride and groom out here."

Raoul took Christine by the hand and led her through the door and onto the back porch. The others waited inside.

A mile down the tracks, the engineer on 3751 blew the whistle, which Christine could barely hear, and the train started slowly moving. The onlookers applauded and cheered, while still and video cameras recorded.

Christine and Raoul smiled and waved. The back of the lounge car was covered with flowers and a large banner that read: JUST MARRIED. Christine was startled when the cans, buckets, and barrels tied to the back of the train started bouncing and banging as the train picked up speed.

Christine waved until the depot was out of sight. Frankie and Carlos stepped onto the porch as the train slowed to a stop and Julio pulled up in a pickup, towing a trailer.

Carlos hugged Christine and kissed her on the cheek. He shook hands with Raoul. "Take care of her, man."

"I will," Raoul said.

Frankie and Carlos unhooked the chains that held the barrels and cans and Carlos hopped off the train as Julio began gathering up cans. Several agencies had signed off on the barrels, but insisted they be removed shortly after leaving the station and before picking up speed—a fifty-five-gallon steel barrel being dragged behind a train at speed could do serious damage.

The train started to move, and Christine waved. "Bye. Thanks for everything."

Christine watched Carlos and Julio for a moment, and then stepped back into the lounge car.

"You can use this as a sitting room," Frankie said. "It's all yours, along with the *Estelline*. Everyone will give you your privacy unless you invite them back here."

Christine and Raoul followed Frankie through the lounge car.

"Breakfast is ready," Frankie said. "Are you hungry?"

"I'm starved," Christine said.

"I can imagine."

Christine poked him in the back.

They walked through the *Estelline* and two other private cars until they reached an elegant dining car, specially chartered by Franklin because it had one very long table down the middle, with chairs on both sides. It was filled with people, mostly family, who immediately burst into applause.

Christine blushed and covered her face.

"What's wrong?" Raoul asked.

"They know what we did last night," Christine said.

"I should hope so."

Christine pulled her hands away from her face and waved.

"Right this way, madame," Frankie said.

"Ugh, I'm no longer a mademoiselle."

Frankie guided Christine and Raoul to their seats in the middle of the table, between Johnston and Maria on one side, Jim Bob and Zoe on the other, and directly across from Chantal, and Raoul's parents. Frankie, Meg, Sue, and the twins were nearby, along with Alfonso and Tegan.

Breakfast was quickly served, and Christine dug in.

"Where are we going?" Christine asked.

"One night stopover in Chicago, and then on to New York," Frankie said.

"I thought we were going to Saint-Tropez."

"We are but it will take a while to get there," Raoul said.

Christine thought about it for a moment. "Oh, now I get it," she said, suddenly excited. "We're going on the *QM2*."

Frankie laughed.

"What's so funny?" Christine asked.

"That was just a ruse," Frankie said.

"I thought you said your grandmother doesn't fly," Christine said to Raoul.

"I don't, but I didn't come over on the *QM2*," Chantal said.

Raoul pulled out his cell phone, tapped on the screen, and then showed it to Christine. "She came on this."

Christine looked closely. "What is it?"

"Our yacht," Chantal said. "It's the only civilized way to cross the Atlantic now that the great liners have given up the trade."

"I didn't know you had a yacht," Christine said. "Why didn't I see it when I was in Saint-Tropez?"

"It was in dry dock in Toulon, being refitted," Raoul said.

"It was in what, where, being what?" Christine asked.

"In the shop, being remodeled," Frankie said.

"The family's previous yacht was requisitioned by the Nazis during the war, and sunk at Toulon by Allied strafing, so this is the replacement, built during the late forties," Raoul said. "Dad thought about buying a new one but decided to go old school and refit this one. It's not as fast or sexy as the ones owned by the Russian billionaires, but it's oceangoing, and we like it."

"It's beautiful," Christine said.

"I had lots of good times aboard when I was your age, but now it's time for a new generation to make memories on her," Chantal said.

"*Grand-mère* asked me to choose a new name after the refit," Raoul said.

He poked at the screen and showed a stern view of the yacht.

Christine gasped. "*Sofia*," she said.

"We have always named our yachts for great characters from opera," Chantal said. "She was previously the *Leïla*."

"From *Les pêcheurs de perles*," Christine said.

"Yes," Chantal said, turning to Raoul. "She's a keeper."

"It's perfect," Christine said, wiping a tear and then kissing Raoul.

"I hope you don't mind a few extra people along on your honeymoon," Hannah said.

"Not at all," Christine said. "All I need is a bed and a boy."

"Any boy?" Chantal asked.

"This boy," Christine said, putting her head on Raoul's shoulder. "Is everybody going on the yacht?"

"Just us," Hannah said, "Maria and Johnston, Zoe and Jim Bob, and Sofia, of course."

"I promised Zoe a honeymoon, but we never got around to it," Jim Bob said.

"Frankie, are you and Meg going on the yacht?" Christine asked.

"No, we're staying in New York for a few days, see some shows and then run up to Boston. We'll load up and head over later, once the honeymoon is over."

"That may take a while, but come on over whenever you like," Christine said.

"I'm going to hang with Frankie and Meg, if that's okay," Sue said. "You don't need me on your honeymoon cruise."

"I'll always need you," Christine said. "Are you sure you don't want to go on the yacht?"

Sue grinned. "I met a boy. At the reception."

"No way," Christine said. "Why didn't you tell me?"

"I didn't want to harsh your vibe on your wedding night."

"You could never do that. You should have told me. Does this boy have a name?"

"Carter," Sue said.

"We totally hooked her up," Addison said.

"He's a sophomore at Harvard," Kendall added.

"We've known him since we were kids."

"His mom is old Boston money."

"His dad works for the Foreign Service."

"So he disappears for a couple of years at a time."

"And comes back speaking another language."

"He has a thing for Asian chicks."

"He speaks Mandarin."

"Better than I do," Sue said.

"Great," Christine said. "But you are coming to Saint-Tropez, right?"

"Definitely," Sue said.

"Bring your boy toy," Christine said. "Teegs, what about you and Alfie?"

"We're going to do New York and Boston with the gang and then stowaway on whatever method of transport Frankie has lined up to get us across the pond. We want to go to Cannes while we're there and check it out in case we ever have a film in the festival."

"It's about a ninety-minute drive," Raoul said.

"Drive? How bourgeois," Chantal said. "We'll take the *Sofia* of course and arrive in style amongst those ghastly Russian speedboats. I have friends in Cannes, and they know all the best clubs."

"Score!" Addison said to Tegan.

"You'll love Cannes," Kendall said.

"And Cannes will love you, *mon cheri*," Chantal said. "You remind me of Brigitte when she was your age."

"Brigitte?" Tegan asked.

"Bardot," Chantal said.

31

ANGEL

CHRISTINE AND RAOUL sat in a love seat in the lounge car, holding hands, as the train rolled along. The twins, Sue, Frankie and Meg, Alfonso and Tegan, were nearby.

"Do you lovebirds want to be alone?" Sue asked.

Christine shook her head. "No, we're fine."

"Are you sure?"

"I'm sure. He needs to recharge for tonight."

Frankie laughed.

"We'll be alone then, doing our thing, or I guess I'll be doing his thing," Christine said.

Sue covered her face and shrieked. Everyone else laughed. Christine leaned forward and looked out the windows as the train slowed but didn't stop.

"Is this Albuquerque?"

"Yes," Frankie said.

"Where are we going?"

"Belen. I promised to take you there, remember?"

"Where is it?"

"South of Albuquerque. We'll drop off the steam locomotive at the BNSF yard there."

"You're taking a whole train full of people to Belen, just so I can see it?"

"Not really. We're going there anyway."

Christine pulled up a map on her phone. "Okay, I'm no expert, but we are totally going the wrong way."

Raoul looked at her phone. "She's right."

"Oh, yeah," Frankie said. "You were otherwise engaged early this morning."

Christine smiled.

"There's a wildfire between Raton and Trinidad," Frankie said. "Amtrak suspended operations over the pass until the fire is out and they can inspect the tracks. Dad polled the car owners and they agreed that instead of waiting indefinitely we should take the Belen Cutoff, through Clovis and Amarillo. They were all quite excited about it, actually. If Amtrak is forced to abandon the Raton line for financial reasons, which is a distinct possibility, this will be the new route, so everybody wants to check it out."

"Works for me," Christine said.

"It's also the route Daniel Senior took that night aboard the *Scout* with the young opera singer, in that very car." Frankie said, pointing toward the *Estelline*.

"And I'll be sleeping with a young opera singer in the same bedroom, right?" Raoul said.

"You won't be doing a lot of sleeping," Christine said, grinning.

Frankie laughed. "History repeats itself."

Christine looked at her phone. "What time will we be in Amarillo?"

Frankie checked his watch. "Well, let's see. There's an hour time change, so probably around six. Why?"

"I want to stop there. Can you make that happen?"

"The old Santa Fe depot is still there but there aren't really any facilities for a passenger train."

"If anybody can do it, you can. Work your magic."

"Why in the world do you want to stop in Amarillo?"

"For dinner," Christine said, thumbing her phone.

"We'll have dinner on the train."

"We'll also need a ride," Christine said.

"No problem," Frankie said, chuckling. "I'm sure they have limo services in Amarillo, or at least shuttle buses."

Christine studied the map on her phone. "Call Angel. He can give us a ride."

"You want Angel to drive all the way to Amarillo to give you a ride to dinner?" Frankie asked, incredulous.

"Yes. Tell him to bring that limo bus thingy, and his wife."

Frankie looked at Raoul, who shrugged and said, "Send me the bill."

"Can he get there before we do?" Christine asked.

"If he hauls ass," Frankie said.

"Sue," Christine called out.

"Yo," Sue said.

"Do you have your violin?"

"Of course, and my horn if you need it."

"Nope, just a violin." Christine looked at Frankie. "Does this train have Internet and a printer?"

"This train has everything. What do you need?"

"I need to download some sheet music," Christine said. She looked at Raoul. "Unless you think you can wing it."

"Uh-oh," Raoul said. "Wing what?"

Frankie enlisted the help of his dad, who loved a challenge and immediately went to work. It helped that several railroad executives were aboard. Amtrak had previously used the alternate route on occasion when there were track problems on the Raton route, but stopping the train in Amarillo, where Amtrak had no facilities, would require calling in some favors. Franklin was up to the task.

RAILFANS FROM AROUND the world had converged on northern New Mexico. That the occasion was the wedding of some teenage girl who was reputed to sing a bit, and a wealthy French nobleman, or boy, was of no concern. What mattered was that the wedding was cause for assembly of the longest string of private varnish any of them had ever seen, or even heard of. From the time 3751 was attached to the private train, railfans were busy chasing, ogling, photographing, and filming, with expensive drones flying overhead. While Christine spent a blissful wedding night aboard the *Estelline*, railfans set up their cameras in anticipation of the arrival of the rest of the train, led by 3751, and its departure for Chicago over the Raton Pass.

As they chased the train south out of Santa Fe they were surprised when the train switched to tracks headed for Albuquerque instead of Lamy. A flurry of phone calls, text messages, and emails revealed the situation at Raton, where several railfans had positioned themselves. The westbound *Southwest Chief* was holding at Trinidad, waiting out the wildfire. The eastbound *Southwest Chief*, having just left Gallup, still had options, and time to reroute.

Either the private train was returning to Los Angeles, or taking the Belen Cutoff through Clovis and Amarillo, and on to Chicago. Confirmation came when the train arrived at Belen and, after a brief stop to uncouple 3751, headed east. Railfans were thrilled. They were chasing a long, historic private train over the Abo Canyon, through Clovis, and on to Amarillo. That Amarillo was once headquarters for the Santa Fe Railway's Texas subsidiary was a happy bonus.

The railfans at Raton immediately loaded up and headed southeast on US 87 to intercept, while those who had chased the train to Belen quickly checked maps and were ecstatic to discover that from Fort Sumner to Amarillo, more than 150 miles, the private train would be running parallel to US 60, much of the time east of the highway with the sun high in the western sky.

THERE WAS A THRONG of onlookers, railroad employees and their families, along with civic leaders, the media, and an enthusiastic group of railfans, as the private train rolled into the old Santa Fe depot in Amarillo, where no passenger train had called for decades. Railfans were ecstatic when the train stopped—they had expected it to only slow down through the yards and then pick up speed as it left town. They were over the moon when the doors opened on several private cars and the owners invited them aboard.

The railfans were oblivious to Christine and her entourage as they stepped off the train. They also took no notice of Angel and Alicia standing beside the door of the limo bus parked trackside. The train was the thing.

"Thank you so much for coming," Christine said as she hugged Angel.

"How could I miss it?"

He pulled a checkbook out of his pocket and handed it to Johnston. "Juanita said she hoped this is the right one."

Johnston opened the checkbook and looked. "This will do."

Angel, as usual, had already scouted his route, and quickly arrived at their destination, only blocks away. The press, who had followed them from the depot, were turned away at the door of the homeless shelter.

There were murmurs and stares as the well-dressed and hardly homeless strangers stepped inside. Many people sat at the long tables, eating, and others stood in the serving line.

"Do we sit together, or mingle?" Addison asked.

"Mingle, of course, and do try to be cordial," Chantal said.

A gray-haired man in his seventies stepped forward. "Good evening. I'm Thornton, a volunteer here. This wasn't my shift, but I came in as soon as I heard."

Frankie shook his hand and made the introductions.

"And you must be Christine," Thornton said.

"Yes sir," Christine said.

"I'm sure you don't remember me. You were just a little girl at the time."

Christine threw her arms around his neck. "You gave me soup."

"Yes, I did."

She pulled back and looked at him.

"It was the best soup I ever had. It was so cold outside."

She hugged him again.

"I'm sorry to hear about your father. He was such a gentleman."

"Yes, he was. I miss him so much." She took Johnston by the hand. "This is Johnston Caldwell, my adoptive daddy."

Johnston and Thornton shook hands.

"And my new husband, Raoul," she said, smiling.

"I hope we aren't imposing," Johnston said.

"Not at all. We are well-prepared, and you are certainly welcome. We have plenty of food. Thank you very much for the generous donation."

"Donation?" Johnston asked.

"A food service truck was here a couple of hours ago and unloaded a massive amount of food. Our coolers, freezers and shelves are full, enough to feed our clients for days."

"I didn't want you to run out of food because of our group," Frankie said. "But that wasn't the donation."

Thornton was confused.

"You gave food and shelter to Christine and her father when they desperately needed it, and in a way, helped bring her into our lives," Johnston said. "We will be eternally grateful."

"And laundry and a bath," Christine said. "That was a pretty big deal at the time."

Johnston smiled, pulled a check from his pocket, and handed it to Thornton.

"This is our donation, from all of us, Christine's extended family."

Thornton was stunned when he looked at the check. "Oh, my."

He looked closer to count the zeros. "I don't know what to say."

He shook Johnston's hand. "Thank you so much. This will allow us to help so many more people."

"Don't thank me. Thank Christine. Even when she had little or nothing herself, Christine worked as a street performer to raise money for the homeless, so it's the least we can do."

Thornton hugged Christine again, both now in tears.

"Let's eat," Frankie said. "We have a train to catch."

Thornton gestured toward the serving line. Christine took Raoul by the hand and led the way.

Christine and Raoul sat across the table from a young couple with a little girl. The others spread out wherever there was room. Chantal sat down beside a dirty, hairy young man and introduced herself. He was leery at first of this strange, elegant woman who spoke English with a distinct French accent but was soon conversing like she was his own grandmother.

Sue and the twins found a table filled with young men wearing various articles of military clothing on their bodies and vacant stares on their faces.

"You look like that Disney chick," a scruffy young man said to Tegan.

"I get that a lot," Tegan replied.

When they finished eating, Angel and Alicia made their way to the small stage. Few noticed.

"May I have your attention, please," Angel said.

Some turned toward the stage, but most were not interested.

"My name is Angel. This is my wife, Alicia."

He looked out over the room. "I see some veterans out there. Thank you for your service. I have been where you are. I did two tours in Iraq and one tour of homeless shelters and VA hospitals across the country."

The veterans and many others now turned and listened.

"Six years ago, I was hitchhiking my way across the country. I was messed up, strung out, and headed nowhere fast, but generally west, where I hoped it would be warmer."

Some of the veterans nodded.

"It was winter, and horribly cold. There's a joke I never can get right about a barbed wire fence north of Amarillo holding back the cold, but it blew down that night."

There was some laughter, mostly from the staff and volunteers who had lived in Amarillo for years.

"It was snowing sideways. A trucker dropped me off on the Interstate and somebody gave me directions to this place." He pointed to the front door. "I opened that door right over there and came in out of the cold. I was cold and hungry, and all I wanted was a hot breakfast and I would be on my way west."

He wiped tears and Alicia quickly took his hand and squeezed.

"As I opened the door, I heard someone singing. It was the most beautiful voice I had ever heard. It was truly the voice of an angel, and for a moment I wondered if I had frozen to death."

He now had everyone's attention.

"There was a young girl, about eleven or twelve, standing right here on this stage, a beautiful child with blonde hair. She was singing, accompanied by a man, who I later learned was her father, playing violin. She looked right at me. I'll never forget those blue eyes. Actually, she was probably looking to see what fool had opened the door and let in the cold."

He paused for laughter.

"I was convinced she was singing just to me. She saved my life." He put his arm around Alicia. "Well, actually, this woman saved my life, but it was the young girl's singing that convinced me to stop running, stop drinking, along with other things, and start living. I made it as far as Albuquerque where I got clean, got sober, got straight, got a job, and met this wonderful woman, who did the rest."

He kissed Alicia.

"That young girl is here today. She's all grown up, on her way to Chicago, on her honeymoon, actually, but she wanted to take time to stop here and thank the staff for helping her and her father when they were in need."

Christine whispered to Raoul, "Come on, Daddy. We have to pay for our dinner."

"Ladies and gentlemen, the vicomtesse Christine Daaé de Chagny, accompanied on violin by her new husband, Raoul."

There was a smattering of applause, mostly from friends, family, and staff, as Christine and Raoul took the stage, followed by Sue, who quickly opened her violin case and handed Raoul her violin. She then placed the sheet music on the music stand and sat on the edge of the stage.

Christine smiled and then turned to Raoul and nodded. He began to play, and Christine sang.

As usual, Christine tried to look at everyone in the audience, or at least in their direction, but she took special notice of the young man sitting alone in the corner, hunched over his plate, with a dark hoodie pulled over his face.

Tears rolled down Erik's disfigured face as he listened to Christine sing "Angel."

ABOUT THE AUTHOR

C. David Stephens is a screenwriter whose best-known work is *Cabin by the Lake*, USA Network's highest-rated original movie. He has several screenplays in various states of development, including *Granny*, a horror film co-written with the late Blake Snyder, *An Affair of Honor*, a tragic love story set in France and North Africa in 1940, and *Every Mother's Son*, a coming-of-age story set in a small town in west Texas in 1969. His teen comedy *Wish List* was featured in *Written By*, the Writers' Guild magazine, as one of the best unproduced comedies in Hollywood.

He served as a counterintelligence agent with the First Cavalry Division (Airmobile) in Viet Nam from 1969–1970. He lives in Lubbock, Texas, on the Llano Estacado.

ABOUT THE TYPE

The text of this book is set in Dante, a typeface designed by Giovanni Mardersteig (1892–1977) founder of the private press Officina Bodoni. Dante, while not a true revival, was influenced by the types cut by Francesco Griffo (1450–1518) working for Aldus Manutius in Venice. The punches for Dante were cut by Charles Malin (1883–1955). Dante derives its name from the first book in which it was used, *Trattatello in Laude di Dante*, published in 1955 by Officina Bodoni. After the death of Malin, a young Matthew Carter cut the punches for additional weights. Carter would go on to become one of the most influential type designers of the second half of the twentieth century.

Soon after its introduction as a foundry type Dante was adapted for machine composition by Monotype. The typeface was eventually digitized for Monotype by Ron Carpenter, which is the version used here.

Chapter titles are set in Dante Titling.